THE
FINAL
OUTBREAK
M.L. BANNER

THE FINAL OUTBREAK

M.L. Banner

ISBN: (Paperback) 978-1-947510-06-7
Version 1.04, March 2019

THE FINAL OUTBREAK is an original work of fiction.
The characters and dialogs are the products of this author's vivid imagination.
Most of the science and the historical incidents described in this novel are based on reality, and so are its warnings.

Published by

www.toesinthewaterpublishing.com

To my wife, Lisa.
For your unending love and support,
even during my times of MADNESS.

Part I
MADNESS

"If you gaze long into an abyss, the abyss will also gaze into you."

Friedrich W. Nietzsche

"It's a plague of madness that has infected most animals...
a ticking time bomb, which could go off at any moment."

T.D. Bonaventure

PROLOGUE

Santa Cruz de Tenerife, Spain
1712

A scream sent him into motion. Aldolfo Suárez raced up the face of La Gomera, sure his son was seriously injured. He bounded deftly over the volcanic rocks, focused on not catching his sandals—there was no helping his son if he too were injured.

Halfway up the summit, his fatigued legs forced him to stop and find rest under the ancient umbrella of a dragon-tree. While trying to satisfy his oxygen-starved lungs with fitful gulps of the foul, sulfur-filled air, he took in the world's surreal textures.

Besides being colorless, like a charcoal drawing, it was soundless, not unlike a dense snowfall. Gray ash, instead of flecks of snow, quietly floated down from the murk, spotting the landscape.

He glared over his left shoulder to examine its origin. Only the thick plume of La Palma's volcano was visible now. An unending boiling geyser, belching ash from the depths. The townspeople blamed the eruption on God, saying that they were being punished for the sins of their past. Aldolfo knew it wasn't a vengeful God; evil was at the root of all of this and it was getting worse.

In the week since the eruption, the looming clouds thickened with each passing night. Daily, the sun's life-giving warmth was quelled by this cloak. And the skies grew more violent, with darker shades of crimson each afternoon.

He caught a glimpse of several sheep by his *granero*, the only building up on the hill. They had spread out from their normal confines, now testing the farthest reaches of his vast property. Sheep preferred to remain together for safety and not spread apart.

A tortured screech and several sheep dashed below him, not even slowing down, as if he wasn't there. They always stopped to gather around their shepherd.

Puzzled by this, he carefully studied them as they scurried along the well-trodden path, then around a corner into one of the two caves on his property. They disappeared inside.

However odd and troubling this was, he thanked his good fortune. At least those animals would be easier to gather.

Bleating pulled Aldolfo's attention once again back toward his *granero*. Above this, an undulating cloud of black dots fell from the sky, disappearing behind the building. Then the cloud rose again, where it clung to the air for barely a second and then tumbled downward. The chaotic dots then circled back to some unseen spot behind the building.

Movement to his right.

A winged shape emerged from the gray gloom. Black and angular. Bright red eyes. It flapped furiously, arched, and then dropped onto the back of a frantic sheep, which cried a labored bleat and burst past him. Its normal coat of alabaster—his flock's wool was well known throughout the region—was covered with tawny splashes. The winged shape rode on its back like death bridling a horse of the apocalypse. It lifted its head and shrieked back at him. Something fibrous hung from its orange beak.

Aldolfo gaped, dumbfounded.

Then he understood. The shapes, the clouds: these were *cuervo negro*, a black raven common around the island. Except their normally coordinated flights and wonderfully sinuous formations were erratic. Almost angry.

There were more shrill cries coming from behind the building. He ran again, to the sounds of his distressed animals. Making no connection to the birds, he became sure that one of the neighbor's mad dogs was attacking a few of the wandering herd. It had already happened twice this week. He clutched his staff, getting ready to wield it against the attacking *perro*. There'd be no warning this time; he'd beat the devil out of the animal, and demand payment for his injured or killed sheep.

Aldolfo arrived breathless, just off the side of his *granero*, and was once again frozen in his steps. What he witnessed stupefied him. For the first time, fear raced up his spine, faster than a cold December chill.

The *cuervos* were swarming three of his sheep; each lay in a dying heap on the rocky ground, wailing in pain. The birds pulled at the bloody flesh, frantically ripping at and plunging their heads into the moribund bodies.

Finally, the good shepherd in him reacted. Aldolfo jumped up, hollered a command at the offending fowl and swung his arms wildly.

The birds reacted instantly, the cloud breaking free from the mostly still carcasses—they were once his beloved animals. The haze of *cuervos* barely rose from the ground before quickly changing direction and flapping frantically, this time toward him.

They no longer seemed disorganized.

He yelped as each *cuervo* pelted him. One after another they hit, causing him to lose his balance. But he righted himself and swung at the thickening cloud, now swarming him en masse.

Their wild screeching was so loud he thought he might go deaf, if he even survived this.

Some of the birds fell from the swings of his staff, and a few others broke away, just avoiding being hit. But there were far too many. Each momentary hole in the black clog filled up again, as they continued their unyielding barrage.

Spikes of pain flared all over his body, and he caught momentary flashes of his own blood with each swing. A flood of panic rushed over him, causing him to thrash wildly. Losing his balance again, he dropped his staff and started to tumble toward the ground when he saw perhaps his only outlet of salvation.

The door to his *granero* was slightly ajar. If he could only make it inside there.

Using his headlong motion, he drove his legs forward, pushing through and into the comforting darkness, landing hard. Several cats bolted past him, yowling their own displeasure, and disappeared outside, just before he kicked the door closed.

The frame of the large building rattled and then, for a moment the world was a muffled quiet but for his own harried puffs for air.

A shaft of weak light nudged through the *granero's* single dirty window, illuminating a small lump in the middle of the floor, as if God Himself had reached in with His invisible hand and left a foggy thumb-print of light that split the darkness. The thumb-print crackled with movement.

His *granero* was not used much anymore, so the building should have been empty right now. He squinted at the abyss, fighting an inability to see anything in the dark.

One of his eyes wasn't working. He spat mental curses at the devilish birds for what they did to him. The back of his hand trailed over the nonfunctional eye, tentatively confirming nothing was blocking his vision. It felt sticky and moist. He purposely forced both eyes closed and attempted to reopen both again, hoping it might improve his vision. It didn't.

It was only then that he realized he wasn't alone.

With his one good eye, Aldolfo refocused on the illuminated lump in the center of the structure that he had first assumed was something his son had left there—he often didn't put things where they belonged. Maybe it was some more of those damned cats that were everywhere.

A spell of dizziness rocked him, and only then did he know how badly he was hurt. Yet he fought back the wooziness: he needed to know what this lump was. He felt drawn to it. An unshakable feeling, however irrational, that whatever the lump might be, it would offer him comfort.

He attempted to pull himself deeper into the building, using his elbows to propel his body forward.

A painful ringing crescendo in his brain, which already felt as if it might pop at any second. And yet above the internal din, he heard something else.

It was a dull murmur, coming from the illuminated mass.

The benign image of a litter of puppies jumped into his head; its edges fuzzy, like after a dream.

His son had watched over the neighbor's newborn pups, long before they had become vicious. Back then they were adorable, but when it came time to feed them, they showed their inner animalistic self, attacking their food, ripping at it and gnawing each morsel with untamed abandon. Their gnawing sounded like what he was now hearing, only raw.

As if something covering his ears were removed, he could hear better, the ringing barely noticeable. At the same time, the image became clearer. He halted his progression and focused. He could now see and hear this lump in motion.

He convulsed uncontrollably.

It was chewing sounds he was hearing, along with sounds of tearing and ripping at flesh. It was the evil *cuervos* eating from the mass...

They were eating his son.

His boy must have attempted to escape the birds inside, just like his father.

Aldolfo gave up all fight, fully accepting his fate. There would be no escape for him, just as there wasn't any for his son.

He watched the cuervos race toward him and wished at that moment, he could have once more told his boy he loved him.

Before everything went black, he marveled at the redness of the *cuervos'* eyes.

DAY ONE

WE DIDN'T KNOW IT AT THE TIME, BUT IT ALL STARTED TODAY... THE BEGINNING OF OUR END.

01

Madrid, Spain

The red-eyed beast came out of nowhere, moving so fast they had no time to think, only react. And if it hadn't been for TJ seeing the creature and calling it to their attention before it struck, one or both of them might have suffered serious injury or a far worse fate.

Two days would pass before they'd come to realize that this was just one of many signs of an apocalypse that was about to befall the world. Until then, they would chalk up this event to just another part of the normal chaos that comes with travel these days. Technically, the chaos began over a week ago.

When they had boarded their transatlantic flight, they were mildly aware of some travel disruptions that had started earlier when Iceland's Bardarbunga volcano began spewing ash into the atmosphere. The volcanic ash plume slowly ballooned out toward Northern Europe causing flight delays and diverting air traffic across the continent—the thick particles of ash played hell with jet engine rotors.

This very thing had happened years before, and so neither Ted nor TJ Williams gave it much thought as they luxuriated in their first-class flat-bed seats and happily discussed their upcoming transatlantic cruise from Malaga, Spain back to the US. Their flight attendant added to their self-imposed detachment by topping off their glasses with seemingly endless sparkling wine.

An hour before landing, Sicily's Mount Etna blew its top as well, diverting more flights and adding to the already heavy air traffic coming into London's Heathrow Airport.

When they arrived, they received their first taste of the travel problems that lay ahead of them. Many flights had already been canceled, and further cancellations were mounting by the minute, as flights around Europe and Asia were being grounded. Their next flight was one of them.

Ted and TJ had only one more leg left on their journey to Malaga before Regal European's *Intrepid* would set sail at five tomorrow afternoon. Although Ted's agent set up the trip, TJ had done all the detailed planning, as she normally did for any of their vacations.

Now anchored at the American desk, outside their arrival gate, they were both scrambling for options. The gate agent busily searched for other air-travel possibilities on American, while they also searched on their phones for other available flights on competitor airlines.

"How about Madrid?" Ted spoke just below a shout, to be heard over the commotion. "There's a BA flight leaving in thirty. Ah... flight number 6-2-8-0." His eyes met TJ's for confirmation that this would work for them.

Instantly her face was awash with excited expectation. "Yes!" She turned to the gate agent. "Can you find us two seats?"

The agent furiously tapped at her keyboard, eyes drilled into her screen. "I have two bulkhead seats in coach, but at least they're next to each other," she announced with pride.

"We'll take them!" TJ threw back, without hesitation. In other circumstances, she might have been disappointed as a Platinum member of American's frequent flier program who just lost first-class seats on a canceled flight. But she was pretty sure they'd have no other choices if she waited even a few more seconds. This flight didn't get them to Malaga, but it brought them to within driving distance.

Once she heard the printer below the desk spit out their tickets, she asked the next obvious question. "Do you or anyone else have anything from Madrid to Malaga?"

"Sorry, there's nothing available. This may be the last flight in or out of Madrid," the gate agent responded fairly quickly, still not looking up.

Ted handed TJ his phone. "Here. I'll get our tickets. This is Cynthia with Hertz in Madrid." He flashed a Keanu Reeves sort of smile, which then broke into a grin. The curl of his handlebar mustache—the one part of his made-up British author persona she'd like to change—lifted high on his face.

At any other time, she might have smirked or said something about his appearance, made more out of place by his Cubs ball cap. Instead, TJ beamed at him, accepting his phone. After twenty years of marriage, he still loved making her smile.

They had to run to the gate to make the full flight to Madrid, with barely a few minutes to spare. Ted pulled their luggage, while TJ secured an economy car with Hertz in between harried puffs for air.

Relief turned into worry after they landed at Madrid's Baraja.

They made their way to baggage claims and customs, pacing silently, taking in news snippets from each TV they passed—most were tuned to BBC. The results of Mount Etna's eruption were devastating: it was the largest eruption in over a hundred years; several hundred perished in a giant swirling pyroclastic cloud that swept through Fornazzo; and air travel throughout Eurasia was now at a standstill.

They were the lucky ones, indeed.

At the Hertz counter, where lines of frantic travelers received the bad news, they were evermore thankful they had booked their car when they did, and that it hadn't been given to someone else. Yet a sinking nervousness gnawed away at their bellies. Something much greater than an immediate disaster was occurring and they were about to get their first taste of it.

Ted had volunteered to drive if TJ would navigate. She was far more adept at that than him, calling out approaching signs and anticipating their next turn. He didn't need a GPS when he had her. TJ was his GPS.

With both of their doors opened, they flashed each other smiles over the roof of the car. They had a five hour drive to Malaga, and maybe then they could relax a little.

That's when TJ called out, "What the hell is that?"

Ted's head snapped to where her finger pointed. "Get in the—" he yelled, cutting off his own command, as he threw himself into the driver's seat, and pulled the door closed behind him.

TJ, normally the one to react to a potential threat quicker than Ted, seemed frozen by bewilderment. It was fear. Her hesitation negated her ability to jump in on time. Reflexively she ducked behind the door's glass window, just as what looked like a dog made impact.

Both TJ and the dog yelped.

She remained fixed for a long moment, until Ted hollered, "TJ!"

Reacting as if being punched, she finally sprang inside, slamming her door behind her.

They watched in stunned silence as the German shepherd righted itself and shook its head violently, spewing blood and saliva across TJ's side window. The animal momentarily scrutinized them, its eyes an unnatural and angry red. It seemed rabid with rage—without the foaming of the mouth—and yet befuddled at the same time.

Then the animal caught sight of something behind them, out of their periphery, and hurriedly limped away in that direction.

"What was that?" Ted squeezed his wife's hand to comfort himself, as well as her.

Time held its breath as they waited for their hearts to slow.

TJ, unable to find the right amount of air needed to reply, left his question unanswered. She didn't have an answer, even if she had had enough air.

Ted gazed at her and considered what must be going through her head right now. It was, after all, a dog attack that almost killed her and left her physically and emotionally scarred. Now just about any animal, big or small, caused his wife to freeze in fear. It had become such a liability to her now, she could no longer operate as a Bureau field agent, spending most of her time behind a desk. Even working out for her had to be done indoors, where there were no alleyways or streets where dogs could be potentially lurking.

She peered through her glasses at the side mirror, searching for the wild animal that just tried to eat them.

Finally, she turned to him. "Let's get out of this nightmare."

But their nightmare was only just beginning.

DAY TWO

WE WERE LOOKING FORWARD TO A PHYSICAL AND EMOTIONAL RESPITE: GOD KNOWS WE NEEDED IT. BUT MALAGA WOULD OFFER US NEITHER.

02

Malaga, Spain

This time, she didn't duck and the rabid-like dog got her. This time, he couldn't do anything to save her. He was forced to watch from a distance. The crowds of people swelled around him, holding him back, as she lay there alone and dying. When he finally broke free and made it to her, he knew he was too late. Her life-giving blood was everywhere, her eyes welled up in agony, pleading to him to answer why he wasn't there for her; why he couldn't have stopped this?

Then she was gone.

Ted sat up, swallowing back the bile that filled his mouth. He snapped his head to her side, desperately hoping she was there.

He couldn't see her.

But it was dark and he couldn't make out anything, really. A weak shaft of light from the coming dawn illuminated an unfamiliar desk on the other side of this foreign room.

He heard the distant sound of a car horn, which didn't make sense because they lived in the country.

Then he heard her.

She exhaled soft puffs of air, her breaths rhythmic and restful. She was asleep beside him.

And then it all made sense. She was fine. They were in their hotel room in Malaga, Spain. He didn't lose her. This time.

Ted continued to dry-swallow the bitter nastiness lingering in his mouth and the burn in his throat, while trying to keep from hyperventilating. He drew comfort in his wife's peaceful breathing and started to calm himself.

Many recent mornings he woke from a similar horror, with only the circumstances changing. Last week it was her drowning in their lake; the week before, she was being run over by a truck—that was the most common one. In each nightmare, a suffocating crowd flooded around him, holding him back with debilitating panic, so that there was no way to save her.

For over twenty years he'd been having this same damned nightmare, his author-mind only creatively interjecting different causes of death. But in the end, the result was always the same: some outside force caused her to die and he was held back by a swell of people.

He began to feel his breathing accelerate again, just by thinking about all the people.

"Same dream?" TJ asked, her voice heavy from sleep.

"Yeah," he huffed.

She slid over to him and wrapped her arms around his trunk, squeezing him tight. "Well, I'm very much alive, I love you, and we are now in the beautiful town of Malaga. Let's get up and go see the city."

"Sounds like a terrific idea."

And they did just that.

After checking out of their hotel, they stowed their bags in the trunk of their parked rental car and meandered through cobbled pedestrian thoroughfares bustling equally with tourists and locals.

Interspersed were city workers push-brooming away the fine layer of volcanic dust which had settled everywhere. Likewise, the Williamses pushed aside their worries about home, work and their travels, quickly wiring themselves into the vibrant culture and ancient history of Malaga, Spain.

Hand in hand, they walked quietly, each focused on their own thoughts. They were not unlike any couple who had shared twenty years of respect and love through marriage. Only as a couple, they rarely spent much time together, at least not lately. With TJ's and Ted's disparate schedules, they found themselves frequently apart. TJ worked late hours and often had to travel to other Bureau offices, sometimes for a week or more at a time. And Ted's agent often had him traveling around the US and the UK for book signings at small bookshops and radio and TV interviews. His schedule was especially busy around new book releases. His latest was apt to be his biggest. The cruise was to be their calm before their stormy schedule, already packed full of travel and appearances. And it would be a celebration of their anniversary.

Threading the needle of their already ballooning calendars, Ted's agent had recently booked this trip. He would have never chosen a cruise, because of all the people. But TJ insisted that they could spend most of the time in their cabin and it would give them some needed "us time." He relented, knowing their chances to be together would go away in less than a month.

At the *Teatro de Roman*—an ancient Roman theater excavated in the heart of *Ciudad de Malaga*—they turned right and ascended the centuries-worn ramparts leading up to the stone entrance of the Moorish palace known as Alcazaba de Malaga.

Originally built in the 11th century and continually expanded upon through the 14th, it was an impressive fortress pridefully peering over its Malagan subjects. The palace's occupants included Muslim rulers and Spain's infamous Queen

Isabella and King Ferdinand.

And though the trek up from the city center was a calf-burning distance, the rewards were breathtaking vistas, flourishing gardens and ornate fountains which gushed sparkling streams, engineered into cascading outdoor water courses running through stairwells and walkways. An Andalusian Garden of Eden.

Just inside the towering defensive walls, they stopped to admire an impressive column of seagulls, which had corkscrewed up and into the complex, like one giant organism barking its excitement as it swooped overhead.

They passed tourists, young and old, including an elderly Spanish couple, their withered hands clasped together, their supportive canes on opposing sides, clunking against the polished stones in perfect synchronicity. Ted glanced at his wife, to see if she had the same thought as he, but she was preoccupied, as she had been the last several days.

Continuing along, just inside of the fortress's protective walls, they found themselves gazing up at a long walkway that crowned the top of the wall's buttresses, spanning the distances just five feet below the wall's lip. Bisecting the walkway periodically were lookout towers.

TJ couldn't help herself and took off like a jackrabbit, ascending a stairwell up to the closest tower's door. "What do you suppose is inside this tower?" She tugged on the obviously locked rustic door, which looked as ancient as the rest of the structure.

"Not sure you should even be up there," Ted stated tepidly, always amazed that someone in her profession so easily played fast and loose with other people's rules.

"Don't see a sign that says 'Don't enter.' Besides, it's locked."

Just as a large mouth might sense a new meal, the tower's knotty walnut door retracted inward. It was like a dried-up tongue pulled back to reveal a blackened opening surrounded by rotten stone teeth. The weathered appendage disappeared into the darkness, stopping with a clank.

A bearded man wearing official-looking work clothes of white and yellow stepped from the gaping orifice and jerked to a stop on seeing TJ there.

She quickly flashed her usual bright smile and added a warm, "Hola."

"Hola, Senora," the man replied, far more reserved than her.

"Can we, I mean, *podemos...*"

"You want to see inside?" the worker asked her, and then beckoned to both with his hand. "It's okay."

"Gracias, Senor," Ted replied from below, expending pretty much the totality of his limited Spanish vocabulary in one sentence.

TJ quickly stepped into the dark tower opening while Ted started up the brick steps, stopping just before the small doorway to glare at some point off the horizon, over Malaga.

"Come on in, Ted, you've got to see th—" TJ halted mid-sentence after gathering in her husband's demeanor.

She couldn't see what he saw because he was looking at something outside, past the tower. She bounced a little as she waited for him to tell her what it was, so she could resume her exploration.

Only a few hundred yards away, the same column of white seagulls continued its aerobatics, swooping around and around above them all, like a giant living corkscrew-shaped light fixture in the sky. But another larger swarm of gulls barrel-rolled from the west into the natural chandelier of birds above Alcazaba's grounds. The larger group of aggressor gulls broke through their brethren's columns, attacking each of the scattering birds.

Ted's chin started to sag. What he was seeing looked like a WWI dogfight between birds of the same feather, directly above. At first a surreal fascination, it quickly turned gruesome.

After biting, ripping, and clawing at their panicked kin, sending their damaged bodies plunging to the ground, the aggressor gulls sought out new targets.

The people below.

Like a tsunami, panicked screams started to roll in, first one, then two, then four, as Alcazaba's visitors scattered to the four winds, each flailing at the terrorizing birds. The elderly couple they had passed hobbled toward an exit but then tumbled to the ground as one gull after another pounced on them,

That sight tore Ted from his moorings. He sprinted the rest of the way into the dark safety of the tower structure, nearly sending TJ—who was just making her way back out to see what was keeping him—to the polished brick floor.

"Close the door!" Ted yelled at the worker. "They're attacking."

The confused worker asked in Spanish what the crazy tourist was making such a fuss about.

"Per favore, close the damned door!" Ted hollered. He crawled along the floor and pushed with a shoulder to close the opening.

The worker, his foot blocking the door's closure, craned his head into the outside light, wanting to see with his own eyes why this tourist acted so loco. But then just as quickly, he pulled himself back inside and thrust his palms into the hard wood. Just before it loudly clasped shut, two thumps, like deep tremors, vibrated from the other side, causing both men to jump and exchange knowing glances.

"What the hell is going on out there?" TJ yelped.

"The birds; they're attacking!" Ted answered.

TJ was about to toss back a sarcastic comment about the Hitchcock classic, but held back after seeing Ted's face, and then hearing the screams outside. "What birds?" she stuttered.

"*Mira*," the worker said, now pointing to a long slit in an opposite wall, a few feet away from them. TJ studied the place where defenders used to shoot their arrows at attacking invaders centuries earlier. When the tower was open to tourists, this deep cleft afforded limited views out over the Puerto de Malaga and the inviting blue of the Med. Now, through the opening streamed terror-filled screams and shrieks from gulls, some of whom streaked by in flashes of white, gray, and blood-red.

The three of them tentatively ambled toward the opening to get a better look. TJ reached it first and stuck her face into the top of the six-inch-wide space.

Before the other two could reach her, she screamed and flopped backward onto the hard floor. A gull crashed into the opening with a thump, stopped short by its extended wings.

The men gasped at the red-eyed bird as it thrashed to gain traction with its claws and broken wings, but then fell away from the opening, out of sight.

"*Mierda*!" the worker panted.

They remained fixed in their places, for a moment, before TJ jumped back up. She quickly snatched up a pile of coveralls on the floor and shoved them into the opening. Ted and the worker followed her lead, snagging drop-cloths from a pile and completely sealing the opening.

They listened to the muffled shrieks from the birds and the occasional scream from a human, until there were no more of either. Waiting for what seemed like an hour, but was more likely just a few minutes, they carefully pulled the makeshift stopper from the opening.

They watched and listened for a longer period before they dared to brave the door.

Whatever had just happened was over now.

"Se terminó?" the worker asked them, still breathless.

"I think so," replied Ted, the first of them to tentatively descend the stairs, followed by TJ.

The cobbled walkways were carpeted in bloodied and mostly dead seagulls and a few other birds. Every fifth or sixth carcass flopped or fluttered with weakening brays. Splatters of blood were everywhere.

As they hurriedly navigated the ancient path out of the castle, Ted and TJ clasped their hands, clutching each other so hard their knuckles turned white. So fixated were they on the sky and getting out of Alcazaba, and then Malaga quickly, they didn't even notice the old couple they had passed on the way in. The two ancient lovers who had drawn Ted's admiration were slumped in a dark corner of the entrance, the first human casualties of the attack.

03

Puerto de Malaga

"Leave it," TJ demanded, her voice all wobbly. "We'll call the rental company from the ship. We can mail the key in when we get home. It'll cost, but I don't want to spend another moment in Spain."

Ted was already out of the car, double-parked outside the port entrance, and gathering their bags from the trunk. "How far to the ship?" He asked this partially out of a nervous need to say something, as he could plainly see three cruise ships in the distance. But the port also looked pretty big and he didn't want them to take a wrong turn. And although it was the first time either of them had been to the Malaga port, he knew she'd studied the map and knew by asking she'd be focused on where they needed to go next so they wouldn't dawdle out in the open.

"I know this is the way."

He slid a rollered bag into her hand, and they scurried across the street and into the vast Puerto de Malaga.

They walked in hurried silence down a long, straight

pedestrian street filled with shops on their left, bustling with people. On their right, the boarded walkways of a dock ran parallel. Small but expensive boats were intermittently tethered, each gently swaying to the Med's incoming tide.

Their eyes continually darted toward the dark sky, tracking on any bird that fluttered above.

On their left, a small delivery van stopped in front of a store, making a delivery of supplies or perhaps picking up the few baubles that didn't sell well.

Glorious aromas of coffee from the street-side restaurants fought against pungent scents of decaying sea-life pushed in by the cold waterfront breezes.

It all felt normal.

Those not milling around the shops seemed to be ambling in the same direction as them, although at a much more leisurely pace: probably passengers on their cruise ship or one of the others.

As they passed each clog of tourists—all pulling giant bags on rollers—they'd attempt to catch a bit of their conversations. Only a few spoke English, and none of those spoke about anything of importance. All seemed jovial and unconcerned.

Ted and TJ maintained their constant pace in silence.

Their ride from Alcazaba had consisted of short bursts of navigational instructions, but no other words. The whole time to the port and even now, both their minds were mentally racing to keep up their anxious desire to get to safety, away from the outside, sure another attack was imminent.

But no one here was anxious. There was no panic.

It was human nature to discount an event that went against all measures of normalcy. And both were doing this in their own ways. Perhaps what they experienced only occurred at Alcazaba and nowhere else. It had to have been an anomaly, based on what they were seeing now. It might have been terror-filled, but only incidental. As their minds continued to discount the enormity of what they witnessed, the adrenaline stopped pumping and fatigue quickly caught up to their steady march. The endorphins had long since ebbed, and now they felt tired. Yet they didn't slow.

They found themselves coming up to their ship, the Intrepid. As if they needed any prompting to board, it let loose a long horn blast.

Between them and their destination was a giant terminus where a few other passengers calmly lolled inside. Most of the passengers, they suspected, were on board, as they had chosen to check in as late as possible, to as TJ said, "give them more time to enjoy Malaga." Of course, the bird attack scuttled that idea.

Only when they were forced to slow their pace, and feeling the safety of the giant building beckoning them inside, did TJ start to breathe just a little easier.

Ted's breathing increased the moment he saw the huge crowd inside. His eyes appeared to nearly pop out of their sockets; his posture stiffened, while almost shrinking.

She knew this look: he was about to go into a full-on freak-out.

Every time this had happened it broke TJ's heart. She couldn't imagine the pain her husband felt losing his first wife and child, all because of his enochlophobia. But she wouldn't let it run its course. She wouldn't let it conquer him. Not this time.

She snatched his hand and dragged him and their bags—leaving one bag with a porter—through the horde and the port security.

TJ did most of the talking for them at check-in, while he focused on his breathing.

They might just make it through without incident, or so they thought.

After receiving their Seacards they were told to head up to the gangway, which led to the entrance of the ship. They were definitely among the tail-end of the incoming passengers. Purposely avoiding most of the crowds was by TJ's design. And Ted was thankful for this.

Just inside the gangway entrance, they stopped at the rail to allow a small clump of passengers to move past them.

It was their first moment of inactivity since Alcazaba.

Each examined the other, faces still drawn tight. Ted brushed a lock of TJ's hair away from her cheek and flashed a warm smile. He breathed a deep and exaggerated breath. "Whew, we made it, huh?"

She returned his smile. Even though the gangway was mostly covered, she still felt anxious. Part of it must have been Ted, she reasoned.

They watched their fellow passengers, also in the gangway, slowly process onto the ship. The awaiting crew welcomed them on board with beaming faces.

Below them, a few of the ship's crew pushed carts of baggage into a much larger entrance. One cart even held kennels containing a variety of dogs: pets of the passengers who paid for the privilege of sailing the Atlantic with their animals.

It was all the normal hubbub of a cruise preparing to leave port. No one, not a single soul, appeared to reflect any of the angst or fear Ted and TJ had been feeling.

"It's almost like what we witnessed never happened, isn't it?" The ship's horns sounded again, with two long blasts, which were deafening this close, even inside their enclosed gangway. TJ watched the lazy movements of a couple more passengers ambling behind them, and still others being welcomed inside.

After a while, TJ noticed that Ted had not answered her. She turned to him, concerned that maybe he was still not dealing well with the crowds, even though they weren't that large at all.

That concern changed focus quickly when she saw him;

he had that same look he'd had at the castle. "Ted?" She wasn't really after an answer.

He clutched her forearm, not diverting his gaze.

She followed his gaze, squinting to see what he must have been staring at. Her glasses were in her purse so she couldn't quite focus that far.

She felt the presence of a few other passengers on the gangway and noticed that they too were also seemingly mesmerized by something going on outside the port entrance where they had just abandoned their rental car.

She blinked harder and squinted tighter, wishing her eyes worked better.

In the distance, in front of a few plumes of smoke coming from the city center—which normally might have drawn a curious glance—there was a growing haze. The haze clung to the ground, like a smoke cloud rolling toward the port entrance.

It reminded TJ of the occasional haboob they'd see in Arizona, near where they lived: a growing billow of dust that would consume everything in its path, dumping tons of sand on homes, businesses, vehicles, people, and pets. This swelling wave was similar in that its dusty mass seemed to consume most everything in its path. Only this cloud didn't appear to be anywhere near as tall as a haboob. In fact it couldn't have been more than a few feet above the ground, whereas a haboob could reach a thousand feet, or more.

Also peculiar, this cloud was only moving down Paseo Reding, into the traffic circle of Fuente de la Tres Gracias. When they arrived, they'd noticed the streets of Malaga were covered in a fine gray dust, which had seemed foreign. Their hotel's concierge said this was from the Mount Etna eruption. A wind blowing the dust could create this rolling cloud. But that didn't explain why the dirty billows were tracking along only a couple of the streets.

At the traffic circle, connecting several streets, the cloud noticeably turned and blew into the port entrance.

It wasn't a weather event.

"Look, it's moving toward us, almost ..."

"... like it was sentient," Ted finished.

"What is it? It doesn't look like the birds up on the castle," she stammered.

As their hearts accelerated, they gawked in horror as this undulating mass of murk quickly churned down Paseo de la Farola, the main street through to the port—parallel to the one they'd just walked on.

A man crossing the street, seemingly unaware of the oncoming cloud, turned to look—it must be making a noise—and in his surprise, he tripped and fell onto the pavement. A small van veered off the road to avoid the man, crashing into a building.

The wave didn't hesitate. It blew closer, consuming all in its path.

Now, the pedestrians on the parallel street were running. Their frantic screams arrived in breeze-filled wisps.

Ted squeezed TJ's arm tighter and flashed a puzzled grimace at her.

TJ couldn't stand it. She had to see what this was. She snatched her glasses from her purse with her free hand and banged them onto her face.

She quickly averted her eyes and peered into his. Hers were filled with puddles. "Oh my God, Ted. What the hell is going on?" But neither of them could understand what was at the root of the cloud and why the people and cars were reacting this way. Dust blowing over you would not cause the fear these people obviously felt.

Finally, TJ could see what caused the clouds, and it sucked her breath away.

A younger woman beside Ted shrieked in horror.

But it was Ted who announced the cause of the pandemonium. "No! Those cannot be rats. What ... what are they doing?”

“Attacking,” TJ answered, her voice cracking.

“What? What are they attacking.?”

It was a rhetorical question, because each of them watched the wave of rats attack everything with a heartbeat: men, women, children, dogs.

When the bile rose in his throat, Ted seemed to be the only one to understand what this meant to them. “Um... I think,” he announced in a loud voice, “we should all get on the ship.” He backed away from the railing, pulling his wife with him. They bolted toward the ship entrance at the end of their gangway, a very long hundred yards away.

But he and TJ were the only ones moving.

At least ten passengers lingered on the gangway, holding fast to the railing, gawking. Two even held up their cameras in an attempt to chronicle this oncoming spectacle. TJ shouted, “Let’s get going, people, before the rats get here.”

Apparently, the use of “rats” in a sentence had the same value as shouting “Fire!”

That moved them.

The final passengers trotted behind Ted and TJ, their heavy footfalls and squealing baggage wheels a deafening swell as they bounced toward the ship entrance: their mutual finish line.

“Slow down, folks,” commanded a crew member who thrust out his palms to hold back the wave of worried tourists coming his way.

They slowed, with Ted and TJ still leading.

A muffled din grew in the background.

A few terror-filled screams ripped through their frenzied calm, breaking down their usual decorum, and they pushed forward faster.

They panicked when they could hear the cacophony of little squeals and the scampering of thousands of little feet, like heavy raindrops on a metal roof.

"They're coming," someone yelled and pushed past TJ and bounded into the crew member, sending both tumbling to the ground.

Other security crew members emerged from the door, thinking a fight had broken out.

Ted and TJ held at a bridge connecting the port's gangway with the ship's opening. Ted yelled to an approaching security guard, "We need to get on board and you need to close up the doors. See that? It's rats." He gestured behind them to where he could hear the roiling mass.

The guard could see a wave of movement stream up the gangway stairs and toward them. The remaining guests slipped past him, some abandoning their bags.

He blinked twice in sudden comprehension and pushed Ted and TJ toward the opening.

With everyone in, the guard halted at the entrance and glared at the open hatch.

"Can't you close this?" TJ asked, her voice growing more unsteady.

The panicked guard turned his glare to her and said, "Only the OOD, security director, or captain can announce the command to seal up early."

"Then call the fricking captain!" Ted howled.

04

Captain Christiansen

"Staff Captain, what am I looking at?" bellowed Captain Jörgen Christiansen.

All heads of the bridge crew rubbernecked in the same direction. They gawked through their starboard windows, down the gangway below, fixated on the fast approaching wave of just what they didn't know. None paid attention to the ringing phone, its light indicating it was from their starboard main guest entrance. It would ring when they wanted to close up, or if there was a problem.

"Sir..." Staff Captain Jean Pierre Haddock hesitated through his binoculars, "I think they're rats."

Captain Christiansen didn't need any other prompting. Jean Pierre confirmed what his own disbelieving eyes were telling him. He learned long ago not to worry about the reasons why something was happening. He dealt in facts, and not in what was unexplainable. He had no idea why waves of rats were streaming in their direction, but he did know he didn't want those damned things invading his ship, just as they appeared to be invading the port. "Sound the call to close up and to pull away from the dock."

The officer on deck or OOD, Urban Patel, didn't hesitate, slapping a big red button on a panel below him, which sounded the horns announcing their departure. The deep blare of their ship's horns was loud even in the protected confines of the bridge.

Usually Security Chief Spillman, who was MIA at this moment, would ring the second officer on duty at the gangway entrance. So Wasano Agarwal, the first officer of security and now senior on the bridge, followed protocol and picked up the ringing phone. "Close up, now! Pull in everyone waiting to board; everyone else who comes after will need to wait."

He hung up the receiver and picked it up again, punching another button on the comm's console. "Close up, leave whatever baggage isn't already on board... No arguments. Do it now!"

"I can confirm the doors are closing," said Jessica Eva Mínervudóttir, first officer of navigation, watching her panel. "The passenger door is closing. The freight doors are already closed."

"Release from the dock now," encouraged the captain.

"What about the pilot boat, sir?" Jean Pierre asked.

"We'll wait just off the dock. I don't want any of those rats on my ship." The captain's head and binoculars were one, aimed like a gun barrel pointed at the leading edge of the first wave of rats fast approaching along the gangway. They seemed to be surging toward them even faster.

He moved over to the exit onto the starboard-side swing deck, to get a better look and to hear what he was seeing. The bridge was soundproof as well as waterproof to protect it during the gales of the heavy storms they sometimes encountered at sea.

The moment the steel hatch cracked open, the frantic sounds of Puerto de Malaga poured into the bridge. The crew peered in the door's direction. For only a few seconds, they paid little attention to their monitors as the outside blared a violent torrent of screams, car crashes, frenzied horns, and something else.

It was a haunting sound: an escalating frenzy that built upon itself; a horrific drumbeat of hundreds of thousands of scampering feet and their corresponding squeaks. A crescendo that grew with each passing second.

The captain could only stand the nightmarish sounds for so long. But before he turned back into the bridge and sealed them once more into their orderly bubble, he caught a quick glance of a sight that would haunt his nights, perhaps for the rest of his life: a couple of dock workers and at least one crew member overwhelmed by blankets of rats.

He had once witnessed the decapitation of a crew member, back when he was a first officer. He always thought that was the most horrible sight he would ever see. This was worse.

Jörgen stepped back onto the bridge and slammed the door, sealing out the chaos. It was the one space over which he had some control. Outside, he had none. He felt the troubled eyes of his crew on him, all wide, and close to panic.

But the quiet was like a balm to their frayed nerves. And the strength of their captain was an elixir.

Captain Christiansen only momentarily flashed anything resembling worry before his usual stern presence stood before them. "Report, how many on board?" He didn't know what the hell was going on out there, but he knew his crew would be able to focus on their duties if he directed them. That would give them all a much-needed sense of control. Duties now; discover what's happening later.

"They're still counting the last few who squeezed aboard when we closed the doors." Jean Pierre fixated on his tablet. It flashed up-to-the-moment details about the ship, its passengers, and its crew. He kept his eyes glued to it for a prolonged period before giving the count, as if staring at it a little longer would somehow increase the dismal numbers. "*So far*," he stressed, "728 guests and 501 crew. Only one cart of luggage didn't make it. And we're fully supplied."

The ship was supposed to have 1525 guests and 700 crew. Most of the missing could be easily attributed to the many flight cancellations. But he also knew others didn't make it because of the rat attacks—still, it seemed utterly ridiculous to even consider that supposition.

"Captain?" Jean Pierre asked. "What should we do now?" This kind of thing—rat attacks and departing early, leaving passengers and crew behind—was not part of their training or experience.

"First Officer Mínervudóttir, call the harbor master and tell them to get the pilot boat here in two minutes or we're plowing through the harbor without him."

"I'm on it, sir," Jessica fired back.

Jean Pierre held his gaze on the captain. "No, sir. I meant what do we do about the missing passengers?"

Captain Jörgen Christiansen looked at each of his crew, who returned his steady glare with apprehension. He'd served with these five men and one woman for almost four years now, and they'd been through a lot, including one hurricane, one rogue wave, even an attempted boarding by terrorists. But none of them had ever been through anything like this.

He learned a long time ago, as he was making the ranks on his way to becoming captain, to deal with what you know. These are the only actions over which you'll ever have control. Don't focus on those things you have no control over. They'll take care of themselves.

"We're going to do our one job now, which is to take care of our current passengers and crew. OOD Patel, please contact corporate and let them know, so they can get help on the ground and make arrangements for the stranded guests. We'll get through this together, okay?"

"Aye, Captain," they responded together.

"Mr. Haddock, can I see you in my ready room?"

~~~

The two marched in and sat at the same conference table they'd met around hundreds of times to discuss everything from the highly significant, like which crew member to fire, to the insignificant, such as whether or not they should give a free spa package to a certain guest to keep them happy. The gravity of what they needed to discuss now weighed heavily on both.

Jörgen hovered for a moment over a side table, slowly pouring equal measures of coffee into two mugs from a carafe that was always kept full and hot by one of his crew. He mindlessly set the full cups down on the conference table. "I wanted to speak to you before the rest of the crew about some troubling issues ahead of us, which are going to come to light soon." He took the seat beside his number one, grabbed his Uffda coffee mug and sipped the hot liquid.

"You mean more troubling than a swarm of rabid rats attacking our guests and crew?" Jean Pierre didn't want any coffee. He was fully amped up at this moment, his body providing all the natural stimulant it needed, and so he certainly didn't need caffeine. Besides, Jean Pierre was barely hanging onto his wits, by the edges of his fingernails. He was mere seconds away from drowning in waves of his own fear. He took in quick shuddering breaths, trying to calm himself down.

Jean Pierre knew that it was important to look strong and decisive in front of the rest of the crew, especially on the bridge. His captain had taught him this. But in here, in the captain's ready room, Jean Pierre knew he could be himself, speak his mind, and let his hair down (assuming he had any).
~~~

"Captain, what the hell is going on? If you have additional information, please tell me."

"That's what I wanted to talk to you about," Jörgen paused and gazed at his staff captain. "I don't mind telling you that I'm terrified of what we'll be dealing with in the next few days."

This caught Jean Pierre by complete surprise. He had never thought his captain was afraid of anything. Crazed terrorists proved that to him. Plus, he wasn't speaking about what just happened; he was speaking about what was going to happen.

Jörgen turned on his tablet, scrolled down the screen, and started to read off a laundry list of subjects which normally would be terrifying for any cruise ship, but seemed mellow by comparison to what they were witnessing right now in Malaga.

"We've already spoken about the Icelandic volcano, which is still erupting, and so is Mount Etna. We know these are causing all sorts of navigational difficulties to the north and east. And we must be prepared for the sea traffic, which will be abnormally heavy. But what has me most concerned is the report of tremors on two of the Canaries. There was one report that stated that La Palma might blow any day now. Here it is." Jörgen read the report dispassionately, like he was reading off the daily fuel numbers.

Although he had just said otherwise, Jörgen seemed completely calm. And it was having an effect on Jean Pierre. He could feel his blood pressure simmering and he pushed up straighter in his chair. He no longer felt the uncontrollable panic that was overwhelming him only moments ago, in spite of the terrifying news.

Just then, Jean Pierre realized this was by design.

Jörgen knew him that well, that he obviously saw he was about ready to break. This short time in the ready room was to enable them to take stock of what they knew, as well as what they didn't know. To focus on the ship-related issues and the corresponding actions they would need to take. It was all bad news. But it was factual. They could apply their years of experience to each of these data points and come up with the best solution available. And when new data arrived, they would render similar or different judgments. They would figure it out, together. Just like they always did. They would figure this out too.

"What do the reports for Gibraltar look like tomorrow?" Jean Pierre asked, preparing himself for the worst.

Jörgen tapped a corner of his screen and scanned through the summary provided by Jessica, who besides overseeing navigation looked at weather, currents, ship traffic, and anything else that might affect their successfully making it to the next port on time.

"Looks like smooth sailing. Since we're leaving a little early, we can take our time getting there and assess the situation in the Canaries as we get closer," Jörgen resolved.

"Okay, I'll ask about the horse in the room—"

"—you mean elephant?" Jörgen corrected, smiling at Jean Pierre's misstatement.

Jean Pierre was always trying to improve upon his American idioms, but he still had a ways to go. Since Jörgen was a lover of American culture, he taught Jean Pierre many he hadn't yet heard. This slip would be fast forgotten—Jörgen often kidded him about his slip-ups—because Jean Pierre was not on his A-game. *Another idiom.*

"Yes, the elephant, or rather, thousands of crazy rats..." Jean Pierre trailed off, unsure what to ask.

There was a knock on the door. It was Jessica.

"Sorry to interrupt." She nodded first to Jörgen and then Jean Pierre. "We've released from the port, but we had to abandon our stern line because the dock was overwhelmed by... by the..." She paused, her eyes welled and her lower lip quivered. She recalled the mental picture of the dock workers being attacked, and of the rats running up the line toward the ship. She shook her head. "Sorry. Also, there's no answer from the harbor master—or anyone at the port authority, for that matter. As far as we can tell, the port operators have left the harbor. But there is little to no large traffic right now. Just a few small craft. So I'd recommend we go, while we can." Jessica hesitated at the door, like she held a secret that she wasn't supposed to reveal. "And Staff Captain," she said to Jean Pierre, "Mrs. Williams and her husband did make it on board."

"Thank you, First Officer. Unless there's anything more, we'll be just a minute more," Jörgen replied and waited for his first officer to leave and close the door behind her. When the door clicked closed, he continued. "The rats at this point don't matter, Jean Pierre. I fear it's not the worst thing we'll witness during this cruise." He let his words sink in before continuing.

"But our job is still the same: to keep everyone safe, comfortable and happy. In other words, I want us to do everything we can to keep our guests and crew thinking about anything other than what's going on in the outside world."

"Aye, Captain."

"And find me Spillman!"

05

Robert Spillman

Security Chief Robert Spillman had a secret he was desperate to keep under wraps. His professional life depended on it.

Before his appointment, he waited for the monitor room shift change. When the incoming monitor stood in front of the MR door's small inset window, the outgoing monitor got up and left the room to "pass the baton" or hand over the MR key just outside the door. This process ensured that no more than one monitor was in the room at a time, which Robert argued helped to protect the ship's privacy policy. Actually, Spillman's procedure promoted the breaking of the ship's privacy policy, and that was on purpose.

Usually, the outgoing monitor took the opportunity at this point in the key exchange to also pass on stories about the passengers who did stupid things because they didn't realize they were being watched and recorded on one of the four hundred and sixty cameras spread throughout the ship. Discussing what passengers did on camera during work was against Regal European's policies. But that never stopped

them.

Like Robert, the monitors attempted to keep their "non-work" activities outside the ever-present cameras' purview. Since there were no cameras just outside the MR doorway, the exchange provided the monitors ample opportunity to trade stories and pass notes as to where to find the discussed videos. All video feeds were copied and retained in a multi-terabyte hard drive for the duration of the cruise. The drives were swapped out during the turnover, when a new itinerary started. And then new stupid passenger feeds would be copied and stored again.

While the two monitors were occupied with each other, Robert made sure he wasn't seen and flicked a switch that turned off all the deck 2 cameras. He was purposely quick and stealthy about this, as he only had a few minutes today before the captain noticed he was missing. He also knew the discussion outside wouldn't last as long, as there were no stories yet to tell about this cruise: the passengers were just getting on board.

Once the passengers' lips had become more pliable after the application of the ship's overpriced alcohol and they had tested out the boundaries of the ship, the stories between the incoming and outgoing monitors would be longer and more animated.

He closed the monitor room behind him. His two men's heads snapped to attention, their lips falling quiet at his presence.

He enjoyed this.

"Don't mind me, gents. It's pretty quiet right now, and I won't be back for a while." That was code for, *Screw off as much as you'd like, because I won't be watching over you.*

That would also give him at least ten minutes to do what he needed to do before being seen.

"Thanks Security Chief," they both acknowledged, having difficulty holding back their grins.

Robert took the public elevator down six floors to deck 2 and quickly moved forward through the port-side hallway to the first wall panel, using his master key to open a metal cabinet. Inside, multi-colored wires ran up and down the left side of the long foot-deep enclosure, some stopping midway at a circuit board. This was where various electronics for this hallway were connected to the ship's main lines. He reached in and without hesitation grabbed a blue wire and yanked it out of its board, leaving it just off its connector, as if it had somehow jostled itself loose on its own. This would disable only the port-side, deck 2 hall cameras aft of the elevators.

Soon, his on-duty monitor would notice that deck 2 cameras were black. After flicking them back on, if he was paying attention, he'd notice cameras 63 through 68 were still dark. Once it was confirmed that only these deck 2 cameras weren't working, and it wasn't a connection in the MR, maintenance would be called to investigate. Robert figured he had at least thirty minutes now.

He wouldn't need that long.

He shut the panel and casually walked aft, toward cabin 2071.

A couple lurked around their cabin entrance, in between him and his destination, causing Robert to stop in front of a restricted doorway. Using his card, he unlocked and pushed open the door that warned "Crew Only" and hung inside the small well which gave crew access to a separate elevator and stairwell. It was similar to the passengers' access, but far more utilitarian in design.

He pushed his back into the door, like he was holding it open for a crew member, and listened just out of view for the couple to leave or go back into their cabin. He craned his head forward and cupped a palm around an ear to block out the active chatter coming from above and below him.

The guests closed their door and he heard a female voice say something in German.

He waited for them to turn and exit to the public elevator, a few steps away. They shouldn't even pass by this doorway.

Robert examined his watch, feeling each minute ebb away deep in his groin.

"Hello, Security Chief," sang one of the seventy-five or so room attendants, who came from below and turned to ascend the stairwell like a light breeze on his way to a higher deck. Robert didn't recognize the young Croatian man and guessed he was one of the new crew members, reporting in late. His supervisor would cut him some slack this time, because several of the new crew were late or simply didn't make it because of the flight delays.

"Excuse me," a heavyset man said—everyone who took a cruise was heavyset in Robert's opinion. "Where pool?" The man had a distinctive German accent and obviously a poor command of the English language. There would be a lot of Germans on board this cruise, as the cruise line heavily advertised in Germany.

He almost grunted his reply, but corrected himself quickly. "Take the lift you just passed on your left, and go up seven floors to deck nine. Then walk aft maybe fifty steps and it's right there." Robert said this with a fake smile, pointing down the hall. He wanted to say to them, "Can't you read a fucking map, you stupid krauts?" He didn't like German cruisers much. They expected perfection from everyone, except themselves.

"Danke," said the woman, who had to be at least twice the man's size. They both waddled away, clutching their room towels. Cruisers always brought their room towels to the pool, even though the pool provided towels for them so that they wouldn't ruin the ones from their room. Not that they cared.

He closed the crew-access door and waited for the unbearably slow German couple to exit.

Finally, they left the hallway.

Robert moved abruptly, like a thoroughbred horse bursting from its starting gate.

Better yet, a stud seeking his mare.

There was no one else in the hallway, plus he had very little time now. He was anxious to get started and not suffer through any more delays that would lessen his time of pleasure. He almost jogged the hundred-yard space to the cabin door, tossing a quick glance at the mostly hidden camera above, which he knew wasn't working.

He pulled out a different card he'd retained from a fired employee and slipped it into the door, the lock blinking green, telling him he could enter. He let the door shut on its own. The cabin was mostly dark, with both the curtains and the sheers drawn. A small electronic candle pulsed a flicker from the desk area, casting just enough light to see the outline of the bed. This was funny since he didn't need any mood lighting. He just wanted sex.

"You late. You get in my bed now," said Chen Lee in her poor impression of a sultry voice.

He slipped off his clothes and slid into bed, instantly feeling her warmth as she wrapped her arms and legs around him.

He had barely fifteen minutes now, so their lovemaking would have to be quick.

06

Deep

"Dammit!" croaked Whaudeep Reddy, or Deep as the other crew called him, banging the flat-screen monitor, as if that would make it work again.

He grabbed the radio microphone, switched to the channel monitored by maintenance and said, "Hey, this is Deep in security. Buzz, are you there?"

"I'm here," crackled Buzz. He had a longer name that none of the Anglos could pronounce, and since he was the expert at making all things electrical work on the ship, everyone called him Buzz. Both were on their ninth contracts and they'd worked together on the Intrepid all nine years. "What's up, Deep?"

"The deck 2 hall cameras are down again. I thought your guys had fixed this." Deep wasn't accusing his friend, or his mates. But he did want him to know his level of frustration over one of the many things that didn't seem to work on their fifteen-year-old ship. And this was even after their ship had just come out of dry-dock, where so many things had been replaced and cleaned up.

"Sorry, Deep, I did too. I'll check it out myself this time."

"Thanks, Buzz. Hey, I have three for the game tonight."

Deep and Buzz had an ongoing card game almost every night in the crew living room, especially when they were on the same shift, as they were on this itinerary.

"Excellent. See you after the change. Buzz out."

Deep almost jumped out of his seat when he realized the staff captain had quietly entered the MR while he was on the radio. Or was it before? He immediately felt his mouth dry up like the desert: the second in command of the ship just heard him talk about their card game. They were not allowed to gamble on the ship, so they used a system of old ravioli noodles, colored to represent different denominations. Either Buzz or he kept a tally of winners and losers. All who played that week would settle up each Friday at the Slop House—the crew's mini-market—where the loser would buy the winner the equivalent number of desired products using their Regal European Seacards. They played the game in plain sight, so that everyone thought they were just playing for the fun of it. But he always wondered when one of their superiors would find out.

"Sir." He stood up to greet the ship's second in command, his right knee banging loudly against his work table. "I'm sorry, I didn't hear you come in." His voice cracked.

"Please sit down. I didn't want to interrupt you. What's going on with the deck 2 cameras?" Jean Pierre now stood over the young man and glared at the deck 2 monitor, which was black and then flashed images of the starboard cabins, then the forward cabins, aft, then it was dark again.

"Don't know exactly. When I came onto shift, the switches were off for Decks Two and Five. When I switched them back on, deck 2 never fully came on. We had this same problem yesterday and the day before. So I'm having maintenance look into it again. Well, you probably heard that part."

Jean Pierre seemed to think about this for a moment and then asked, "Is the security chief around?"

"Ahh, I saw him up here right when I came on shift, but I'm not sure where he went. Do you want me to call him for you?"

"No, that won't be necessary. Actually, I wanted to see the tape on deck 7, the aft suites, for the last hour or so. Can you pull that up for me?"

Deep tossed him a curious glance before working his magic. The staff captain almost never examined video recordings. That's what the security chief would do, and usually only after one of the passengers had done something to warrant the attention. Deep wanted to take advantage of this rare opportunity to show off his talents to his superior and he started to relax a little, thinking maybe he dodged a bullet on their illegal card game. He knew right where to look for this video, having brought up passenger recordings thousands of times at the insistence of Fish, who had the shift before him, especially tapes of the pretty ones.

Fish, or Fish-Eye as he was called by his mates, had already made a listing of the times and camera numbers for the feeds Deep needed to examine to see the beauties who had checked into their cabins. Today's listings were for the deck 7 aft and deck 8 forward cameras. Deep hadn't planned on taking a look at these until after he'd been on his shift for a few hours, when he knew no one else would be checking in on him.

"Here sir," he said, setting the video replay on 4X, so they could cover the span of an hour in fifteen minutes. Any faster and they'd miss something.

Less than five minutes later, the staff captain had him stop and view it in real time. Yes, Deep thought, just as his friend Fish told him. *She is beautiful, for an older woman. And she is blond!* He loved blondes.

07

TJ and Ted
4:27 PM

Without missing a step, she flicked her blonde hair back over her shoulder.

They marched aft, down the long hallway, over the ridiculously-colored carpet. Ted trailed behind, their rollered bags squealing their displeasure behind him.

"I just want to get to our room and drink heavily," Ted said.

"I think 7652 is right down here," she mumbled, glancing at her Seacard once again for confirmation, even though she knew only the last two digits appeared on it.

"So the last thing I want to do is clink glasses with strangers tonight, or with the captain tomorrow, and all the while pretend everything is good with the world."

"Here it is right here, corner balcony," she emoted, all too chipper considering what they just went through.

"Have you heard a word I've said?"

"Yep, every one." She slid her card into the card reader.

A little green light pulsed a confirmation that it was the right one, and she pushed the door open a crack.

"Fine, I'm dumping my bag and bellying up to the Irish pub I saw on the ship's map."

"Okay, if that's what you want to do," she said, not even allowing a wisp of emotion to salt her words. She took her bag from him, pulled it through the narrow doorway into the room and let the heavy door flop back, like a Venus flytrap. It thumped closed on her husband.

A few seconds later, the lock clicked open. Ted withdrew his card and pushed open the door. "Man, you piss me off sometimes." His voice imitated hot, but he wasn't really that fiery.

"I know, that's why you love me." She flashed a playful smile at him.

She was very familiar with this game. Ted often played the victim in circumstances such as these, when he didn't want to deal with other people, especially a lot of people. The victim thing—which he played rather poorly—was in hopes of garnering enough sympathy from her to release him from tonight's dinner with a table full of strangers or that he'd be let out of his obligation with the captain tomorrow night. But she needed him to keep up appearances and although she rarely participated, she couldn't completely shut him down now as she often would in these kinds of circumstances.

She snickered again, and then suppressed her smile, pretending serious. "Look, if you want to go on a binge or continue your anti-social behavior on my vacation, and on our anniversary, I'm not going to stop you. We can order room service tonight, but don't think you're going to abandon me to a dinner that was set up in your honor tomorrow. And don't forget the captain is a big fan of yours. You wouldn't want to let one of your biggest fans down, would you?" She batted her eyes at him for effect.

Then she did turn somewhat serious.

"And as far as the drinking goes, I'm the one who's going to be pissed if you don't take me with you drinking. After almost getting eaten by Cujo, then a flock of fucking seagulls and then a billion damned Bens, I need to do some heavy drinking myself."

Ted didn't say anything in rebuttal, pretending to examine the couch, while she quickly started the process of unpacking. She often would do busy things when she was anxious.

She paused and glared at him for a long moment before continuing.

"And before we both get slobbery drunk, you need to make sure I can call Mom. I can't figure out the damned ship's cell service. Even though we texted our families, I just want her to hear my voice before she reads about any of this, whatever *this is*."

Ted plopped into the couch and just nodded. They'd been married long enough for him to know when she was releasing her pent-up worries, it was best to just let her finish before he said anything.

She wasn't done, but flicked her hair once again, not for show but because it bothered her. It wasn't tied up into her normal ponytail, the way she liked it. She was trying to be a little more dolled up for their cruise.

"Finally, and speaking of almost getting eaten, are we going talk about what we've witnessed the last thirty-six hours and what's going on?"

Ted removed his ball cap and ran a hand through his thinning black hair. That was his tell that he was deliberately considering what she had said, and he was choosing his words carefully.

"Can we decompress about all of this later? I still need to consider a few things. Maybe tomorrow?"

It was the way Ted's mind processed things—like an engineer, very methodically. He never rushed to judgment. He was always stable like that. And although it was what she preferred, she sometimes wished he'd act irrational, just a little.

"Fine. I'm going for a run, then." She moved toward the bathroom, mumbling something unintelligible about needing a busy activity to occupy her mind and an errand she needed to take care of before dinner.

He watched her reach into her bag and precisely find and snatch out her running shorts and sport shirt, as if the bag had handed these items to her.

She disappeared into the bathroom, leaving Ted to himself.

~~~

Ted marveled at her organization. Even though their main checked bag, with all their formal clothes, hadn't arrived yet—he wondered if it ever would, based on their abrupt exit from the port—she packed exactly what she needed in her carry-on, and had it placed exactly where she needed it. She'd probably be fine if their main bag never arrived. His stuff was separated unequally between the checked bag and his carry-on; he couldn't even say what was in each. He'd unpack later.

Far more interesting to Ted was what awaited him on the small built-in desk/dressing table. It had mirrors and compartments too small to hold anything useful. More practical was the desk's center, where three bottles of red wine were displayed on a tray. And beside it, a leather-bound notebook.

"All right, now we're talking," he said, mostly to himself, since TJ was out of earshot.

A noise like a muted rocket ship engine blasted away from inside the bathroom. He couldn't help but break a smile at
~~~

the sound of the turbo toilet, wondering how startling that must have been to some first-timers who used it. TJ had been on many cruises before they met, so that noise was probably old hat to her.

Enough of this. Time to drink.

He turned his attention back to the wine mirage and plucked an envelope sandwiched between two of the bottles. After noticing the RE logo on the top left corner, he pulled out a hand-written note card and paraphrased it loud enough so that she could hear him inside the bathroom. "The captain wants to welcome us on board with these three bottles of wine."

Using the corkscrew—also monogrammed with the solid white on dark blue Regal European logo—he yanked out the cork, and poured half a glass of the red cab. He'd prefer she'd join him in this, but knew she wouldn't have one until after she finished her run. He couldn't wait that long.

In the small open area of the desk, he unfolded his iPad, turned it on, and loaded a copy of his second-to-last book, along with all of his notes.

He sipped the wine and glanced down at the healthy streak left on the side of the glass. It was a bit harsh, but it would do just fine thank you. He took a larger sip.

With eyes focused on his iPad, he went directly to the Research area of his Scrivener program, and opened the document on toxoplasmosis.

Another sip of wine.

"Oh shit," he muttered.

He swallowed the rest of the glass of his wine, no longer tasting it or feeling its warmth in his belly. His ball cap came off again; he put his glass down and massaged his aching temples.

TJ popped out of the bathroom a new woman: her lipstick freshened, her hair pulled back into a tight ponytail, and her slim figure perfectly highlighted by her running outfit.

Ted watched her move with quick determination, briefly

admiring his wife's athletic physique, before he turned his attention back to his iPad.

She thrust the clothes she'd been wearing—folded neatly, almost creased—into the already opened small closet, laying them neatly on a middle shelf, and walked over to Ted. "Save some for me, dear." She smiled and pecked him on the lips, turned and marched out the door.

He needed more wine.

~~~

TJ had intended to head up to the sun deck, two decks above them, and go for a run. Then she had a meet-up with a ship's officer. But she only made it three steps out of their cabin before she stopped dead. There were dogs barking.

Her head snapped in the direction of an open crew access door. A small man with a big smile was pushing a service cart her way. She wasn't paying him any attention, because her mind was busy attempting to confirm what she thought she had heard. Before the rats attacked the port, they had seen the dog crates being ushered on board. But only now did it connect: these dogs were on her ship, that was their barking, and they could be loose.

That's when the memory flooded back all at once. She had thought she had long since suppressed this, burying it deep down where it would no longer hurt her. She squeezed her eyes shut and desperately tried to think of anything else. Still the memories came: the images, the sounds, the smells... and the fear.

TJ had been in Chicago as part of a larger investigation of Cleavon Drummond, or *Cleavon the Cannibal*, as the media later called him. One of Cleavon's victims was from Tucson and so TJ had flown out to work with their team in Chicago. The
~~~

next day, they had a warrant for one of Cleavon's suspected locations. Her Chicago equal, Agent Little, and she were going to cover the back of the property. What their sources never told them was that Cleavon owned several vicious dogs tied off by the exit. Unfortunately for Agent Little, he surprised the dogs. More unfortunate was TJ's deathly fear of animals, and most especially dogs, since it was a dog which had viciously attacked her years earlier. She had hung back behind a dumpster when the animals struck. Even though she was supposed to cover him, she froze. She even retreated farther behind the dumpster to get away from the animals.

The dogs tore the agent apart, and she did nothing.

His screams were heard for blocks and other agents came running.

But it was too late.

Agent Little died on the scene and TJ remained in her spot, cowering behind the dumpster, shaking like a leaf in October.

A Chicago PD officer helped her up, though not before commenting, "I sure as hell wouldn't want you backing me up." Turned out that wouldn't be a problem anymore, because after that, TJ had been relieved of her fieldwork.

She froze, and Agent Little died.

"Ms. Williams," called a voice in the distance.

TJ blinked her eyes. She came out of her vivid daydream and found herself nearly hyperventilating.

"Ms. Williams, are you all right?" begged the little man standing in front of her. He'd swapped his willful smile for genuine concern.

"Yes. Thank you." she answered, in a voice that didn't sound like her own. "I'm sorry..." she tried to focus on the man's badge, but was having difficulty."

"I'm *Jagamashi*, but you can call me Jaga."

He was an Indo, she thought. She started to feel a little more... normal. *"Ah, terima kasih, Jaga,"* TJ replied.

"Sama-sama, Ms. Williams. *Senang sekali bisa ngobrol dengan orang yang bisa berba-hasa Indonesia."* Jaga smiled genuinely. (Thank you, Ms. Williams. It's so nice to speak to someone who understands Indo.)

"Bahasa Indonesia saya tidak terlalu bagus." TJ chuckled quietly and shrugged. (My Indo is not that good). She was surprised the language had come back from her time in Indonesia.

She took a deep breath. "Thanks Jaga. Speaking to you in Indonesian really helped. Ah, before you go, check in on my husband. He has some questions about room service and I know he'd like some ice."

"Of course. *Sama-sama*, Ms. Williams."

"Makasih, Jaga." She smiled and then jogged past Jaga in the direction he had come, tossing a side-glance at the now-closed crew access door. She was glad she had some work after her run. She needed to focus on anything but crazy dogs.

08

The Dogs

Allegro Palmigren Ramgoolam—guests were thankful he went by, Al—loved what he did, especially at times like this.

When he entered the giant thoroughfare known as I-95, the internal "road" which traversed the *Intrepid* from bow to stern, he only heard the muffled mechanical thrum of the ship's powerful engines. Maybe two hours earlier, these spacious halls had been a buzz of activity as many of the officers and crew found their way to all parts of the ship, out of sight of the ship's guests.

A noxious combination of grease and oil filled Al's nostrils. He shot a scornful glance at a chin-high box filled with mechanical parts and gave a tug on the master leash. His canine charges were unrulier than usual.

The box was one of many organized discards which awaited recycling when they ported in Miami fourteen days from now. Even though the cruise had just started, this stretch of hallway was already lined with pallets of various items slated for the same purpose: corrugated boxes, strapped tight into a human-sized square; a multi-colored rectangle of pressed aluminum cans, which reflected dull spikes of hallway light as he walked by; and maybe a dozen other various boxes, the contents of which he didn't know. By the end of the cruise, every square meter of wall surface throughout this vast network of hallways would be crowded with recyclables and other discards.

A crash and a series of thumps in the distance drew his and the dogs' attention.

An unruly toy poodle barked at the unseen clatter and it shot forward, pulling the collection of dogs and Al with it. Al gave a mighty tug on the master leash, which was connected to all the individual leashes, which were connected to each dog's choke-chain. "Heel," he boomed his command.

The pack halted instantly.

The little white poodle, the perpetrator of this undisciplined instigation, coughed twice and then sat its haunches on the gray laminate floor, panting its displeasure at being restrained roughly. The other dogs followed suit.

And so ended the first lesson in tonight's series of lessons, for Al to establish himself as the pack's alpha dog.

"Hello Al." A tall Croatian crew member in a black jumper strode by. The mechanic's head snapped forward after admiring the pack's obedience, and then he turned into a connecting hallway, the echoes of his black Dickies already trailing off into the expanse. Al didn't know the mechanic, other than he was probably from engineering based on his uniform. But the mechanic obviously knew Al.

A chasm-sized smile of bright white spread across Al's face.

Having one of the few pet kennels on any cruise ship, filled Al with a large measure of pride. He often enjoyed boasting on phone calls or on social media to his family and friends in Mauritius, as well as to other crew members, that he had the most unique job among all cruise lines. This wasn't an exaggeration, since other than RE's *Intrepid*, the only other cruise ship that could claim a pet kennel was the QE2.

Al was also prideful of how well he did his job, the proof of which was evidenced by the generous tips he often received and the many positive comments sent into corporate about him and his pet spa. Regal European responded with elevations in title and pay, lots of praise, and recognition among his shipmates. Corporate even offered to give Al a number of staff befitting his position. He had heard that some in corporate felt a second officer shouldn't be walking dogs, or cleaning cages. But Al preferred to do this job himself. So he operated solo.

But the real secret to Al's success was in how he handled the guests. As he told his mother many times on the phone, it basically came down to giving guests what they wanted, at least in their minds.

Usually the guests stressed over their pet's wellbeing while on the ship, and this was where it would seem (to the guests) that Al focused most of his attention: what food the animal was eating—he ordered food in advance from many specialty outlets all over the world, for which RE charged a generous mark-up; how often they were being fed—he was very careful with this; whether they were getting enough sleep-time—"It's their vacation too," he'd tell the owners; if the other animals were being mean to their pet—"Absolutely not!" he'd insist to them; whether the animals were watching the right programs on TV—"Because they all had their own favorite programs," he'd mimic in a comedic voice to his family through their laughter; the number of times they saw a picture of their "mommy" or "daddy"—the pet's parents always had a specific number in mind; and so many more requirements imposed by the guests on him for the care of their pets. But this was where Al had a secret which helped him excel.

He learned to take copious notes of the guest's instructions and concerns and he made sure to repeat them back to the guests. That way the guests believed their wishes were going to be fulfilled to the fullest measure, even if Al was lax on some of their standards. As he had told his family, "What they don't know won't hurt them." And he could tell pretty quickly what he could get away with and what he couldn't, based on the pet and their owner.

And as a trained and certified vet, Al was also adept at caring for the animals' medical needs.

Most of these animals—typically dogs—were very pampered by their owners, and almost all just wanted attention: they suffered from separation anxiety, especially after being dumped at the kennel. But they also suffered from a sense of being the most important entity in the owner's household, sometimes to the detriment of the owner's own children. It was this pet-centric thinking and the lack of training that led to the pet's overall lack of discipline.

And so the first walk of the cruise was critical.

He always conducted the first walk late during the first night of the cruise. That would allow him to take control over his boarders without any interference from the pets' owners or any well-intentioned crew who might wander by and offer scorn for his seemingly rough methods. He never did anything to harm an animal. It wasn't in his nature. But since most of his boarded pets were undisciplined, just like their owners, he often needed to be aggressive by showing them who was in control.

And there was always that one pet that didn't do what it was told.

This time it was the white-colored toy poodle, owned by a wealthy Brit traveling to one of her homes in the states—he had yet to meet her. Her equally pampered dog, Monsieur, had its own ideas about where they should go. To prove this, the poodle rose and attempted to take off again. But Al wouldn't have it. Snapping back on just Monsieur's leash caused the little dog to once again gasp for air.

It would eventually learn.

Al looked up, and saw the signs pointing to various crew rest areas: The Living Room, the Slop House, and so many other areas all dedicated to the crew. From this point forward to the bow of the ship, he'd experience more crew than he wanted: he just didn't want to find himself under the scrutiny of others while he was training the dogs. And he still had a lot of work ahead of him. Al glared at the poodle, about ready to wander off again.

"Heel!" He tugged hard on the master leash. Two of the dogs yelped in surprise and instantly came to attention. Monsieur went the other way—again.

"Dammit!" he hollered as the little rascal once more tried to dart toward another hallway. *This dog has some of the worst shiny ball syndrome I've ever seen.*

Al did a quick 180, making sure what he did next wasn't seen. He reached over the other dogs' leashes to make sure he grabbed only the poodle's leash and gave an enormous tug. Like a giant rubber-band had broken, little Monsieur snapped back into the air and then tumbled to the feet of the others. A Shepherd in the group unceremoniously stepped on top of the dog—Al would have sworn it was vindictive. The little dog yelped and then attempted to dart away in the other direction, tangling all of their leashes into a web of leather spaghetti.

"No!"

He'd have to untangle this mess quickly, before he lost further control of the situation.

One by one, he unleashed a dog, untangled the leash and reattached the dog to the master leash. When he unhooked Monsieur's leash, the little dog unexpectedly bolted through Al's grip. A flash of white scurried away, then down the hall it had been angling toward the whole time.

Al knew why: this hall contained all the food storage on the ship.

Thinking quickly, he attached the master leash to an orange strap binding two boxes bursting with discarded wood furniture pieces. He trotted after the poodle. The dog, already out of sight, seemed to be hot on the trail of something: no doubt some of the ship's food.

That little dog is about to experience the wrath of Al, he thought as he stomped off after the mutt.

As Al came around several pallets of canned food, he found the poodle. It had stopped in front of the opening of the butcher's area, and was growling a face full of little teeth.

Al proceeded toward the beastie, figuring he could grab it while the dog's attention was on the doorway.

Cold from the refrigerated area met the warm hallway air, condensing it into billowing clouds of dense fog, making the inside invisible. The dog seemed fixated on what was inside.

Now was Al's best chance.

He slowed his pace, meticulously placing one foot in front of the other, to not startle the animal while it was preoccupied with the fog. When he was a couple of feet behind the unsuspecting pooch, he leapt. At the same time, Monsieur decided to dart inside the milky murk.

Al didn't even lay a finger on him.

He glared at the opening shrouded in white mist. He couldn't see a thing.

He had never been inside the butcher's area where they stored the ship's beef, in which one butcher cut up all the meat before sending the cuts to one of the ship's three galleys. Al was a vegetarian, so he'd never had an interest in venturing inside. Now he wished he had.

As he stepped into the vapor, he immediately ran into a table with lumps of beef randomly strewn around it. An icicle of pain dug into his hip.

It occurred to him then that the butcher couldn't have operated in this near invisibility. One of the freezers inside must be open and none of the lights were on. Al squinted his eyes tighter and could only make out that there were one or two large shapes further away. Their images were fuzzy, almost ethereal.

"Hello?" he begged, thrusting his hands out to block anything he might run into, and continued around the table. Now he could only make out the dark sticks of his arms and the two approaching shapes. Then he wondered how he would even see Monsieur. By every measure, he was blind.

"Monsieur," he called out as he moved deeper into the room. He remembered overhearing that it was three rooms in one: a preparation room that he was walking through, one refrigerated storage room full of meat, already prepared and ready to be cooked, and one freezer. He couldn't tell which or if both were opened.

The two shapes, he suspected, were by the cold storage. They were also bigger than he'd thought.

And they almost seemed to be... moving.

Al felt his way around until he reached one of the two shapes. His heart rose up as he touched it. Cold.

It was a side of beef, hanging from the ceiling.

Taking in a breath of the room's arctic-like air, and feeling more confident, he pushed forward to what he guessed was the open freezer.

It was a good thing he held his hands out like bumpers, because both his feet tripped over something—*probably another side of beef on the ground, only defrosted*—and he cartwheeled forward. He would have hit the hard floor face first, but his palms and elbows took the fall, and banged loudly.

Electric jolts of agony shot up from his elbows.

He breathed out a puff of frothy air, relieved that only his elbows absorbed the landing, and not his head. Then he gasped.

Just in front of him was a small object. At first, he thought it was another piece of meat that had fallen to the floor, only smaller. He still couldn't see anything in this white soup.

He reached out with a finger and touched it, retreating

back instantly, as if the object had snapped at him.

It was warm, and furry. Not what he expected.

Panicked, thinking it might be Monsieur, he unhooked his feet from what had tripped him up and scurried forward on his elbows to get a closer look.

"Mon-sewer?" he begged, his voice cracking. He didn't want it to be true.

"Yip-yip-yip," shrieked a reply from the murk.

Al caught a flash of movement in front of him, then over him, and then behind him—a frightened sounding yip trailing behind, and then exiting the door both the dog and Al had entered.

He tried to turn toward the escaping animal to get a glimpse, to confirm his hope. He still couldn't see past his knees. But he was pretty sure it was Monsieur. He is all right.

The chill of the floor and the frosty air all around started to seep into him, making him shiver.

He had almost forgotten about the soft furry thing he had thought was Monsieur, but now confirmed it wasn't. Then he was jolted with the thought that what had he touched wasn't the dog, but something else entirely.

He turned back with trepidation to see and was rocked once more.

It was a dead rat. Worse yet, half a dead rat. Its head was cleaved off.

Al shrank back in revulsion, pushing himself up so that he was again standing. More like wobbling.

Rubbing feeling back into his legs and hands, he tried to get his mind around what a still warm beheaded rat was doing inside the near-frozen butcher's area.

Scurrying sounds and an unmistakable squeak yanked his head up toward the open freezer.

Like a thunderbolt, Al exploded from the floor.

He wasn't much of a runner, but he was quite sure that it took him less than a second to find the exit, and close the solid door behind him. This was despite his tripping again over the body of the dead butcher—his mind didn't even offer an alternative to it being anything other than a fallen side of beef.

Al remained in front of the butcher's door, bent over puffing, his lungs gasping for air.

When he heard a muddled whimper below him, his heart practically leapt out of his body, thinking it must be another rat. But right away Al could see it was the toy poodle. It rubbed up against him, acting like it had done nothing wrong.

Then he saw the blood.

He reached down and scooped up the animal, and noticed that the little guy's paw was bleeding, although not badly. He did a quick wrap, using one of the plastic bags he carried to pick up any of the feces his boarders left during their walk. He'd have to clean up the dog's wound tonight and cover it. And less savory, he'd have to explain to the owner what had happened when she visited tomorrow.

"Come on, you little monster. Quit complaining."

He connected the leash to Monsieur's collar and ushered the pack back in the direction of the spa.

He was so focused on the dogs, he didn't even think to report the rats and the open freezer until the next day. It wouldn't have mattered if he had. A few minutes after Al and the dogs departed, an unsuspecting member of the kitchen crew tasked with getting a few more select cuts of meat for a specialty restaurant would open the sealed butcher's door and find a terrifying surprise.

09

Crew Mess

Flavio Petrovich from Romania—as it said on his name-badge—was headed to the crew mess carrying with him a giant attitude and an even larger headache.

He had just finished his shift, after being stuck training the world's dumbest person: *Chichi Vega from Chile*. Chichi had zero experience in the dining room, while Flavio had years of it. Naturally, the powers that be stuck them together for the rest of this itinerary, and maybe the rest of his contract. And to make matters worse, Chichi spent most of her time gabbing with the guests, instead of doing her job. She'd "Ooh" and "Ahh" at the guests' stories about rats and birds, while Flavio had to do his job and hers.

He had no appetite, but knew if he didn't eat, his migraine would get much worse. With his head down, seething with anger, he marched to the mess.

It was late. And as expected, the only sounds he heard were the echoes of his rapid footfalls, marching with him down the giant hallway. It was his preferred time to eat: long after the MDR shut down and most of the crew had already eaten and moved on to either their next shifts or their bunks to get some needed sleep before their shifts started again. Eating now meant that he missed out on many of the food options offered to the crew during the prime time. And there were quite a few, although not as many as what was offered their guests above. It was okay though, as Flavio didn't care for most of the offerings by this head chef, who was English. Flavio did not care for British food, and cared for this chef even less. He often stated flatly to his fellow crew, "How many culinary schools do you hear coming from London versus Paris?"

Eating late did have its benefits, though: there were fewer crew members around, which meant it was quiet. And after a day of noisy guests and dealing with Chichi from Chile, he could use some quiet time. It also gave him the chance to watch what he wanted on the satellite TV without having to haggle with the others over what should be on. One thing he always found interesting on this ship was that the crew had far more options on their satellite TV then the guests had on their own, including the news. But tonight, he wasn't interested in the news. He just wanted to get a little spicy Thai food (there was always an offering of Thai food, no matter the time of day), eat in quiet, and then return to his cabin and get some sleep. He was exhausted.

He considered what the captain announced to the crew, about many of their fellow crew not making it onto the ship because of flight cancellations and other oddities. Flavio felt pretty sure this was just some bullshit excuse the cruise line used to take advantage of workers like him, who were already working extra shifts. He was always telling others how the cruise line was trying to screw him and his fellow workers.

He realized his headache was really killing him. He might have to take his food back to his room and eat in the dark.

Flavio pushed through the door marked "Pub," which led to a combo pub and lounge area with comfy chairs and a giant flat-screened TV. It was a great place to get a drink, if he did that, and hang out with friends—he didn't have many. The beer was cheap: about a euro versus the eight euros the ship charged their guests. At least this was one way the ship didn't take advantage of its crew.

As Flavio stepped inside, he immediately saw something odd: there were dozens of crew here, even though it was so late. Usually there were only one or two, at the most. All were clustered around the flat-screened TV on the wall. Also odd was that they weren't watching the usual American soap opera or what they called "Reality TV." They were all watching the news.

He gazed at the screen showing Fox News with several people arguing about something he couldn't really hear over the crew's chatter, while a crawl of news points slid across the bottom of the screen...

"Animal attacks continue throughout Europe: four confirmed killed in Paris dog attacks... Rats attack city of Malaga, Spain..." Report after report spoke about animal attacks, over several places in Europe.

He hmphed in disinterest, and then turned back to the mess entrance to get his Thai chicken. The animal attacks were a concern, but not a big one to him because he and the others were on this ship for the next two weeks, headed to America and then the Caribbean, not Europe—where all the attacks were occurring. Now if they had this problem on the ship, then it might draw his interest.

When Flavio entered the crew mess he felt his anger grow even more. The trays that were supposed to hold assortments of food were empty. Other than a bowl of fruit and some desiccated Danishes, there was nothing. He saw a skinny dark-skinned man wearing the white uniform of a sous chef shoot him a glance before returning to his busy work.

"Hey, what am I supposed to eat?" Flavio was almost surprised to hear he was yelling at the man, who kept his back to him, clanging pans and pots. "I'm talking to you. Do I look like some monkey? You must think so if I have only bananas and other fruit to eat."

The skinny man finally acknowledged Flavio, but he kept his back to him. "You miss dinner time. We all closed up. Come back in morning."

There was a commotion in the pub area, probably some numbskulls fighting it out over what channel to watch.

He was too tired to fight with this man, not that it would make any difference nor get him his food. He'd go up to one of the main galleys and grab some of the food offered to the guests. Crew weren't supposed to do that, but the kitchens were supposed to feed him too. The ship's worry, not his.

Flavio pushed back through the crew mess entry and halted in the doorway, momentarily stunned.

Rather than the futile brawl he'd expected, he was shocked to see that the men and women who'd been sitting in chairs passively gawking at the TV were now spasmodically dashing around the lounge, like some wild version of musical chairs—without the music—attempting to get away from... What were those things?

Rats?

He hated rats.

They were dirty and disgusting animals. They brought disease and filth with them, and they most certainly didn't belong on his ship.

He withdrew a knife—he always kept a steak knife sheathed to his body—and held it in a reverse defensive grip.

Flavio blinked back his headache and marched toward the melee. He'd kill every last one of these things if he had to. Then, he'd get his meal.

DAY THREE

THE CAPTAIN'S MORNING ADDRESS BLARED, JUST OUTSIDE THE CABIN. NOT WANTING TO MISS IT, I RACED TO OPEN THE DOOR.

THESE WERE HIS WORDS, MORE OR LESS.

"GOOD MORNING, GUESTS OF THE INTREPID. THIS IS YOUR FRIENDLY CAPTAIN, JÖRGEN CHRISTIANSEN, COMING TO YOU FROM THE BRIDGE.

"WE ARE PRESENTLY LOCATED AT 36 DEGREES, 30 MINUTES NORTH BY 4 DEGREES, 30 MINUTES WEST AND ON A SOUTHWESTERLY COURSE AT TEN KNOTS. AS WE SLICE THROUGH THE OCEAN, JUST OFF THE SPANISH COAST TO OUR NORTH, WE WILL PASS BY FUENGIROLA SHORTLY. AT THIS CURRENT PACE, WE WILL ARRIVE AT THE BARBARY COAST TOMORROW AS SCHEDULED.

"TODAY SHOULD BE A CALM DAY AT SEA, WITH THE CURRENT TEMPERATURE OF TEN DEGREES CELSIUS OR FIFTY DEGREES FAHRENHEIT. AS WE ATTEMPT TO GET AHEAD OF THE CLOUD LAYERS WHICH SEEM TO BE KEEPING OUR TEMPERATURES DOWN A LITTLE, PLEASE ENJOY ALL THE ACTIVITIES IN ALL OUR LOUNGES. AND TO CELEBRATE OUR FIRST DAY AT SEA, TEQUILA SHOTS WILL BE ON SALE ALL DAY LONG FOR ONLY $5—I MIGHT HAVE ONE OF THOSE WITH YOU... JUST KIDDING.

"HAVE A FANTASTIC DAY ON THE HAPPIEST SHIP ON THE OCEAN, THE INTREPID, REGAL EUROPEAN'S SHINING STAR OF THE SEAS."

10

All Access Tour

The All Access Tour was supposed to have taken place near the last day of their cruise, but it ended up being pushed up to the second day for reasons unknown. Only later would they realize the tour would save their lives.

Last night, while eating, Ted confided in TJ that there were only three activities on this cruise which interested him: his time with her, the periods of ocean-churning inspiration while writing on their balcony, and the All Access Tour. The tour offered an exclusive look inside the bowels of the ship, a behind-the-scenes peek into what made a cruise ship tick. And only a few people were given this opportunity, if it was even offered during a cruise; because of security concerns, the tour was considered a privilege that did not come cheap. On this ship, participants would have to pony up $160 US, per person. Ted would have gladly paid more.

After they finished their room service, a call on their house phone informed them that the tour would take place at "9 AM sharp, tomorrow," their two spots were reserved, and it was gratis to them.

Anxious for the superficial respite before bed, they argued over the reasons for the free passes. Was it a gift from the captain, "because the captain is your biggest fan" as TJ loved to chide? Or was it additional compensation, as Ted argued, for his giving a lecture in a couple of days? They'd ask the captain to settle this dispute when they saw him at tomorrow's dinner.

Neither of them slept well that night. Ted spent more mental time puzzling over trivial matters—any excuse to avoid their larger worries. Before he settled into a fitful sleep, he wondered why he was so excited about the tour. He wasn't particularly interested in ships, or cruising. It was only because of his agent, and later, his wife's insistence that he even agreed to go on this cruise.

When the "restricted" doorway opened into another world occupied only by the ship's crew, Ted hearkened back to a childhood memory when he gazed into the glass ant farm, a thin layer of soil between two panes in a wooden frame. He remembered the thrill he had, with face pressed against the glass, knowing that he was witnessing the buzz of activity usually unseen by mere humans above ground. He felt the same sudden excitement now witnessing the unseen buzz of crew activity—the ship's worker ants.

Almost immediately, the apocalyptic worries of the outside world were forgotten, or at least pushed aside for later. They were replaced by the surge of questions he and his fellow tour-takers hurled at Stephanie, their All Access Tour director, about all that went into this working ship.

The efficiency of it all was the most surprising.

Then he saw the first kink in the ship's machinery.

Just off the main "highway," what they called I-95, they were supposed to turn to the food-storage area. It was on their tour itinerary and Ted was anxious to see it. But as they approached, Stephanie announced that they had to skip the food-storage areas for now because of a "hazard concern."

This struck Ted as something odd to say, and he wasn't alone, as he saw his wife cock her brow and flash him a glance that said, "That was a bullshit excuse." Their mutual supposition was vindicated when their group was rushed past the hallway which led to the various food-storage areas and Ted caught a glance that screamed "Problem!"

It was just a glimpse, but it was enough. An area halfway down the food-storage hallway was blocked with yellow tape, like a crime scene. The partially closed doorway to a room oozed a white mist that obstructed the view inside. If he had had more time, maybe he could have seen inside. But the oddest part of the immediately visible scene was the bloody boot prints.

At least that's what it looked like to him: boot prints leading away from the foggy entrance. Maybe that was just Ted's macabre sensibility. TJ always joked to him and their friends that she needed to sleep with one eye open after reading his first end-of-the-world book. Besides, it was just a glimpse.

Several steps past the suspicious hallway, Ted glanced over to TJ to see if she noticed the same thing he did, to confirm his own questions. But her pert features were entirely focused on their tour guide, who was now describing the recycling they did and how the ship used all the funds they derived from recycling to give back to the crew for new equipment for their living room and other leisure areas.

She must not have noticed what he did, as TJ seemed absorbed in the tour and what Stephanie was saying. Not bloody boot prints.

Ted immediately discounted what he thought he saw in his glimpse. And normally that would be that. But nothing was normal right now, no matter how much he wanted to not deal with it.

He gazed at TJ, now completely ignoring the tour. At

least she finally found something to focus on other than the bizarre animal behavior currently going on outside of their micro-managed environment.

Ted must have become so absorbed in watching and thinking about his wife, he was startled to find that Stephanie was leading them down a small hallway of luxury cabins, with very regal placards: Princess Suite, Prince Suite, Queen Suite, and so on. They abruptly stopped at a plain entrance, whose placard simply proclaimed, "Bridge."

Ted had completely lost track of what deck they were on. He shot a glance back to where they had been and then forward again to see if he could catch a room number or something that would indicate where they were. Then, when his attention fell back to his wife, he noticed something odd.

TJ was no longer focused on Stephanie, who was speaking to the other three people in their tour group. Instead, TJ appeared to be looking past their group to Ted's right, at something or someone down a connecting hallway that he couldn't see. Then she mouthed something.

Ted inched up closer until the subject of her attention was visible past the edge of the connecting hallway's wall. It was a bald officer with four stripes, and he was mouthing his own silent words, back to Ted's wife.

Ted must have been staring—all too overtly—at this odd spectacle, because both the officer and TJ stopped and turned to him. Ted's cheeks flared heat, feeling like he was the one caught doing something he shouldn't. The officer offered up a warm and practiced smile.

As if on cue, Stephanie addressed their group now. "And I'm pleased to welcome the ship's staff captain, Jean Pierre. He is the second in command of the whole ship and we are privileged to have him, rather than one of the second officers, give you a tour of the bridge."

All the heads of their group now turned then to the staff captain, offering a golf-clap. Jean Pierre still held Ted's glare, for a long an uncomfortable moment, before finally turning his attention to the group. He thanked them all for coming, and for Stephanie's contribution to the All Access Tour. Then he told them they were going to be given a special treat and warned them to be quiet while they entered into the designated public area of the bridge, as the officers were on duty working. Finally, before turning to the door, he told them that the captain would join them in a couple of minutes as well.

He opened the narrow door, and one by one, their group crossed the bridge's thick threshold.

"Mr. Williams?" Jean Pierre whispered, just before Ted stepped through.

"The captain would like to speak to you personally right now. Could you please walk to your left"—he pointed in that direction—"and join him in his ready room? It's the first door on that side of the bridge."

Ted stammered, not sure how to respond, "Ah, I don't want you or the captain to make any special arrangements for me." Ted could feel the eyes of the other tour passengers and his wife on him.

"It's no trouble," the staff captain said.

Ted nodded and stepped through the metal doorway into a new world known as the bridge.

It was a vast room that felt surprisingly dark, because it was almost completely lit by the outside light pouring through the giant window-panels. Those slanted up and away, and spanned the 180-degree arc of the semi-circular chamber. Curiously, five of the most forward of the thick-looking panels had human-sized windshield wipers.

Ted's imagination immediately played scenes of the wiper-blades furiously beating back a tempest. He'd gotten lost again in his thoughts, and looked back to his group on the right. TJ was now whispering amiably in Jean Pierre's ear, cupped so that only Jean Pierre could hear her.

He turned toward the other direction, as he was

instructed, and marched up to a line meant to block out the public. Beyond it, the only door on a wall. It was open and an older man with one more stripe than the staff captain beckoned him forward into the tiny room.

Ted stepped past the roped area.

“Mr. Williams.” The captain, distinguished in his highly starched uniform with his crown of impeccable white hair, offered his hand. “Please come in for just a moment.”

Ted proceeded forward, with his own hand extended. But he couldn’t ignore the feeling he was just called to the principal’s office for something he did wrong. He felt “off” and not entirely himself today.

The captain clasped Ted’s hand and shook firmly. “Mr. Williams. I’m Jörgen Christiansen, captain of the Intrepid. Welcome.”

When Ted entered, the captain immediately closed the door and drew the shades. Ted felt his heart start to beat faster.

“Please excuse the theatrics,” the captain continued, “but I wanted to ask you something, privately. And I would ask that you don’t mention our conversation to anyone, other than your wife, of course.” His face was stern and focused.

Ted was definitely taken aback, and now wasn't sure what to say without knowing what the captain wanted. “Please tell me how I can help, Captain, and call me Ted.” The captain cocked his head and flashed just the slightest look of confusion, as if he had perhaps expected someone different, before regaining his composure.

“Very well ... Ted. I have just been made aware of a very serious problem that affects everyone on board this ship and I think you might be able to help.”

Ted’s mind instantly recalled the bloody footprints from the misty room. “Should I sit down?” Ted asked.

“No, I don’t want to keep you from the group. I’ll be quick. I wanted to know if what you wrote in your book,

Madness, is actually possible, or if it's all just a well-crafted story entirely made up from your imagination."

Before the captain spoke, Ted seriously thought that he was going to ask for the ship's wine back, or to tell them that the cruise line was sorry that their bag didn't make it, or something entirely trivial. But to be asked whether or not what they were experiencing was some sort of apocalyptic event, just like what he had written about in his second-to-last book, was the last thing he expected. And it terrified him to his core. This was no longer just his own supposition. It was real. His heart raced like an express train.

"I-Ah... I honestly don't know." He couldn't think of what else to say. He was wondering this very thing, but he hadn't come to any conclusion. It had seemed too impossible. But the very fact that this obviously sane man, who captained a ship carrying nearly two thousand people, was asking the same question he was asking himself was hard to comprehend. He felt dizzy, and drew in rapid puffs of air. He thought he might have a full-on panic attack.

There was a knock on the door, and then it opened a crack and the staff captain stuck his head in the door. "Sorry to bother you, sir, but Doctor Chettle has the autopsy results for you."

"Thanks, Staff Captain. I'll be right there."

Jean Pierre nodded once and closed the door, sealing Ted and the captain back in.

"Again, keep all of this between us. There appears to be an uncanny similarity between what you've written about and what is going on outside of this ship. I need to know what we have to look forward to in other ports, and I wanted to know if my concerns were valid, or not.

"Please consider all of this, and if it's okay, I'd like to call on you again during the cruise, if needed. Further, if you have any information that you feel might impact this cruise or anyone on it, would you please contact our staff captain or me?" He handed Ted a business card.

Ted almost missed grabbing it: he thought he saw two cards. He needed to get outside. Fast.

"This has my contact number on the bridge. Call it from any of the ship phones and they'll put you through to the staff captain or to me." Ted slid it into his pocket, without looking at it.

The captain opened the door and offered his hand again.

Ted quickly shook back, whispering, "Thank you, Captain," and rushed past him, in his attempt to beeline it outside. He didn't even think to talk to TJ, who was still on the bridge with the rest of their tour. He had to get to fresh air.

As Ted brushed past the security posted outside the bridge hatch and turned to the exit, all the enjoyment he had felt during the tour was forgotten. It was at that moment he knew they were all in big trouble.

11
Eloise

Eloise Carmichael made her money the old-fashioned way: she married it. The rest of the story, as Paul Harvey used to say, was that she had outlived three previous husbands, all of whom died of "mysterious causes."

It wasn't that she was some sort of black widow who purposely sought out wealthy potential husbands, with the plan to kill them for their money. At least the premeditated planning part wasn't true. She just got bored with them quickly. And divorce wasn't an option, with prenuptials and all. So she found an easier solution each time.

Months after her last husband's death, a cloud of questions stirred up by his siblings clung to Eloise like flies to a dead body. Frustrated at their persistent haranguing and their constantly calling the police on her, she'd had enough. So she sold her last husband's mansion and sought greener pastures in Paris.

It wasn't that she was interested in French men. Though she did love their beautiful-sounding words—like songs—when they whispered their desires to her, she just didn't want to have to learn how to speak it back. She was too damned old to learn another language. Yet Paris was where Eloise believed her next husband would be found.

She had read about the few *arrondissements* where wealthy English ex-pats often lived. So she set her sights on their Parisian haunts and within twenty days, she had already found a suitable candidate: Sir Edgar Carmichael—the title part was an extra bonus. One month later, they were married.

Like the others, just as quickly as they had wed, Eloise became tired of poor ol' Edgar. It would be during their honeymoon that she would seek out Number Four's "accident."

It was purely a stroke of luck that Edgar told her of his love for transatlantic cruises and suggested that option for their honeymoon. Eloise didn't care for cruising, but she thought the open sea would present her with ample opportunities for Edgar's demise; after all, they were going to be in the middle of the fricking Atlantic Ocean.

While planning their honeymoon, Eloise immediately discovered a behavior that just wouldn't work for her: Edgar was cheap, even insisting that to get what she wanted, she'd have to spend some of her own money. It was one more reason why he'd have to go.

When he first offered to buy her a transatlantic cruise, Eloise suggested the QE2 because it fulfilled her one non-negotiable: the ship had to have an onboard kennel, so she could take her "baby" with them. The second requirement, although not an absolute, was only natural for newlyweds with substantial means: they should also have the best cabin on the ship. But Edgar became furious when the agent told him it would cost him 45,000 euros per person for their Grand Duplex suite on the QE2.

When she thought her intractable demands might scuttle the whole thing, and thus her opportunities, she went along with his recommendations of Regal European, as they were the only other one with kennel services. She pressed for RE's best cabin, even though Edgar made her pay for her share—she'd get it back from him one way or another. So for the bargain price of 10,000 euros each, his agent booked the Royal Suite for Eloise, Edgar, and Monsieur, her toy French poodle.

Once it was settled, she got to work on her plans to find the most dangerous place on the ship, or on one of their excursions. Everything was falling into place, until just before they checked into their suite on the Intrepid.

It was her little Monsieur. She was concerned because he was not acting himself lately. After their flight from Paris, just before going through customs in Malaga, Monsieur actually growled at her. She had been anxious to check on him since then and decided to do so now, before they got ready for dinner. She left Edgar at their cabin for his daily nap and set off to find the kennels.

After getting directions from one of the better-looking younger officers—she only spoke to the senior crew members and rarely dealt with the peons on the ship—she was told to take the aft elevators. She glared at the officer for this.

It was the third cruise she had been on and it bugged her to no end why they just didn't call this "the rear" part of the ship. If you had to explain that the aft actually meant rear, why the hell not just say "rear" for the guests?

She felt her temperature start to boil a little when she exited onto deck 1, only partially accessible to guests.

The deep thrumming of the ship's engines rumbled underneath her, adding to the already unsteady feel of walking with heels on a moving ship—another reason she didn't care for cruises. Now, she almost felt dirty, just thinking about how close she was to the ship's mechanical parts.

Finally, she found the Regal Pet Spa. *At least that sounds better than "Kennels."*

She pushed open the door.

Regardless of where she was, whenever she entered a room Eloise expected that all men's heads should snap to her attention. To aid in this proper response, she had donned her stilettos to announce both her approach and arrival. And to complement this effect she wore an ensemble so tight-fitting, she looked vacuum-sealed in it. All were designed to reveal her God-given—albeit often enhanced by top plastic surgeons—assets.

It was therefore almost an affront to her whole persona when the spa's only human occupant, a small dark-skinned man, didn't even acknowledge her entrance. Further adding to her indignity, as she waited an intolerable amount of time, the man paid her no more attention than he would to a warm breeze. He was purposely ignoring her. She even slammed the door of the kennel to demand his consideration. Nothing.

But the sting of this personal injury quickly faded when she heard the growling and barking from the farthest kennel. The bark's high cadence was very familiar to her. And so when the realization hit her like a punch to her liposuctioned gut, she knew it was her Monsieur.

She clip-clopped over to the small man, who was outfitted in standard worker clothes, not epauletted like an officer. She actually didn't care about that right now. This man, regardless of his lowly status, was trying to calm her dog. However, it became instantly obvious to her that he didn't know what he was doing.

"You're just scaring him more," she whined, pushing him aside and positioning herself in front of her pup's enclosure.

Her indignation swelled to epic proportions when she saw that Monsieur's front paw was wrapped in some sort of bandage. That meant her baby had been injured on Regal European's ship, and most likely under the supervision of this little man.

Then she nearly fell backward, the shock rocking her whole body. Instead of seeing her normally well-mannered Monsieur, there was a terrifyingly wild animal behind the windowed enclosure. His face was scrunched up in an angry scowl; his lips and cheeks were drawn back to reveal a surprising number of nightmarishly pointed teeth; and his eyes flared a ferocious red, like blazing rubies. She shuddered.

"Monsieur?" she begged, hoping to coax her beloved puppy to come out of this horrid looking one. "It's Mommy."

Monsieur growled a violent-sounding warning, like he was possessed by some feral animal. It was not the loving pooch she'd known for the last five years, who had comforted her through the trauma of her last three husbands' passings.

Eloise shot up, pulling down her skirt, which had hiked up too far, and preened over a rogue lock of her hair. "What did you do to my dog?" she barked at the little man.

"Ah, Mrs. Carmichael," Al stuttered. "Ah, this was how I found Mon-sewer this morning." He wanted desperately to avoid bringing up last night's events. "Have you noticed any behavioral problems before this trip?"

As if slapped, she recoiled, her own anger boiling over at this man's insolence. Still, his words rang true. Monsieur had been confused before they left Paris and then he acted a little aggressive yesterday morning when he was checked onto the plane. Maybe her baby was just scared of traveling. She knew she would often get tired and cranky after waking up from a long day of travel, like now. It's probably worse for an animal traveling in a cage, something she would otherwise never do to her Monsieur. Perhaps this man wasn't to blame after all, though he would have to explain what happened to his foot. Still, she was sure he didn't know how to calm her pup.

She'd try what always worked when he was frightened.

"Leave us alone for just a moment," she said to the man. When she spoke to Monsieur, her voice went up an octave and down a few decibels. "Monsieur's mommy knows how to settle him down."

The worker, whose name tag listed an unpronounceable name and indicated he was from Mauritius, nodded and walked back to the front of the room and sat down at a small desk she hadn't even noticed when she pounced on him from the door. She knelt back down and tried to relieve her tiny boy's anguish, talking to him in baby talk as she normally did.

Monsieur emitted a long rolling growl, punctuated by a sliver of saliva hanging from its mouth.

A better idea struck her like a thunderbolt, and she almost shuddered at her own brilliance.

A guilty flash at the little dark man confirmed he wasn't looking her way. Feeling safe, Eloise opened her Hermès and yanked out a prescription pill bottle from her own stash of narcotics. She kept an ample supply for just about every occasion. Her doctor had given her these particular babies for her anxiety—she'd been having more of it lately, although she didn't know why.

She pulled out two large, white capsules.

She was allowed to have two of these at any one time. So one, for a dog maybe one tenth her weight, should more than do the trick. *Okay, maybe Monsieur is more like a twelfth of my weight, but who's counting?*

She flashed a glance once more at the little man and when she was sure she was alone in her next crime, she tossed one tablet into her mouth, then opened the door to Monsieur's enclosure just enough to thrust her hand inside. She kept her eyes glued to the man and blindly held her hand out for Monsieur, insisting he take the second tablet out of her palm, the way he'd usually take treats from her. When she felt the tablet drop out, she attempted to withdraw her hand—and Monsieur bit her.

She yelped, clicked the door closed, and bolted upright, clutching her injured hand. She gave a deep scowl at her dog for adding to her indignity. With her throbbing hand held at her side, she clamped down on it with her other, so the man couldn't see it.

"Are you all right?" He was bounding in her direction.

"Yes!" she blurted.

She glanced back down at Monsieur because he'd finally stopped growling. At first she was shocked to see the droplets of her own blood on and around the pill. A trail led to and pooled under her hands. Her dog's next action disgusted her.

Monsieur busied himself licking up her blood like some sugary treat, and with the blood, he ingested the pill. The sight turned her stomach. Holding back her nausea, she felt some measure of relief knowing her mission was accomplished. That downer should calm him pretty quickly.

She turned back to the man, keeping her body between her hand and him. "And I think Monsieur will be fine pretty soon, too."

With her back to him, she snatched a silk handkerchief from her purse and tightly wrapped the wound. She wondered if she needed medical attention, or if just a band-aid—*perhaps many band-aids*—would suffice. *No-no, a band-aid would not look right with this evening's special gown*, she thought. It was her fondest hopes that the gown alone would be enough to stop Edgar's heart. That wouldn't happen if her hands were covered in band-aids. Presentation was everything to her.

When she returned her attention back to the little man, she noticed that he was staring at her ass—at least he had a pulse, which is something he couldn't say about her Edgar—and then, startled at his own dalliance, returned his own gaze up to her eye level.

She sashayed past him and strutted to the door. "Thank you... Ahh ..." She acted out a harsh squint in the direction of his name tag, but wasn't going to even try to figure out what to call the man.

"Al is my name, Mrs. Carmichael," he said with a very sweet grin. *He is kind of cute, in a small-man sort of way.*

Eloise snickered at this and his chosen nickname.

"Thank you, Al." She gave him a genuine smile and paraded out the door, knowing where his eyes were now. Her smile grew even larger.

She hesitated after the door closed behind her, holding up her throbbing hand. The damned thing hurt a lot now, and it was still bleeding. She couldn't very well go to dinner bleeding all over the place. She caught a glimpse of the Regal Medical sign, conveniently located right next door to the Pet Spa. Perhaps the doctor had a skin-colored bandage. Then she remembered she had some white gloves she could wear over the bandage.

She didn't want anything to spoil her grand entrance tonight.

12

T.D. Bonaventure

T.D. Bonaventure, as he was known to his millions of readers, asked everyone at the captain's table to refer to him as Ted, and to his wife, Theresa Jean, as TJ.

Captain Christiansen still couldn't get over the disparity between "Ted" and "T.D." He had presumed someone different. Although T.D.'s stories dealt with one apocalypse or another, his writing style was literary, almost like poetry. And he often injected British idioms into his prose, which had led Jörgen to believe that T.D. was British, perhaps even belonging to the aristocracy, as he remembered reading something about a Bonaventure family in a British historical novel his wife had once given him. When he briefly met Ted on the bridge, and more so now, he could see he was completely mistaken.

His image of the aristocratic Mr. Bonaventure clashed greatly with the real-life Ted, in spite of Ted's handlebar mustache. Besides using a name some would consider uncivilized, instead of his given name of Theodore, he spoke with the coarse parlance of a common American, attaching primitive colloquial phrases to otherwise well-thought-out sentences. Yet, in spite of the clash with his assumed persona, Jörgen actually liked him better as "Ted." He was far more real.

"I'm so glad you've chosen to join us. I've been looking forward to speaking with you about your books."

Captain Christiansen spoke with jovial animation. Ted wondered if it was the same man he had met earlier on the bridge. But he reasoned that the captain was just keeping up appearances, and was attempting to play down what they both knew were growing problems closing in fast. Ted feigned a smile, trying to play along too. "Thank you, Captain. It's an honor for us to be invited to your table."

Being in the giant dining hall was already pushing Ted's limits. But sitting at the center of this fishbowl was almost unbearable. It took almost a bottle of the gifted wine to ply his nerves to a manageable enough level and get to dinner, albeit late. He'd need another bottle to make it through this.

His stomach was already in knots over reliving the events leading to their cruise. Ted felt his nerves ramp up even more now, eager to deflect the attention from himself. Before he considered the implications he blurted, "I'm curious, Captain, were you able to get most of your crew and guests on board before you had to depart early?"

This was the one conversation Jörgen had hoped to avoid while at the dinner table. His turn to deflect. "First, Mr. Bonaventure—"

"—Ted, please, Captain. Besides, you know Bonaventure is just my nom de plume. My British roots are pretty far removed from the Ted you see here."

"Yes, of course, Ted. I just wanted to thank you and your wife for your assistance in alerting the guests and some of my crew, so they could get on board before... we had a bigger problem."

"And thank you, Captain." TJ interrupted, "for the wine." She held up her glass of the wine served at their table, the same wine as their cabin gift.

Ted noticed that she was enjoying the wine as much as he was.

"It's my honor, Mrs. Williams." The captain raised his glass with a smile.

"Oh please, call me TJ. Everyone does."

"Theresa Jean sounds much better," Jean Pierre interjected, with a wider smile.

"Just TJ, please." She flashed a sloppy grin in return.

Ted noticed once more the familiar comfort they had with each other, and that they held one another's gazes for longer than normal.

"If you don't mind," the captain continued, "I'll call you Theresa Jean, which sounds far lovelier to me, too." He offered his own grin to her, but Ted found it to be more practiced, expected.

"To answer your question, Mr... Sorry, Ted. We have a total of 738 guests on board, and we had bookings for 1325. We're short 195 crew, but because of the lower guest number, we're in good shape. The good news is you can have seconds of everything!" The captain announced this with laughter. Again, practiced.

Ted caught the staff captain mouthing something to TJ. Ted glared at her, and she flashed him the look of a Cheshire cat with a canary still in its mouth. It was not like his wife to flirt with another man, except for her job, and certainly not in Ted's presence. But this was more than flirting. They knew each other and yet both were pretending otherwise. It was one more puzzle he did not want to have to solve.

"Excuse me Mr. Bonaventure?" Zeka, the ship's cruise director chimed in, interrupting his mental meanderings.

"Please, just Ted."

"Oh, ah yes, Ted. In your first novel, *Bugs*, how did you come up with the story of insects taking over the world?"

"Didn't you know?" TJ said with laughter in her voice.

"He's actually an entomologist."

"Retired," Ted cut in.

"Yeah, he studied the mating rituals of praying mantis, or is that manti"—she flashed her sultry grin and raised her glass in his direction. "Anyway, he studied praying manti and other interesting shi... stuff."

"Of course, a praying mantis ate its mate... after." He clicked a smile and raised his glass.

"Touché, dear," TJ said clinking his glass.

"And what do you do Theresa Jean?" Zeka asked.

"Just TJ."

"Oh, don't you know," Ted said in his fake British voice, "My wife is a secret agent for the US government." He offered a smirk, exaggerated a look upward, while twirling his mustache.

"No, really?" asked Zeka.

TJ leaned forward and said, "But if I told you, I'd have to kill you."

There was a break in the table's conversation as food was being served. But it also seemed that an invisible bubble separating them from the rest of the guests had been pierced. At that moment, the din of the main dining room or MDR flooded their ears. The MDR's dinner guests were abnormally loud in their conversations. And there was little doubt about what they were discussing.

Although earlier the captain had publicly announced that they had set sail without problems, at their table he had just let on—loud enough that many around them could hear—that several of his crew and several hundred guests had not made it on board.

Ted was sure that this, along with what they had witnessed earlier in Malaga, was the subject of the nervous chatter rumbling around the room.

Many heads were glued to their phones, mouths reporting what their eyes saw. Because of the ship's proximity to the coast, many still had Internet or texting capabilities by connecting to nearby cell towers, in addition to those who ponied up for the ship's high-priced Internet service. Besides the stories around the Internet, word was bound to spread with communications from worried friends and family back home.

Ted's eyes wandered from table to table and took in the uneasy faces. It was like worry had taken on a palpable presence of its own, as it floated from group to group, like some dark cloud that rained down disquiet upon each table, and then moved on to the next one.

The person with the phone at each table, after sharing their news to their table mates, then shot dark glances in Ted's direction at the captain's table to see if they shared in their same worry.

Then everything changed.

Another presence commanded the attention of all those with eyesight at the MDR.

It was Eloise Carmichael.

A very attractive woman with long black hair strutted along the port-side walkway running through the MDR, an elderly man in tow. Even though it was the first formal night, it was not unexpected to see all manner of formal and wildly informal dress every night of the cruise. But formal nights often brought out the most outlandish. This woman's dress, or lack of one, was what drew everyone's gaze. Men and women, guests and crew, all gaped at what they saw.

Every curve was visible through her sheer gown, which looked as if she had delicate white lace flourishes painted directly onto her arms, shoulders, breasts, torso, groin, and legs, all of which conspicuously covered just barely more than a sheer negligee might. As she approached their table, it appeared to Ted that the dress's long skirt and train—also nude-colored—hid everything from her hips down. But everything else above this was all her.

TJ's elbow found Ted's gut, in a not too subtle chide. "You're staring, dear," she huffed.

"Everyone is staring, dear," Ted chortled.

"Good God Almighty, what is that?" quipped Urban, one of the captain's first officers, who was known among his fellow crew members for his often prudish comments about guests and their poor taste in clothing.

"That would be Eloise Carmichael, and her fourth husband," announced Zeka.

"I'm sure she married this one for love," TJ offered sarcastically.

There were a couple of snickers, but Zeka ignored the comment and continued, seemingly more mesmerized than the others. "I have that same dress. J. Lo wore it to the '13 Golden Globes. Hers and probably this one are by Zhair Murad. Mine was a knock-off from China. Besides, I don't look like that."

Most of the dining hall gawked at Mrs. Carmichael as she paraded to a table for two in the middle of the two-story hall, only one table away from the captain's.

"Fourth husband? That's a lot of divorces in a short time. She doesn't look that old," Ted mused out loud.

"The other three died of quote *mysterious causes* end quote," said Jean Pierre, who seemed more interested in Ted's wife than Mrs. Carmichael, now directly behind them. Ted looked at Jean Pierre and then around to the Carmichaels' table.

Carmichael made eye contact with them, flashed a big smile, and waved a white-gloved hand in their direction. She paused while her husband waited for her to sit, but she changed course and headed in their direction, leaving her husband waiting for her.

"Oh look, dear, she's coming over to meet you," TJ continued to tease her husband.

"More likely Captain Christiansen," he responded, but he felt his panic increase as he watched her advance and stop directly in front of him.

"Mr. Bonaventure," she said through an exaggerated smile accentuated by oversized lips. She daintily offered that white-gloved hand. "I'm a huge fan. I'm Eloise—"

"Mrs. Carmichael," Ted said in a somewhat British accent. He stood and accepted her hand, although he was unsure if he was supposed to give a peck on a knuckle or shake it. The dilemma and the pause made him immensely uncomfortable. He hadn't even wanted to come to the damned dinner, preferring the anonymity of room service. Their checked bag arrived and with it their formal clothes. Without any more excuses, TJ insisted, and so they came and he was thrust into this situation. But then something caught his eye.

"Mrs. Carmichael? I'm sorry, but I think your hand is bleeding." Ted released her. The back of one of her gloved hands looked padded, like it was full of wads of cotton balls. On the top of the padding was a moist semi-circle of red, apparently from a wound that had bled through. *That explains the gloves*.

"Ah, thank you, Mr. Bonaventure," Eloise said, covering her injured hand with her other, shrinking back from him. She stared past her hands for a moment, seemingly befuddled. She snapped back to attention. "I better go back to the doctor," she announced. "Captain," she nodded in Jörgen's direction.

"Mr. Bonaventure. Until later, I hope." She turned and left, following the same parade route she had arrived on. This time was not for show. She hurried, not even waiting for her husband who attempted unsuccessfully to catch up.

"See, Mr. Bonaventure, your fans even bleed for you," TJ snickered.

"Before you sit down, Ted, would you offer a toast?" boomed the captain.

Ted, already completely out of sorts, was now mortified to see he'd not only drawn his table's eyes, but those of the entirety of the dining room.

TJ leaned toward him, whispering just loud enough for him to hear. “And don’t fuck it up.” She smiled, knowing it was probably exactly what he needed to hear.

He just glared at her. But his glare turned into a winsome smile. His wife always knew which buttons of his to push at the right time.

Ted reached down to grab his wine and noticed a flute of champagne at each of their place-settings. He hesitated only a moment before raising his, waiting for everyone from their table and the dining room to follow. A character from one of his books was in a similar situation—if that was even possible. And from it he offered this toast:

"*May the wind be at our backs and the seas ahead be calm as we sail on to our next port of adventure.*"

“Cheers,” the table said in unison, followed by the entire dining room.

All clinked their glasses, sipped their champagne, and the MDR’s chatter built back up. Finally, Ted sat down, shrinking into the more comfortable confines of his own chair.

“Captain,” TJ asked, her voice almost inaudible through the din, “Do you think Mount Etna's eruption will affect our itinerary?"

“In a way, it already has, Theresa Jean.” Captain Christiansen sipped a coffee. He was about to say something more, when the head waiter handed him a note.

At first, the captain’s stately poker-like mug held. The distinct lines of his ruddy features were like deeply chiseled navigational marks carved over forty years of working on ships. Then they did a course correction, only for a moment. But others were watching. So they steered back to their normal intensity.

He grabbed the shoulder of his staff captain, and when he stood up he whispered something that changed Jean Pierre’s demeanor in an instant.

"I'm sorry, but I have to leave you, but we have a few

things we must attend to. I'll be in contact with you shortly," he said to Ted. "Theresa Jean and Ted." He smiled and nodded to both of them. "Thank you for your enjoyable company."

He still acted like there was nothing wrong in the world, yet he hurried to a back exit. The staff captain followed, but hesitated as he passed by TJ, casually thrusting his hand out into TJ's. "Charmed, Theresa Jean... Ted." He then bounded quietly after the captain.

While Ted and the MDR watched them leave, TJ glanced down into her palm. In it was a crib note: "Tomorrow @ 6:30 A.M."

13
Jaga

"Taufan?" Jaga whispered, fearful of letting anyone outside his quarters hear him.

"Taufan?" the young man called again, rummaging through the belongings around his bunk.

He stood back up and glared at his bunk area, scratching his disheveled hair, forcing himself to think of what he must have missed.

"Jaga, what are you doing?" boomed his best friend, who had quietly entered and snuck up from behind.

Although startled, Jaga was also relieved that it was just Yakobus and not someone else. Then, Jaga's features drooped, like a slice of cheese on a hot sandwich. He leaned over to his friend's ear. "Yakobus, I can't find Taufan anywhere. He's not in his box."

Yakobus nodded calmly, and quickly stepped over to the open door of their shared quarters, closing it tight. Putting an ear to the door to make sure what they said would not be heard, he whispered, "Could he have gotten out?"

"I don't know." Jaga moaned while trying to massage the worry from his temples.

They both knew Jaga would be fired for hiding his pet ferret on board. Their superior, the assistant chief of housekeeping, was okay with the infraction, if it was kept quiet and no one else outside of his roommates knew about it. If their secret left their inner circle or if Taufan happened to spring free to another area of the ship, Jaga's years with Regal European would end abruptly.

His roommates would never break Jaga's confidence, not only because they too loved Taufan, but because they believed the little guy brought them luck. They also felt sorry for him. Besides being small for a ferret—not that ferrets were big to begin with—Taufan often shivered when scared. It was both pitiful and cute at the same time. Taufan apparently had a much lower than normal body temperature and pulse rate, compared to a typical ferret. So he often shook as a reflex to the outside temperature. Jaga had even hand-stitched a little covering out of athletic socks to keep him warm. Although it looked ridiculous, his roommates agreed the ferret-suit was perfect for Taufan.

Jaga first noticed Taufan was missing when he found the empty sock covering on his bed. When Jaga noticed it was somewhat torn, he became alarmed and started his search.

At night Taufan normally slept with him under the covers. And when Jaga arose, before he left for the day to start his duties, he would put Taufan in a giant shoe box, with holes poked into it for air. Inside was a small rolled-up towel, which acted as a bed, and even a little litter compartment, separate from Taufan's sleeping area, for him to do his business. At night Jaga left the box open and Taufan would crawl in and use the ferret-bathroom or he'd crawl up and say "hello" to his roommates, or just prowl around the room. Usually when Jaga woke up, Taufan was by his side, often snuggled into his neck. But during the day, he stayed in his box. No exceptions.

Today, when Jaga had returned, Taufan was gone and his box's top was askew.

There were previous occasions where Jaga had thought that Taufan had broken free from his box. Items under his bed, where the box lay, were moved and the box top was not quite on right. Yet he had never caught Taufan outside of his box during the day, until now.

Yakobus pulled Taufan's box from under his bed and poked around underneath with his flashlight.

"I already searched there," Jaga snapped.

Yakobus shot back a glare and then took a long breath and said in a soft tone, "Jaga, I'm just trying to help. You might have forgotten something."

Jaga hung his head, feeling sorrow for his momentary spike of anger directed at his friend. It was obvious Yakobus had his best interests in mind. Mostly he just missed his little friend.

The door crashed open and Asep bounded through, like the big, bumbling fool that he was.

Yakobus and Jaga both spun on their heels, their eyes meeting Asep's, who halted mid-motion. This was the roommate they liked the least. Worse, Asep was assigned to several of the concierge class rooms on deck 8 of the ship and always reminded his roomies of this.

"What's going on, brothers?" Asep asked, eying each suspiciously from under his flawlessly coiffed hair, which hung just above his eyes. He sported a crooked smile, perfectly chiseled into his olive features, which had never shown a blemish. He was working on a dark stubble, even though he had shaved a second time at noon.

Asep was always calling them 'brothers' even though they had no direct relation—that they knew of.

Jaga hesitated answering, intent on measuring his reply so as to not reveal too much. So Yakobus jumped in. "Jaga has lost something. I was trying to help him find it."

"It wasn't that silly rat of yours, was it?" Asep was always calling Taufan a rat.

"Have you seen Taufan?" Jaga pleaded.

Asep looked over his shoulder first, apparently making sure no one was listening, then back to his roomies. "I came in here about twenty minutes ago to get something I had forgotten. Anyways"—he always started his stories with *anyways*—"sometimes, when no one's here, I would say 'Hi' to your rat. He's my buddy too, you know."

Jaga nodded, now understanding why Taufan's box top and some of his own belongings had been moved at various times.

"Anyways, when I came back to the room twenty minutes ago, I visited with Taufan. But he jumped out of his box and bit me." He held out his hand to lend support to his story.

"Did he escape?" Jaga wasn't interested in Asep's superficial wound.

"Well, no. Anyways, I closed the door right away, as you had asked, and he ran around the room, all crazy-like. Anyways, he stopped on our desk." Asep pointed to the common desk they all used. "And I was standing there." He pointed to where Yakobus was standing now, in front of an open locker.

Asep paused, like he was trying to gather how to explain what he was going to say next. "Anyways, your rat just stared at me and his eyes were red, and... well, I swear he growled at me."

"Ferrets don't growl," Jaga snapped back.

"Anyways, he made weird noises—it sounded like a growl, *okay*. And then he ran at me and then jumped for me. His mouth was open and I swear to you he was going for my face..."

"What happened, pretty-boy?" Yakobus prodded, impatient to conclude the story. Asep loved to draw out a story forever, especially if it concerned his "perfect olive complexion." Besides, they all had to get back to work soon and certainly couldn't be standing around here all day long listening to another one of Asep's stories.

"Anyways, Taufan tried to attack me—I swear—and I just reacted. So I fell to the floor." Asep demonstrated, collapsing down to his hands and knees.

"Anyways, Taufan missed me and landed inside the locker there." Again Asep pointed to where Yakobus was standing.

"You opened this locker?" Yakobus asked, looking at the closed locker.

"No! It was open when I got here. Catur must have left it open. Anyways, Taufan had landed inside Catur's locker. And you know Catur is a pig and so Taufan couldn't get out because he was trapped in all of Catur's stuff. So I spun around and slammed the locker door shut while he was flailing around inside." Asep demonstrated Taufan's movements, convulsively waving his hands and arms, like someone having a seizure.

"You left him in there?" asked Jaga, somewhat incredulous about Asep's whole tall tale.

"That's why I came back here again, I wanted you to know that I—" Asep glared at Yakobus, who was opening the locker door. "Don't do th—"

Yakobus yelped as Taufan leapt out of the locker past Yakobus and made a beeline for the entrance to their quarters, which Asep had left open.

Asep reached for the entrance door, just one second too slow. As the door seemed to shut in slow motion, they all watched the flash of Taufan whipping around the door frame's base and down the hallway, out of sight.

They stood silently for a moment, unsure what to do next.

Jaga leapt for the door, opened it, swept through, and ran after Taufan, anxious to save his ferret and his job.

14

Al

The speed with which Al had lost control of his boarders, and therefore his career, was mind-numbing.

After a quick nap, he was woken in his room by a call from the hotel captain, "We're getting complaints on decks 2 through 4 about some full-on ruckus involving dogs."

Al could hear them long before he stepped into the Regal European Pet Spa. Inside, the barking was so loud he had to cover his ears. He hollered at the guests. "Hey-hey-hey. What's all the barking about?" It was a rhetorical question, because he knew exactly what was upsetting all the animals.

He marched down the spa's walkway, passing each pet-suite. If he had looked through each floor-to-ceiling glass door, he'd have seen each resident scurrying around its space, barking its discontent at the last suite at the end of the walkway: The Presidential Pup Suite.

Al halted in front of this double suite, which looked even bigger because of the diminutive size of its occupant. He just glared at the pup.

Not acting its size, the white toy poodle stood resolutely behind the clear glass, with all the bluster of an animal ten times its weight. It snarled erratically through its teeth. Then, upon seeing Al, it focused an ascending growl at him, as if seething with pure hatred. Its eyes were a crimsoned fury. Its gnarling rumble crescendoed and, like a coiled-up spring releasing, it leapt at the door. Ignoring any tenderness it must have felt from the injured paw—there were three stitches under those bandages—it pummeled the glass boundary with its front paws and jaws.

Al could do nothing but gawk at the poodle, driven mad by something absolutely mysterious.

The poodle's behavior had him completely flummoxed. After its owner had left, the dog had almost immediately fallen asleep in its bed, without so much as a whimper. And he figured the poodle had finally settled down.

Then this morning, when Al came in to clean the suites, Monsieur's personality rapidly changed. First it was confused, bumping into the walls and barking at the air. Then, it became outright hostile. When Al attempted to take the animals for their morning walk he had to muzzle the poodle and leave it to stew about its behavior. It wasn't his first time dealing with an aggressive dog. And so he assumed this pampered pooch was no different.

Al had learned long ago that he had to act quickly so as to wrestle the behavior out of the animal before there was a chance it would bite him or any of the others. It was simple: he'd quickly muzzle the offending dog, and that dog would learn its boundaries. Dogs were smart and pretty quickly figured out what was acceptable and what was not. An Aggressive would settle down soon after that. Once its behavior was more passive, he'd remove the muzzle as a reward. If it didn't play nice at that point, he'd muzzle it again. With the more combative breeds such as pit bulls or chows, he'd sometimes have to muzzle the animal as many as three times before it had learned its place. With Monsieur, it had already been four, and was about to be five. It was only then that he started to doubt whether this behavioral modification technique was going work at all with this boarder.

Al pulled the clipboard out of its sleeve, just off the door, and reread Monsieur's details. Maybe he'd missed something.

He hadn't.

Then he considered the injury to its paw. He'd thought the dog had cut it on one of the many sharp objects in the butcher's area, but maybe it was something else. A horrid thought hit him: what if it had been bitten by one of the rats and the rat was rabid?

Although the dog now displayed many of the signs common to rabies, there was the problem of incubation period. From his veterinary training, he knew the typical period from exposure to onset of clinical signs was weeks, not twenty-four hours or less. No, it had to be a behavioral issue. Al made a decision.

He flipped a switch on the wall, and the Presidential Suite's glass door went milky-white. Its snarling occupant disappeared from his sight. He wasn't sure how the door worked—something having to do with electrical poles and filaments—but it seemed to mostly silence the animal's tirade. Rather than growling, it seemed to busy itself, probably with one of its many toys.

Al turned and walked back toward the front of the spa, flipping each of the suite's door switches as he passed, until he reached the first door. The spa's din rapidly became muted, and then blinked out. It was time for their walk, and Al thought it would do them good to get out and walk out their agitation. He'd muzzle and leave the poodle once again, for punishment. One last shot with that one.

One by one he pulled out each dog and attached their leashes to the master harness, making them sit and stay by the door. Although two of the dogs acted confused, they all behaved. When it was time to deal with the poodle, he flipped the light/door switch. His mouth drooped open and his jaw went slack.

The double suite was utterly destroyed: the bedding ripped to shreds, the toys similarly disemboweled, pictures from the walls knocked down and torn, and finally, bloody paw prints everywhere. The little dog stood transfixed by itself in a cracked mirror on the opposite wall, foaming spittle pooling below it.

Al shook his head once and regained his composure. Now was the time to muzzle the dog, while it was preoccupied. Al acted quickly, but the dog was quicker.

He swished the door open and took three rapid steps to the dog, who was still glowering at its mirror image. It appeared frozen but for its rapidly heaving chest. With his left hand, he reached for the dog's collar, and with his right he moved to slip on the muzzle. But before his left touched the collar, the animal snapped its head back and sank two of his canines into Al, who reacted by dropping the muzzle. Monsieur then dashed out the door, toward freedom. Al leapt for the crazed animal, futilely attempting to get a hand on it. But the dog was gone.

Al scuttled out of the suite on elbows and knees, just as Monsieur hopped on top of the giant German shepherd named Max, the same dog who had stomped on Monsieur last night.

Max, like Al, watched in sheer disbelief as the toy poodle, who was maybe a twentieth the size of the shepherd, sank its itty-bitties into the massive shepherd's neck. The shepherd shrieked and then clawed at the air and flung its head and body sideways to detach the small ratlike dog. Monsieur flew several feet before sliding to a stop against a wall. But it wasn't dissuaded. The poodle righted itself and leapt into the pack of dogs, chomping at anything near its mouth.

All the dogs were panicked now, snarling and barking at

the pint-sized terror. But size didn't seem to matter in this crazy world. Little Monsieur viciously targeted the next dog in the group, a gray schnauzer with white legs. Once again, the smaller but far more ferocious dog had no trouble overpowering the larger one.

Al was panicked himself, as he raced to break up the melee. The little dog was drawing blood, lots of it. And the other dogs were going crazy trying to get away from the little devil. All the dogs were going to be seriously injured if he couldn't stop this. And... he glanced down at his throbbing hand and saw that he was gushing blood everywhere from a larger than expected gash.

~~~

Eloise Carmichael stumbled on the last step of the stairwell, nearly falling over before one of her five-inch heels caught the sheer material, partially tearing the train of her $20,000 dress.

She righted herself and inspected the damage, pulling the train's folds forward and contorting at an odd angle. From what she could see, she assessed it was only a small, unnoticeable tear. Most eyes shouldn't be on that part of her dress anyway.

She stood erect and automatically preened her hair, certain some of the strands must be out of place. She stared forward at nothing. She felt lost and now, thinking about it, she'd completely forgotten why she was on this deck in the first place.

Her eyes searched for some sign and she found herself before the deck 1 elevators. Both sets of doors were framed by a golden metallic material, polished to a nearly mirror sheen. Eloise now saw her own reflection. Better do a systems check, as husband number two or three—she couldn't remember
~~~

which one—used to say.

She scrutinized her face. After her second most recent facelift, she looked pretty good. Her fingers patted at her throat, causing some small tremors in the little wattle that hung below her chin. She would need to have them work on that soon, but otherwise...

Passable.

She touched at the ends of her hair, which had held well throughout the evening.

Passable.

Next, she examined her figure, wonderfully accentuated by the dress. She stood up straighter still and held her hands below her bust, pushing up and letting go: the dress didn't have any bra inside to lift and support, although, after the $30,000 augmentation by her plastic surgeon, her puppies held firm.

More than passable.

Just then, she caught a glimpse of her hand, her clutch dangling from her wrist. It throbbed worse than before and now a large red stain glared back at her.

She reached into her clutch, considered the four pills she'd had earlier, hesitated, then yanked out another three Valium and dry-swallowed them. She was tired of the pain.

It then occurred to her that this was one of the reasons why she was down on deck 1: to see the doctor again. But there was another reason, and it was related to her hand. *What was it?*

She couldn't seem to hold her thoughts as the night dragged on. Maybe it was the alcohol or the Valium or that she was second-guessing herself about killing Edgar. She just felt off tonight.

Then, she remembered: her dog bit her. That's why she was bleeding... *And, what?*

She was going to see if Monsieur was okay. That's also why she went to deck 1. *And what?*

To tell the little man... *Al something... That's it!* She was going to give Al a piece of her mind for letting her dog get injured and go crazy.

She was startled by the clip-clop of her own heels on the hard floor, surprised both by the clatter it caused—it was the only guest floor in all the ship, besides the outside decks, or the dance floors, that wasn't carpeted—and by not remembering that she had started to walk.

And I'm here because why again?

She had forgotten already.

Eloise found herself standing—no, swaying—in front of the Regal European Pet Suites door, scowling at it, as if it were alive and she was daring it to talk back to her. If it did, she'd rip the door's head off... *but that's silly because it doesn't have a head. What the hell is wrong with me?*

She turned the doorknob and pushed open the door, expecting to find that silly little man on the floor again, but instead the giant mug of a German shepherd was right there at face level. Its dirty paws punched against her clavicle, knocking her backward onto her keister. Husband Number Two, the first Brit she'd married, always called her rear her keister. And so there she was, tumbling hard onto her keister.

Her world crept into slow motion as the massive mutt leapt over her, screeching and whining, as if in pain. The other dogs immediately followed, jumping over her, en masse. She had been falling slowly, but these dogs were moving like the wind, treating her like she was the stationary center of some cruel dog-trick, as part of some dog show: the "watch the dogs jump over the flailing lady on the floor" routine.

For a moment, she thought the lights had gone out. But then she realized the dogs had blotted out the ceiling lights above as they passed over her field of vision.

The horde bounded past her, trailing a single long leash, and then down a side hallway, which she could swear hadn't been there before, opening into the crew-only area.

Another much smaller dog sprang out of the room. Like

the others, this dog bounded over her. The realization of which dog this was struck her like a cold slap across her face: it was her little baby, her Monsieur—*that's why she was here, to check on her little Monsieur!*

The cruel dog show continued as Monsieur bounded down the same side hall, less than a dozen steps behind the others.

"Monsieur? Are you all right, my baby?" she called out to her white toy poodle, covered in red splashes. He didn't even stop to acknowledge her, instead chasing the other dogs while growling viciously.

She watched the pack scamper into an opening and then veer into a wide hallway out of sight, their yelping and cries of fear following them. Several crew members braced themselves against the hallway wall, trying to avoid the frantic animals. Little Monsieur furiously scratched his way around the same corner, growling behind them, seemingly determined to close the distance.

Adding to her insult, Al was out of the pet spa next, leaping over her. "So sorry, Mrs. Carmichael," he said, while dashing into the crew area. "I'll get Mon-sewer," he huffed, before he disappeared out of sight.

It was her husband's fault that they chose this discount cruise line over the QE2, because he was too damned cheap. He was the reason she was lying there on the ground, in her favorite gown. Her chest filled up with air like a giant dirigible until it reached its limit and she let loose with a roaring scream, as she had never done before. It was an exhalation of all the built-up frustration and anger, and something more primal that she neither understood nor cared about. She knew one thing: she was more determined than ever to kill her damned husband, and she wanted to do it now.

She attempted to jump up, but something was holding her legs to the floor. This incensed her even more. She thrust out her legs much harder this time, pulling with all her might on the hall railing until she felt something give. It was just a little at first, as when a stuck zipper lets go and then slides all the way down to open effortlessly, like a knife through butter. In this case, there was a rude ripping sound. But she was standing.

Eloise attempted to move forward, but her ankles felt restrained and she was falling forward, a return run to the floor. Before she tumbled, she grabbed the railing, with both hands this time, dropping her purse in the process. She then glanced down her legs and saw that the lower part of her dress at her waist had ripped completely off, and it was still wrapped around her ankles. A thought flashed in her mind—she should have worn underwear. But that wasn't important now. Her legs just needed to be free.

She scissor-kicked the fabric away and then stood upright. Seeing that nothing else was keeping her from her needed chore, she thrust forward, high heels clacking.

A few guests, walking up or down the aft stairwell from decks 6 through 2, swore that a half-naked woman in high heels, somewhat conspicuously covered in white lace, was running up the stairs between 10 and 11 PM, growling the name Edgar.

But most who heard this story attributed it to that evening's two-for-one Long Island ice tea special.

DAY FOUR

THE CAPTAIN'S MORNING ADDRESS BLARED ONCE AGAIN RIGHT AT SIX O'CLOCK. THIS TIME I WAS READY AND I TURNED THE VOLUME CONTROL TO THE MAX SETTING ON THE LITTLE SPEAKER BOX, WHICH WE HAD GUESSED EARLIER WAS THE SHIP'S INTERCOM SYSTEM FOR DELIVERY OF THESE KINDS OF MESSAGES.

"GOOD MORNING, INTREPID," THE BOX ANNOUNCED, "THIS IS YOUR FRIENDLY CAPTAIN, JÖRGEN CHRISTIANSEN, COMING TO YOU FROM THE BRIDGE.

"WE ARE PRESENTLY AT A HEADING OF 36 DEGREES, 8 MINUTES, 44 SECONDS NORTH AND 5 DEGREES, 21 MINUTES, 47 SECONDS WEST, OR MORE COLLOQUIALLY, WE'VE ARRIVED AT THE PORT OF GIBRALTAR, WHICH THE CUTE AND LOVABLE BARBARY APES CALL HOME. WE'LL START THE DISEMBARKATION PROCESS IN THIRTY MINUTES ON THE STARBOARD SIDE OF DECK 1.

"IT'S A COOL 9 DEGREES CELSIUS OR 48 DEGREES FAHRENHEIT OUT THERE TODAY. SO BRING YOUR JACKETS AND DRESS WARMLY. THEN DRINK A PINT FOR ME AT ONE OF THE MANY FINE PUBS THE TOWN HAS TO OFFER. BUT DON'T STAY TOO LONG, BECAUSE WE WILL BE PULLING OUT OF THIS PORT AT 4 PM AND HEADED OUT TO SEA, AND WE DON'T WANT YOU TO HAVE TO SWIM AFTER US."

I REMEMBER HEARING A COUPLE OF LAUGHS IN THE BACKGROUND. WE SNICKERED, TOO. IT WAS THE LAST TIME I REMEMBER LAUGHING WITH TJ.

"HAVE A FANTASTIC DAY, AND WE'LL SEE YOU BACK ON

THE GRANDEST SHIP ON THE OCEAN, THE INTREPID, REGAL EUROPEAN'S SHINING STAR OF THE SEAS."

15

TJ

TJ adjusted her compression shorts and started a morning run that she would never finish.

The ship's outdoor trek stretched one quarter-mile around the main pool, the most popular area on the ship at midday—at least on sea days—when the sun's rays would normally have warmed the sea air to a satisfying 22 degrees centigrade. That was when the weather was normal. Nothing seemed normal in the last few days, least of all the weather.

It was downright cool out. The sun, a bare ghost in the sky, appeared more distant today, as if it were embarrassed to be seen. TJ rubbed warmth into her arms.

Menacing clouds undulated above and around her. They weren't the typical storm clouds, heavy with water and ready to burst. She tossed a glance behind her to confirm they weren't the plumes of smoke from the ship's single giant smokestack blowing onto its decks. They weren't. She peered then to her sides and saw that these clouds were everywhere: out to sea, around the port, blanketing the sky, covering the top of the Rock of Gibraltar, overlooking the town.

These clouds were also astringent, rather than water vapor, biting at her lungs, causing her to involuntarily gasp. The smell gave it away: it was sulfur. She instantly flashed to their time at Yellowstone when she labored to breathe the foul air.

She also hadn't noticed, until now, that a gray layer of dust coated the track, the chairs, maybe even the people. It muted the color out of everything, like death.

TJ ignored these unpleasantries and focused her attention on the near-empty running track before her.

Even without the weather anomalies, she knew early morning above deck was usually a ghost town. And during days at port, like today, even those hardy few who would otherwise be up here were most likely already queued up and waiting to leave the ship. Because of her husband's phobia, she and he would be the last to leave. To be honest, she preferred avoiding the crowds too.

Only a few walking dead stumbled about the track. In her previous cruises, those usually using the track at this time of day were the ancient folk barely able to walk, or the excessively obese. The obese were the most common, fooling themselves into believing that walking a few steps around a rubberized track constituted exercise. Most barely expended a dozen calories in the process of trudging their ballooning bodies around the small oval, just before heading inside to one of the fifteen restaurants, ready to start the first of their half-dozen daily ten-thousand-calorie meals. The gluttony of a cruise ship often got to her, especially when she worked so hard to keep her own weight off.

She sprang forward, her muscles instantly feeling tight from the cold. She should have worn warm-ups.

As if on an obstacle course, where the obstacles were moving in slow motion, she darted around multiple targets, each seemingly tasked with slowing her down: a fat man wearing a straw hat and muscle shirt that said "Grand

Cayman"; a beach ball-shaped woman wearing overly stretched-out running shorts, hiked up to just below her mountainous breasts; and then there was an elderly couple, walking hand in hand. A juxtaposed reflexive image hit TJ just then, a brick wall that blunted her energy.

After gliding past the couple, she stopped and stared back at them, rubbing her watering eyes. She wasn't sure if it was the lack of sleep, bad dreams, or just the growing feeling of utter terror: these two looked *exactly* like the couple they had seen at Alcazaba two days ago, and then more prominently in recurring images from horrific nightmares.

This same couple was getting pulled to pieces by wild seagulls. She'd always wake up when one bird started snacking on an eyeball.

TJ shook the nightmare away. That's all it was, she reasoned with herself.

She watched the old couple hobble by, their heavily lined faces carrying their own share of worry. Upon closer inspection, she realized they weren't the same couple she had seen. And she was merely reflecting her own worry on them. Their lines were softer, and looked less like concern and more like contentment. Their facial creases folded into their smiles. It was joy they exuded, buttressed by a mutual understanding and an unflappable peace. No doubt all of this was born from their many years together. Oh, they looked physically feeble, but they were undoubtedly strong in their resolution, as if they could deal with anything, as long as they were together.

What the hell is going on with me, and with the world?

Although she was prone to psychologically analyze people—her job demanded this—she never personalized her targets, not that this couple was a target. She approached everything from a fair and analytical view. But lately, she'd felt very... *Emotional!*

She shook her head in disbelief at her own obtuse thoughts. *Were not the events of the last two days enough to make anyone emotional?* She reasoned.

Like one of Rodin's marbles in his sculpture garden, she remained a statue, contemplating the old couple's life and her own. Now she had become the obstacle in the middle of the track to the oncoming zombies. Her eyes remained fixed on the backs of the old couple, until they disappeared around the bend of the jogging track.

Worries about her mom sprang up again. She'd always looked after her mother, ever since her father's violent death, before she left for school. Last night they had talked for a couple of minutes—at ten bucks per minute she kept it short—and she sounded fine, but she still worried about her.

TJ jumped to attention as if she'd been defibrillated. She was here for two reasons.

A quick twist of the wrist to check the time. Her watch said it was 6:28 AM. She'd still make her rendezvous, but the run was out of the question now.

She jogged a few dozen more steps before finding the stairwell Jean Pierre had told her about, a little farther forward, "just past where the jogging track turns..."

She ducked into an alcove, underneath an outdoor stairwell that led to another sun deck, if she remembered the ship's map correctly. This area wasn't viewable by anyone else, unless they walked up on her, while she waited for him.

Less than two minutes later, Jean Pierre—also dressed in running gear—jogged down the same track. He looked nervous, checking both sides, to see if anyone—guest or crew—saw him. He even wore a hat, pulled low on his head so that he was less conspicuous, what with his polished dome being so recognizable.

Just before the alcove, Jean Pierre stopped and reached behind a towering steel beam to stretch a cord out and across the walkway, connecting it to a concealed hook behind another beam on the other side. It clicked home, effectively blocking anyone from walking their way and ensuring that they wouldn't be interrupted.

Jean Pierre immediately saw her turned away from him, behind the stairwell.

He stood before her while she was straightening her little jogging outfit and flashed him an embarrassed smile.

"We don't have much time before the captain needs me back. I'm sure you can guess we've been a bit busy up there."

"No problem. What do you have for me?" she said with a smile and a wink.

~~~

It was a jarring screech. If anyone was around him, on another balcony or in another cabin, they would have no doubt compared it to nails on a chalkboard. On a normal cruise, to Ted, this would have sounded like music.

Other than yesterday's All Access Tour, this was the other activity Ted had longed for.

The veins on his head bulged as he dragged the heavy table closer to the balcony railing, until it clinked metal to glass, announcing it had reached the balcony's limit. Next, he pushed the mesh chair closer to the table. Both were now ready to accept him. He then ducked into their cabin to retrieve and lay out the rest of what was needed: his iPad tablet, the Internet passcode in an envelope, a pot of coffee (ordered the moment they had awoken), creamer and a cup, and finally his iPhone containing some notes he'd dictated to himself earlier.

Except for the briny air and clatter from the port, this setup was not unlike what he had at home where he'd do his writing in the morning. He'd envisioned doing quite a bit of writing at this very spot while on this trip. He had imagined the inspiration that would be fostered by gazing out across the water as the ship's screws churned up the seas, leaving a white
~~~

foamy wake. Even parked at one of the two ports on their itinerary, he had looked forward to his creative juices flowing, unleashing a flurry of words.

There would be none of that today.

He needed to know more about what was going on in the world and to do that, he needed more information. From all he had witnessed or heard, buttressed by the knowledge he had gained while researching his second-to-last book, Ted thought he might know some of what was going on. He hadn't let on to the captain, when Christiansen asked if he thought that the story of Madness could be coming to life. His answer was "I don't know." But he thought he did know.

And if he was correct, what that might mean for their lives and the lives of everyone on this planet absolutely terrified him.

His wife kept insisting on talking to him about the animal attacks, but that was the last thing he wanted to do. Talking about it would only make it real. Similarly, his fictional tales, floating around in his conscious brain and his subconscious nightmares, became real—at least to his readers—only after he wrote them down. That was fiction.

This was not.

If he was being honest with himself, he'd have to admit that part of this research effort was to avoid dealing with the consequences of making this real. But he knew it was also wise to double check his information before panicking the whole ship. So he'd excused himself from discussing this with TJ once more this morning when she brought it up, until after completing his research review. But he really didn't need to, because the more he thought about the whole concept of *Madness* and the research behind it, the surer he became that he was correct.

He was just going through the motions now.

First, he'd check his email, and procrastinate even more.

He logged into the ship's WiFi network, another freebie

because of his upcoming lecture on the ship; he would never have paid the twenty dollars per day they charged for this service. He paused before clicking open his email program app and instead opened a browser and pulled up Google News. On a hunch, he typed "animal attack" in the search box, and tapped the ENTER key.

There were hundreds of stories, and he scanned through several of them.

"Good morning!" blared Captain Christiansen's voice from the loudspeaker.

Ted shuddered and then reflexively examined his watch. It was 6:45 AM.

"We should be letting all of you loose in a few minutes. You're welcome to proceed in that direction.

"I would ask that you return a little earlier than planned. We'd like you back on board by 3 PM. This is one hour earlier than we expected. Again, 3PM is now the time you must be on the ship.

"Have a wonderful day in Gibraltar, before you return to the most wonderful ship in the Mediterranean, Regal European's Intrepid."

Ted considered the captain's rosy message for a second, then returned his gaze to his tablet's screen and refined his search to "animal attack Gibraltar."

The first story in the results demanded his attention and so he opened it and felt an electric shiver crawl up his spine with each word he consumed. On a hunch, he refreshed his search and a new article popped up which he opened in a new tab. Halfway through the article, he slapped his iPad and keyboard closed, grabbed his key-card, and dashed out of the room.

He had to see the captain, and he had to see the captain now.

16

Bollocks

"Hey, little guy. What's your name?" asked Boris, a Brit with a pale face that resembled a plastic bag stuffed with dinner rolls. He offered the visitor a wide grin.

Boris carefully balanced a plate loaded with six chocolate croissants stacked up like some monument to the God of Chocolate Gluttony. In fact, they were a favorite of his wife of ten years—one of many surprises he'd planned to bring her during their anniversary cruise. He shot a quick glance at the monument, glad he hadn't attempted to make it bigger with one or two more on top of the pile. He didn't want to lose the whole lot and spoil his surprise.

He hesitated for just a second, and then carefully plucked a small morsel from the chocolate tower to offer up to his new friend.

He didn't want to scare the little bugger away, so he clenched his teeth and carefully bent his knees to get closer to the ferret, who seemed to be patiently waiting for its prize. Boris feared that he might not be able to get back up if he crouched down any farther—his knees weren't used to many, if any, ups-and-downs and he'd already accumulated some extra pounds since their holiday had begun. So he struggled to push back up, tensing the muscles in his face. As if on cue, both his knees buckled. The plate of pastries tumbled toward the ground and so did he.

Boris attempted to slow his fall, using his right elbow against the bright colored carpet and his right shoulder against the wall.

He came to rest in the middle of the hallway, like a jackknifed tractor-trailer blocking a large roadway. Thankfully this roadway had no traffic, minimizing his embarrassment. Unfortunately, his load—the appetizing morning snacks he'd secured for his wife—was now spilled all over the carpet.

Not one of his finer moments.

"Bollocks!" Boris grumbled under his breath, mad that he'd tasked his already shaky knees too much. "I hope you're happy, mate." He scowled at the ferret, who just stared at him with its creepy red eyes.

Funny, Boris thought. He didn't remember ferrets having red eyes. His brother in Camden had a ferret, and its eyes were brown, not red like this one.

A moment of panic set in as Boris realized that he really was utterly alone, as everyone was trying to get off and see the sights in Gibraltar. His wife would not come to his aid, and the ship's crew might not come across him on the floor for a while. He glanced past the ferret, down the hall, and then tried to turn his body around so he could look the other direction, but he couldn't twist far enough.

"Double-bollocks!" He looked back at the ferret. It had moved closer to him. With Boris' own face almost ground level, the ferret was literally staring at him red eye to bloodshot eye.

Still, the ferret didn't move, as if it was considering its options.

"You know it's rude to stare, mate? Here, take this

morsel." He shook the piece of Danish he still clutched in his right hand. Maybe he should save it, since it was the only piece of Danish that hadn't touched the carpet. He glared back at the glorious chocolate croissants scattered over the carpet, taunting him. The five-second rule had long since expired.

He glanced back at the ferret, who was sniffing him, like a blooming dog. It opened its little mouth—he was glad it was little because it was filled with lots of ferocious-looking teeth. Just then it looked like the little guy was planning to take a chunk out of his nose. Instead, the ferret reared back on its hind legs and peered over Boris' head as if it saw a better offer behind him. Then the little thing hissed, turned and quickly scurried away.

At the end of the hall, the ferret turned back and looked once more at the silly human dumped all over the hall, hissed again, and then disappeared out of sight, where the hallway veered off to the right.

This was all very strange behavior for a ferret, not that Boris was any expert. Although at this point he recalled when one of the neighbor's dogs once stuck its wet nose up against the front window to inspect his brother's ferret, which was running around the living room while they were watching the telly. His ferret—named Charles, after the Prince of England—hissed at the dog, just like this one did.

He had a horrific thought, which he knew was incongruent with reality: what if a dog was behind him? That was, of course, ridiculous because pets weren't allowed on cruise ships. Though he was also remembering something his wife had said on the day they boarded. It was right before the craziness with the rats happened, she said, "Look there, Boris, among all the hand luggage: there be pups in those crates."

The three-tone chime of the ship's intercom rang out loudly, startling him.

"We are all clear to Gibraltar, and we'll be releasing everybody in a few minutes on deck 1. Please have your sea-pass ready as you visit the land of the Barbary apes."

The rumble of the ship's engines had stopped some time ago, after they had made port—and yet, it sounded like there was a rumble, almost like a growl. But this wasn't coming from below him. It was coming from the hallway behind him.

The skin on the back of his neck crawled and became prickly. He let go of the bit of croissant that he'd been holding this whole time, and threw his arms around his head in an attempt to roll around in the other direction, knowing he couldn't just turn his head. He grunted at the effort and felt a shot of pain pierce his hobbled knee. He waited for the pain to subside, his face contorted—the rolls in his cheeks sucked in as if they had been eaten—and then he opened his eyes.

The pain had made him forget for a moment why he went to such effort to turn around, but when his eyes opened, they instantly focused only a few meters ahead, fluttering several times to bat away any foggy obstructions. He could see that his situation was much worse than he had thought.

A little white toy poodle, covered in blood, like some miniature hound from hell, stood a few feet away from him. Its eyes glared an angry red, and then it leapt at him.

"Oh, bollocks."

~~~

"I need to see the captain, please," Ted pleaded as he bounded down the hall, toward the bridge.

A Brazilian member of their security stood between Ted and the entrance to the bridge.

"I'm sorry, but the captain is very busy right now. If you want to see him, please go to Guest Services. They will arrange a tour fo—"

"—Look..." Ted cut the man off and took another step
~~~

closer, almost in his face. "I appreciate what you're doing, but I really need to see Captain Christiansen *now*." Ted looked down and patted his pocket for the captain's business card, only remembering at that instant he'd been given one and could have called ahead first. But Ted was in such a hurry to personally share what he'd learned with the captain... He looked up and realized his stance appeared too aggressive to the security guard, who had adjusted his posture. He risked landing himself in the ship's brig, assuming they had one—not surprisingly, that wasn't part of the ship's tour. He took a step back and said, "Tell him it's Ted Williams, or maybe you should say, T.D. Bonaventure. He asked me to contact him if I found something. Please!"

The man wasn't moving.

Better the brig than to do nothing.

"Tell him *every* passenger on this ship may die if he doesn't act right now!"

The guard's eyes grew wide, and without hesitation, he yanked out his radio, mumbling some words in Portuguese, and then in English, he blurted, "Code Alpha! I repeat, Code Alpha!" The Brazilian fixed a stern gaze upon Ted, but it was masking the concern that he had just encountered a madman. The guard thrust a palm into Ted's chest and shoved him backward, away from the entrance and back down the hallway.

Ted knew he pushed it too far, but continued his pleas, while being forcibly moved backward, farther away from the bridge entrance and the captain. Several more reverse steps down the halfway, Ted backed into a human wall of very substantial proportions. The wall clasped him on the shoulder, and a hand like a vise clamped down uncomfortably hard.

"Come with us, sir," said the booming voice that belonged to the hand, thick with a harsh Slavic overtone.

Ted felt something hard press against his side. A quick downward glance confirmed it: a stun gun.

He regretted his decision altogether now, wondering if

he could get out of this. “I’m sorry, I have the captain’s business card. I’ll go back to my room and call him directly.”

The two guards continued to firmly pull him down the hall, one step at a time, not answering or even acknowledging his new request. In fact, the Slavic guard squeezed harder, if that was possible. Discomfort was fast turning into pain.

“Captain Christiansen knows me and will want the information I have. Please, I’m begging you. Let me go back to my room and I’ll call him.”

They nearly had him out of the hallway and into the aft stairwell.

“Ted? Is that you?” the captain called down the hall.

They all stopped and gazed forward.

“Captain. Oh, thank God. I need to talk to you,” Ted bleated.

“Code Blue, gentlemen. I repeat, Code Blue,” Jörgen bellowed.

The giant Slavic security officer opened up his mitt, releasing Ted. The Brazilian moved out of the way. “We’re sorry, sir. We were just following orders.” His voice had turned timid.

“It’s all right.” Ted pushed past the Brazilian and dashed back toward the captain.

Overhead, the loudspeakers announced that passengers could now start leaving the ship and enjoy the warm hospitality of Gibraltar.

Ted was face to face with Jörgen, the two guards trailing not far behind him. “Captain, please tell your security not to let anyone off the ship. They’re not safe in Gibraltar.”

Jörgen shot Ted one glance. It was quick, but for a man who seemed to rely on his crew and making quick decisions, Jörgen only needed a second for this one. To the guards behind Ted, he barked, “Tell Patel to hold up the passengers until further notice from me.”

The Brazilian, who must have been senior of the two

guards, repeated the message on his radio.

"Please come in and tell me why we're going to ruin our passengers' day in Gibraltar."

17

The Barbary Apes

Over three hundred Barbary macaques of Gibraltar represented the sum total of the wild monkey population on the entire European continent. Only today would the town realize how wild they'd become.

Because they were tailless, they were often referred to as "apes." The Spaniards called them *monos* or monkeys, which was technically a more correct identification. Regardless of their label, for years they'd been favorites of visitors, who reveled in the monkeys' acumen for stealing bags belonging to selfie-focused tourists from park benches and unattended food plates from tables at nearby cafes.

For the most part though, the Barbary apes stayed out of the town, choosing to remain at the Gibraltar Nature Reserve as the star attraction. And other than some occasional petty theft and a few cases of minor property damage, the *monos* had been good neighbors. They didn't fear humans, learned through their daily intermingling, and were never considered a menace. Yesterday, that all changed.

One of the apes attacked a tourist. Then, another attacked and killed a British pub-owner. This morning, there was another attack. And because it was still too early for the rumor mill to fan the flames of worry, residents and tourists continued their activities as if nothing had happened.

It wasn't until the *Intrepid*, Regal European's shining star of the seas, pulled into Gibraltar's port and announced its arrival with its throaty horn that all the apes appeared to go crazy.

Each ape, having ten times the strength of a human, easily tore through people and property, without pause. Most bit wildly at anything with a pulse: store owners, just starting their day; residents and pets enjoying a walk during the morning coolness; and visitors, eager to consume their first espresso at a street-side cafe. Most of the town's occupants seemed unaware of the approaching ape mob until a wave of screams hit their ears.

When the apes entered the more populated areas, some stopped to take larger chunks out of their victims or just tore at limbs, which came off easily. Although they acted crazed and independent from one another, all the apes seemed to be charging through town in one direction: toward the port and the only cruise ship currently docked there.

The mass of apes wasn't yet visible through Captain Jörgen Christiansen's binoculars, as he scanned for some visual vindication to his decision. Moments ago, he had made the announcement to cancel this port of call, explaining to his frustrated guests that it was just too dangerous, and that they'd be leaving port shortly. Ted, who had just left the bridge, made far too compelling an argument. Still, Jörgen scanned the farthest reaches of the town with his binoculars, both wanting and not wanting to find visual verification. And while his crew busied themselves, they anxiously glared at their captain's head and awaited his next order.

"Do we still have the refueling ship available?" Jörgen

barked at Jean Pierre, who was standing patiently beside him. The staff captain hadn't agreed, but backed the captain's decision.

The refueling ship was still tied to a berth on the other side of them. They had waved it off earlier, with their plan to refuel in the Canaries. But that was before Ted's report and their decision to leave.

"Yes, sir." Jean Pierre snapped to attention, repeating the information they had already discussed. "They only have heavy fuel and it's heated higher than your preferences. And I have confirmed your calculations with the chief engineer that we're already 20% over needed heavy fuel until the Bahamas."

"JP"—the captain rarely used first names, much less nicknames on the bridge, without titles—"I fear we might need more fuel than we're guessing. Please fill us to capacity. If I'm wrong, we can replace with MGO before we pull into US waters, and still satisfy their environmental standards."

"Aye, Captain," Jean Pierre confirmed, and then quickly turned and picked up the outside phone line to the harbor master. He wasn't sure what the captain was thinking, but he trusted his judgment.

Captain Christiansen didn't know what lay ahead, but he was going to ensure they had more supplies than they needed. He had learned this back in 2005 when twenty-eight hurricanes hit during the season, cutting off supplies and stranding them at one or another of their ports while they waited for a refueling ship. Generally, he kept his ship's fuel supply at 20% over the calculated maximum needed amount for their long route, in case he had a problem with a supplier. This afforded enough leeway to move to the next port and refuel there. It wasn't hurricane season, but with everything going on, a voice inside told him he'd need every drop he could get right now.

Jörgen watched from the swing deck with controlled nervousness as the refueling barge sidled up to their ship's port side, while remaining tied to the berth. It only had to move a few meters before it was in position. It was maybe half the length of the *Intrepid*, but only a couple of decks above water level. It was completely full of heavy fuel, something akin to crude oil. He kept one eye on his crew and the tanker's two crew members racing to connect the giant hoses; with the other he gazed at the digital fuel gauges, mentally pushing them upward. Deep down, in the pit of his stomach, an apprehensive worry burned like fire. A part of him felt sure they had very little time left.

~~~

Nigel James blew warmth onto his hands and vigorously rubbed them together in a vain attempt to get feeling back to his digits. It wasn't the abnormal temperatures outside; the pipe fittings were ice cold. Touching them seemed to leach the coldness directly through the thin material of his gloves. Then almost instantly the reverse happened, as the heated fuel cascaded through their barge into the ship. He felt the fittings change from cold to warm and then to hot. Now he started to sweat and stepped back to wait until he was told they were done. He looked at his mate manning the controls, who nodded at him. Then Nigel gave thumbs up to the two crew from the cruise ship, who were already stepping inside their hatch, eyes wide, like they were worried they were going to get docked pay for cavorting with sludge-sloppers like him. Most crew from cruise ships were cordial. The *Intrepid's* was not, which was very strange.

Nigel glanced up at the top decks of the sparkling cruise ship, admiring its recently painted hull. Several decks had lines of balconies, some with passengers—no doubt on holiday—luxuriating. His eyes scanned for a pretty female until he found one in a sumptuous bathrobe. Then he imagined himself in that
~~~

very room with that pretty lassie. He remained fixed in her direction, not so much as leering, but watching his mind play out the narrative of his daydream...

They had just made love before having their morning cafe out on the balcony. He could almost taste its bitterness and the smooth sweetness of the milk stirred into it. He'd have had several by this point, while he planned his day with his super-model girlfriend: where they'd go, what they'd buy at the store—

"Nigel, is our seal still strong?" his mate hollered from behind him, rudely interrupting his reverie.

He hated this job, but he needed to keep it. So he bit his tongue and didn't tell him what he could do with the bloody seal. Nigel shot a glance at it. "Looks good here."

He furtively glanced back up to the balconies, searching for the woman. She was gone. There were more passengers now on their balconies, all looking over Gibraltar. Many were pointing at the town.

"As if there was anything that interesting in this bloody town but a few bloody monkeys on a hill," he snickered.

A scream drew his attention to a passenger more forward from where he'd been gawking. He squinted and found the screaming passenger also pointing with one hand, her other clutching her mouth. Beside her, an elderly man was gazing through binoculars. Nigel heard a muffled, "Oh my God."

He now turned his attention in the same direction that she was pointing.

"Perhaps the Rolex she wanted was no longer in the window of her favorite store," he grumbled.

But there was something going on in town. Some sort of commotion. He wished he had some binoculars too. But he was close enough that it didn't take long for him to figure it out.

Not far away from them, just outside the port, was a street lined with outdoor restaurants. Nigel had daydreamed plenty about drinking unlimited pints of Guinness out there, instead of drinking a local brew at a pub much farther inland for about a fifth of the price. Outside each of these restaurants were little tables and chairs, which would be soon bustling with visitors from this ship and at least one other that was due to arrive later. There were only a few people there now, but they weren't sitting. They were moving away from the street, slowly at first. Then, they darted inside as several objects moved down the street, mostly ignoring the restaurants. One of the objects, a brown and gray blur, dashed inside and then moments later bolted back outside, carrying what looked like a rolled-up towel that sprayed liquid.

It was still very hard to make out at this distance with the naked eye.

"Hey, what is that?" Nigel called out to his mate.

"Don't know," was the reply.

Another scream. This time, more of a screech, not as distant. And he could just barely make out the objects now: the brown-gray objects were actually those blooming monkeys. And that one monkey that had come out of the restaurant wasn't holding a rolled-up towel.

It was holding up someone's severed arm, like a macabre trophy. Now it was swinging it in the air, while it cried out to the other monkeys.

They all seemed to be headed to the cruise liner terminal... in his direction.

~~~

"Give me the number!" Jörgen bellowed from behind his binoculars. He did his own calculations on the port-side swing deck of the bridge, while glancing at the pandemonium in town drawing perilously closer.

"Ninety-two percent," Jessica snapped back, her eyes
~~~

glued to one of the many large tilted computer screens in the middle of the bridge.

"That's good. Cut loose and let's get out of here." Jörgen scanned his entire port side before his gaze fell on the two barge workers, who appeared to be watching not their stations, but instead the town. Then one of them reacted abruptly and ran toward his bow, slipping down into an open hatch below. Both workers were needed to disconnect so that they could leave.

He wondered if they had waited just a minute too long.

~~~

Nigel looked back up and noticed the *Intrepid's* captain was outside, gazing down at him, before turning and ducking inside his bridge. Nigel glanced back for his mate, but he was gone too. Probably went down below deck.

The two Regal European crew members who had made a hasty retreat earlier were back outside, yelling orders at him. "Disconnect! We need to leave *now!*"

Nigel was about to panic and bail: jump into the water and swim away. He then imagined how cold that water would be; he hated the cold. Then he reasoned that maybe he and his mate could get away in the barge and he'd be dry, if only he could do what they asked and disconnect.

More screaming, again from the balconies above. This time he ignored them all and examined the connected hose.

There was a blur to his left side for just a second, and then it was gone. Nigel looked over in that direction and saw two monkeys crawling on the tie line connecting the barge to the dock. The monkeys were headed for them. They couldn't leave until they were disconnected, and he couldn't disconnect until the flow had stopped. Nigel made a quick decision and
~~~

darted to the outside control panel, where his no-good friend should have been.

He punched the emergency stop button and dashed back to the hose coupled to the big cruise ship. One of the crew from the ship was already trying to pull it off, but it was too soon. The man had to wait until the pressure was equalized, which wasn't going to be for another moment or two. He desperately clawed at the fittings, shooting a glance at Nigel, just as Nigel pulled up to him. His eyes were wild with terror. And he was bleeding.

"The apes. We've got to go!" he yelled. Letting go of the coupling, he leapt up to the hatch at the same time as a monkey jumped up to greet him.

Nigel watched in disbelief as the monkey attacked the worker, who was trying to escape into the ship. He couldn't help the guy. He had to disconnect now, if there was any chance of leaving. He lunged for and unclasped the coupling and it burst off, spraying black oil everywhere. He had pulled it off too early, but he didn't have the luxury of waiting any longer. Part of the nozzle still held to the fitting. So he yanked once to pull it free and lost his footing on the oil already covering the deck.

All of his one-hundred-fifteen kilos tumbled hard onto the deck of the barge, his head hitting harder, and his vision exploded in fireworks.

He lay there for what was probably only a couple of seconds, but seemed like forever, as he tried to clear the daze that held him. He watched a monkey viciously bite and tear at the Intrepid crew member above. His crewmate, already behind a sealed door, stared through the porthole.

Then Nigel saw people above him, on those nice balconies, looking down at him.

One passenger was smoking a cigar.

What an idiot, Nigel thought. Didn't your ship tell you it's against the rules to smoke?

He watched the passenger move over him, unable to tell which was moving: the cruise ship or his own barge. Then he saw the cigar do somersaults in the air, seemingly on a wire, guided right at him. While he heard more cries and screams, Nigel gazed incredulously as the cigar bounced off his chest and landed on the deck's oily surface beside him.

Nigel knew he still had a minute or two to abandon ship, as the heavy oil shouldn't explode like the MGO. But it would burn very hot.

He attempted to right himself, but he couldn't get a foothold. The oil looked a lot like black blood.

He felt a rush of heat and knew that the oil was already catching. He'd forgotten that heated oil burned quicker, and their oil was heated high. This was usually good for them because heated oil took up more room, which meant they could sell less of it for the same amount per liter and make more money. It wasn't good now. The boat's owner's money-grubbing ways were going to get him killed.

With all his effort, he found himself standing hunched over, head craned up sideways like Quasimodo, glaring at the cruise ship as its bow passed by him. He knew what he needed to do to save himself. Only five feet separated him and the barge's edge, and therefore the water. He put one foot in front of the other, slowly at first, then a little quicker, even though a searing pain swept up his legs—his pants must be on fire.

Three feet.

His hands started to burn.

Two feet.

A blanket of heat covered his arms.

One foot.

A blaring screech hit him at the same time as a large brown object, sending him back onto the smoldering deck.

As Nigel's face started to singe, a gruesome ape, mouth agape, screeched at him. Before it sank its giant fangs into his face, he noticed its eyes. They were red like blood.

18

Ted

For Ted, the unfolding of the last two days' events was akin to watching a painter throw together a watercolor canvas on one of those PBS shows. But this version was even more excruciating.

The artist always started with a blank white canvas; what it would become was only known by the artist. First came the foundational colors: splashes of blues, browns, and blacks. Even after all of these were applied, the canvas revealed nothing to the audience. The blurry mess could have been anything, or nothing at all.

As the artist added flourishes to specific locations on the canvas, images started to take shape. On one corner, mountains burst upward out of the browns. On the other, low cloud formations billowed from the blue skies. And among the darkest portions of the canvas, a single boat emerged from the murk, like a ghost.

Each of these disparate images had its own story, which should belong to separate canvases. Or so it seemed. Of course, it was obvious to the audience that they must be somehow related, because of their single but most crucial connection: They were attached to the same canvas.

The animal attacks and the volcanoes were seemingly unrelated anecdotes splashed upon the same grand cataclysmic landscape taking shape before the eyes of the world. It should have been obvious to all that they were related. But Ted suspected few if any were connecting these anecdotes. He was instantly overwhelmed by a fear that by the time the world's audience perceived this connection, it would be too late.

Near the end of the PBS show, the television show painter would toss a few quick strokes of his brush onto the canvas and instantly connect all the images into one: land, sky, and sea all seamlessly woven together into one symbiotic mosaic. Only then did the reason or theme of the painting become obvious. Those final flourishes were all that was missing to provide that ah-ha moment.

Ted was trying to speed up the process to get to that ah-ha moment so that he could understand why the animal attacks were connected to the volcanoes. If he did, maybe he could help to save his wife, his ship, maybe even humanity.

He sat heavily on the small couch of his cabin, facing the open slider and shrinking view of Gibraltar. His head was back and his eyes closed while he considered this real-life apocalyptic canvas that he and all his shipmates had found themselves splashed upon.

Something had caused animals to go all wonky in Spain and other parts of Europe. And whatever was doing this drove those animals into attacking other warm-blooded creatures. He was pretty sure he knew the root cause of their madness. After all, he had based a fictional book on this. But something had to instigate this mass bout of rage with the animals. Some sort of inciter.

In his book, it was a virus created by an insane anarchist.

He doubted this real-life story had a human antagonist behind this. He wasn't sure what logic was driving his thinking, but he believed this had to be natural and caused by the volcanic eruptions, he just didn't know why. If he was at all correct, what would become of them was terrifying. And would this disease of madness remain only in Europe or spread elsewhere? And if he could even solve this part of the puzzle, would there be any way to stop it? The possibilities of more than half of all animals in the world being afflicted were too scary to even consider right now.

Ted sat up, still holding his binoculars, but he hesitated to raise them to his face, fearful that seeing it would make it real. TJ and he had traveled to Gibraltar once before, as part of a tour of Spain. He had been looking forward to seeing Gibraltar again, in spite of the large ship-spawned crowds: the majesty of its "Rock," easily accessible by tram; the humor of its infamous residents, the Barbary apes; and its uniquely British feel, bursting with pubs serving Guinness on tap along with more tasteful twists to traditional British food, or what they'd call *flavour*.

Ted and TJ swore that they'd come back again. After the hordes had disembarked the ship, they'd take a little time to stroll its cobbled streets, enjoy some of its food and imbibe a pint, or two. That wasn't going to happen now, and perhaps not ever again.

He considered the magnitude of this epidemic, with the numbers growing daily: three days ago, a couple; two days ago, several more; yesterday, an explosion of them. Today, the international news blogs and TV stations were abuzz about the animal attacks in Europe.

He considered two primary commonalities: the animals seemed crazy and their eyes were red. From as far north as Iceland to as far south as Egypt, and from Portugal in the west to Turkey in the east, birds, dogs, cats, and rats (and monkeys) were going mad.

From *Le Figaro* in Paris, yesterday:

"Packs of dogs roaming the Latin Quarter attacked other dogs and people. Seven deaths have been reported."

From *La Vanguardia* in Barcelona, a few hours ago:

"Twenty-five people were treated for injuries sustained from what several victims reported as 'rabid cats, with red eyes.'"

From *EL PAÍS* in Madrid, two days ago:

"Five people at a Hertz rental car parking lot were mauled by a German shepherd. Two died on the scene."

And finally, from the *Dario Sur* in Malaga, yesterday:

"Fifteen people were attacked by seagulls in the Alcazaba castle area. An elderly couple was found dead at the scene."

These last two prompted Ted to look specifically for stories from the next few scheduled ports. So far, there were no reports of attacks in the Canaries, although he had read a few mentions about recent earthquakes and worries about one of its active volcanoes erupting. But in Gibraltar, he found one small news story on a local blog site. It was the one that had prompted him to warn the captain. Then a minute later, it was backed up by a UK paper.

"British tourist mauled and nearly killed by one of Gibraltar's infamous Barbary apes."

In a way, he wasn't too surprised, and this alone didn't cause him worry. Frankly, he always wondered why more people weren't injured by those monkeys, whose evil charms and proclivity to steal from unattended bags earned them favor among the tourists. If one of them wanted to get violent, there wasn't much that could be done to stop them. And at least once before, several of the more "aggressive" monkeys were relocated to a wildlife park off Gibraltar.

But it was the report that had popped up in the UK's Daily Harold that made him grow cold.

"Molly Adams of Lancashire was expected to make a full

recovery after having her nose reattached. She couldn't offer comment, because of heavy sedation. However, one of her nurses had reported that Ms. Adams kept screaming about 'their evil red eyes.'"

That's when he knew the captain couldn't risk exposing the passengers of the Intrepid to more potential animal attacks. Christiansen seemed unsurprised by Ted's reporting and responded with conviction, immediately canceling disembarkation and sealing up the ship. Now they were sailing out of port after topping off their fuel.

Ted felt good about this, but he knew to his bones that this was just one more vignette of this apocalyptic canvas unfolding all over Europe, and perhaps elsewhere. He hoped that he would be proven wrong, even though it would mean that he alone was the reason for everyone missing out on Gibraltar.

Please be wrong.

But he knew in his gut he wasn't.

The whole time he had been back at their room he hesitated to look upon Gibraltar as it faded in the distance. He just didn't want to confirm his thinking. Finally, Ted brought the binocular lenses up to his eyes, which were assaulted with both the surreal and horrific.

There were several fires burning, including a scary black blaze at the port they'd just left. Stores were damaged, cars had crashed, and in between each were glimpses of monkeys jumping onto people, running after others, and killing still others on the ground. A startling bright red-orange light burst filled his field of view, as if he had pointed his binoculars directly at the sun.

Ted jumped, his heart skipping several beats. A deep thumping boom shuddered his suite's back slider and their living area mirror.

Ted gulped back his surprise and watched in awe as a rolling ball of black smoke and fire spun upward. Something big had just blown up in the harbor.

Their cabin door opened and then slammed shut and TJ strolled in, her arms full of plates of food and two Stellas.

He had wondered what had happened to TJ as she had been gone the entire time Ted had done his research, convinced the captain to leave Gibraltar, refueled, and then returned to his cabin. It had been hours since she had left for a run. He even started to fear that she had somehow left the ship, even though the captain had confirmed no one had. He was immediately relieved to see her.

"I heard what you did and figured we needed some sustenance," she said, her face grim.

She seemed unaware of the explosion, or the monkey attacks, but she was aware of his efforts to convince the captain to avoid Gibraltar—or was she?

"How did you hear?" he asked, laying the binoculars down on the vanity.

She set the plates and beers down on the coffee table and wrapped her arms around him.

She hugged him hard, and then released him, her face painted with a bright coat of anxiousness.

"We need to talk."

19
The Talk

They had closed the slider, sealing themselves in, and talked for more than an hour. It was a tough talk. TJ first admitted to him the truth about their cruise: it wasn't part of his book tour. It had all been set up by the Bureau because of her job, not his writing.

She didn't tell him the entire purpose of the cruise or the number of times she was meeting up with Jean Pierre. She couldn't yet.

He suspected some of this, but he had to admit he was a little disappointed. Yet none of that really mattered. Regardless of the reasons behind their trip, or TJ's long disappearances, or the secrets, both they and the ship had far greater concerns.

He told her everything he knew, and as he did, he became more and more convinced that he had predicted the crazy animal crisis they were experiencing today. He felt the need to hold back some of the details, because he didn't want to scare her too much, but she needed to know what was basically happening, and talking about it out loud helped him to see if there were holes in his theory. To TJ's credit, she accepted everything in a very measured manner, treating every point logically and not emotionally as he expected. It was after all an animal apocalypse, and she was frightened of animals.

"So why volcanoes? I mean, what do they have to do with the spread of this disease that makes animals crazy?" she asked.

"I don't know. I haven't figured that part out yet. But they have to be connected."

"But you think most animals that came in contact with the discharge from a volcano could be affected?" TJ took a final swig of her Stella Artois. She wished she'd plunked down another twenty for two more.

Ted was tapping away on his iPad, almost as if he was ignoring his wife's question. "Yes, I believe so, if my theory is correct," he said without looking up. Finally, after a minute of silent scrutiny of his screen, Ted looked at his wife. "Um, sorry. I just had a thought. I wondered where the trade winds would blow the discharge from the Iceland and Mount Etna volcanoes." He swung his tablet around to show TJ. "This is a picture of the ash cloud over eleven days during the 2010 eruption, and remember this was just from the one volcano, from Iceland."

"That's all of Europe," her eyes followed the progressive lines of the ash cloud. "...half of Asia, and part of the US."

"And again, that's just one volcano..."

"The Canaries look like they may be in the covered area. Did you check to see if there were any reports in La Palma?"

"There was nothing as of a few minutes ago." Ted rose from the couch and stretched. They'd been sitting the entire time. "I need to take a bathroom break and I think I hear our room steward. I'll drop our dishes outside for him."

"Cool, do you mind if I do some searching?" TJ pulled the iPad onto her lap. "And see if you can get him to bring us some more beer."

"Sure, on both." Ted gathered up the tray of dishes and their two empties. He padded to the door, balancing the tray in one hand and opening the heavy door with the other. A whoosh of wind whined through the cabin. It was a wind-tunnel blaring from their back slider—they'd cracked it open a few minutes earlier to get some air movement—through the open front door. Ted let the door close with a deep thump, forgetting for a panicked moment whether he had his key on him. Then he remembered it was in his back pocket.

He looked in both directions and didn't see Jaga's cart of supplies, so he leaned over and set the tray down by the door. He'd call room service for the beers and ask that they pick it up. His head snapped to his right toward a rapid motion, and he froze, still holding the tray.

"Hey there," he said to what he at first thought might be a very large rat, and then he realized it was a ferret. He figured someone must have brought it on board and it got free.

He froze.

The ferret didn't move, and just gazed at him with blood-red eyes.

Ted was still bent over. His face and neck were completely exposed to this animal, if it attacked. His heart beat a countdown to what he thought would be the ferret's eventual strike.

Ted's fingers softly glided across the tray's surface where he remembered seeing a metal fork, which he could use as a weapon. He felt his chest pound, as he remained frozen. Nothing else on him moved, other than the tips of his fingers, brushing slowly across the tray. When his hand found the fork, the ferret popped up onto its haunches and made sniffing sounds with its nose.

Ted thought that was the signal, and he waited for it, freezing in place and bracing for imminent impact. Instead, the ferret lowered itself to the carpet and then raced past him, down the hallway. It turned right and dashed down another corridor.

He let out a long series of puffs and lifted himself up, clutching the fork in his left hand. Then he considered the ferret's behavior.

He had been sure the ferret would go all honey-badger on him when he first saw the red eyes, but then he realized the animal wasn't crazed, like the other animals. It was thinking, considering. The mad animals seemed to lack all reason: they just attacked.

"Mr. Williams?" asked their room steward, Jaga, "can I get you something?"

Ted was startled, completely lost in his thoughts and what he thought was going to be his violent end. "Ah, hi! No, we're good, thanks." He turned, slid the key into the door, and let himself inside their cabin. With a *whoosh* and a *thunk*, the door slammed behind him.

"Thought you dropped into a black hole. Come here and look at this." TJ pointed to the iPad. "Never mind, I'll just tell you about it. There are still no reports about animal attacks in the Canaries, at least not recently. However, there were a rash of attacks in the 1700s. There's a book on Google, a history of the Canaries, and it talks about one period—which by the way was days after a volcanic eruption—where, and I quote, 'a dark period fell over the islands, where people and animals were said to have gone crazy.' Coincidence or harbinger?"

Ted had found his place back on the couch, while he listened to TJ's findings. "Good find. By the way, do you know anything about the typical eye color of a ferret?"

She looked at him like he was the one who had gone crazy, especially with what he held in his hand. "Ah, no. And what's with the fork?"

He glanced down and saw that he was still unconsciously clutching the damned fork he had been about to brandish at the ferret.

He hesitated and then decided to tell her about the

ferret he'd encountered when a double pulse-tone reverberated throughout the cabin.

It felt to them like the dreaded phone call often received in the middle of the night, carrying with it the news of a family member's illness or death. Both TJ and Ted glowered at the phone, feeling their chests leap and their stomachs turn over at once. It rang again, but neither of them budged.

Being closest to the phone, TJ finally picked it up.

"Hello?" she answered, her face steely and serious. "Oh hello, Jean Pierre," she said, now much friendlier.

She nodded, looking down at the desk, where the phone was located. "Ted too?" She looked over to him. "Both of us?" Once again, she looked away. "Okay, thank you. We'll see you shortly."

20

Taufan, the Ferret

Taufan finally zeroed in on the source of the scent it had first gotten wind of.

The ferret had never been outside of the three-meter by two-meter chamber its owner shared with the other roommates, so every square meter of the ship was new to it.

Taufan didn't understand what was going on, and certainly couldn't comprehend why. It was a ferret, after all. It only knew that it was confused, lonely, and very hungry, all at once. These feelings were as foreign as the hectares of ship it'd already explored. Until today, it'd only experienced its little belly being filled when it wanted food, and the love of its owner and its owner's roommates.

Now it had felt the pain of hunger all day long and was unable to find any food. Twice, it thought it had a chance of getting fed. Earlier, a big man tried to feed it, but a larger animal chased it away. And then a man looked like he might offer it something on a tray, but then Taufan smelled something far more appetizing.

A crew member had left a restricted doorway open. And through that doorway, down a stairwell, is where it caught wind of the glorious smells of fish. Lots of fish, along with other foreign but equally tasty aromas. Taufan wasn't finicky. It only knew the taste of fish, and it was so hungry right now. Even the humans it raced by looked like food, though it had never thought of its owner and his roommates as food before. It was then that Taufan became frantic. It burst into the vast main galley where all the food was being prepared for the ship's guests.

Because the ship was missing half of its kitchen staff, and dinner was still expected on time, many of the kitchen crew found themselves working two jobs. And amid the craziness of everyone racing around the kitchen, no one even noticed the small ferret scurrying inside and then working its way toward the aromas it'd been attracted to the whole time: the fish prep area.

Taufan had only experienced cooked fish, from the tidbits that Jaga and his roommates would bring it each day from their own dinners. Jaga was a fish fan himself and therefore so was Taufan. But the smell of fresh salmon was almost too much for the starving ferret. Like a guided missile, Taufan rocketed as fast as its little legs would accelerate it to its target, working its way around all impediments with ease.

It hopped onto a bucket beside a haphazardly abandoned cleaning cart and followed the makeshift staircase up the cart and onto a counter, bringing it belly-level with the kitchen crew. It remained unnoticed.

Without pausing, it scurried up several pots to a long shelving unit that stretched across the many stainless-steel food prep areas, almost the entire length of the kitchen. At the end of this shelf was the fish prep area.

The kitchen crew took great pride in making sure that they followed rigorous safety procedures for handling food. That way there was no chance of contaminations, which could lead to infections or outbreaks. But with the short staff of this cruise, including the loss of their safety officer (who never made it back from Malaga), mistakes were being made. Those mistakes were like dominoes, which started a cascading effect of failures that not only allowed a ferret to find its prize, but something much worse.

A bucket of dirty water, left by one of the short-handed cleaning crew who had to run to clean up a mess in the auxiliary galley, was precariously perched on the edge of the same shelf that Taufan was scampering over. This type of infraction was absolutely unheard of on cruise ships, especially those run by Regal European. During normal times, food would be discarded immediately if there was any chance that it touched the same place this bucket did. Again, these weren't normal times.

At the moment Taufan brushed past the bucket, which was partially blocking his route, a large ocean swell caused the ship to roll in the same direction, and the bucket started a long tumble to the floor. One-third of the way down, it hit another cart, also carelessly parked below. Because of the surge, this cart had also started to roll toward the opposite side of the main kitchen walkway and the produce prep area. The bucket struck in such a way that most of the blackish water—a disgusting combination of old fish parts, slop from the floor, and other sludgy unmentionables, all ripe with bacteria—splashed outward toward the table of leafy greens.

Just before this, Samuel Yusif from Somalia, standing behind one of the prep tables, carefully adjusted his yellow scarf, earned from his two earlier contracts. He scanned his area for the green tub he absolutely needed for his next step. It was gone. He had already chopped up everything that would need to go into the special tub, which would be used to transport the greens to an area occupied by other yellow scarves to prepare that evening's salads. Normally, the tub was brought back to him by another crew member, usually one of the green scarves. But several of the greens hadn't made it on board in Malaga. He hmphed under his breath, knowing he'd have to find the darn tub himself.

Leaving his area, Samuel barely acknowledged the sound of the crashing bucket behind him; he had just spotted one of his missing tubs and was focused on grabbing that and getting rid of his greens before his supervisor yelled at him for taking too long. As Samuel grabbed the tub, the falling bucket splashed its blackish contaminated water all over his freshly chopped lettuce, and then bounced unnoticed under his prep table.

When Samuel returned and scooped his chopped greens into the tub, he never even noticed the little specks of food particles and dirt that peppered his lettuce. The wet floor was odd, but that only sharpened his focus on not slipping and dropping his Romaine.

He quickly walked his tub over to the salad preparers who were waiting for it. They then assembled the leafy greens with other freshly prepped ingredients into each bowl. Another yellow scarf added the freshly made croutons. Each was beautifully presented, as always. Only one of the yellow scarves noticed what looked like pepper flecks, but she didn't think to mention it, as their new head chef was always trying new things.

Flavio breezed in from the service elevator, turned the corner into the main kitchen aisle, and pulled his cart over to the salad prep table. Immediately, without a spoken word, the yellow scarves loaded it with the freshly prepared salads. When his cart was full, he swung it around and pushed it quickly back toward the elevator.

As he turned the corner, directly past the smelly fish prep area, he witnessed what he thought he'd never see in a clean kitchen: an odd-sized rat was gorging himself on one of the large planks of fresh salmon. He hated rats and thought he'd already taken care of the ship's rat problem. This pissed him off.

He looked to his left and right and didn't see anyone in that area. So he decided to take matters into his own hands. He was tired of this ongoing issue.

Flavio withdrew a steak knife from his sheath; in his position, he always needed a knife, and the steak knives were versatile and plentiful. It didn't have the balance of the throwing knives he carried back home or his Morakniv carbon knives that he kept in his cabin, but it would do.

In the rat's direction, he hollered, "Hey rat!"

Taufan glanced up at the yelling human, while it frantically chewed a mouth full of delightful salmon.

The waiter paused just a moment—knife poised to be released—as he considered this odd-looking thing: its body was longer than a normal rat and the ones he encountered yesterday. But like the others, its eyes were as red as Ukrainian rubies. The red eyes were just too much to take. That momentary pause was all the creature needed.

Flavio let loose the knife. It had the perfect speed and arc, and it was on target. But it hit right when the long rat had jumped from the table. The knife clattered off the surface, cleaving away an additional piece of the ruined plank of salmon.

He *humphed* a momentary frustration at his miss before putting his weight again into the cart. Hungry diners were waiting for their salads. Somebody else would have to kill this rat. He reached under the cart and grabbed a replacement steak knife and sheathed it. He'd have to remember to sharpen this one. He hated dull knives.

Just before he entered the elevator, he spotted the senior assistant chef, Jon. Just the man to whom he needed to report this egregious infraction.

"Hey, Jon." His Romanian accent and limited English vocabulary kept him from expressing the indignities he wanted to articulate, but his mind screamed them. *How could you allow a rat to even exist in this kitchen, which up to now has been pristine? How could planks of fresh salmon be left unattended? And how could you allow a galley that was so well run go to shit?*

Flavio already hated this assistant chef because he was English, just like the head chef—he really hated English food. But this was all too much to stomach.

He had served more contracts than this fool, and from the staff captain on down, he was very well respected among his crew because of his skill and work ethic. Still, the assistant chef was his superior.

When he had Jon's attention, he spat out, "You have a rat eating the salmon planks, and no one is there to see it. You need to take better care of your kitchen."

He didn't wait for a reply.

As he pushed the deck 6 button, which would lead right into the MDR, he watched with both disgust and a little delight as the strange-looking rat scurried around the kitchen, chased by Jon and two yellow scarves.

21

The Rabid Toy Poodle

"It was a blooming rabid toy poodle, I tell you!"

Boris sat up from his infirmary bed, cheeks rosy with agitation. "The thing is vicious. And it had red eyes, like a little devil." He pointed to his eyes and clenched his teeth to make himself look scarier. "You've got to warn the captain."

"Settle down, Mr. Thompson. We'll tell everyone who needs to be told. Let's make sure you're fine first." Dr. Chettle turned to his nurse, and whispered the order to take Mr. Thompson's temperature once more.

Her last reading was 97.02, which was far below normal. He assumed that she didn't do it right the first time. She'd never served on a ship before, and at this moment he couldn't remember her qualifications. *But she should be able to take a damned temperature.* At least he thought so.

He suspected that Boris Thompson was in fact fine, other than very superficial puncture wounds from three dog bites and a few minor abrasions from the carpet, which broke his fall. There was very little tissue damage from the punctures, which hadn't penetrated more than a couple of millimeters of epidermis. Infection was the biggest worry. Thompson's blood pressure was slightly elevated, but this was normal considering his current level of agitation and his weight. They'd already cleaned and bandaged him up fairly quickly. Mr. Thompson could be released once Chettle had an accurate temperature for his records.

More concerning to Dr. Chettle was that this was the third dog bite he'd treated in the last twenty-four hours, and it was only the third day of the cruise. So he'd tell his superiors about this incident, and even include Mr. Thompson's colorful commentary. Not because he believed in the story of a rabid toy poodle; he believed that Al was not taking care of business at the pet spa. If Al allowed a toy poodle to escape, imagine what would happen if he didn't keep the kennel's larger dogs contained, especially next door to the ship's clinic?

In truth, Dr. Chettle despised having a dog kennel on the ship, and was so blinded by the chance to catch his colleague in a mistake, he missed any connection between dog bites and the several cases of rat bites on the ship, including those on the body of their butcher, who died from a trip and fall accident.

He tapped out a couple more notes on his tablet and then attached the file to an email he had already started. He read it over again, changed "second" to "third," and then sent it to the staff captain. He looked back up to Mr. Thompson, who was sitting up again and slinging animated words at his nurse.

"No, your bloody thermometer is not broken. My temperature is naturally low, so what? You're wasting time. You need to warn the captain, and he needs to warn the crew and passengers about this crazy dog. We're not safe!"

~~~
~~~

"I think he went this way," said Yakobus, who knelt by a pallet of crushed cardboard and pointed down the throat of a junction off the I-95 hallway.

Jaga and Catur stopped short behind him and looked around, pretending to have a good reason to be there, one that didn't involve chasing after their illegal ferret. Whenever a ship's officer would approach, they tried to act normal. Any crew member ranked lower than an officer wouldn't care what they were doing loitering along I-95. They had been looking for Taufan for hours now, and when they heard that a "really long rat is loose in the kitchen," they came running. They picked up Taufan's trail on I-95. And then they lost it.

I-95 was the busiest and longest thoroughfare on the ship, stretching from bow to stern. And because it was used by all crew to trans-navigate the ship to get to their shifts and transport supplies outside the scrutiny of guests, Taufan could be anywhere now.

An engineering second officer strolled past them for a second time, glancing at the curious room attendants, who seemed out of place.

"Sir," they all said in unison.

"And I think you should report the missing clothes to the laundry," Yakobus hollered at Jaga, much too loudly, acting as if they were caught in mid-conversation when the officer passed.

When the second officer was no longer visible and out of earshot, Jaga knelt down to where Yakobus had been pointing and saw the droppings, plus something else: a fish bone. This had to be from Taufan, when that nutty ferret reportedly raided the salmon in the kitchen. Jaga couldn't blame his buddy for going after fresh salmon. *I'd have done the same if I was in his shoes... I mean, paws.*

"Hey guys," warned Catur. He had popped up like a tower, and like Yakobus beside him, he was facing straight down the long hallway junction toward the vast provisions areas. Both wore looks of shocked anxiety.

Fifty feet away, in front of a pallet of bottled waters, was a pack of dogs barking and scratching at the containers. Some of the offending bottles had burst and still sprayed water like fountains. All the dogs appeared crazy, consumed by some rabies-like frenzy. And Jaga could see the object of their fury.

In the middle of the pallet, surrounded by the water bottles on all sides, was a small man cradling himself, and rocking back and forth. Beneath the pallet was little Taufan, attempting to shrink into the dark recesses to evade the dogs. The dogs didn't see him.

"What do we do?" To Catur's shock, he watched Jaga already tentatively walking on the balls of his feet, approaching the pack of wild dogs.

Jaga hugged a wall and quietly stepped closer to the pack, attempting to look small and not make any noise that might attract their attention. He had no idea what he would do when he got there, but hoped he'd figure something out before the dogs attacked him.

He halted halfway to the snarling pack. Before him was the crumpled form of a man lying behind a box of bundled papers waiting to be deposited at their next port. Jaga reared backward a couple of steps, almost losing his footing. The man appeared lifeless; his skin color matched his gray work clothes. A puddle of blood expanded slowly from his neck and sought escape under the box. The man appeared to have tried to hold together his mangled neck in a failed attempt to stay alive. Bloody bite marks spotted his body, and gory paw prints made it clear; the dogs were the killers. It must have just happened.

"Oh my God," Catur yelped, having just left Yakobus behind and caught up to Jaga, and now seeing the body. He said this much too loudly.

The pack of dogs abruptly halted their ravenous clawing and barking and turned its collective attention away from Taufan to the trio.

"Oh crap," Catur yelped once again.

Jaga wanted to kill him, but instantly knew they would be next.

A crazed little poodle scurried around the edge of the pack, and despite its tiny size issued a terrifying, high-pitched screech.

Jaga sucked up a scream when he realized the chase was over. There was no way they would be able to run away from this pack. He made a quick decision and leapt out to the middle of the hall, and then ran toward the pack, waving his arms and screaming the vilest swear words he knew in Indonesian at the top of his lungs.

Catur stood dumbfounded as he watched his friend Jaga charge the pack of crazed dogs in an attempt to divert their attention from them to him alone.

The dogs—all but the poodle were leashed together—charged after Jaga, with the toy poodle trailing. Both Jaga and dogs were converging quickly, with barely a second or two separating them. Just before they crashed into each other, Jaga dove into one of the wide-open refrigerators.

The pack of dogs didn't see this coming and attempted to change course immediately, but their feet—slick from the blood and the water-bottle attack—slid across the hard floor. Each attempted to regain its footing, some doing somersaults and others flailing at the air. But no amount of effort on their part could stop their momentum. Finally, they stopped.

They spasmodically righted themselves and bounded, as one tangled group, for the open space of the refrigerator. Jaga, unseen inside, seemed insane himself as he yelled more Indo curses at the oncoming pack, which bounded through the door almost at the same time.

There were multiple crashing sounds, followed by breaking glass, barking, and chaos. Then Jaga burst out of the refrigerator. He pivoted quickly and pushed with a grunt at the massive sliding door. It clicked closed just as the muffled sounds of the dogs pounded and scratched on the other side.

Jaga, practically hyperventilating, searched around the walls for something and made a small sound of satisfaction. He lumbered to the other side of the closed refrigerator, took down the notice about an upcoming crew party, flipped it around, and with his Sharpie wrote “Don’t open! Crazy dogs!” on the back and slid the notice into the handle: a warning to the next person who might be tempted to open this refrigerator.

Jaga then mustered the last of his strength and sprinted to the pallet of ruined water bottles. Finally, Catur and Yakobus caught up. They checked on the rocking man and helped him out of his faltering water-bottle containment. “Are you okay?” they asked.

“Come here, Taufan,” Jaga called into the dark space under the sloshing, dripping mass of eviscerated water bottles. Yakobus and Catur quietly plodded behind him and the three listened, hoping Jaga’s pleas would be rewarded.

A barely audible squeak blurted back in reply, and moments later a soaking wet Taufan waddled over to them and leapt into Jaga’s arms.

None of them reveled in their joy at finding their little friend and not dying in the process. Rather, they turned and left the area quickly. All three averted their eyes when they walked past the dead body. They would head back up to their room and put Taufan back, safe and unseen, into his bed. Only then would they report the dead body and the locked-up dogs.

They turned back onto I-95, Jaga cradling Taufan while his friends draped their arms around him, heaping praise upon him for his heroics.

A few seconds later, the warning sign Jaga had made slipped off the door and fell to the floor, note-side down.

22

Edgar

Edgar trudged through the bedroom to close the slider, but left it slightly ajar. It had been open the whole cruise, despite the cool temperatures. He liked it cold, and she didn't mind. But in her state now, it seemed right to close out the cold.

He'd checked the one in the living room, and it remained shut behind the sheers and drapes, which were fully closed. She wanted it that way, having no interest in seeing the outside.

After making sure that their cabin was secure, he sauntered back into their bedroom and paused at their bed, studying her and wondering what he should do next. More accurately, what he should do about her.

Eloise had come home last night after a late-night bender. He was in their lavatory dealing with an upset stomach after that evening's meal. He heard her clumsily rumble through their cabin, yelling his name, and then she was quiet. A few minutes later, when he exited the loo, he found her face down on their bed in much the same state she was in right now. He had turned her over once, just to make sure she was breathing. She was. She'd had been passed out for hours now. For this, he was glad.

At this moment, he had the best of both worlds: she was unconscious, which was far better than her annoying conscious self, and she was almost completely naked, and he did enjoy looking at her body. What was not to appreciate after she'd spent so much money attempting to perfect it? And if he was being truthful, her looks were what attracted him to her in the first place.

He harkened back to when they met, and she had come on to him.

He had not been with a beautiful woman since secondary school. After he graduated from college, he'd married a respectable woman of fine lineage; it was Martha who he had faithfully been with the entire time, until her death last year. Martha may have been homely on the outside, but her beauty was deeper and evidenced by her kindness to others. Eloise was the opposite.

He rehashed the images from that night when he first saw her at a pub he and a few of his friends frequented, near his Parisian home. She was wearing a bright red dress that was quite revealing and clung to her curves. He could also see she'd had way too much to drink. She staggered toward him and then halted a few feet away, wobbling such that she had to steady herself on a bar stool. She was searching for something in her designer clutch and then pulled out what looked like car keys. He remembered thinking, *You're not going to try and drive in that state, are you?* He couldn't let her do it. He excused himself from his mates and approached her as she was trying to figure out which of the three keys went to her car.

He insisted that he drive her home. She responded with measured resistance, but almost immediately agreed and dropped the keys into his open hand. He had put an arm around her when she almost flopped over, just to steady her, until they reached her Mercedes. But before he could drive her, she'd passed out in the passenger seat. Without an address—her little purse held only a wad of euros—he carried her to his home across the street and placed her in one of his five guest bedrooms. The next morning, he woke to find her in his bed.

The rest was a blur: the sex, the whirlwind romance, the small wedding—she wanted it small—and now the cruise/honeymoon. But the more he got to know his new wife, the more he realized he simply didn't like her. Oh, she was beautiful on the outside. But something was very wrong with her, like a delicate red apple with a spoiled core; you didn't know it was bad until you bit into it. It was only after the wedding that her true self came out, and the sex stopped immediately. He suspected then that her whole purpose was to get to his money, which was funny because she seemed to have lots of it herself.

And now he found himself on this cruise, married to a woman he didn't love, and didn't even really like. Other than her being great in the sack—before she put a stop to it, anyway—and being movie-star beautiful, she had nothing he wanted anymore. He no longer wanted to be with her. He had insisted on a prenuptial agreement, and that was good, because he decided then and there, while staring at her unconscious body, that when this cruise was over he'd tell her he wanted a divorce. She could keep what she had and he'd keep what he had.

He glanced at her beautiful body, lying peacefully in their bed. She was so arousing though, and he was an old man, not likely to ever have a woman who looked like this, unless he paid for it. He felt himself tighten up, and a wicked thought grew in him. This was probably his last opportunity to lie with her. She sure wasn't going to have him when she was conscious.

That little part of him that was still good, that last part that she hadn't yet destroyed, protested. *This is wrong!*

He considered her once more: drool ran from the corners of her mouth toward her ears; her healthy chest—only her nipples were covered by the fine flowered embellishments of her damaged dress—was now heaving up and down rapidly; her lower half—where the dress was torn completely off—lay fully exposed and beckoned him.

He decided to do it.

He dropped his trousers and quietly walked around to the front of their king-sized bed. Her legs were bent at the knees, draped over the edge of the bed. Her thighs waited. He pushed his large, tangled comb-over to the other side of his head, and then parted her legs. He pulled her closer to him and mounted her.

At one point, he thought he heard her moan. Otherwise, she slept through it all.

DAY FOUR Cont...

LA PALMA, SPAIN

IN 1971, CUMBRE VIEJA, ON THE ISLAND OF LA PALMA AT THE WESTERN TIP OF THE CANARY ISLAND ARCHIPELAGO, ERUPTED FOR THE SEVENTH TIME IN SIX HUNDRED YEARS. COMPARED TO SOME OF ITS PREVIOUS ERUPTIONS, THIS ONE WASN'T VERY LARGE AND DIDN'T LAST VERY LONG. THE ERUPTION IMMEDIATELY PRIOR TO THIS ONE, IN 1949, LASTED THIRTY-SEVEN DAYS AND SHOT LAVA THIRTY METERS INTO THE AIR. BUT EVEN THAT ONE WAS SMALL IN COMPARISON TO THE ONE IMMEDIATELY PRIOR TO IT IN 1712. AND STILL THESE WERE NOT CONSIDERED "MAJOR" ERUPTIONS.

WITH EACH YEAR THAT PASSED WITHOUT A MAJOR ERUPTION, TOP SEISMOLOGISTS WARNED, "THE BIG ONE IS COMING." PAPERS WERE WRITTEN, BUT MOST VOICES ONLY RECEIVED PEER REVIEW AND NOT THE ATTENTION OF WORLDWIDE MEDIA, EVEN THOUGH THE POSSIBILITIES OF A GIANT ERUPTION WERE GREAT. AND THE EFFECTS OF SUCH AN ERUPTION WOULD BE MONUMENTAL... "APOCALYPTIC," SOME WOULD EVEN SAY.

UNLIKE THE THREATS FROM MOST VOLCANIC ERUPTIONS, WHERE BLACK ASH, PYROCLASTIC CLOUDS, OR EVEN MOLTEN LAVA WERE THE PRIMARY CONCERNS, CUMBRE VIEJA POSED A MUCH GREATER THREAT TO ITS NEIGHBORING CANARY ISLANDS AND EVERY COASTAL TOWN ON ALL SIDES OF THE VAST ATLANTIC SEABOARD: A GIANT TSUNAMI.

A MASSIVE SLAB OF ROCK, TWICE THE VOLUME OF THE ISLE OF MAN, HUNG FROM THE NEARLY TWO-THOUSAND-METER-HIGH MOUNTAIN, BARELY CLINGING TO ITS ROCKY BASE BY ITS NAIL-THIN ROCK ANCHORS. EACH YEAR, THOSE ANCHORS WERE WEAKENED FURTHER. BECAUSE OF THE SLAB'S ENORMOUS SIZE, EXPERTS SAID THAT THE NEXT LARGE

ERUPTION WOULD MOST LIKELY DISLODGE IT, CAUSING IT TO SLIDE INTO THE OCEAN. THE ENERGY FORCE CREATED BY THIS WAS PEGGED BY ONE SOURCE TO BE THE EQUIVALENT TO SIX MONTHS OF ALL THE POWER GENERATED BY ALL OF AMERICA'S POWER STATIONS. THE RESULT WOULD BE A MASSIVE TSUNAMI, LARGER THAN ANYTHING EVER RECORDED.

ESTIMATES VARIED WILDLY. ONE SAID THAT THE RESULTING INITIAL WAVE COULD ATTAIN A LOCAL HEIGHT OF 600 METERS AND PEAK AT 1600 METERS, OR ONE MILE HIGH. THE MOUNTAIN-SIZED WAVE WOULD TRAVEL AS FAST AS 450 MILES PER HOUR, OR NEARLY THE SPEED OF A COMMERCIAL JET AIRCRAFT.

A WAVE THIS SIZE WOULD FLOOD THE COASTLINES OF AFRICA IN AN HOUR; THE BRITISH ISLES WOULD BE DELUGED IN THREE TO FOUR HOURS; AND EVEN NORTH AMERICAN COASTS WOULD BE SWAMPED IN SIX.

THE DEVASTATION WOULD BE UNIMAGINABLE.

AT 5:40 PM, THE UNIMAGINABLE HAPPENED.

23

Bridge Trouble

It was the second time in a few hours that Ted had been up on the bridge. Neither visit was pleasurable.

"Please wait here," said the first officer, Jessica, who ushered them to the entrance of the ready room.

They stood with their backs to a wall, ready room on their left, active part of the bridge on their right, and quietly watched the bridge crew do its thing during what was probably one of the most stressful times any of them had ever experienced. The nervousness was palpable and hung like humidity during a hurricane.

During his previous visit to the bridge, as part of the All Access Tour, Ted had not spent more than a moment to really take in the bridge, even though that was the tour's purpose. Now, while they waited for the captain, he studied all that was going on around him.

The *Intrepid's* bridge was an expansive mélange of old and new, hierarchical and exclusive, functional and symbolic. This was demonstrated by all the systems and the personnel working on it. Each member of the bridge crew proudly wore two bars or more on their shoulders, signifying the bridge's obvious importance. And yet, its purpose was somewhat archaic. He remembered hearing one surprising fact from the tour: 95% of all ship functions, including all maneuvering, could be handled by Ivan, the operations room chief, and his crew, three decks below. There were other seemingly anachronistic elements in this "modern" bridge.

A captain's chair stood up high and resolute in the middle of the room, giving the captain a 180-degree view of everything outside the ship. Of course, there were no other chairs, because no one sat while on duty, least of all the captain, who seemed to spend most time eyeing a monitor farthest back, and away from the most forward view of the ship.

Eating up a lot of the floor space were maybe a dozen bulky platforms, each rising to chest level, each with a tilted computer screen blinking multitudes of data relevant only to the five crew members bustling around them. One per each crew member would have been sufficient, as surely each of these had the same conning and ECDIS software and would have been connected to the same computing power available to those in the operations room

Finally, a vestigial remnant from the past lay in front of them: a gigantic back-lit table, which would have held navigational maps on an older ship, took up a large portion of the bridge on the port side, where they waited. Instead of paper maps—replaced by the ECDIS system—there were now permanently fixed schematics of many of *Intrepid's* deck plans. Different from the public deck plans displayed on every deck, these revealed protected details like locations of restricted hatches. As an afterthought, in the middle of the table was a large to-scale-model of their ship, encased in a glass display.

Ted and TJ couldn't hear what exactly was being said, but they could tell that the crew members were treating each decision like it was one that concerned life or death for them and everyone on board.

The first officer who asked them to wait was a young woman with model-like features, including Icelandic-blonde hair that starkly showed off the three bars on her pressed white uniform. She couldn't have been more than thirty and looked like the youngest of the bridge crew. She leaned into the captain's ear and said something, no doubt concerning them. The captain flashed a glance their way, nodded and said something more to the first officer, who proceeded to another area of the bridge and glared at two computer screens with a feigned indifference, as if this were her normal day.

The captain's shoulders were pointed in their direction, but his head was focused on Jean Pierre, the staff captain, to whom he barked off some orders. Jean Pierre's bald head spun around, searching for someone or something, before he responded subserviently.

The captain nodded back and barked something more, before finally walking in their direction. Ted thought that Christiansen looked like he was carrying the weight of the world on his shoulders.

"Thank you for coming, my friends. Please join me in my ready room." He thrust his left arm out, toward the door. TJ opened it and the three of them walked in.

"Time is precious right now, and I'm sorry to lay my burdens upon you, our guests. But I suspect you know why you're here. So, I'll cut to the proverbial chase. Thanks to your warning, Ted, we avoided a catastrophe in Gibraltar, but our problems have just begun."

~~~

The monkey had worked its way up and over the metal railing
~~~

of the crew's outside cigarette break area on deck 4. Because its hands and feet were slick from the fresh blood, it slid down almost an entire deck before regaining some traction on an opening in the metal. It didn't hesitate, as it was overwhelmed by a hunger for more. It had to have more.

A human voice called out, catching its attention. A man appeared just above and called out again to someone behind him.

The monkey didn't need any more prodding. Nails and digits scratched up the side of metal and glass, its rapid clattering over the ship's surfaces mirroring its frantic desire. It scurried up one of the windows framing the Windjammer Cafe. On the other side of the thick glass, ten-year-old Ashley Brown watched with wonderment, a giant spoon of ice cream shoved in her mouth, while her eyes tracked the monkey as it slipped by the window and pulled itself up to the next deck.

One foot slipped, and so it took a moment to regain its footing and glance back up. The back of its prey's head was still in sight, so it leapt the last five feet. But the man stepped away just before the monkey could sink its claws and teeth into his skull. Instead, it clutched air and started to fall.

With nothing to stop its progression downward, the monkey flailed in the air, skittering and bouncing off Ashley Brown's window—she dared not blink for fear of missing it pop up again. She needn't have bothered... With one final reach before its unobstructed plunge into the ocean below, it frantically stretched out one bloody hand and hooked itself on a deck 8 balcony. It yanked itself up like a shot over the railing, smashing back-first into the large balcony's arranged set of table and chairs.

An old man sleeping on a lounger outside rose to a sitting position, unsure what awful noise had woken him. His wide eyes glared at the balcony's shadows, floppy comb-over having come un-flopped, dangling in place on the side of his head. From behind an overturned table in the corner of their balcony, something flailed and banged against metal. It rose onto its hind legs. A furry beast, almost invisible in the dark shadows, its red eyes glaring like stoplights, fixed... on him.

He planted his feet on the balcony's non-slip surface, sprang up, and darted as fast as his legs would take him. He shot through the drawn curtains, over several of his wife's discarded pumps strewn over their bedroom, past his buck-naked wife still sleeping off her Valium hangover. He bounded through the bedroom door, pulling it closed behind him, not daring to look back. The door weakly rebounded off the frame, and came to rest slightly ajar. He skittered through to the reception area, where he turned the corner and scurried to their suite's exit. Almost there.

He clawed at the door handle, frantically attempting to push it down and simultaneously pull the door open, but he missed. Off balance, he stumbled to his knees.

A whimper burst from his lips as he bolted up again, grabbed the handle with both hands, twisted and yanked at the surprisingly heavy door. It sprang open. He thought he might make it.

He lunged for the opening's safety just as an immovable weight piled on top of him, driving him into the entry foyer's welcome mat. His head was smashed hard into the "te" of "Royal Suite." He lifted and turned his head to scream, but the beast shoved his face back into the floor and simultaneously sank its teeth painfully into his left scapula. Out of one eye, he could see a room attendant turn a corner, only a few feet from their suite entrance, and then stop in front of another cabin. The attendant opened the door and slipped inside, but never turned his way. The old man tried again to lift his head, perhaps his last chance to plead for assistance. But he couldn't, under the weight of the beast's foot. He groaned, "Help!" but it didn't come out much louder than a dull crackle.

The door of the same cabin popped back open and the attendant's hand wedged a towel underneath it to hold it open.

The old man felt the beast leap off him and watched it bound toward the partially opened cabin. It hopped inside, its foot tangling in and dislodging the hand towel, causing the door to flop closed. He heard a muffled scream and then a pounding against the door.

The old man managed to push with his right arm and move his damaged body backward out of the path of the door. Parts of him felt broken, but he thought he might actually survive this ordeal, if he could just get the door closed.

With one final effort, he spun around and pushed himself up to a sitting position, dislodging himself from the door, which swung quickly and slammed with a thud. After some time collecting himself, he felt the back of his shirt become wetter and he feared he wouldn't have long. He stood, his legs wobbly and unsure. He bent forward, forcing himself to stagger in the direction of the reception area, his feet scraping over the carpet. Once in their bedroom, he halted at the foot of the bed, his eyesight now foggy. He hesitated, while swaying from side to side, ready to topple. He knew he needed to wake his drugged-out wife, and risk her getting him to the ship's doctor, although he suspected she might not.

Finally, he grabbed her bare leg and aggressively shook while he groaned her name. She woke abruptly, screeched at him once, and then everything went black.

24

The Captain

"The animal attacks are not just in Europe; we've had several here on this ship. And there have been casualties: we've lost three crew members and two more of our crew have been bitten, along with three guests. This havoc has been wreaked upon us by rats, dogs, and a Barbary ape, and that's just in the last two days."

Ted and TJ were seated in two of the eight cushy leather chairs surrounding the cherry wood conference table, which had undoubtedly never witnessed a discussion like this one before. They listened attentively. TJ's mouth uncontrollably drooped open.

"Were their eyes red?" Ted asked, seemingly unfazed by the captain's revelation.

TJ's hand clenched his under the table, with almost viselike compression. Her mind then registered her husband's question and she reflexively nodded her head, even though she did not want to hear the captain's answer.

"Yes, I believe so," he responded, while examining his

tablet. "There are at least two reports of this: one regarding the dogs and one for the rats. In both, witnesses stated the attacking animals had 'red eyes.'"

"Did any of your reports include a ferret?"

Both the captain and TJ looked at Ted.

"No, why?" the captain asked.

"I saw a ferret outside of our door, just before your first officer called us."

"You weren't bitten, were you? Wait, why didn't you mention this?" TJ huffed.

Ted winced a little as she squeezed harder. "No, I wasn't bitten." He tried to pull his hand away, but she wouldn't let go. "The ferret wasn't aggressive, like the other animals. It seemed more... confused and... hungry."

He softly laid his other hand on top of their mutually clenched ones. "I didn't mention it because I was still processing this, and I didn't want you to freak out at the prospect of a potentially wild animal on board this ship. I feel pretty sure now that this particular animal is not a threat. But I am sorry for not telling you."

"And yet it had red eyes, like the animals who've been attacking people?"

"Yes, and that's what's puzzling. It seems obvious that the animals affected by whatever this is exhibit not only the red eyes but also a crazed desire to kill and feed on flesh. This ferret's behavior was thankfully aberrant to that of the others. Or it means something entirely different."

"Couldn't it mean the mad, aggressive tendencies will pass?" TJ was fishing in a very small pool of hope that most animals in the world were not trying to kill them. Ted wished he could cast his line into that same pool.

"I just don't know. But we also have to consider that this tells us that not all infected animals exhibit the aggressiveness. The fact is, we don't know enough to say if we're at the beginning or at the end of this thing." Ted pulled off his ball cap and rubbed his temples.

Captain Christiansen sat down, finally. They noticed the uncharacteristic bags under his eyes, and his shoulders sagged. He laid his tablet on the table and asked, "What do you think is causing this and more importantly, is it contagious to humans?"

"I believe it's some combination of an infection most animals already have, along with something else that was caused and/or spread by the volcanic eruptions. I have no idea if there will be any effects on humans, but perhaps you should isolate those who have been bitten until we know more."

"That sounds like a fair suggestion. We'll do that." He tapped his forefinger on his table.

"Where are the animals, you know, the ones that attacked on the ship?" TJ sank deeper into her chair, her death-grip on Ted unyielding, and if possible, squeezing harder with each revelation. Ted's head turned back from her to the captain. He wanted to know this as well.

"The rats are all dead. One of our crew members killed them all, before they could do much more than bite a couple other crew. The monkey attack occurred outside the ship; we closed the hatch before it could come in. The dogs, on the other hand, are still loose somewhere on deck 1. The good news is that all the exits to that deck are being closely monitored. In theory, the dogs will be contained there. I'm convinced, we'll find and subdue them soon enough. So other than the ferret, there shouldn't be any more animals unaccounted for. I think we're safe, at least on this ship."

TJ's grip relaxed somewhat.

Ted continued to stroke her upper hand with his free one. "Any thoughts on what you'll do with the dogs when you catch them?"

TJ pulled that hand free. "You need to destroy them all!" she declared adamantly, pounding the table for emphasis.

"Remember, they belong to the passengers." The captain averted his eyes. "But that's probably what we'll do to avoid further infection." Jörgen and Jean Pierre had been discussing this very point earlier. Jörgen knew this to be the right answer, no matter how many times the ship would be sued for it. He was hoping for an alternative.

"But..." Ted smiled at TJ before returning his attention to the captain. "I'd like to get a look at one of them before you do—you know, after you catch one."

TJ firmly gripped Ted's hand again with both of hers and she tugged at him, so he was again facing her. Her face said it all. He had known his wife long enough to know she did not agree.

"Look, Ted, I understand your interest here, especially with all the research you did on this subject. But I don't like it. We don't know if this—whatever it is—is contagious. And until we do, then you should stay away from these animals even after they're captured."

The captain added from behind them, "Once they're found, they'll be contained at the pet spa, where they had been before they were accidentally released."

Ted nodded, and then looked deeply into TJ's agitated eyes. He squeezed her hands back, albeit tenderly. "Only after they are secure, I'll go see the pet spa guy—what's his name?"

"He goes by Al. He's already aware of your thoughts on the animal attacks outside of the ship. And I'll let you know when they've captured the dogs so you can go."

TJ nodded slightly. "Yes, that all sounds fine, Ted. But you're just a sci-fi author. You're not a vet or an epidemiologist from the CDC. Why do you need to take the risk to see them?" She was both angry and visibly shaken.

Several long moments passed in quiet.

"Your wife is probably correct. I'd rather not put either of you at any more risk. Al is a licensed vet. He will also thoroughly examine the dogs and report his findings to me. I'll make sure you get a copy. Additionally, you can talk to him, someplace outside of the pet spa. And again, that's only after we catch these things."

"Fine, just keep me in the loop then." He didn't want to push her anxiety about the animals any more than he already had.

Ted and TJ's gazes were now firmly fixed on the captain, who seemed more interested in the activities outside the ready room's windows. There appeared to be a commotion on the bridge. Abruptly he rose, pushed his chair away, and pulled open the door.

The quiet of the conference room—obviously well insulated from the bridge—was suddenly filled with the sounds of an agitated beehive of activity and a pulsating alarm.

The staff captain's large frame filled up the ready room's doorway. "Captain, La Palma has erupted and we have radar confirmation of a tsunami coming our way. ETA fifteen minutes."

As if this were the most natural thing and part of the normal course of events on the bridge, the captain replied, without any hesitation, "Sound the alarm. Get everyone to their cabins."

"Yes, sir," Jean Pierre replied, pivoted on his heels and then jogged over to Jessica, who was tapping away at a console in the middle of the bridge. Jean Pierre hollered a command that everyone on the bridge nodded to.

The captain turned to Ted and TJ. "I'd recommend that you two go back to your cabin as well. We've experienced rogue waves before and we'll be fine. But you'll be safer in your room." He quickly ushered them out of the conference room and through the bridge, stopping at a small desk built into a wall. On it was a nest of radios, connected to a charging station.

The captain grabbed one and handed it to Ted. "I want you to contact me if you think of something that might help." He opened the hatch and waited for them to file out. "I'll be in touch shortly. And thanks for your help."

"We will, Captain," Ted said, following TJ into the hall. They both turned to see a guard was posted by the closing hatch. Just before it shut they heard the first officer state, "Radar has the wave at over fifteen meters, and grow—"

Ted and TJ stared at each other and then started jogging down the hallway to the most forward stairwell and elevators. Their plan to take the stairs was jeopardized by the flood of passengers in semi-formal clothes, filing down for early dinner seating. Just then an elevator opened in front of them.

"Let's grab this," TJ said, pulling on Ted's arm as he was about to check the deck-plan to confirm which was the quickest route back to their cabin. "We'll take it down to six, walk aft and then up one to our deck."

"How have you already memorized the entire deck-plan?"

"I just don't want us to not be in the room when a fifty-plus-foot wave hits our ship."

They stepped into the elevator just as a double-horn sounded on the ship's intercom system. "This is a shipwide alert. Attention, we have a tsunami alert. In ten minutes, we expect a tsunami wave to hit this ship. To prevent any injuries, all passengers are instructed to go directly to their cabins and put on their life vests."

The elevator doors closed and the elevator started its descent.

"Attention. This is a shipwide al—"

The overheads flashed off, sending their tiny room into darkness, and the world around them abruptly stopped.

25

Chen Lee

Chen Lee stopped to blow her nose and then made sure she still looked good before continuing.

She wore his favorite traditional kimono with her hair put up precisely, held in place by black chopsticks with white pearl inlay. Underneath her kimono, she wore nothing at all.

She had no intention this time of giving him what he wanted. Instead, she was going to show him what he would be missing, and then maybe she'd stab him to death with one of her chopsticks. She was that mad right now.

Earlier today, she was speaking with Lana, a girlfriend who also worked in the spa part-time because of the staff shortages. Normally, she worked at the photo gallery. Chen found Lana in the crew mess and they got around to the subject of men. Lana gloated right away that she had been seeing the head of security, Robert Spillman, and that they were having sex all the time, and in fact, they had a rendezvous set today for four.

Chen was ready to tell Spillman it was over, when he left

a message that he had a meeting at four, but could they meet in a new room at five instead?

The last thing she was going to do was participate in his sloppy seconds. She recalled all the times he had been conveniently unavailable over this past month. That's when she got real angry and decided to get even. She figured the best gotcha would be to show him what he would be giving up by sleeping around. She knew neither Lana nor any other woman could give him what she did. She worked at it. She couldn't wait to see his face. Just a few minutes more.

The new room—he was always changing rooms around—was a luxury suite on deck 8 that wasn't going to be used until the Canaries, when several maintenance crew were being added to help with some of the systems that hadn't been fixed yet while the ship was in dry-dock. That's what he told her.

Robert said he changed the location because he could no longer hide their meeting at the cabin they had been recently using on deck 2. Something about the ship's maintenance fixing everything and he could no longer disable the cameras. And that meant they might be caught if they didn't switch their meet locations. In his position as a first officer, he said, they couldn't be caught, or it would mean his job.

For this meeting, he told her that he had found a cabin which was just outside the view of all but one camera, and he would take care of that one. Robert gave explicit instructions to wait until right at 17:00 and then to ascend the outside forward crew stairwell and exit port side on deck 8, to cabin 8504.

She couldn't care less where it was. She knew he was interested in only one thing, and so was she. Before finding out about his infidelity, she had been happy to give him what he wanted because he promised her a life in America after this cruise was over. So she'd played the part of the demure geisha, even though she was Chinese, offering sexual favors in whatever form he desired. Then when they were married and she had her citizenship, she could do whatever she wanted. Even at the time, she knew he was using her, so she didn't think it was wrong to be using him too. But that had all changed now. She'd find another officer after him.

She tilted her watch—a gift from him—and saw it was time. She bounded up the crew stairwell, the hem of her kimono clutched tightly in both hands and held close to her body to shield her private parts from anyone who might walk underneath. No one was going to get a free show, least of all Spillman.

The stairwell lights blinked twice and then she was covered in darkness. She felt hot and had started to panic when the lights flashed again and remained on, but considerably dimmer than before. She continued up the stairs.

At the entrance to the hallway, she felt light-headed. Maybe she was coming down with a cold. She held her fingers to her forehead to see if she was running a fever. She was warmer than normal, but that was probably because of the kimono. Perspiration streamed down her neck and the small of her back, so she loosened the heavy garment to let in some air. She hated the damned thing, and him more.

The hallway had a murky feel from the orange glow of the backup emergency lights. The power must be out, probably part of Robert's plan. She marched forward, wanting this to be finished as quickly as possible.

When she found the cabin, it was as if something inside her snapped. The door was supposed to have been propped open by a room attendant, but it wasn't. Spillman had given her someone else's key-card, but he said it should be used only as a last resort. He didn't want evidence of her being there and so he'd have the door propped open. As she pulled out the stolen card, her anger completely overwhelmed her reason and she imagined slicing his face up with it.

She thrust the card into the door and yanked it out after

a green light told her it was unlocked. She shoved the door open with a crash, her anger pouring out.

None of the lights were on. Nothing happened when she flipped on the light switch. This angered her more. Only the hallway light provided illumination enough to see partially into the room.

She jumped, startled by someone on the farther of the twin beds. He sounded like he was eating, but in a crazed sort of last-meal-like way. The small figure had his back to her and he was near the corner of the room, where the meager hallway light couldn't penetrate. He seemed oblivious to her.

At first, she was angry at Robert for screwing this up and sending her to the wrong room. She was going to apologize, but then felt the urge to take her aggression out on this person for being in her room.

She let go of the door, and simultaneously flipped on the light switch, already forgetting that she had tried this before and the power was out.

The door flopped closed loudly, its frame shuddering. With the hallway light cut off, the room fell back into complete blackness.

Behind the closed cabin door, a muffled high-pitched scream leaked out, and was immediately consumed by the carpet before it had a chance of being heard.

26

Robert Spillman

Robert Spillman's career problems were mounting, and to protect himself, he'd have to put the whole ship in jeopardy.

Captain Christiansen and Staff Captain Haddock were already suspicious of his disappearing one too many times. Then the damned maintenance guys fixed the cameras in such a way that he couldn't disable just the one camera. And then, to add insult to injury, he found out that the one area on deck 8 that he thought was a hole in their camera system wasn't a hole anymore, as the maintenance men also swapped out the nonfunctioning camera #387. Once again they had eyes on every corner of every hallway on the ship. And Chen Lee was going to be walking by 387 and into the cabin he had set aside for them in less than two minutes. A cabin that was supposed to be empty. He had to do something quick or they'd be caught.

Shift change wasn't for another two hours and now he only had one minute ten seconds, if she followed his instructions. Desperation was setting in, and so was his longing for her body; hers was far firmer than Lana's. He did the only thing he could think of: shut down a portion of the ship's power, and most of the cameras.

Oh shit! I'm going to Hell for this, he thought and then he pulled the lever.

The lights went out, and he waited for the emergencies to flash on. Then he shot out of the confines of environmental and dashed out and around to the entrance to the monitoring room, where he met Fish at the door.

"Fish, go check the breakers. I'll hold up here and check with the bridge," Spillman commanded, holding up his radio.

"Yes, sir," Fish said and dashed out of the room, heading down the path Spillman had just come from.

Robert smiled at his ruse. But he only had thirty seconds at the most. He reached underneath the work table and opened a panel revealing all the circuit boards. Next, he pulled out a folded piece of tin foil, unfolded it, and pressed it against the back of the main circuit board, which he knew controlled all the cameras. From what he understood, this would work. He'd been waiting to try this trick, but only when it was necessary, or when he was desperate. Like he was now.

He left the panel open and then stood up, waiting for the power to come back on. He had flipped a switch that only controlled two decks and shouldn't affect any of the other areas of the ship. At least that was what he remembered from his research.

If this didn't work, he was pretty sure he'd find a way out of this mess, just like he'd always done in the past. Even when he was fired from his department for watching porn videos in his patrol car, he worked his magic by having a friend change his employment record and remove the reason for his termination. That gave him the freedom to tell his next employer it was mutual. Most prospective employers wouldn't dig further. Certainly, Regal European didn't.

The bright overheads flashed back on and the

emergency lights darkened. Almost immediately, the monitors flashed on. At the keyboard, he toggled to camera #387 and saw Chen walking to their meeting place. She was wearing the kimono he adored.

Then all the monitors flashed again and went dark. There were sparking noises inside the panel and the smell of something burning.

Quickly, Robert reached back into the panel to grab his foil, but it had melted to the circuit board, which was melting too. *Oops. Better think quick.*

He grabbed his walkie and hollered into it, "Attention, this is Security Chief Spillman. I need at least two security personnel to appear at the monitor station, on the double."

Just then Fish strolled in and said, "Sir, someone had flipped off the master power lever. I flipped it back..." He wrinkled his nose. "What's burning, sir?" he asked, but his superior didn't reply.

Three security guards arrived at the door and Spillman let them in.

"Okay, Fish, admit what you did and we'll go easy on you," Spillman demanded.

Fish shot him a confused glance. "Sir, what do you mean?"

"Don't play games with me. This is your last chance."

Fish swung around to see the guards come up behind him. That's when he got nervous. "Sir, I really don't know what you are talking about. But I assure you, whatever it is, I didn't do it." He thought maybe he was about to be busted for his card games with Deep and the other crew.

"So you didn't flip the master switch off and then pretend to switch it back on—"

"—what? Wait, you just asked me to check it out."

"And the whole time, you set up the monitors to crash? Why? Who's paying you to do this?"

The guards grabbed his arms to restrain him.

"What are you talking about? You saw I was here... Wait, you're trying to pin something on me, aren't you? What did I ever do to you?"

"Take him to the brig. We'll let Captain Christiansen sort this out.

"You," Spillman said to one of the guards. "You stay here. I'll be back in thirty minutes."

Spillman bounded out the monitor station's door and into the hall, where several other crew members had assembled and were nervously talking to each other.

"Go about your business!" he yelled at them, barely slowing.

He charged out a crew exit, turned two hallway corners and found himself in front of the cabin in less than a minute. He pulled out his keycard and opened the door to the cabin.

It was pitch dark; this time not even a flickering candle waited for him.

"Chen Lee, are you here?"

He flipped the switch and it didn't work. A scary thought flashed across his mind: what if his efforts caused power to go out in more than one area? The lights should have been on; only the cameras should have been disabled.

A crazed scream curdled his blood. It came from the back of the room and it was rushing in his direction.

He had pulled out his phone to engage the flashlight app on it. He flicked it on and caught a flash before he felt his eye explode.

27

The Bridge

"Bring us around to a heading of two-zero-nine point five. We're going to go straight into the wave at full speed," the captain announced.

"Can't we outrun it?" pleaded First Security Officer Wasano Agarwal, voice fluttering. He bit his lip before it quivered to hide his fear from the others. Even if he wasn't the most junior officer on the bridge, he would have been forgiven. The others were just as frightened. They merely hid it better.

"Afraid not," Jessica cut in. "It's traveling at over four hundred knots, and of course, our top speed is only twenty-five. And even if we could travel faster, there's no place to hide. No, we have to go directly into it."

She tapped away at her keyboard and then a window popped up on all of their display screens. Inside each of their pop-up windows were three numbers telling them all they needed to know at a glance: the wave's current height, now 29.58 M; the speed, 418.61 K; and finally the time to impact,

00:09:47:53. All three numbers fluctuated rapidly. The first two kept increasing. The last and largest number ticked down much too quickly for the crew's comfort.

Jean Pierre hung up one of the multiple phones on a wall at the back of the bridge, and then padded over to the captain while examining his tablet. "Engineering is preparing to give us full power on all engines so that we can slice through this bad dude. Also, the shipwide announcement has gone out and is being repeated every two minutes."

Wasano added, "I'm already getting reports from my security officers." His voice grew stronger, more resolute as he too stared at his tablet. "Passengers are proceeding to their rooms in an orderly fashion. There's at least one security posted at each stairwell on each deck to help whoever needs it."

Jean Pierre nodded to Wasano and then added, "Hotel captain reports that they've started the process of storing away glassware and other breakables. But he said there's not enough time to secure everything. There will be damage."

Urban Patel, the deck officer, added, "And shipwide, the crew are taping up windows and binding tables and chairs to limit damage and potential injury."

"I hope these are our biggest concerns," said the captain, voicing what they were all thinking. He scanned the bridge area. "And where the hell is Spillman?" he yelled at Wasano.

"He's still missing, sir. My men were looking for him before the tsunami alert sounded."

"Captain?" Jessica hollered, sounding very alarmed.

All eyes turned toward Jessica.

At first it wasn't immediately obvious to any of them since there was little lighting on the bridge. This enabled them unhampered views of their screens and everything beyond the bridge windows. The black screens should have been the biggest clues, followed by the absence of the muted illumination from the recessed lights.

The crew understood the problem at the same time... their electric power was out.

"Where's my power?" yelled the captain.

Jean Pierre had one of the ship's phones at his ear almost immediately. "You too? Merde! Call us as soon as you do.

"Sir," he hollered from the back of the bridge, "engineering reports loss of power as well. They have comms, with no controls. Chief Engineer Ivan Pavlychko has already given the order to set up for manual. That way, we'll have manual controls if computers remain offline, to steer through the tsunami. They'll report to us as soon as they're done.

"He also reported that the stabilizers will be stuck on until we get our power back. We may not have all the speed we need." Jean Pierre was stating the obvious to the captain as he glanced at the screen for the current speed, but it was still dead. Only seconds ago, they were doing just over fifteen knots. It felt like they were going faster, but still much too slow. If they didn't get more speed, the giant wave could capsize them.

The lights flashed once, and the crew held their collective breaths.

Then they flashed again, but remained on.

"That's emergency power, but we still have a shipwide outage," Jessica announced. More stating the obvious, but that was the protocol. Cold comfort, if any.

The windows in their screens appeared to be resetting, indicating their computers were rebooting, which meant they might regain helm controls. Each screen finally updated its numbers: 33.87 M, 423.18 K, 00:05:56:21

Jean Pierre wasn't a praying man, but at that moment he looked up to the sky he couldn't see and said a quick prayer for his ship, her crew, and her passengers. They would need some divine intervention if they were to make it through this one alive.

28

Ted & TJ

"Here it is." TJ's disembodied voice poured out of the dark opening in the elevator's ceiling above him. A few seconds later, a grunt and scraping sounds preceded a ladder unrolling from the hole, reaching its end a foot from the floor.

"Great find," Ted stated earnestly, as he quickly planted both feet and then his hands, carefully moving up two rungs at a time. "This looks pretty heavy-duty, like it might even hold me. How did you know?"

"I didn't, but I guessed they must have something up here, for emergencies." She smiled at him when he popped his head through the opening. "And it's an easy ladder up half a deck to 6."

"What do you suppose happens if the power comes back on?" Ted mumbled.

"I guess we'll be able to better see the elevator when it runs over us, then."

"Ha-ha. Not funny," Ted deadpanned.

The emergency lights inside the elevator shaft flickered, and the elevator under their feet shuddered, moved—and then stopped.

Then the lights flicked back on.

They exhaled and shot forward, scurrying up the ladder's rungs and into the recessed safety of the deck 6 doors before the elevator moved again. An easy release on the inside gave them their exit—Ted thought they were going to have to find an ax or something else to pry open the doors, like in the movies.

The alarm horns blared twice again, followed by the message about heading back to their rooms.

"What I don't understand is if their engines are running, and they provide the power needs of the ship, how can the power go out?" TJ asked.

"I was wondering the same thing too. How much time do we have?"

TJ glanced at her watch, her face instantly twisting in a grimace, before she glanced up at Ted. "Um, less than five minutes. Let's run."

~~~

Hugo from Philippines dashed up to the first refrigerator in the hallway and tugged on the handle, making sure it was properly sealed and didn't budge. It was secure.

He jogged to the next. This one held the spirits, wine, and beer. As he stopped in front of the huge door, one foot slid on a piece of paper. Realizing he was going to go down, he reached for the only solid surface available to stop his momentum: the door-latch handle. Immediately the door clicked and slid with his forward motion, opening the vast space before he and the door finally came to rest. His heart
~~~

raced at his nearly catastrophic fall, which probably would have resulted in his breaking a bone and losing his contract, had he not been able to grab something. He let go of the latch and lay on the floor to collect himself.

He'd been running for the last five minutes in the vain attempt to make sure all the food and supplies were secure. *Who is going to make sure that I and my fellow crew members are secure?*

He'd lost track of time and wasn't sure how much time was left, but it felt like there couldn't be very much.

A wet blob from above him landed on his forehead with a splat.

Hugo slipped his fingers over the wetness, closing his eyes in the process, and rubbed it. *It's slimy.*

His vision instantly shot upward. The ceiling lights were blotted out by red and brown... and it was panting.

It was a large German shepherd spotted in red-brown, like dried blood, as if it had been in a dogfight. The dog was shivering, and there were other dogs behind it, connected to it.

"Hey there, dogs, what you are doing in the liquor supplies... having a drink?" He smiled at his humor. Then his smile slid off his face when he remembered the staff captain's warning to the whole crew about crazy dogs on the ship.

Hugo spider-walked backward, his butt sliding. After a little distance, he pushed himself onto his knees. He kept his eyes on the dogs the whole time and tried to remember what had been said about them. Animals were going mad on the mainland, and they were to watch out for several dogs that attacked some of his fellow crew and passengers. He couldn't remember their breeds or how many. But when he was eye level with the shepherd, he remembered the most crucial trait. He remembered his skin crawling at the thought, just like it was now.

Their eyes were red. Red like the color of fresh blood.

~~~

“One minute, twenty seconds,” TJ called out, as she stretched out each stride like a gazelle. Ted huffed and puffed behind her, his heavy footfalls clobbering the grotesque carpeting into submission. He sounded much heavier than someone who weighed two hundred pounds.

She held up, just before their cabin. Ted stopped beside her, hands on the wall, struggling for air. Clattering sounds pulled at their attention, where their hallway T’d and connected with an outside doorway. On the threshold were two feet, wiggling, and their owner was groaning.

Ted arrived first, leaning over the elderly woman, whose walker had skidded outside across an open deck. “Can I help you, ma’am?”

“Oh, aren't you sweet,” she replied.

“I’ll get your walker,” said TJ, who slipped past them as Ted tried to attend to the woman.

“Are you injured?” he asked.

“Oh, mercy no. Just my pride is a little beat up, and my shins.” Her voice was all Southern belle.

“Where is your cabin, ma’am?”

“Only two floors from here. Just wanted to see the giant wave.”

Ted helped her to her feet and steadied her against the door frame. “Well, you’re going to have to stay with us until this passes. There’s not enough time to get you up two...”

Ted’s voice trailed off as he fixated on his wife, who had just unhooked the elderly woman’s walker from the railing and was gazing forward, toward the horizon. Her mouth was agape, as if her jaw no longer had the will to hold it closed. Her face tensed, her brow furrowed. He’d seen this look only two other times: when she was almost attacked by a pit bull, several
~~~

years ago, and when they were almost attacked by the German shepherd, three days ago. She was terrified, and now so was he.

From the distance a deep rumble like a Cape Canaveral rocket launch tumbled through their hallway. The salt air felt motionless and heavy.

“Ted... Run!” she yelled.

Ted was already moving the elderly woman, slowly at first and then picking up speed. TJ blasted through the hatch and pulled it shut behind her. Before it clicked closed, the rumble outside had already built to a terrifying crescendo, and now the muffled roar vibrated under their feet.

TJ discarded the walker in the hall and caught up to them, grabbing the woman’s free arm. The three of them pushed themselves the last few feet: the last leg of a three-legged race.

The three-member team from Tucson and someplace South fell over the finish line of their open cabin door just as the tsunami struck.

29

The Tsunami

"Withdraw the stabilizers," the captain stated in an almost matter-of-fact way. His eyes drilled forward. He no longer needed binoculars to see what was about to hit them.

Second Engineering Officer Niki Tesler, brought on the bridge because of *Intrepid's* power problems, touched the control that immediately withdrew the two mid-ship fins. "Done."

"We're at twenty-one-point-five knots, sir, and rising," declared Jean Pierre, while lowering his binoculars.

There was not much more they could do. The ship had been straightened and was headed in a perfectly perpendicular angle to the giant surge. All power from the ship's four engines pushed the ship's two screws to their limits. They hoped to coax them up to twenty-five knots, which was well past the ship's rated maximum. If they could only gather enough speed, they might be all right. Might.

Only minutes before, they had regained helm controls after Buzz found and corrected the electrical outage problem:

some odd wiring problem with the alternators. And it was deliberate. But learning who the perpetrator was and what their criminal intentions were would have to wait for after. If there was an after.

The important thing was that they had control. And for the next few seconds, they could steer the ship precisely. That was, until the moment the wave reached them. Then their fate was in the hands of the sea and God.

That moment was now.

It took only milliseconds for the one-hundred-fifty-eight-foot wall of water to travel from bow to stern, but like an old reel-to-reel film, the individual images of this movie flashed by each actor one by one, as if slowed down to the speed of a slide presentation.

The captain glanced at their speed. He blinked once at the odd number.

"-190.2."

The controls were supposed to be reading the ship's speed compared to the water around them. Now it read the leading edge of the currents generated from the wave.

Jean Pierre blinked at the sea and sky becoming one, as if some leviathan of unfathomable size—too large to even see—had appeared from the depths and swallowed all in its path.

Their bow. Eaten.

Followed by their open forecastle. Gone.

Urban squinted at the bridge windows. He wanted to ask if they'd handle the force of the impact. Even if he had the time to ask the question, it would have been pointless: none of these officers, not even the captain, had ever experienced this before. Urban's vocal cords and oral cavity got as far as forming "W—" before the rumbling monster ate the bridge too.

Jessica flashed an image of her ten-year-old son, who was waiting for her with her husband back home in Iceland, after her contract was up in two months.

Niki reflexively shut her eyes, in anticipation of the water's impact.

It was so quick, none of them could even register its breaching the farthest port-side window of the bridge, left unlatched earlier by Urban when he didn't believe the frigid outside temperature reading, wanting to test it himself.

The immense pressure from the unstoppable surge buckled the window, cracked its hinged panel, and then broke free, shot inward along with thousands of gallons of salt water through a one-foot by three-foot opening. It stormed through the captain's ready room, destroying everything in its path, including the captain's favorite *Uffda* coffee mug. The to-scale model of the *Intrepid* broke free from its glass case, and rode the wave. With nowhere else to go, the water was diverted inward, a mini tidal wave that rocketed through the bridge, catching each of the officers mid-gape and sending them to the floor to scramble for traction.

And then it was all over.

Had this enormous swell hit land, its immeasurable power would have leveled anything standing in its way. Every structure would have been scrubbed away, without exception. But Regal European's *Intrepid*, just like a surfer diving into the full force of an oncoming curl, pierced the towering crush and came out the other side mostly whole.

The damage was still substantial.

The monster took with it all the ship's antennas and satellite dishes, disconnecting it from the rest of the world.

The single smokestack listed backward, like a giant scab about to come off, barely covering an open wound, which now bled its black exhaust from its exposed base.

Two of the three zip lines were torn from their moorings; their steel cables had been cast forward, driving their bulky connectors, with whip-like precision, through the pool area's glass windows and walls at nearly the speed of sound.

Her decks had been scoured of the few remaining tables, chairs and loungers left top-side, gobbled up like the leftovers from a Thanksgiving meal—the deck crew had stowed away the rest.

It was miraculous that there were only a few fatalities, and much of the credit was rightly given to the assistant safety officer's efforts to button up the ship. But it would take a day to do a head count before they knew the final number.

The fatalities seemed odd at first, but were clear upon closer examination: the occupants of two forward cabins failed to close their outside balcony sliders.

In one of the deluged cabins, the newlywed occupants had been too busy with their lovemaking to bother heeding the ship's multiple warnings. During one breathless moment, the new bride said, "What's that rumble?" To which her spouse quipped something about the power of his loins, but was interrupted by a large portion of the Atlantic crashing through their cabin. At least they'd drowned in each other's arms.

The other cabin, just starboard of the bridge, on deck 8, and therefore partially protected, sustained only minor water damage from a slider being left ajar. Its occupants were already under investigation by the FBI, but their whereabouts were unknown and no crew had been inside the cabin for the last two days.

Not until the next day would the horror of what was behind the door of cabin #8500 be seen and understood.

30

After Effects

The announcement blared through the ship's loudspeakers—at least those which were still functioning.

"Attention crew and guests. This is Staff Captain Jean Pierre." His Belgian accent was thicker than normal.

"The tsunami struck, but your ship, the Intrepid, fared quite well. Now you'll have something exciting to tell your grandchildren: the wave that hit us was almost fifty meters high, or over one hundred fifty feet.

"Although there was some damage, what concerns us most are your injuries. For everyone's safety, please stay in your rooms until further notice. All restaurants and guest areas are closed until we've had a chance to check on every passenger, and then assess the damage.

"If you have minor injuries and you can walk, please go directly to the Wayfarer Lounge on deck 6 and our medical staff will treat your cuts and bruises.

"If your injuries are more serious, please report these

immediately from your cabin phone. Just dial zero. To assist us, please do not use your cabin phone for any other purpose. We have limited staff to attend to your calls. So again, please use the cabin phones only for extreme emergencies.

"Additionally, our crew will be making a room-by-room check to make sure everyone in your cabin is safe and uninjured. To assist us, if you're not going to the Wayfarer Lounge, please prop your cabin door open with one of your life preservers. That way, we'll know you're in your cabin. We will check on all the open cabins first.

"If your room is damaged and you feel you cannot stay there, you are also welcome to come to the Wayfarer Lounge on deck 6. Our crew will ask you about the damage to your room, and either schedule immediate repairs or get you placed into another room.

"For everyone else, please remain in your cabin until the morning, again with your cabin door propped open. There will be an announcement first thing tomorrow morning.

"Thank you!"

~~~

Right after the wave had passed, Al, the pet spa director, got a call from Hugo: his dogs had been found shivering in the giant refrigerated storage room that held the ship's liquor. He rushed over to find all the dogs, calm but confused. He carried each of them individually to the pet spa, mostly because they wouldn't respond to his commands, and some had sustained injuries. He breathed a hearty sigh of relief when he had them all behind their doors.

Two of them were pretty badly injured and had lost a fair amount of blood. He bandaged both and for one, he had to set up an IV. All the dogs were now heavily sedated. He was
~~~

taking no further chances with their escaping or attacking one another.

Strangely, even though they had been exhibiting the aggressive signs of rabies earlier, none of the animals was aggressive now. If it was some strain of rabies, they'd still have been aggressive. Stranger still was their eyes.

Each of the dogs' irises appeared crimson-colored, like the blood vessels had exploded. He had only heard of this affliction in albinos, who have extremely low quantities of melanin, and cursed his computer because he couldn't connect to the ship's Internet to research it further. He was sure that it was related to their rabies-like behavior, which now appeared gone. The other odd symptoms could be explained away.

Before being sedated, each dog was confused. That symptom could be a result of the stress each had experienced, as could the labored breathing. Each dog, although sedated and unconscious, was breathing heavier than normal, as if its metabolism was working overtime.

His original theory that each had come down with some sort of virus was knocked out when his initial tests indicated their body temperatures were below normal. Without a fever, his virus-borne disease theory had to be thrown out.

Al opened a document and started typing up the details. Without access to the ship's intranet, he couldn't open a new incident report, which he'd eventually be required to fill out for corporate to explain what had happened, not that he could state that with any clarity or certainty at this point.

As he typed out a chronology of events, he was coming to believe that whatever aggressive tendencies had affected the dogs must have passed, in spite of the eyes and the confusion.

He wiped the sweat from his head with a towel. The air wasn't working—probably related to the tsunami—and it was starting to get hot in the pet spa.

Propping open the front door provided instant relief.

Somewhere on the ship, there were windows and doors open to the outside, and this air was immediately cooling off deck 1. Lucky for him and everyone on board, the outside temperatures were cool enough that it did the job of their nonfunctional air conditioner systems.

When his radio called to him, he realized that he forgot to update the bridge regarding the dogs. They had asked him for updates on the hour.

He stepped back into the spa and snatched the unit from the charging stand. "This is the pet spa director. Hello, Staff Captain."

Jean Pierre's voice poured out in a fury. "Report on the dogs. We understand you have them. What's their status?"

"I am very sorry for not reporting sooner, sir. All dogs are sedated and stable in their rooms. Sir, I believe the trouble has passed. They are no longer showing aggressive behavior. When I retrieved them a couple of hours ago, they were confused, but certainly not aggressive. I believe the incidence of aggression is only temporary. I am typing all of this up in detail, but I cannot file an incident report because there is no connection with the ship's intranet."

"That's great news on the dogs, and better news on the Rage Virus."

"Rage Virus, sir?"

"That's what the news is calling it."

"I don't believe it's a virus, sir."

"Regardless, can I report to the captain that the danger is over?"

"I believe so."

"Thanks, Second Officer. Staff Captain out."

~~~
~~~

"Glenda Biggins, 82," as she announced proudly in their introductions, would not entertain having the medical crew look at her injuries, which she said were so minor, they didn't warrant anyone wasting any more time over one foolish old woman.

After having thrown the kindly Southerner into their room just as the wave hit, Ted and TJ stayed with her until the announcement, minutes later.

She preferred to go back to her cabin and wait for the crew to come by and check on her. She did not want to trouble them any longer. Ted and TJ escorted the slight woman back to her cabin and said their goodbyes. She thanked them profusely for saving her life and invited them to come visit her at her home on the beach in South Carolina. Again, she apologized for her silly exercise of attempting to gawk at the huge wave.

Ted didn't have the heart to tell the woman that her home on the coast of South Carolina was probably already gone, or at least severely damaged, one of the millions of tsunami casualties. He wasn't sure TJ had considered this, either. That was fodder for another day.

On their way back to their cabin, they came across one person after another who needed some sort of medical help. Surprisingly, none of the injuries were bad: only cuts and bruises. But there were quite a few people who appeared in some state of shock. Some couldn't remember their names and where they were, and some were almost completely non-responsive to Ted or TJ's questions or to those of the crew.

Each injured or confused person was escorted to the Wayfarer Lounge to be attended to by the ship's crew.

The medical staff shared with them that they too were encountering quite a few confused guests, but they attributed this to the stress and shock of the giant wave. The Williamses also heard, indirectly, about the young couple drowning in their cabin, because they hadn't closed their slider before the wave hit. But those were the only two deaths they'd heard of. And if that was the extent of the deaths and injuries, the Intrepid could consider herself very lucky indeed. Luckier still for everyone was the news from Jean Pierre.

He called the Williamses to report that the dogs had been found and were currently sedated at the pet spa. The vet was typing up a report on what he'd observed, but said that he thought that the dogs' aggressive tendencies had passed. He added that the vet believed the rage affliction was only temporary.

It was after one in the morning when both Ted and TJ finally lumbered back to their cabin. As they lay in their bed, they were filled with hope that they would wake up to a new tomorrow where the animal attacks were subsiding and volcanoes would stop erupting. They fell asleep almost as soon as their heads met their pillows, their thoughts turning into dreams, and then their dreams quickly turning into nightmares, which didn't end, even when they woke.

DAY FIVE

THE CAPTAIN'S MORNING ADDRESS BEGAN PROMPTLY AT 07:00. THAT AND THE BLARING TONE THAT PRECEDED IT WERE THE ONLY SIMILARITIES TO THE ADDRESSES OF PREVIOUS DAYS. EVERYTHING ELSE WAS DIFFERENT. GONE WAS THE JOVIAL BANTER OF A MAN WHO ENJOYED EVERY MOMENT OF THE JOB HE WAS DOING. HIS TONE WAS ALL BUSINESS NOW. I IMAGINE ANIMAL ATTACKS AND A TSUNAMI LEADING TO THE DEATHS OF PASSENGERS AND CREW MEMBERS WOULD DO THAT TO A CAPTAIN.

THE INTERNAL SPEAKER UNITS IN OUR CABIN DIDN'T SEEM TO WORK ANYMORE, NOR DID OUR PHONES. MORE TSUNAMI CASUALTIES? WE DIDN'T KNOW. BUT THE DOOR WAS PROPPED OPEN WITH OUR LIFE PRESERVERS, AS REQUESTED BY JEAN PIERRE, SO THE CAPTAIN'S MELANCHOLY VOICE WAS CLEAR, WITHOUT OUR HAVING TO GET OUT OF BED.

"INTREPID, THIS IS CAPTAIN JÖRGEN CHRISTIANSEN COMING TO YOU FROM THE BRIDGE.

"WE ARE PRESENTLY AT A HEADING OF 35 DEGREES, 37 MINUTES, 3 SECONDS NORTH BY 14 DEGREES, 58 MINUTES 21 SECONDS WEST. OUR COURSE IS 28.6 DEGREES WEST BY NORTHWEST. WE HAVE STARTED OUR TRACK ACROSS THE ATLANTIC TO THE U.S.

"YOU ALL KNOW ABOUT THE MONSTROUS WAVE WHICH TOOK US BY SURPRISE. WE WERE LUCKY THAT MORE PEOPLE WEREN'T HURT. AND IN FACT, MOST INJURIES WERE MINOR, JUST A FEW CUTS AND BRUISES.

"THE WAVE WAS THE RESULT OF THE VOLCANIC ERUPTION ON LA PALMA. WE ARE NO LONGER IN DANGER, BUT WE HAD TO CANCEL OUR STOPOVER IN THE CANARY ISLANDS.

"OUR SATELLITE AND INTERNET ARE DOWN BECAUSE OF DAMAGE TO OUR ANTENNAS. THERE ARE SOME OTHER SYSTEM ISSUES AS WELL. BUT OUR TIRELESS CREW IS AWARE OF THESE AND THEY'RE WORKING TO FIX THEM AS I ADDRESS YOU. PLEASE BE PATIENT, AS IT MAY TAKE A FEW DAYS TO GET ALL OF OUR SYSTEMS BACK ONLINE.

"NOW, LET'S FOCUS ON THE GOOD NEWS. THREE OF OUR RESTAURANTS ARE OPEN, AND WE HAVE MANY WONDERFUL ACTIVITIES PLANNED FOR YOU TODAY. ONE ACTIVITY I'D RECOMMEND YOU ATTEND IS THE OPPORTUNITY TO MEET THE FAMOUS AUTHOR T.D. BONAVENTURE. HE'S AN EXPERT IN POTENTIAL APOCALYPTIC EVENTS AND HE MAY EVEN OFFER A WORD OR TWO OF EXPLANATION ABOUT WHAT HAS HAPPENED WITH THE VOLCANOES AND THE ANIMALS, AND WHY WE THINK THE WORST OF THIS CRISIS HAS PASSED."

THERE WAS A LONG AND SOMEWHAT UNCOMFORTABLE PAUSE—FOR BOTH OF US—BEFORE THE CAPTAIN CONTINUED.

"EVEN WITH ALL THAT HAS HAPPENED ON BOARD, TRY TO ENJOY YOUR TIME WITH US. LET US WORRY ABOUT TOMORROW'S PROBLEMS SO THAT YOU CAN ENJOY TODAY.

"FINALLY, I'M VERY HAPPY TO REPORT THAT WE ARE OUT OF THE SHADOWS OF THE VOLCANIC CLOUDS, AND WE EXPECT SUNNY SKIES FOR THE FIRST TIME SINCE THIS CRUISE STARTED. WE'RE ALSO EXPECTING WARM TEMPERATURES, AROUND TWENTY DEGREES CENTIGRADE THIS AFTERNOON. CHAIRS AND TABLES HAVE BEEN RETURNED TO OUR SUN DECK. TAKE TIME TO ENJOY THE SUN THIS AFTERNOON AND VISIT WITH YOUR FELLOW CRUISERS. I'M SURE EACH OF YOU HAVE SOME INTERESTING STORIES TO TELL ABOUT WHAT YOU WENT THROUGH LAST NIGHT.

"THAT IS ALL, FOR NOW.

"HAVE A BLESSED DAY ON THE SAFEST SHIP ON THE

OCEAN, REGAL EUROPEAN'S INTREPID."

THE CAPTAIN WAS OBVIOUSLY...

31
Anniversary

"What are you writing?" TJ mumbled, her voice heavy with sleep.

"Oh, nothing important." Ted flashed her a smile and closed the leather-bound book, clutching it to his chest.

TJ leaned over and kissed him. "Morning." Then she abruptly disappeared into the bathroom.

They had remained in bed—both were exhausted—during the captain's address and for several minutes afterward. The door had been propped open the whole night, as was advised. TJ never woke once, not even during the crew's wellness check in the wee hours. A splash of light on her face from the crew member's flashlight, to verify she was in fact uninjured, didn't cause her to stir. Ted understood perfectly; it was the first time she didn't feel anxious in the last four days, and he certainly didn't want to upset that. Only when the captain's address blared through their doorway did she even stir, barely registering his words, before she rolled back over and stretched out her slumber some more. Ted, on the other hand, bolted upright in bed, terrified of what the captain had announced.

It really didn't bother him that he'd been asked to assume the role of the ship's ad hoc PR officer by delivering the captain's message that the animal attack problem had gone away, even though he wasn't yet convinced of this. It was simply that he'd have to do this in front of hundreds of people.

Far more than crazy animals attacking, or volcanoes spewing ash clouds, or even one-hundred-fifty-foot tidal waves, it was getting in front of a crowd of people which absolutely terrified him. The doctors called it enochlophobia, explaining it was a form of agoraphobia. He only knew that he'd been fighting panic attacks most of his adult life, induced by this very type of public forum. Therefore, he avoided such things like the proverbial plague.

In a former life, when he had worked as a scientist, his work activities were perfectly suited to someone who didn't like to interact with people. Ted did everything he could to not be stuck in large public places, even going so far as to do his work research at home.

When he chose his later-in-life author career, the prospect of scheduled public appearances—such as book signings or radio or TV interviews—meant he had to find a way to make them work with his needs. So his agent chose very limited venues, with only a few people or a space that allowed him to leave quickly if he felt a panic attack coming. Regardless, Ted would not take meds, although alcohol did offer occasional comfort. Instead, he'd work through his affliction.

When his agent contacted him with the idea of this cruise—turned out it was his wife through the FBI, who set everything up—Ted agreed to do the Q&A only because the venue was to be very small. He and TJ had even scouted the room on the way to the All Access Tour, and confirmed he had a quick exit if he couldn't deal with it. It was all just as his agent had said. But that was before the captain had intervened and invited the whole damned ship to come. He knew that the room would be packed with people, all crowding him, touching him, questioning him... The pounding in his chest made it hard to breathe.

To get his mind off his looming lecture and Q&A session at 08:00, he started the journal.

The whole hand-written journal thing was new to Ted: all of his writing was done on his iPad tablet or on the desktop at home. But along with the wine, the captain had given him the beautiful journal as a gift. After the captain's announcement, when he felt panic take over, and he got out of bed to pace, he finally examined the book.

It was exquisite. Fine leather protected its blank, parchment-like vellum pages. "Regal European" was richly etched in gold lettering on its dark blue cover.

He brought it back to bed and gazed at the first blank page and considered what he might scratch onto it. He started to think back over the last few days' events. That's when it hit him that it might be useful—to whom, he didn't know yet—to jot down some of the details about what they were experiencing. At this moment, he wasn't sure what the journal's purpose would be, or if it would ever be read by anyone but him. His apocalyptic mind kicked in, just for an instant, and wondered if it would be used as a historical record for some dystopian future, long after they were gone.

He shook away this thought and opened his bedside table drawer. He snatched out one of his Ultra Fine Point Sharpies, which he used for scribbling inscriptions inside his books during book signings. He brought a bunch of them everywhere he went, especially when he was potentially meeting some of his fans. This book deserved something better, but Sharpies were all he had. He popped off the pen-cap and poised the hard felt-tip over the expectant page, waiting for the words to flow out of him like a stream. He'd focus on writing slowly and smoothly so that others could read what he wrote. His cursive was nearly illegible, so he opted to write in controlled block letters and made sure that each letter was finished.

Far from being sure how best to approach this, and how much detail he should include, he just started at the beginning... "Day One." He wanted to catch up, so he wrote only a few sentences for each, intending to return with more detail, until he reached today, Day Five. His writing flowed easily and quickly, only pausing when TJ had woken.

Their cabin door clicked closed. Ted looked up to find TJ standing beside his side of the bed, wearing a big grin and clutching a small colorful object.

"Happy anniversary!" she stated jubilantly, thrusting out the colorful object. She was practically hopping. An excited squeal leaked from her pursed lips.

Dammit. He'd been so preoccupied—he had planned to surprise her with his gift first, right when she'd woken up. But she had beaten him to the punch.

He put aside the leather journal on top of the small bedside table, slid open a drawer below this, reached in and pulled out a similarly colored box. He held it out for her, offering a *you got me grin.* "Happy anniversary," he said back.

Every year, each of them had gone to great lengths to surprise the other with a small anniversary gift. It was never huge or super expensive, just a little something special to memorialize that anniversary. This being their twenty-year anniversary, he was elevating his game. He had been waiting for most of a year to give this to her.

She threw her arms around him, snatched his gift from his hand and replaced it with hers. She eyed her gift, but then looked up, flashing another big smile. "You first." She plopped down on the edge of the bed and eyed him expectantly.

"Okay-okay." He slipped off the bright red ribbon, ripped open the festive wrapping paper, and flashed a quick glance at the Mont Blanc box and then up at her.

"When I saw you writing in that journal, I was so excited to have you to open this..."

From the box, he pulled out a jet-black Mont Blanc pen, with two gold bands. *T.D. Bonaventure* was etched on the cap. He'd always wanted one, but could never justify spending the money for something like this. But as an anniversary present from his wife... *it was perfect.*

"It's perfect. I love it. Thank you." He leaned toward her and they exchanged a kiss.

"My turn," she said, almost with a giggle. She ripped into her box, quickly exposing a similar black rectangle, only a little bigger. She cracked open the top, revealing a rich blue interior. Nested inside was something that sparkled. She flashed him a stunned look.

"It's Orion, the Hunter. Only this version is a warrior woman, kind of like my gorgeous wife."

She pulled it out of its box, letting the necklace dangle from its thin gold chain, eyeing it and then him as he spoke.

"Each diamond is a star in the constellation Orion. I know it's a bit more than normal, but I found it in London last year and knew you had to have it."

She handed it to him and turned her back to him. "Put it on me, would you?"

He did and she bounded from the bed and padded over to the full-length mirror across from the bathroom door, where she stopped and studied herself and the necklace.

She dashed back to his bedside and once again threw her arms around him, squeezing tight. "It's absolutely the best gift you've ever given me. I love it. Thank you."

She kissed him hard, like her embrace, and then looked into his eyes.

She leaned in and kissed him again, only softer, more passionately. She pulled back, smiled at him, and softly batted her eyes, fluttering them seductively. Her smile grew impossibly large as she lifted her arms in the air, beckoning him to pull her top off.

He obliged.

32

Satellite Down

TJ moaned under her breath as she slowly let her head roll around her neck, her hair snaking a trail over each shoulder blade. Her new necklace bounced playfully against her chest. Her hands were mounted above her hips, her right barely covering the large scar, a marker of a time that changed her, from when she nearly died from a dog mauling several years back. Her fingertips rested above the edges of her black Jockey briefs, legs splayed on the carpet for stability. “Geez, every part of me hurts, like after a marathon.” She flashed him a smile. “What about you?”

Ted averted his eyes from her and swung his feet out of the bed. “Yeah, I can hardly move.” He flashed an even larger grin at her, and she continued her stretching.

He snatched up the remote and clicked on their TV. It was a little tube-job from twenty years ago, with a screen not much bigger than his tablet. He knew the result, but he was still curious to see what would happen after the captain’s announcement.

Before the tsunami, when they'd turn on the TV, the same info channel appeared, either replaying the previous night's talent or variety show—last night's show was understandably canceled, so he didn't expect to see this—or a talk show hosted by Zeka, the ship's cruise director. The talk show, often recorded late on the night before—they guessed this based on the lack of sunlight and the small number of people in the background—gave an overview of the upcoming port of call or that day's activities. He was hoping they would have done something like this to give them more details about what had happened to the ship.

There was no picture whatsoever.

The TV displayed only white static, as if it were a closed-circuit TV's view of an outside blizzard and they were in Alaska and not a more southern latitude in the Atlantic. He glanced at the outside balcony to mentally confirm this wasn't the actual weather: partly cloudy, but certainly not snowy.

He poked the channel-up button once. Then again, and again, one channel at a time. Each displayed the new channel number, but the same white snow.

"Well, the captain said the satellite was down, and this confirms it."

"So is the Internet," TJ said, surprised, and scowled at her cell phone, which she had grabbed while Ted was playing with the TV. He figured she had in fact slept through or had forgotten the captain's message about connectivity.

They both jumped, as if hooked up to electrodes, when the house phone jangled at them.

~~~

"Well," Ted said sarcastically, "at least we know our phone works."
~~~

TJ was already there, receiver in hand, having moved her stretching exercises over to the more spacious middle of their cabin floor. "Hello?" There was the expected pause as she listened.

"Oh, hello JP." She smiled at Ted and nodded, agreeing with something Jean Pierre must have told her.

"Yes, we're fine." She cocked her head at an angle and crooked her brow, as if what she was hearing was painful. Then her face changed again.

"Yes, he's here. Do you—okay." She averted her gaze and nodded again.

"Yes, I'll let him know." She pulled her gaze back up at her husband, but she hadn't made eye contact with him yet.

"What? Oh yeah." She feigned a smile this time, which didn't hold. "I think he was hoping no one would be interested."

Ted eyed her back suspiciously, watching her every reaction.

"Oh, he'll be there." She laid the phone back on the cradle, but didn't say anything as she sashayed over to the chest where they were keeping their clothes and pulled out her running uniform.

"Well?" Ted thrust his hands up in the air. "Are you going to tell me what all of that was about, or are you going to hold on to your little damned secret?"

"Jean Pierre was passing along a few messages from the captain. First, the pet spa director has printed his report and one of the crew will hand you a copy this morning. He said he read it and they're breathing a sigh of relief."

TJ had already slipped on her shorts and long-sleeved sports shirt. She slid on her first running shoe, stopped before tying it, and gazed up at Ted. "Do you think this thing is really over?"

He locked into her eyes, not wanting to elevate her fear, but not wanting to lie to her either. He chose the best answer—the only true answer. "I don't know. Did he say when I'd get to read this report?"

Ted searched for his clothes, thinking that he'd have to dash out and meet this crew member who had the report. Finding his well-worn warm-ups, his preferred outfit at night and in the morning, he slipped them on over his underwear and stood up.

"Ahh, you might want to wear something else."

"Why? I don't care if someone sees me in this."

"It's not that... Remember your talk, at eight? That's where the crew member will hand you the report."

"Yes, of course I remembered, even if I didn't want to." He looked at the digital clock-radio nestled against the journal on his bedside table. It was seven-fifteen. He had forty-five minutes.

"There's one more thing..." TJ hesitated, and then looked down, knowing what she said next would consume her husband in terror, far more than any potential crazed animal attack would have consumed her. "They've moved your venue to... the main theater."

"What!" Ted hollered.

"Well, it appears," she said in an even voice, her best attempt to be calming, "that people really want to listen to your talk about the apocalypse, especially after the captain's announcement this morning. They decided to make sure you had enough room."

"But the theater?" He groaned, closed his eyes, and fell back onto the bed, his breaths becoming shorter and more uneasy.

She moved over beside him and stroked his head. "There's more. The captain wanted you to stress the point that the whole animal craziness thing was just temporary and that everyone on board is safe right now. You could just say a few words and then take questions. You'll be into it quickly—I know you—and you'll forget the audience in no time."

She thought about the story he had told her about the death of his first wife and young child on a French vacation, deaths he was sure he had caused.

As she watched him breathe, she tried to imagine what it must have been like: watching the crowds building around him in the public square and his enochlophobia causing a full-on panic; then seeing his young wife cradling their child, walking across the street toward him; then his glancing up and seeing the madman barreling through the crowds in a truck; then Ted realizing his wife and child would be next, but because he was frozen from fear, he couldn't do anything, except watch them die.

She still couldn't imagine how devastating that was for him.

But that was so long ago, and he had been doing much better lately.

This cruise, and especially the main dining room, were big tests, which he passed with flying colors. This next one would be much bigger. Perhaps it was too huge for him to bear.

"Just tell me you'll be there," he groaned, his eyes still closed.

She didn't answer.

He lifted his head and glared at her. "Really?"

"You told me you didn't want me to come to this; I'd be bored and so on, remember? Besides I have some work-related stuff after my run.

"You mean your *work-related stuff* with Jean Pierre?" he countered.

"Yes, Bureau work, Jean Pierre is helping us with. I told you, it's the main reason we're here."

"Fine, guess I don't need to do this talk then," he huffed.

"Ted Williams, don't be selfish. You agreed to do this, regardless of venue size. I'll miss only the first part of your talk, and then I'll be there."

"Guess it's settled then." He sprang up and darted to

the bathroom. “I’m jumping in the shower and going to go get a stiff drink. That way, I can really make a spectacle of myself.”

She thought about saying something more, but she had already said too much. She knew he had to deal with this in his own way. At least he was dealing with it, versus just hiding in their room. She could hardly have been surprised if he did. She just didn’t want to compound his problem.

As the muffled spray in the shower sounded, she slithered her other foot into its shoe and quickly tied both.

Guilt about leaving Ted to fend for himself swept over her. She had set up another meet with Jean Pierre, while Ted was giving his presentation. She decided then that her husband had to come first; she’d tell Jean Pierre that she could no longer do what she was doing. She was going to spend the rest of the cruise with her husband. She’d not waste this opportunity, feeling like maybe they’d all been given a second chance.

She stood up, truly excited. She was anxious to get going and finish this, so she could support her husband. And knowing that the threat of wild animals roving the decks of the ship had been handled, she could enjoy her run as well.

~~~

Two decks above them on the other end of the ship, completely forward, Catur, the room steward, pounded once more on the door of cabin 8500. Its occupants had not been heard from for over two days, and they did not prop their door open as requested by their staff captain last night. He had waited as long as possible, wanting to offer the couple their privacy. The Do Not Disturb card carried lots of weight for most guests on the *Intrepid’s* transatlantic cruises, as some guests rarely left their cabins. This was especially true with the Royal
~~~

Suite. But the time for privacy had passed. And the hotel captain now required that each room steward account for every one of their guests, DND card or not.

Cabins with doors propped open by life preservers had already been inspected and their occupants' wellness checked. Cleared cabins received a green sticker on the lock assembly. Catur had just three non-green sticker cabins. One deck 7 cabin was a disaster and a tragedy. When he first did his wellness-check rounds last night, he saw water pouring out of the bottom of 7512. He opened it to find that the slider had been left open during the tsunami, and the cabin was utterly destroyed. In a heap, among all the other debris, he'd found the beautiful honeymoon couple, naked and drowned. It was awful.

The next of the three was cabin 8504. But it was empty, so he didn't bother to check it. That left one more suite. And he had put this one off to the very last minute. He desperately didn't want to find any more dead guests.

He pounded again. "Housekeeping. This is Catur, Mr. and Mrs. Carmichael, I need to come in and check on you."

Catur pressed his ear to the door and listened. He could hear a grunt and a rumble inside the cabin. He panicked then and thought that maybe one of them was severely injured and couldn't get to the door. Mr. Carmichael was much older, and so it was very possible that he had fallen and broken something. Falls were common with older guests.

The guard normally stationed in front of the bridge entrance at the end of the hall wasn't where she was supposed to be. Probably better that security didn't see what was going to happen next. Catur imagined accidentally interrupting something he just didn't want to see: two old people having sex. Although the wife was a looker, the old man was just scary-old. He tried to shake away the ghastly image, knowing it would be something he could never unsee. He'd have to offer that mental image to Asep and Jaga, and let them share in his discomfort.

Catur smiled at that idea and rapped with a balled fist on the door, harder this time, while he fumbled with his master key-card. Almost dropping it, he regained control, slipped it in and out of the slot, and upon seeing the green light flash, he cranked the handle and pushed in hard.

It was dark inside, and only a bare channel of light flooded in from the hallway. He was immediately overwhelmed by the most horrid smell. It smelled like spoiled food. Food that had been bad before it spoiled.

He tried the light switches, flipping them on and off, but to no effect. *One more thing that isn't working.*

He took one tentative step inside and stopped, still holding the door open for light, his foot sloshing on the carpet. For a moment, he thought he saw something in the far corner of the room. Squinting, he mentally cursed the guests for leaving the curtains and sheers pulled so tightly across the slider windows.

Swift movement. A shadow, now by the couch.

Then it was closer, and Catur could see the movement was coming toward him.

"It's Catur." His voice wavered. "Mr. and Mrs.—" Something struck him in the chest with the force of a moving truck, knocking him hard into the side of the door, which he had still been holding open. At the same time, he felt something inside him break. He tried to scream, in hopes that someone would hear him in the hallway, but whatever hit him knocked his wind out. Some crazed animal screeched at his face with a warm foulness he'd never smelled before, nor did he want to. He clenched his eyes tight, afraid to look as he tried to pull in a painful breath through his mouth and nose. He'd belt out a cry for help. But he gagged at the horrid stench. Once more, he pulled in another breath—this time using just his mouth and ignoring the smell—when it felt like his entire throat had been ripped away. His gurgled half-breath bubbled out of the new opening.

Catur's dying body was released by his attacker and collapsed into the doorway, keeping the door propped open. The beast chewed the fresh piece of flesh in its mouth, heard someone else and dashed toward the call for "Housekeeping" down the hall.

33

T.D. Bonaventure

Ted—T.D. Bonaventure, as he was introduced—was being peppered with questions. Although many of the questions were coming from people who had read his books, most of the questions came from those who had no idea who he was. They had come for answers, and heard that Ted was the one on the ship who had them. For Ted, it was a catharsis. He stood in front of a huge crowd, calmly answering questions, without any fear whatsoever. He'd have to thank the captain personally for this. And Vicky, the bartender.

Ted had worked himself up to almost a full-out panic before eight. He marched over to the Anchor Bar for a drink or two to relax him. They technically didn't open for another hour. Thankfully, he was able to coax a stiff shot of whiskey out of *Vicky Smith from England*, the bartender who was setting up for the day. She said she remembered his name, although she only read romance novels. Doubtless, she took some pity on the author who admitted he was scared shitless to be giving a speech in front of hundreds of people at the theater. Ted just hoped the drink would give him enough confidence to go through with it. Turned out he didn't need the drink.

It was just a few words, offered by Vicky, a bartender's simple platitude about human fears. On any other patron, her little pearl of wisdom would have been lost. For Ted, it was exactly what he needed.

"You know why you're bloody scared of your talk?" she stated, momentarily moving her gaze from the heavy tumblers she was balancing to Ted.

He bit. "Okay, why?"

"Because you're hiding from some other shit that bothers you more."

Better than a dozen shots of heavily fortified Tequila or a doctor-prescribed sedative, her little bromide not only removed his anxiety, he almost forgot his talk altogether. He dashed down a couple hallways and a flight of stairs, before arriving at the theater, one minute late.

At the theater's performer entrance, a crew member had been waiting for him and delivered a copy of the vet's report on the crazed dogs. Because this was germane to his talk, he explored the vet's detailed findings. But he was still chewing on Vicky's words.

Ted skimmed the very thorough report for its major points, until he arrived at and slowly read the conclusion, "I recommend keeping the dogs isolated from their owners until the conclusion of the cruise, during which time I will continue to observe their behavior. It is my belief that the aggressive tendencies we saw earlier have passed, and that the dogs are no longer a threat."

Ted had rolled the report up into a tube after rereading this passage once more. Then he fist-pumped the air with it. "Yes!" he said, under his breath. His brain yelled, *I sure hope you're right*, and then he stepped through the entrance.

"I'm told he's here now," bellowed the amplified voice of Zeka, the cruise director from the theater. "Some of you know him from his international best-selling books. Others of you might be looking for answers about what's going on outside. But all of you need to welcome the Authoritative Author of the Apocalypse, and your fellow passenger, Mr. T.D. Bonaventure."

Right on cue, he stepped through the curtains, a big smile enveloping his mustached face. He pulled his pipe from his lips and waved to the crowd.

"Thank you, my friends," he said into a microphone handed to him, his British accent—practiced for public venues—rolling off his tongue as if he were a London native.

His heart was beating like a set of bongos, and the welcome feeling of adrenaline pumped through his veins. He couldn't see most of the people because of the stark spotlight, which blinded him, and that was a good thing. He tried to imagine it was only a few dozen, even though the introductory applause sounded like hundreds. The vast room had become quiet very quickly.

"Let's see," he said, scratching his head for effect, as he looked up to the ceiling, "a giant tsunami, volcanoes erupting, animals attacking, and chaos everywhere... And you want me to talk about apocalyptic *fiction*?" He flashed a wide smile for the crowd.

The response from the audience had been a dead-quiet nothing, laced with a couple of nervous snickers, and an elderly man near the front hacking up what sounded like a lung. He'd seen jokes from comedians thud like this.

He took a puff from his pipe and decided to deliver the captain's message to set his audience and himself at ease.

"First, I have a message from our captain. We have several dogs on board with us, and like the other animal behavior we read about and many of us experienced firsthand on land, there were reports of several passengers and crew getting bitten."

Gasps billowed throughout the audience, and a woman

had started weeping.

"Hang on. Before you get all twisted with worry, I'm happy to announce that the dogs have been apprehended and are locked in a protected area. Furthermore, the ship-board vet has observed their behavior and reports that all the animals' crazy behavior has passed. They are currently sleeping.

"Let me put this another way. Even though we haven't been able to communicate yet with the outside world to get further confirmations, it appears that the danger—at least on board this ship—has passed."

At first there had been just a few claps, but then the entire theater erupted in applause. The guy handling the lights turned them up on the audience and down on the stage. Ted could see the entire theater was packed to its limit and every single person was on their feet, cheering.

He clapped too. He couldn't help it. Part of him felt like maybe this thing may have passed, and he was ready to embrace this hope just as quickly as his fellow passengers were.

When the clapping subsided, Ted raised the microphone again. "Okay..." He waited for a few more slow ticks of the clock for the clapping to stop, and then said, "Okay, because this situation is unique, rather than me rattling on for a while on subjects I choose, like why you all should buy my next book, I'm going to open it up to you. What would you like to ask me?"

The early questions came from some actual fans and were centered on *Ring of Fire*, his series about the ring of 452 volcanoes in the Pacific, several of which erupted, causing a new Ice Age. They asked, "Did the rogue wave mean anything bigger?" And, "Are we going to experience more volcanic activity, and even a new Ice Age?"

By this point, even though the lights were still turned up on the house and he could see everyone clearly, Ted felt at ease. He again attempted some humor and reminded his audience that although he did a lot of research for his novels, he was not a geologist or volcanologist. Those points were not entirely true, as he had studied a lot of geology in college, and almost chose that field for his vocation. But he didn't want any more added responsibility and found it was often better to deflect.

So far, so good.

Then someone went for his jugular, and it changed everything for Ted.

A gruff-looking man wearing a red Ferrari sports shirt—Ted had seen one just like this, on the worst day of his life—stood up. "Why do most people in this room believe that a paperback writer of fictional tales could tell us anything about crazy animals?"

It wasn't the nature of the question. It wasn't even the questioner, but the shirt he was wearing and the words of Vicky Smith from England, which transported Ted out of this theater, back to that moment years ago when his life changed.

~~~

It had been a beautiful day in Nice, France. Promenade des Anglais was bustling with Bastille Day celebrants. In the middle of it all was Ted, soaking up the culture and sun, waiting for his wife and toddler son to finish up in a restaurant bathroom across the street.

He was alerted to an odd noise before it seemed anyone else was: a large vehicle's engine being gunned, somewhere on this street clogged with people. Before he saw the truck, Ted observed his wife and their toddler exiting the restaurant, beaming a smile at Ted.

A man in a red Ferrari sports shirt bumped into Ted and scowled, as if Ted were the cause of their collision. It was then that Ted noticed the throng of people had grown. Worse, they
~~~

now separated him from his young family. He couldn't easily get to them.

In a flash, the truck, its engine roaring, was barreling through the crowds of people. Without slowing, it was headed straight for his wife and son, who remained blissfully unaware and unmoving in its path.

Ted sucked in large gulps of air, while the enveloping crowds pushed at him, obscuring his view of them and seemingly taking him farther away from any possibility of saving them.

He had a scientific mind, and he understood cause and effect. His mind had already calculated, based on speed and the direction of the vehicle, what was going to happen: he was going to watch his family die.

It was a gut punch of a realization.

And rather than doing anything, he just watched. More so, he shrank back, away from warning them; saving them. He let the hordes overwhelm him.

~~~

"Hey! So what makes you an expert?" a distant voice hollered.

Ted shook his head, aware that he'd been lost in his own thoughts. His breathing had escalated, and he was uncomfortably hot. He glanced at the giant crowds in front of him—not unlike the crowds of that Bastille Day, when he watched his wife and son die. But he no longer felt possessed by the overwhelming anxiousness he always felt when he faced crowds of people. Something was different.

It was something he had not paid attention to until this flashback: his wife and boy were doomed, regardless of the crowd around him. It wasn't his fear of the crowd that caused their deaths; it was a crazy terrorist.
~~~

Vicky had said his fear of crowds was just his "hiding from some other shit that bothers you more." Ted needed to feel guilty about their deaths, and his fake disease was what he hung onto as the reason he couldn't save them. But no one could have saved them, certainly not him.

He really wasn't scared of crowds. In fact, at this moment, in front of this large audience, he felt damned good. Having TJ here would have only made it better... And taking down this little prick with the Ferrari shirt.

"What's your answer?" demanded Ferrari Shirt.

Ted focused on the man now, and his question.

When Ted had first opened up the room to questions, there were side conversations, like little brush fires that erupted around the room. At times, the room had become so loud and electric, Ted had to stop until the din quieted down. It was understandable, as everyone had their own opinions about the seemingly apocalyptic events they'd all experienced, and feeling more at ease, they wanted to share their opinions, sometimes at the same time. Now, the room fell back into its natural state of nervous silence. Literally, Ted thought he could hear a pin drop, if it weren't for the puke-colored carpet. All eyes were on Ted as he considered his answer.

He didn't want to let on that he wasn't yet convinced that this thing was over, any more than he didn't want to mute the possibility that it might be. But this guy was a heckler calling into question his abilities at getting the science right, and Ted knew the science that went into his book and the reasons for the animal population's madness were correct.

"Imagine"—he looked around the room as he spoke—"that a single-cell organism could take control of an animal's mind and reprogram it so that the only purpose of its host's existence was to kill, feed, and propagate for that organism.

"Imagine further that this organism could live dormant in the animal's brain for as long as the animal is alive, just waiting for the right stimuli to then take control of the animal and demand that it attack and follow its new programming.

"Finally, imagine that these protozoa had already infected as many as three-quarters of all animals on the planet.

"This isn't fiction, folks. This is real. That protozoa is called *T-Gondii*, and this puppet master has already been proven to be behind the aggressive behaviors of both animals and even people for many generations. Further, I believe, it's the root reason why animals appeared to be more aggressive recently."

Ted paused momentarily to study his audience. All faces, without exception, were serious and staring at him. Husbands and wives clutched each other's hands; tears streamed down the faces of some of the children; one individual literally shook with fear. Ferrari Shirt had found his seat and was attempting to disappear.

Ted had gone too far to make his point. He'd allowed his own pride and excitement at conquering his greatest fear to trump what the captain had asked him to do for the good of the ship.

His book *Madness* theorized what would happen if a small protozoa, which already infects most of the Earth's animal population, made its hosts insane. But it was still fiction. It had to be. And there was something big that he had failed to mention.

"But this was just a novel, folks! A fictional assumption of what could be. Yes, there has been some strange behavior from animals in Europe. We've even experienced it on this ship, but I'm not sure that that has anything to do with what I wrote about in a book.

"Besides, my book had anarchists manipulating the T-Gondii to make its host animals crazed, so as to usher in the downfall of humans. That's not what is going on now. It made for great reading and sold a lot of books, but it's no more real than the evil clown in a Stephen King novel... That's a bad example: some clowns are evil."

He could see some of the same people who looked terrified moments ago now wrestling with their smiles. They wanted to believe that the danger was over. And so did he.

"You're telling me that you believe that bloody rats ripping out some poor mate's eyes out of his skull is just fiction?" This came from an overly rotund bald man wearing a Manchester - MANC AND PROUD T-shirt and shoving potato chips into his mouth.

A young woman with puffy red eyes, being comforted by a man of similar age with his arm around her, squeaked, "I heard on a newscast that there was a pack of dogs in Paris attacking people in the Latin Quarter,"

A teenager grasping a hardback copy of T.D.'s book featuring the object of the Williamses' own nightmares, stood up and bellowed, "I saw some birds attack someone in Malaga."

Ted thought of when the publisher's cover artist and he went to blows over the cover. Ted wanted something scarier than what was offered. A week later, it was perfect, and almost exactly what was on the current published book: a crow with red eyes and a bloody, severed index finger held in its beak. Talk about fiction coming to life. This was the real-life image he had seen in the Alcazaba palace, the image that caused him to shiver when he'd recall it. As it was doing right now.

"Well?" bellowed Manchester, crumbs tumbling out of his mouth. "What about the bloody birds?"

He so wanted to be calming, for his audience and himself. But he was the "Authoritative Author of the Apocalypse," as he was described by his agent and the media. He was paid to think up the scariest shit and make it real, to cause people to lose sleep over thoughts of their own mortality. He wasn't someone who dished out calm, and why the captain thought he'd be able to was beyond him. But he also knew that a panic wasn't going to benefit this ship. His ship. So he tried to think of something positive to say.

"Yeah, what about the birds?" another voice warbled.

"Ahh, sorry," Ted said, snatching the rolled-up report from under the podium. "I, ahh... I mean, my wife and I saw the same thing at the Alcazaba palace in Malaga, three days ago. And I have to tell you, that was terrifying.

"But again, we now have proof that this aggression doesn't last." He held up the report he had mangled and rolled into a tube. "Until we know—not guess—otherwise, I think we have to assume that we are now out of danger."

Ted flashed an image of his dead wife and child. And a gnawing anxiousness about finding TJ and making sure she was safe burned in his stomach.

It was time to finish this talk.

"I'd suggest that all of us, me included, take advantage of today's drink special, two zombies for the price of one, and we soak up the sun, which the captain said we'll be able to see today for the first time on our cruise.

"What I am saying is, we have very little time on this big blue ball. Let's go and enjoy it.

"Thanks for being such a great audience, the largest I've ever had the privilege to speak to. I almost feel like one of the Beatles.

"God bless!"

Ted waved once and made his way back out the way he had entered.

In front of the theater was the display for him to sell his books—he'd forgotten completely about this and the long process of scratching personalizations inside the cover to each and every person. He glanced at the growing line of people already snaking from the front of the table, along the hallway, around a corner, and out of sight. One of the crew waited for him at the table, ready to ring up sales of his pre-signed books.

Conspicuously absent was his wife. TJ had said that she'd miss only part of his talk, not the entire thing. Now he was getting worried.

Before proceeding to his table to give a feeble excuse why he couldn't stay to the clamoring crowds, Ted snatched the radio the captain had given him, attached to the back of his belt. He flicked it on and turned up the volume so he could now hear the chatter, in case something important was reported.

A raspy voice interrupted, "Mr. Bonaventure?"

Ted looked up and then lowered his gaze to find an elderly woman held up by a carved wood cane looking at him over wire-rimmed glasses. Even measuring to the top of her wild hair, she wouldn't have made it to five feet nothing. He guessed she didn't want to wait in line with the others.

"I'm so sorry to be disruptive, sir. Besides being a fan of your work, I am a microbiologist—well, retired, technically. I believe you did a fine job in your book regarding toxoplasmosis."

"Thank you," he said, looking past her at the many expectant faces waiting for him to finish this business and move on to his table.

"I know what has caused the *T-Gondii* to do what it is doing, and it certainly was not anarchists. Moreover, I'm afraid the vet's thinking that this is over is terribly wrong."

A panicked voice called out on his radio, over-modulated and unclear. Ted wouldn't have heard what was said, if he had held the radio's speaker directly to his ear. He let it pass.

"What is it?"

"Thermophilic bacteria!" she stated resolutely.

For the first time, he seriously considered this woman while she readied herself to give details, her face turned up to Ted's, intense blue eyes amplified through thick lenses. It was a face carpeted by a lifetime of wrinkles. Her whole persona spoke of wisdom and decades of scholarly research. She seemed sure about what she was about to tell him.

"You, sir, I believe are completely correct on the toxoplasmosis! But the *T-Gondii* was hijacked by thermophilic bacteria. You see, these bacteria love it hot, and can even be found around volcanic vents. And as we all know, there have been an irregular number of volcanic eruptions lately. I believe that a strain of thermophilic bacteria has been released by volcanoes, and because this bacterium is wired to look for warm-blooded hosts, it sought out the warmest blood available. And that would be birds, which have an average body temperature of 104 degrees Fahrenheit. It then has been working itself down the warm-blooded mammal food chain.

"With each host, the thermophile triggers the *T-Gondii* in its host to do what it had, as you said, already reprogrammed the animal to do: attack without any personal regard for its own wellbeing."

Another voice on the radio screeched something like, "Where is it?"

"So you believe that birds must have been the first animal genus affected and they spread the thermophilic strain to other animals?"

"That's one possibility."

Ted pursed his lips, about to ask another question, but he stopped when the radio blared again, this time with a panicked woman's voice. The voice said two words that made Ted take notice: "monkey" and "killed." He held the radio to his ear.

"Hoy," a voice from the book-table line yelled out. "Excuse me, but we'd like to meet T.D. too, and get to the pool before the sun sets."

Ted turned to the voice, then back to the elderly woman, and to the radio in his hand.

"Go on, Mr. Bonaventure—"

"Please, Ted. And you are?" Ted held out his hand.

"Dr. Molly Simmons. It's my pleasure."

The radio blared, "It's been spotted on deck 8..."

Deck 8? TJ was supposed to be on that deck.

Ted lifted the radio and barked into it, "This is T.D.—ah,

Ted Williams, consultant to Captain Christiansen. Are the staff captain and Mrs. Williams up there, on deck 8?"

"Mr. Williams? This is Intrepid Security... I haven't seen the staff captain or Mrs. Williams up here. And I recommend you don't come to deck 8, either. There's a wild monkey up here. In fact—" The transmission stopped.

Ted clipped the radio back to his belt. "Thank you, Dr. Simmons, for the info. I really have to go. Can we talk later?" He moved away from her, as if a force at his book table were magnetically pulling him toward it.

"Yes, Guest Services can look me up for you."

Ted nodded and dashed over to the table. He quickly gathered in the clamoring line of people. "I'm sorry, folks," he hollered so that they could all hear him. "Something came up for the captain. I'll try to be back. In the meantime, all my books are half-off, they're all pre-signed, and this gentleman can take your payments." He pointed to the crew member, who looked a little panicked.

Ted didn't wait for a reply. He slid behind the table and darted down the long hallway of people waiting in line, away from the theater. He had to get to the forward section of the ship on deck 8 and warn his wife.

34

The Monkey

"Don't puke. You are not going to puke!" Lutz Vega of Lisbon told herself again.

It was no use. Something had gotten to her. She'd been feeling yucky all morning, and the feeling had been getting progressively worse as each minute slowly ticked by. As the guard who was stationed at the bridge's only interior entrance—*for the next four hours*, she confirmed by her watch—she could not leave her post, no matter what. Even if she were puking toenails. But wouldn't she get into trouble if she puked up her breakfast right in front of the bridge? It was a "lose-lose proposition" as her good-for-nothing boss Robert Spillman liked to say.

Lutz tried to consider her options, but there really weren't any good ones. Then she remembered the assistant director's report this morning. Included in the report was the status of rooms for each deck assignment, including vacancies. She pulled out her folded page, which listed the names of each occupant and the vacant rooms. She glanced at the starboard side, down the small bisecting hallway, and knew that cabin 8504 was right there, just out of eyesight now, but there. It was vacant. If she had an uncontrollable bout of nausea, she could just run down the hall and puke in the unused washroom, and be back before anyone noticed she was gone.

The more she thought about it, the better it sounded. She might even go there now. She could drink some water and splash some on her face, and she'd feel better. Maybe she'd even just force herself to puke up whatever was bothering her, and be done with it. Back in her bulimic days, when she was trying to fit in with her police department, she could do it on command. And although now it was more difficult, the way she felt, even without the bout of nausea, she thought it would be easy.

She looked aft, down the long highway, and then starboard again, at her destination, and didn't see anyone coming. Further, the captain's meeting in 8000 was expected to continue for at least another half hour. So this might be the best time to time go. She hesitated, and then another wave of nausea rocked her body. She ran.

Fumbling with her key-card, Lutz turned the corner and held up right at the door, card out and ready to deploy. She was a mere second or two from puking. But she stopped, the wet hairs on the back of her neck prickling. She swung a glance back forward and saw that the Royal Suite's door was propped open. Then she saw why.

She doubled over and heaved violently, tossing the remnants of breakfast, then her dinner, and probably every other thing that ever visited her stomach. A disgusting mix of yuck spilled out of her, all over the already puke-colored carpet. And then, while she was retching, she started to laugh a little at the thought that that's probably how they made this carpet: thousands of workers puking up colors that didn't belong together into one carpet. *Be serious, girlfriend,* Lutz told herself, and then stared again at what lay in the doorway of the

Royal Suite.

It was Catur. The room attendant who always smiled at her in the crew mess. He was... It was too ghastly to even look at his injuries. He was literally ripped apart.

She jumped when the door to cabin 8504—her destination before she puked—shook from someone pounding and scratching on it. But this room was supposed to be empty.

"Who's in there?" she called to it.

More banging, and something else... it sounded like moaning.

"Are you all right?" She became sure that someone else was injured by whatever did that to Catur. But just in case...

She lifted the long Maglite wand from her belt and held it like a baton with her right hand while she slipped her key-card into the lock with her left. The lock flashed green, and she clicked the handle down, but hesitated. The Maglite lifted higher into the air, ready to come down on whomever or whatever, might come out.

"I'm opening the door now," she said into the thin, dark opening.

She pushed a little more and saw five hairy digits crimp around the door's edge and pull inward. The thing vaulted at her with an ear-piercing screech.

She tilted sideways and swung the Maglite, connecting with the monkey's skull, sending it hard against the hallway wall.

She spent no time contemplating the oddity of a monkey in the hallway of her ship. Having heard about the carnage in Gibraltar, and knowing she'd lose a battle going to toe-to-toe with this beast, she did the one thing that came to mind.

She dove into the cabin's darkness and simultaneously kicked the door shut. It slammed hard and continued to shudder, as the monkey, now on the other side of it, pounded on it, shrieking its anger at her through the two and a half inches of steel and plastic.

Two things occurred to her as she huffed and puffed, on her back, in the dark. First, she was sure the door would give way, as the beating it was taking was incomprehensible. Next, she realized that the inside of this room smelled so putrid that the nausea that she had momentarily forgotten about was back again in full force.

"Oh God." Something or someone else was dead in this cabin. Her skin cooled and she started to shiver, even though the air was decidedly muggy.

The pounding outside had stopped, and so did the beast's howling. She sat up and leaned forward until her ear was pressed against the door, doing her best to ignore the rancid smell. She heard the monkey breathing and something else. There was the sound of scraping against carpet, like something heavy was being dragged across the floor. The noise grew and then trailed off, becoming softer. Another revolting image popped into her head: the monkey was dragging Catur away. She was instantly sure this was true.

Although a part of her breathed a sigh of relief at knowing the killer monkey was not after her any longer, she knew she had to do something to stop it. It was wrong.

The radio!

Between her panic and desire to get away from the animal, she forgot she had a walkie. Using the door handle, she hoisted herself up to her knees and yanked the radio off her belt. Adjusting the squelch till voices could be heard, she clicked transmit and spoke over whoever was talking. "Hello! We have an aggressive monkey on deck 8. It has already killed a room attendant." She paused a moment, but still held the transmit button down. "Repeat, very dangerous and strong monkey on the loose on deck 8." She let go of the transmit button and listened.

There was an immediate response. "This is T.D.—ah, Ted Williams, consultant to Captain Christiansen. Are the staff captain and Mrs. Williams up there, on deck 8?"

That was the passenger-author, she thought. *What's he doing on the ship's private radio?*

"Mr. Williams? This is Intrepid Security," she chimed back, a little miffed that he was using their radio for unofficial business. "I haven't seen the staff captain or Mrs. Williams up here. And I recommend you don't come to deck 8 either. There's a wild monkey up here."

A shuffling sound in the room.

"In fact—"

A moan, followed by the sound of an object clattering to the carpet, sounded from behind her.

She spun around, held up her flashlight up and clicked it on, sending a cone of light to the floor midway through the cabin, toward the sound. Only a few feet from her, at the foot of the bed, was the body of a man—she could tell by his shoes.

She moved the light up, illuminating his body, and then gasped.

The chest and stomach were gone, emptied. It was like his trunk had exploded outward and his gore was everywhere around him. And... she caught the epaulet on his shoulder. Three bars. It was Spillman.

Another noise and Lutz moved the light up farther, casting it on the whole room.

What she saw shocked her so badly she dropped her flashlight. It bounced twice and went out.

35

TJ & Jean Pierre

"Did you hear that?" TJ asked. She shuffled over to the door on bare feet, putting an ear to it. "I swear I heard something out there."

"What? I didn't hear anything. Come back here," Jean Pierre pleaded.

She paused to wipe the sweat from her face with her palm, miffed at how hot this interior cabin was. All because the door was closed, so that no one could hear them from the hallway, or accidentally wander in, forcing them to explain what they were both doing there.

She glanced again at Jean Pierre, feeling guilty about being here and not with her husband. Her hand brushed against her Orion necklace, causing her body to shudder.

She just realized how late it was. She had missed Ted's talk, completely. "I'm going," she announced.

TJ marched over to the bed and collected her personal belongings. "I'm tired and I need to go, now."

He finally glanced up at her. "But what about, you

know...?"

"I really don't care at this point. Look," she squeezed his shoulder tenderly, "I really appreciate all you've done, I just can't do this cloak and dagger bullshit anymore. And the not telling Ted everything kills me, especially since he trusts me implicitly."

"You think he would still trust you if you told him that you were in a cabin, sweating with a single man?" He smiled at his rhetorical question.

She slapped his naked dome. "You're evil. But yes, he would still trust me, even after that!"

"You Americans are so—"

"—Hey, wait. Holy shit! Did you see that?" TJ pointed at Jean Pierre's laptop screen.

He turned back around to look at it. "I know, that's what I've been trying to show you."

~~~

Ted bounded up the stairs, taking two at a time. When he cleared the deck 7 stairwell, he saw another man coming up from the other side, matching Ted's pace.

"Flavio?" Ted huffed, ascending more stairs.

"Mr. Villiams." Flavio exhaled, still countering his pace.

Each rounded deck 7 and, now side-by-side, were vaulting up the next set of stairs to the half-deck.

"What are... you doing?"

"Kill monkey. Same as you," the Romanian head waiter declared.

They turned to their separate stairwells, Ted on the left, and Flavio to his right, and made way for deck 8. They cleared the last step at the same time, but Ted turned right this time and Flavio turned left, crisscrossing each other to different
~~~

sides of the deck's two hallway entrances. "I think monkey this way, Mr. Villiams," he whispered, while withdrawing a large cooking knife from a sheath with his right hand. It was polished to a mirror finish. He held up at the port-side hallway entrance.

"How do you know?" Ted whispered. He bent over, grabbed some breaths and shuffled back across the hall to Flavio.

"I do not know. I just think it this way."

"I'm not here to get the monkey. I'm here to get my wife, before the monkey gets her."

"I'll lead then." He turned right and stridently marched down the hallway, stopping only occasionally to consider each and every sound.

It was the same hallway Ted had walked down earlier with the All Access Tour group, leading to the bridge all the way forward. The tour's route began at the forward stairwell versus their mid-ship start. Now, they needed to walk halfway across the span of the *Intrepid* just to get to the bridge from here. TJ was nearby in cabin #8511. It felt like an impossibly long walk, with a crazed monkey on the loose. And now he remembered, based on the cabin numbers, the cabin he was looking for was on the starboard side of the ship.

Ted tried hard to moderate his breathing, but it was difficult because he was winded from the stairs and he feared for his wife's safety. He concentrated on taking long and deep inhalations, one for every five footsteps.

Almost every doorway they passed had a green sticker on its handle and several were still propped open, as all the passengers had been advised to do earlier. Their occupants were either away or had forgotten it was okay to shut their doors now that they'd been cleared. Worse, each open doorway presented another opportunity for a hiding, crazed monkey to leap out and kill them.

When they made it to the forward stairwell, without any sight or sound of the wild monkey, Ted bit his lip and turned right. Flavio seized him by the shoulder. "Why?" he whispered.

"My wife is in 8511."

"Dat's your cabin?"

"It's not ours... But she's there now."

"Vait." Flavio swiftly withdrew another knife from a sheath on his other hip, flipped it around with precision, and handed it to Ted, handle first. "In case you see monkey. I come around by bridge and meet you at room."

Ted nodded and pointed the shiny knife blade outward, almost more afraid now of cutting himself than getting attacked. Almost.

He studied the starboard hallway, looking in both directions. There was no movement or noise, other than an indistinguishable voice or muffled cough. But there was the blood. A lot of it.

A line of blood led from one end of the hallway to the other. It looked fresh. Leaning over, he touched a forefinger to the wetness and pulled back, his fingertip coming up red. His thumb rubbing the crimson around his forefinger confirmed it. And no coagulation meant it just happened. He shuddered just a little and clutched the knife handle even tighter. Then, he turned the corner, immediately coming upon cabin 8511, which abutted the stairwell.

He contemplated whether to knock or holler. Either would make too much noise, and he suspected if the monkey was somewhere on this floor, the noise would attract it. Deciding a short double-rap would be best, he raised his clenched fist.

Then the door opened.

It was TJ, who looked as surprised as he. Behind her was Jean Pierre.

"Ted? What are you do—"

Ted put his hand over her mouth and forcibly pushed her and the staff captain back into the room.

As Jean Pierre backed up, he caught a glimpse of the

very large knife Ted was nervously brandishing. “Ah, Mr. Williams, Theresa Jean—I mean Mrs. Williams—and I were doing nothing wrong. In fact—”

“Shhh.” Ted glowered at the stammering officer as he let the door close softly behind him.

Ted glanced quickly at the room and its occupants: pages of papers taped to the walls, including schedules with times and dates; two laptops, his and TJ’s; the staff captain, his bald head and face glistening with sweat, one tail of his shirt untucked. Then he noticed the bed behind him had been hastily made. For just a moment, his mind wandered, until he glared at TJ.

“Before you think anything further, I’m gay. I have no interest in her.”

Ted ignored him and wrapped his arms around TJ, and hugged her tight. Upon release, he said, “I’m sorry for being such an asshole. I’ve been taking things out on you because of my own guilt with my first wife and son dying, and I’ve been shrinking away from you, and that’s wrong. Please forgive me.”

She hugged him back. “Of course, I forgive you.”

A smile grew on Ted’s face. “Also, I no longer suffer from enochlophobia.”

They kissed for a long moment, while Jean Pierre waited uncomfortably.

Jean Pierre continued to scowl at both of them, before he finally shook his head and said, “Oh, you already knew what she was doing here and you knew it the whole time?”

“Yeah, she confessed to me about the whole... Affair?” Ted snickered at his pun. “I know this cruise is an FBI setup, so that TJ could work undercover—though I thought it was all about me—to catch Eloise Carmichael, because the rich son of one of her victims has a Senator uncle who pushed the FBI to send someone on this cruise, before she killed her seven-hundredth husband.”

“We may be too late on that one,” TJ cut in. “We were

just about to open her cabin when you arrived. We were watching video recordings from her living room, when we caught a glimpse of... So did you come here just to apologize and tell me you loved me?"

Ted's face became grim. "I don't want you to freak out, but one of those damned Barbary apes got on board and was spotted on this floor. I came up to warn you both."

"Oh shit," she breathed. Her features tensed, then relaxed. "But I thought that the aggressive behavior passed after so much time."

"Me too, but the guard I spoke to on the radio said that a crazed monkey was on this deck, that it had already killed someone. There's a long blood trail just outside, spanning much of the hallway. Someone or something has been seriously injured."

Jean Pierre broke out of his gaze and grabbed his radio from his belt. It had been turned down the whole time, while they were monitoring Carmichael's cabin, in an effort to be covert. He turned it up and they heard a flurry of voices.

"Come on, let's get this over with," TJ said and bounded out the door, with the two men following.

Only a few steps later, they arrived at the Royal Suite, cabin #8500. The blood trail appeared to lead right up to and under the door, and a puddle of vomit lay off to the side of it.

Jean Pierre tentatively opened the door using his key-card, revealing the slaughter.

~~~

It hit TJ like a shot to the head—the carnage and the knowledge that this gory mess was from an animal attack. At that moment, TJ recalled the scenes of the blood and gore from Chicago, when her actions led to a partner's death, and then to
~~~

the more vivid moments from the day she was attacked.

They popped into her head in rapid succession: the vicious dog coming out of nowhere; her hand pressed against her damage; doing 180's, watching and bracing for the next strike she knew would come at any moment; the shock and dizziness from the blood loss; the extensive pooled blood and gore just inside the stables; the attack that followed.

The fear she felt from those moments ate at her every day.

It was now overwhelming.

She steadied herself on the doorjamb, reflexively snapping her head back to make sure the monkey wasn't there, before returning her gaze to the gore before her. She squeezed her eyes closed before opening them again, trying with all her will to ignore the terror that wanted to consume her. She didn't want them, most especially Ted, to see this. They needed her.

~~~

"Good God, what the hell happened here?" TJ whispered, her voice scratchy. She didn't wait for an answer and stepped over the pool of blood and muck.

"Do you think that's wise?" Ted asked as he carefully navigated the large puddle of red soup: a mixture of blood and other unrecognizable organic material in it. A disgusting human bouillabaisse, Ted thought. Bile rose up in his throat.

Each of their steps into the cabin splish-splashed, indicating it too was swamped by the tsunami. Jean Pierre pulled open the sheers and curtains, to let in some light.

TJ yelped, startled as someone popped out of the bedroom. "Flavio? What are you doing here?" she asked.

"Mrs. Villiams... Mr. Villiams... Staff Captain." Flavio nodded at each, stopping in the reception area, where the
~~~

gathering group held up. “Monkey not here. Also, dead man in bedroom.” Flavio pointed.

They all rubbernecked, and then one by one made their way through the thousand-square-foot cabin, complete with grand piano, full-size living room, office, and giant bedroom. On the bedroom floor, among some debris, were the bloody remains of an elderly man.

Pulling a tissue from her pocket, TJ crouched beside the body and pressed it against the dead man’s face. “Based on the body’s morbidity, I’m guessing he’s been dead more than a day.”

“Just as the dark video confirmed.” Jean Pierre stated while hunched over the other side of the body. He stood up and addressed the others, “We’ve been keeping an eye on Mrs. Carmichael during the cruise. But the video had gone dark, like much of the ship. Then we had just seen a flash of what we thought was Mrs. Carmichael. That’s when we had decided to enter the cabin.

“I’m no expert, but these sure don’t look like claw marks.” Ted pointed to the man’s stomach and chest.

TJ used her tissue to examine one of the cuts, pulling at the sliced clothing surrounding one of the stab wounds. “You’re right. Eloise is probably responsible for both murders.”

“I only see one body,” Ted murmured, searching the shadows of the room. “How do you know all the blood at the door wasn’t the husband’s?”

“Besides the trail of blood in the hallway, the gore in the entrance is... fresher.”

Jean Pierre moved to the living room and used his walkie to call security to find out where his guards were, including the guard who was supposed to be posted in front of the bridge. He also wanted someone posted here, to protect the crime scene, and to get an update on their crazed monkey.

“Come here. Now,” Flavio said from the hallway.

They trotted out of the cabin, again carefully stepping

over the gore in the entry, and found Flavio pointing down the hallway with his knife. "I think monkey drag second body this way." He didn't wait for them, stalking along the side of the corridor, just outside of the blood trail.

"How can one of those little monkeys drag an adult down a hallway?" Jean Pierre asked.

"That little monkey is many times stronger than you or me," Ted answered. His exasperation was growing. "So I guess now we're searching for both a woman serial killer and a crazed monkey?"

"It would seem so," Jean Pierre said.

"Even you wouldn't make something like this up in one of your stories." TJ turned to Ted and kissed him. "I forgot to thank you for coming up to warn us."

"Gee, shucks. Here." He handed her Flavio's knife. "You know how to handle this better than I do. And I have a feeling we'll need it where Flavio's taking us."

They caught up to Flavio, who had stopped outside of a cabin door. "Blood trail goes this way. Different blood here, into this cabin."

Flavio was right. The long blood trail almost appeared to fork a few feet from cabin 8531, with one prong, mostly blood droplets, at the threshold of the cabin and the other, more pronounced, going into a restricted crew-only doorway.

Flavio put his head to the cabin door, and then announced, "I hear nothing."

Jean Pierre had opened the restricted access door that led into the crew's mid-ship elevator and stairwell. From below, they heard distant screams.

Flavio brushed past his staff captain through the door, the others reluctantly following.

Once inside, they froze.

36

The Monkey

"His name is Catur. He's one of the room attendants," Jean Pierre said softly to the group.

"I see no knife wounds though, just bites and ripped flesh." TJ once again had another tissue out, while Jean Pierre held a flashlight on the body.

"So the monkey killed this one and Eloise—" Ted was interrupted by a terrified scream from downstairs. All heads turned.

"Enough talk," Flavio whispered and then quickly proceeded down the stairwell, using the scream and the monkey's small bloody footprints as his guides. The other three followed close behind.

They tracked the bloody marks all the way down to deck 1. When they opened the door onto I-95, everything was quiet. This was an oddity, since even during early morning hours, the area was normally abuzz with activity. It should have been bustling right now.

"Look, blood goes there," Flavio said, and then he

continued his pursuit, leaving the others to ponder their next move.

"Is it just me, or is Flavio a badass?" Ted tried to crack a joke, but it fell as flat as his others earlier today.

TJ just scowled at him and then caught up to Flavio, clutching the knife Ted had given her.

"That looks like the crew's break area," Jean Pierre whispered to Ted and pointed down I-95 to where the gory impressions stopped, collected and then continued on. "It's where they can smoke and get some fresh air, outside of the view of guests."

As they continued, several crew peeked out of doorways, fearful of coming out any farther. Jean Pierre motioned for them to stay where they were. Ted would have preferred to have been in any of those places, rather than out here tracking a crazed killer-monkey. But if TJ could be tough, tracking a wild beast when she was terrified of most animals, he figured he should at least back her up on it. He had fallen behind and scurried to catch up with the group.

At the exit marked "Open Deck" and "Smoking Permitted," they examined the crimson splashes that also included boot prints, running away from the door, out of sight, toward the crew recreational areas. Flavio tentatively stepped through the door and came back out shaking his head. There was nothing. They continued along the trail, listening for any sounds that might cause them to change direction or spring into action.

They started down the smaller hallway leading to all the crew areas: recreational, admin, and even a convenience store. The hallway didn't connect with any other arteries, and the footprints only went one way. The monkey was down here.

Jean Pierre lifted his walkie to his face and spoke softly. "Security, this is the staff captain."

"Staff Captain, this is Deputy Chief of Security."

"Wasano, we've found a dead body in the deck 8 aft

crew stairwell. We've followed a blood trail down to I-95, and finally to the crew rec areas. Send personnel to secure these areas. And we need a weapon or two down here to deal with a crazed monkey. Get down here on the double. I'm now off comm." Jean Pierre turned his volume down again, and trailed behind the other three, who followed two sets of fading bloody footprints: one human and one primate.

At the Slop House, the crew's mini-market, the group held up as Jean Pierre slipped in and grabbed two sets of silverware. He was about to exit when a meek voice wobbled unseen behind the counter. "Sir? You have to pay for that."

Jean Pierre grabbed his Seacard and flicked it over the counter. "Don't lose it. I'll be back." He grinned at this: even in an extreme emergency situation, they were following the rules. "No exceptions!" the captain had drilled into them.

He rushed to the group. "Here, Ted." Jean Pierre handed him one of the sets. "Didn't want you not to have some protection."

"Thanks," he said, examining the cutlery, "I'm pretty vicious with a fork on Prime Rib Day."

"Inside," Jean Pierre said as he opened the packaging, "you'll find a rather substantial steak knife."

They pulled their knives out and carefully followed behind Flavio and TJ, tracking the blood-trail to the living room, where the crew went to relax, watch TV, and play games. They held up for the next body.

It was a crew member. But other than that, it was hard to tell who it was. There wasn't the slightest amount of Regal European blue or white showing on his ragged uniform, as it was covered in blood. The poor young man's throat was ripped out and all that remained was a ragged opening.

The body also looked like it had been chewed on.

"Come on. He's dead. Monkey in here," Flavio announced and rose to proceed into the room.

"Flavio," Jean Pierre whispered, "I've called security.

They're bringing real weapons. I'd suggest we wait until they get here. We'll keep the monkey in there."

"Don't want to lose more crew, sir. I go in, you stay." Flavio pushed through the swinging double doors. One by one, they followed him.

The cavernous room appeared empty of crew, and certainly held no monkey. The only sounds were that of an old movie playing on the large flat-screen TV at the other end and distant tapping.

Once inside, they all took knees and huddled closely. Flavio suggested he'd walk through the room slowly and they would back him up by spreading out. He wanted to make sure there was no crew inside. They agreed, and Flavio slowly advanced, making a trail bisecting the room, passing by a foosball table, a drum set, and a video gaming area, before he'd end up behind the couch in front of the TV.

TJ followed Flavio part of the way and held up at the foosball table, while Ted stepped carefully over to the gaming area. He tested the weight of his newly gifted steak knife and wished he had kept Flavio's more substantial one.

Jean Pierre remained at the door, so he could quietly direct security when they arrived with their weapons.

Ted noticed evidence of the crew being here besides the TV, as he negotiated his way past a couple of tables. One of these was obviously abandoned quickly, with cards splayed haphazardly across the table and on the floor. Curiously, multi-colored ravioli shells were in three tight piles in front of three pushed-out chairs, one overturned.

Ted's heart almost burst out of his chest when he saw movement underneath the table. He was ready to hoof it in the other direction, but after a moment it registered he saw no fur—only a small man, curled up in the fetal position, eyes as big as dinner plates, staring at him.

It was probably unnecessary, but Ted held a forefinger to his lips.

Ted turned back toward Flavio and almost guffawed at the movie playing on the TV. It was the original *Planet of the Apes*, and Charlton Heston was demanding, “Get your hands off of me, you damned dirty apes.”

There was commotion coming toward his end of the room. Ted stood up from his squatting position to see Flavio frantically pointing at a brownish form in the corner, previously obstructed by the couch. It was the Barbary ape, and it was much bigger than what Ted remembered of these monkeys.

It was violently scratching at a cabinet, growling at it. A muffled whimper wafted through the slats of the beaten cabinet door. Someone had escaped the monkey and was hiding. But that door wouldn’t hold it back much longer.

A pinball machine spontaneously sang out its rhythmic sounds, followed by a ding-ding-ding.

The beast turned in its direction. That was also their direction, and the monkey instantly saw Flavio.

Flavio reflexively tossed his knife, which sailed in a perfect arc and struck pay-dirt, hitting the beefy part of the monkey’s bicep, which had moved in front of its chest, as it turned to leap in his direction.

It screeched a terrorizing racket and raced at Flavio.

TJ was next and threw her knife, but it rotated one revolution too many and hit the monkey handle-first in the face. The monkey diverted its path and headed for her, as she panicked and flopped onto her rear. She had no protection.

Ted jumped, unsure what he was going to do but knowing he wouldn’t be able to throw a steak knife effectively. He did the only thing he could think of. Clutching his knife, he leapt toward the monkey, who was completely focused on TJ. He connected shoulder and knife blade into the monkey’s chest, just before it could get to her.

The monkey bounced in one direction and Ted came down hard on a guitar. A thud, a twang, and a crack, which was either one of his bones or the guitar neck breaking.

The monkey hit the wall on the other side of the room, knocking down a shelf of books. It shook its head. Ted's steak knife still protruded from its chest, Flavio's from its arm. Then it focused its red, violent eyes at Ted. It snarled its anger and leapt the short distance between them.

There was a loud explosion.

The monkey's head disappeared behind a spray of red, saturating Ted and everything around him. Its limp body crashed into a chair beside him, coming to a rest for good.

By the front entrance, Deputy Security Chief Agarwal lowered his rifle.

Ted let out a long sigh of relief.

37

Falling Apart

"I heard what happened," Captain Christiansen said, offering his staff captain a steaming cup of coffee. "Thank you, Jean Pierre, for mitigating the problem, before it got much worse."

Jean Pierre accepted his cup and sank into the sumptuous chair, one of six surrounding suite 8000's dinner table. The plush cabin, contiguous to the port side of the bridge, was unoccupied during this itinerary. Its $9,000 price tag wasn't a problem for its prospective Parisian occupants; they just never showed up. With the ready room damaged by the tsunami, the captain pressed this one into service.

The message Jean Pierre received said this meeting was "important," but no other information was given except that a similar meeting would follow with the remainder of the ship's first and second officers. The implication was huge. On the other hand, it might have simply been an opportunity to refocus the troops, and to thank each of his officers for a great job during difficult circumstances. Jean Pierre had no idea which it was. He hoped it was the latter. Still, it felt odd to know that other than him, the captain and the two lone officers on the bridge, all the ship's brass were waiting in the hallway, outside this luxury cabin's door.

"Actually, sir, it was one of our head waiters, along with the Williamses and Deputy Security Chief Wasano. They all came through and saved countless lives."

"Yes, of course. Still, I'm proud of the work you did." The captain lifted his cup of coffee to his lips and sat beside his friend. The bags under his eyes were bigger, darker. "Did you find out what happened to Spillman?"

"He was a casualty too, along with one of our masseuses and one of our guards. The three were found in cabin 8504. We're not sure what happened, as some of their wounds seemed to be self-inflicted, and there were lots of bites, too. Our best guess is that the monkey was accidentally locked in the room with Spillman and the masseuse; maybe it followed one of them inside. I'm sure you are aware they've been having an affair since the last itinerary. And I had just learned that Spillman, in an attempt to cover his tracks, was messing with the security cameras. We're also pretty sure he was the one who shorted out the electrical, and blamed it on one of his security monitors, who has since been cleared of all charges. Anyway, they were killed by the monkey and the guard must have heard it, went inside and was attacked as well, and in the process, she must have let the monkey out. Yet... some of what we saw is impossible to explain."

"Like what?"

"We found the guard's and the masseuse's bodies together, propped up against the door—this made it really hard to enter the cabin. The masseuse's body had multiple wounds, and substantial blunt force trauma to the head. It was dark, and so we believe that the guard thought the masseuse was the monkey, and because the guard's throat was ripped mortally, she must have panicked and killed the masseuse with her flashlight."

Jörgen shook his head and then said, “Okay, that mostly makes sense. So what was impossible to explain?”

“The masseuse had skin and muscle tissue in her mouth which corresponded to the bite to the guard’s throat.”

Jörgen looked at his friend like he’d lost his marbles; for a moment his mouth dropped open, as if he wanted to ask a question. Then his mouth closed, and his expression changed from incredulous to grim. “So our total casualties from the animal attacks and the tsunami stand at nine crew and three guests?”

Jean Pierre gazed into his coffee, and then back up to Jörgen. “Yes, sir. I’m afraid so.” He’d learned of the numbers, and who the casualties were, only minutes ago, and he almost fully accepted all of this. He had to. But hearing it from his captain’s lips made it seem so much more... horrible. On all the ships he’d served, after all these years, the most crew or passengers he’d lost on one ship had been two passengers. And they were fairly old folks who died of heart attacks.

Yet the *Intrepid’s* circumstances were so extraordinary. And from that standpoint, any one of these issues could have caused many more deaths. It was horrible, but considering what they had gone through, they were lucky.

Jean Pierre added, “We’re still looking for Mrs. Carmichael. But we think she might have gone overboard during the tsunami, after she killed her husband. Her body will probably never be found. Even considering all that’s happened to us... we were damned lucky.”

Jörgen was quiet. He seemed lost in his own thoughts.

Jean Pierre knew that as bad as he felt, his friend was burdened even worse for being the captain. But there was more to his friend’s look than just the weight of their losses. He knew that Jörgen had something even more serious to say. That had to be the reason for this meeting, before the one with the other officers. His stomach started to churn when he asked, “We are through the worst of it, right?”

"I'm afraid not," Jörgen responded as if receiving the verbal cue he had been waiting for. He handed Jean Pierre the TV remote and looked him straight in the eyes. "No one on this ship, except me, has seen what you're about to see."

Until that moment, Jean Pierre hadn't realized they were facing the TV. But now he knew this, too, was on purpose. "But I thought we didn't have sat..." He didn't need to finish his sentence, and clicked the "On" button. This was the reason he was here, alone with the captain, with the rest of their officers waiting outside. Jörgen had been building up to this.

When the giant screen flicked on, Jean Pierre nearly dropped his coffee.

There were eight separate news channels in boxes, all displaying similar images. The volume was on for the first box, which was the Fox News Channel, but set very low, almost inaudible. Tucker Carlson was reporting about fires, mass deaths and vast damage to property. The lower-third crawl reported the numbers of dead in various countries. Every channel appeared to be discussing similar chaos and mayhem: cities damaged, fires burning out of control, people dead or dying. Intermittently among the pictures of destruction were reports of animal attacks: incidents of most every kind of mammal attacking people and other animals.

Jörgen spoke over the low chatter of the TV. "The tsunami devastated every coastline on the Atlantic, with those closer to the source suffering the greatest damage: Lisbon, Portugal; Brest, France; and Bristol, England, for example, were wiped out. The damage decreased as the waves spread farther. Large portions of Bermuda were destroyed, because it's so low-lying. The Bahamas and most of the East Coast of the US suffered significant damage, but nowhere as bad as other places. Then there are the animal attacks. They are exploding all over the world: Europe, Asia, and Africa. America has a few reports sprouting up, but not too many at present. The places least affected appear to be out of the reach of the ash cover from all of the volcanic eruptions."

Jean Pierre continued to sink deeper into his chair, letting the sounds, sights, and stories from the Chyron crawls of each program wash over him.

Jörgen said nothing more. He wanted to be sure Jean Pierre had a few minutes to process the enormity of what he was seeing. He had had all night to come to terms with this new reality.

Jean Pierre turned his watery eyes to Jörgen and said, "We need to get to Florida as soon as possible."

"I thought the same thing. But I don't believe it would be safe there, either. I used our sat phone and spoke to several port masters in Florida and one in Charleston.

"All East Coast ports are closed from tsunami damage, though all are working on repairs and should be back open soon. They haven't yet heard reports or seen incidents of animal attacks at their locations, only north of them. And perhaps the Rage disease—as the newscasters are still calling it—might not spread there, but then again it might. If when we arrive we're allowed to disembark, what if the animal attacks have started? We are safer on this ship, waiting it out. So I came up with a plan, and it was accepted by corporate.

"We were already scheduled for Nassau, Bahamas, as our last port before heading to Miami, Florida. Their port sustained only moderate damage from the tsunami. They expect to have it open again in forty-eight hours. So far, there are no reports of animal attacks on Nassau." He was going to add, *Though I wouldn't count on that by the time we get there,* he left that part out. "So our plan is to still port in the Bahamas, but we won't go ashore until we can guarantee this Rage thing has passed or the area remains unaffected. I'm still hopeful that this thing has a short fuse and will burn itself out in a matter of days. Either way, we can try to resupply and sit it out until it does."

Jörgen paused to make sure Jean Pierre didn't have any

other questions. The staff captain was still in the shell-shock phase. He continued, "In the meantime, we say nothing about this to the rest of the crew and guests. We'll be in Nassau in five days. We'll use those five days to watch and carefully plan what we'll do next. I'm going to tell this to the first and second officers, right after we're done.

"The good news is, with the route I've plotted outside the ashfall, we should have sunny skies most of the way, and it's warmer outside. I intend that we all put on our best faces for the guests, and make sure they enjoy their cruise. Happy guests are manageable guests."

Jean Pierre was sitting up straight now. He turned his chair toward Jörgen. "What do we say about the TV reception and the Internet?" Jörgen could see Jean Pierre had fully accepted his plan and was already preparing himself for the days that lay ahead.

"We lie. Maybe tell them we won't be able to fix the satellite and Internet service until after we have made it to Nassau and get new equipment. We should know for sure what we're facing when we get that far. Then we can tell them the truth. But not before then."

"What about the Williamses?"

"Tell them. Keep them in the loop, as you would other first officers, at least until this crisis passes. And update the two officers on the bridge too."

Jean Pierre nodded. That was it. There was nothing more to say. Jean Pierre trusted that Jörgen had considered their options and, as he said, received authorization from corporate. They'd have five days to watch, wait, and then figure out all the details. In the meantime, their job was to make their guests feel safe. He could deal with the next five days. They'd worry about after when "after" came.

Jean Pierre stood up, straightened his uniform, cleared his throat, and saluted his captain. "Sir!"

Jörgen rose, returned the salute, and warmly shook the

hand of his friend and Number One. “Thanks for being someone I can always count on.”

Jean Pierre offered a small grin. “Should I let in the other officers?”

“Yes, please. Then can you go ahead and make sure all our guests have a great time today?”

“I’ll do my best.”

38

Sunshine and Lollipops

It was a day full of contrasts: small puffy clouds, set upon a deep blue sky; a sun revealed, now pouring out its warmth upon the cold salt water sloshing around the main-deck pool; multi-colored swimsuits covering blanched bodies swollen from this morning's breakfast; a general acceptance that all was good among the ship's guests when there were signs of potential doom all around. Otherwise, it was a day that almost seemed perfect. Almost. And if something violent was approaching, no one seemed to notice, or even care.

Once the *Intrepid* had charted a course along a diagonal arc that appeared free from volcanic clouds of soot, and the sun reigned supreme again, air temperatures rose quickly and by eleven, it was a comfortable 20 degrees Centigrade out, with the forecast of it going even higher. The crew had already cleaned up most of the debris from the public areas of the ship. The broken windows pool-side on deck 9 were cleaned up and boarded so that no one would attempt to walk through the empty frames. Only a few areas were cordoned off, not available to passengers. The passengers quickly accepted these minor inconveniences, which they were told would be fixed either in Nassau or at the end of their cruise.

All the remaining deck loungers, which had been put up before the tsunami, were laid out and were already one-third full of guests who were just happy to gather some warmth from the previously hidden sun and drown their troubles in the saltwater pool or one of the multiple Jacuzzis and the daily drink special: half-priced, double-rum zombies. It had been Jean Pierre's idea to ramp up the alcohol content

The crew expected the remaining chairs to fill up quickly once word spread that the sun was out and the world wasn't going to end. What few crew knew was that most of the guests were ill from yesterday's dinner salad, which had been tainted with a nasty mix of bacteria and other microscopic monsters.

The Williamses were among those who had decided to take temporary advantage of the warmth, finding two lounge chairs which offered sweeping views of the sun deck. Jean Pierre had wanted to meet with them up on the bridge at noon, not only to personally thank them again on behalf all the crew, but to also update them on the captain's plan for the coming days of the cruise. They had a little time to kill and it seemed like a perfect opportunity to take in some sun and reap one of the bennies given to them for their help in saving the ship from a larger disaster.

They raised their drinks in a silent toast. Some sort of red-orange rum concoction, compliments of the pool-side bartender, who informed them that all their drinks were free for the remainder of the cruise.

Ted brought the drink down to his lips and sucked down a large portion of the sweet liquid, while glancing over the entire deck and the guests who littered its surface: a multitude, lounging in chatty happiness.

After swallowing another mouthful, he said, "You know, it's funny how quickly the human spirit desires to move away from pain and tumult and set itself upon anything pleasurable. To look at the people out here, you wouldn't have even known, unless you were paying attention, that anything bad happened over the last five days. It's all sunshine and lollipops now."

"I was thinking the same thing. How quickly everyone wants to forget." She sipped her drink and then glanced tentatively up at her husband. "Is it really over?"

Ted held the bridge of his nose, fighting brain-freeze from the slushy beverage. "Not entirely. If the effect is only temporary, then maybe this will pass. I hope we'll hear of more signs from the outside that it's over with. I have a feeling one of the reasons Jean Pierre wants to talk to us is that they've made contact with other ports, and he has more of those details."

"I hope they're the details we want to hear."

"Me too." Ted finished his drink, furtively eyeing the bar only a few lumbering steps away. He decided it was better to meet with Jean Pierre with a semi-clear head. With some luck, there'd be plenty of time for drinking. He set his glass down, folded his hands into his lap, and shut his eyes, relishing the warmth on his skin.

TJ was only teasing her drink, twirling her straw around it, as if it still wasn't mixed entirely. She was worried sick about her mom and hoped that Jean Pierre would offer some way for her to call. Surely, he'd find a way.

Then she remembered the other question she had. Glancing back over to Ted she asked, "So explain to me how the volcanoes tie into the animal attacks?"

He didn't open his eyes. "Well, this is just a hypothesis. But it's the best one I've heard. They're called thermophilic bacteria. These little guys love it hot, like most bacteria do. However, this particular bacterium loves it *really* hot, even hanging around volcanoes and steam vents. They have some sort of special cellular protections that normal bacteria don't have so they can survive extreme temperatures, and they're hard to kill. When several volcanoes erupted they sent their trespassing thermophiles into the atmosphere. Those thermophiles are constantly searching for heat, and it's not too warm in the upper atmosphere. So in their search for hot, they find themselves attracted to birds, who have among the highest temperatures of all mammals. The infected birds bite other animals and transfer their infection to those other animals, who go after others, and so on."

"Wait, I thought your book was about T-something messing with an animal's brain, causing it to go all crazy-mad. What does that have to do with thermo-bacteria?"

"Right. The *T-Gondii* is a parasite already present in almost all animals and most humans. But it sits dormant in most of its hosts. The theory is that the thermophilic bacteria, once it got into the bloodstream of the infected animal, woke up the T-Gondii, which then commanded the animal to do what comes naturally, without any sense of worry about its own welfare."

"What comes naturally?" TJ asked, but she knew the answer the moment her question left her lips.

"Killing, of course."

"Thank God it doesn't affect humans too."

"Yeah, that actually puzzles me. I'm not sure why it doesn't—affect humans, I mean."

"Maybe it's because our body temperatures are different." TJ glanced at her watch and was shocked that it was already almost noon. "We need to get going to the bridge or we'll be late."

Ted didn't move. He seemed frozen in place, eyes almost glazed, staring off toward the horizon.

"Did you hear me?" TJ set her nearly full glass down and squeezed his shoulder. "Ted?"

"Sorry." Ted shuddered a little. "Your comment just got me thinking." He stared at the horizon a moment longer, and then returned his wife's gaze. "Yeah, let's go."

~~~

A cloud of darkness hung inside the bridge.

Ted and TJ didn't notice the darkness immediately when they were ushered inside: they were too taken aback by the damage. A boarded window on the port side spoke of the causeway. Together, their eyes followed what they suspected was the path from the sudden inflow of water: through the ready room—currently roped off, its windows blown inward; then into the rest of the bridge. Half of the consoles were detached from their normal places and now rested against the port-side window-wall, useless artifacts. Holes where the consoles had been were occupied by small men in black jumpsuits. Some were all the way in their holes; the rest were half in and out, all of them talking frantically back and forth in a foreign language. Bundles of wires snaked out, across the floor and into each of the holes. It looked as if they were rewiring the entire bridge.

The first real signs of trouble came from the two bridge crew members, at their posts: They looked sullen, almost dumbstruck. The Williamses hadn't expected to see anyone being overly cheery, knowing that several of their fellow crew and three of their guests had died over the last couple of days on their watch. But surely their spirits should have been lifted today after having avoided so much more death, and with the prospect that all the troubles of the last few days would pass. Not to mention the fact that even after what should have been a devastating tsunami, they still had a ship in working order—minus some obvious damage which they were still fixing—and lots of supplies. But the crew's dark mood was quickly obvious to Ted and TJ. They knew something was wrong.

Jean Pierre interrupted their mutual contemplations. "Welcome, my friends." He held out his hand and shook each
~~~

of theirs warmly. "Let's go out to the starboard-side swing deck, where we can have some privacy." He walked them through the bridge and led them outside through a side hatch.

"My apologies for not offering something more comfy. I didn't realize the captain would still be in a meeting with many of his officers."

They didn't mind. In fact, they preferred the outside salt air and the stiff breeze, though the north side of the ship didn't offer any sunshine.

Neither of them wanted to hear what they suspected was coming next.

Ted deflected, partially from curiosity. "Tell me first, since both of you are here... Whatever became of Mrs. Carmichael?"

Jean Pierre looked at TJ, who looked at him. "You should explain this, since it was your investigation."

"Yeah, well we don't know what happened to her yet. We suspect she was washed overboard by the tsunami. And before that, we think she killed her husband. As you also witnessed, we found him dead in their cabin, with multiple stab wounds. As far as I'm concerned, and therefore as far as the FBI is concerned, she's on our Most Wanted list, and will remain there until she's ruled officially dead in a year."

TJ looked over to Jean Pierre to see if he wanted to add anything more, seeing the staff captain had stepped over to the north-facing railing. "This reminds me. The finger later found in their cabin—did Dr. Chettle offer any guesses on who that belonged to?"

Jean Pierre's back was to them. His binoculars were glued to his face, pointed at some wispy black cloud on the northern horizon that appeared to be moving in their direction.

"Sorry." He lowered the binoculars and turned back to them. "The finger appears to be Mrs. Carmichael's. And based on the teeth marks, it appears she chewed it off herself."

~~~

The door rattled, stopping Paulo in his tracks. He tugged on the waistband of his borrowed black overalls, feeling his cuffs being restrained by his heels.

Paulo glared at the door, daring it to make another noise. Down the hallway, a similar shuddering sounded. He huffed, now discounting what he heard as coming from the movement of the ship, which would naturally cause things to vibrate.

He tugged once more at his pant legs and felt the pending scorn of his supervisor if he didn't hurry along. He was summoned to the bridge to assist with all the electrical problems they were having there. It wasn't his normal job—he was a janitor—but they needed all the competent able bodies on fix-up. And because he was pretty good with electronics, and after getting a recommendation from Buzz, he received a promotion today and was now a mechanic. They told him they'd find a uniform more his size when they reached their home port in Miami.

The door to cabin 8531 was once again jarred furiously from the inside. It clattered so violently, he thought it might come off its hinges.

"Are you all right there?" he called out to the person who must have been behind the door.

The response sounded like a muted grunt, and so Paulo put his ear to the door and listened carefully. Again, he called out, "Are you all right?"

Another rattle, and a longer, more pained-sounding grunt. The person behind the door was obviously in distress and couldn't answer. The previous wellness check on the guests must have missed this one. Or maybe their condition had worsened.
~~~

Panicked, Paulo looked up and down the hallway, searching for any crew member who could take over responsibility. He assumed this floor would be a buzz of activity, but it seemed empty now. There was no other crew to be seen or heard, though he did hear some more rattling far down the hall. Its hollow echoes only added to Paulo's building anxiety.

He was certainly overdue on the bridge by now. But he couldn't ignore the cries of a potentially injured guest. He withdrew his new Seacard from his pocket, not convinced it would work on this door. But with the elevation in title came increased access.

"Hello! I'm going to come in and help you, okay?"

The drumbeat rattle on the back of the door continued, more furiously, followed by another long groan.

Paulo slid his card in-out, the lock flashing its green acknowledgment.

He pushed the handle down and nudged at the door, just enough to crack it open. "I'm coming in to help," he hollered louder, so that the injured occupant and anyone else around could hear.

There was pressure from the inside, so he pushed harder, but the pressure was building by an equal portion, as if the injured guest was working against him.

Maybe the guest was pressed up against the door and couldn't move.

Paulo, as determined as he could have been, dug his heels into the carpet and pushed low into the solid door.

When he had it wedged half open, he stuck his head into the black opening.

Lights must be burned out here, too.

Paulo focused on the floor, figuring the injured guest would have been there.

He was startled to see bare feet and legs, and as his eyes continued up, the pelvis of a naked female. He blinked his eyes and moved his head upward, attempting to avert his gaze. Instead, he caught a glimpse of the woman's mostly exposed breasts. He pawed on the door, intending to push himself away from it and the woman.

"Ah, oh my," he stammered. "I'm so sorry, miss. I didn't know. I thought you were hurt. I—"

A vise-grip clutched his hand, clamping it to the door.

It was a female hand, bloody. It was missing a finger.

Paulo yanked his own hand loose and skittered backward, his legs and cuffs tangling. He was going to fall. He glanced up, his eyes meeting hers. They were bright red and so angry.

She screeched an unearthly noise.

He attempted to scream back, but was cut short.

No one heard Paulo die, as all around the ship, the doors began to rattle.

Epilogue

"Is that a ship, out there to the southeast?" The man pressed the binoculars to his eyes and focused all his attention on the ship south of them. His vision was blurred, but the image was clear. "It's a blooming cruise ship!"

His partner bounded over to him, causing their little aluminum boat to pitch violently.

"You idiot. Do you want to toss us over?"

The smaller man immediately sank to the floor, his rear splashing in a couple of inches of water. "Sorry, Thomas," Phillip said, looking down at his pants. They had finally dried out and now they were sopping wet again. He glanced at the distant ship, ignoring his friend's gaze. "Yeah, I can see it. But it seems... broken."

Thomas glared at him for a moment longer, before returning to his binoculars and the cruise ship in the other direction off their bow. The ship was already plainly visible without the help of the binoculars, but he couldn't see clearly since his glasses went overboard. "It's the smokestack. You're right, it's bent over. They must have survived the tsunami, but it still got busted up. You want to see?" Thomas held the binocs behind him, expecting Phillip to snatch them from his hands. He turned back to find his friend sitting in the water gathering in the bottom of their little boat, staring downward. "Phillip, what's wrong?"

Phillip looked up. "I miss our friends, and I don't feel well."

"Me too." Thomas thought about what they'd been through, the only two out of a crew of twenty who survived the tsunami. How he and his friend Phillip made it, he had no clue. But somehow, after it passed, he found his friend and then this boat, floating beside them. The boat had no oars, but at least they were out of the water. That was, until it sprang a small leak, which required them to bail constantly. If they could stay ahead of it, they'd stay afloat long enough to be spotted. And they had a good chance of being spotted since they were floating in one of the busiest shipping lanes in the world. At least, it had been the busiest before the tsunami.

Thomas turned back to the cruise ship.

It looked like it was headed in the normal westerly route all transatlantic ships took from Europe, when they were first headed to the Azores. Unfortunately, their little skiff was probably too small and too far away to be seen by anyone on that ship. Just in case, he put the binoculars down and held up the broken oar they had found in the debris of another destroyed ship. With a T-shirt tied to its flat end, he waved it furiously from side to side.

"Will they see it?" Phillip asked, and then dry heaved over his lap. "I don't feel too good." He moaned and then slowly hoisted himself back up on the second seat in the battered rowboat to get a better look.

"Doubt it. But we gotta try. No telling how many ships survived the tsunami."

"I sure am thirs..." Phillip's voice trailed off.

"I'm thirsty too, Buddy. But what I'd *really* love is one of those rum-filled drinks that they serve to all their guests. You know, one of those fruity things with the umbrellas in them?" Thomas closed his eyes and licked his lips, almost tasting its cool yumminess. "A zombie! That's what it's called. Remember when—"

Thomas turned back to his friend, wondering why he hadn't heard a peep from him while he was yapping on about the rum drink. Phillip had loved those things when they stopped at a beach bar on holiday in the Canaries a couple of years ago. He found Phillip staring into the heavens at a giant black cloud that moved rapidly over them. This cloud screeched and crackled.

"It's a flock of blackbirds. Probably coming from the Canaries," Thomas said, as he watched the swarm of them pass overhead, all flying toward... the cruise ship he'd been watching.

"Philip?" Thomas begged, pointing back behind his friend, who was stooped over in his seat.

There were dozens of stragglers, flying irregular patterns, rather than the normal sinewy lines of a flock. In fact, the flock had looked rather irregular as well. The stragglers were flying lower too, so he could hear their cackles more prominently. Several of these seemed to be flying toward them.

The attack was quick, and before either of them knew it, they were overwhelmed by the demonic-looking blackbirds. The birds screeched at them and dove into Thomas, burying their beaks into his flesh, followed by clawing and ripping.

Thomas got turned around while swinging at the offending birds, when he heard gasping and cries from Phillip, and then a scream. But it wasn't a scream of terror. It sounded like frustration, or anger.

Thomas batted away two of the birds, and this gave him enough of an opening to turn to see his friend Phillip—his buddy since childhood—leap off his seat and land on top of him. Phillip dug his fingers into Thomas' skin, and his friend opened his mouth wide, like he was going to take a bite out of him. "What are you do—"

Shock stopped his words as he saw Phillip pull away from him with a chunk of Thomas' own skin in his mouth. This part horrified him, as did his friend's insane behavior. But what made him piss his own pants was his friend's red eyes.

Part II
PARASITIC

"He who fights with monsters should be careful lest he thereby become a monster."

Friedrich W. Nietzsche

PROLOGUE

Fifteen Years Ago

The dog came from out of nowhere, completely silent, rather than the usual vicious pooch announcing its terror long before it reached you. It crashed into her right side like a freight train. She only heard the briefest sound of the monster gulping one last bit of air before it struck.

When she hit the ground, she heard the animal grunt from their impact and then growl as it attempted to get a better grip on her side, so that it could set itself to ripping her flesh.

If she had any time to think about her situation, she would have probably panicked. This was where her training kicked in. Her gun was already unholstered, and so she quickly fired off a shot. But it was from the same side as the mutt. She missed. Quickly, she switched hands and shot once more from her left.

A long moment of quiet passed. Not more than maybe twenty heartbeats.

They both lay in a heap, but only she was panting.

Upon quick inspection, she concluded this was not your back-yard, shit-bird variety of pit bull; this was a pure-bred Vizsla: slick, muscular, and very powerful. The Bureau already knew that the dog's owner had bought a half-dozen over the years from a breeder in Jackson, about ten miles south.

Of course it never occurred to her superiors in the FBI, who put together this raid, that the dogs might be a threat, only their owner.

Well, they screwed the pooch on that one, she thought.

"Sitrep, people," blared her earpiece.

"Taggert here... Wren here... Anderson here..."

With some effort, TJ pushed herself onto her knees. She

lifted her mangled shirt edge to inspect the wound. It looked pretty bad.

"Sitrep, Williams."

Her black FBI jacket came off—*damned thing was too hot anyway*. She pulled off her shirt with a grunt and groan, thankful she was wearing her sports bra and not one of the frilly Victoria's Secret-things Ted bought her. Folding it lengthwise until it was a long, thick strip of fabric, she wrapped it around her side, making sure both ends of the wound were covered enough. Holding the ends of the jacket arms, she spun it around, turning it into a cord, with most of it bunching up the middle. It too was placed over the wounded area. Finally, she tied the jacket's arms tight around her other side, cinching it down to hold the field dressing, and hopefully stem the flow of blood.

It would have to do until this was done.

"Williams, report," her earpiece hollered at her again.

"Williams here. Damned dog frickin' bit the shit out of me. Had to shoot it. I'm good to go. 10-76."

"Roger."

She should have called in 10-52, Ambulance Needed. But then she'd have to walk ten times as far back to their mobile base, and she really wanted to get this sonofabitch, especially after now learning he was training vicious dogs.

She drew her weapon again; it had been holstered while she'd rendered herself aid.

Each step forward elicited a painful grunt, and she could feel a warm trickle of blood drip down her backside.

Worse yet, she felt a building anxiety, giving way to a constant need to check her twenty for another crazed animal.

The ranch house was only a hundred yards away, and no doubt their perp would be looking out his window in her direction. So she had to approach it covertly, which was damned hard to do without much natural cover. With any luck, he'd think her gunshots were from a hunter, illegally shooting on the Yellowstone National Reserve property, contiguous to his. He had often called in complaints to Game and Fish about this.

The worst case scenario would be the guy coming out, guns blazing, and then they'd have another Waco on their hands. And that they did not want. The guy may have been a murderer, but they didn't want his dozen-member family hurt too. They were the reason TJ had to keep going.

It was because the kids hadn't been seen for several weeks, and all of them missed the first two weeks of the fall semester that a couple of deputies from the Jackson Sheriff Department were dispatched to check on the family. Upon arriving on the scene, there was a single panicked radio broadcast from one deputy. The dispatcher claimed the caller said only, "He's crazy." Nothing more. An hour later, the FBI stepped in as they were not coincidentally investigating two missing hikers from Prague, who were last seen wandering in the same direction as TJ was now.

She stopped to regain her breath, and to readjust her field-dressing, which was already coming loose. She was sweating like it was ninety out, when it wasn't much more than sixty. She pressed her palm to her bicep. Her skin felt cool. *Do not go into shock*, she told herself. As if one could coax oneself into not doing so.

She cinched her jacket-pressure-bandage even tighter, moaning at the pain, while she trudged forward the last few steps.

The moaning continued, but this time it wasn't her.

"This is Williams," she whispered. "I'm at the southwest corner of the corral fence-line, about fifteen yards from the home. I'm hearing some sort of... moaning. Going to investigate."

"Hold up Williams. Wait for your team."

The rest of her advance team reported in, but much farther away. She would be there long before the others, which meant no backup. Yet, if the moaning was from an injured family member or the hikers, waiting longer might end up killing one of them. To buttress her argument for moving forward, she was feeling queasy. It occurred to her, she'd have to finish this pretty quickly, before she passed out. The last thing she wanted to do is blow the whole operation passing out before they got 'em. She'd rather accept a verbal tongue lashing, if it meant they could catch this SOB.

Maybe I could claim delirium from the dog bite. It wasn't too far off, she thought.

She'd press forward, moving along the back fence line.

Within a minute, she heard the moaning sound again, only it was more of a groaning. It was coming from the dark opening of the barn, diagonally across from the corral.

TJ slipped in between the rough slats of the split-rail fence and yelped when she saw where she stepped. She thought for a moment it was another dog. But it wasn't.

Below her foot and against the fence lay a dead horse. Practically gutted. A dark stain circled the carcass; the blood had mostly seeped into the corral's soft dirt. There were multiple small round puncture wounds and deep gashes in its throat and sides, like it had been mauled by a wild animal.

Her head pivoted, searching around her twenty for the wild animal that did this. Her breathing accelerated, to the point of hyperventilating. The perp had more dogs. What if they were just as vicious as the one that attacked her? She felt a chill shoot across her spine.

TJ bent over to catch her breath. It was either the blood loss or her hyperventilating or both: her dizziness turned to double vision. At any moment, she felt certain she'd either panic or pass out. Touching the lower edge of the bunched-up shirt against her side, her fingers came away very wet and dark red. She was losing too much blood. She needed to call it. Losing any more blood, she'd surely lose consciousness, maybe even die.

A low growl, like a dull echo, pulled at her. Her head drew up, attempting to find the sound, and she instantly saw it.

Or rather him.

Their perp, Jim Tanner. Father of ten. Multi-millionaire, ranch owner. Perhaps even mass-murderer. Was the one growling. And running.

He was running toward her. In his hand, he brandished a metal rod, like a piece of rebar.

"Subject is running toward me, yelling," she warbled over their comms.

More like screeching, at her. He sounded and looked like some crazed wild animal. An insane thought hit her: maybe their perp, and not one of his dogs, mauled the horse.

"Mr. Tanner. FBI. Freeze!" she demanded, but it came out a weak croak. She raised her Glock 29. He was sighted in, with only the slightest of twitching. Good thing, there were at least two of him coming at her.

He kept coming, only faster.

"Mr. Tanner, I'll shoot you," she hollered. Her own voice sounded distant, like it was someone else's.

TJ dropped to her knee, not just to keep her gun hand steady: she was seeing three of everything now.

"Stop!"

He didn't.

She fired. Three times. One for each of him.

Then she tumbled to the ground, her strength leaving her.

"Subject down. Officer needs assistance," she whispered over her comms, and then passed out.

~~~

Present Day
~~~

Even though this incident had long since been paved over by years of other forgotten memories, the abject fear of attacking animals born from it clung to TJ's daily consciousness.

Only now did she consider that moment. Not for what she would have done differently, but for one important detail about that crazed dog, and equally crazed man. It only occurred to her on this day that the man they were going to try to arrest, the man she ended up shooting and killing, had one physical attribute that she had completely forgotten, until now.

Yet when the memory burst into her head like the pain she often felt from the physical scars to her right side, she knew it was important.

His eyes were blood red. Just like the animals they were seeing today.

The Journal of TD Bonaventure

DAY FIVE Cont...

... THE DAY I LOST MY WIFE.

THERE WAS SO MUCH WE DIDN'T UNDERSTAND AT THAT MOMENT.

FOR INSTANCE, IT WASN'T JUST THE ANIMALS WHO WENT CRAZY. THIS POINT SHOULD HAVE BEEN OBVIOUS TO ALL OF US. BUT BY THE TIME WE FIGURED IT OUT, IT WAS TOO LATE.

EVEN AS WE STARTED TO RELAX, OUR ONLY CONCERNS WERE FOR THE ANIMAL ATTACKS. AND THOSE, WE THOUGHT—IT WAS MORE LIKE HOPE—WERE POTENTIALLY EBBING. THAT'S WHEN PROVERBIAL HELL BROKE LOOSE ON OUR SHIP.

TJ AND I WERE BEING UPDATED BY THE SHIP'S STAFF CAPTAIN, JEAN PIERRE. THE INTREPID DID IN FACT HAVE SATELLITE. THEY HAD TOLD GUESTS OTHERWISE TO KEEP THEM IN THE DARK, SO THEY WOULDN'T PANIC—LIKE WE WERE DOING WHEN WE HEARD THE REST. THEY HAD BEEN MONITORING THE GLOBAL NEWS NETWORKS. IT WAS BAD: EUROPE AND PARTS OF ASIA HAD DEVOLVED INTO CHAOS, AND ANIMAL ATTACKS WERE SPREADING LIKE WILDFIRE OVER EVERY CONTINENT, EVEN IN NORTH AMERICA.

WE HAD WITNESSED SOME OF THIS FIRSTHAND ON OUR TRANSATLANTIC CRUISE: FIRST, AT MADRID, IT WAS A RABID-LIKE DOG; THEN, AT MALAGA, IT WAS THE BIRDS, FOLLOWED BY THE RATS; THEN, AT GIBRALTAR, THE MONKEYS; AND FINALLY, THE DOGS, BROUGHT ON BOARD BY SOME WELL-HEELED PASSENGERS, HAD GONE CRAZY TOO. ALL WERE SYMPTOMATIC: BLOOD-RED IRISES AND MOST HAD AN ABSOLUTE DESIRE TO KILL, EVEN WHEN MORTALLY INJURED. UNTIL THEN, WE HAD THOUGHT THE TROUBLE, LIKE THE

VOLCANIC ERUPTIONS, HAD RUN ITS COURSE AND WOULD BE EVENTUALLY OVER. BUT THIS WAS BASED ON INCOMPLETE INFORMATION.

THE PET SPA'S VET FOUND HIS WILD BOARDERS AFTER THEY HAD GOTTEN LOOSE AND BELIEVED THEY WERE NO LONGER AGGRESSIVE. AND WHEN I RAN ACROSS A RED-EYED FERRET OUTSIDE OUR ROOM—THEY SUSPECTED IT WAS BROUGHT ON BOARD BY ONE OF THEIR CREW—IT WAS ALSO NOT AGGRESSIVE. BECAUSE OF THESE EXAMPLES, WE ALL HAD ASSUMED THAT THE AGGRESSIVE TRAITS OF THIS DISEASE WOULD PASS. WE DIDN'T KNOW BEING SYMPTOMATIC DIDN'T AUTOMATICALLY MEAN AGGRESSIVE IN EVERY CASE.

AND HELL, THROW IN A MONSTROUS ONE-HUNDRED-FIFTY-FOOT TSUNAMI IN THE MIDDLE OF ALL OF THIS, JUST TO DIVERT OUR ATTENTION FROM THE REAL PROBLEM. AND WHEN THE SUN PEEKED THROUGH THE VOLCANIC CLOUDS, WE WERE ALL READY TO FORGET THIS, AS WE WOULD WITH ANY BAD DREAM. BUT THAT WAS OUR NORMALCY BIAS… AND OUR IGNORANCE.

IT WAS THEN THAT THE BOOM WAS DROPPED ON US BY JEAN PIERRE.

MY WIFE TJ WAS PROBABLY THE TOUGHEST WOMAN I'D EVER MET, AND YET SHE WAS ABSOLUTELY PARALYZED BY A FEAR OF BEING ATTACKED BY AN ANIMAL. IT WAS UNDERSTANDABLE WHEN HER HEAD DROPPED DOWN IN ANGUISH, AND A WELLSPRING OF TEARS FLOWED FROM HER FACE.

I TOO FELT GUT-SHOT. I HAD FEARED THIS VERY THING FROM THE MOMENT THE FIRST SIGNS OF THIS RAGE DISEASE (AS THE MEDIA WAS CALLING IT) SPRANG UP. AFTER ALL, I WROTE A DAMNED BOOK ABOUT SOME VERSION OF THIS MADNESS. OF COURSE, I HAD WRITTEN ABOUT MANY POTENTIAL APOCALYPTIC EVENTS. I NEVER REALLY EXPECTED ANY OF THEM TO COME TRUE. THIS ONE APPEARED TO BE WORSE THAN EVEN I HAD ENVISIONED: IT WASN'T TERRORISTS

OR ANARCHISTS WHO HAD WEAPONIZED THE T-GONDII PARASITE, WHICH ALREADY INFECTED MOST MAMMALS AND REPROGRAMMED THEIR BEHAVIOR AGAINST US; IT WAS SOME BACTERIA FROM VOLCANOES THAT IGNITED THE T-GONDII PUPPET-MASTER TO PULL THE STRINGS OF ITS MAMMAL HOSTS AND SET THEM AGAINST US, EN MASSE.

AND AS BAD AS IT APPEARED IT WAS GOING TO GET, WITH MAMMALS OF EVERY STRIPE ATTACKING HUMANS EVERYWHERE, WE HAD NO IDEA THAT IT WAS ABOUT TO GET SO MUCH WORSE.

YOU SEE, IT WASN'T JUST THE ANIMALS, IT WAS THE HUMANS TOO.

THE REPORTS OF HUMAN ATTACKS SO FAR WERE INFREQUENT AND BLENDED IN WITH THE OTHER CHAOTIC STORIES AND WERE NOT RECOGNIZED AS A SIGN OF THE GREATER PROBLEM. AT THIS POINT, THE WORLD WAS RUNNING FOR THEIR LIVES FROM THE ANIMALS AND NATURAL DISASTERS, AND SO FEW HAD TIME TO ANALYZE THE DISEASE'S PROGRESSION LEADING TO ITS ULTIMATE HOSTS: HUMANS.

BY THEN, IT WAS TOO LATE.

OUR SHIP WAS IN FACT A PERFECT MICROCOSM OF THE T-GONDII'S EVOLUTIONARY PROGRESSION: FIRST ANIMALS WITH HIGHER BODY TEMPERATURES, THEN DOWN THE BODILY TEMPERATURE-SCALE, UNTIL FINALLY HUMANS WERE AFFECTED. BUT WE DIDN'T KNOW ANY OF THAT YET. AND I'M GETTING WAY AHEAD OF MYSELF.

THE DAY THAT EVERYTHING FELL APART, THIS DAY IN FACT, STARTED WITH JEAN PIERRE'S SIGHTING OF A CLOUD OF BLACK BIRDS THAT WERE HEADED OUR WAY.

39

The Birds

It was like a gut punch.

TJ Williams had doubled over, grabbing her side right where the dog had gotten her years earlier. It almost felt like the dog had hit her full force once again, pushing all the air from her lungs.

But it wasn't the dog.

It was the piece of a missing memory. Something she had forgotten entirely. Until then.

Those damned red eyes!

"Are you alright, Hon?" Her husband Ted asked. He clasped a comforting hand onto her back and bent down beside her, no doubt thinking she was not dealing well with the future prospect of unending animal attacks. He wasn't altogether wrong.

She rose up and Ted matched her movements. His eyes poured out deep concern for her. She so wanted to alleviate his anxiety; to tell him "Yes, I'm fine." But she wasn't fine.

Her fingers reflexively brushed over her necklace. It was

something she found herself doing constantly, even though she'd just received this anniversary gift from him. It was representative of his view of her, and in fact what she wanted to be: a fearless warrior. But that wasn't her at all. She was plagued with fear. And it was all because of that day.

Those dark images from the past, the ones she had been hiding from, all at once flooded her mind. That horrific moment in her life that had shaped her; that had molded her into the weak person she had become, so that now she practically hid from her own shadow.

Because of the pain that moment caused, she had long since repressed those images and their accompanying feelings of terror. Yet the terror always remained.

And somehow she'd forgotten that the dog's eyes were the color of blood?

And yet, as troubling as that was, it wasn't the gut punch. That came the moment Jean Pierre mentioned "people": that was when she remembered the man that she shot, the one who was about to attack her.

He had had red eyes too.

"As I was saying," Jean Pierre's voice had boomed over the stiff headwind which was whipping through the swing deck where the three of them had been standing. He had paused to get a better look at a black cloud off their starboard bow, getting closer. "It's spreading everywhere, to animals of every stripe—especially dog populations... and people..."

It was his people comment that was the key that unlocked the red-eye memory she'd buried.

She blinked back the pain to see Jean Pierre had pulled his binoculars away from his head to examine them, as if there was something wrong the eyepiece, or his own sight.

After a very long pause, he finished his thought, "...and people are getting attacked in larger numbers."

He paused again.

TJ's mind was a jumble. While Jean Pierre focused on

the fast-approaching cloud, TJ thought more about what he actually said, not what she thought he was going to say.

Jean Pierre had kept his back to them the whole time while he peered through his binoculars at the building black cloud, delivering the bad news in large doses. He had told them that they'd been hopeful that the animal attacks had run their course, as their firsthand experience had demonstrated. But the reports coming from the outside world pointed to an escalation, not a cessation.

During this elongated break from Jean Pierre's delivery, TJ had looked past him to regard the growing cloud coming their way fast—anything to avoid considering what she remembered.

Far from a normal formation, it was in stark contrast to the blue sky, and it appeared headed right for their ship, almost course-correcting for their own movements.

Her anxiety burned in her gut, until it turned into fear.

"Now we've lost all communications with Gibraltar. We can only assume that… Oh merde!"

He lowered his binoculars and flashed a glance at them, his face and bald head paler than normal. Then he burst from his stance and dashed past them. In one motion, he opened the hatch and then leapt from the swing deck into the bridge.

TJ couldn't tell yet what he saw, not wearing her glasses, and so she glanced at Ted to confirm he couldn't either. But they could both guess. And with the same abruptness, they moved fast to the hatch opening, just as Jean Pierre made his announcement to the bridge crew.

"Attention everyone," the staff captain bellowed. "There is a giant flock of black birds headed right for our ship. I've been watching them the last few kilometers. My guess is they're coming from Funchal, Madeira. Sound the alarm. We need to warn the ship."

All but two of the crew moved toward the port side windows of the bridge to see for themselves.

Safety Officer Ágúst Helguson didn't hesitate after receiving the order from his superior. He turned aft and punched a big red button on the control panel behind him, which took up a large portion of the aft bridge wall. A light flashed on the panel and on all their functioning console screens, pulsing in sync with deafening horn blasts which began blaring outside and around the ship.

Officer of the Deck Jessica Mínervudóttir also remained at her post, eyes carefully monitoring the periphery of the ship from the bridge windows and the EDISC software on her console.

All of them waited for their staff captain's next command.

TJ glanced behind her, momentarily forgetting she was still outside. She moved quickly inside the bridge, not wanting anything to do with the crazy birds, which were now almost upon them. Ted held up momentarily, half in and half out of the swing-deck hatch, to gawk at the massive cloud of black dots descending from above. He stepped inside, pulling the hatch closed behind him, cutting off the piercing horn-sound from the bridge.

"Thank you," Jean Pierre said to him.

"What should I announce to the crew and guests?" Ágúst asked. He wasn't sure what to tell them, other than stating the obvious.

"Tell them to get inside ASAP."

Ágúst was already poised in front of the ship's intercom system microphone. He punched the transmit button. There was a crackle and squeak coming from the bridge's speakers. Ted imagined it was similar ship-wide, on all the public and cabin speakers outside of the bridge.

All heads turned to face the oncoming birds, now everywhere outside their port-side windows.

In anticipation of the question, Jean Pierre spoke in a hushed tone to Ted and TJ, "The general alarm stops when there is something transmitted over the ship's PA system."

"Attention! Attention, guests and crew. There is a large flock of black birds coming from our port side. We believe they are aggressive. Please move indoors quickly. You will be safe inside the ship. Attention. Please move inside the ship immediately. You are in danger outside." He let go of the transmit button and the horn blared again, everywhere except on the bridge, its head-hammering tone repeating over and over again.

The first wave of birds hit, just outside the bridge windows, pile-driving themselves into the outside speakers.

Deputy Security Officer Wasano Agarwal lifted his portable radio to his lips and called inaudibly to his security guards to get out to all the sun decks and make sure the guests were helped off the decks to safety.

Jean Pierre tapped away at his console screen, adeptly pulling up the camera views from several of the outside cameras focused on the Sun Deck one deck above them. Jessica did the same for hers and the other two functioning consoles. All the bridge crew, Ted and TJ turned their attention to the screens.

They all watched in horror.

At least two hundred guests were milling about in and around the pool and Jacuzzis. Many of them had wandered to the ship's port railings, presumably to get a better look at the birds, even before the announcement. Only a few were moving to the exits. None were moving fast. Some even appeared to be not moving at all. A few looked like they were vomiting.

"Can't they hear the alarm? Why the hell aren't they moving?" TJ whined.

Then almost everybody did.

They'd crowded around the consoles, each displaying four different views of the sun deck, but with little clarity. From the cameras' perspectives, it was just billowing plumes of black descending upon the entire ship. Each of them looked up at the bridge's windows to confirm what their screens were showing: the entire ship was enveloped by clouds of black birds. Some were pelting the ship, just outside of their view, their soft thuds unheard.

The open decks of the ship looked like an ant city that had been sprayed with pesticide: rapid movements, erratic convulsions, general panic, and even death.

They all gasped.

A large swath of the guests and crew were headed to the forward exits, but there were bottle-necks at each doorway. Hands swatted at birds; splashes of red were either seen or imagined—it was hard to tell.

"They're getting murdered out there," Ted yelled. He broke for the bridge exit.

"Ted," TJ yelped. "Where are you going?"

"I can't just stand here and watch." He opened the lone bridge exit.

"Sir?" Wasano pleaded to Jean Pierre.

"Yes, of course. Yes, we need to go. But OOD Jessica and SD Ágúst, you both need to remain on the bridge. We'll be in contact by radio.

"Aye, sir," Jessica snapped. Ágúst nodded, and then transmitted the announcement again, even though it felt superfluous now.

On the way out, Jean Pierre grabbed a radio for himself, and handed two more out to TJ and Second Officer Urban. "In case any of us get separated." He saw that Ted still had his. "Ted and TJ, we'll go aft, to the mid-ship Sun Deck exits. Wasano and Urban, update the captain—in case he hasn't heard the alarm in 8000—then head up to the forward Sun Deck exits."

"Aye, sir," Wasano and Urban responded in unison.

Jean Pierre and the Williams bounded out of the bridge and made their way aft through the Deck Eight port-side hallway.

Wasano and Urban followed behind them, stopping just off the bridge entrance, and pounded on cabin 8000's door. Urban closed the bridge exit, safely sealing the two lone officers inside.

"SD Ágúst?" Jessica called out, "Check your monitor... the mid-ship one, looking aft. Ahh, camera nine-fifteen."

"What am I looking fo..." Ágúst gasped. "I'm... Am I seeing this correctly?"

"I think so."

40

8000

Jörgen had pulled the edge of his hat forward so as to block out the remainder of the cabin's light from his closed eyes. But he'd been unsuccessful in his attempts to find sleep.

First he'd tried picturing the image hanging on the wall of his quarters: his wife Katrin beside him, their three fully-grown kids in front of them, and their four grandkids seated in front of them. When this didn't work, he'd tried to picture where Katrin and he would travel after his retirement next year. With the kids out of their home and no other responsibilities, they'd spoken endlessly about their plans to see so many new places; or take the time he'd never had to visit family and friends near their home in Lyngor, Norway; or to simply watch time slip by while sipping Udfa coffee with Katrin.

Yet with each tick of his watch, he had felt increasingly sure those dreams would never come. And neither would sleep.

Then his attention fell on the meeting he'd concluded

moments ago. He had put off the conversation for as long as he could—or as Jean Pierre told him, *he should stop beating around the tree*: it was obvious that the outside world was devolving further into chaos and not likely getting better as they all had hoped. So he knew he had to tell his crew, starting with his number one, Jean Pierre, and then his first officers and many of his second officers. They all took the news as well as could be expected.

After it was done, and he had found himself alone in this suite, knowing Jean Pierre had the bridge, Jörgen figured this was his best chance to at least rest his frayed nerves, even if sleep wouldn't come.

That's when he contemplated several contradictions from the meeting: what his crew had reported with what Ted had told him about the red-eyed ferret and the airborne manifestations of the so-called Rage disease.

~~~

"It appears that many of the reported cases of illness are from food poisoning," Dr. Chettle told the group in his usual measured voice, while referring to the notes on his tablet. "We've had sixty-eight reported cases of this; some are in the temporary infirmary we set up on deck one. I suspect three times as many guests and a number of crew have been afflicted with some form of amoebic dysentery."

"How the hell did this happen?" Captain Jörgen demanded.

"Our new chef said he believes it was some dirty water that contaminated last night's dinner salads. He said it was a combination of being short-staffed, a few errors by newer staff, and, I quote 'a ferret that somehow got into the kitchen.'" Dr. Chettle lowered his tablet and scowled at their ship's vet and
~~~

pet spa director, as if he were the cause of this embarrassing episode.

Jörgen glared his own discontent at his ship's sole doctor. He was angry about the doctor's feud with the vet as well as the food poisoning. But these were small concerns that he'd save for another day. His focus was on keeping his guests and crew healthy now, until they could figure out what to do when they arrived in the Bahamas in a few days. "Anything else we can do to mitigate this?"

"Other than the typical good hygiene—you know, washing hands—there's not a damned thing we can do but wait until this passes. The damage has been done. The good news is that it does not appear to be very serious, although it feels like it to everyone who's sick from it, and it's not contagious." Chettle usually preferred to overstate these kinds of things, sure that everyone he spoke to, including Jörgen, was clueless when it came to diseases. The doctor often grew short when answering similar questions again. So it was obvious the man was glad to have the floor in front of a larger audience.

"Well that *is* good. The last thing we need, after all that's happened, is another Legionnaire's Disease outbreak." Captain Jörgen consulted the next item on the checklist from his own tablet. "What about those in isolation from the dog bites?"

Chettle's attention was now drawn to two of the officers at their meeting, who looked ill, probably considering whether they needed to go to the infirmary.

"Doc?" the captain prodded.

"Sorry, sir. We had five crew members, including our vet Al..." Chettle paused to shoot another dismissive glower at Al—Jörgen had heard the doc didn't like Al because the man cleaned up after pets—before returning his attention to the captain. "...and four guests, who reported dog or rat bites. All but Al here and one guest remain in isolation. The guest refused. None of them show any symptoms similar to the animals, and other than mild infections and slight elevation in temperatures, they look fine."

"So," Jörgen now looked at Pet Spa Director Al, "was the Rage disease transmitted from one dog to the other by their bites?"

"That's our best guess, sir," Al answered. "We just don't have any way to test this. But our evidence is that one or more rats bit a toy poodle, who was already somewhat aggressive. Then the poodle turned rabid-like and bit the other dogs. Those dogs later became aggressive. It would seem that it is then spread by bodily fluids."

This was contrary to Ted's theory that it was something in the air.

"How long from bite to becoming aggressive?"

"The dogs appeared to become symptomatic within an hour or two after being bit."

"And what's the status with the dogs now?"

"They're still quarantined in the Pet Spa. And they're heavily sedated, so that I can continue to observe and run tests."

Chettle jumped in, obviously disliking Al taking over the floor from him. "If what Al says is correct, I'd suggest we release all our patients from isolation."

"That's fine, Doc. You have my approval."

Jörgen knew the next item, without looking again at his tablet. *Just give it to them. They can handle it,* he thought.

"The main reason why you, my top officers, are here is to tell you some bad news...The world as we all know it is changing for the worse. This Rage disease, as the media is calling it, is spreading like wildfire. In many of the main cities of Western Europe, and all of our prospective ports, and even our US home port in Florida, there are rampant animal attacks being reported. Many basic services have been disrupted. In other words, it is simply not safe for us to go ashore any time soon.

"We are not telling our passengers or any other crew about the outside world. Our hope is that this improves by the time we reach the Bahamas. Assuming it's safe, we'll port, resupply and then decide where we go from there.

"I need each of you, my most trusted officers, to work on keeping everyone's spirits high and to focus on the safety of our passengers and your fellow crew on board. Really, this is the safest place we could be at this time.

"We will continue to monitor the situation, and if anything changes, I'll report back to each of you.

"Remember, what's going on outside this ship is to be kept quiet. I don't even want you discussing it among yourselves, because I don't want others to become unnecessarily alarmed and increase their anxiety among everyone else, including our passengers. So mum's the word, and let's go take care of our passengers and continue to keep them feeling safe and comfortable.

"Do any of you have..."

~~~

The horn blared and Jörgen sprang from his seat, his captain's cap falling off in the process.

This was the general alarm. *What the hell is going on now?*

There was deep pounding on the door, followed by the high-pitched chime of the suite's doorbell.

A moment later, it clicked open, both Wasano and Urban bounding through. The horn, located just outside in the hallway, now blared so loudly it was almost impossible to hear anything else.

Wasano let go of the door, so that it clasped shut. "Sorry to interrupt sir, but—"
~~~

"—Why the alarm?" Captain Jörgen asked as he marched in their direction.

"A swarm of birds are attacking the passengers on our Sun Deck. We're trying to get everyone inside. The staff captain and the Williamses went aft to assist guests at the Solarium exits. The deck officer and I were headed to the forward exits."

Captain Jörgen pulled open the door again and yelled into the blare of the horn, "Let's go then."

They rushed the short way down the hallway, turned left into the hallway and immediately hit a wall of people..

41

Sun Deck

Most of the guests saw the birds before they heard them, pointing at the odd cloud formation and articulating their puzzlement: "What is that?" "Is that a cloud?" "Are those birds?" More fingers pointed and more bellies found the edge of the port-side railing on the pool-side Sun Deck and the open deck 10, above them. They all spoke in hushed tones, curious but not frightened. Not yet.

Not one guest, whether sucking on a zombie, basking in the sun, or sharing war stories about the previous night's tsunami, even considered asking the question that needed to be asked: Were these birds coming their way a threat? And yet, every guest had heard about or witnessed attacking birds firsthand.

Those guests and crew who bothered to take notice of the swarm of birds headed right at them still chose naive ambivalence over learned logic. And many were about to pay a stiff price for their chosen ignorance.

Even when it became obvious that the frenzied flock of

birds was about to descend upon them, their reactions—trained from years of normalcy—were more of shock or surprise than of fear.

It was only when the birds struck that full-out panic gripped the majority of the Sun Deck's passengers and crew members.

Frau Wankmüller's reaction was similar to most. She marveled at what she first thought was a hail storm, though she had never seen hail stones as large or black as these before. She watched them violently collide with deck chairs, loungers, railings, and people. When the dark hail squawked and screeched, she still held firm to her lounger, not wanting to mess up the pleasant buzz she felt from the uncountable number of rum drinks she'd consumed. She only reacted to the bird melee after one buried itself into her leg. At first she was jolted by the impact, but immediately discounted the attack to her fuzzy vision playing tricks on her brain. And when the offending fowl yanked out something that looked vitally important to her wellbeing from the newly formed bloody hole in her appendage; that's when she finally screamed.

Besides now flailing, the only other resistance her addled brain could come up with was to toss her empty drink glass at it. Missing the bird completely, the decorative glass connected with and shattered off of the elbow of a fellow passenger who was busy battling beasts of his own on the deck flooring in front of her. Before Frau Wankmüller could scream again, she was knocked out cold, when another bird hit her in the back of the head with such force that it broke its own neck against hers. She flopped forward and then back into her lounger unconscious. Now that her body was still, it was too much for other nearby birds to resist. Within seconds, a mass of black was feasting on the soft flesh of her eyes, neck, and stomach.

Like several passengers, her daughter hid underneath the lounger beside her, gazing wildly at the birds as they made a meal out of her mother above her.

The blaring ship horns only made matters worse, as no one could hear anything above them or the pandemonium topside.

Only the birds seemed to give the horns any notice, as dozens pelted them like kamikazes giving their lives for some greater bird cause.

A few passengers had the good sense to attempt to make a run for one of the entrances inside the ship. Those close to the entryways were also being coaxed inside by crew members and fellow passengers. But just like when a plane crashes or a ship is sinking, most passengers blindly ran forward, rather than first looking to find the best route. Illogic born from panic drove most folks forward to a cluster that had collected before the entrances, where many had stumbled or stopped to fight off their attackers.

Inside, large crowds had developed behind the forward stairwell entrances and the deck-to-ceiling glass walls surrounding it and the Windjammer cafe on both sides. With the first wave of the bird attack, before those outside thought to find safety inside, those already inside seemed to understand that it was not good to let the birds in, so they had shut the big sliding doors. Even the crew members, whose job it was to open doors for passengers who needed the help, were pushed aside by those who sealed the openings and resisted every attempt to open them back up. When the occasional bird bounced off one of the glass panes, those closest yelped in surprise and tried to step back, but instead were pushed more forward by the growing swell of gawkers behind them.

The crowd inside stood gaping at the onslaught outside, feeling safe behind the glass enclosures.

With each passing second the hordes of people inside grew, fed by more passengers streaming from upper and lower decks. Most were coming to the Sun Deck to catch some sun or get some food at the cafe, oblivious to any problems until the general alarm sounded. Now they collected en masse and gawked.

Crew members from inside the ship attempted to get outside and help. But they couldn't get by the swelling crowds, protected by the closed doors. And instead of being fearful, they pushed and shoved forward to the glass to take in the amazing spectacle outside.

As the assemblages collected and grew, the swell pressed against those up front, restricting their movements and making it impossible for anyone outside to come in, even if the doors were open. Passengers outside pleaded with those inside to let them in.

Even with what was going on outside, those inside felt protected by the heavy glass keeping them separated from the onslaught.

A screaming bikini-clad woman came out of nowhere, as if she just materialized from the darkening murk outside. She banged hard into the port-side window-wall. Several of the crowd collected behind the window shrieked and then screamed when they saw the woman was covered in an undulating mass of black, pecking away at her face and exposed body parts, now raw and bleeding.

Other outside passengers followed, some covered with birds, others not. All banged on the doors and windows, demanding entry. But the crowds behind the glass walls held firm, unable to move away from the horror.

Holding back the mad birds from the mid-ship stairwell was a two-story observation glass wall. Before the tsunami, its floor-to-ceiling windows bathed the stairwell in light. Now, a large eight-foot-wide by ten-foot-high section, broken from the tsunami wave, was filled with thin plywood, a temporary fix this morning by the crew, with the intent of replacing the broken windows either in Nassau (if they were available) or more likely upon return to their home port in Miami. Other than restricting the passengers' view out, they would have been solid enough for the occasional children's hand or gust of wind. They were certainly not intended to hold back panicked passengers.

Because none of the inside gawkers could see through the plywood paneling, there were only a few behind it and therefore nothing to buttress the thin material against the immense pressure being brought to it from the other side. Outside, a mad crush of passengers, insane with fear, intuitively sensed the wood wall's weakness. They beat and pushed against it. When their force was far more than the temporary wall could hold, it shattered inward. With a way inside, the outside mass of people poured in. And so did many of the black birds.

The inside crowd joined in the panic, now pushing the other way. They flooded the stairwells, the elevators, and the restaurant entrances. All attempted to get away from the oncoming threats.

Passengers trampled fellow passengers, while the inside din of screaming grew to such ear-splitting loudness, it surpassed the decibel levels of the ship's blaring horns. All of this noise and movement attracted still more birds inside.

At some point during the rampage of birds, something changed. Amongst the panicked crowds many passengers and a few crew members started attacking each other.

42

Boris

Before the Sun Deck's insanity started, Boris Thompson and his wife Penny did mostly what they were told: they soaked up the sunshine by the pool. The captain had directed them and everyone else on the ship to do this in his morning address. Yet the ship's doctor told Boris to remain in the infirmary because of the dog bites he'd received. Supposedly, they wanted to "observe" him. Choosing which command he'd follow was easy: he wasn't about to miss the first sunny day of the cruise. Besides, as far as Boris was concerned, a ship's captain had a higher rank than the ship's doctor, who had earlier annoyed Boris with comments about his weight and abnormally low body temperature.

Each time he thought of the doctor and that damned little dog, he reflexively scratched around one of the six bandages covering his "superficial wounds" made by the insane dog. He felt lucky not to have been hurt worse and was still pissed at the doctor for not believing that it was a toy poodle. If he were making it up, he'd have said it was a Great Dane or a

German Shepherd, something much more macho than a blooming poodle. Still, thoughts of the attack terrified him.

Boris glanced around the deck, trying to remain on guard if the evil little pup were to show up again. He just didn't believe they'd caught 'im.

"You keep scratching at that, it's going to start bleeding again," Penny droned on; at the same time she was scratching at a raw part of her belly that had formed at the top edge of her bikini bottoms, already stretched to their limits. He had warned her that the damned thing was not her size.

"Bloody hell, woman," he snapped at her.

She busied herself with her second rum drink, sucking away its final frothy remnants.

Boris remained calm, reminding himself that it was their anniversary. He was attempting to make every effort not to say anything cross to his wife during this momentous celebration. "Sorry love. It's just the damned things are itchy as hell." It still annoyed him that first the doctor was on his fanny about his wounds, and now so was Penny. He bit his lip, hating that every inch of his body felt anxious.

Something brushed against his elbow.

This startled him so much, he jolted his arm forward and away, knocking his own full drink glass onto the exo-skeletal leg brace protecting his knee. It catapulted its flavorful contents all over his other leg, the chair and then onto the rubberized decking of the jogging track before them. He pivoted at the same time to prepare himself for what he was sure was the attacking mad poodle's next assault. Boris' opposing arm cocked back, ready to unleash his balled-up fist on the red-eyed devil before it could take a seventh chunk out of him.

Directly in front of Boris, a mere moment before he'd administer his pummeling, was the bum of an elderly man. The man's rear thrust upwards and farther toward him, now bumping up against his shoulder. The old man's only sounds were the squeaks of his chair.

"Now look what you did," trumpeted an old woman's voice, raspy and condescending, "you made that man spill his drink."

Boris couldn't tell where this disconnected voice was coming from because the backside of the man's knickers, now thrust into his face, filled up his whole field of vision.

The offending backside spun around, pivoting on furry slippers, and then Boris could see daylight once again.

"Damned ship put our chairs too close together," the old man croaked back to his wife and then faced Boris, a grimace etched into a swarthy mug, ancient and wrinkled like a bed-sheet at dusk. "Sorry son." He scowled at the reddish-brown liquid splashed everywhere and then back to Boris. "Can I buy you another... whatever *that* was?"

Boris wanted to be angry, but this man couldn't have weighed more than forty kilos, and seemed genuinely embarrassed by his bump. He stood patiently waiting for an answer, stooped over, loose skin waggling in the breeze.

"Are you buying the man a drink?" demanded his equally stooped-over wife, impatiently waiting for her husband to finish up with her chair.

The elderly man ignored her, a grin forming. It was a curiously happy look that said, *That's just my old woman. You'll understand this, if you make it to my age.*

Boris liked this old guy instantly, and now he wanted to buy him a drink, not the other way around.

"It's nothing, sir," Boris said loudly, so that the old man's wife could hear. "I'm just a little jumpy and I'm a bloody klutz. Can I get drinks for yah? We have one of those all you can drink packages, so it costs us nothing."

The old man wanted to say no, but then scratched his cheek, more of a habit than his attempting to dispense with an itch. The deep fissures of his face moved around his burrowing fingers. Boris could tell the old guy was programmed to react with a "no!" Probably pride more than desire. But the man continued his hesitation, obviously wanting one.

To make the old man's decision easier, Boris pushed himself up and out of the clutches of his lounger, ignoring the sticky liquid coating his left leg and his right leg's inability to cooperate. "Come on, sir. Let me get you and your wife a drink. Our treat. Tell me what you're both drinking. We're having the ship's special: some tasty rum drink called a zombie."

The man's wrinkle lines went vertical, and a grin now covered his whole face. "Mercy no. We're whiskey folks. Both my wife and me. Thank you, we'd love to take you up on your offer. I'm David Cohen." David thrust out his withered hand, gold Rolex dangling off his wrist.

Boris returned the shake and noticed immediately David's forearm had a series of numbers stenciled on it: A-18523. It was almost unreadable, but he knew immediately what it meant: David had spent time in the Auschwitz concentration camp. Boris and Penny had just visited that horrible place last year and it made such an impact on Boris, he remembered everything. Boris quickly averted his eyes from David's, feeling guilty for staring at the tattoo, and more so for guessing what it meant. "I'm Boris, Boris Thompson, and my wife Penelope."

Penny waved with one hand, her other clutching her drink glass, her lips glued to its straw.

"Evie—hi." David's wife waved back.

"Very pleased to meet you, sir. I mean, David."

"Pleasure's all mine, Boris. And sorry again about the chair."

"It's just like the airlines, where they pack us in like sardines—"

"—Don't forget mine, Boris," Penny interrupted, holding out her empty as proof.

Boris just smiled and began his waddle toward the bar, the temporary brace on his injured leg squeaking. He had to move around several people, who seemed to be slowly milling around, pointing out to the sea, as if they saw something important.

He ignored them, focusing on not falling on his face again and fulfilling the first half of his mission: get Penny's drink and one whiskey for David's wife. Penny and he had the bar package, which allowed them to drink as many alcoholic drinks as they wanted, only one at a time. But the pool-side bartender—he had forgotten the man's name already—took pity on the hobbled Brit, and allowed him to carry two at a time, as long as both Seapasses were swiped. Boris wasn't too sure if the bartender would allow him to get two and immediately fill another order for two more, so that he could get all four of them drinks. He'd worry about that after he returned to get David and his drinks.

"Hi Boris, back for another round?" asked the slight man from the Philippians. Doe was his name—he just remembered.

Boris was about to belt out his order to Doe when the ship's horn, directly above their foreheads, blared so loud Boris thought his head would explode.

Doe too seemed jolted from the horn sound. But then Boris watched the bartender's face go from confused to shock and then something more: it looked like fear.

Boris twisted around and glanced at the pool below them on deck 9, and then the upper deck where they were, but he didn't see anything that would warrant concern.

All at once the outside turned dark from a thick cloud that passed over them.

Then it fell down upon them, like it had lost the ability to stay up in the air.

The upper sun deck and lower pool deck looked like they were holding a giant rugby scrum, involving the whole population of the ship. Most were either running or flailing away at the enveloping cloud. An ear-piercing cacophony of horn blaring, squawking and screaming filled the air.

A grunt and scream beside him caused Boris to twist

back, where he saw Doe fighting with two black birds.

The cloud was birds!

Doe howled again, this time from pain, as one of the black birds ripped at his cheek.

Penny! Boris thought. She was in danger from these birds.

He spun too quickly, his braced knee not moving the way his brain thought it should, and he flopped hard onto the decking.

In front of Boris, also on the deck, a woman covered her face, curled into the fetal position, as birds mercilessly pummeled at her head and arms with their beaks, bringing up blood with each head-plunge.

Boris got up onto his knees and spotted a wadded-up beach towel beside him. He snatched it up and heaved it at the birds, connecting with one. Two others fluttered above, squawked at her, and then continued their assault.

Boris pulled himself all the way up using the fixed bar stool, grabbed a dirty plate left on the bar, stumbled over to the woman, leaned over her and swatted at the twin fowls, connecting so hard the plate broke in two. One broken piece and the two birds thumped off a railing a meter away.

Boris stood erect and fixed his sights back on his Penny. She was so far way. He clutched the large plate piece harder, brandishing its ragged edge outward, ready to use it to chop and slice at anything that stood in his way. He hobbled forward toward his wife, periodically swinging at one bird at a time. He'd get to his Penny, not fall in the process, and kill as many of these damned red-eyed monsters as he could.

~~~

Penny wondered what all the commotion was about in front of
~~~

her and below her on the Sun Deck. But she didn't wonder enough to task herself with looking up. She was too focused on her book and her drink. When the ship's horns blared and she was jolted by a bird landing in her lap, she looked up. The lap bird flapped its wings in a frenzy, like it forgot how to fly. Then it screeched at her and tried to right itself, glaring its bright-red eyes at her.

Even in her slow to react state, Penny sensed its evil intentions. She belted out a scream and swatted at the bird with the back of her book hand. When another hit her in the shoulder, her screams grew several octaves louder. She gave up swatting, and instead covered her head and closed her eyes when it had reared back and was about to go for her face. She waited for the pain. She heard a loud squawk and then a dull thump, but felt nothing more. She quickly flashed her eyes open, catching a glimpse of the offending bird sailing end-over-end over the railing down onto the next deck and into the pool. Then she felt pain.

She glanced down at the one on her lap, which had dug its talons into her leg, and caught the dark arc of something flashing by her, connecting with this bird, knocking it away.

Casting a shadow over her was their new friend David. His hand was out, the other clutching a thick hardback book, newly coated in blood and feathers.

"Follow me. We're going inside," he demanded.

She flashed him a look of confusion, as he quickly withdrew his hand, gripped his book with both hands and yelled, "Duck!" He swung at her head just as she threw herself to the decking.

David then dropped to the deck himself and grabbed something from a tray before pushing himself back up.

"Make a soft fist," he commanded above her, his voice no longer raspy or frail.

When she glared at him with more confusion, he bellowed once again, "Stick out your hand and make a soft fist.

Now."

She thrust out her arm, wrist all floppy-like. She turned her head away from him, to check out a woman screaming directly behind her and felt something being wedged onto her hand. "Wha—"

"Now tighten your fist, like you want to punch something," David explained. His voice was calm, but still loud enough to be heard over the craziness going on around them.

She saw it was a heavy drink tumbler, not like the decorative glasses used for her rum drink. She complied, feeling the glass around her fist tighten.

"When you see one of those birds, punch at it with your new fist. Now let's go." He tugged on her elbow, intending to lead her toward his wife, who had sought protection under a lounger.

A bird hit beside Penny's feet. At first she yelped and pulled away from David's grip. But then she felt the weight on her fist, cocked her left arm and drove her heavy fist at the bird, pulverizing it into the decking. Pulling it away, she marveled at the glass, now colored red. "I'm like the bloody Iron Fist," she proclaimed.

~~~

"Oy!" Boris yelled from behind Penny.

She smiled at him and proudly showed off her blood-soaked glass fist.

Boris tossed a blue-striped towel over her head and then yelled, "David. For Evie." And he tossed him the other.

David snatched it from the air, tugged Evie out from under the lounger and laid the towel over her head, pulling her behind him. As they moved in front of Boris and Penny, David hollered, "We're going aft, toward the mid-ship entrances; the
~~~

traffic's lighter there."

Boris pushed his wife forward, and he took the rear of their human conga line to safety.

Every once in a while, when they'd slow or stop to work their way around people, Penny would punch at the air yelling something like, "I am the immortal Iron Fist."

Boris couldn't help but smile at this, as he was picturing himself as a cricket batsman—the best on the planet—each time he'd take a giant swing at one of the birds.

Another run for the batsman.

The oddest part of their mad journey across and around the jogging track to their exit to safety was the fact that none of the birds seemed to bother Boris. They swarmed most everyone he saw who was moving.

What he couldn't see because he was too focused on continuing their track was that he wasn't the only one untouched by the birds: others, some hiding, some running, some just sitting in shock, were also completely ignored by the birds.

43

Wasano

Wasano Agarwal halted at the turn of the railing of the half-deck stairwell, unable to move any farther through the swarm of passengers. He may have been *Intrepid's* new Director of Security—he became senior director when Robert Spillman was gutted yesterday—but he didn't feel like it. He'd already lost sight of his captain.

Wasano craned his neck forward, attempting to catch a glimpse of Captain Jörgen, but it was impossible to see past where he'd turned from the half-deck and somehow slipped through the throng and up the stairwell toward the next deck. Wasano, on the other hand, hit a wall of people attempting to push down the blocked stairwell. This crushing mass oscillated like agitated cockroaches, trying to get out of the light. He could barely move, much less get forward.

"What do you see, sir?" Wasano yelled out, doing his best to project his voice over the alarmed passengers and a few crew. Some of them were screaming, attempting to push down the stairs to get away from the sun deck and what he imagined must be awful outside. Some were bloody, but thankfully those passengers appeared to be only slightly injured. He was more worried about the majority, who were in some form of shock, their faces drawn and pale. A few were even non-responsive and looked like they might fall over. The crowd appeared to hold them up and shove them along. Other than these zombie-like passengers, everyone seemed to be infected by some form of panic. He knew he was. But it was the panic-filled screams that brought him back.

They reminded him of the Express train platform in Mumbai, and his father.

Amit Agarwal was a second generation coolie, and Wasano was destined to follow in his footsteps. After school, Wasano would help his father, to earn a little money for himself and his family, but to also learn from Amit, so that he could become just like him. Wasano even had his own license, which was required of all coolies. And he proudly wore the uniform: bright red shirt and yellow turban. Porting heavy bags for passengers from one train platform to the next was back-wrecking and neck-breaking work: most bags were carried on their heads. Wasano was always smaller compared to his friends and other coolies, so he became determined to make himself stronger and to work harder, just like his father. It was all planned out for him, until his father died.

That day was a particularly busy one, with passengers crowding Amit's platform, not unlike this mid-deck. Wasano struggled with half of one passenger's load; his father, farther out front, had the remainder. Then something happened. A ruckus in the crowd caused people to rush, with little room to do this. Amit attempted to move along the edge, but the stammering crowds pushed him and his load pulled him over. He tumbled onto the tracks. Wasano dropped his bags and tried to make a dash for Amit, but he couldn't get past the crush of people, who all seemed to be going the other direction. He yelled his father's name, as the Tejas Express arrived. Even over the screeching of the train's brakes, he heard his father scream.

The inhuman screeching sounds, followed human screams, were in front of Wasano now.

Somehow, he had gained a little ground on the mid-deck by inching forward, and he could actually see the stairwell open up to the next deck. He could also see the source of both the screeching and everyone's panic. In response to his captain, whose head he could barely see, and to Urban, who was behind him, he hollered, "I see the birds!"

Deck Officer Urban Patel had been following Wasano closely. He too must have given up moving against what felt like a stampede of sheep.

At the start of the half-deck, just ahead of them, a large man tripped over his own feet and tumbled forward, taking down a half-dozen others in front of him. Still others, attempting to hold up, were driven forward by the swelling horde behind them, causing even more to tumble on top of the now-writhing pile.

"People! Please slow down. You're safe now," Wasano yelled, hands held up. He didn't believe it though, and instead he and Urban tried to move through the crowd and to help up those who had fallen.

"Please folks, don't panic," the captain bellowed above them, still mostly out of sight. And then, "Wasano, I need your flashlight."

Wasano found an opening in the crowd that formed where the pile of toppled people stopped and the others still on their feet had continued downward around them. At the inside rail, he slipped around the edge where it moved up the stairwell. Now he could see Captain Jörgen reaching down to him. Wasano slid the large Maglite out of his belt loop and stretched it out over several bobbing heads, until Jörgen snatched it from him and plowed back through the bottlenecked crowd. They were milling on and above the stairs, twisting and turning to look back at where they had come from. Jörgen then began swinging at any bird within reach of his new weapon.

Wasano gazed at the hordes still frantically attempting to move as far away from the Sun Deck as possible. They pushed forward, only gaining room when those at the edges of the pile toppled over into it. They still looked either panicked or forlorn, but some of the faces were twisted with anger, spitting out profanity-laced commands demanding others move.

The pile of people continued to grow, with many flailing around, desperately trying to get loose of the others. Some were clawing and kicking, and hurting others in the process.

Wasano was always amazed at how illogical people became when they panicked. He felt the panic swell that day in Mumbai, when others seemed to be pulled into the well and tumbled into the tracks right after his father. If the people had remained calm, no one would have needed to get hurt, not the least of which his father. If they had just done what they were supposed to. Like these people.

He saw a woman at the top of the pile and he reached down and helped her onto her feet.

Urban worked his way through another opening, over to the other side of the large half-deck separating the two stairwells. Urban lunged for a large man covered in blood in a vain attempt to help pull him up. But when he grabbed the panic-stricken man's arm, the man clawed him with his other hand, gouging bloody nail marks across his forearm. Urban let go, reared up and clutched his arm, to stem a trickle of red starting flow. "Dammit, man. People, settle down," he demanded.

Seeing that this was getting worse by the second, Wasano pulled guests up and out of the pile more aggressively now. He was worried there would be more serious injuries if they didn't mitigate this immediately.

Another crew member arrived, and started to help them

pull people from the top of the pile collecting on the half-deck.

With more room up and down the stairs, and along the railings, passengers began to flow around the obstruction at the half-deck landing. They processed down the stairs, relieving some of the tension against the human barricade, which also appeared to thin. This had a calming effect on everyone, even with the screeching and screaming above.

Then something happened.

It was as if a panic switch was flipped on once again, but elevated to a nonsensical level.

A surge in the middle of those still on the stairs pushed out hard, causing more to flop back into the pile. The screams started up again, loud and piercing. They were panicking again. Many turned and ran back up or tried to shove their way by the pile and continue down. More people fell, some tumbling down the stairs. Others were stepping on top of those in the pile.

At least a couple of people in the pile—now numbering thirty or more—yelled animal-like screeches, and more were flailing, causing more harm to those around them.

Urban was fighting with the same large man who had scratched him. Now this man appeared to focus all of his anger on Urban, as if he were the cause of this problem. The man must have become insane, because he ignored an open compound fracture to his own forearm: it was bent at an odd angle. When the large man lunged for him, Urban was careful not to touch the man's broken radius, shooting straight up out of his skin like a flagpole. Instead, he tried to block the man's shoulder, but he missed and fell forward into the man. The crazed man's head hit Urban's neck and then something ratcheted down hard onto his scruff and ripped. It was Urban's turn to panic. He yelped when he saw the large man pull away, face crazy, bloody mouth full of organic tissue—his tissue. The large man's eyes were a crimson fury.

44

No Help

The crush of people was almost overwhelming.

Ted focused on Jean Pierre's back as the three of them swam up the mid-ship stairwell against the sea of humanity racing past them. Equally reassuring was knowing TJ was behind him, her vise-like grip on his shoulder to keep her from getting separated.

He had definitely not thought through this action, like he normally did with anything he did. Had he thought about the prospect of rushing out to face thousands of bloodthirsty birds to save some people, especially after seeing their panic firsthand, he probably would have chickened out of the whole thing. But everything was set into motion.

Focus on Jean Pierre, he told himself.

They halted at deck 9.

Jean Pierre snapped his head from side to side, scanning the flood of people frantically milling past them.

Ted eyed the doorways leading outside to the pool and Jacuzzis. They were clogged with people stopped by the doors from streaming inside, and others holding up just inside the doors, waiting to continue up and down the stairs. A good number were going into the Solarium's two entrances, just off both sides of the stairwells. This made sense to Ted because the Solarium was a separately enclosed giant atrium, with a large indoor pool and spa as its centerpiece, surrounded by tables and chairs, and a small restaurant completely forward, just above the bridge. It had two smaller doorways which could easily be sealed, whereas the entry/exits leading outside from the stairwell in between were large sliders and he heard one radio report that at least one of these leading to the Forward stairwell and elevators were stuck open. There was no way to go against the crowds, and no way to go outside, at least until they thinned.

Obviously, Jean Pierre was thinking the same thing, because he led them through the throng of people and into Solarium's starboard side entrance. It seemed like a good strategy, as they could close off the Solarium from the birds and help those people first, before then moving out to the pool decks when they cleared out.

Upon entry to the Solarium, Ted was struck with the sheer number of people there. It appeared that at least half the passengers from the pool deck and sun deck above were now here. Cruise ships and their schedules were designed in such a way that passengers were segregated—of course they never knew it—so as to not congregate too many in one place at one time. Only during muster drills at the beginning of a cruise did you get the full sense of how many people were on the ship at one time. But musters were well organized. This was chaos.

With so many panicked people clustered into one area, even one with a two-story windowed-atrium, the echoing din was almost deafening. And a few of the crazed birds had found their way inside as well, continuing their relentless assault. Shrieks from passengers marked their location.

Jean Pierre hopped off to the left, in the direction of one

of the screams, while Ted felt drawn toward another.

Ted felt a tap against his back and realized it was TJ. He had been so intently focused, he didn't remember her letting go of his shoulder. She handed him one of two serving trays she had collected from an abandoned cart they'd passed. He was only momentarily unsure why, and then understood: she was intending for him to use it as a weapon.

He tossed a quick glance at her, first catching the glint of her Orion the Warrior necklace he had given her for their anniversary—was that only yesterday? They needed her warrior side right now. He then found her eyes: piercing blue, intently fixed on their target up ahead. Ted couldn't help but flash a smile at how well she was handling the prospect of dealing with more wild animals. Only moments earlier, up on the bridge, she seemed overwhelmed with the news and seeing the incoming birds. Her FBI training must have kicked in, and she somehow pushed aside her abject fear of animals. It was like something in her had changed and the fears that had possessed his wife no longer had control over her.

She stood resolutely, wearing her body-hugging running outfit. A Nike swish on the hip of her compression shorts confirmed her body language: "Let's do it!"

A man and woman screamed beside him, and Ted turned that way. A black bird had clawed its way into the woman's hair, screeching and pecking at her head, clawing its way for her eyes—*they seemed to be always going for the eyes*. Her husband or boyfriend attempted to dislodge the bird from her, reaching up to grab it, or swat at it, in an attempt to get it away from her. But he was too slow: with each swipe the bird got him, drawing blood and profanities from the man.

Ted lunged forward, tray clutched and drawn back.

"Watch out!" Ted yelled at them, but realized that was a dumb command, because he really wanted them to duck. The man seemed to understand his Ted-speak by ducking, just as Ted swung. Ted's tray connected with a *thunk*, and the bird shot outward, spinning in the air and then splashing into the pool.

The man remained crouched low, just behind and below the woman, which was good, because she collapsed into his arms, as if she lost all strength to stand. Either her injuries were greater than they appeared, or she had just fainted. The man shot a glance up to Ted. He didn't verbalize his thanks, but his face said it.

A scream behind Ted, pulled him away from his momentary feeling of triumph. He spun around, expecting TJ to be right there, but she wasn't. Farther away than he expected, he saw two women entangled... struggling.

One of them was TJ.

He dashed in their direction.

Clawing at TJ was a rather large, pale woman in a pastel-colored onesie. A small older man was cowering under a table, eyes dinner-dish wide. TJ was barely holding the pastel woman back as the two rolled on the wet decking. Partially out of shock, but also because he couldn't see a way into the scuffle, Ted stood before both of them, hesitating, with arms drawn back; a home-run slugger, about to rip the cover off the baseball, if he were just given the right pitch. Then he saw his opportunity.

TJ flipped the pastel woman around and held the woman above her. For a moment, it almost looked to Ted like Pastel Woman was trying to get away from TJ. Just a moment's hesitation, and in that moment, upon seeing Ted Pastel Woman squealed her frustration at him, just before he silenced her.

He released his swing, swatting the woman's forehead with the flat end of the tray. She buffeted back, momentarily confused as TJ slid out from under the rotund woman. Then Pastel Woman snarled again at Ted, her face twisted and bloody. He momentarily wondered if he had caused this, but saw flecks of organic material around her mouth. Her skin was pale and sickly, as if she had a really bad fever. Her movements were erratic, like a confused animal; her guttural grunts, like some hellish beast and not the sounds he would have expected from an older woman; her eyes were shiny red and wild with insanity: they were the same eyes as the dog, as the birds, as the rats, and as the ferret.

The infection had crossed over to people.

"Holy shit," he mumbled.

Pastel Woman sprang up on her feet and lunged for Ted, knocking him down. The woman grabbed him with such force, he would have thought her to be a male body-builder not a flabby woman who was older than him and most probably hadn't even seen the outside of a gym in decades. He could feel the putrid warmth of her breath on his neck, and he thought for a flash this might be it. She was about to get him.

Then he heard a deep thwack and the woman released her grip, and her weight tumbled off him. His wife's voice trumpeted, strong and absolute as she stated, "Get your hands off my husband, bitch!"

She must have swung her tray edge-first, connecting hard across Pastel Woman's face, because that woman lay in a heap, unconscious.

Ted glanced up at his wife. TJ stood triumphantly above him, hand thrust out. She was breathing heavily, her face still intense, but mostly unreadable. At some point she'd put her sunglasses on. Then her lips curled and a grin formed. He accepted her hand and she pulled him up easily.

He quickly cast his gaze upon the Solarium's convulsing crowds.

Only then was it obvious to him: close to a dozen people—passengers and crew—were attacking other passengers and crew inside the atrium.

"It's crossed over to the people," he yelped. "We need to get out of here."

45

Infirmary

A crewman struggled to carry an unconscious woman who wore shorts and a t-shirt coated in splashes of red. A blood-soaked beach towel was strapped around her calf with a man's belt. "Where can I put her?" bellowed the crewman.

Dr. Chettle pointed to a corner of the room, where there was an open spot on the floor. Its occupant had been released a few minutes ago. He watched the crew member lay the woman down and one of his volunteers, charged with triaging the incoming patients, quickly checked the woman's vitals. The volunteer peeked under the injured woman's makeshift bandage, pulled out a red marker and drew a single red line across her forehead: her injuries were life-threatening, but they could probably save her. At least it wasn't a black marker, which would have meant death was eminent.

He'd had two patients with the black marks of death in the last few minutes. He didn't want any more.

The day, like the patients coming to the ship's ad hoc infirmary, had quickly gone from green (minor injuries) and mostly food poisoning illnesses, to yellow (non-life threatening injuries) from bird attacks, to red and black because of the more serious and yet very odd injuries.

He moved over to the newly-delivered bloodied woman in the corner and examined the loose red bandage wrapped around her leg. His nurse, Chloe Barton, joined him on the other side of the injured woman, having just finished suturing one of the many bird-bite wounds they had had in the last few minutes.

"What do you need for this one, Doctor?" she asked.

He glanced up from his patient to find Barton already slipping the cuff of their electronic sphygmomanometer around the woman's forearm, obviously taking a cue from the woman's red designation. Chettle's view of Barton's abilities and usefulness had grown exponentially in the last 24 hours. She'd been an enormous help to him and the injured. It was like she'd taken a common sense pill: pressure seemed to forge her into one of the better nurses he'd worked with over the years. Perhaps she needed a hectic atmosphere, like an ER. When this whole mess settled down—if it settled down—he'd recommend that she work in an ER, rather than the day-to-day boredom of dealing with the cuts and bruises of stupid or drunk passengers on a cruise ship. Her talents were needed in an ER setting. But at this moment, he was very glad to have her here.

"I don't know, I was just..." Dr. Chettle halted and glared at the exposed wound, a fresh stream of blood pooling around its edges. "We're dealing with human bites now." He looked at Barton, almost to confirm what was an obvious but still unbelievable fact: this was the fourth human-bite case they'd witnessed in the last half-hour.

He looked around for the crewman who brought the woman in, wanting to find out what happened. But the man had already left. Chettle had only picked up a few dribbles about the pandemonium up on the pool and sun decks. And based on the injuries, as crazy as it sounded, he could at least explain the bird-bites. When the human bite cases started to appear, he had no explanation. Human bites were almost always reactionary, a means of defense.

He'd only seen offensive attacks such as these in drug abuse cases. If there was only one case on the ship, perhaps he could explain it. But four? He needed to find out what was going on. He caught another crew member steadying a new incoming patient, this time an older man, but with a similar looking bloodied arm. The old man weakly held a red towel against his wound.

Chettle turned to his nurse. "Completely clean, suture, and dress the wound"—he paused to consider all the cases—"and make sure there are no other wounds. I'll be right back." He stood up and turned away from the injured woman and Barton, who was already removing the towel from the wound, while clutching a bottle of Hydrogen Peroxide.

"Hey you," Chettle bellowed to the crewman across the room. "What's happening up there?"

The crewman's eyes darted to him and around the room. Right away, it was obvious he was both scared and confused.

"It's okay. You're safe here. Now please tell me what's going on topside?"

The man looked down and up again. "Ahh, they're attacking each other?"

"Who? Who's attacking?"

"The people."

"How..." Chettle turned his attention everywhere around the room and yet nowhere. His eyes fell upon the spots of two of his earlier patients who had been feeling really sick from the same food poisoning that hit maybe forty percent of the ship's passengers and similar numbers of crew. Both patients were confused and one was drooling and almost unresponsive: the one with the Hawaiian shirt, who was no longer in his bunk. Three different types of incidents: food poisoning, then animal bites, and now human bites. All, within days of each other and all seemingly unrelated. And yet something in his gut told him they were, even though that didn't make a lick of sense.

"Hey Doctor. Can my brother go now?" hollered a hulking German man, two beds down. Chettle stepped over to the bed, where another much skinnier German, bare-chested with a blanket around his shoulders was sitting up, alert. The beefier version of the man—if Chettle remembered right, they were brothers—was standing beside him. The beefy one gazed at the doctor with scornful eyes. He was the one who asked the question.

Chettle flipped through his charts, searching for the bed number. Franz Litz and his brother Hans. Franz was bitten by a dog. He supposedly tried to pull away a crazed dog that was attacking another passenger and was bitten in the process. Franz had been disoriented for a few hours, but seemed alert now. They'd long since cleaned and dressed his wound. Chettle knew he'd need more bed space, especially now. So there appeared to be no reason to hold this man. "Yes, you both can go. But—" Chettle stopped mid-sentence, his head drawn to the other side of the infirmary, where there was a flutter of colorful movement.

"Great!" exclaimed Hans. He yanked at his brother's arm, pulling Franz out of his makeshift bed. "Let's get out of here and go to the pool to take in beer and bikinis..." his voice faded off as both brothers gazed at the flash of commotion away from them.

The man in the bright Hawaiian shirt, who had earlier left his bunk, was now stooped over another patient—a woman who Chettle had sedated after multiple bird bites and who was finally resting. She was now screaming in a perfect soprano pitch. Hawaiian Shirt almost appeared to be growling back at the woman, and the woman was pushing at him and kicking, trying to keep Hawaiian Shirt away.

Chettle started after Hawaiian Shirt, not sure what he would do, but knowing he had to intervene in some way. "Hey," he yelled at the man. "What are you doing?"

Hawaiian Shirt hesitated and was kicked to the ground by the screaming woman, but he immediately pushed himself up from the floor and leapt at the kicking woman, who had wiggled out of her bed and was now trying to stand. Her voice broke into an even higher pitch, if that was possible.

Chettle reached the man, who was chomping his teeth like some comedy routine where he was mimicking a Great White chowing down on a lowly fish.

Just as Chettle reached Hawaiian Shirt, the man's chomping teeth found the flailing woman's hand, clasping down on it like a vise, cracking tendons and bones. Her screech reached glass-breaking levels when Chettle tugged at the man's Tommy Bahama, pulling the woman his way too.

~~~

Hans' face turned from scowl to shock upon seeing the same thing Franz had: the bloke in the colorful shirt had turned his chomping-act onto the doctor.

Franz had felt wobbly at first when his brother had so abruptly pulled him out of bed. He was alert now and standing upright. And although he felt plenty warm now, he pulled the blanket he'd been wearing more firmly around his shoulders and gazed at the scene.

The threesome of the doctor, the injured woman and the colored shirt guy all struggled on the floor; the doctor was now the one doing the yelling; there was so much blood.

Another scuffle occurred right beside them. An oriental crew member appeared to be fighting with another patient,
~~~

and both were flailing around on the floor. The oriental was pounding the patient's face with balled-up hands, like a machine whose only purpose was to pummel objects: a machine that was screaming... *no, screeching*, like an animal. "*Was zur Hölle?*" Franz yipped (What the hell?).

"*Der Mist*. The Americans call it a 'shit-storm,' little brother. Let's go."

Franz could see the woman who had been bitten on her hand—it looked bent at a funny angle—was now pounding with her other hand on the crazy guy with the colorful shirt, who was busy trying to chomp down on the doctor's neck. "But... but shouldn't we help?"

He didn't look up at Hans, totally transfixed by what he saw.

The infirmary's noises had now grown ear-splitting, as most of the room's occupants or visitors were rushing in panicked dashes for one of the two exits.

"That *Drecksau* (dirty pig)?" Hans said about the doctor. "No, we go now."

Franz felt his big brother yank his arm back and pull him toward the closest exit. He did nothing to resist, while his arm was nearly dislocated in Hans' anxiousness to get them out of there.

The whole time, Franz watched the "shit show." He caught another glimpse of the colorful-shirt guy's mouth finding the doctor's jugular, sending a geyser of blood in the air.

But what drew Franz' gaze, just before he exited the infirmary, what made him shiver from a growing cold inside of him, as he glanced at each of the multiple scuffles involving people screaming, growling and attacking, were the evil red eyes of the crazy-looking ones.

46

Flavio

Flavio Petrovich was awakened by a rattle and crash. He lifted his head slightly, eyes ratcheted open, scanning his cabin. Not that he could see anything, his cabin was pitch-black. Even if he had left his lights on—he remembered turning them off—he wouldn't expect to see anyone or anything because he didn't share his cabin with another crewmate. That meant the noise had to have been made by some other damned rude person outside his cabin. Another crash and a heavy bang against his door set Flavio on a boil. He couldn't get a moment's rest. It wasn't bad enough that he had to deal with all of the stupid crew members, and the obnoxious German guests, and then the crazy red-eyed rats, but now his fellow crew wouldn't let him sleep.

Why can't they leave me alone, in peace?

"Is that too much to ask?" he bellowed at the murk.

His fingers fumbled through the darkness, finally finding and flipping his phone around to see the time. It was 13:42. He'd only slept three hours. Now he was really pissed. He was going to give this person an ear-full.

Flavio tossed back the covers, slid his feet into his slippers and marched over to the door of his cabin. Admittedly, he was glad to have one of the few private cabins for non-officer crew members, because of his seniority with Regal European. Although he always felt it was their way to try and placate him, instead of paying him a higher wage. He slapped the handle, twisted it violently, and threw open the door.

Inside the doorway, he held up and froze.

As this was a deck three, crew-only hallway at the far aft of the ship connecting mostly officer's cabins to other crew areas, the last thing he expected to see was trash. But right in front of his door was an overturned cart, just like the ones used by room attendants to clean up rooms. Half of the contents of a bag of trash attached to the back of the cart was spilled across the orange-carpeted floor. A crushed tampon box stood up like a sign-post of all that was wrong, right before his slippered feet.

"Vat da holy hell is this?" he blared to no one.

A scream to his right.

He turned to see a running room attendant, gaping mouth hanging, in full stride bounding over the cart and the trash, as if it wasn't his place to deal with this. He probably was the one who made the mess.

Flavio was about to yell at the man's back, before he was out of earshot, when he heard another scream... more like an animalistic screech.

Again, Flavio turned to face the noisemaker: it was another crew member running right at him. He wore a black jumpsuit and roared like a tiger whose cubs were poached. The man looked as angry as Flavio felt. More. *Perhaps you should have picked up the trash,* Flavio wanted to instruct the attendant, who was probably out of the hallway by now.

The jumpsuited-crewmember didn't belong here though: his uniform indicated he worked in the engine room, and he certainly didn't have a cabin in this hallway. Jumpsuit Man attempted to run by Flavio, dead-set on the attendant, and didn't seem to notice Flavio, much less the large obstruction in the hallway. Instead of jumping over it like the attendant, he plowed through it, without any success. Jumpsuit tripped and fell hard, face first. There was a crack that Flavio knew all too well: the man had broken a bone.

"Whoa—whoa there, crazy man. Settle down," Flavio instructed as he took a step into the hallway.

Jumpsuit didn't "settle." He convulsed and flailed, no doubt causing more harm to whatever part of his body he broke.

Flavio stepped closer to the man. "Are you crazy?"

Jumpsuit twisted back to glare his anger at Flavio. The man's eyes were a fire-like red and he had a deep gash in his cheek that seeped blood. Jumpsuit's arms were thrashing in the air and against the carpet: a cross between trying to get traction and a temper tantrum, but the man's brain couldn't decide which, so he did both without any control.

A couple of years ago, the crew members like Flavio who dealt directly with guests were given a security seminar on what happened when someone was shot with a stun gun. Some of the security guards were getting them. Corporate said they were non-lethal and wanted to show the crew. One of the old-timers, Eddie, who worked with Flavio in the MDR, volunteered, acting as if there were nothing to it. When Eddie was hit by the electrodes, or whatever they were called, he convulsed violently on the floor just like Jumpsuit Man. Unfortunately for Eddie, no one knew about his heart condition. He died, along with the stun gun program.

Jumpsuit finally gained a little traction on the garbage, squishing beneath his feet liquids, soaps, creams, and other unmentionables, all disgusting discards from people's trash.

Flavio reflexively took a step back toward his room, thinking it was a safer place to be than in this hallway, with this convulsing freak.

Jumpsuit found his footing, although one foot wasn't working too well: it was bent at an odd angle.

Flavio could have sworn he heard a grinding sound and imagined bones upon other bones, breaking and grinding inside the man's mangled ankle. But Jumpsuit ignored what had to be excruciating pain. It was as if the man no longer felt pain, or he felt it and just didn't care. Then again, maybe he did feel the pain, because Jumpsuit brayed an unearthly sound which was a mix of a tormented scream and a vengeful battle cry. Flavio had heard both before, but in a much different theater.

Flavio stutter-stepped backwards when he realized Jumpsuit was somehow moving toward him fast on his broken ankle.

Flavio's heel slid—*on the damned tampon box*—and he started to fall backwards into his room. At that moment, for perhaps the only time, Flavio wished he had had a roommate, because there was no one there to help him. He looked up, just as Jumpsuit landed on top of him.

47

Deck Eight Falls

Just outside of cabin number 8531, a nearly naked woman, known to a few on the *Intrepid* as the woman who liked to marry and then murder her husbands, and to the rest as simply Eloise—this was before she was *purged*—straddled a man in black overalls and plunged her digits into the man's eye sockets, burying two of them up to her first knuckle. Her forefinger, already chewed off at the second knuckle, pressed into the man's temple, generating pain for her, and more anger. Eloise palmed the man's head like a bowling ball, screeched an anguished cry, and drove her mouth into the man's cheek. As she bit down and pulled back, enough skin, muscle and tendons ripped free to expose the man's teeth. After she chewed on his raw tissue, the man who'd just been promoted to mechanic bellowed a final howl before Eloise tore into his throat to silence him for good.

An alarm blared an ear-rattling tone, drawing Eloise's attention. She glared a serpent-like gaze at the speaker with headlamp-like anger and howled at it in reply; her newfound food burst out of her mouth.

She sprang up, intending to attack the speaker with equal abandon, when a rotund man from cabin 8520 brushed past her, his terrycloth bathrobe and black boxers fluttering as he dashed down the hallway.

Eloise brayed at the man's back, a guttural scorn for disrupting her focus. Bathrobe Man raced forward, unabated down their starboard-side hall, toward movement a couple of dozen cabins away. She cast her eyes back down at the man in the black overalls below her, holding her gaze on the dying man.

The decimated mechanic would never get a chance to tell his wife that he would have been bringing home more money for his family because of his promotion. Instead, he lay in a growing pool of red, gurgling, shallowing puffs of air bubbling out his newly enlarged mouth and opening in his throat. His eyes were now growing bowls of crimson, their soupy liquid pouring over its corners like tears down his face. Finally, his last breath—barely half a puff.

Eloise turned back to the speaker, no longer blaring horn sounds, but the voice of a man commanding them to do something she didn't understand. She spun back to glare at Bathrobe Man, who had tackled a couple of German tourists running the other way. The trio thrashed and wailed together. This drew Eloise's interest. She responded with an anticipatory snarl and leapt off the dead mechanic, dashing toward the rising din of screams.

~~~

Asap jumped again at the screeching sound, somewhere close, out in the hallway. Between the crazed dogs and rampaging monkey earlier, his skin crawled with each new sound that
~~~

didn't normally belong on a cruise ship. To make matters worse, he was way behind on his duties. He needed to stop being so damned jumpy and focus on getting all of his port-side rooms cleaned. He had maybe half his normal time to get his rooms clean because he spent so much time consoling his roommates over the death of Catur. It was still weird to think that someone he knew got killed on this ship.

Yacobus and Jaga were more affected by their roomie's death than him. Asap figured Catur probably did something stupid to get himself killed by that monkey. He would miss him, at some point. But he wouldn't mourn him. This thought felt... foreign, like it wasn't his own. He used to be more caring. Now it just didn't seem to matter.

He fumbled with his key card, almost dropping it. The lock clicked open, but Asap didn't move. His eyes found the green sticker, confirming what he had thought he'd forgotten to check. The green-stickered rooms were the ones cleared by the crew hours ago. And as his roomies reminded him, it was a non-green room that supposedly contained the crazy monkey that had leapt out and killed Catur. All of Asap's rooms now had the distinctive green stickers on them. So they were clear of any crazy monkeys. Further, he should have been lucky as all of his cabins should have been empty, since all passengers were supposedly topside, enjoying the pools. Of course, he wasn't that lucky.

Several of his guests were ill from something they ate, and some were in their beds or in the bathroom, puking toenails; often they missed their toilets, which meant he'd have to clean it up. But as much as that annoyed him, what was most disconcerting were the others.

Some of his passengers were in a weird state, like a drunken daze. They were either confused, babbled some gibberish, or they were completely out of it. He could slap them and they'd do nothing. The weird ones were now taking up two out of every three of his cabins.

He knocked again on the cabin door in front of him and listened. *This was taking too damned long and he didn't want to see another one of those weird ones!*

The only consolation was that he couldn't clean the rooms the passengers were in. So other than a little puke, he didn't have to do much more with these. He'd freshened up their towels and let them be. With each cabin door he closed, he was one step closer to being done with his mid-day duties. That's at least how he should have felt. But really he thought he'd never finish. And that pissed him off.

"Better to be pissed off than pissed on," Catur used to say. Thinking of this incensed him even more. Asap felt his anger reach a boiling point, to the point of it becoming overwhelming. He couldn't remember feeling uncontrollable rage before, like he was feeling now.

And with each room, his rage grew, now manifesting itself in a desire to commit violence to whomever was behind this door, if only because they didn't answer him. More than wanting to tell his needy guests to stuff their requests for more towels, or tissue, or lattes down their fat traps, he now wanted to rip their sniveling throats out or break things over their heads.

When an image of what this might look like came to mind, Asap was taken aback. He was always frustrated by others, but he rarely thought of violence as a response. Now that was all he felt: an absolute need to commit violence.

His shock slowly bled into a feeling of empowerment. It was as if he was no longer a pawn of this ship and its owners, and the guests he had to incessantly coddle. He felt like he could finally stand up for his rights. He could finally do something about the injustices constantly poured out on him.

His fists were balled up, waiting to pounce on something, but he couldn't remember what. That was something else going on recently inside his head, and it too bothered him.

He was forgetting things. Lots of things. And he never forgot things before. This was just another example.

He stood in front of this cabin door, and tried to remember why he was in front of this one... He also couldn't remember if he had one more cabin or two to finish after this? Then, was he going to report all of his sick rooms to Chettle, or just let them die? He was leaning toward the latter: if they were dead, he didn't have to service their rooms again.

Oh God, what's going on?

He glanced at the door, and then the placard that told him the cabin number. *You're on Deck Eight*, he mentally yelled at himself, momentarily wondering this because he wasn't sure.

What was I supposed to do next?

The door rattled, almost in answer.

He violently pushed in the heavy door, as if it were the reason for his memory lapses. It clanged off someone standing behind it.

What an idiot to be standing behind the door.

He remembered the cabin belonged to a single man—Asap couldn't remember the man's name anymore—who stumbled back a little from the impact. The man glared at Asap, his eyes full of fury. Then he screamed a jumble of unintelligible words and ran through the doorway, knocking Asap down. Then the man dashed down the hallway.

As Asap prepared to push himself back up, he realized that there was lots of screaming and other noises everywhere, including much door rattling.

He righted himself and watched with fascination as a guard ran his way. Asap started to move out of the guard's way, so the man would have easy passage, but then stopped. He had as much right to the hallway as this guard did. So Asap stood his ground, facing the guard head-on.

The guard ignored Asap and punched past him, almost knocking Asap down again. The guard was grunting and groaning and seemed fixated on the loud voices he heard coming from within the bridge, just out of sight at the end of the hall.

That's it. I'm done with my work!

Asap was now standing before another cabin door, feeling his anger grow even more, but part of him knew he needed to figure out what was going on. Something bad was happening around him and maybe even to him. He could feel he was different inside, but he didn't want to think about it.

The cabin's door was ajar, kept open still with the life-preserver wedged in it, as was advised by the staff captain last night. That meant this cabin was empty: perhaps its occupants—again, their German names escaped him—were in the infirmary or topside on one of the decks. He could only hope.

There was a scream (he guessed) from inside the bridge. The voice sounded familiar. It was Jessica Something, the real pretty bridge officer so many of his male crewmates spoke of when they were talking about female crew they'd like to have sex with. He then heard some sort of struggle.

Asap decided to take himself out of this. He kicked the life-preserver out of the door and shut it behind him. Bent over and out of breath—*why am I breathing so heavily*—he looked up, saw himself in a mirror and gasped.

He took great pride in keeping his complexion perfect by using the right soaps, rinses and conditioners. And he kept his hair carefully groomed. The man that looked back at him was pale, almost to the point of death. His hair was standing up and out in all sorts of directions. "And my eyes," he whimpered.

There was a grunt on the other side of the cabin.

Asap turned and for the first time saw he wasn't alone.

A thick German, face covered in blood, eyes matching the rest of him, stood over the lifeless body of what Asap guessed was the German's wife.

The German man screeched a horrible-sounding cry.

Asap screeched back.

48

Bridge Troubles

"Be OOD for a moment, would you?" Jessica asked. "I need to use the head."

"Sure," said Ágúst, her only other bridge mate, and the ship's Safety Director. He then grinned wildly. "But don't be gone too long, or I may steer us to Barbados."

"Maybe I'll take my time then," she said, loosely manufacturing a smile as she dashed through the door closest to her.

The smile immediately slid off her face once she closed the door to the bridge's only bathroom. She stared at the light pouring in from the gap below the door. It was far from an air-tight hatch; this was just an area built into the bridge for the officers' convenience. Being only separated by thin materials off the bridge, it offered little protection to life's need for private moments like this one. But there was only one head for the entire bridge crew, set up so they could remain on a secured bridge until their shift ended. A slight convulsion jolted her.

With her head drooped, she let her slacks slide down to her ankles and waddled over to the toilet, attempting to muffle the sobs breaking free from her palm. When seated, she held her phone up to her face and gazed at its screensaver: a selfie with her husband and child, taken five months ago, just before she boarded the *Intrepid* to start her most recent ten-month contract. It felt so long ago. Much too long. A few of her tears splashed the screen, but she didn't wipe them away. She continued to stare at the glistening picture, willing it to come to life in her mind.

There had been no word from them since they'd left Malaga. Were they alive, and if so were they still at home? She had no idea. Meantime, there had been no emails or texts from them either. And the two times she tried to call them, a computerized voice told her the circuits in Reykjavik were busy.

She kissed the screen, clicked it off, and flushed the toilet. After splashing some water on her face she opened the door back onto the bridge. She pushed the pain deep down. Immediately, she was alerted to an alarm coming from her console, bringing her back from her momentary respite with her family. It was a navigation alarm she had set for herself: a reminder to reset their coordinates.

To stay on the path somewhat cleared of volcanic ash carried by the jet-stream, as the captain requested, she had to get creative with her navigation. The captain's plan made sense, as he'd felt sure that getting out of the ash clouds was paramount to mitigating their exposure to whatever was infecting most of the animals.

Her solution was a course that required corrections. First, they'd set in their coordinates to Sao Miguel in the Azores. This took them into the middle of the jet-stream's cone, with volcanic clouds to the north and the south of it. Once in the middle of the area free of the clouds, she could set a straight heading to Nassau, Bahamas, their next port. They were now in the center of this area.

She'd also calculated that this was the most fuel-efficient point to reset their coordinates. And efficiently using their fuel was important to corporate's bean counters.

At this point, all she needed to do was enter the new headings and then tell the ship's computers to follow the new coordinates. She set the alarm because if she forgot, and they didn't correct their path, they'd ultimately crash into their current set destination of the Azores in a couple of hours. Not that she would have forgotten.

"My turn," Ágúst announced, practically running to the head. He'd had an upset stomach all day, but didn't want to leave his post, especially in light of all that was going on. Unfortunately for him, he had the same stomach bug afflicting many others, from what was believed to be accidental food poisoning by their British chef. He should have told the captain and have been relieved by someone else. But she understood his dedication. It was one of the many reasons she liked working with Ágúst.

Jessica nodded at him as he breezed past her, and she moved to her console, pulling up the coordinates she had worked out. Just two more key strokes to get the *Intrepid* pointed in a more south-by-southwesterly heading. But before she executed the new commands, as always she would recheck her numbers and make sure they were absolutely correct.

Another alarm rang out, making her jump. But this alarm was more like a buzz. And then she understood it was just the intercom. She glanced at the door to the head, hearing Ágúst puke again through the paper-thin door. *There can't be anything left inside the poor guy,* she thought. She'd have to deal with the intercom first, then her calculations. She had plenty of time.

As she made her way to the hatch, one of the many ship's rules sprang into her brain: it was the one where the OOD always had to have their eyes on the console and their bow. Because she was the ship's OOD at this moment, she was breaking that rule by answering the door.

The intercom chimed again, and this time she heard a voice. "Help! Please! They're coming to get me."

"Who is this?" she hollered into the box that was fixed a few inches above her mouth, forcing her to stretch up to the box. She had projected her voice loud enough so that Ágúst could hear what was happening as well, and hopefully finish his episode.

"This is Second Officer Brian Murphy. Please let me in. They're attacking us."

That was all she needed. She saw what was going on outside through their screens. She put her body into the locking latch, clicking it home, and then tugged on the hatch. The Second Officer was obviously helping, because it became instantly light.

When it flopped open, Brian rushed in and brushed past her before he turned and puffed out, "Oh thank God. I thought I was done for." He bent over, holding himself up at his knees, not looking up while he collected needed air in short breaths.

While he did, he gazed at her. The fear hadn't left his face, but he looked like he was starting to feel safe. Then his face twisted up and he yelled, "Close it. They're here."

Jessica turned away from Brian and flashed a look into the doorway. It was filled with a guard, who barreled through the hatch and crashed into her, knocking her onto the deck.

49
Flavio

Flavio was beyond upset: Jumpsuit Man had piled on top of him and was attacking him for reasons he didn't know; his sleep was interrupted; and to top it off, he had another splitting headache.

He tried to push Jumpsuit Man off him, but the crazy guy kept thrashing, and something so strange… It appeared as if the man was trying to bite him. Why would someone from engineering try to bite him? The man was obviously insane, but why the biting?

Flavio braced himself and then when Jumpsuit Man lifted up to get a better angle of attack, Flavio placed a foot under the man's stomach and shoved with all his might, sending Jumpsuit across the room with a crash.

Flavio fixed his gaze in that direction, but he could barely see the man, because his cabin lights were still off. The only available light was coming from the hallway, through his open door. He was thankful that he'd taken the spring off the door, or it would have shut off all light.

He had heard the man's head hit the floor and the opposite wall hard, and now the man was spasmodically flailing around, just as he was before in the hallway, trying to right himself. Flavio could also feel the crazy guy glaring his weird red eyes at him. He couldn't see the man's eyes, but he could feel them. He knew the man was going to attack again.

Flavio had enough of this shit. He spun around and reached up above his desk, snatching from the wall his employee of the year award that he'd received for saving a guest from drowning. It was a useless piece of wood and a thin piece of metal, which only graced his wall for that occasion where a senior officer might visit his room, though that had never happened. It served no other purpose, but it did have some heft to it.

Flavio spun around, just as Jumpsuit was coming at him. Extending his arms back, while clutching the award, Flavio swung just before the man was upon him, connecting directly with the man's head. The award split in two, just like he suspected the man's head did as well. The man now lay in a heap beside his bed, the hallway light illuminating enough for him to see blood trickling out of a good-sized gash to his forehead. He was unconscious but not dead because Flavio could also see the man's chest rising and falling rapidly.

Flavio squeezed his eyes shut, a weak attempt to push away his migraine. Then he opened them back up and huffed a huge sigh, glaring scorn at the unconscious man bleeding on his floor. Another annoyance he didn't want.

And who would clean up the blood?

Flavio popped up, stepped over to his bed and flipped the light switch on, while keeping his gaze on the man. He humphed at the growing pool of blood being soaked up by his carpet. That was not going to come out easily.

He glared at the man, trying to decide what to do with him, and then made up his mind. He needed answers, which meant waking the guy while he still could.

He yanked off a pillow case from one of his six pillows—he needed many pillows to help him sleep. Then from a drawer, he pulled out some paracord, and using one of his many knives, he cut off two separate two-foot sections. Grabbing Jumpsuit's legs but avoiding the man's broken foot—he didn't want to wake him yet—he gave a hard tug. Then, with the precision of an American cowboy roping a steer at a rodeo, Flavio hog-tied the man's legs and then his arms. The pillow case slipped over the man's head was a final measure: he did not care to see the man's eyes until he had to.

He stood up and padded over to his open cabin door, but hung in the doorway. He poked his head out into the hallway, for one final confirmation of what he thought he had seen: that it wasn't some sort of weird flashback to his time in the army. With the headaches often came flashbacks of that day the Russians invaded his beloved country. But there was no time for this.

The overturned cart was still there, along with the garbage strewn in the hall. And although he could hear a commotion in the distance, out of sight, he didn't see any more crazy people.

Then he heard it.

It was the same angry bray he'd heard from the crazy man on his floor. Something had happened. It wasn't just this one crazy man; others were crazy. He knew it wasn't just the crazy rats and dogs; this was bigger. But was it the whole ship or just his area here? He needed to find out more, and find out if the captain was still in control of his ship.

His migraine crashed an agonizing drum-beat inside his head, as if to answer him. "Have you forgotten about me?" *No, I have not*, he thought, while rubbing his temples. It would be so easy to cast Jumpsuit out of his door, close himself in and go back to sleep. Whatever was going on was going to continue with or without him. Especially if some plague of craziness had struck the ship.

But his captain and the officers, even if they were talking heads for the corporation that owned his ship, might need his help. It's not like their two-bit security officers knew anything about fighting: they were overseen by a washed-up American cop. This was *his* ship and *his* people, and if he didn't do something about what was going on, then who would?

For just a moment, he allowed himself to think about the family he'd lost in the war. When the Russian troops invaded, it would have been easier to have given in to them. To lock his doors, ignore his superior's call to report to his regiment, and instead go about being the man of his household, protecting his momma and younger brothers and sister, like he had since his father had died. But just as he felt the calling now to right a wrong that was going on, he knew he had to stand up against this regime. If he didn't, who would? Turned out it didn't matter, as the rest of his adopted Ukrainian Army folded over like wet towels. And the bombing and crossfire of their short, one-sided battles ended up killing his family. If he was there when it happened, he'd have been killed too. And a big part of him felt like he should have been there to protect them. At least, unlike so many of his countrymen, he stood up for what was right. And he would do it now as well.

His migraine would have to wait, as it always did.

Flavio slammed his cabin door, grabbed a bottled water from his mini-refrigerator and knelt before the silent man. Whisking the pillow case off his head, he splashed some water on the man's face and watched him spring to life. Instantly, the man became crazy again; red eyes drilled into Flavio with fury, mouth screeching animalistic brays. He was crazy all right. Flavio knew what he had to do.

He slipped the pillow case back over the man's head, causing him to thrash even more. Folding the top of his own digits toward his palm, and stiffening his hand and wrist, Flavio waited and at the right moment, chopped with the side of his stiff hand just below the man's ear, making him quiet again.

Time to go to war again, but this time against an unknown enemy. Regardless, he would have to dress appropriately.

A rudimentary plan started to form in his mind, while he slipped on his camouflage pants and long-sleeved olive shirt and laced up his boots. He'd get to deck 8 and the monitor room. There, he could communicate with all the parts of the ship, so he knew better what he was up against.

He remembered Jumpsuit's chomping mouth and attempts to bite him in the neck and thought he'd add extra protection. He tied a heavy scarf around his neck and pulled out his leather work gloves to protect his hands. Last, he pulled out his two carbon Moriknives, with plastic sheaths, and slipped one on each side.

A thought occurred to him and so he considered it, nodding acceptance and stepping to his closet to get what he knew was perfect for this mission. He had found a giant wrench, left on I-95 a year ago. It was almost two feet long and was heavy. It was the perfect blunt weapon, he thought as he glanced at Jumpsuit, lying in silence, chest still heaving.

Slipping each glove on, he lifted the wrench-weapon and threw open his door and rushed into the hallway. Checking both ways, Flavio dashed forward, turned a corner and headed toward the nearest crew elevator.

If Jumpsuit had been conscious, the crazy-man would have heard the *thump-thump-thump* of boots double-timing away, followed by an animal-like screech, then immediately by the *thwack* of Flavio's wrench-weapon striking something soft, followed by the *thump-thump-thump* of his boots, as Flavio headed into his next battle.

50

Deep

Whaudeep Reddy of India, or "Deep" as his Regal European name tag declared, stared in stunned silence at the monitor room's screens. It was like watching a T.D. Bonaventure horror movie in HD. Only this was real, and it was live.

Deep was so fixated on the monitor room's screens, he didn't even blink once as he moved his focus from one screen to the next, holding his gaze just long enough to see each camera's passing three-second image. Then it moved onto the next camera view. Each of the nine screens displayed one scene or another of the same type of rolling images. All revealed the ship in complete chaos.

The firsthand experience with the monkey attack was beyond scary. This was worse. Ironically that was the reason Deep was here: Fish was so freaked out by almost getting eaten by the monkey during their card game in the Living Room, Deep had volunteered to take his shift. This shift.

And what a shift it was. First he watched birds attack the guests and crew. At that moment, it was the most bizarre thing he'd ever seen. He did nothing of course; what could he do? So he just watched helplessly as passengers and crew were running for the exits, or beating back the assaulting birds with whatever they could get their hands on.

Even on the little screens, he could see the blood, and the terror on their faces. But that was nothing compared to the next wave.

It had come out of nowhere. The first indication was odd but still explainable: a couple of passengers rolling around the deck and he assumed they were simply trying to get up and release themselves from their entanglement, or they were fighting a bird attack in an uncoordinated fashion. But that was all he could gather during the camera's three-second glimpse, before it cut away to the next camera view.

Then Deep caught another similar scene on a screen showing the mid-ship, starboard deck 5 cabins. There were two passengers also on the floor. But one was on top of the other whaling on him with his fingers extended like little knives, rather than fists, as Deep would have expected in a fight. He thought knives, because he could have sworn in the three-second vignette he'd seen, blood coating each of the assaulting man's digits. Then that camera cut away again.

Within minutes, most camera views showed either passengers or crew running in a panic, or in a fight with one another. It was impossible to make heads or tails of what was going on though, because the view of each of the ship's 460 cameras continually changed every three seconds, like 460 irritated eyelids blinking back what they didn't want to see. And then each fluttered, revealing the next three-second scene. All nine of his screens blinked from scene to scene at a dizzying pace, but none of the vignettes provided enough information to really know what was going on. Deep had had enough.

He typed a command to show the continual streams of several specific cameras. He called up cameras, 28, 57, 98, and on the same deck 99, 247, 394 and 395, 421, and finally 422. This gave him the uninterrupted views of the areas he had seen the most activity around the ship, just before and after the bird attacks.

His jaw fell open.

Each of the cameras he had chosen showed the same thing: scores of people had gone crazy like the birds and the dogs, and were now attacking other people.

A scene in the Solarium told him the whole unbelievable story. A very large woman in a multi-colored dress had been bent over heaving the contents of a recent meal. Deep was watching her, because she was right in the center of the camera's view and at least two other people who appeared to be overcome by this crazy-disease ran right past her.

Why were the crazy people attacking other people who were running away, but ignoring this big target that wasn't moving? It made no sense to Deep, and so he watched.

Then Deep was surprised to catch the streaming video of that very pretty blonde with the pony-tail, dressed in her tight running outfit. Her author-husband was in front of her. They stepped quickly by the big sickly woman; the husband—he couldn't remember their names—seemed to be fixated on helping someone on the ground, just out of the camera's view.

Deep watched the blonde pass by the sickly woman, and like a switch had been flipped, the sickly woman sprang up and attacked the blonde. *Or was the sickly woman attempting to attack the husband, but the blonde was in the way, and the two got entangled?*

There was a loud thump on the door, which made Deep shudder.

He cocked his head over, while remaining seated, and saw a pale-looking crew member in the small window inset in the door. The crew member glared at him with strange red eyes, like they were bloodshot from a three-day straight shift, but even redder.

The crew member opened his mouth, like he was intending to mouth words, knowing Deep couldn't hear anything through the heavy door. Instead, the mouth of the pale man opened wider, and then wider still.

Deep turned his shoulders, fully intending to run the other way and hide. It was so creepy, his skin crawled.

But then Deep remembered that that door was as solid as they came. It was a specially reinforced hatch meant to secure the monitor room and its recordings from terrorists. Part of some of the upgrades during its time in dry-dock.

He sat up straight, feeling safer now that he had thought through his position.

The pale crew member seemed fixated on Deep, mouth stuck open, a line of spittle growing off his chin. Then the crew member's head spun, like he heard something. His mouth closed and he moved away from the window, out of sight.

Deep glanced again at his main screen—his mind processing what he just witnessed firsthand—desperately wanting to see what was happening to the pretty blonde. She was holding the sickly-looking woman—who wasn't acting very sickly now—back, and having some difficulty because the larger woman was flailing around so much. The larger women appeared to be trying to bite the blonde. For a moment, Deep thought that the blonde wasn't fighting the larger woman, but holding onto her. Then the blonde's author-husband bashed the large woman in the head with a serving tray.

Deep wanted to watch what happened next, but another camera caught his attention. It was one of the bridge. There were only two officers there: Jessica, from Iceland and the most beautiful of all blondes on their ship, and their safety director, Mr. Helguson. Deep watched Jessica open up the hatch and a second officer he didn't recognize rushed through the opening and was frantically telling Jessica something.

"Dammit! I wish I could hear what you're saying!" Deep spat at the screen.

While Jessica was focused on the other officer, someone rushed through the hatch—she didn't close it—and ran into Jessica. It was one of those crazy people.

Deep rose from his rollered-seat abruptly, sending it across the span of the small room and crashing into the other wall.

"I can't help you, Jessica."

51
Bridge

At first Jessica was only startled, thinking it must have been some sort of mistake: this man didn't mean to run into her. But just as suddenly as she was slammed into the bridge flooring, she knew she was now fighting for her life.

The man on top of her seemed enraged to the point of being crazy, and she desperately tried to push him back, her hands clasping around and then slipping off his sweaty upper-arms. His mouth chomped at the air in an exaggerated way.

He's trying to bite me.

His mouth moved closer, and she exhaled a brief scream; she'd forgotten to breathe, holding it much too long, and then she tried to gulp back needed air.

This seemed to stir up the crazy man even more, his mouth chomping rapidly in anticipation of reaching her. A wad of his saliva plopped onto her neck, right below her Adam's apple.

The crazy person was telegraphing his next target.

She was equally disgusted and petrified at the same

time. And yet she was able to react to his movements, mostly keeping him at bay.

Fatigue was already bearing down on her, aiding the crazy's unending assault. If this battle persisted much longer, she suspected she'd lose, even though the slight man didn't weigh any more than she did.

He was so close the heat from his putrid breath felt scorching.

She turned away, seeking help from Brian Murphy, the second officer who entered their bridge with this crazy person in tow. But Brian was cowering behind a console. He stared wildly at her and the crazy man on top of her.

"Help me!" she begged. However, expelling the air to say this only gave the crazy man more ground. And she knew she couldn't hold on much longer.

Her words seemed to shake Brian from his moorings. Maybe it was the man's ingrained chauvinism or maybe he forgot himself. She didn't care; she was just glad that he seemed to be heading her way, though way too slow. She knew she only had a little fight left in her.

She couldn't look at the crazy, who kept chomping his mouth and teeth, like she was some piece of meat. She was used to being treated this way among the men in her profession, but it was always figuratively, not literally. *This was insane.* "Help!" she bellowed again.

Brian disappeared and then reappeared, now holding up a model of the *Intrepid*, a to-scale rendering of the ship. He held the model back and then arced it around in an attempt to knock Crazy Man off her. But he was too high and he didn't have a good grip on the ship model.

It connected and then bounced off Crazy's head, only snapping the man's head back, but at least momentarily stopping his chomping. Crazy reacted instantly, turning his anger on Brian, who appeared perplexed at becoming the focus. Crazy Man sprang off Jessica onto Brian in a single bound.

The springboard off her stomach took all of Jessica's breath away, and for a long moment, she remained on the floor, physically and emotionally paralyzed, while she gazed out the side of her field of vision in amazement. What happened next shocked her back into action. Crazy Man's mouth clamped down on Brian's neck, brutally. She launched like a rocket and leapt onto the two men in an attempt to pull Crazy off her now gravely injured comrade, but she tumbled off them. Crazy doggedly held onto Brian.

Jessica found the ship model on the floor. Rising to her knees, with all the strength she had left, she picked the model up and brought it straight down onto the Crazy Man's head, cracking it open like a melon.

But she feared she was too late.

Brian gurgled a hollow scream while pushing off the now unconscious, or even deceased Crazy Man.

Oh God, I think I killed him!

With the dead man off, Brian clutched his torn-up neck and blurted another weak scream.

She'd never seen so much blood, not thinking it was possible for a human to expel that much blood and still be alive.

Oh God, Brian was going to die!

Jessica was at once swept with feelings of overwhelming sadness and terror, and the strongest of desires to crawl into a corner and cry. But there was no time.

At the hatch, two more crazy people bounded through. One instantly locked onto her and pushed off the other to try and redirect his movement in her direction. But their legs tangled and they both tumbled to the ground in front of her.

Run.

There was no way she could make it to the hatch and exit the bridge: the crazies were between her and it. But she might be able to make it to the starboard swing deck.

If I leave now.

She bounded up, glancing once at the flailing tangle of crazies, desperately trying to right themselves and get at her. One of them was almost up already.

She focused on the swing deck hatch, putting all her effort on this. It was her only chance. Then she remembered Ágúst: he was in the bathroom still. She flashed a glance at the door, seeing the sliver of light shoot out the bottom. Then she remembered the navigation instructions, and she turned to look at her console; its warning light—the one she set to make sure she entered in the course correction—was flashing at her, giving her a countdown to their collision course into the Azores.

She turned back to the swing deck hatch, knowing she had one chance to make it out alive—the only chance she'd have to see her child and her husband, if they were even still alive.

She pumped her legs, but like a nightmare, she was too far away and going way too slow. She could hear the crazy behind her, snarling and huffing.

She chanced a glance back, knowing that it was the wrong thing to do, but unable to keep herself from doing so. She had to know.

He was right behind her, and he was reaching his hand out—

She smacked hard into the starboard window-wall, just to the right of the hatch, surprised that she was off her mark. *I should have been facing the door.*

She reached over to the hatch mechanism and pulled herself to the door, just as crazy man hit, head to metal.

Jessica put all of her fifty kilos down on the handle, the hatch clicking its response.

She chanced another glance, amazed that the crazy man, who should have been knocked out or at least dazed by his head connecting with the metal, was still doggedly after her. The crazy refocused on her much too quickly and even though his head was now gushing blood from the impact with the bridge's steel window-wall frame, he was clawing his way toward her. She still had to open the door, slip through, and close it tight. *She wouldn't make it in time.*

Jessica squealed, moments before the crazy was upon her, when a black-laced shoe hit the crazy mid-chest, sending him past her to the ground. She glanced below her and saw Ágúst there, now wearing his sunglasses, panting and trying to right himself.

"Let's go," he hollered, and she obliged, pulling the door open that Ágúst could slip out, followed immediately by her.

We might make it after all. Maybe I will see my family.

They yanked on the handle, four hands intertwined as one, sending the hatch shut with a *thunk*.

They released and scuttled back on their butts as the hatch's window was filled with the pale face of the red-eyed crazy man, silently snarling at them.

With their backs to the rails of the swing deck, they panted mutual "whews" at their just making it out of the bridge alive.

They glanced at each other, unable to form words from panting uncontrollably, large smiles covering their faces.

And then they heard the screeches again.

These were outside.

Both their heads snapped aft, to the solid wall end of the swing deck. There, only a few feet from them, were at least a dozen black birds, fighting over the torn-apart carcass of a seagull.

They had interrupted the black birds feeding. Now the black birds focused their red-eyed attention on the two officers. It was as if their fiery eyes were telling them, "Why fight it?"

Jessica glanced back at the bridge and now saw two crazy men silently growling out of frustration that their meal that got away, clawing their raw fingers at the closed hatch that they couldn't figure out how to open.

Unheard by either of them, an alarm rang out on her console. Its display read…

1:30:00

1:29:59

1:29:58

52

Crazy People Too

"Run to the Spa," Jean Pierre yelled.

Ted and TJ both knew the place and immediately moved in that direction, leading the way, and Jean Pierre following close behind. Ted briefly paused to snatch up a little table that had scooted out into their walkway, brandishing it by two of its legs. He liked the weight of it and that he could use it to keep the crazy people's mouths away from him. He also scooped up a pointed butter knife and slipped that into his back pocket, wishing he had one of Flavio's knives, or even one of the ship's steak knives they'd hurled at the monkey earlier. But as there was no meat being served in the Solarium—*except the raw human kind,* he thought—this would have to do.

"Come on," TJ insisted, also holding up. Her sunglasses flashed as she whipped her head from side to side to check out her perimeter for any potential threats to them. Her abrupt movements from side to side caused her Orion necklace to flop around onto the small of her back.

To Ted, she now looked like a living rendition of the

warrior Orion, at least the necklace's version. And yet she acted anxious. *Of course, who wouldn't here, now.*

Ted couldn't help but take in the surreal landscape of the Solarium. It truly was stranger than fiction.

One of the performers in the cruise ship's drag show was there, dressed in full costume. He was attempting to escape one of the crazed people by jumping into the spa pool. The performer's dazzling feather-headdress hit the sloshing water first; his sparkling platform boots entering the water last. The crazed person didn't seem to care for the water much, immediately redirecting his fury at someone else less wet. That poor SOB was a passenger who was completely caught off-guard while gawking at the flamboyant performer's leap into the pool. The crazed person tackled the unsuspecting passenger, driving both of them into the slick and yet very solid pool decking. Both their heads hit hard, and the crazed person harder. Yet the crazy man rose and continued his assault on the now-dazed passenger.

The soaked drag show performer saw his opportunity and popped out of the water, sans headdress, white makeup sliding off his face. Mixed with the red of someone's blood, his was a macabre mug. He clutched his knees, panting and grinning. He must have known his luck wouldn't be so kind if he held there any longer, and he dashed off.

Passing in front of Ted and TJ was an obese man with frazzled white hair attacking a very small oriental woman. The woman appeared to be holding the crazed man back to protect her husband, an equally small person on the floor, wearing bright orange pants and white slip-on loafers. The man was screeching in a sopranic voice, sounding almost like a waterfowl. The frazzled-hair man was overpowering the much smaller woman, biting her and scratching at her, until she fell to the ground.

The crazed man then turned his attention to her orange-trousered husband, who tried to duck walk away without much luck. The crazed man caught up with the smaller man right in the middle of their path to the Spa.

Ted had a thought. He wasn't sure where it came from, but like many of his thoughts, his subconscious mind figured shit out before his conscious mind could give reason to it. But as usually was the case, he knew he was right. Just before his wife was about to thwack the white-haired man with her tray, Ted yanked out the butter knife and holding the blade-end, he whacked one of the table legs multiple times, generating echoing ping-noises, as if it were a musical instrument.

Apparently the *ping-ping-ping* sound was so loud, even TJ stopped in mid-swing, almost acting like the sound was piercing and hurting her ears. But it also had the desired effect.

The crazed man's head swiveled in Ted's direction, and he course-corrected, pushing off the oriental man.

Ted wasn't sure what he was expecting. He knew subconsciously that the loud noise would affect the crazy-person, he just hadn't thought through what would happen after he'd done it: it was not like they had time. Certainly, Ted hadn't expected the man to move so quickly, because he had barely enough time to push the table forward, using the top of it to deflect the man away. Luckily for Ted, inertia—both his and the man's—caused the frazzled-hair man to shoot past Ted and onto the floor.

When the crazy man bounded up, both Ted and TJ were ready. Before the crazy man could take more than one step, both pummeled his head multiple times, until he crumpled to the floor and lay unmoving.

They briefly flashed each other smiles, before TJ moved forward, Ted following. Jean Pierre still brought up the rear, swiping wildly with his own drink tray at a bird that seemed absolutely fixated on his chrome dome.

A flash of movement to Ted's left pulled at his attention. He didn't know how, but amazingly the oriental woman who was brutally attacked and bitten sprang up. She looked a bloody mess, but without hesitation, she sprinted toward a couple cowering in a corner of the Solarium under one of the larger tables.

Was it a bite that did that to her? he wondered. But that made no sense from what he understood about this parasite.

Ted must have not been paying attention, because he crashed into his wife, who was trying to hold the spa door open.

She said nothing, but scowled at him. Ted shrugged his shoulders as Jean Pierre breezed by them inside. Ted and TJ rolled in, clicking the spa door closed behind them.

The three of them stared out of the spa's double glass doors, chests heaving for air.

"Did you see that the people are crazy too?"

Ted and TJ swung their gazes at Jean Pierre. They didn't have to say anything; their looks screamed, "No shit, Sherlock."

TJ turned to her husband. "Is it the bite that turns them... crazy?"

"I wouldn't have thought it, but it seems so. Did you see that oriental woman bound up after being attacked?"

TJ grimaced behind her Oakleys. "Yes, but how? Why?" She reached around her back and pulled her Orion charm around her necklace chain, rubbed it a couple of times and let it drop just above the neckline of her soaked sports shirt.

In quiet, they studied the Solarium's chaos, while catching their breaths. Jean Pierre decided to check out the spa.

Ted hadn't answered TJ. And TJ didn't press him, as she knew he was chewing on the new sets of facts. "Did you see how they responded to sound?"

"Yeah, and you almost made me deaf."

"It wasn't that loud," he lamented. "Besides, I have a theory. The infected animals and now infected people are attracted to sound. I saw it with the birds: they attacked the loudspeakers while the alarm was going off, and then they stopped when it was no longer blaring. The screaming of the uninfected seems to draw the attention of any crazy humans or animals."

"Once infected, they don't seem too human. And did you notice they don't seem to care about their inj—"

A screech from the back of the spa stopped them both cold.

"Psst."

Jean Pierre was in front of one of the individual spa rooms, his hands waving them forward.

They quickly scooted in his direction.

Jean Pierre pushed open the door, and out poured Zen music: some sort of Indian musical montage, obviously meant to help their spa clients meditate or feel relaxed or something of which Ted had no idea, not being a spa-guy.

Jean Pierre slipped in through the door, followed by TJ and then finally Ted, who pulled the door behind him.

The three of them froze.

Inside were two couples. One of the two men, a bare-chested older man with wrinkled olive skin, brandished a heavy hardcover book, covered in splotches of blood and feathers. He was poised like a baseball player at the plate, about to swing for the fences. Then the older man's jaw dropped at seeing Ted.

He brought the book-weapon he had been holding up down to face level, pulled out a white handkerchief from a back pocket of his khakis and whipped off the gore from back cover—not even flinching at the blood and guts. He let the hankie drop to the floor, while glancing at the back cover, and then turned up his face again at Ted, his scowl building into a grin.

Ted recognized the older picture on the back cover: it was his big stupid-looking smile, complemented by a handlebar mustache, his deerstalker hat tilted down to block out the sun, and the ocean surf spraying behind him from the balcony of their aft cabin of his first transatlantic cruise, some years ago. He never liked the picture, but his agent said it made him look like a "real person."

"Greetings, Mr. Bonaventure," said the man. "I'm David Cohen." He thrust out his hand as if he were at a book signing, and nothing else was going on in their world. All thoughts about adding more gore to his book-weapon were forgotten.

The Zen music was almost loud enough to drum out the screaming outside their room. Almost.

53

Collapse

All they could do at this point was run. It wasn't what Jörgen and his crew were trained to do, but who was trained for a riotous horde of crazed people, driven by an absolute desire to kill?

Somehow, they were able to pull Urban away from the crazed man who had taken a huge chunk of flesh out of his neck. But there were others now. What seemed like scuffles within the crowd were passengers and some crew attacking others. Both Jörgen and Wasano attempted to break up the attacks, but it was no use. In rapid fashion, they were being overwhelmed.

There may not have been any policy for dealing with riots like this one, but there was the rule about protecting your fellow crew members when invaders had boarded your ship. And this crazy disease had boarded their ship and was attacking it and his crew. And with Urban's injuries looking more serious by the second, Jörgen and Wasano thought it better to retreat to safety for now, while they still had a chance.

They followed the panicked passengers down the half-flight of stairs and then turned into the first crew access they could find, figuring that the numbers of frenzied people would be smaller, if only because of the smaller ratio of crew to passengers. They were correct.

Although there was some screaming in the crew stairwell below them, it certainly wasn't the all-out melee of the more public areas. They could stop here and collect themselves and figure out what to do next.

They found a cart of linens in the stairwell, abandoned by a room steward, and fashioned a make-shift compression bandage around the left side of the nape of Urban's neck. This they tied around his chest and under both arms. A lot of tissue was missing in his wound area, and more important, he had lost a lot of blood. His blanched features and sunken eyes were alarming. But all of this was alarming.

In the back of Jörgen's mind, he couldn't help but wonder if the Urban's bite-wound would turn him into one of those lunatics. It didn't matter. If he did, they'd deal with him. Right now, he was one of their crew and as his captain, Jörgen knew that he would do everything he could to protect his officer to the bitter end, no matter how or when that might be.

"So where now, Captain?" asked Wasano. "Officer Patel needs medical attention."

Jörgen wanted to get onto the bridge. That's where he belonged. From there he could captain them through this crisis. But Wasano was right, Urban needed immediate medical attention.

"Give me your radio."

Wasano handed him his walkie.

"This is Captain Christiansen. Repeat, this is Captain Jörgen Christiansen. Doc Chettle, report. Bridge, report. Engineering, report." He let go of the transmit button and turned up the volume.

Static and screaming sounds were followed by "Captain, this is Assistant Engineering Director Niki Tesler. Sir, we cannot get to engineering. This whole floor is overrun by these insane people…" she started to breakdown. "They ate Ivan, sir. It was horrible. I didn't know what to do…"

They thought she had stopped transmission, because they couldn't hear anything else. Then… sniffles. She still had her transmit button depressed.

"I'm sorry, sir."

Background static now, as she was done.

"It's all right, Niki." He almost never referred to someone by their first name in public, and certainly not on the radio. "Are you safe? Where are you?"

"I'm just off the control room, in Ivan's—I mean the Chief Engineer's—private office. I have two other crew here. We've been hiding and trying to keep quiet. They seem to be attracted to noise. But the place is overrun. So we're not going anywhere."

"Have you heard from the bridge lately?"

"No, sir."

"What about the engine room?"

Static silence. Niki was keeping off the air to let someone from the engine room chime in.

"Captain…" the speaker crackled, "this is Max Borne, from ER. I'm stuck in an access duct, port side aft of the main engine room. This place is a madhouse, sir."

"Sit tight, Mr. Borne, until this blows over." He said this, even though he doubted this would blow over any time soon. "To anyone else, do we have any control over this ship?"

Silent static.

Niki chimed in again. "Sir, I believe all those not affected by this have holed up somewhere, for safety."

There was a screech directly above them. It was close.

Jörgen turned the volume down and clicked transmit. "We're going off comm for a little bit. Sit tight, officer, and anyone else listening. Captain out."

Safety first, he thought. Then medical assistance for Urban, then figure out how to wrestle back control of the ship later. Everything should be on automatic, so they should be good for a while.

"Ye Olde Tavern," Jörgen whispered. It was only two floors down from where they were, and if they could make the turn quickly enough, and there weren't many frenzied people in the area, they might be able to escape inside. They needed to get to someplace safe to attend to Urban, who now appeared to be going into shock. "Ye Olde Tavern would be closed, and no one should be inside," he whispered once more, not wanting the frenzied person below them to hear.

Jörgen and Wasano hoisted Urban up, on each side of him, and they lumbered down the two decks, practically carrying the nearly unconscious man.

Holding up at the exit, they gave each other a quick glance. The low lights of the crew access stairwell masked their concern. At first, Jörgen didn't want Wasano to see his alarm. And Wasano had the same look, probably thinking something similar. At this point neither cared.

Urban did his best to just stay lucid. But he continued to lose blood, in spite of their best efforts to suppress the flow from his wound with their linen compression-bandage. It was obvious he was teetering between consciousness and unconsciousness. They couldn't get to Ye Olde Tavern fast enough. And even then, he still needed medical attention and they were moving much closer to Chettle's infirmary.

Ye Olde Tavern's door was immediately contiguous to the crew access door they were lingering behind. If the coast was clear, they could quickly unlock the door and close themselves in. No one else should be there.

Wasano carefully pushed open the door, just a crack and peeked out. An ocean of screaming and yelling poured through.

“How does it look, Wasano?” whispered Jörgen, inches away. He couldn’t see a damned thing, and it was killing him not to be the eyes, but he wanted to honor his new head of security by ceding this part of their mission to him.

Wasano remained motionless, other than his head, which turned slowly, like a lighthouse beacon, taking in everything. “I think it looks clea—hold on.” Without saying another word, Wasano bounded through the door, his feet squeaking on the floor.

Jörgen took over his position in the door and glanced out. He whispered to Urban, “Don’t move,” and then dashed out the door as well.

~~~

Urban wasn’t sure if any time had passed, or if he had lost consciousness or not, because the world was swimming in front of him. His captain said something he didn’t catch, before disappearing. Using his uninjured arm, he grabbed the doorknob above him and swung himself to the other side of the door, twisted the knob and peeked through. He now understood where his captain and security director went.

An older woman was fighting against a much younger woman wearing a spa bathrobe. The older woman kept beating the younger woman with her cane, but the younger woman was unrelenting, screeching anger and scratching at the older woman, who had her back up against the Ye Olde Tavern entrance.

The security director yanked the younger woman away, tossing her easily to the floor, while the captain helped the elderly woman up. She was trying to tell them something when several people burst out of the Ye Olde Tavern’s door. The elderly woman must have been trying to hold the door closed
~~~

when she was attacked.

The Spa Woman was already up and fixated on the security director, while captain and the elderly woman were racing back toward the opening Urban sat in. Urban used the last of his strength to move out the way and hold open the door farther to make passage easier. He hoped no one else would come through, because he wouldn't able to do anything. The captain, security director and elderly woman bounded through the opening and slammed shut the door, and the only thing holding Urban. He flopped to the floor, hearing his head clunk against the floor and the door being pounded on from the other side.

Another wave of dizziness hit, but he forced himself to stay conscious.

"My-oh-my. You gentlemen were just in time. Thank you!" said the old woman in between shallow breaths.

"It's our pleasure ma'am," answered Wasano.

Jörgen helped Urban up.

"I'm fine, sir," Urban responded.

"I guess Ye Olde Tavern was open already..." the security director stated what was obvious to all of them.

"How about the life boats, sir?" Urban croaked.

Both the security director and the captain shot each other glances, and then back to Urban.

"That's a terrific idea. There's a first aid kit for you, as well as provisions, and because they're locked up there won't be any passengers or crew there. We should be safe," the captain stated triumphantly. "And we're on the shady side, which should have fewer passengers, because of lack of sun. Wasano, would you lead us?"

"Yes, sir," the security director said and then took them down the stairwell and out a hallway that led to a separate crew access door out on the starboard Promenade deck, right in front of lifeboat #35.

A quick check both ways, and it appeared to be clear. So

the four of them rushed out the door and across the rubberized decking to the locked gate. The security director already had the proper key ready, driving it in with purpose, and they were in.

The captain had his arm wrapped around Urban, who could no longer move on his own. The elderly woman seemed more agile than she had appeared at first. The security director closed and tried to lock the gate, but the tumbler seemed broken.

He threw open the door and hesitated momentary. When they heard a scream on the promenade deck, very close by, the four of them poured into the life boat and clicked the door closed.

Before Urban lost consciousness for good, he caught a glimpse of a large, hulking man standing in back. Then he was out.

54
Swing Deck

"Birds!" screamed Ágúst.

If just their presence didn't seem to do it, Ágúst's screaming did the trick. The dozen or so birds thrashed at the air, desperate to get to them as quickly as they could.

Jessica looked around for something to hide behind or to use to defend themselves with, but there was nothing on the swing deck. She had already slunk under a console, but there was nothing she could use to block the oncoming birds.

She'd read about horrific events, like a car crash, when everything appears in slow motion. She understood the science behind it: all of your senses becoming aware of everything at once; the firing of so many neurons to catch the input of a billion pieces of stimuli around you; your brain just trying to catch up. Still, it was something she had only read about. Experiencing this firsthand was amazingly intense as the birds came at Ágúst and her. And at that moment, which had slowed to a crawl, something very strange happened.

Images of her husband and her seven-year-old flashed

in front of her. She had read about this too; it made sense. It was the human mind's escape mechanism, a way to cope with the unbearable. She suspected it would have been natural for her to accept these images, just as it was to not fight the inevitable about to hit her. But she was a fighter.

In fact, the images made her mad: she wasn't going to let these birds take her away from her family. She would at least try.

She looked up, remembering just then that there was a slide-out table above her, with keyboard. She clicked off the locks and slid the table out and off, the keyboard falling off its cradle and onto the deck. The birds hit at the moment she held out the table like it was a shield. They pummeled the table, as if individual fists were punching at her, pushing back her shield toward her. She pushed harder, locking her elbows, as they drilled down on her.

She felt one peck at her leg, out of sight and she kicked at it and the others flapping nearby. She couldn't see any of them. One attempted to come around and attack her side, but she was able to deflect its advance before it could get her face—they seemed to be going for her face.

She held back the assault of what felt like hundreds of birds, but she knew it was probably still only some of that dozen she'd just seen a millennia of moments ago.

Then she felt pecks at her fingers, followed by pain. Lots of pain. Several connected directly with her legs, despite her thrashing at them.

She was starting to feel pain everywhere and more so, a sinking dread that she couldn't keep this up much longer, when she heard *ping... ping... ping.*

And still the assault continued, but now with fewer birds than before.

Again she heard *ping* and something else. It was a grunt and then another *ping*.

When she no longer felt the birds attacking, she

ventured a look over her keyboard table-shield.

It was Ágúst. He was standing in front of her, huffing and puffing, holding a small fire extinguisher. Before him were the dead bodies of at least a dozen birds.

He'd killed them all.

"You all right?" he begged, dropping the fire extinguisher and holding out his hand.

She thrust out hers.

"Oh no, your hands," he said, his face twisted with concern.

She pulled them back and examined them. Her hands were beat to hell. But they were still functional. She slid out from under the console and glared at the sky, sure another attack was imminent.

Other than the occasional bird in the distance, there didn't seem to be any interest in them. At least for now.

She glanced at Ágúst and was surprised to see he didn't have any injuries. She knew she must have looked like hell. She glared at her bloodied legs and then back at Ágúst. He didn't have a scratch on him.

"Don't worry about me," he said, watching her.

Then she remembered their larger problem. She spun on a heel and now focused her attention on the swing deck's console. It was supposed to have had ninety percent of the bridge's controls. She'd only used the swing deck controls for some basic system checks, since all the controls she needed had been on the bridge. But now she needed them.

She flicked the power switch on, but none of the monitors flickered on.

She toggled the on/off switch back and forth, but the screens remained black. "Dammit!" She pounded the middle of console with a balled fist.

"What's wrong?" Ágúst asked behind her.

"I left the bridge before I was able to reset our navigation. I was hoping to do that here."

"So we don't get our efficiency bonus this year by blowing through more fuel than scheduled. I can live with that," Ágúst snickered.

"You don't understand. Because I wasn't able to reset the controls, we're still scheduled to *run into* the Azores in an hour or so."

He gulped back a breath, spun and dashed past the bridge hatch, sticking his face against the glass, cupping his hands around his head. He pulled back and glared at her, his face slackening.

"What?" she asked.

"Look," he answered.

She did.

Inside the bridge were the two crazies, gazing slack-jawed at her console. It blared an alarm tone that warned there was 1:18.53 left until they'd run into one of the islands.

"Okay, so how do you fix this?" Ágúst begged.

Jessica ignored him and instead dashed to the most forward point of the swing deck. Reaching under that console, she found a set of binoculars.

She pulled them to her face, glanced through them, and then handed them to Ágúst so he could understand what she did.

Sao Miguel was just ahead and there was nothing they could do to stop them from running into it in a little more than an hour.

55

How Could It Get Worse?

"Please just call me Ted." Ted accepted the bare-chested man's hand and returned his enthusiastic handshake, attempting with difficulty to match the man's firm grip. He immediately noticed the Auschwitz tattoo on his forearm and thought, *This man lived through the Nazis and is probably a tough customer.* Ted suspected he would find this out firsthand, if they made it through the day.

David continued pumping Ted's hand, while his words tumbled out. "I'm a big fan, although I'm a little behind on my reading. Never finished your last one so I was starting it again, but was interrupted by the damned birds. Nice talk, by the way."

"I'm Evie," said an equally skinny woman, sitting on a massage table, towel around her shoulders, with two other passengers who looked nervous. Evie waved her palm tentatively. "My husband won't let you get in a word in edgewise; he's a bit of an author groupie."

David tossed a scowl behind him at his wife obviously

practiced over the years.

Ted waved back at Evie and couldn't help but smile at how odd life was: they'd just barely escaped with their lives, and now were in a spa room filled with Zen music, while making small talk with a concentration camp survivor, who was also a Bonaventure groupie. He couldn't make this shit up.

"Enough of the meet-and-greet," demanded a rotund, bald British man seated in the back of the room, with an equally large pale-faced woman clutching his hand. He ignored Ted and David and focused his attention on Jean Pierre. "Staff Captain, what's going on out there? Is the captain still in charge?"

David's expression changed almost immediately, as did Evie's, a scowl finding what Ted suspected was a normal place on David's face.

Jean Pierre pushed past Ted and addressed the room. "Hello…"

"Boris and my wife Penny," said the large Brit.

"Hello Boris and Penny, and David and Evie. I probably don't know more than any of you. You saw the people attacking other people, didn't you?"

Ted suspected Jean Pierre had said this for the same reason Ted wanted to ask: it just didn't seem real.

"Yes, we did," stated David, his face very serious now. "That's why we're here, hiding from them, like you."

"You saw this coming, didn't you?" puffed Penny, glaring at Ted.

This comment took Ted by complete surprise. He didn't know this woman. And yet he'd been asking himself this very question over the last twenty-four hours. "Ah, no." His voice was weak. His eyes darted around the room furtively. It felt very small inside at this moment and he could feel his pulse take off again. "My book was fiction, and in it only the animals were crazy. Plus, it was a terrorist that caused it all in the book, which I don't believe is what we're experiencing."

Ted realized then it wasn't the woman's question that got his heart racing; it was his wife. She had been completely silent this whole time, and usually she would have said something snarky about David's adulation and certainly in response to the woman's accusatory comment. He turned to look at her.

"You're being somewhat coy about this, Ted, aren't you? I live with a man who's guarded about most things," Evie lobbed a knowing look back at her husband, "except when it comes to meeting his favorite authors." She returned her gaze back to Ted. "Please share what you think is going on."

Ted ignored her question, as his eyes had not left his wife since he had turned to look at her.

TJ was standing in the corner of the room, away from everyone. Her hands were planted on her hips, as she often did after a run. Likewise, her chest was heaving, mouth wide open to get air. Besides the oddity of her wearing a splash of blood across one of her arms, bare belly and cheek, she was still wearing her dark sunglasses inside. Further telegraphing her mood, her shoulders were hunched and head pointed at her shoes. She was upset about something, whereas she seemed fine after dealing with all the crazies in the Solarium.

"Hey Yank, do tell us what you think. Why have so many gone all barmy? Will we go barmy too?"

TJ looks distressed, he thought. "Hon, are you all right?"

All attention turned to TJ, and she seemed to know it. She caught her breath and tilted her head up to meet Ted's gaze, and shot him a weak grin. "I'm fine... Just a little freaked about the birds and the crazy people."

She huffed once and then stood up tall. She wasn't going to say anything more, and neither should he push her to answer, until he had her alone.

Jean Pierre seem to sense the awkward moment, and so he repeated the question, "Ted, please tell us what you think is going on."

Ted took a breath, turned to face the others, and started.

~~~

"It's a parasite; that's what's causing the fits of rage we've seen first in the animals, and then the people." Dr. Molly Simmons stood again, adjusted her skirt, and sat back down, readying herself for more questions.

"A parasite, you mean like a tapeworm? You think a tapeworm caused these people to go bonkers?" Hans shot a scornful frown at the elderly woman, as her fingers played with the contours of her odd-shaped cane.

She mostly ignored him. "Tapeworms are but one of tens of thousands of species of parasites. In fact, there are five times as many parasites as all other organisms on earth.

"This particular parasite is called toxoplasma Gondii or T-Gondii—"

"Sounds like a fauking sexual disease, raweyet?" Hans blurted and held his hand up for a high-five from his brother Franz, who also ignored him, and then readjusted the blanket around his shoulders. Franz kept his attention on the smart old woman, as if his life depended on it.

Molly disregarded this comment too, pushed her coke-bottle-sized specs further up her nose and continued, "And we are only just starting to learn how the T-Gondii rewires human and animal behaviors to do its bidding."

"Wait, Dr. Simmons," the captain barked. "Are you saying this T-Gondii planned this? Why would it want animals and humans to go insane and kill each other?"

"Yes, Captain, you're correct on the 'planned this' part"—she made quotation symbols with her two hands in the air— "of your comment, but not in the way you and I would
~~~

look at it." She removed her glasses and rubbed away an invisible smudge on one lens and then polished the other, using one of the top ruffles of her long skirt. After a quick examination to make sure they were clear, she popped them back on her face.

It was her way of collecting herself when she was nervous—this time she was scared beyond reason. But unlike an academic lecture in front of a boisterous classroom or a presentation before her peers, this talk was about the scariest parasite she thought she'd ever encountered. Parasites had killed maybe a billion people over the years. This one might end up killing all the rest, making what they were all experiencing an extinction event.

Focus Molly, the captain, and others are counting on your knowledge.

"The T-Gondii is... a single-cell organism. So it doesn't have a brain, like you or me. But like us, the T-Gondii has DNA that tells it what to do, and we've seen many cases in the parasitic world where the organism transfers some of its DNA hard-wiring to its hosts, so that their hosts will do what it wants."

"But to what end?" the captain asked. "Why direct animals and people to attack and kill each other? Wouldn't that lead to every host's death?"

"Sounds like a stupid fauking bacteria," Hans chortled, raising his hand up toward his brother again in another attempt to get a high-five from him. After the moment lingered, when Franz avoided acknowledging him entirely, Hans lowered his hand and looked down.

Typical bully, Molly thought. *But at least this bully is listening to you.*

"No, sir. Far from stupid, in fact." She wanted to say, "unlike you," but such a comment would be juvenile, like him. "The protozoa has DNA, much like our own: a complex network, interconnected. It's very much like what goes to make up our own brains, at least for some of us." She couldn't help the small dig, but thought better of carrying it any further and inciting the large man."Whereas a bacteria is just a bag of loose DNA and proteins, this particular protozoa is very smart, indeed. And like all other organisms—to get to your question, Captain—T-Gondii wants to survive and thrive, and to do that, it must take out all threats. Only those who are not infected are a threat. Somehow each host infected with T-Gondii knows who's not infected and desires to kill only those people or animals."

"What are you, some kind of damned expert on parasites?" the big German stated. It wasn't a question.

She turned away from the captain to address the man she had instantly disliked when they had arrived at this lifeboat: a skinhead, who must have instinctively known her Jewish roots. She assumed his brother was of similar ilk, although he wasn't as bellicose as his Aryan brother. "In fact, sir, I *am* an expert on this subject. I'm a parasitologist." She left off the "retired" part.

She returned her gaze to the captain, then across from him to the unblinking eyes of the ship's security chief and, head resting against this man's shoulder, the severely injured man, who was listening with his eyes closed. This one looked very pale.

"So I suspect that everyone who is not infected with T-Gondii will be attacked. Everyone who is infected will be mostly left alone."

"That makes sense, Captain," chimed in the security chief, addressing his superior. "Remember some of the passengers were not getting attacked by the birds and others were?"

Captain Jörgen considered this, and then looked back to Molly. "Please, no disrespect, Dr. Simmons, but how could you possibly know this with the limited anecdotal evidence we've seen?"

"You are correct, this is a supposition of mine, based on limited observations, but also a lifetime of studying parasites, like this one. This is what parasites do."

"So..." Captain Jörgen, looked upward to remember something, and then, as if he plucked the thought from an imaginary mental file cabinet above his head, he continued, "...explain how thermophilic bacteria plays a role in all of this."

"Yes, of course, you would have spoken to our author-friend." She grinned, just a little. "You cannot have the one operating without the other. Not on the scale we're seeing. You see, most of the time the T-Gondii doesn't appear to be active in most hosts. When it is active... Well, this is why, before this recent wave, we've been seeing more and more incidents of aggressive behavior by both humans and animals. But it still affects everyone it infects, having already done most of its work of reprogramming their brains, and then it lays in wait, for what we never knew. But I always believed it was waiting for some inciting stimulus to activate the T-Gondii and turn on the new programming in its hosts."

"*That's* where the thermophilic bacteria comes in," exclaimed the captain, nodding his understanding.

"Exactly. I don't know why, perhaps no one will, even if by some miracle our race survives this. But the thermophilic bacteria was just the inciter that the T-Gondii was looking for.

"And this bacteria was already unique, without the normal soft cell-walls of most bacteria. This thing is tough as nails—almost indestructible. And when it infects a host that is also infected with T-Gondii, it appears to set the T-Gondii's new programming off, so that the hosts then do what the T-Gondii told it to do: kill or destroy every non-infected species of mammal."

"Sorry, Ms. Simmons," interrupted the security head—she couldn't remember his name, nor see far enough to read his name-tag. "You said, 'if our race survives this.' There must be some way to stop this?"

"It's Dr. Simmons, actually." Molly wasn't one for titles, but she didn't want her words to be taken lightly. "And it is I who am sorry. I'm not sure there is any way to stop this. We've known for decades about the Plasmodium parasite that causes malaria and kills two to three million people a year. And yet the best we can do is practically kill the patient with arsenic. So instead, the medical community had been focused on prevention, because we simply don't have a cure. I don't suspect we'll ever find a cure for this either."

The six occupants of lifeboat 35 fell completely silent, weighed down by this shocking piece of information.

A loud tone startled all but the security chief and the captain. The security chief reached around his belt and unclipped his radio, and to Molly, he said, "Someone has put out an 'all hands' call on the radio. Mine was turned down so as not to attract the attention of any of the crazy people."

He turned up the volume.

"… Repeat. This is First Officer Jessica Eva Mínervudóttir. We are stuck on the swing deck. I'm asking for any officers to respond, or anyone from engineering."

The radio responded right away. "Hello, First Officer. This is Staff Captain Haddock."

The security chief held the radio to his mouth. "This is Acting Security Director Wasano Agarwal. I'm here with Captain Jörgen, Deck Officer Urban Patel, and three guests."

"Jörgen, you're safe, sir?" bleated Jean Pierre.

Wasano handed Jörgen the radio.

"Yes, we're safe. But Deck Officer Patel was seriously injured. Where are you?"

"We're holed up in a room in the spa. What about you?"

The captain quickly gazed at Molly, and then Hans and Franz before speaking. "Staff Captain, we're in life boat 35, with *three* passengers." The captain's tone had changed like he was reminding his officers to keep up their radio decorum. Molly was a widow to a ship's captain and understood protocol very well. "First Officer, who's OOD?"

Oh-oh!

There was a long silence, before Jessica—*the one trapped on the swing deck*—answered, in a much more obtuse manner. It was as if she knew, after the captain's subtle reminder, that there were passengers within earshot.

"No one is, sir. And I didn't get the new navigational instructions into the ECDIS. We are still on a 296 degree heading, at fifteen knots, and we'll hit our destination in just over an hour."

~~~

Jean Pierre let his head droop down, his chin practically coming to rest on his chest, the walkie held suspended in the air, where he'd been listening. After a deep breath, he stood up straight, radio finding his ear. "Have you been able to raise anyone from engineering?" He suspected he knew the answer, but he had to ask to confirm this.

Jessica answered, "No, sir. Since Safety Officer Helguson and I were chased off the bridge, we've been trapped on the swing deck by a couple of those crazy people. I've been trying to raise someone for the last fifteen minutes."

"Merde," was the only thing Jean Pierre could think of saying, before he let his body fall into a soft chair, pushed up against the wall of their spa room.

Ted stepped over to him. "Did I understand your first officer's veiled point correctly?"

Jean Pierre looked up to Ted and then over to the four passengers who heard much more than he wanted to have to explain, but he knew he had to now.

"We're all in this together now. Best tell them what we just heard," Ted exclaimed, while rubbing a temple.
~~~

"Yes, JP," TJ huffed, the first words any of them had heard from her in awhile. "Spill the damned beans."

"If we don't find some way to get to either engineering or the bridge and change our course, in just over an hour, we will slam into Punta Delgado at fifteen knots."

56

Eye in The Sky
A few minutes earlier

Deep had been watching and listening to everything, but that's all he could do.

When he first saw the ship's captain and the others about to make a break for Ye Olde Tavern, Deep tried to warn them on the radio that this would be a problem with all the crazies running around that very public deck, and those in the bar. But his base unit wouldn't transmit, even though it was receiving most everything, albeit weakly.

Best he could figure was that the connection to the radio's antenna, which ran up through one of the conduits and out to the antenna outside—so he and the bridge, just forward of him, and engineering, below and aft of him, had the best radio reception—was broken, no doubt from the tsunami. The fact that he was receiving anything seemed a miracle. Worse, like an idiot, he'd forgotten his portable in his cabin. So while he'd glanced at each of his monitors, he was busy fashioning an improvised dipole antenna for his base unit, using strands of wire from a coil pulled from a dead generator.

After a few minutes of watching the captain's group, the staff captain's group, the bridge, starboard swing deck, engineering, and a few other key areas, it was obvious to him that they had lost control of the ship to the crazies. This was, of course, bad. But he wasn't immediately worried, because he knew everything on this ship, including navigation, was on autopilot.

They still had some time. At least that's what he was thinking.

Now, all Deep wanted to do was tell everyone with a radio that he was right there with them watching.

He thought about some American news programs, which received periodic reports about traffic accidents and safe routes for morning commuters, all coming from a news helicopter, which called itself their *eye in the sky*.

He would be the ship's 'eye in the sky' and maybe point out possible routes to safety for crew members and passengers. He also wanted to promote the conversation further among the officers and crew about what was going on and how they could fight against it, together.

Deep keyed the microphone, "Hello, this is Deep, speaking from the MR. I'm putting a call out to all officers. This is Deep in the *Intrepid's* Monitor Room. Do you read me?"

"What was that?" asked the staff captain, his signal weak and scratchy. "Something just cut you out, like someone was transmitting over you."

"Dammit!" bellowed Deep. The steel surrounding the MR was too great. His antenna wouldn't be enough to transmit his signal outside the MR and then to each location, many of whom were also deep within the ship's bowels. This is why his base unit was connected to an outside antenna. He needed to get his new antenna outside. But he had no idea how to get it outside while he was stuck inside the MR.

Deep stepped to the MR entrance and glared out the

small window to the outside world, currently owned by the crazies.

He heard a muffled animal-like screech and saw a shadow shoot by, the beast's screech-sounds trailing behind it.

"How will I get an antenna out there?" he wondered out loud, shoulders drooping. It seemed impossible. He wished he could talk to Buzz, their know-everything-electronic fix-it guy, more than anything right now. Buzz always knew what to do.

Deep was lost in thought, staring through the window, when something large consumed all light in the window.

He stepped back and saw it was a man in a head waiter's uniform. The name tag flashed by before he could see it, but he saw the colors of the flag.

Ukrainian or Romanian, he thought.

There were others huddled around the waiter.

Deep caught a brief view of the side of a ferret cradled carefully in someone's palms, followed by the faces of his friends Jaga and Yacobus and one more familiar face behind them. They were mouthing something.

Deep disengaged the lock, and the four men and one ferret poured inside, with the waiter slamming the door shut behind them.

"Tha-thanks for letting us in, Deep," Buzz stammered.

"You are exactly the person I needed. So glad you're here, and you're safe."

Deep turned to his other two friends, wearing chasm-sized grins. "Hello Jag—" Deep nearly bit his tongue when he caught the full-view of Jaga's ferret, cradled against Jaga's chest. The ferret was eyeing him. Exactly like the other crazy animals, Jaga's ferret had blood-red eyes.

"Don't worry about Taufan; he's fine, even though he has those crazy eyes."

"Enough pleasantries. You contact bridge? What is status of crew?" demanded the big Slavic waiter. This man was serious looking: more like a general in the military than a waiter. The uniform looked too small for him, like it had shrunk or he had grown out of it.

Deep wondered, even though the accent sounded right for his nametag, if this man killed the waiter whose uniform he was wearing: it was coated in splotches of blood. There were other oddities: long sleeve shirt, leather work gloves duct-taped around his sleeves, and large bandanna bunched around his neck. Finishing his ensemble were two sheathed knives—one on each side—and a large wrench clutched in his hand, also covered in blood. He was ready to do battle; rather, he had already done battle.

"This is Flavio," said Yacobus. "He helped us get here safe. He wanted to get to the MR too."

"Hello Flavio," Deep offered, making direct eye contact with the man who towered over all of them.

Flavio didn't change his expression, blurting, "Status please?"

Deep knew who was in charge, in spite of the uniform. He obliged the man. "The ship has crazies everywhere, including on the bridge and in engineering. And I haven't been able to reach anyone on the radio yet, because my connection to the antenna is broken."

"How do we connect?" Flavio asked. He scooted closer to the video screens, his arms now folded and cradling his blood-soaked wrench. His eyes flitted from screen to screen.

"Well, I don't exactly know. But I'm hoping Buzz here could help us figure that out." He turned to Buzz, whose eyes had been searching around the MR, "So Buzz, I've constructed a dipole, but it won't work in here because of the heavy steel around us. Maybe we could—"

Buzz cut him off, "Actually, that's simple. You have plenty of coaxial cable. Connect that from the radio to the dipole antenna you created. Then someone needs to get outside the crew areas, where you're not dealing with the thicker steel skeleton around the MR, for instance, inside the atrium."

Deep's mouth dropped. He was going to suggest some way to connect with the broken antenna, or push wire through the conduit. This was so much better. And yet it was impossible.

Who would be nuts enough to volunteer to leave the safety of this room, and then snake a coax line from there through the crew access hallway into the atrium, where there were bunches of crazies waiting to murder him?

Flavio turned to Buzz, with the same serious expression he had when he came in. "Thought you said this was simple."

"Simple, yes. Easy, no."

"So, if antenna is placed outside in public area," Flavio tilted his head upward to do the calculations, "roughly eighteen meters away, assuming you have enough of this cable, we can speak to the crew?"

Deep's mouth snapped shut before he spoke, "Yes, I have more than thirty meters of cable."

"Okay, I go, now."

"But..." Jaga looked out the window of the MR door and watched another two crazies pass by. "There are so many of them out there. We just barely made it. How will you get through them?"

"I can handle it." Flavio hoisted his bloody wrench in the air and tapped the handle of one of his knives with his free hand to demonstrate his intent, which was already obvious to the others. He didn't blink an eye as he studied the screens, especially those on deck 8—their deck.

Flavio tracked Deep who had returned from the other side of the room with a roll of black cable and another roll of thin metal cable and said, "Would be better if you can make diversion noise, but I can still do it without."

Deep nodded and quickly twisted the two wires connecting the coaxial cable with the antenna. He grabbed a roll of electrical tape and spun it around and around the splice, cut the tape and smoothed out the edges.

While Deep was focused on the antenna, Buzz paced around the room, stopped suddenly, and then addressed Jaga.

"Say, does your ferret still do that *run-away-and-return* game?"

At that moment, Jaga started fidgeting as he did when he was nervous. He knew exactly what Buzz had in mind.

~~~

"This is stupid idea," Flavio told them. "My life is depending on big rat?"

Jaga flashed the big man a scornful glance, but Flavio had already turned away to receive instructions from Buzz on how to set up the dipole antenna so that it would work throughout the ship. Jaga returned to reassuring his ferret Taufan, while Deep adjusted the animal's straps. Attached to the straps was one of the two portable radios Deep had retrieved from the lost and found. They were almost his, as the guests who left them ten months ago hadn't requested their return. After twelve months, lost items would go to the crew in an auction, held once a month. The funds from the auction were used to add supplies to their crew recreational areas. Deep had already told the potential bidders that the radios were his. The auction was to have occurred in a couple of days, if the world hadn't ended.

Oh well, maybe the radios will help to save us, he resolved.

"Taufan will do as he's told," Jaga announced, while looking up at the hulking Slavic. "Are you sure the angries won't eat him?"

"Angries"—Flavio smirked at this—"only attack people or animals not like them. Can't promise it works for big rats,
~~~

but I guess better than nothing... unless one of you want to be diversion?" Finally, Flavio's small grin evaporated, as if it never existed before.

"It'll work, Jaga," Yacobus insisted. "Remember how he was with those dogs? They weren't after Taufan; they were after that man hiding behind the water bottles."

Jaga seemed to accept all of this, deciding absolutely that Taufan would do this. It was certainly less risky than one of them going out there, as Flavio had joked.

Jaga leaned over to his ferret. "Okay Taufan. When I tell you to run, you run, all right?"

Taufan seemed more interested in preening himself than anything else. And at that moment, all but Jaga felt dubious the ferret would follow his commands.

Flavio humphed a sigh, and then grabbed the rolled-up cable and attached antenna. "Make sure your rat goes in right direction. Don't want crazy people chasing both of us."

"He's not a rat. He's a ferret." Jaga rose and stood tall, in defiance. But his face was not even close to that of the larger man.

Flavio grinned again, just a little more this time. "I know." Then he turned serious again. "Let's do this, now."

Deep stood ready at the MR exit and when he received a tepid nod from Jaga, he slowly unlocked and cracked open the door. He turned his ear to the opening, while the others waited directly behind him. Deep must have felt safe, because he pushed his head outside just enough that he could see in both directions of the hallway. Then he withdrew himself back inside and took a knee.

"Okay, now!" he whispered and threw open the door wide enough for them to do their part. Jaga darted into the hall, facing forward, laid Taufan down and held him pointed away, so that he'd run in that direction. Then he commanded, "Run, Taufan. Run."

Taufan took off, and Jaga withdrew back through the

door. Their door clicked closed.

Jaga lifted the second portable to his lips and yelled, "Run!" And then clicked on the emergency button that comes with these radio units.

Even muffled, all of them heard the loud tone echo down the hall, followed by the louder tone's reverberation from their walkie. The sound changed slightly, telling them that Taufan had just turned down the U-shaped hallway, that followed around them. It would be out of view of their cameras, until he returned or ended back up front.

All but Jaga glared out the window. He didn't want to see this.

Several shadows dashed by their window, running forward, in Taufan's direction.

"They're taking the bait," exclaimed Deep.

"Open door, quietly," Flavio commanded.

Deep obliged and Flavio slipped out, clutching the loops of coaxial and antenna cable in his left hand and clutching his heavy wrench with his right. He held up at the edge of the doorway.

Two more crazies ran by, screeching their dislike at the loud noise, but running toward it just the same.

Flavio shot an eye aft, holding for just two seconds. Then he darted in that direction, letting loops of cable fly out of his left hand. His wrench was held up, ready to strike. He didn't look back, even though he should have.

Yacobus held tight on the other end of the coaxial line, while Deep clicked the door shut, although with some difficulty because the thick coaxial jammed open the bottom corner of the door.

"Not yet," Deep insisted to Jaga, who held the radio at his lips, ready to issue the next command.

"Okay, Jaga, turn off the tone."

Jaga let go of the button.

"Now."

That was Jaga's invitation to call his little buddy back.

"Return, Taufan. Return." Jaga let his hand, squeezing the radio, drop to the floor, and he sprang up to look out the window with Deep. They waited.

No sign of Taufan.

They were startled to see several crazies running past their window, headed aft. They were headed toward Flavio and their antenna.

Jaga, Yacobus, and Buzz crowded around the small window to the insane world outside the door, with Jaga bouncing from heel to heel.

Deep stepped back. He knew there was nothing he could do, other than hope the ferret and Flavio made it.

He dashed over to his table and gazed at the lone camera located at the crew entrance to the hallways around the MR, but didn't see Flavio or the ferret. Really, he had only one measurement for success. He turned up the volume to his base unit, and waited to hear voices.

It was nothing but static.

57

A Flawed Plan

Their plan had been full of flaws. After ten minutes, both Flavio and Taufan were still missing. No signs of either. And with the infected running past the MR window, in both directions, their hope had ebbed further away with each tick of the clock on the monitor wall. The staticky blare from the base unit's speakers, turned up high so that they wouldn't miss anything, had been only occasionally interrupted by distant incomprehensible voices, before they too had bled back into the radio's static murk.

Yacobus and Jaga had stood vigil at the door, glad it was more of a reinforced hatch than a regular door, even though there was a little opening at the bottom where the coaxial snuck through. They took little comfort in their wall of protection. It had kept the infected out, but it also kept them locked in. They knew they couldn't stay there forever.

Jaga's angst had been the heaviest. "I don't know what to do. I'm afraid to call him again: I don't want to risk any more noise and attract more angries to him."

Yacobus had put his arm around his friend and offered reassurance. "He'll be fine." But his words didn't sound believable when they had come out.

They had continued to stare out the window and anxiously tapped at the floor with their heels.

Buzz had made himself useful by working on a burned out circuit board, the one which had caused two of Deep's monitors to not function perfectly and had seemed to set up a chain reaction in other systems. It wasn't a high-priority task. But it was all he had thought he could do while they waited.

Deep had simply focused his gaze at the base station's speakers, as if that would improve the reception.

Still nothing.

Then it had come.

As if someone had thrown a switch to give them instant reception, the speaker's constant crackle had been replaced by a mélange of voices seemingly speaking over each other. Then the sonorous sounds of the most beautiful officer on the ship, Jessica Eva Mínervudóttir, the bridge's navigational officer, sounded over all others.

Deep would have known that voice anywhere. He was in love with Jessica, even though she was already married, with a child. Even when he would occasionally bump into her in the crew mess, she talked to him about her husband and son constantly. It was Deep's little secret that he never shared with anyone. And upon hearing her voice, his whole persona changed. All he could think was, *Thank God, she is safe.*

Then his heart had sunk upon hearing her plight.

He could only imagine what she was going through on the swing deck, and that she'd be terrified not knowing what happened to her husband and child. Or with the outside world in chaos.

Deep was then knocked out of his lapse when he realized he had an audience. Jaga and Yacobus had sprung up behind him, knocking their knees into the back of his chair.

Buzz laid a palm on his Deep's shoulder; a sort of *attaboy* for Deep's accomplishment. All of them had silently gawked at the speaker when they heard the familiar voice of their staff captain, followed by the booming voice of the captain. They were all just connecting for the first time.

When the captain had asked Jessica who was on watch, their hearts sunk further. They knew the answer, but they were hoping they had somehow hoped they heard it incorrectly. Jessica then destroyed that hope.

What she said next was at first confusing, and then shocking: "we'll hit our destination in just over an hour."

They were supposed to be in the middle of the ocean, and their next port of Nassau was at least four more days away. It was the use of "*hit* our destination" that was so jarring. It was code.

When the radio paused, as the officers chewed on Jessica's response, Yacobus and Jaga whispered, "What did she mean by that?"

"It's code," Buzz answered. "They know passengers might be listening and don't want to alarm them."

Deep went slack-jawed when he got it, and in case the others didn't, he said it out loud. "Jessica just told us that we're going to crash into land in an hour, unless they can take back the bridge or engineering and readjust our course."

While his friends gasped, Deep didn't waste another moment, clicking the transmit button. He also didn't waste time mincing his words.

"This is Whaudeep Reddy from the Monitor Room. I read you, First Officer, and you, Captain, and you, Staff Captain. I can provide you eyes above in your efforts to get to either the bridge or engineering. But I'm afraid there are many crazies between you and both locations."

~~~
~~~

"This is Captain Jörgen. Thank you Mr. Reddy."

Jörgen clicked transmit once more. "Staff Captain, can you try for the bridge and help the first officer, and we'll head to engineering?"

"We'll do it, sir," Jean Pierre's voice crackled back.

"First Officer, do you have an exact time of arrival?" asked Jörgen, his voice as steady as normal.

"I would have to guess forty-seven minutes, sir. The bridge consoles and the swing deck console are all dead. Punta Delgado is close enough to see without binoculars."

Jörgen immediately set the timer on his watch for forty-six minutes and released it. The second hand exploded forward and raced toward a finish line that seemed impossibly short. He clicked transmit once more. "Not to worry, the staff captain is coming to get you. And I'm heading to engineering, just for insurance." His words were offered with the same steady cadence his officers had come to expect.

"Mr. Reddy," barked Jörgen. "What is our clearest route to engineering, then report the clearest route for the staff captain's group to the bridge?"

The static barked back.

Jörgen's heart skipped a beat as he wondered if they had lost communication with the MR. But when Deep finally responded, Jörgen knew the man was simply checking his monitors for their safest route.

"Captain, I'm afraid I don't have a clear path for you. Outside of your emergency craft are at least five or six crazies… they're ah… murdering a crew member. If you can get past them—maybe you can if you don't make any noise—then take the crew access stairwell above you on Deck 6. Walk forward to the crew stairwell, which appears clear right now, up to deck 7. Then go aft, down the hallway for the senior crew quarters. You'll have to exit the main hallway, where you'll probably encounter more crazies. At least they're intermittent. Again, if you're quiet, it should be a few steps to the mid-ship crew stairwell. You can then take that all the way down to engineering. Getting inside engineering is another problem. The whole area is swarming with them. Sorry, sir."

"Thanks, Mr. Reddy. We'll tell you the moment we're set to go. Then, if you can, keep watch for more of the... what do you call them, crazies?" He hadn't heard the term before, but it was appropriate.

"Aye, sir. As for the staff captain, the news is worse... I don't see—"

"—Don't worry, Mr. Reddy," interrupted Jean Pierre. "We have an idea. We're going to take the zip line across. If you can get us the best route to the aft access, we'll take it from there."

"Sir, I don't think that's a good idea," Deep pleaded.

"Thanks, Mr. Reddy. Are we clear from the crew access to the stairwell and finally the crew exit to the zip line?"

"Hold on, sir... I thought I saw a crazy running around the spa... I don't see him anymore. Stay on guard for him. Otherwise, you're clear."

"Thanks again, Mr. Reddy. We'll also tell you when we're headed up. And we also need you to eagle-eye our passage too."

"Aye, sir."

Jörgen glanced over to Urban. His face was slack and ashen, motionless. Then he looked at Wasano, who shook his head in answer to the question he knew he didn't need to ask. Urban Patel, First Officer and member of his bridge for three years, was dead.

"Wait," Hans exclaimed, popping out of his seat. Jörgen figured the man's addled brain just connected the dots to Jessica's obtuse message. "You mean there's no one driving this thing? Don't you have a baby-captain or something?"

Jörgen ignored him and looked back to Wasano. "You

ready?"

~~~

Jean Pierre clipped the radio to his belt and gave an unsure glance at his group. "All of you wait here, and either I or someone else—"

"I have your back," TJ barked and stepped forward, sunglasses glinting from the overheads.

"So do I," Ted stated, although with much less surety than his wife. "It sounds like you'll need at least a couple of sets of hands."

"We're not staying here," declared David. "Besides, if two sets of hands are good, four more are better still."

"Don't we get a vote on this?" begged Penny, anticipating her husband's response.

"We're both going too," Boris croaked.

Jean Pierre opened his mouth to say "no," and then hesitated. Under normal circumstances, he'd never have allowed guests to participate in something that was bound to result in one of them getting injured, or worse. But if they didn't reach the bridge, and the captain didn't reach engineering, in forty-five minutes, they'd all be dead. No, he *did* need all the help he could get. "Fine. But you all must do exactly what I say. No exceptions. Anyone who disobeys me will be left behind with the... the crazies. Am I clear?"

All heads nodded, except TJ's. She was already at the door, clicking it open.
~~~

58
Abyss

The zip line spanned almost three hundred feet, easily one third of the length of the ship. Falling the thirty or so feet from the line to deck 10 would normally cause serious injury, perhaps worse if you landed on your head or if you plummeted the additional twelve feet to the sun deck and pool. Today, falling from the line would certainly result in death, as both decks 9 and 10 appeared full of crazy people, infected by a disease of madness, all of whom appeared to need to kill anyone not infected. And lest they forget, there were dozens of crazy birds still buzzing around outside, searching for the opportunity to nibble on any human stupid enough to slowly work their way across the zip line.

Ted, like the rest of his group, considered this insurmountable span and their mission. He mentally climbed the entire span of the line from the porthole they looked through to the broken antenna tower and out of sight to their final destination, the bridge. Even if they made it there, they still had to somehow lower themselves from the outside into the nearly impregnable shell of the bridge that mostly withstood a giant tsunami. And if they managed to make it inside the bridge, they'd have to battle more crazies to save two officers and wrestle back control of their helm. And because that wasn't enough pressure, added to an already near-impossible situation was the fact that they had to do this in around forty minutes, or they'd crash into an island and die.

"So are we all ready?" TJ bellowed.

This elicited a scowl from everyone.

Ted's wife often demonstrated acts of fearlessness that surprised him, in spite of her rabid fear of animals. But bravado now seemed reckless in this situation. Then again, a lack of fear would be welcomed: Ted felt practically paralyzed by it at this moment.

He stared at his wife, wondering what was going on in her head. Curiously, she was standing away from everyone, staring at her feet while rubbing the Orion necklace he'd just given her. Maybe she was trying to call up her inner warrior.

"Please, Lassie. You go right ahead," quipped Boris. He waved his palms in the direction of the zip line, a taunt to her, obviously viewing her as some sort of *rah-rah, I-can-do-anything, body-Nazi*. Ted guessed the rotund man was just as scared about this as he was. So what came out of Ted's mouth next, surprised even him.

"I'll go fir... first... to help everyone off," Ted barked, though he heard his own voice warble a little at the end. He instantly hated his volunteering to go first. He had no interest in doing this at all, but he felt every second evaporate and knew if they didn't do something quickly, everyone on the ship might die anyway.

Jean Pierre, thankfully asserting his authority, stated, "I'll go first. Penny, you follow, and then Bor—"

"There's no blooming way I'm going across that," Penny cut in with a nervous chortle. Then her face crumpled into a panicked scowl. She appeared close to tears.

"I second what she said," protested Boris.

"Fine. Anyone who wants to sit this one out, stay here," Jean Pierre peeked out the porthole, no doubt eying a couple of birds fluttering over one of the corpses on the pool deck. "Just stay inside here. When we've secured the bridge, we'll send someone back for you."

"I'm going too," David stated resolutely and then turned to Evie, "but I want you to stay here with Boris and Penny."

"Wherever you're going, so am I," she responded, equally resolute. Evie's arms were wound around her chest like a tight garment that constricted everything. It was her way of saying she was intractable on her not going.

He softly squeeze one of her arms and gazed into her eyes, "I'm worried you won't make it across the *one hundred* meter span, upside down, especially with your arthritis." He spoke almost at a whisper. "You were having difficulty holding onto a pencil this morning. This is far more difficult. And if you fall, I'll never forgive myself. *Please* allow me to go and help these people, and I'd ask you to stay and look after our new friends."

While listening to David's plea, she slowly released all of the tension in her arms, until she finally let go. "Okay," she huffed, "Just promise you'll return to me."

He wrapped his arms around her, "I'll do my best."

David let go, turned to Jean Pierre and said, "All right, let's do this." Even though he sounded resolute, gravity pulled at his wrinkled face abnormally. He looked very tired and very old, completely different from when they first met in the spa.

"All right then. I'll go first, then you Ted, then David, and TJ will bring up the rear. How's that?"

Everyone nodded.

"Wait until the person in front of you is halfway across. I don't know if the line could take more than two of us at a time."

"Guess I shouldn't have eaten that full breakfast then,"

Ted joked. His voice had raised at least an octave over normal. He glanced at his wife, who usually laughed at his jokes, no matter how stupid they were. She was stoic. No, focused, and now eying the other side, almost like she didn't want to be here, with them. Everyone else ignored him too. He couldn't blame them; there was a lot riding on their success, or failure.

They filed out of the hatch, one by one. TJ stopped upon exit and double-slapped the portal window, a signal to lock them out. A heavy thump sounded behind the door.

Jean Pierre, already at the edge of the platform, grabbed the line with both mitts underneath. Then he curled one leg around it, followed by the other so that he was hanging.

Like a piece of meat on a spit, Ted thought.

Ted turned to his fellow adventurers, just to confirm that he didn't actually say it out loud. He didn't.

He turned back to watch Jean Pierre dangle just above the edge of the tower skirting they were all standing on. The wind whipped at Ted's clothing and batted at his eyes. As Jean Pierre slowly crawled upside down, one hand and foot over the other, sliding along the line, Ted let his mind wander. He, the storyteller, had difficulty imagining what lay ahead of their little group on this life-or-death mission. Harder still was imagining what promised to be their new world, even if they miraculously got command of the helm of the ship and steered it to safety.

They talked around the periphery of this larger question inside, but Ted hadn't until this moment considered what it might be like to live in a world where fifty percent or more of the human population might be so crazy that they wanted to kill everyone else who wasn't infected. Then add a trillion infected mammals, picking off the survivors. This truly was an apocalypse, more vast and horrible than he could have ever imagined. Worse than all of those he had conceived, combined.

In his book called *Madness*, he'd only considered fifty percent of the animal population going crazy. That logically would result in a near extinction-level event for humanity. But in this real-life scenario, it was not only most of the animals, but half of the humans too. How could they possibly survive this one? Would they?

He was jolted from his daydreaming when he heard his name. He looked up and his wife was beckoning him forward.

"Ted, you're next. David will follow you and I'll be behind to make sure everyone gets across safely." She expressed this without a hint of emotion.

A bird squawked above, raising their heads. It flapped about a hundred feet away, folded its wings into its body and barreled downward, aiming right for Jean Pierre, who was more than halfway across the line.

It zipped past the line and buried itself into the lifeless corpse of a passenger floating on the swaying surface of the reddish pool water.

At that moment, Ted panicked. He wasn't ready yet. "But..."

TJ shot him a glare, through her sunglasses. It was her, and not the stoic person who'd been possessing TJ's body the last thirty minutes or so. Her look said, "Not a good time to wimp out on me, buddy."

Ted didn't say anything more. He swallowed hard and did what Jean Pierre did. And within a couple of minutes, he was a third of the way across the line. That was when he made the big mistake of looking down.

A momentary wave of faintness washed over him. While dangling, he felt himself being blown around by the stiff breeze and swayed by the rocking of the ship. He shot a glance ahead of him, in a vain attempt to gain a solid visual footing. He saw an upside-down Jean Pierre move all around his field of vision, making his nausea worse.

But that feeling went away the instant Ted's phone sang out the William Tell Overture—it was his text tone.

He couldn't see it, and was glad for it, but he imagined

the Azores were close enough now that his phone was picking up one of their cell towers. And even though his phone was nested deep in his jeans, the sound was loud. Too loud.

In response, he heard and then eyed several crazies below, screeching up at him.

They want to eat me.

Like some macabre choir taking their lead from the music coming from his pocket, the hordes below howled their rapturous reply. They growled and screeched, all while congregating underneath him, willing him to let go, to fall into their clutches.

Ted drilled his eyesight back down the metal line, aft to his wife, where he had started. She was still glaring at him.

Was that concern for him, or disgust at him?

He couldn't tell.

He carefully moved one hand after another, one foot over the other, not slowing down even when he felt the pinprick-bites as his hands scraped over some sharp surfaces in the line.

Then he felt a steady hand on his shoulder. It was Jean Pierre helping him off the line.

He'd made it.

Ted gave the thumbs-up to the rest of his party and was surprised to see David already crossing.

It all looked like it might work.

The growing hordes below growled in contempt.

David was halfway across, pausing for a moment to glance forward at Jean Pierre and him, when a loud cracking noise sounded.

It reminded Ted of the sound of ice breaking off a glacier.

The two men looked around the glass flooring underneath them, thinking maybe it was breaking underfoot.

"We couldn't break this if we tried," Jean Pierre stated emphatically. Yet he didn't know what it was either.

When part of the zip line snapped back at them, they understood at once.

Somewhere in between TJ—she was already swiftly moving across—and David, two of the line's three metal strands broke free. With the tension released, the broken ends snapped back to their starting points.

When half of the line shot by David, under her legs and through his arms and hands, it tore through his skin, knocking his hands away. His top half fell, but his legs and feet remained curled around the remaining strand, holding him.

This final strand groaned at the undue strain of two humans pulling at it, even two skinny humans.

TJ ignored her own pain from her own cuts, the slickness from her blood coating the surface of their life rope. She raced across the remaining distance between her and David. "I'm coming, David. Hold on."

The roar of the breaking lines and their commotion brought more crazies into a foaming frenzy just below them. The crazies' dinner bell had just been rung. A few of the birds, previously occupied with the dead, took flight, and made way for the human beacons calling to them.

Ted motioned like he was going to hop back on the line, but Jean Pierre held him back. "I don't think the line can stand any more weight, Ted. If anyone can get him across, it's your wife, TJ," insisted Jean Pierre.

David seemed stuck, dangling by his legs, thirty feet above a horde of crazy people, feverishly hoping he'd let go and drop.

When TJ slid over the area that broke, she saw that the single line that held the both of them up was frayed too. It wouldn't be long before it also would snap. She slithered the remaining distance. Now ignoring how loud her voice projected, she yelled out, "David, I think this line is going to break soon. Can you reach up and grab or do you need a boost."

This did it. He swung his arms back and then forward, grunted and stretched upward with one hand just hooking the line. He pulled himself up the rest of the way until he had both hands on the line. He didn't hesitate then, he bolted.

TJ held back a little, giving David some room and then mirrored his speed. David shimmied the remaining amount of the line and reached out one bloody hand to Ted and then the other to Jean Pierre, both clasping David's wrists.

It was then that final strand snapped and TJ went flying.

For a moment, TJ looked weightless, as if still suspended in the air. Then she was falling, even though she was still clutching the line. She was falling too fast to shimmy up in time. She curled one arm around the strand and gripped hard. As she swung down, her forward and downward motion drove her into a trellis beam. She hit like a rock, bounced once, and then she let go.

She fell into the gathered horde of crazies that brayed at the expectation of killing another human.

"Noooo!" Ted screamed as he watched his wife disappear in the crowd of crazies that swarmed over her.

She didn't scream even once.

59

Jörgen

Captain Jörgen felt the weight of his command now more than at any time of his career. Before this, he would have thought he'd dealt with every conceivable problem, including a terrorist boarding. Was he ever wrong.

Besides the absurdity of mad dogs and birds attacking his guests and crew, he now had zombie-like crazy people roaming his ship, each with an insatiable desire to kill. And because the outside world was in total chaos, they were entirely on their own. And finally, they only had forty-three minutes to race to engineering and change the navigation or they'd all die. And yet, he liked his odds.

In spite of everything being stacked against them, he had the best crew in the world. He had every confidence in them to find a way around whatever problems were thrown at them, no matter how impossible they seemed. And as long as he was still breathing, with his crew's help, he would captain his ship to safety. He'd already lost an uncountable number of crew and guests. Whatever power he still possessed to change their fortunes, he'd make sure no more lives would be lost.

He asked Wasano again, "Ready?"

His current head of security nodded resolutely.

Jörgen then glanced at the two German boys, and they half-nodded. He didn't want to take them, but the older one said he wouldn't stay, and he just didn't have time to argue. He nodded to Dr. Simmons, who looked dejected and just scowled at him. She didn't like being left behind, but they had little choice. She would have slowed them down and there was no way she could do what they needed her to do next.

He held his glare one final time at Urban's body, covered with one of the emergency boat's blankets, resting peacefully on the most forward bench seat. Jörgen would make sure he was accorded a proper burial at sea, when they got through this.

If they got through this.

Wasano cracked open the door and slipped out, followed by the Jörgen and the two German brothers. Dr. Simmons held the door to the lifeboat open just a crack, enough so she could watch them. She promised she'd lock it the moment they were out of sight, or any of the crazies came close.

Their plan was to quietly exit the secured area, walk a few feet to a ladder attached to the inside wall and climb up ten feet to a large steel strut supporting the ceiling. From this, they'd climb over to a deck 6 crew access balcony, hanging cantilever on the other side and just above the promenade deck they were on. Their plan depended on two of Dr. Simmons' assumptions. First, that it was sound that caused crazies to react. So they'd have to sneak by the crazies without them hearing. Second was the assumption that the crazies wouldn't climb up after them to the balcony, because they seemed to lose some motor functions after turning into whatever they were now. Those were two giant assumptions which must be true for their escape plan to work, and he hated to assume anything.

They slipped out of the gate of a jail-like structure that protected the lifeboats, each of them holding it for the other to pass through. Hans, the last out, turned to deal with the gate.

Jörgen eyed the cluster of crazies tearing apart one of his crew. It was even gorier than what he saw with the rats and the dock workers in Malaga. He couldn't help but wonder what possessed them to do this. It was one thing to hear about this from their resident expert on parasites; it was another to see it front and center.

Wasano had swiftly climbed up and over and was already beckoning them from the other side. Jörgen would go next, followed by Franz and then his brother Hans, who boasted he could climb anything.

Jörgen may have not been as nimble as he was years ago, when he was on the Norwegian gymnastics club team, but he was healthier than most sixty-five-year-olds. Up was simple, but over became difficult with his dress shoes. Rubberized soles like those worn by his crew in the galley would have been much better for this kind of task.

When Jörgen's foot slipped a second time, he took a moment to examine his footing and just happened to glance behind him. That's when he saw the gate was still open.

The gate to the enclosure was supposed to have been clicked closed by Hans—t*hat was the boy's only damned job, except to not slow them down.* But the gate was not only wide open, it was starting a slow swing inward.

Maybe with a little luck, it would clasp shut on its own.

Then it stopped, as the ship swayed to starboard, and the gate picked up the sway and began to swing the other direction.

It gathered speed, until it reached its limit and clanged loudly against its metal frame.

The sound was so jarring it startled Dr. Simmons, who was hanging out of the lifeboat hatch to get a good look at them. She lost her grip, fell out and landed face-first on the hard deck. The crazies heard all of this too, screeching their displeasure—or was it pleasure? He wasn't sure.

Jörgen peeked sideways at the crazies racing toward the lifeboat and Dr. Simmons, who lacked the physical capabilities to retreat back in the lifeboat in time. At the same time, he watched Hans flash the oncoming crazies a wide-eyed look, then Dr. Simmons—who was squinting back at him and the crazies. Just as they were a few feet from him, Hans decided it was every man for himself. He jumped up on the ladder, going around his brother, who had just grabbed a rung. Hans scurried up two rungs at a time.

Dr. Molly Simmons was one more passenger who was going to die if Jörgen did nothing. He wasn't going to let that happen.

Jörgen jumped, landing squarely on the lead crazy's back, just as it was passing underneath him. He heard something crack, like a bone, and hoped it wasn't one of his. His muscle memory from his gymnastics days kicked in immediately. Somehow he rolled and landed on both feet.

A definite 10.0, especially on the dismount.

He must have spent too much time relishing his success, when another crazy blindsided him, knocking him backwards.

Before getting flipped around, Jörgen caught a glimpse of Wasano leaping off the balcony and racing toward him. Close behind was Franz, who raced after two crazies who were headed toward Dr. Simmons. He guessed Hans was hiding.

Jörgen felt a sharp pain on his wrist. He was shocked as he rolled once more that the crazy's mouth was clamped down on his left wrist. While continuing to roll, Jörgen balled up his right hand and punched the crazy on the side of his head. Each punch caused more excruciating pain, as the crazy bit down harder, holding on like a pit bull.

Still Jörgen kept pummeling him, until the crazy lurched to get a better hold with his teeth and instead received a solid blow. The crazy's head wrenched back at the same time Jörgen's shoulder hit something solid.

With the crazy dazed, Jörgen pulled his right elbow back and delivered one final blow, sending the crazy man's head sideways, into the metal panel he'd found himself against. The crazy's head bounced hard and he was out.

Jörgen recognized the man who had just attacked him. He was from Florida, some sort of banker who, with his wife, had taken a picture with Jörgen just before the dinner in the MDR. He couldn't remember now if that was one or two nights ago; it seemed a lifetime. Now this man, who had gone crazy, lay in a heap, bleeding. Maybe he'd even killed the man.

A snarling bray, followed by a scream, pulled Jörgen's attention back toward the lifeboat. Molly was whacking at the head of one of the crazies with her cane, while Franz tugged the feet of another trying to get free and attack the old woman. Wasano was dashing toward them to help, after he had just dispatched another.

Jörgen pulled a handkerchief from his back pocket and wrapped his mangled wrist and stepped toward the lifeboat to assist. He knew this thing was going to hurt like hell when his adrenalin wore off.

In a flash, Wasano was up the stairs and beating the crazy man attacking Dr. Simmons.

Jörgen held up in front of Franz, rolling around with another crazy, thinking maybe he could use his dress-blacks for something useful, rather than ceremony. While Jörgen waited for an opening, he noticed something interesting. This crazy wasn't trying to bite Franz. In fact, to the crazy, Franz was nothing more than a clutch of seaweed it had accidentally gotten entangled in. It simply kicked and wriggled, attempting to free itself, only gnashing its teeth wildly when it caught sight of either Wasano or Molly, who was now being helped up.

When Jörgen saw an opportunity, he looked at the crazy like he would a football, and not the American kind. He lined up, took one step and drove his foot through his target. *Score!*

Jörgen was also a pretty good footballer in his day, stepping past the delirious man to get to Molly. "Come on, Dr. Simmons. You're coming with us now."

"Thank you, Captain, but please call me Molly."

They all turned and scowled at Hans, who had wandered back to the enclosure, examining his feet.

With one arm around Molly, Jörgen announced, "Let's go. I hear more coming."

60

Outside The Bridge

"A little farther," huffed Jean Pierre. There was no response.

"Did you hear him?" David brayed at Ted.

Ted nodded, though he was staring in the other direction. He released some of the tension on Jean Pierre's leg, causing the man to slide down farther. David did the same.

Each held one of Jean Pierre's legs, who was stretched out, face-down on the long slope of the bridge's windshield. His target was the area where the window had broken from the tsunami a day ago. The area was temporarily covered in plywood until they could make home port, where it would be replaced. It was there that they thought they'd make their entry into the bridge. Deep had told them the crazies were on the starboard side of the bridge and they might be able to enter unnoticed. Getting in without a sound would be difficult at best.

As he slid closer, Jean Pierre noticed one of the windows beside the broken one was left partially open. If Jean Pierre could reach the window, he could slip his hands inside and manually crank it open far enough for them to slip in.

"Almost there. Maybe a foot more." He said this with his head tucked back, so that he was facing them, and a palm directing his voice away from the opening, so that the crazies inside didn't hear him.

"Hey Ted," David cracked. "Please get your head back into the game. Your wife would want you to survive this."

Ted mindlessly nodded and lowered Jean Pierre as far as they could. Now he and David held onto each of the officer's ankles.

"Make sure you've got his weight supported by his ankles and not his shoes," David directed.

Ted wasn't listening. His mind kept flashing the images of his wife's expression as she fell into the horde below. And then their undulating mass on top of her in an instant. He couldn't believe she was gone.

"You're losing him," David barked.

It was too late.

Jean Pierre's foot slipped out of the black dress shoe Ted had been clutching. Jean Pierre's body started to slide down sideways, David's grasp providing the only resistance. But as Jean Pierre's body started to twist, David who didn't have full function of his hands because of cuts from the zip-line, lost his grip as well.

Jean Pierre pressed his palms hard against the glass in an attempt to slow his progression. Their squeaky protests were no help. He slid faster.

Now he was both sliding downward and fishtailing around; his feet were moving faster than his upper body. He eyed the direction he was headed. That's when he saw his one chance to stop himself and avoid slipping off and crashing five decks down onto the forecastle. All he had to do was snag the bottom of the open window.

His slide sped up, as his heart pounded painfully. With his eyes drilled onto his target, he waited for the right moment.

Then he sprang outward, extending his left arm and fingertips to their limits.

His pinkie brushed by the low edge of the window, and his heart sank as he thought he'd just missed it. But somehow, he hooked the bottom of the open window with two fingers. It was just enough.

With his downward progression abated, he swung under and was now able to grab with his other hand, giving him a firm grip.

"Made it," he breathed.

When his motion stopped, he pulled himself up just enough so that he could venture a better peek inside the bridge. With all the squeaking, he'd thought for sure it would have brought all the crazies to his port side. But he didn't see any there.

Hauling himself up farther, he looked to his left, toward the consoles on the starboard side of the bridge, where most of their work was done. That's where two crazies were taking out their anger, pounding away on one of the consoles. It was Jessica's; the one emitting an alarm. He knew it was the alarm she had set to warn her to change the ship's navigation. It had been blaring the whole time. Both crazies were beating with their fists so hard against the console that glass, skin, and bones were breaking. Each fist lifted revealed a red pulpy mess, and yet they were completely focused on their mission: stopping the alarm. This was their opportunity.

While the crazies were occupied, it was their best chance to surprise them.

Jean Pierre heard a noise from above. It was Ted and David trying to make sure he was okay. "Yes," he mouthed. *In spite of your letting go of me,* he thought. It was Ted, but he couldn't blame him. He was surprised the man was functional at all after watching his wife die. But they all had to focus right now on the task at hand. With a little luck, there'd be time for mourning.

Jean Pierre reached inside and worked the hand crank slowly to open the window wider, one centimeter at a time. Just a few more turns and he could slip in all the way. Each crank, though, creaked a loud chirp, and so with each squeaking crank, his nervousness grew. While he turned the crank, he glared at the crazies, willing them to not turn his way.

When the crank stopped cranking, Jean Pierre examined the opening. It was plenty of room. Glancing once more at the crazies—they were still pounding away at the offending alarm—he slid in head-first.

~~~

Jessica watched wide-eyed from the starboard swing deck. Ágúst was at the opposite end, because he'd vowed to take out any more crazy birds that showed up. She gave him the thumbs-up and he returned it, without the smile she expected. He adjusted his sunglasses and then re-glued his face against the swing deck windows to watch Jean Pierre and the others take back the bridge.

She was surprised by her staff captain's brash plan. And it might just work. The crazies—they were all calling the infected people this now—appeared to be dead-set on beating her console to death. And that is what concerned Jessica more than just their presence on the bridge: she still needed that console functional to change the computer's navigational instructions, and she had maybe thirty minutes left. She sure hoped her staff captain would stop these crazies from their equipment pummeling. They'd tried to do this themselves and it almost got her killed.

First Ágúst and Jessica pounded on the starboard bridge windows, and for less than a minute, it seemed to work: the crazies stopped pounding, and momentarily glared at them
~~~

with their creepy red eyes. But their pause was brief as the two crazies returned to assaulting her console and its non-stop alarm. Each subsequent attempt to divert their attention by pounding was ignored by the crazies. Then she tried something stupid.

Ágúst was against it, but she insisted. They cracked open the hatch and she screamed at them through the opening. The crazies ignored her. It's like they knew they couldn't get to her. She slipped through the door and screamed some more, and still they did nothing. But when she took two steps toward them and screamed, that drew their interest. They darted toward her, much quicker than she expected. She turned and jumped through the door. In mid-dive she could feel one of them swipe at her shoe, but it couldn't get a hold on it. When she hit the swing deck floor, Ágúst slammed the hatch. They agreed that neither of them would try that again.

Probably ten minutes passed since then and now they just watched and discussed what they saw.

The root of the crazies' fury appeared to be the console's alarm. And Jessica and Ágúst pounding on the windows just wasn't a loud enough substitute. It was only when she was yelling close enough to them that they turned away from the alarm. They confirmed this with Deep on the radio, who told them of other witnessed occasions when crazies attacked the loudspeakers inside and outside during the general alarm. Just like the birds did.

Jessica would have loved to have gotten more feedback on the radio from Deep, but he said he wanted to keep the radio open for emergencies and to steer the captain's group and staff captain's group to their appointed targets. So they waited, and watched the crazies pummel her console. Until the staff captain slid into the bridge.

They held their breath as they watched their superior slide inside the bridge window, their eyes floating from him to the crazies and back. He must have been quiet enough because the crazies continued their unceasing pounding.

When he was all the way in, after also confirming the crazies were occupied, he slipped the top half of his frame up and through the half-opened window and signaled his team above. That's when something happened.

From the outside, they couldn't really hear the alarm or the crazies' pounding, so they couldn't tell what happened. But all at once, they stopped their pounding. They glared at the console, like it was telling them something. Both crazies held their fists halfway up in the air, in between putting them down, or raising them to continue their pounding. It was as if they didn't know what to do next.

"Is the alarm still going?" Jessica asked.

"I'll check," Ágúst said, already running forward to the leading edge of the swing deck and the beginning of the bridge windows.

"No! I think the alarm is off. The screen looks dead. I think they killed it," he reported, hands cupped around his face, sunglasses pressed to the glass.

"Oh no!" Jessica breathed.

Then she screamed, "No!" and started pounding on the bridge windows.

"What?" Ágúst begged. But then he saw.

61
Infected

Jean Pierre signaled David and Ted. It was their turn. David gave a slight wave and whispered, "You're up" to Ted, who gave a weak nod.

Ted glanced down the course from below his feet to where the top half of Jean Pierre was beckoning out the broken bridge window, some twenty feet away. And beyond that, an abyss. If Jean Pierre didn't grab him, or if Ted slid down wrong, he'd careen off the bridge's bank of windows onto the forecastle, at least thirty feet down, to certain death. Yet he wasn't at all nervous about this. And for just the briefest moment, he considered taking a dive down the twenty-foot window span, purposely missing Jean Pierre's grasp, followed by the thirty foot drop. Then he might be where TJ was right now.

Why not?

Something squeezed his arm, vise-like. He turned and saw David, gazing at him with compassion. "Look Ted, none of us would fault you for sitting the rest of this out. But you need to decide right away."

David was right, of course. He couldn't just sit this out. They would probably need another body on the bridge to help take it back. Mourning for his dead wife would have to come later. And if there wasn't a later, so be it. At least he'd try to make TJ's death matter.

Ted glanced back at David, took a breath, and said without any bluster, "I'm good. I need to do this." David gave a weak, unbelieving smile back.

With his back to the bow, Ted knelt down and thrust out his hands, and David gripped them firmly.

Ted extended his legs and arms, and David lowered him over the bridge windows face-down. Ted's tennis-shoe'd toes squeaked against the glass. Once David's arms were outstretched and he was on his own belly, he shot glances at Ted and then Jean Pierre. Ted waited for the moment of release, trying to guess when that might be from David's face and body language. And although everything in him told him he should try to flip over on his back so he could see, he stuck to the plan, held his breath and braced for it when David nodded.

And then he let go.

Ted's slide was very slow at first, as he pressed his hands and sneakers against the thick glass for traction. But just like Jean Pierre had sped up, so did he. He realized too quickly that traction was impossible because the windows were coated with a layer of salt that made them slippery.

Ted accelerated with no control.

He told himself that it was out of his hands: he'd either be stopped by Jean Pierre, or he'd sail over the edge. When it felt like he had traveled at least the estimated twenty, Ted was about to panic. Then he felt Jean Pierre clasp onto his legs and tug.

Weightless, as if he were floating, but only for a moment, when he hit hard Ted did all that he could to take up most of the impact with his knees, but he felt one of his ankles give way and he tumbled to the bridge's solid floor.

Muting a painful grunt—ice picks in his ankle—he glanced up and watched their plan go completely to hell.

Two crazies screeched and dashed toward them—he assumed his loud landing must have drawn their attention.

He'd written about and even read about situations like these in books and stories, and it was true. Everything around him slowed down to a snail's pace. And it was during this elongated moment that he had three thoughts all at once: he'd never see his wife again, this plan was a bad one, and he knew what he had to do next.

A quick head-snap back confirmed to Ted that Jean Pierre was more concerned with Ted's hard landing than the crazies running toward them. Only when one of the two crazies brayed did Jean Pierre's features change. But his reaction would be too slow.

Ted returned his gaze to the first oncoming crazy, and at the same time he leapt upward. His left ankle screamed for him to stop, but he sucked in the pain and hobbled two more stutter-steps forward. That's when his ankle gave up completely, sending Ted sailing forward, toward the first oncoming crazy. Keeping his arms up like goal posts, he tucked down his head, and braced for impact.

The first crazy didn't anticipate this, and because somehow Ted was able to snag the crazy's legs, it flipped over him and hit the decking with a deep *thunk*, just before it could reach Jean Pierre. Ted held on. The crazy convulsed violently, all in an attempt to flip itself around again—*some part of the infecteds' brains must have been turned off, or confused. They weren't able to control or figure out some of their normal motor functions.*

Ted let go and spun out from under the crazy who, now free, fairly quickly turned itself around. And faster than he would have thought, it now scuttled its way toward Ted.

Ted wasn't sure what he was expecting: maybe the

crazy would stay down when it hit the ground. And it was why Ted remained on his belly when the crazy barreled toward him.

Again he didn't think; he just reacted.

He spun himself around and onto his back, taking a cat-like defensive posture. If he had thought about it, he probably would have tried—albeit unsuccessfully—to run. When the crazy fell on top of him, Ted was able to deflect it using his legs and arms. His left ankle roared in pain. But he ignored its pleading. He had bought another few seconds.

Jean Pierre was now in motion, but in the other direction, while Ted watched, still on his back.

For a long moment, Ted thought he was running away. Even more surreal, he grabbed a large model of the *Intrepid*—the plaque read 1:50 scale—from the floor. Clutching the model—its smokestack looked damaged just like the original—with both hands, Jean Pierre took two long strides to the crazy, who was once again trying to right itself. But before it could, Jean Pierre swung and connected solidly, sending the crazy into the wall just below the window they'd just entered. The timing was perfect, because David slid in hard, landing right on top of the crazy, taking him out, perhaps permanently.

That left one.

Ted spun around again, not sure why the other crazy hadn't struck yet, but then he saw why.

Jessica was wrestling with the other.

The crazy was moments from biting her when Jean Pierre and David arrived. They pummeled the crazy—David with a foot and Jean Pierre with the ship model—until the crazy no longer moved.

Jessica squirmed out from under the unconscious crazy and dashed to one of the consoles. It appeared to be the same one Ted and TJ had seen her working on earlier today.

Jean Pierre bounded over to Jessica, while David stepped over to Ted. No one thought to look after Ágúst, who had disappeared from sight.

David hoisted Ted up off the floor. Ted swung his arm around him and the two men slowly moved to the back of the bridge without making a peep. The last thing they wanted to do was interrupt the officers' attempts to do what they needed to do. From what they saw, it didn't appear to be going well.

"David," Ted whispered, a quiet call to his human crutch that he was about to let go.

Ted released himself and sat heavily in one of the bridge's only two chairs, behind a long console of computer and radio equipment. The other chair was the captain's, at the very front of the bridge.

David must have realized that the bridge's hatch was still open, because he dashed the ten or so feet and locked up the bridge. He then grabbed a tape dispenser from inside a glass bookcase and darted over to each crazy and wrapped their legs up tight. Perhaps he thought they would wake up, even though Ted suspected they were both dead.

Inside, they were safe, but outside…

Ted pointed to the bow, past the captain's empty chair.

David, now standing behind him, followed Ted's finger forward. He shuddered, instantly understanding it wasn't the bow Ted was pointing to. He was looking beyond the bow.

When they were up top, although their view was even better, they were more focused on their mission: to get into the bridge and regain control. Now that they had to wait impatiently for the two officers to do their work to regain the helm on one of the broken consoles, they couldn't help but plainly see the perfectly framed Sao Miguel Island. It was so close now that it occupied a good portion of the bridge's windows.

They needed to fix the navigation problem quickly.

Jessica tossed a glance and some hurried words in their direction. "Can one of you go check on Ágúst? He has a nervous stomach and ran into the bathroom."

Ted only half-heard her, because at the same time the

pretty Icelandic officer was speaking, he was wracked with overwhelming grief. All he could think of at this moment was that he would never see his wife again. Even if they somehow got themselves out of this mess, she was still gone. Forever.

He dropped his face into his hands and wept.

~~~

David glanced down at Ted and immediately felt sorrow for this man. Ted was cocooned, head cradled in his hands on the table-top. He watched the man quietly sob; small convulsive quivers buffeted Ted's body every few seconds. The shock phase had passed, and this was the first moment the man had been allowed to mourn. David understood quite well what it was like to lose a loved one to a horrific fate. He'd lost more loved ones than he could count to the evils of this world.

"I'll get him," David said. He glanced back at Jessica and Jean Pierre. They were frantically working away at the console. Neither was going to respond.

David had never been on the bridge of a cruise ship, and he suspected the makeup of the bathrooms—*didn't they call them heads on these things?*—was probably different than what land-dwellers like him were used to. At first, he wasn't sure he'd be able to find it, but since there was only one other doorway besides the entrance and the ruined doorway to some room on the other side of the bridge, he assumed this was the bathroom. A small sliver of light stabbing out from the bottom of the door was the exclamation point to his assumption.

David approached the door and tapped on it lightly at first. He waited a few seconds and then put a little more authority into his tapping.

There was no answer.

"Hello, sir. Are you all right?"
~~~

Still no answer.

David grabbed the handle and was about to open the door, but then wondered if this was the smartest idea. What if this Ágúst was one of those things now?

While clutching the door, David turned back and glanced first at the staff captain and then first officer, now working on a different console without lights. Then he glared at Ted. "Hey Ted! Ted, please!" David's words came out in short puffs of air. He wanted only Ted's attention, and not the others.

Ted slowly released his head out from under his own clutches. He lifted his face up, his teary eyes meeting David's.

David put aside his compassion for the man. "Sorry to interrupt, but I may need you to back me up..." These words came out even quieter. "In case... You know."

Ted nodded and pushed himself up, using the table while holding up his injured ankle. He put some weight on it and immediately pulled it away, his face screwing up. But then he tried it again, as if he were testing it.

Ted nodded again, this time more resolutely.

David nodded back and pivoted back to the bathroom door. He gave one more light tap and then twisted the handle.

He pushed the door open.

A bright splash of light shot out, causing David to squint and hold a hand up to hold back some of its brightness.

Quickly his eyes adjusted, and he saw the officer.

Safety Officer Ágúst Helguson was lying on the floor in the fetal position.

For just the briefest of moments, David wondered if the man was dead. Then he saw the man's rapid breaths. And slight convulsions.

Was he crying?

This wasn't the action of a crazy, and immediately David's demeanor changed from alert to feeling sorrow. He was feeling lots of that lately. He offered his hand and said, "Hey, Mr. Ágúst. The crazies are all incapacitated." He thought of saying "dead" but wasn't sure if this man would be able to take the added stress: he obviously wasn't dealing with the attacking crazies very well. Who would be except Holocaust survivors like him and his wife?

"Are you hurt?" He thrust his hand out farther, palm up.

The officer seemed not to hear him. But he was definitely crying. Again, always being alert—that's what kept him alive all this time—David became more convinced this man wasn't a crazy, but someone ill-adjusted to a world where people kill other people.

David took another step toward the officer. Then another. Now standing over him, David knelt down a little.

"Sir?" David tapped Ágúst on his shoulder, causing the man to shudder.

Ágúst lifted his head slowly and eyed David.

David's first reaction was to run.

He shuffled back the few steps to the door, not lifting his eyes from Ágúst's.

Ted had advanced closer to the door, now holding a pen in one hand as a stabbing device and a clipboard in another. Ted's face twisted from anticipation to confusion, now begging the question, "What is it?"

"Ah, folks," David bellowed as he continued back-stepping out of the bathroom until he bumped into Ted. "We have a problem."

Jean Pierre and Jessica both turned from their broken consoles. Jean Pierre had been talking on a handheld and he continued to hold it out in front of him, while they both gave David their attention and then the bathroom doorway.

Framed by the doorway, Ágúst was slightly hunched over, silhouetted against the bathroom's bright lights. His hair was disheveled and sticking straight up, his shoulders hung low. And there was something else they couldn't quite see. That was until Ágúst took a step into the bridge.

To the two officers who knew the man well, it was

almost like a birthmark they'd never noticed before. Then it was obvious. And now it was the only thing they could see.

It was Ágúst's eyes.

They were blood red.

62

TJ

The experience had been surreal.

TJ would have sworn it was someone else, not her. Someone without fear. Someone without anxiety. Someone who didn't feel fatigue or pain. Someone fully alive. Someone—anyone—but her.

But it was her.

No, it was a *new* her.

She felt like some meta-human, chronicled in a graphic novel; this person who couldn't be her had not only lived through the hard fall from the zip line, but the horde of crazies below. She didn't feel injured. And somehow, she was surviving, even now.

No, big correction—she was thriving.

It seemed impossible, but the horde of crazy people had not hurt her.

She was covered in blood. But she knew, just as she did about so much more, it wasn't her blood.

And yet, she couldn't explain why, but the coat of blood

she now wore felt to her like a new protective skin, a skin made from the blood of all of these crazy people.

She felt impenetrable as she beat and kicked and punched and elbowed every crazy around her. One by one, the crazies around her fell to the ground. And she did it all without a weapon.

And then there was the swearing.

Like a drunken sailor on shore leave, she was hurling profanities as rapidly as she landed each swing. And behind the profanities was her anger.

She didn't know where any of this came from. She only knew that she was filled with the most putrefying outrage: she was angry at the line that broke and deposited her unceremoniously on top of these crazy people and then this deck; she was furious at these insane people, who at first seemed dead-set on killing her and now didn't seem to care about her at all; she was resentful of her husband, for leaving her to deal with these crazies; she was irate at her weaknesses, or previous weaknesses; she was infuriated at her being angry. She was filled with an uncontrollable bitterness for everyone and everything. And with each crazy she slugged, her heated desire to cause more destruction to everything that affronted her grew, like a wellspring of hate that had pooled up from the darkest part of her soul.

Her fears were completely gone now; they were replaced with her bountiful anger.

Her fear of animals... gone—she hated them now; her fear of hurting herself... non-existent—her previous aches and pains pissed her off even more; her fear of being weak... history—she felt completely intolerant of all fear.

Instead, she had an uncontrollable need to hurt these crazy people, who were mindlessly flailing around her, keeping her from something she needed right now, but just didn't understand.

The new TJ felt like for some unknown reason, these

crazies were the cause of all her woes, previous and current. And so she took it out on them.

With even more fury, she pounded away at each crazy, leaving a trail of unconscious and broken people and sometimes the occasional bird still fluttering about. Everyone and everything in her path suffered her wrath.

Before long, she found herself inside the ship running.

It was as if she had blinked in the middle of her battle royal and transported herself seconds or minutes later to where she was galloping to her destination.

But what destination?

She had no idea where she was going, but without the hindrance of the crazies standing in her way, she only knew she had to get there.

With several possible routes to her goal, she turned and darted toward an open crew access stairwell she'd never been in before. Oddly, she seemed to know it was the shortest route to where she was going.

Another thought struck her, and it was odder still.

The new TJ felt as if she were being controlled—a marionette, and her master tugged at her strings, making her lurch in one direction, and then another, all setting her upon this unknown course. Yet she almost didn't mind that she had little control over this. In a way, her life had felt out of control for a long time now. This somehow felt better, like she had a purpose. Whatever that purpose was.

Just as she blew in through the doorway, she held up momentarily to take in the most exquisite smell. She'd never smelled something as glorious as this before. And when she turned her head to examine the source of the smell, she was both shocked by what it was, and even more, her reaction to it.

It was a small cowering Filipino crewmember, curled up and literally shaking in a fetal ball. His wide eyes glared at TJ, and then he reflexively shrank even farther from her. He was utterly horrified... of her.

But it was TJ who felt all at once horrified. Not of the Filipino's reaction to her, but her reaction to him: she was possessed at that moment with a desire... no, a complete need, to kill him. To pummel him to death. To rip him to shreds. To bite and tear and to... drain him of his life-giving blood.

At that moment, the shock of these feelings was too much to handle. The repulsion of these desires was enough to push her away from this fearful little man.

She stutter-stepped back from the Filipino. And although her maddening desires were still there, just as pronounced as they were moments before, she could now gather herself and instead refocus on the other desire that still pulled at her, the one that tugged at her from the opposite side of the ship.

This other force she also didn't seem to have control over. But this force seemed like a good one. With the almost uncontrollable urge to kill now gone, she followed the other urge, which gathered strength as she found herself dashing down a stairwell in leaps, three stairs at a time.

An old image filled her head. It was the Iron Rattler roller-coaster in Texas. She and... it was someone whose name she couldn't remember, even though he was important to her. They were on this roller coaster. Their roller coaster soared down a multi-story drop, and she was momentarily flying—like now. A small part of her allowed herself to feel the fear she would have once felt, along with the desire to get off. But mostly the feelings were exhilarating: the feelings of not knowing where this coaster was going next. And the whole time, she screamed with joy. Like she did now.

She felt that same abandoned exhilaration of the unknown, as she popped out of the stairwell and dashed down the hallway. She sprinted by a group of crazies beating on a partially-open cabin door. Its occupants losing the battle of holding these crazies back. The crazies screeched their desire to get in. And it was like she understood why, and she could have joined them.

But she had another desire.

None of the crazies turned their heads or even acknowledged her, even when she bumped shoulders with one of them, almost knocking it down—it was as if the new TJ didn't even exist to them.

I'm not a threat to them, she thought.

Another crazy was feasting on the body of another guest. Her old self would have stopped, though she wasn't sure why. The new TJ didn't slow one bit. She leapt over what her old self would have thought was a gruesome sight. But now... she just didn't care. Her puppet master seemed to be giving her two options. And this unknown path was the one she wanted to continue to follow, even though she still didn't understand it.

And yet the hallway she was running through was very familiar. She didn't think about the why. She was only aware and knew that finding out the why wasn't important. Not right now. Only getting to her destination was important. And the not caring part felt so freeing. Once again, she screamed her joy to no one but herself.

She arrived at a door and reflexively pulled something out of her back pocket and slashed at the door with this object. The door opened and then it closed itself.

She turned, reached down and pulled on another door and leapt inside, where she hit the cool floor and a wall of what she instinctively knew was a bathroom.

She had come to rest, having found her destination and unfolded herself from the heap she had landed in. Breathing labored breaths now, she remarked at how rapidly her chest heaved, so much so she thought her lungs might explode.

Finally, after many minutes, she pushed herself up from the floor and pulled herself up farther by the counter. She glanced at the woman staring back at her. She wasn't sure if this woman was the new TJ or the old one. This person looked like the victim of a horrendous homicide: every square inch of her was covered in blood, some dried and some bright red and dripping from places like her nose, chin and ears.

Her undone hair was no longer blond. Parts of it were sticking to one side; the rest looked ragged: a homeless wreck of a person.

She held herself up, elbows slightly bent, and scowled at her image for the longest time. And still her breathing was rapid and irregular.

A thought hit her and she reached up with a forefinger and hooked her sunglasses and gave a small tug; they didn't want to let go. They were caked into her face and matted hair. She gave them a larger jerk, and they fell from the bridge of her nose, but still clung to a dangling lock of hair.

She ignored them and stared at her face.

To get a closer look, she pushed her nose up against the glass, smudging the mirror. Her gaze held onto the woman staring back at her. Her focus fell to one of her eyes: gone was the familiar blue ring of her iris resting delicately on a round white eyeball. Instead, the blue color was now replaced with a vibrant red; its color almost mirroring the blood seeping off her.

She pulled back a little and gathered in both eyes. One of her irises was the same color as the crazies she'd just battled with. It was the tell-tale symptom of what made the crazies crazy. She had the same crazy red eyes—well, one of them; the other was more pinkish. If she had the same eyes, she was now a crazy too.

At that moment, all the strength she had felt left her.

She collapsed onto the cool surface of the bathroom floor.

Everything went black.

63

Engineering

"It's nonfunctional, sir," Jean Pierre reported on his walkie, eyes glued on Jessica's console, in case something changed.

"Have you tried..." Jörgen closed his eyes and went through a mental checklist of all the possibilities Jean Pierre had told them they'd tried, just in case there was something they might have missed. But Jean Pierre was always so thorough, as was Jessica. There was nothing else they could do. The only previously fully functioning console on the bridge was officially beaten to death by the crazies. And there was nothing they could immediately do to resurrect any of them before they ran into Sao Miguel Island. There was only one hope for his ship now.

"I guess it's up to us then," Jörgen stated, his mind whirling.

"What's your status, sir?" Jean Pierre crackled over the handheld.

Jörgen gazed at Wasano, Molly, and his two German troublemakers. Then he thought about what he'd say and clicked transmit. "We're just outside the deck 2 crew entry. We're still waiting on Deep to give us the all clear"—that was a reminder to him for an update—"and then we're going in."

"Sorry, sir," Deep chimed in immediately, his voice solemn. "There are still three or four of them hanging around that entry."

Jörgen rose from his crouch. "We don't have any more time to wait, Deep. I'm going—"

"Hold on, sir," barked Wasano. His heavy flashlight lifted, ready to strike at whomever or whatever they all heard, fast approaching them.

A large shadow arrived from a connecting hallway. Their skin crawled, until they saw the man attached to the shadow float in and then kneel in front of them.

It was Flavio.

"Let me go first, sir," he huffed, breathing in long, measured puffs. Flavio looked like he was dressed for some macabre Halloween party. He wore goggles, rubber gloves taped to long-sleeved arms, and his ankles were taped around some sort of extra padding. Everything was coated in blood, as if he had just butchered a live animal. His eyes were serious and mostly dispassionate, except there was a hint of annoyance: as if the world was conspiring to keep him from what he should be doing, which was most certainly not this.

Adding further to his surreal costume, in one hand Flavio clutched what looked like a long work glove—the kind used with heavy equipment. Each of the glove's black fingertips hung heavy, as if weights were inside. Upon closer inspection, recent splashes of blood cleft off the glove's finger-tips sprinkling the floor below where he held it suspended. In his other hand, he clutched a two-foot long wrench, its heavy end also coated red. Two sheathed knives, one on each side, were tilted at the ready.

"I go in and distract them in one direction; you go the other, to engineering."

Jörgen shot Wasano a look of disbelief, and then quickly studied Flavio; his immediate thought was, *Isn't this guy a waiter? Looks like he's better suited to security. No, the military.* "Yes," Jörgen said and nodded. "You take them port-side, and we'll go starboard, to engineering."

"Roger-dodger, sir." Flavio said. He leapt up, opened the door, burst through it, and mostly closed it, leaving a small crack so they could see through and know when to move.

"Hey, you crazy bastards. Come get some of this tasty Romanian meat," the macabre ex-waiter taunted.

Even louder, "Hey crazies. Come herrrre."

This deck 2 area had a reception-like desk just inside the door that separated two hallways: one going to the left to a couple of engineering offices and other equipment rooms; the hallway to the right led to engineering.

Several screeches and groans responded from both hallways: one crazy from the port side and two from the engineering side hollered their anger at his taunts. Flavio turned to the crack in the door. "When they've followed me down port hallway, you run to engineering. I can give you one minute. Don't waste time."

Flavio didn't wait for a reply. His eyes were on a single crazy coming from his left, just turning the corner. He leapt toward that crazy.

Flavio's movements were precise and fluid: he swung the weighted glove backhand with his left hand, connecting with the crazy's head and knocking it sideways and off balance. Then almost simultaneously, with his right, Flavio brought the wrench down hard on the crazy's Achilles' tendon, collapsing it to the floor, where it screeched its absolute hatred at Flavio.

Flavio took a knee behind the writhing crazy, ignoring its screeches, seemingly unconcerned with its movements toward him, while he glared at the other hallway. He rose up, standing tall, and waited stoically for the other two screeching crazies to arrive. He didn't flinch as these two beasts burst out of the hallway, turned at the reception desk, and barreled toward him.

Flavio held his position, a statue of the ultimate bad-ass man: *a rarity this day, for sure,* Jörgen thought. Flavio's gaze was fixed on the crazies, up to the moment before they were on him. The anticipation of their eminent conquest was almost too much for them to take. Each crazy groaned in anticipation.

Just before they reached him, Flavio stepped sideways. The crazies reached for him, missed, and tumbled over each other, entangled legs and arms clawing, colliding and one of them breaking with a loud crack.

Flavio immediately sprang down the left hallway, holding up after twenty steps. "Come on, you stupid crazies. You missed me. Now you got to kiss me," he bellowed. He almost seemed to be enjoying this.

Jörgen's group edged farther through the crack of the door, waiting for the right moment for their dash to engineering.

"I love this faucking guy," huffed Hans, behind them.

"Shhh," demanded Wasano. He didn't even look at the German, not wanting to miss their opportunity.

"Captain," stated Dr. Simmons, "did you see how they don't think about their movements? They're clumsier than children. Wonder if they'll have to re-learn their basic motor skills?"

The doctor was almost mumbling, more or less talking to herself, like a scientist in a laboratory dispassionately studying a dissected animal, while dictating observations into a recorder for future study.

Franz was quiet, as he had been almost the entire time. He looked like a smaller, more demure version of his brother. "Hey! Shouldn't we get going?" he whimpered.

"Go now!" Deep crackled through their radios. He was obviously following their every move, and was on top of their plan once Flavio had sprung into action.

Jörgen yanked open the door and Wasano led, followed by Dr. Simmons, Jörgen, and the Germans.

They raced down the right hallway, only slowing when they'd reached their destination, engineering.

So far, so good.

The small and simple placard on the door seemed to belie the importance of this area, especially now.

Knowing their time was short, Wasano immediately swiped his card and pushed the door open upon its clicked acceptance. He slipped into the doorway first, heavy flashlight raised above his head, ready to strike anything or anyone who rushed him from the shadows. He snapped it on because the overheads were off and the room was murky. While dousing the room with a cone of light, he worked at the switch to the overheads, confirming the lights weren't working—little on their ship seemed to be working now. At least the computers seemed functional: all the monitors were blinking their minimal light, coating the room in misty Regal European Blue.

Most important, there were no crazies.

The room was fairly compact, with one long row of three monitoring stations, crowded with half a dozen flat-screens per station, and a single desk in the left corner of the room, with its own flat-screens. On both sides of the room, connected to the ceilings, but tilted so they were visible to the whole room, were giant flat-screens with multiple views of the ship's engine room areas, various mechanical areas and the bridge. All the walls were papered over with multiple layers of deck-plans, charts, schedules, and other items Wasano didn't really understand, nor did he care to. This place was all about utility. There was nothing else to it. Certainly no place for crazies to lurk.

All three stations were abandoned, their chairs spun around. The butts which had occupied them must have left in a hurry.

"It's empty, sir," whispered Wasano to Jörgen and their

group. They all quickly moved inside and clicked the door shut behind them.

Jörgen immediately went to work on the middle console, thinking if one didn't work, he'd move over to one of the others.

"Tell JP we're here," Jörgen said while tapping on the keyboard.

Several monitors sprang to life, blinking from murky blue to blazing white, removing more of the room's ghostly shadows. Jörgen brought up the Electronic Chart Display and Info System or ECDIS and saw their position: only 8.64 kilometers from the island. A red light flashed its concern about their proximity. Their ETA was still twenty minutes, probably because with the stabilizers out and down, providing maximized resistance, their overall speed had crept down to 14 knots. Their ride was much choppier, but it had bought them time. Just not enough.

First step was to engage the ship's rudder and steer them away from Sao Miguel Island. Jörgen brought up the Navigation and Command System or NACOS, which would allow him to steer the ship using its rudder.

There was a knock on the door, and Wasano prepared to answer it, holding his flashlight up high. He felt a little stupid, because he didn't see any evidence that crazies would knock first. But he wasn't taking any chances. Dr. Simmons stood fast, while the Germans shrank back deeper into the room.

Expecting Flavio, Wasano was startled instead to see a blonde-haired woman, wearing large designer sunglasses, an orange swimmer's nose-clip, and a crooked smirk.

"Are you going to leave a lady hanging outside, or do I have to beg to come in?" she said, her arms folded over her chest, acting impatient to be let in.

Jörgen turned from the keyboard—he had been waiting for the computer's program to respond to his commands—to take in the woman at the door, whose voice sounded somewhat familiar. "Hold on." He erupted from his seat. "Theresa-Jean?" he called out. "Is that you? Let her in, Wasano."

All eyes watched the athletic woman, clean and sporting a fresh coat of makeup, stride in and wait for Wasano to close the door. Her sleek jogging outfit appeared pressed and perfectly fitted to her form; her ponytail glistened. She looked like she had come from the spa, refreshed after a treatment, and certainly not someone who they had heard had fallen two stories from the zip line and then tangled with a horde of blood-thirsty crazies.

The oversized sunglasses and the swimmer's nose clip seemed out of place on her. And other than her sporting a clean bandage covering part of one wrist, she looked good. Really good. She certainly didn't appear deceased, as they had all assumed, including her husband Ted.

"Thanks, Captain. Did my husband and JP make it onto the bridge?" Her smirk was gone, crossed arms still in place over her chest, which appeared to be rising and falling rapidly. Her voice had a more nasal quality than usual.

"Yes, they did."

"I must talk to Ted and let him know I'm alive. I lost my radio in the fall." Her words were rushed and she offered a smile, but it seemed forced. She was not at all like the jovial woman he'd witnessed at dinner. She wasn't right, even though she more than looked it.

Jörgen said nothing, and simply beckoned her to the seat beside him, where a microphone telegraphed at an angle, waiting.

When she sat and rested her elbows on the long counter, Jörgen overtly pressed the transmit switch to the left of the microphone, now a few inches from her lips.

A cacophony of voices burst from a small speaker in front of her.

She shuddered slightly and pulled away. But when

Jörgen nodded for her to go ahead, she leaned forward into the microphone and spoke.

"Ted?" Her head remained frozen, her lips closed, as she waited. Then she spoke again. "Ted, are you there? This is TJ."

Jörgen, sensing she was done, visibly clicked off the button so she could take over, while he continued with the ship's controls.

Radio static bled through the speakers for many long moments. Even the crew who had been just speaking were quiet.

"TJ?" a shaky voice answered. "Is… Is that really you?" Ted's voice raised an octave with each word. "My God," he said, his voice cracking, "how?"

"What can I say, I'm—"

Jörgen abruptly put his hand over the microphone and bent the flexible boom in his direction.

"Sorry, Ted. This is Captain Jörgen. I need the radio back. She looks fine. In fact, she seems almost completely uninjured. Let's hope you two have plenty of time to catch up. Jean Pierre, can you hear me? We still don't have any helm controls here. Unless we can discover some other way to gain control or reverse the engines in the next twenty minutes, we will collide with Sao Miguel."

64

Sao Miguel

São Miguel Island, although the largest of the Azores Archipelago, was still nothing more than a tiny spot on a map of the vast Atlantic Ocean. Its closest landmass, Lisbon Portugal, was over nine hundred miles away. To the *Intrepid*, it was supposed to be a transitional point on their navigational compass. Almost as if a harbinger of what was to come, São Miguel burst out of the ocean depths from a violent undersea volcanic eruption many millennia ago. Now, the island's three-thousand-foot high peak filled up the bridge windows from port to starboard, a looming target which grew larger with each eye blink.

This sub-tropical island had been a growing favorite stopover for Europeans and transatlantic cruise ships. If the *Intrepid* had intended to port here, its crew would have long switched its controls to manual, slowed its engines to less than ten knots and guided the ship around the island's southern exposure, and then north into Punta Delgada, the island's cruise port terminal and the archipelago's chief port. But that was not their destination.

Jessica had programmed the Intrepid's nav computers to take them directly into Nordeste, the easternmost town on São Miguel. Unfortunately for them, Ted heard that Jessica always hit her mark.

Of course, Nordeste was only meant as a reference point. Several miles back, they were supposed to have changed their course, resetting their heading for Nassau Bahamas. It was all part of the captain's simple plan to track along the path of the least dense cloud configurations, those coming from the ongoing volcanic eruptions. Because some in the media had suspected the volcanic clouds as the root cause for the Rage disease, striking first the animals and now people, the captain had thought it would be good to stay out of the clouds and have the added effect of keeping their passengers happier by giving them warmer temperatures and sunshine. That was before they lost control of the ship.

Now, with dark clouds thickening above and around them, and with the island growing closer by the second, the *Intrepid* crew sounded as if they were in a full-on panic.

The NACOS had automatically adjusted their stabilizers, and that had slowed the ship somewhat. But without helm controls, they were fast running out of options.

The team on the bridge and the one in engineering were shooting ideas back and forth over the radio. With staff captain Jean Pierre and first officer Jessica still working on their consoles, Ted manned the radio and repeated their words from the bridge to the captain in engineering. "The staff captain asked if you were able to reach anyone in the engine rooms?" His words were careful and without any emotional inflection.

Ted repeated Jean Pierre's words and waited. But he wasn't really listening.

Ted was jumping out of his skin. More than anything, he needed to be with his wife, TJ. Besides just the simple desire to see her, a part of him relented that they were probably going to crash. And if that was their fate, he didn't want to waste any more time being apart from her. He wanted to leave this world holding her.

But he also needed to confirm she was really all right: his logical mind told him it was impossible, replaying as evidence the scenes of her falling from the zip line and then disappearing into the writhing pack of crazies. *There was no way she could have survived this,* his mind argued. And yet, he had heard her. And so she did survive, his emotional side debated back. Even with the captain's confirmation, he still needed to verify this with his own eyes. He just needed her, and he needed her now.

He beat his fist on the table, demanding his logical mind's silence. *Focus, dammit!*

There was still a chance, no matter how small, that they could come out of this alive. But to do so required that he pay attention and not miss all that was going on. He could play a role in helping their success. But if he screwed up or delayed the crew's efforts, it could lead to all of them dying.

Did Jörgen just say, "No!"?

The captain continued on the other end of the radio conversation, "I'm going to go down myself and hit the automatic shut-off. But we have another problem." Jörgen paused. When Ted heard nothing but squeaks coming from the speakers, he twisted the volume control to its limit.

No one on the bridge could see the captain furiously scribbling computations on one of the flat-screen monitors with a wax crayon.

"Please, sir. Don't try both shut-offs on your own..." Jean Pierre hollered from the other side of the bridge, in between rapid puffs of air, "...with all the crazies out there..." Ted watched him, as he dashed across the span of the bridge; with Jessica in tow, each clutching paper navigational charts.

"What problem, sir?" Jean Pierre huffed.

Jean Pierre and Jessica were now on the port side of

bridge, spreading their navigational charts out on the long table. Jessica pointed enthusiastically at some point on the chart. Ted's heart was racing uncontrollably. For just a moment, he stopped thinking about his separation from TJ.

Ted had the microphone open, but he feared the captain didn't hear what was just said. "In case you did not hear that, the staff captain was worried about your going at it alone and attempting both shut-offs, especially with all of the crazies out there. Though I don't know where those are, I'd agree about the futility of such a lone endeavor because of the crazies. They're now both examining some paper charts... Oh, and the staff captain asked what was the other problem you mentioned?"

Ted let go of the button and turned up the volume to its highest level. He didn't know how much time they had left, but he looked forward out the bridge windows and was shocked at how much closer the island was to them, just in the span of the last minute.

Two ridiculous thoughts leapt out of Ted's mind simultaneously: *it was so close, they could swim from here. And why don't they try that?*

He looked back down at the radio, unsure he'd let go of the transmit button, even though he could hear the background sound from the captain's own microphone being open.

An echoing voice from he guessed the security director said, "I'll go with you, Captain." It sounded like it was meant for the captain and not their consumption. But then Ted heard TJ's voice. His heart skipped a beat, and he gulped back his breath, as he heard her say in a colder than normal voice, "One officer should stay here; I'll go."

The microphone remained open for several seconds and some hushed words were barked, and then the booming voice of the captain erupted. "Thanks. But even if we're able to stop the engines, we still need helm control. Otherwise, we're too close to the island and we'll have too much speed: at this point, we'll still hit."

Oh shit! Ted thought. Or maybe he said it out loud.

"We could use the anchor," hollered Jessica from the opposite end of the bridge. "What do you think?" She said this facing Jean Pierre.

Ted punched the button. "Jessica, I mean the first officer said we could use the anchor?" Ted repeated, but it came out as a question, even though he knew it wasn't meant as one.

"That's not a horrible idea," Captain Jörgen answered in a flurry of words. "If it weren't for the depth... We'll need all twelve shots just to scratch the surface, and by then, it would be too late, because we'd be too close."

Static.

"But what about the Nordeste Bank?" Jean Pierre barked. A quick glance to Ted told him to repeat quickly. He held up his finger like he wanted to add something.

Ted kept his eyes on the staff captain, while clicking transmit. "The staff captain wants to know what about the Nordeste Bank? There's something more..." He waited for his next instruction, still maintaining eye contact and still holding the mic open.

"Tell him..." Jean Pierre trotted over to the base unit, stopping on the other side of the workstation and leaning over, "Sir," he yelled, "it's as little as 245 feet deep nearly two miles offshore. That should be enough, if you can use the stabilizers to nudge us over it. Jessica figures we only need to change our heading by two degrees to starboard, but it must be done right away."

Static.

Jörgen clicked open the mic and mumbled to himself, just barely loud enough that Ted and Jean Pierre could hear. "...if we dropped the aft anchor at the tail end of the Nordeste Bank, assuming the automatic release wasn't engaged, as it was designed to be, severely damaging the ship... It might be enough to stop us, if we can also cut off the engines…" Finally, Jörgen puffed out a loud breath, his mouth up against the mic. "That's a great idea. But get someone there right away, and I'll work on the stabilizers."

Ted knew from the All Access Tour that the release was on deck 1, and on the other side of their long ship. It seemed too far a distance for someone from the bridge. Engineering was right there. Someone from their team should be going.

The radio's pulsing static droned on while everyone listening waited for some heroic volunteer to go on this newest suicide mission.

Ted would have volunteered, if only to break the silence, but he couldn't get there quickly with his bum ankle and he didn't know which buttons to push; they didn't tell him that part on the tour. And thinking it through further, that was the key: knowing what buttons to push or levers to pull and when. And other than the captain, no one from their group in engineering would know what to do. It seemed impossible.

And while Ted waited helplessly, as time raced by, he once again considered belting out, *Why don't we abandon ship?*

"Sir?" pleaded a meek voice from behind Ted.

It was Ágúst, who'd been sitting on the floor, arms resting on top of his knees. David had been watching him like a hawk the whole time to make sure he didn't become a threat: none of them still understood why someone infected and symptomatic wasn't violent.

The officer shot up abruptly. David countered with a two-step back, taking a defensive posture. Ágúst glared at his staff captain with his odd-colored eyes. "I'd like to volunteer for that."

Jean Pierre had since walked around the table and was also now standing beside Ted. Jean Pierre didn't hesitate. He spun around, punched the mic and stated, "Captain, First Officer Helguson volunteered to go now." He glanced back around, while touching the transmit button, to scrutinize the Ágúst.

"Should he go alone?" asked the captain. He asked this, but they knew he wasn't really looking for an answer. There was no time to question the decision. He would have to depend on Jean Pierre making sure this was the most viable option. And of course they'd all have to stake their lives on Ágúst.

Again, Jean Pierre didn't hesitate. "Trust me when I say he'll be fine."

Ted immediately knew this to be the best solution. So did everyone else on the bridge. Ted had explained to them earlier that the crazies seemed to ignore those who were also infected, even those like Ágúst, who were infected but hadn't become violent like the others. He'd be perfect for this, assuming he remained sane, and they had enough time. He didn't want to even look out at their looming target.

They could all *feel* its proximity.

65

Becoming

Jörgen busied himself on his console, focusing on the only thing he had control over at this moment. He had had an idea. And it seemed to be working. Like other helm controls, he didn't have manual controls over the stabilizers. They were automatically being controlled by their systems. But he was able to feed false compass data into their NACOS, causing it to automatically adjust the port stabilizers and move them slightly to port. If he'd thought of this sooner, he might have been able to steer them completely away from the island. But they were too close for that now. With a little luck, it should be enough to place them over the Nordeste Bank, a low-lying underwater mountain of sand and rock, barely two hundred feet from the surface. His ECDIS display, as well as movement of the island across their bridge windows, told him this was working. *Thank God, at least these controls are still functioning,* he thought.

With the port stabilizer no longer providing resistance to the port side of the ship, and the starboard stabilizer continuing to provide the only resistance, he could feel the ship's stutter through the water beneath them. His eyes were glued to the ECDIS display, eyeing their speed and heading, his mind going through the computations to make sure it was enough. It was. He could leave now.

Jörgen spun in his chair to face his acting security chief standing guard at the door. "Wasano, if you're ready, let's get an update from Deep on the status of our hallway."

"Captain," TJ demanded from the back of the room, stepping closer. She had found a back wall in engineering after the captain had cut her off from the radio. "You need me to go—"

A double-pound sounded from the other side of the door.

All heads but one turned to the door.

TJ cast down her gaze, huffed out a frustrated *humph*, and ratcheted her arms around her chest.

Wasano cracked the door open, his flashlight raised, just in case.

This time, it was Flavio, who slipped inside, pushing the door closed behind him.

The former waiter, and now the ship's chief bad-ass, was a little more scratched up than before, and wore a few new splotches of blood, but he otherwise looked fine. He had halted just inside the door and quickly flashed glances at the captain, the German brothers, Dr. Simmons, Wasano, and then finally TJ. "Are we... Mrs. Villiams? Good to see you," he said to her.

TJ half-nodded a confirmation, without any smile or show of emotion. This was different than the Theresa Jean that Jörgen had met with several times. But on the other hand, she'd just escaped certain death.

Flavio continued, returning his gaze to Jörgen, "Sir, what's our status?"

TJ jumped in, "We're basically fucked. We've got ten minutes to get someone to the engine room now to stop the engines. Wasano volunteered and so did the captain. I told them both I should go, if someone would tell me where to go."

Flavio ignored her and responded with an immediate flurry of words to the captain. "No, captain must stay here and run ship. I get to engine room. Someone tell me where is stop controls. I am only one who can do this." Flavio's hand was already on the door handle, his body pointed in that direction.

"What makes you think you can get through all of those crazy people and make it to the engine room in time?" Wasano asserted.

"I deal with crazy passengers all the time, and now everyone crazy. No time to discuss. You and I go. Captain and others, vith Ms Villiams stay." He twisted the knob.

"Wait!" bellowed TJ. "I am going with you." Her arms were down, her shoulders squarely pointed toward Flavio.

"Absolutely not," the captain, now standing, demanded.

"We don't have time for this," Wasano yelled, taking a place behind Flavio, almost pushing him forward.

TJ stepped in front of Flavio and pulled off her sunglasses.

Wasano jolted backwards, hoisting up his flashlight to strike.

Everyone in the room either gasped or loudly caught their breaths.

Jörgen squinted and now understood why TJ seemed so different.

Flavio didn't flinch. "Okay, you come then. We go now. Follow me, I know shortcut to engine room." He dashed out the door.

~~~

Only moments ago, Eloise had felt satiated. Fulfilled. But she
~~~

had also known that she still needed… something.

She had had her fill of food and felt better in what she'd become. It was a warm feeling, like a… *soft blanket* came to mind; this made no sense to her, though the thought felt right. And although she had a strong urge to sleep, she fought it. She just didn't know why.

She could have slept right where she stood. This part made sense. She was exhausted. But at the same time she felt exhilarated. It was better than after sex. That was one thing she remembered very well, and another urge she needed to fulfill. But she would satisfy that urge another time. Sleep was needed now.

She glanced at her misshapen wrist and the missing digit on her hand. She understood instinctively that her body needed sleep, if only to repair what was damaged. Her wrist was swollen. She remembered that it was called a sprain—she'd had had one of those before… she couldn't remember where. Her finger wasn't bleeding anymore. Another instinctive thought instructed her that her body was already healing. This instinct also told her that it wasn't yet the right time for sleep: something else needed to be done.

But what? a voice in her head yelled.

She started searching, first with her eyes. Then her search moved her and she lumbered around the open Promenade deck.

The public deck was littered with discarded cups, towels, purses, splotches of blood, and an occasional body. She had no idea what she was searching for amongst the debris. Only that like everything else that now came to her, she knew what she was searching for would come to her soon. She stumbled around, one foot shuffling after another, until she tripped over a corpse.

No, it was another person like her. This person was resting, just as she wanted to be doing.

Eloise took a few more slow steps and stopped over the

body of a pretty officer, lying on her back, eyes opened, pupils dilated. Eloise knew instantly several things about this woman: she wasn't someone who had become like Eloise, and that was the reason she was dead.

Eloise examined the dead officer more closely, sensing she'd find a clue to her search.

She started her inspection with the dead woman's hair. At one time, before her rebirth, the old Eloise would have been interested in how this woman prepared her hair—what was this called? She would have thought it cheap-looking, but still pretty. The new Eloise had no interest in such things. But she felt there was something else important about this officer. So she continued her examination.

Eloise scrutinized every part of the dead officer, knowing now what she was searching for was here. It must have been something she had glanced at that made her stop. The dead woman's mouth was wide open—a scream interrupted: her jaw slack and silent; her neck a ragged mess, but no longer releasing her life's blood; her chest unmoving; the tag above her breast told others that she was Cruise Director; her ripped shirt was made from a cheap polyester material, just like her faux leather belt; the radio…

That was it!

Eloise snatched the radio from the officer's belt and fumbled with the controls. She'd never worked one before, but she knew she could figure it out. She twisted a miniature knob marked "V" and the radio came to life.

People were speaking on it. They were people who had not become like her. They were the Other People who she needed to kill.

They were talking about stopping the ship. They were saying that they needed to stop the ship before it hit an island.

Eloise realized right then that she needed to be on that island. She needed to get off this ship and get on the island. Her mind searched for the reason why, but there wasn't any.

Nor was there a struggle with this decision. Once again it came to her intuitively, just like how to hunt, or eat, or kill. She knew that this ship was now useless to her. Most of the people had already become like her, or they would eventually; everyone else on this ship would be dead by tonight. But on the island, she felt... No, she knew, there would probably be many more Other People on the island, rather than on this ship. So she had to get there.

Right at that moment she knew what she must do: get off this ship and get to the island. And to do this, she needed to stop these Other People talking on the radio. She didn't know how, but she knew this, just as she knew everything else, and that this too would come to her. She listened intently to everything the radio told her.

A scream from an Other Person—she definitely knew this was not one of her people—forced a small tick in Eloise's face, but she didn't turn her head from the radio or adjust her position. She remained mostly still, crouched down beside the dead officer. After another terror-filled scream, she reluctantly lifted her eyes from the radio, and glanced sideways.

It was a woman in a one-piece bathing suit, perfectly sculpted to her body—a Ballet Maillot by Amaio, with the French mesh. This wasn't one of those things that just came to her intuitively. It was an old memory, from the old Eloise... She had had one just like it. Before becoming. The old Eloise would have stopped this woman and told her how good that suit looked on her. The new Eloise only wanted to kill the woman. But she'd leave that to one of her own people.

The woman raced by Eloise, a feline yowl escaping from her rapid puffs for air, her strides choppy but quick. The woman's head snapped to her right, just as two people who had also become tackled her to the floor. The woman screamed once more, and then was silent.

Eloise returned her glare back to the radio when she heard one of the ship's officers say they were going to deck 1 aft... Eloise knew for some reason that she was already aft and near a crew stairwell that went to deck 1. She remembered now that one of the officers told her about the aft stairwell—she glanced at its door a few feet away from where she was at that moment.

Someone on the radio said that First Officer Helguson was going to disconnect the anchor automatic release. He was already headed that way. Again, she didn't know why, but she knew that she had to stop this person. Somehow by preventing this Officer Helguson from doing what he was about to do, she could get onto the island.

Eloise quickly learned not to question these thoughts, where they came from or why. She just accepted them. It was all part of her becoming.

She sprang from the dead officer, surprised at how quickly she was already at the crew access door and inside. She felt so alive and so full of anticipation once again.

66

TJ

"This way," Flavio stated in his usual matter-of-fact tone. He grunted as he struggled with a large hatch in the floor. It moved an inch, but then his wrench slipped out of one of his hands and he lost his grip. The door and wrench *thunked* back to the decking, with a deep thunder-like tremor.

TJ pushed past Wasano, who was doing nothing but stand in her way, grabbed the handle and heaved. The thick metal door flew open, its metal clanging hard against the steel frame. Flavio shot her a stunned glance, one that said both "What the hell?" and "Damn, you're stronger than you look."

TJ turned away, wincing at the pounding reverberation in her head: a throbbing echo of the hatch's banging sound. Her features bunched up, as if she were in horrible pain, while she focused on quelling something worse than pain that wanted to come out: a darkness, more loathsome than the most abhorrent pain she'd ever felt. And like her body's previous responses to pain, she felt jolted and unable to stop its coming. Also like pain, which she used to just accept, this dark urge didn't give her the luxury of choosing. It rose up and demanded her acceptance. But she couldn't. If she did, she would lose control over that urge. So she dug her fingernails into her palms, nearly piercing skin, and pushed it back harder.

Then she stopped to listen. They all did.

The sound echoes from the hatch-banging must have vibrated throughout the metal structure of this hallway, as there was a growling response forward from them, just out of sight.

TJ looked up at Flavio, who was studying her with suspicion, just as he had been since they left engineering. "Are you going down first or am I?" she flared. They had so little time left and she wasn't sure she could hold it together much longer.

"Follow me," Flavio said, grasping the ladder with both feet and one hand—the other now clutched both the bloody wrench and glove-weapon. He slid down the ladder with dogged determination, until he hit the deck 1 flooring with a teeth-rattling *thud*.

TJ followed, sliding down in one fluid motion, her landing cat-like. She waited until Wasano was with them, after shutting the hatch. "You see, the... crazies, as you call them, are both attracted to and hate loud noises." She whispered this not only for their benefit but for her own. She was desperately trying to understand all that was going on in her and around her. Recalling the clang-echo which had thankfully started to fade, she continued, "It's like ringing the dinner bell, but at the same time, you're rattling their mental bells. In other words, when you make a loud noise, you might as well be calling them to you."

"You know this because you're one of... th-the infected?" Wasano stammered, his voice a little too loud and shaky. He didn't want to hear her answer. His eyes darted around the area in which they were standing, in an attempt to gather in any movement: it was a narrow utility hallway, marked with emergency lights that faded into the darkness in both directions. Flavio continued to study TJ, his demeanor also jumpy, but in a different way. She sensed no fear in him; he was simply ready to strike her down the moment her actions became aggressive.

Yeah, she *knew* the whole sound-thing quite well. And while she culled some of this from recent observations and suspicions, she mostly perceived it instinctively, like so many things she seemed to just fully know, ever since her... *what, rebirth?* When she had the time, she wanted to mentally explore and understand why a simple loud noise made her head scream. And not the dull banging pain that she'd always felt... *no, scratch that, pain she used to feel in her head and side since the dog attack.* This wasn't pain. The urge that she pushed back was rage, pure and simple. She wanted to wallop on that hatch for making that noise, but also on everyone around her, including Wasano and Flavio. So yes, she understood this, because she knew exactly what the crazies felt.

She glanced back at Flavio, still scowling at her, and she motioned to the aft-side of the darkness. He nodded and then held out his two makeshift weapons, in preparation for combat against more—*dementeds* came to her mind and seemed like a better word than crazies. Crazies felt demeaning, and far too close to home.

Flavio waddled into the darkness, with her close behind.

"Okay, fine. Don't answer me," Wasano whined. He kept a couple of paces behind TJ, watching her more than anything else.

Flavio abruptly stopped and turned to face TJ. He leaned in so close TJ could feel his breath. She reflexively twisted back a little at the move, almost as if she were repulsed by his breath. She couldn't smell him. Mostly. With her nose plugged, she couldn't smell anything. But it was reflexive, because she knew what he smelled like and that terrified her.

He breathed, “You’re not going to try and eat me, are you, Ms. Villiams?”

Once again, she had to suppress a natural emotion. This time, it was something she hadn’t felt since all these changes took place: laughter. She gulped it back, but enjoyed the moment and said deadpan, “I do have a weird hankering for rare Romanian meat right now.”

At least I haven’t lost my sense of humor.

“Humph,” was Flavio’s only response.

He turned back and continued walking a few more steps before stopping once more, this time less sudden. He pivoted to face a sealed hatch in the wall pulling up the latch with his glove-whacker hand until it clicked. Then he pulled at it.

A shaft of light shot through, illuminating them.

Flavio gestured at the thin opening. “What is it you Americans say… Ladies first.”

She nodded and slipped through, the hatch swiftly closing behind her.

Almost immediately, she thumped twice from the other side.

It was their agreed upon all-clear signal. There were no dementeds on the other side.

Flavio cracked the door open again and whispered through it, “Nothing?”

“Nope,” she said.

“Do you smell them?” Wasano breathed.

“More like, I don’t smell them. But I do smell both of you, ah… very strongly.” She positioned the orange nose-clip back over her nostrils and squeezed.

“It’s my manly scent,” Flavio quipped, as he slid past her and continued his track aft.

“What do we… non-infecteds smell like?” Wasano glared at TJ.

She suspected he would be less likely to ask this question if she’d taken her sunglasses off and he had to stare directly into her eyes. "If I told you, you'd freak out." She moved past him and caught up to Flavio, leaving Wasano with that thought. For the second time since her change, she felt her cheeks crease into a smile. It felt good, even though she had to work hard not to think about what both of them smelled like. Again, thoughts of a dinner bell came to mind. In truth she was more afraid of freaking herself out.

Flavio held up at another door. He leaned forward, beckoning them both to come closer, so they could hear him.

"This starboard engine room," he told them. Then he faced Wasano. "You must enter security key."

Wasano tapped in the numbers on the pad below the handle. It clicked and so did a solid lock in the door.

A blast of heat and noise pushed through the door and spilled into their hall.

TJ didn't wait for the offer. She pulled off her nose-clip, letting it dangle around her neck, and slipped her head and part of her body in, stopping midway. She tilted her head back and whispered, "Wait here for a moment." She silently stepped through, clicking the door closed behind her.

Flavio put an ear to the door, while Wasano eyed him and waited to glean something from his facial reactions, or for some sort of report from him.

Wasano shrugged his shoulders. *What?*

"I hear struggle. I hear thump. I hear another thump. I hear nothing."

Two knocks on the door.

Flavio pointed to the door lock again, and Wasano quickly entered in the code and the door once again clicked open, sending in a blast of heat.

TJ stuck her head through, nose-clip on. "Okay, there are no more dementeds... at least conscious. Find the shut-off quickly. We have little time."

Flavio stepped past her and glanced at the two human shapes lying silently on the metal flooring a few feet in front of

them.

"Did you kill them?" Wasano asked as he slipped by her.

"No, of course not. They're still people, you know... Please, the shut-off?"

"Yes, of course." Wasano nodded and then took a few quick steps to an opposite wall with his back to Flavio and TJ, who watched him attentively. Wasano's head fixed on an unseen point on the wall, then darted around, before he pushed his radio to his ear and yelled something they couldn't hear.

"What's the problem?" TJ asked Flavio.

"Don't know. I know ship's deck plan well. Never been in engine room."

They both rushed over to Wasano to ask what was wrong and why the engines weren't powering down.

Then they saw.

A large electrical-like box hung by wires from where it obviously once fastened much higher to the wall. On its face, now bent and distorted, was a hole and below it a placard announcing that this was the "Emergency Shut-Off." Pieces of bright red plastic littered the floor below the now nonfunctional device. It was destroyed. And that meant that someone, or more likely something, had sabotaged the emergency engine shut-off.

67

Ágúst

First Officer Ágúst Helguson scampered down the stairs, out of control, as if something were chasing him. In reality, he was running from himself.

He turned a corner and dashed through a crew doorway, barely slowing. When the door swung back and slammed shut, he twisted his head to shoot an angry glare at it for making so much noise. Still barreling forward, not watching his path, he pile-drove into a rotund passenger.

It was like hitting a wall. A soft wall.

Ágúst bounced off the much larger man, and tumbled to the floor. He glanced up at the moving shadow above him, and was surprised to see it was one of those lunatics, and it was snarling at him. *Oh God, I ran into that?*

The beast wore a Hawaiian shirt, with one panel ripped and hanging open, revealing a huge belly with deep scratched troughs that were raw and oozing. The beast roared bear-like at Ágúst, spewing flecks of dark coagulated blood from its mouth, while the thick gold chains that ringed its neck flopped in a frenzy. Then it stopped and just bored holes in him with its fiery eyes.

Ágúst reflexively pushed away from the loony, but he realized almost immediately that he wasn't scared of the man at all. In fact, he felt angry at this thing for snarling at him and being in his way. The feeling passed.

Ágúst stood up, ignoring the beast, who now seemed to have grown disinterested in him as well. So he continued his race once again. He didn't care about the loonies anymore; they certainly weren't going to bother him, unless he ran into them. He had to get to the aft anchor. His staff captain asked him to do this.

As he zipped through the large expanse of the deck 5 public areas, he marveled at everything he observed: all seemed out of place, and at the same time, just right. With each stride, he gathered in the scenes around him: objects that seemed different or that he'd never noticed before—it was his job was to notice things—or people running in terror, or the loonies running after them. With each object or person or loony he studied, he came to know more of what was happening to himself.

When he leapt over an overturned table full of useless pamphlets about the ship's various spa treatments, he knew he was stronger than he could remember. He felt like he could take on anyone and anything; he could beat up anyone, even that big loony he'd just ran into. He felt indestructible, like a superhero.

When two loonies were stumbling in his direction, he knew he was no longer afraid of them, and the loonies didn't pay any mind to him either. It was just as the author had told him would happen. And it wasn't just the fear of loonies that had left him; he no longer had any fears, about anything. He scoffed at himself, at how he used to shiver at night, thinking about what others would say about him. Even when he made first officer, he was sure he overheard others talking about him.

None of that seemed to matter now.

And the smells. He wasn't much of a foodie, as Jessica called it, so the smells coming from their mess never turned him one direction or another. Eating was just something he had to do. But now there was a bouquet of both the most foul and most delightful smells, and none of them he recognized. He felt like he could smell something many meters away too, even though he didn't know how that was possible.

His eyesight seemed better as well. He noticed this in the darkened hallway and again when he dashed by blackened windows of the Computer Center. He often gazed in to see who was there, but he could never really see inside, even when he stuck his face up against the glass and cupped his hands around to block out the light. Now, as he breezed by, he could clearly see inside. Further, at some point he realized his glasses had fallen off and he didn't seem to need them anymore. But along with the better eyesight, everything seemed so very bright. The overheads felt like they burned holes into his skull. He found himself squinting and looking down while he ran.

But the biggest change of all was his anger. He was so angry now. And the smallest things made him angry. It was worse than simple anger. He felt almost insane with rage right now. He knew it was all part of the disease. But he also really didn't care. It felt strange that this didn't bother him. He would have been paralyzed by all of this... Before.

Really, nothing bothered him now... except for the urges. Those bothered him a lot.

Before this, he lived a life of regimentation and planning. He didn't have urges or yearnings. He took pleasure in his work and that was all he needed. His one desire in life was to improve to the point that others recognized him. In everything else he was careful and hesitant, never wanting to make noise. Now, he had overwhelming urges that he felt compelled to pursue, and with wild abandon: sex, violence, murder, and the hunger... For what he didn't know.

During all of this, he never connected the dots, assuming his urges, no matter how bothersome, were something that would pass. Then he came across a slight woman—he remembered her from the spa. She was hiding underneath a table, eyes owl-like, obviously hoping no one would see her. At first, he didn't see her; he smelled her.

He tried to ignore it, even running past her, but the glorious smell was too much to ignore. He halted, desiring to know what that smell was. No, he desperately needed to know. He pivoted on his heels and followed the unknown scent until he was upon the table. The woman's head swung up to catch a glimpse of him. She shrank back in terror. He shrank from her too when he realized what the scent was: he was smelling her, and he knew right then what he wanted desperately to do. And this so disgusted him, he almost puked right there. He pedaled back farther, away from the woman and her hiding place, just as another loony reached in and grabbed her.

Ágúst turned and continued his run, daring himself not to look back at that sight. He didn't want to admit it. He wouldn't acknowledge it. But he knew it, like everything else: he was a loony too.

Now on auto-pilot, he zoomed from hallway to stairwell to hallway, until he crashed through a final entrance and dashed the final stretch of hallway before he would be at the entrance to the aft anchor area. He could almost see it.

That was his whole purpose. He had only one mission, and that was the only thing that mattered. He was to drop the anchor and make sure that the auto-release mechanism didn't engage and the anchor chain held, slowing or stopping them before they hit the island. The whole ship was depending on him.

He rounded a pallet of recyclables and was five short strides from the door, and the realization of his mission. But he abruptly held up, stopping just short of his goal.

In front of him, blocking the entrance to the aft anchor

area, was a completely naked woman.

68
Engines

"You're kidding, right?" TJ huffed, as she first heard and then watched the group of demented rush toward them. *They didn't have time for this.*

She exhaled and then ran at them, targeting the first demented, who was oak-tree-sized, and like the others, wore a black jumper. Her immediate thought was that if she'd make like a bowling ball and knock this one pin down, some of others would tumble behind it. *With a little luck, because this demented was so big, maybe he'd take out all of the others.*

This supposition was more of the combo of intuition and observation. For reasons unknown to her at this moment, she had more dexterity and control over all her motor functions than the dementeds did over their own. Most dementeds appeared to be either lumbering or spasmodic, with the spasmos acting like they were running downhill and were easily tripped up. Rather than take them on one on one, and risk any of them getting through to Flavio or Wasano, she knew it would be better to trip up the whole group of them.

Just before she was in striking distance, TJ threw herself up and somewhat sideways into the air. But at the point of leaping, she twisted her body hard, reacting to another crazy who had pulled up quickly beside the big one—*the two pin was off kilter now and wouldn't automatically fall when she took out the one pin. She'd settle for a one-two split.*

She wasn't sure where these thoughts were coming from, or what exactly they meant, only that they were correct.

Her body moved more slowly in the air than she would have thought, and so she had to gesticulate more to get the second one. But this caused her to lose sight of her second target as her head and torso rolled around to face Wasano and Flavio, who gaped at her actions. When her right foot connected, she couldn't really see the impact, but she felt the hard bone of her ankle connect with the soft jowls of the number two demented's face, almost at the same time as all her body weight smashed into the big one.

She expected her forward motion to continue, toppling the big one, but was instead jarred to a sudden stop. Her body was forcibly wrenched down and then sideways. She felt the beast's giant arms clamp down around her, and then deftly fling her away from it and the rest of the horde. She was airborne again, this time traveling in the opposite direction.

Once more, she wasn't anxious or fearful about any of this—more like surprised. Just before she crashed hard against a wall of pipes, she saw the big demented barely acknowledge her. The beast turned only slightly, and then continued its barreling toward Wasano and Flavio, with others close behind.

A splash of stars filled TJ's field of vision; her head had struck the steel exterior ship-wall.

What just happened? she wondered. *The dementeds weren't supposed to move that way. They weren't supposed to react so quickly.*

Her legs were above her in an awkward position, her body contorted at an odd angle. She swung her feet down and around until they slapped the floor.

Droplets of liquid slid down her face. Blood? A disconnected set of her fingers wiped above her brow, her wet fingertips held up for inspection and confirmation that it was only her sweat. It was hot down here... At the same time, rather than the expected feelings of fatigue or injury, she felt invigorated. More so, she was enraged and ready to do battle, more than any time in her life.

The engine room roared its unstoppable rumble all around her—a mind-numbing rattle that infuriated her even more. And with this was a chorus of other sounds too: screams, growls and grunts, all coming from the horde attacking and the two men now fighting this band of dementeds. She glared at the hubbub like she wasn't a part of this, but her mind still analyzed her best target.

Upon seeing the big one beat down on Wasano with its giant paws, this vision lit a fire under her. She resolved then that they would lose, and therefore she would lose, if she didn't immediately help.

She quickly pulled herself up, using her elbow, already hooked around a cross-beam. The wooziness was sudden and struck all her senses. And yet she fought through it. Oddly enough, there wasn't any pain. Shouldn't I be in pain?

Before all of this, if her head had connected as solidly, she would have just stayed down and taken her time, making sure she didn't have a concussion—she was most certain that she did now, and yet she should have had deep flashes of pain. She felt none and had no worries about this or any of the other injuries she must have sustained. Instead of pain or worry, she was filled with more overwhelming waves of irrational anger: killing and maiming were the only things that seemed to offer her comfort. She would oblige these feelings.

Right beside TJ was a fire extinguisher, as if the ship handed it to her. She grabbed it, hoisted it high, and focused her sights on the biggest demented. The beast towered over the much smaller security man, who would lose this battle in seconds. She sprang forward, almost fell over before straightening herself up, and rushed to the back of the horde, ready to strike.

When she reached the group, she pile-drove the extinguisher's hefty base into the first demented she came upon—one away from the big one—striking the back of its head. She knew she hit hard, because she felt the crack through the extinguisher, and watched the demented crumple to the floor.

She lifted the extinguisher up high once again, intending to now target the largest demented's head. Using the unconscious body of the one she'd knocked out as a vault, she catapulted herself up and came down on her target, striking its head with much more violence than the last one.

Her body rattled back, and she landed on her feet directly behind the giant. The huge demented stopped, but didn't fall. It swung around and glared at her, as if the horrendous knock on the head was but a light slap from a fly-swatter. It fixed its red eyes upon her and howled a spittle-laced blast of air into her face.

~~~

"We'll be approaching the Nordeste Bank at any moment," boomed the captain over the radio microphone. This was an announcement to Wasano and his team to let them know they needed to do whatever they could to get to the engine shut-offs immediately. It was also meant for Ágúst, in hopes that he would chime in and let them know how he was doing on the anchor. Finally, he wanted to update Jean Pierre and Jessica too, even though they were busily working on a different console, with Buzz over the radios adding some instruction—
~~~

they were onto something, but Jörgen feared none of it would matter. They were all just about out of time.

Jörgen had finagled the stabilizers to steer them slightly north, toward the Nordeste Bank, but with half the resistance offered by one stabilizer, they were picking up speed again. If the engines didn't get shut down and the anchor dropped properly, they'd only have one option left: they'd have to brace for impact.

"What's their status, Dr. Simmons?" he asked.

"They're still stuck battling with the parasitics," Molly stated in her measured tone, eyes drilled into the big TV screen tilted from the far wall. It was far enough away that Jörgen couldn't see each of the little screens within a screen clearly. "I still don't see the officer by the anchor-thing."

Hans watched attentively from the entry of engineering, his back to the door. Earlier, he had been asked by the captain to check the door and make sure it was locked. The captain didn't—for good reason—trust that the man had properly secured the door after Wasano, Flavio and TJ had left. Hans had simply glanced at the door, assumed it was good, and then flipped around so he could watch what was happening next on the large monitors, and the console where the captain was working. His brother Franz was busying himself in another seat next to the captain, disinterested.

Jörgen furiously typed in commands. He still wasn't able to wrest control of the helm, and was fearful of turning off the automatic systems because they were the only ones running. He just didn't know what the hell was going on with the controls. There was a loud bang beside him. He stopped, fingers poised over the keyboard, and glared at Franz, who was spinning himself around in circles in the leather chair beside him, like some little kid bored to be visiting his father's office during *Take the Brat to Work Day*.

"Oops, sorry." Franz shot a demure glance at the captain. He rapped his feet onto the floor and stared at the screens in front of him. A red blinking light attracted his attention. Franz knew he probably should say something to the captain, but was fearful of garnering more ire. He'd already been a nuisance. A second red light started flashing in unison with the other.

~~~

TJ shot a glance at both men: Wasano was now swinging his large flashlight at other dementeds, connecting with one, and Flavio was knocking one wiry demented away with his wrench, while thwacking another with his work-glove weapon. Other dementeds attempted to push through openings in the melee to get at the only two non-infected people there. But there were too many for them to handle.

She glanced back at the big tree-of-a-demented, roaring at her, unfazed by her strike. She wished that she were battling an overweight blob of a passenger, rather than...

That's when it hit her. A latent memory flashed in her mind, back before she had become. It was a classic sci-fi movie called *The Blob*. Its star, Steve McQueen, used the cold of a fire extinguisher—like the one she held—to stop the blob. He froze the blob so that the other characters could get away. *Maybe this would work too.*

She flicked the safety pin out, clutched the handle, pointed the hose and squeezed. A white spray of liquid billowed out, splashing the giant demented directly in the face.

The demented became statue-like, his mouth gaping, now full of foam. Its head then listed, as if it was disconnecting from its neck. Then it righted itself. Its mouth closed, squishing out the white chemical spray. It slowly fixed its sights back on her, but she sprayed again, catching him once again right in the face.
~~~

It worked.

She held down on the lever and sprayed the giant demented again, just for good measure, followed by each demented in the horde, one after the other.

The results were the same: one by one the dementeds received a blast of cold white spray, first on their heads and then on their faces as they turned to see what this was. And one by one, after receiving the blast in their faces, they stopped, as if each of their internal go-switches had been flipped off.

Finally, she released the handle, stopping the spray.

The two men were no longer fighting. They watched, stunned like the dementeds. Their faces were almost clown-like: clenched and serious, but covered in splatters of white as well; their weapons fixed in the air, eyes riveted on their near-motionless targets.

"What are they doing?" Wasano huffed. He was mostly covered in white spray, over red splotches of blood; one of those splotches oozed red over the white.

Wasano remained still, back almost pressed to the wall. But Flavio marched forward to examine the dementeds himself, as if he had to convince his eyes what he was now seeing.

Except for their rapid breathing, each demented was stationary on its feet, though wobbling from side to side, looking as if they might fall over at any moment. Their faces were slackening with each second, mouths slinging open. Their reddish eyes glazed over. Their chests heaved unabated, faster even. "It's the cold," TJ replied.

One by one, the dementeds started to fall to the floor, their eyes closing after they hit. And then, as if it were normal, they all fell into a sleep. *They were hibernating.*

"I should announce on radio," Wasano breathed several long breaths, "the cold stops them."

"We must get to other engine," Flavio said as if this

were the normal course of their mission. He stepped over each of the sleeping dementeds and shuffled down the metal walkway. TJ followed, still holding the fire extinguisher, with Wasano behind her on the radio.

Very quickly, they were through another hatch and into the next engine room.

Wasano identified the shut-off button and rushed to it while Flavio and TJ kept an eye out for more dementeds, even though TJ said she didn't smell anything.

Wasano held up his palm to slap the big red button, but before he could hit it, the rumble of the engines hitched and then shut down.

The engines did this on their own, without their help.

69

Down With The Ship

"I think they were successful, Captain," Dr. Molly Simmons announced jubilantly. "The two men are high-fiving each other. The symptomatic woman, Mr. Bonaventure's wife, looks... bored."

Jörgen didn't look up. He didn't need to. The shuddering, followed by the absence of rumbling below his feet, told him the engines were powering down. He glanced up at the same monitor Molly had been studying and caught the screen showing the aft anchor. It should have been released by now. "First Officer Helguson, please report." He bellowed into the radio. Staticky feedback was the only reply.

"What does that light mean?" Franz begged from beside him. He'd been as quiet as a church mouse since being scolded.

Jörgen glanced at a screen beside his and its two flashing lights. On his screen, he pulled up the data, but the reason for the lights didn't immediately make sense. *We've run out of fuel?*

"Captain? Ah, you need to see this," Molly alerted, her

voice fluttering.

"Oy, what is that guy doing?" asked Hans, who had stepped away from the engineering entrance and padded closer to the screen, a couple of feet from Molly.

All eyes studied the monitor, and the images none of them expected to see.

Jörgen squinted, thinking he wasn't seeing clearly. He typed in a quick command and brought up the questionable video feed onto his own screen. The video images now filled up his entire monitor. His mouth sagged.

It was Ágúst Helguson, the first officer on whose actions their very survival depended. He was standing hunched over the anchor release assembly, staring into space, drooling. In his hand he held something.

"Another light is blinking, captain," announced Franz.

Jörgen craned his neck back at that monitor, to his right, and watched a number accelerate…

50—150—350.

It was the counter announcing the length of aft anchor chain spilling out. But it wasn't stopping, as it was supposed to.

He turned back to his video feed of Ágúst. He zoomed in farther to look at Ágúst's hands and confirmed what he was holding. "It's the release pin."

Jörgen was gut-shot with realization. His first officer not only released the anchor, which he was supposed to do, he also pulled the pin that would prevent the anchor chain from stopping when it hit its max length. The anchor would now automatically release all of its chain, as it was designed to do, so as to prevent any damage to the ship. That meant even if the anchor had snagged the Nordeste Bank, as they had hoped, it wouldn't then stop and hold. And that meant it would do nothing to slow them down.

There was now no way to avert their crashing into the island's shore.

"Oy, look at the naked woman. She's a looker for a red-eye."

Jörgen slowly turned to look up at the overhead and immediately found the video feed that Hans had called their attention to. It was the feed outside the entrance to the aft anchor assembly. In the middle of the screen stood, slightly hunched over, a naked woman he instantly recognized. It was Eloise Carmichael, the woman who had killed her fourth husband and was presumed to be washed overboard. She looked very much alive and she was staring with determination at the camera.

She is staring directly at us, he thought. It was as if she knew they were looking at her. She was now one of the infecteds, although she didn't look completely crazy. She tilted her head; it was the look of a predator considering its prey, from a distance.

And even though the color was far from perfect in this video feed, there was no question that Eloise's eyes were blazing the same blood-red color that coated much of her nude body.

All four of them were so focused on the monitor and the bizarre vision in it, they didn't even notice, until it was much too late, the two crazies that burst into engineering. The door that was supposed to have been locked by Hans when Wasano, TJ and Flavio left was left open.

The two crazies crashed through the partially open door, screeching animal-like brays and immediately targeted one person: Molly, who was now closest to the door.

The captain sprang from his chair and just before they could get to her, he struck first, tackling both crazies to the floor.

~~~
~~~

Hans dashed the other way, toward his brother Franz, who was already shrinking into a murky area on the other side of the room. Molly assumed because Hans had missile-locked on his brother, he didn't see she was in his way until he was upon her. Yet, using a shoulder, he blasted through her, knocking her to the floor. Her cane clattered against the other side of engineering.

Hans didn't even look back—she knew this because Hans' locomotion spun her around in his direction, away from the attack. He snagged Franz, who still had his blanket wrapped around him, and they both grabbed the darkest corner of the room, in an attempt to hide behind the overhanging end of the large three-station console the captain had just been using.

Stars filled Molly's field of vision, though if her head had hit something other than the rubber strip hiding some electrical cords, she might not been able to attempt to recover so quickly. It was knowing her life was in immediate peril that fueled her to move quicker than she could remember doing over the last several years.

She pushed herself up from the floor onto her knees and did a quick assessment, while her cane-hand blindly searched for its crutch in vain. Her mind reminded her hand that the cane had hit the other side of the room. It wasn't important now.

The two parasitics appeared to be focused on the captain. Both were pounding on him and one, she was shocked to see, looked to be biting his neck. The captain's pleas for help came out as low gurgles, while one of his hands weakly struck at the biter.

That should have been me, she thought.

But she could see the captain was gone, or would be soon, and so would her only opportunity to move while the parasitics were occupied.

She couldn't race for the exit, because she'd have to run around them, and even with her cane, she couldn't outrun

them.

She reflexively turned in the other direction to confirm what she already knew: there was only one way out. She saw the anti-Semite who had just mowed her down when attempting to get away. His eyes were wide, like a little child, afraid for his own skin; his brother was partially covered in his blanket behind him.

There was no getting out of this.

Then the certainty of what she needed to do clicked in her brain, like the solution to a math problem.

She bounded up, wobbled, but regained the leg strength she needed to get to her target, a few feet from the captain. She ratcheted forward, but she couldn't help but throw a quick glance at the captain first. He lay bleeding on the floor as the parasitics tore into him further.

Molly lumbered the last couple of steps to the wall, below the big monitor they'd all been gazing at moments ago. It was on that monitor that she had seen her only salvation, offered to her by the symptomatic wife of Mr. Bonaventure.

Molly had eyed the fire extinguisher on their wall after she witnessed TJ spray the parasitics in the engine room, and then the security man announced on the radio about how cold from the fire extinguisher affected parasitics.

Molly did exactly what she witnessed TJ doing, although she had to clutch the heavy extinguisher against her chest: she pulled the pin, squeezed the handle, and pointed the nozzle and its billowing spray in the direction of the murdering parasitics.

Unfortunately, she just didn't have a good hold on it and either the pressure from the spray pushed at her or the thing was just too damned heavy and she was too damned weak. It fell out of her hands and clanged down onto the floor, and she tumbled over once again. This time, she hit her side on the floor, and she hit hard. It knocked all the wind out of her.

She rolled over onto her back, dazed, expecting that at

any moment, one or both of the parasitics would be upon her.

A flash of a shadow shot past her, but from the other direction. The shadow grunted, as if dragging something heavy.

She tilted her head to the grunting and was surprised to see it was that obnoxious German, Hans, who had knocked her aside moments ago. He finally grew some balls, after she had done all of the heavy lifting. He was emptying the fire extinguisher she'd dropped onto the two already incapacitated—thanks to her—parasitics who had killed their captain.

"Save some for later," she croaked. Her voice sounded strange to her, like it was someone else's.

A loud noise on the other side of the room diverted her attention to the front of the room.

The other German brother, Franz, was standing before the door, which she had guessed had been closed. *Finally*.

Molly laid her head back down and took in a long sigh of relief.

A shadow enveloped her and she screwed her eyes into the dark face staring down at her, features not clear because of the room's low light. She could definitely make out the stupid I'm-proud-of-myself grin plastered over his demented mug. His hand was thrust out, a surprising gesture of help.

"Damn Jew. You're one tough old broad, ain't you?"

Yes, she guessed she was.

70

Rewired

She accepted his hand, and he easily hoisted her up as if her weight was that of a leaf. She wobbled—she was doing a lot of that lately—while standing and feared if the ship pitched or rolled in the slightest, she'd fall over. As much as she hated holding his hand, she had to wait until the wooziness passed before she could let go. Her spine tingled and her skin crawled at the feel of his sweaty mitt.

"Thank you," she said. Her eyes were closed, and her voice barely a whisper.

She felt the familiar form of her cane being placed into her other hand. At first she shuddered at the unexpected act of kindness. But she didn't question it and gladly shifted her weight onto it, feeling instantly stronger.

"How did you know about the fire extinguisher?"

She finally let go of Hans' hand and flicked open her eyes, but didn't make eye contact with him.

"If you hadn't only been staring at the naked woman, you wouldn't have asked me."

“Well, at least I...” Hans finished his sentence in a mumble, or she simply tuned him out.

Her focus was now on his brother Franz, who had paddle-stepped over to the two parasitics, who were in some sort of hibernative state now, just like the ones they had witnessed on the screen, after Mrs. Bonaventure had blasted them with her fire extinguisher. These two were lying beside the barely moving form of the captain.

“Wait,” she huffed, and then waddled carefully over to the captain. Using her cane, she lowered herself down to her knees.

She could see there was nothing they could do for him. He was violently ripped apart and surely dead.

“Wow! Look at that, Hans!” Franz said beside her. “They clawed the ever-living shit out of his neck.” She scowled at the young man, angry at the man’s insensitive comments. The younger man wasn’t interested. With a blanket shrouding his shoulders, he gawked at the captain, just like a typical little boy who’d just witnessed something gory, and liked it.

The radio chirped at them, “Captain, are you there? We need you to try something.”

Molly glanced at the radio and then back to the captain

Again, her spine tingled as Hans sidled up beside her, rubbing his leg against her shoulder. “What now?” the dumb buffoon asked her, as if she would know.

With her eyes fixed on the captain she replied, “Maybe we can’t do anything, at least about the controls, but we can at least tell them their captain is dea—”

Just then, Captain Jörgen gurgled something. His throat was barely held together by the thin strands of tissue that threatened to let loose. She certainly didn’t think he could speak. She leaned over him. "I'm here, Captain," she said, her ear almost touching his lips.

"Tell the... About the fuel... Tell them use... thrust...” His voice trailed off to nothing. She waited, hoping he’d finish, while she held her own breath. After a few long moments of silence she realized he wasn't going to say anything more because he was dead.

"Yeah, that makes sense," Franz said, on the other side of the captain's body. His loud words were jarring. "The gas was off. I mean the red warning light said the gas was off or out."

She had thought the kid was just stupid, but he did have a brain.

"Captain, are you there?" the radio bellowed.

Molly gritted her teeth and clasped one hand onto Hans' arm and the other on her cane, using both as support. Then, pushing herself up and then forward, almost tumbling again, she raced over to the console, falling into one of the three swivel chairs. She spun to face the microphone and punched the transmit button, her face thrust into it. "This is Dr. Molly Simmons. I'm afraid your captain is dead. But he wanted me to tell you that we had run out of petrol, and I believe he said you should use the thrusters, whatever those are."

~~~

Jessica's head was loosely cradled in her hands while she sobbed, "Oh my God, not the captain."

Jean Pierre put a hand on her shoulder and squeezed. Then he let go. He let a few seconds go by before he said in a firm voice, "First Officer Mínervudóttir, I need you to focus on the problem at hand. Now that we have most helm controls, I need you to confirm our fuel supply."

Jessica stared at him, her eyes irritated and watery. She sniffled and asked the question they all thought, "How could we run out of fuel?"

"Have no idea. Doesn't matter right now. Check the
~~~

controls."

"Aye, sir," she snapped, and began typing on the console she had just activated, while Jean Pierre stepped lively to the microphone.

They had both been working furiously for the last few minutes, and even surprised themselves at being able to somehow rewire the only other undamaged console, bringing it back into service. But they still couldn't get control of the rudder. They had limited control of the engines now, but without fuel they couldn't stop their forward motion into the island. "That's it!" she exclaimed. "I think I understand, Staff Captain."

"Go," Jean Pierre gave Jessica his full attention, while he hovered over Ted, who continued his vigil at the radio.

"It's the fuel! I still don't know how we could run out of the heavy fuel." Jean Pierre's head nodded in affirmation, knowing where she was going now. "However, we still have our MGO."

"Do we have thruster controls?" Jean Pierre huffed. *Could it be that simple?*

Jessica smiled, now completely sure of what to do, completing the taps of her new commands into the working console.

"Please explain," Ted begged. David, behind him, also nodded at Jean Pierre.

Jean Pierre held up one hand and punched the microphone button with the other.

"Thank you, Dr. Simmons. Please hang on. We think we understand the captain's command." *His very last command,* the thought burst his bubble of excitement just then.

At that moment, they could all feel the rumble of the ship's engines reverberating through the ship's hull beneath them. And almost as quickly as they felt the rumble, they could feel the gentle nudge of them being pushed forward. Ever so lightly at first, and then more prominently a few seconds later.

"The captain must have realized," Jean Pierre explained to Ted and David as well as the ship, as he also held the microphone down, "that we had run out of heavy fuel for some reason, but that we still had MGO—a different kind of fuel that we also carry—located in a different tank. And if we could get control of our port-side thrusters, we could steer away from the island."

"You mean we're saved?" Ted and David bellowed at the same time, almost sounding as one voice.

Jean Pierre waited to answer this and when they felt the movement hard to their starboard side, a giant grin enveloped his face. "Yes, I think so," he finally answered, and breathed out a long sigh of relief.

Jessica's head shot up and she joined them in watching their view of the island, which had filled the entirety of the bridge windows. The island slowly moved from right to left, until after a few seconds, there was nothing in front of their bow.

They joined in the cheering they heard on the radio. But theirs was far more muted. Still, they would enjoy this hard fought success, but just for a moment. They all knew it would be short-lived. Their next battle would be their hardest.

71

A Pause

They weren't going to take any time to lick their nearly mortal wounds. They didn't have time.

Somehow, they had averted a complete disaster by narrowly avoiding collision with São Miguel. Yet their losses were mind-numbing: their captain and many crew and passengers were dead or missing. Bodies littered the ship, like discarded debris from the morning after an epic New Year's Eve bash.

They had some control of their helm. Having one functional bridge console and the use of their thrusters gave them very limited maneuverability. And for now, they were gliding at just under a knot, with their engines off. Jean Pierre had cut off the supply of fuel to their stuck-on engines—they still couldn't figure out why they were like this—to temporarily stall their screws and with them, their immediate worry about running into any other islands. At least for now.

These solutions felt to all of them like small Band-Aids applied to a giant gaping hole in their collective guts. And if their ship were to ultimately survive this apocalypse, each knew they'd have to eventually deal with their most devastating of injuries: they had lost total control of the interior of their ship, with the only exception being the bridge, engineering and a few rooms or cabins they had radio contact with. None of them had any idea how or when they would regain control anytime soon.

To complicate their troubles, the bridge was mostly blind, and they were unable to regain the video feeds on their two working consoles. At least they could hear what they couldn't see via Deep's regular reporting. He radioed constant updates, laced with many verbal flourishes, describing all of the gruesome images flashing before him from the ship's working cameras.

From his reports, they gathered that it was still chaos outside their secured areas: enraged parasitics—Dr. Simmons coined the term for infecteds appearing violent—still dashed around the public and crew areas. The parasitics chased, maimed or killed their fellow passengers and crew, just as they had done for the last few hours. Some of the parasitics even appeared to be eating their victims.

The only good news was that the incidents of attacks appeared to be dwindling as most of the survivors were now hiding or were hunkered down somewhere, waiting for the crisis to pass. The ship was huge and there were quite a few hiding places for the survivors. It was the survivors on which they now focused their collective attention.

While Jessica was tirelessly working to regain control of another console under the direction of Buzz on one of the portables, Jean Pierre, Ted and David were on the base-unit attempting to identify crew and passengers and to help them find safe places around the ship. Deep continued calling out the potential perils to all involved from the MR.

They communicated with crew members who had radios—many had been listening to the drama unfold before them—and told them what they needed to know about those who were infected, and how to stay away from them. It appeared that if they could get to a cabin or other clear room, simply locking their doors was enough to keep the parasitics back. Ultimately the infected person would grow tired or would so damage themselves from incessantly pounding on the door, it would stop and run to some other location. Many of the crew were trapped, but at least safe. And because it was still insanity out there, they remained where they were until some help could be arranged or they had somehow muted the threat. They would deal with that part later, they all decided.

Ted and David did their best by manning the big port-side table in the bridge with the deck plans. When a group made themselves known on the radio, Jean Pierre would call out the location, and they'd mark down the number of survivors using a black wax pencil. They also marked down reports of those hiding or those still out in the open but headed to someplace identified as safe. These were indicated by an arrow. Reports of parasitics were marked in red with their number. An arrow was added if the parasitics were on the move, showing their direction.

With this system, they were able to track the location of survivors and parasitics, so they could visually keep track of each group. Each survivor was told to hold tight; they'd be retrieved later, when they figured out what to do about the parasitics.

After a while, they were all beginning to feel like they were gaining an upper hand in the chaos. And within an hour, there were few crew or passengers they could help, at least over the radio.

It wasn't long before Ted and David began to feel like third wheels to the process. Because of the few frustrating moments early on, when neither knew a location, Jean Pierre decided to relieve them. He grabbed a portable and took residence at the giant table with now more than a hundred scribbles in red and black pencil littering all thirteen deck plans.

Meanwhile, each time Ted put pressure on his damaged ankle, by moving or just standing, he'd unconsciously grunt or groan. David offered that now would be a good opportunity to thoroughly check out Ted's injury.

They proceeded over to the captain's chair, the only other unoccupied seat on the bridge, and David carefully examined Ted's ankle. Though not a doctor, as a child, David found himself helping his fellow Auschwitz survivors with all sorts of various physical maladies. Because of what he learned, he became pretty good at properly identifying and patching up injuries, using whatever was on hand.

"It's a bad sprain, but not broken," he told Ted.

Using strips torn from a blue bathroom towel, he tightly wrapped Ted's swollen ankle. It wasn't pretty, but Ted could now hobble around, with fewer grunts and groans.

With the added mobility and feeling unneeded, Ted was even more anxious to leave. He desperately wanted to see his wife, who was still somewhere in one of the engine areas. He didn't want to wait any longer to see her. And when he did finally see her, he would hold her tight and not let her go. After thinking he'd lost her, he was practically going mad himself to make this happen.

"It must be killing you to be locked in here, while she's out there?" David asked, mostly to give him a chance to talk about it. David's wife Evie often reminded him that talking out those things you had no control over helped you feel a sense of control. He had done a lot of talking with his wife over the years.

Ted lifted his head and shot him an embarrassed glare. "That obvious, huh?"

David nodded and smiled. He didn't need to say anything more. Besides genuinely wanting to help Ted, he figured talking about it might also help the man better focus on whatever it was they would be tasked to do next. He didn't hold it against Ted that his head wasn't altogether there: if he'd thought Evie had died, he'd be beside himself.

Of course, he didn't know Evie's status. At least not yet.

"I just keep remembering her fall, seeing her fear, and knowing I could do nothing but watch. This very thing had happened to me before... I lost my first wife and a child. And when I thought it happened again, I swore I'd do what I could to protect TJ. And with our spending so much time apart for so many years, it just seems ridiculous now that I know she's alive and she's so close, yet we're not together. I just don't want us to spend another moment apart."

"I get that. Evie and I have had our long periods of separation too, and of course, I really miss her now..." David stopped and glanced down, collecting himself.

"I'm sorry. You don't even know she's safe yet." Ted's shoulders drooped, and his pensive look turned into a glower. "I'm being selfish."

"Nonsense. Evie's alive. She's too much of a pain in my side to pre-decease me." David snickered at this, not sure Ted knew it was a joke. "Guess you spend so much time together as a couple over the years, you feel like a part of you is missing when you're apart."

"Except when they drive you crazy, huh?" Ted said with a wry smile, obviously doing his best to add a little humor to their otherwise serious conversation.

"That's what I love about Evie. She knows what buttons to push. I've long since ceased being a mystery to her and that just suits me fine."

Ted studied him with scrutinizing eyes. "Listen, David. I appreciate what you're doing. But I have to do something—hell, anything—right now or I'm going to go bat-shit crazy just sitting here. Either I find something useful to do to help here, or I'm leaving to go find my wife, regardless of how stupid that may sound." Ted pushed himself up out of the captain's chair, suppressing an under-his-breath-grunt.

"I'll go with you. But let's first ask the staff captain… I'll bet there's something we can do just outside this bridge."

David put an arm around Ted to help him along the short distance to the port-side bridge. Ted gladly accepted and they waddled to the front-facing area of the deck-plan table, where Jean Pierre was slunk with a black pencil touching the white area of the Regal Crown Lounge on deck 11. His ear was pressed against speaker. He nodded every now and then. He wrote the number sign and then "6" with an arrow pointed to the Concierge Club.

He'd just put out another of his many calls to any who hadn't checked in yet.

"Okay. Just remember that curiosity killed the dog." David couldn't help but smile at that one. "You hold tight until we send some crew out there."

After the pause was long enough, Ted asked, "Jean Pierre, do you want us to go up there? If not that, we'll do something else that the ship needs. David and I need something to do. Don't care if it's dangerous. We're going flipping stir-crazy here, just waiting."

David chimed in before the staff captain could answer. "We want to help, but we're kind of limited with our lack of knowledge about the ship."

Jean Pierre looked up, flashing a forced smirk at each man. "You're probably not going to like it, but I do have a suggestion."

"The answer is yes, whatever it is," Ted burst out.

"I need you both to go to the next door cabin, number 8000, on your right." He handed Ted his key card. "You'll need this to get in. It's a luxury cabin and it's one of the only places on the ship that has a satellite connection to the outside world's television broadcasts. It would be good to know what's going on out there, as we'll eventually need to make land at some point."

"Why wouldn't we enjoy luxuriating in the Queen's Suite

and watching TV, just so we can soak in more bad news?"

"It should be a piece of pie, but it would be helpful to know what's going on." Jean Pierre didn't crack a smile, even after his bad idiom. He scoured the notes hand-written all over his table, as if he'd missed something, and then looked back up again. "Please be careful when you leave the bridge: the, ah... parasitics, are still running up and down the hallways."

They both nodded, each remembering the occasional screech running by the bridge's entrance.

"Perhaps, before we step outside, you could ask our eye-in-the-sky if our coast is clear?" David asked and then looked to Ted. "You ready?"

Ted had removed his hat and was scratching his temple, focused in the other direction at something on the bridge. "I was just thinking... Maybe we could secure the area around the bridge entrance and 8000 beforehand, so any of us can come and go and not worry about getting eaten."

"What did you have in mind?" Jean Pierre asked.

"How about those dead consoles? I figure two or three of those, standing side-by-side, should block the hallway access on each side. Maybe we even shore them up with tables or chairs from the luxury cabin?"

Jean Pierre smiled. It was the first time they saw him smile since their ship was overrun. "That's a great idea. I'll help you drag them to the hatch. Then we'll have Deep tell us how it looks and when it's clear for you guys to set up the obstructions."

They all worked quickly, dragging the five dead consoles, and a few heavy pieces from the busted conference table lying in the wrecked conference room. After getting the okay from Deep on the radio, who said he hadn't seen anyone in the deck 8 hall in the last twenty minutes or so, they cracked open the hatch.

Each man carried a hefty broken leg from the conference table, which made a substantial club.

David edged his head out the door first, listening for any sign that he needed to retreat.

He slipped out the door, followed closely by Ted. Both held their makeshift clubs above their heads, ready to pummel any crazy who threatened to attack them. Even though they were just told by Deep that their hallways were clear, David was still surprised at how quiet it was. He wasn't sure, really, what he was expecting… maybe some sounds in the distance or signs of what had been going on the last few hours. His eyes were immediately drawn to a splatter of blood on and around cabin number 8001, right next to their destination 8000.

He turned his head in the other direction, towards Eloise's Royal Suite and saw the slaughterhouse of blood staining the carpet in front, like some macabre welcome mat.

Because of his leg, Ted stood watching and listening at both ends of the hallway split, making sure nothing approached, while David and Jean Pierre hoisted one console after another and placed them into each hallway. One blockade was created on their side of Eloise’s cabin, giving them almost the whole length from stern to an open area contiguous to the bridge. The other blockade was built in between 8000 and the next cabin, 8001.

David and Ted would shore it up a little better with tables and chairs from their luxury cabin destination, 8000. Until then, it was already a vast improvement. All they were looking to do was to fortify each sufficiently to slow down the parasitics enough to allow any one of them to escape back to the safety of either the bridge or the Queen’s Suite.

Jean Pierre left them, not wanting to leave the bridge hatch open any longer than he had to. Plus, he wanted to get back on the radio and see if he could guide more of his passengers and crew to safety. They agreed whomever was on the outside would pound three times on the hatch or use the intercom button when they wanted in again.

David verbalized a suggestion that they use the

mattresses from the cabin to block anyone's view, and to further buttress their blockades. They could then move those aside when someone who was not trying to kill them wanted in.

Jean Pierre nodded in agreement, thanked them and then shut the hatch, locking it in place.

Just after David and Ted stepped into the luxury cabin, Jean Pierre's voice sounded on Ted's radio, asking for an update from Deep.

Because they wanted to get the mattresses out onto the barricades quickly and they wanted to get back, as instructed, to watch for news updates the cabin's satellite TV, neither heard Deep's reply after Ted turned his radio's volume down.

If they did, they would have heard Deep say, "Sir, I can't seem to find any of the crazies. It's like they all disappeared."

72

More Bad News

They double-timed their gathering up each of the suite's two king-sized mattresses, pushing one up against each barricade. Once the suite's door closed, offering security, Ted and David dropped themselves into the lush couch in front of the suite's giant TV. Ted punched the remote's "On" button, filling the cabin with the staticky sounds of a television not receiving a signal, when they heard a loud click from the entrance. Both their heads snapped in that direction, and they sprang from their seats.

"Oh Christ, Officer," Ted gasped, "You gave us both heart attacks." He remained where he stood in front of the couch, a little unsteady on his one good ankle, and took in the officer standing just inside the suite's entrance.

David, in the swift motion of someone much younger, had hopped from his seat, grabbed his table-leg weapon and taken a couple of steps toward the door before Ted's words left his mouth.

It was Ágúst Helguson, from the bridge crew, standing

just inside their cabin, looking almost embarrassed, as if he had interrupted something. But then Ted realized it wasn't embarrassment he was seeing; there was something not right about this man.

"How did you get inside? We locked the door," David bellowed over the TV static. He took another step toward the officer, while he repositioned his hands for a better grip on his weapon. Ted could see he was getting ready for a battle.

The officer held up his key card, in answer. It seemed like a casual *Through the door, you dummies* point, without actually saying this. He said nothing else, keeping his head down, sunglasses on, pointed at the floor.

The man looked pale, like he was suffering from a head cold, and Ted had to remind himself that this man had reddish eyes earlier. He was partially symptomatic with the Rage disease. Had he turned completely and become parasitic like the others? Ted frantically scanned the area around his feet for his own weapon. It wasn't there.

Then he remembered, in his exuberance to get to a seat and take a load off, he had forgotten he had left his club on the dining room table. He glared at it, at least half the distance to the potentially crazed officer. And he wasn't moving very fast right now. If this guy went crazy on them, he'd have nothing to defend himself or David—not that David needed much defending—except for the remote control he now cradled in his right hand.

The officer held up a thumb and forced a weak smile, lifting his head up slightly. Then he burst into the suite's bathroom, slamming the door behind him.

Ted glanced at David and David glared back before giving him a shrug of his shoulders and a smirk. Then they heard the officer heave and both nodded. They understood—the poor guy was just sick, not crazy. They were just learning about the Rage disease and how it worked in humans. Perhaps it simply made some of the infected sick, but didn't give them all the symptoms, including the aggressive part of the disease. He so wanted to know more and felt like their survival would depend on it. Finding out what was going on in the world would help. He wasn't sure what they should do next with the sick officer.

David lifted his head slightly, a half-nod. "Why don't you find a channel that works and I'll stand guard by the bathroom door, in case our officer comes out feeling a little charged up."

Ted nodded back. But rather than sitting down, he hustled over to the dining area table and snatched up his weapon. He heard David try to hold back a snicker unsuccessfully, as Ted lumbered back to his seat. He'd not let go of this until they were free of this threat, or he found a better weapon.

Ted glanced back once more to the bathroom door, behind him. David, whose club was now resting on a shoulder, busily inspected the bathroom door. Feeling satisfied, Ted returned his focus on the TV and the remote.

He remembered the first channel was always the ship's channel, and it was likely to show nothing, especially now without any content to broadcast, nor crew to operate it. The next few channels were cable channels and they had pre-recorded content: movies, television series, and some reality TV show called The Colony. Ted realized pretty quick there were far more satellite channels on this TV than the one in their cabin, even when they were fully operational. He continued his progression forward, pressing the channel-up button until he found a news channel. He let out a deep sigh when the bad news poured in, like a fire hydrant opened up during the summer time.

A big part of him—the unrealistic side—had still held out a small glimmer of hope that it wasn't as bad as his logical side knew it was. He kept telling himself that maybe it was isolated or somehow different outside of their ship.

It wasn't.

BBC World News showed video after video of cities damaged or destroyed: some beat to hell and barely standing, perhaps because of the tsunamis; some still burning, with uncontrollable fires; and some completely gone, as if they were leveled by a nuclear-bomb-like explosion. And then there were the bodies. Most of the videos showed them everywhere. All but one video chronicled the aftermath of what places looked like after the event, whatever it was, that caused the destruction. British reporters described what each saw or vignettes from survivors they'd interviewed.

But Ted wanted more about the infected.

The next channel was CNN. They had some of the same videos, and a few different, but showing the same level of destruction, all while a panel of guests argued the cause of this apocalypse. The consensus was climate change. Ted changed the channel.

On Fox News, the same video was played over and over again, on a loop, all while a talking head with psychology accolades after her name droned on. The video showed people running down a street in London, away from something. At first Ted didn't see it, but then after the third or fourth loop, he caught several of the red-eyed parasitics among the group; they weren't running away, but doing the chasing.

It was confirmation of what he already knew: this disease wasn't just local to their ship and what the media was calling Rage was turning animals and people into crazed killers.

It still wasn't enough. He wanted—no, needed—more examples, more information so they could figure out how to survive this.

He flipped up to the next channel, which was Sky News, hoping they had more videos about the crazies and more information about the infection.

"Any details on the chyrons or just sensationalism like the videos?" David asked, startling Ted, who turned to see he had wandered from the other side of the suite and was now sitting on the arm of a chair closest to the door. His shoulders were still pointed toward the bathroom, while his head was riveted to the TV.

Ted had been trying to read the chyrons while watching the videos too, which is why he'd first missed the parasitics in the video until it had looped back a couple of times. "Only that the mayor of London was killed by one of his aides, who had become parasitic from Rage. They were at first calling it a hate crime because of the mayor's religion, which was laughable..." He trailed off and added, "Really nothing that we don't already know. Anything more from our sick officer friend?"

"Nope. He's been quiet in there. I think he was embarrassed by his queasy stomach. But I'm still watching, just in case—Oh, look at that one." David pointed to the screen. His whole body was now trained at the TV.

It was a live news feed, coming from Paris, from one of their local correspondents. The camera was on her and a street below in the distance, crossing over the Seine. It looked familiar because Ted had been there several times. There was some sort of blockade down the middle of the bridge, made up of clusters of black. But before it could focus on the blockade, the camera swept past to a mass of movement beyond.

It was some sort of mob, which appeared to be moving toward the blockade.

Ted turned up the volume so that they both could hear it better.

"You can see police below us in their riot gear on the historic Pont Norte-Dame." The camera had refocused on the reporter's pretty face, and then it zoomed into the black clusters, which were obviously made up of police in riot gear, standing behind human-sized shields they were holding up. "A large group of Les Fous, which have swept the city, are headed to the Latin Quarter. The Gendarmerie are attempting to hold them back. You can see Les Fous now..."

"What the hell is lay faux?" David asked.

"It means crazy people in French," Ted responded, matter-of-factly.

Les Fous hit the blockade and were momentarily stopped. Then more piled into the line, some climbing over others, the blockade broke, and many of the military police fell, their batons flailing at their attackers.

"Oh dear," bellowed the French reporter. "They weren't able to stop Les Fous. The same thing happened in London earlier today."

Ted and David glowered at the screen as they watched the surreal images of infected Parisians pouring over La Pont, attacking everyone who moved, and even those who didn't. There were just too many of them as they then fanned into the Latin Quarter en masse.

David now was leaning against the back of the couch, mesmerized like Ted, when they heard a loud crash behind them. David spun around, almost hitting Ted's head with his club. Ted sprang off the couch, this time with his own club held high.

It was the front door they had heard.

It was still closed, though the bathroom door was wide open now, and Ágúst Helguson wasn't there. He must have just left.

David was already running for the door, Ted not far behind, as the TV continued to report on the mayhem in Paris.

David yanked open the door and burst through in one motion. And Ted caught up to the door, just before it crashed closed again.

David had stopped just beyond the entrance, first scanning starboard and then forward, doubtless checking out their two blockades. He hollered, much too loudly, "It's the starboard one." Ted could see it too. The officer had pushed aside the mattress and knocked over a console.

David dashed to the broken blockade, which was the only thing slowing down any crazies that might come at them from the starboard hallway.

Ted limped in the same direction, swinging his head forward, until he had passed that blockade. He could have sworn he'd heard footsteps running away.

~~~

"Still, you can't find any parasitics anywhere?" Jean Pierre asked again. It had been over half an hour since Deep had reported their conspicuous absence.

"No, sir. I'm telling you they're all gone. I still don't see any of them running around anywhere. It's like they left the ship."

"We should be so lucky… Okay, Deep. I need you to go back to checking each and every camera feed on the ship and cross off the places you can verify they're definitely not there. We'll do a physical search if we have to. But we must know where they are. Until then, this is for all personnel listening to my voice. Until we know the location of the parasitics, do not leave your position. Repeat, stay where you are."

Jean Pierre let go of the transmit button, considering what else he could say or do right now.

"Staff Captain?" It was Deep, once again. "Hold on." His normally even voice sounded harried.

"Sir… I see a group racing toward the bridge on the port side... I can't tell if they're human or parasitic."

~~~

David and Ted tugged hard at the king-sized mattress, so they could get through, all the while shooting quick glances down the hallway. There was no sign of the officer.

They moved the tilted-over console back into place. It had been moved aside by the one man, even though they struggled nudging it back into place between the wall and the other console. They then righted the mattress, setting it up more snugly on each side, so there was less access room. Finally, they breathed giant sighs of relief. That's when they heard the growing sounds of rapid footsteps. Lots of them.

"They're coming from the other side," David blurted, but didn't wait for Ted's acknowledgment; scooping up his club from the floor, he raced back to the port side blockade. Ted humphed, then attempted to move as fast as his damaged ankle would allow, pulling up to David a few moments later, behind this blockade's giant mattress. Ted peeked through a crack between it and the far port wall and saw at least a dozen people jogging toward them.

"I see at least a dozen people," Ted huffed. "Can't tell if they're parasitic-looking or not. Let's get back into the bridge: it looks like they can move heavy weights easier than we can." He backed up from the mattress a few quick stutter-steps, when David held up his hand, signaling for Ted to stop and wait.

A muffled thump sounded from the other side and the mattress shuddered and started to tumble toward them. Both men put their weight against it and pushed back, involuntarily grunting as they did. They weren't sure now if in fact this wasn't a bunch of parasitics. Both helplessly glanced at the distance from them to the cabin door, which looked much farther away than either remembered.

A woman called out from behind the mattress, "Is someone there?"

Ted's face, a mug of furious focus with sheets of perspiration skidding off, instantly turned into a giant grin. "TJ? Is that you?"

"You were expecting someone else?" she said in that

same playful voice he knew so well. “Are you gonna let us in or do we need some sort of magic password?”

It was definitely TJ, acting as if nothing had happened.

73

Reunited

Ted tugged with one mighty grunt at the mattress, followed by ripping off the additional furniture pieces they'd just piled on top of the barricade. His mind impatiently reunited them, while his physical self caught up. And then his mind wandered. He could almost imagine none of this had happened. A crisp mental picture of TJ materialized. It was from the day of their wedding: her lips had an extra shade of rose-colored gloss, her cheeks shined from a healthy dose of tanning she had done earlier in their backyard, her eyes shined bright blue like the most beautiful sky he had ever seen...

He couldn't wait to see that face. And with each tug of the console to give her enough space to slide in with the others she must have rescued, he found himself hyperventilating, in anticipation of the moment.

He caught a glimpse of her feet and legs and his heart soared, and then somehow jumped several beats faster. For just the briefest of moments, Ted wondered if he was about to have a heart attack and collapse before he could get his arms around her.

The final tug, the space was now clear and Ted lifted his gaze. His eyes skipped past what she was wearing and bulleted to her face, fully expecting the same visage of his beautiful bride he'd been visualizing, only twenty years older.

What he saw struck him with a jolt. He sucked in his breath, tensed and stutter-stepped backwards, so in shock he nearly fell over.

His wife's beautiful blue eyes were now mostly red, like two open wounds; her skin was pale, like someone newly deceased; her lips thinner than he could remember, and lacking all color; and her face and body were covered in giant splotches of blood, as if she had just taken a bath in it.

This couldn't be his TJ.

Oh God, no! She's a parasitic.

Then her eyes met his, and she flashed the coy grin he knew so intimately.

It was her.

He exhaled all his tension.

He didn't know what happened to her or why. At this moment, he didn't give a damn. He needed her embrace. He needed her, no matter her condition.

She slid through the small opening they had made in the barricade and found herself wrapped in his arms. He squeezed her so tight, he almost expected something inside her to break.

She squeezed back, but let go quickly, tensing up as if something were seriously wrong. She pushed away from him, hard. And he looked back to find her strained, her face painfully drawn, as if something revolting hit her senses all at once. *Was she in pain?*

She regained some composure and said unemotionally, "There will be time for us later. Now, let's get the rest of these folks to safety."

Ted held his gaze on her for just a little longer, as she turned from him and focused her attention to the others who had followed her here. She was right. Whatever was going on with her, they could address that later. She was safe and here with him. They needed to get out of the hallway, which was now unprotected.

Ted watched and waited as others, one by one, made their way through the opening in the barricade. Some were injured, with makeshift bandages; the rest looked fine, though every single one of them looked like they carried a heavy load of fear on their backs.

"Yes," David said. "Let's get the rest of you safely into a cabin... Evie? Oh, thank God, you're safe."

Ted wasn't paying any attention to the joyous voices, nervous laughter, the happy sobbing, or the congratulatory hand-shaking. Instead, he found himself staring at his wife, who had taken a position against the stern wall of the hallway. Her face was cast down at her feet and her chest heaved rapidly—*was she out of breath, like him?* Not once did she look up at him. She was obsessing about something, but it was not something in the carpet where her gaze was cast, but something inside. Her whole demeanor and stance were foreign to him.

Ted senses were both overloaded and confused at the same time. He wanted to rush over to her, but she obviously didn't want that. And now, what had become of her? How did she survive? How did she contract the disease? And why didn't she display the other symptoms of the Rage disease?

"Are you okay?" he whispered in her direction, taking a couple of tentative steps closer.

David pounded three times on the bridge hatch, but Ted held his gaze on his wife.

She seemed to wait before acknowledging his question. His heart raced again, this time in fear. Finally, she raised her head up, a grin painted roughly onto her pale features that was meant to say, I'm fine. But Ted read it to mean something was very wrong with her. Her eyes were the exclamation point to this feeling.

The bridge hatch opened and friendly words were exchanged between the staff captain and someone else, but Ted remained riveted.

As her eyes burned into his, he remarked at how one of her irises was sort of pinkish, with a blue hue as if it hadn't completely turned. The other was a bright crimson, the color of blood. They both blazed bright. It was all so surreal.

"Really, I'm fine. Everyone else is in, come on," she said and breezed by him and into the luxury suite, where most everyone had entered, except for Niki Tesler of engineering and part of TJ's group, who joined Jessica on the bridge.

Ted followed TJ into the suite, shooting a quick glance at the already-fixed barricade, before the door closed behind him with a *thwack*.

He had no idea what he was about to walk into.

74

Mixed Emotions

Ted examined the faces of the more than a dozen passengers and crew. He knew there were many other survivors on the ship, but part of him wondered if these would ultimately be the only survivors.

Many he didn't recognize, but some he did. Wasano, the new head of security, was there, and so was Dr. Molly Simmons. Ted vaguely remembered seeing her arrive on the back of some brawny guy who he recognized now as Flavio; Ted could no longer see him as a waiter, after what he had witnessed and how he looked now. Also there were Boris and Penny. Evie stood beside them in the back of the suite, holding hands with David, who was beaming. And then it clicked: Ted remembered the joyous sound of a reunion. It was David and Evie's reunion.

Some sat, some stood, but most were wide-eyed and holding to a nervous quiet, while they listened to Jean Pierre speak with Wasano, Flavio and Molly about the captain, as well as what was going on on their ship.

Al, the ship's vet, was there too. And he appeared to be acting as their temporary doctor, examining the three injured folks' wounds.

Ted briefly watched this before refocusing on TJ. She was once again stoic, her back pushed up against a wall away from the others, head hanging, her gaze fixed at her feet. This time he noticed that she was wearing a swimmer's nose plug on her nose, a pink cord connected to each side and wrapped around her neck. The words rushed out of his mouth, "What's going on with you?"

"What do you mean?" she said, barely looking at him.

Ted just glared at her incredulously.

TJ gave a slight nod. "It's the only reason I survived the fall. I can't explain how it happened, though I'm pretty sure I know why..."

Ted folded his arms around his chest and tried to patiently listen to all his wife had to say, though his mind was darting in a thousand directions, filling up with thousands upon thousands of questions he wanted to ask her.

"It was that dog mauling. That's how I must have contracted the parasite, from that bite. I'd never had cats, and since the dog bite, you know I haven't spent much time around animals much. And you also know I don't eat my steaks raw, at least until now..." She paused again, like she was considering a new thought that hadn't occurred to her until this very moment.

"Yeah... So, I didn't tell you everything about that day. Mostly because I didn't want to remember it. But after I was mauled by that dog, I had to put the perp down—"

"—You told me that already," Ted cut in. This was going too slow. And he desperately needed to ask her some of his questions, if she wasn't going to cover them.

"I didn't tell you about the dog and its master's eyes. They both had red eyes! The target of our investigation had gone crazy. And like his dog, he had rushed me with the intent of killing me. That's why I shot him. This parasitic thing had been going on for a long time before today, Ted. It's just this current iteration with the volcanoes that's new."

He thought about this for a moment and then asked his question again, "So again I ask, how are you? What I mean is do you feel like you want to kill?"

TJ cast her rufescent gaze downward before looking back up again. It was obvious she didn't want to answer this question.

"Most of the time." Her brow furrowed, and her lips pouted, then quivered. "I go from calm one moment to nearly insane with rage the next, and I want to kill everyone who isn't like me..." Her eyes welled up.

"But not now?" He felt like he was breathing almost as heavily as his wife was right now.

Her eyes sparkled through her tears, like two rubies drowning in the deep end of a bright pool. "No, but I fear it will happen at any moment. And when it does, I feel sure I won't be able to regain control again, especially around you, or others."

Ted noticed movement and saw Al was standing nearby, listening intently. He was waiting his turn to say something.

Seeing now that they both acknowledged him, Al held out a thermometer and said, "With the dogs, when their temperature had dropped below 99 degrees, they were no longer enraged and aggressive. I've wondered about body temperatures and this disease after speaking with Chloe Barton, the ship's nurse, who said she picked up the thermometer of one of her patients, who had gone from calm to crazy, when it had dropped out of the patent's mouth. She told me it had read 99.5 degrees, a low fever. So I'm wondering, miss... Could I take your temperature?"

TJ drew the backs of her hands over her eyes to wipe away her tears. Then she straightened up against the wall. "Tell me this one hasn't been used on a dog." She flashed him a weak grin.

"No worries. Just sterilized and previously only touched by human mouths."

She accepted it onto her tongue and clamped her jaw down.

Ted thought she was probably glad to have accepted the thermometer, if only to not have to answer any more difficult questions at this moment. He then noticed Dr. Molly Simmons, the parasitologist he'd met after his talk, and the one who shared with him the fact about the thermophilic bacteria. She had made her way to them and was listening in on their conversation. Ted also noticed everyone else in that room was silent and staring at TJ.

"Hello, Mr. Bonaventure," Dr. Simmons said, looking much older than when he'd last seen her.

"Ted, please, Dr. Simmons."

"Molly is fine, as well. I suspect your wife's temperature is below 99 degrees now. But I also suspect when her temperature rises above this level, she'll feel those urges again to kill. I believe that's the T-Gondii working with the thermophilic bacteria. The thermophilic bacteria are attracted to mammals with a temperature of 99 degrees and above. Further, I believe the thermophilic bacteria cause a fever as well. And when the affected mammal is already infected with T-Gondii, it also wakes up the parasite, which as you know has already rewired the brain of its mammal-host. And that's when that mammal changes, and becomes symptomatic, and that's when the mammal appears to become what you think is crazy."

"What else are they, if not crazy?" asked Jean Pierre, who was now part of their little group surrounding TJ.

"This is all part of their new genetic makeup: to kill those who are a threat, and to do so without fear and the ability to suppress pain, so that it can do its job more efficiently. And then of course, to eat," Molly answered, sounding detached, as if she were reading this from a textbook.

"That's enough," Al said, holding out his fingers to her.

"Let's see what your temp is now."

TJ pulled the thermometer out of her mouth, glanced at it and then handed it to Al, who squinted to make sure he read it right, before announcing to all of them, "98.8."

TJ's eyes snapped back to Ted, sparkling and bright. If it weren't for the red irises, they appeared otherwise normal. They now possessed an aura of excitement. Yes, he knew this look to mean she'd just figured something out.

She turned her head to Molly and Al, and then to Jean Pierre, and then back to Ted. She smiled a chasm-wide grin.

"I know how to save our ship."

~~~

"You see," she projected her voice out so that everyone in the room could hear her clearly, though it wasn't needed because she was already the center of everyone's attention, "it's all about the body temperature. When the infected's body temperature is above 99 degrees, they become symptomatic and aggressive toward anyone and anything not infected, just like the two doctors said. But when the infected's temperature drops below 99 degrees, they lose much if not all of their aggression, even if they retain all of their other symptoms."

TJ paused, but not for effect. She wanted to make sure everyone was keeping up with her and she just didn't want to have to repeat herself again, if someone wasn't paying attention.

"So all we have to do is drop the temperature of each infected to below 99 degrees."

"How ve do that? Give every crazy cold drink?" Flavio asked. He had pulled alongside Ted and Molly.

"No Flavio, but if we could drop the air conditioning down low enough, that would drop their body temperatures
~~~

below the 99-degree threshold."

"That's brilliant, my dear," said Molly. "Just like you did with the fire extinguisher in the engine room."

Ted frowned at TJ, like he wanted to ask her about this, but then turned to Jean Pierre. "Is the air conditioning working well enough to do this?"

Jean Pierre's features twisted and turned, revealing a flurry of mental gymnastics. When TJ had worked with him on the Eloise Carmichael investigation, she remembered that look. He had the answer, he just wanted to make sure it was correct.

"Oui—I mean, yes!" Jean Pierre exclaimed, his face now animated. "Yes. We still have some other issues. But depending on where the crazies were, we could *throttle* the air conditioning down."

Al asked, "Why can't you turn the air conditioning down on the whole ship?"

"Not recommended. It would take a lot of fuel, and we have a very limited supply. But if we needed to..." Jean Pierre turned to TJ, "How low a temperature would we need, and for how long?"

TJ shrugged. "Don't look at me; I just came up with the plan."

"Molly?" Ted begged.

"I was just thinking about this. Based on what Al told me about the dogs getting locked in the refrigerated storage room, which is at what temperature, Staff Captain, normally?"

"I believe it was four degrees, or rather, about 40 degrees Fahrenheit. But I'm not sure I can get the room temperature down to forty degrees with our systems, and definitely not for long."

"Forty would be better, but I'm thinking forty-five or even fifty degrees, for about an hour, should do it."

Jean Pierre paced to the conference table, pulled out his walkie and called into it. Although it appeared that he did this to make his conversation more private, TJ could hear the conversation clearly on Ted's radio, which must have been monitoring the same channel.

"Buzz and Jessica, this is Jean Pierre."

"Yes, sir," Buzz crackled back.

"I'm here, sir," Jessica responded.

"I need to know, without a doubt, if we can run the air conditioning in multiple areas of the ship and drop the temp to below ten degrees? This is a priority."

"Aye, sir," Buzz chirped back. "We'll get working on it immediately."

"Thanks. Deep, you got your ears on too?" Jean Pierre moved the walkie from his mouth to his ear.

"Still on watch, sir."

"Any sign of the parasitics?"

"Not a thing, sir."

"Fine, call me the moment you see something." Jean Pierre adjusted his volume up and clipped the radio to his belt and marched back to the group.

"What do you mean, any sign of the crazies?" Ted asked.

Jean Pierre glared at him and then his walkie, catching on that his conversation was overheard.

"Yes, JP. You said earlier, *depending on where the crazies were*." TJ's hands were on her hips. "Do you not know where the parasitics are right now?"

"I didn't want to frighten everyone, but no, we don't know where they went. And I'm guessing for your plan to work, we need to find their location first, then make sure we get them to a secure area, then assuming the air conditioning works, then we drop the temp to around forty-five to fifty degrees for an hour. Then, we can regain control of our ship."

TJ pushed from the wall. "Sounds like a good plan to me."

75

Divide and Conquer

"So how are we supposed to find these things?" Wasano asked.

"Can't you smell them, Mrs. Villiams?" Flavio insisted.

All eyes turned back to her. It was only then that most of them noticed she was wearing a nose plug.

"Actually, I can't smell them any better than you can. But I can smell those who are not infected." She did not want to tell them anything more than this.

Molly perked up at this. "Okay, I'll bite... Ah, sorry dear. Tell me, what do we smell like?"

TJ looked down again at her feet. She could feel everyone's gaze and she knew she was being obvious in avoiding Molly's question. So she just blurted it out, not caring for a moment, until it came out. "Like the most wonderful food in the world."

"That's some screwy shit," someone in the back room blurted.

"Actually, no it's not," responded Molly. "In fact it makes perfect sense. There are many instances, like in the use of pheromones in insects, where smells are used for hunting."

"Oy," announced a large German, sitting on the couch Ted and David had been watching the television from, "why don't we let the Fräulein sniff out the ship while we sit here and wait."

Jean Pierre scowled at the man before returning his attention back to TJ. "It's not a bad point. Can we use that ability to seek out the crazies? You know, if you smell someone or a group of someones, then obviously they're not a parasitic."

She didn't want to be having this conversation, not in front of her husband. The simple answer was yes, she could detect them or rather not detect them, and therefore know they weren't in a location.

"Yes, I'm sure I can."

"Sir," Wasano cut in, "the ship is a little too large for one person to sniff every single room or cabin. We have a lot of people waiting for us to get them to safety. And they've already been waiting for hours."

"You're right, of course. We'll need to send more people."

"Sir," this time it was Flavio, "if any of these crazies smell people walking around, they could easily be overcome and hurt. Why don't we just kill every one of those crazies?" He glared at TJ. "No disrespect to you, Mrs. Villiams."

"No!" TJ's words leapt out. "No killing, unless it's to protect yourself. We treat these people like people who are sick—"

"—who want to fawking eat us," the German yelled out again from the safety of his chair.

"Enough discussion. We're going to break up into three groups: Flavio and Wasano, Paulo and Igor, TJ and me--"

"—I'm going with you," Ted belted out, like a cough. "I've been separated from my wife, whom I thought was dead. I'm not letting her out of my sight now."

"Sorry Ted, but no." Jean Pierre placed his hand on Ted's

shoulder. “I'm afraid you're too slow and you’ll make too much noise with your bad ankle. It's a risk to all of us, and especially to you. I need you to stay and coordinate with Deep on the bridge radio. And to work with Jessica and Niki on the air conditioning. In fact, since I won’t be there, I’m going to instruct them to follow your lead on this.”

Ted nodded, seeming to accept his fate quickly enough. At his heart, he was a logical man, and pragmatic. He knew it was the right thing to do, even though he hated it.

“I'll go.” David stepped forward, but his wife immediately pulled him back.

“Oh no, you don't,” Evie demanded. “You're staying with me this time.”

David shrugged his shoulders and then mumbled something to her, and she smiled at him.

“Excuse me, Staff Captain,” Molly interrupted, her voice animated. “I suggest you have Hans go with one of your groups.”

Jean Pierre flashed a glare first at Molly and then at the German, who seemed just as shocked to be included. "I'm sorry Molly, but I don’t get why?”

"Yeah. Why would you listen to that old Jew?" yelled Hans, who stood up and squared his shoulders toward the group that wanted to send him out into harm’s way.

Molly smiled. “Because you're infected too. And so is your brother.”

All eyes drilled into the two Germans. A couple of passengers sitting near them shot up and moved away. Franz just sank into the seat lower, pulling the blanket he had been wearing over his head.

Hans took several steps forward, like he was about to pick a fight. “My eyes look red to you?”

“No, you’re not symptomatic. Not yet anyway. But I’ve seen how the parasitics react to you and your brother. They’re not interested in either of you, and you know this.”

Hans acted like he was sucker-punched.

Everyone was so focused on Hans, no one noticed TJ had left her space against the wall and was now standing in front of Hans. She pulled off her nose plug and made a loud sniffing sound. Then she did the same with Franz, before walking back. "Yep, they're infected," she exclaimed.

"Fine! Yes, I know both of us are... infected." He said this like it hurt him. "And it sucks, by the way, because I no longer have an appetite for my favorite food."

"Okay then. If both you Litz boys go with our search parties, I'd be happy to ignore all of the illegal liquor and drugs you brought on board," Jean Pierre commanded.

"Like—like you're really worried about the rules now," Hans stuttered.

"No, I'm not. But at this point I'd be happy to dump you two overboard, for whatever reason I come up with."

Hans scowled at the staff captain, considering whether or not he meant it, and then let his head fall forward. "Fine, we'll go. Come on, Franz." He beckoned his brother to stand up.

Conversations erupted, like little wildfires: several expressed the same concern that an infected could be any one of them and that it was impossible to tell. While discussions were escalating, Jean Pierre grabbed the big German by the arm and pulled him to the group surrounding TJ. He instructed Franz to go with his guards, Igor and Paulo. Hans would be with Flavio and Wasano. He stated something about Wasano not taking any shit from the German and he would keep him in line.

Before exiting the cabin, Jean Pierre gave instructions for everyone to remain behind the cabin door. He asked David and Molly to assist Ted in the bridge and his two remaining officers to monitor the cabin and bridge doors, and just outside, in case anyone else showed up and wanted in.

Jean Pierre then requested his volunteers meet him outside the cabin, while he updated Jessica and Niki on the bridge with their plan.

Ted grabbed TJ's hand and cupped her face with his other hand.

"I'll be fine," she said, her voice soft and emotional.

"I just don't want to lose you again." He leaned in and kissed her.

She accepted, but immediately pulled back.

Even though she had her nose plug on, she could taste him. And she felt an evil urge rise up from the dark reaches of her psyche. She wanted to kiss him, but something even more that she dare not think about.

"Let me do what I can, so we can get through this crisis," she said. Pulling her hand from his, she stepped out the door.

76

Hiding Places

A ding announced their arrival on deck 8. The elevator doors slid open with a slow growl, or at least it sounded that way. Once open, a blast of light from the late-afternoon sun shot in and they had to shield their faces. Hans pressed his hands against his eyes, acting like he was suffering from a nasty headache. Then they heard the sound once more, only fainter.

"Did you hear that?" Hans whispered, shirking back into the elevator. "It sounded like one of those damned dogs. I hate dogs."

"You people have German Shepherds and you're scared of dogs?" Flavio humphed. He stepped out into the hallway, not even waiting for an answer. His fingers squeezed tight around the smaller end of the club—*more like a table leg*—that Ted had given him. It wasn't as hefty as his wrench, but since he'd lost that, it would have to do.

He turned back to see what was keeping the other two and noticed the acting security director roughly grabbing Hans' arm and giving him a couple of tugs until the German reluctantly exited the elevator and they both pulled up alongside Flavio.

Wasano let go and now had both his hands on his rifle, slung in front of him, at the ready. “Do you smell anything?” he whispered to Hans, in between him and Flavio.

Hans grimaced and shook his head vigorously. “Only lots of alcohol.”

Flavio smelled it too. Anyone would. A friend of his family from Romania had a bootlegging operation and made their own vodka, which actually wasn’t too bad, if he drank the stuff. One day, he was invited to visit so he could pick up several bottles as gifts for him and his friends, as thanks for what he had done fighting the Russians. Flavio remembered entering a giant room where his friend bottled the stuff… it had the same gagging smell as this one.

“Let’s keep moving,” Wasano whispered. “We have a lot of decks to cover.”

“And I think we want to find them before sunset?” Flavio quipped. For the first time in memory, he was feeling a little anxious.

Wasano stared at the big man, perhaps picking up on his anxiety. “Why is that?”

“I was thinking... Vampires and other monsters; they always come out at night.”

“Come on,” Wasano huffed, taking the lead into the Crows Nest nightclub and bar.

Flavio had rarely been up here; there was no reason to. They didn’t serve food, the people were noisy and obnoxious and everyone was drunk. He didn’t drink, but even if he did, and he was a passenger, he wouldn’t come up here. A bartender-friend of his, Vicki Smith from England, often worked up here and the Anchor Bar, where they did serve food, and he would hear stories from her about some of the shenanigans that went on at the Crows Nest late at night. By the smell of this place, if the ship had not been overrun by crazy animals and crazy people, he would have thought they were walking into the aftermath of a giant party. "Wow, alcohol smell very strong here," he whispered, mostly to himself.

"I think I smell something," Hans said.

They halted mid-step. "Wait," Wasano breathed. "You smell us, not crazies. So that means you smell more of us?"

"Yes, I think so, but—"

There was a loud thump behind them.

The three swung around toward the noise: Wasano sighted his rifle, finger hovering just off the trigger guard; Flavio lifted his club up into the air, ready to strike; Hans turned his shoulders the other way, as he readied himself to run away.

"Hold on, mate," a female voice huffed. She and an officer were standing behind the large semi-circle bar, holding up full bottles of premium vodka, as if they were ready to use them as weapons for their own battle. "Flavio?" She lowered her bottle.

"You were going to hit friend with hundred euro bottle of Grey Goose?" Flavio huffed.

"Wa-wa-we thought you were one of the zombies," stammered the officer, who lowered his own bottle-weapon.

"Or the zombie-dogs," Vicki said with a smile. She always smiled, even when she was having a crappy day. "Hey, you didn't see them when you came in, did you?"

"No, but we heard a lot of growling," said Hans.

"I think they're gone now." Flavio then sniffed the air, making a show of it. "Vicki, they not have your perfume in gift store?"

"Ha, Flavio! You don't like my eau de Hennessy?" She made a show of extending her head and exposing her neck, ready for nasal inspection.

"Wa-wa-we—well actually, Vicki,—came up with the idea when we heard the zombies could smell us," said the young officer, who acted like he had had one too many cups of coffee.

Vicki shrugged her shoulders. "Tosh. When we heard on the radio about them smelling us, I thought maybe they wouldn't be able to if we dowsed ourselves in some pongy alcohol. Guess we were jammy, because a few of them came in here and left. And then the zombie-dogs—those things creep me out—they came in and scratched at the door with all the people, and then left."

Flavio's eyes were drawn to some movement on the other side of the nightclub room. It was Wasano, clearing the place out further to make sure it was safe. That was the other point of their mission: clear out and secure areas of the ship, for survivors to gather.

Wasano stopped beside a bloody corpse up against a wall. He leaned over, checked the pulse and then continued toward the bathrooms.

Flavio returned his gaze to Vicki. "What people?"

"Oh, there was a large group of people that came here, after the zombies started attacking."

"Why do you keep calling them zombies?" Hans asked, seemingly annoyed by the term.

"I'm a big *Sean of the Dead* fan—sure would love a cricket bat right about now. Plus, they seem kind of like zombies, only the fast kind."

"But they're not dead," Hans continued his needling, definitely annoyed.

"I know, but—"

"Vicki," Flavio interrupted, more irritated at the uselessness of this banter, "where are the people?"

"Oh yes, of course, they're over there, in the loo." She pointed in that direction.

Wasano picked up one of the broken bottles of liquor littering the entry into the ladies' room and then knocked on the door. It cracked open and a mascara-streaked face peeked through the crack.

"It's safe, miss," Wasano said. And then to the officer

behind the bar, "Second Officer Rolland, please lock the doors to this place so that no unfriendlies come in.

The young officer snapped to attention. "Ye-ye-yes, sir." He shuffled around the edge of the bar, on the side near the entry, while fumbling with the keys in one hand, but reluctant to let go of the bottle-weapon with his other. After a few moments, he locked the doors.

Vicky leaned over the bar and whispered, "He's all collywobbles."

Flavio didn't know what that meant, but it seemed to fit the nervous officer.

Wasano had knocked on the men's room door, also announcing to its inhabitants that it was safe. Slowly, passengers and crew exited the restrooms, carefully stepping over the broken glass around the doorway.

"Sorry for that," Vicki called out to them, and then back to Flavio she explained, "After we doused ourselves in the Hennessy, I realized the zombies could smell all the people in the bathrooms. So we heaved several bottles at the doors, hoping they would break and throw off their scents. Seemed to work, but the noise attracted them into the bar. That was my bad."

"No apologies, Ms. Smith," Wasano said, slinging his weapon around to his back. "You may have saved all these people's lives."

"Maybe you should warn others on radio about the dogs and the alcohol. And that we have another safe place now." Flavio held out his hand and laid it on top of Vicki's. "You did good."

"Why, thank you." She curtsied.

~~~
~~~

Jean Pierre turned the volume to his walkie down to its lowest setting and clipped it to his belt before whispering to TJ, "We now have a safe place up on deck 12 forward, in the Crows Nest. And two of our crew found out that alcohol covers human scents, so..." He stopped short. She could see his mind completing the sentence, *so infecteds like you can't smell us.* He was obviously nervous about her transformation and his own role in their mission.

"Looking for an excuse to get a drink?" The words just fell out of TJ's mouth. She was surprised the humor still came so easily, even in her present state. But she didn't want this. She needed to focus so that her mind didn't wander off onto other, more troubling subjects.

A small tremor erupted inside her.

"Ha! You know I don't drink," Jean Pierre whispered. His eyes wandered again to her, and then shot back out in front of him, appearing to search side to side. No doubt scanning for the parasitics she may have missed, even though that was not his purpose for being here.

She didn't reply. Her focus was on the task at hand, which was difficult enough. But then another humorous thought sprang to mind, like the forgotten image of an old friend. "And don't think you can get out of being my guinea pig. We need your—what did you call it?—Yes, your manly scent..."

She was losing her train of thought again. *Skip the damned humor and focus,* she told herself.

Another shiver shook her.

"I know," Jean Pierre said off hand, not really paying attention to his words. His eyes once again glued to her.

When she caught him, he abruptly blurted, "You're really cold, aren't you? Never mind, I can see that." He snapped his gaze to his feet, his cheeks flaring a rosy tint.

Any other time, a comment like that would have brought her utter embarrassment and she would have reacted by covering herself. *But it was only JP. He's not even attracted to women*, she reminded herself. More so, she no longer felt weighed down by the chains of vanity any longer. Part of her changes.

Yeah, she was cold. No, she was *damned* cold. And no wonder, all she wore at that moment was her compression shorts and a sopping-wet sleeveless T that clung to her every curve. It was her own suggestion to pour the bar tub of ice water over her head to cool herself down. Gone were her socks, shoes, and the sleeved shirt she had been wearing over everything before her dousing.

Much more concerning to her than the revealing nature of her ensemble was keeping her core temperature down. Knowing that she might have to do battle again at any moment, she was afraid of her body temperature popping up above the 99-degree-threshold Molly had informed them about. This was especially true after finding out that she had only been a couple tenths of a degree south of this mark when Al had taken her temp.

When she was doing battle in the hot engine room earlier, she must have gotten too hot because she could feel herself losing all control as she beat on the other dementeds. A part of her wondered if she completely surrendered to this beast inside of her, if that was it. Perhaps she'd no longer be human; she'd be one-hundred-percent "crazy," like all the other dementeds. A beast carrying out marching orders by the parasites that battled for control inside of her.

"I'm very sorry, Theresa Jean, that I made that comment. It was rude." Jean Pierre interrupted her mental meanderings.

"It's all right. I *am* really cold right now, but that's better than the alternative. Let's get th-through this."

They had been searching the stern of the ship, from deck 10 down, starting with the At Sea Spa. When they had entered the spa's lower level, they had found several survivors in one of the spa's Zen Rooms. Jean Pierre had done the honors of talking to them, not wanting TJ to frighten them with her scary-red eyes and pale complexion.

Within a few minutes, the spa was cleared, and they decided that it too was a good sanctuary for survivors on the aft end of the ship. When they found other stragglers who were exposed, they would send them there. Jean Pierre had also made this announcement on his radio, just before Wasano made his, so that Ted and Deep, on the radio, could inform those in unprotected areas both aft and forward where to go.

Still absolutely no sign of any of the dementeds.

Next, they would go into the Solarium, where they expected to find more find survivors still hunkered down, per reports from Deep and his eyes in the sky.

Just before stepping out of the Spa, TJ huffed, “Hang on.” Then she spun on bare heels and doubled back, popping into one of the Zen Rooms they had just cleared.

A moment later she exited the room, wearing reflective wrap-around sunglasses. She’d remembered seeing these, obviously left behind by a passenger. Her reddish eyes were now covered—hopefully making her less scary to survivors. Plus, she could better see under the bright lights of the ship’s hallways and the glass enclosure of the Solarium. Bright light was hard to take now.

“Okay, I’m ready to meet my public.” She flashed a smile and pushed through the glass door.

~~~

They continued running, even though they were so tired. And so hungry. Since their release from captivity, their unstoppable hunger was not only for food, but for the need to bite and tear and rip and kill.

The pack could smell all of them, and almost all at once.
~~~

This just fueled their ravenous desire for more.

They dashed down one stairwell after another, following the strongest scent they'd smelled in a while.

The mini-poodle, whose amber-colored coat was now a dark red, led the way as the pack's alpha dog.

At the deck 8 landing, all the dogs halted their progression. Some just stood and some spun around in circles. All thrust their snouts into the air at once, sniffing for the scent again.

It was the scent of their next kill.

They had it now. It was very close to them.

Max, the German Shepherd, woofed his acknowledgment that he knew where the scent was coming from. The little poodle, Monsieur, did as well, only its bark was more of a shrill screech. The two dogs bolted first, and the others followed. They were on the scent's trail.

They raced toward the port-side hallway of deck 8, toward the bridge, where now all could smell something glorious: people-food.

77

The Attack

The attack would be quick but not painless. And by the time any of them realized what had happened, another one of their surviving group would die.

A few minutes before the attack occurred, David and Molly had hunkered over the large map table, on the port-side of the bridge, arguing their options in animated bursts. Although listening in and sometimes offering a comment, Ted was mostly busy on the radio, helping to coordinate with Deep to direct survivors who were not yet in a safe place to the two newly designated sanctuaries on the ship. They had split up the different frequencies used by the different departments of the crew and spread the word up and down the spectrum, mostly warning survivors to stay where they were until they could make sure the parasitics were incapacitated.

The discussion turned to what to do about the parasitics if they couldn't find them right away. The three search teams had been gone for an hour now, laboriously going through each room and crevasse on the ship, and there were many to search.

But there were still no reports of parasitics, as if they all disappeared. Ted listened to the back and forth, but then stood up and stated his case.

He had already advocated for immediately turning on all air conditioners and setting them to their lowest settings throughout the ship. As much as he was worried for the other survivors, his primary concern was for his wife and the three teams out there, who were putting themselves in harm's way.

"If the temps were dropping, would the parasitics not at least be more likely to become lethargic? It may not drop their core temperatures to below ninety-nine degrees, but at least it should help. We don't know if they're hiding out somewhere, specifically waiting for unsuspecting survivors to come by, at which time they'd attack. Turning on all air conditioners to their lowest setting makes the most sense. But we must do it now."

Jessica and Niki had been busily working together on the two functioning consoles, all in an attempt to regain the remainder of the helm controls. When Niki heard Ted's interjection, she turned to him and the group, casting a stern gaze in their direction.

Niki had similar smooth Icelandic features and a striking physical presence as her counterpart, Jessica. That's where the comparisons ended. Niki was almost guy-like. Her checks were more muscular, her biceps more pronounced, and her blond hair was accented by splashes of purple. Jessica, whose natural beauty seemed temporarily masked by lines of worry and an unwavering focus to her duties, had much more of a warm radiance. Even in their turbulent situation, Jessica would occasionally flash a smile, which was more of her normal persona. Niki, on the other hand, appeared to be one-hundred-percent business, lacking all warmth, her mannerisms almost robotic.

Niki's features twisted to almost a pucker, which she held for a moment before releasing. It was like Niki wanted to say something she knew she shouldn't and held back at the last minute. It was obvious she wanted to unload her fury and contempt upon Ted for speaking impetuously. But she restrained herself and became robotic once again.

"The staff captain told me to follow your direction, if he was off comms like he is now. Because you're not a member of this crew, you wouldn't know that if I were to turn on the air conditioners, I'd have to first cycle on both engines, and with it our propellers. This is because we don't have the control to separate the two. This means First Officer Mínervudóttir would have to plot a course so we don't run into another island. Knowing all of this now, are you giving us an order… sir?" Niki's scorn was unmistakable.

Ted was taken aback by both her obvious dislike to have been told to follow his orders, but also because he didn't realize his statement, on the bridge, was akin to giving an order. "Ahh," he turned to look at the others, who just stared back at him, offering no help for his conundrum. "If it wouldn't be too much trouble, Ms. Niki—sorry, I forgot your last name."

"It's First Officer Tesler, sir," she barked.

"Oh, like in the great Nikola Tesla, except a…"

"A woman?" she said, her voice inflecting upward. "Yes, my parents had a sense of humor. I don't."

"That's obvious," quipped David under his breath.

Molly giggled, immediately trying to repress it, but like a sneeze in a crowded elevator, some of it came out.

Niki tossed a scowl in Molly and David's direction before continuing. "My biggest concern about turning the air down below sixty is that it might burn out the compressors." She quickly stepped over to the map table and impatiently waited for Ted to follow. "You see, here." She repeatedly stabbed the table with her forefinger around deck 9, mid-ship, while Ted did all he could to repress his grunting with each of his steps to the table.

"This large section here where we don't have a sealed

area. This further burdens our compressors. That means we'll never get our temperatures low enough, even though our systems will fight to do so, until they fail completely."

She paused and mumbled something under her breath, while air-pointing at each deck. She silently mouthed something else, like she was mentally calculating numbers. "I can return us to zone cooling in most other areas, and get us down to maybe sixty-five degrees *Fahrenheit*"—she enunciated this loudly—"within half an hour. Then I suggest we back off each area that's been cleared by our three teams. This should give us more capacity to lower the temperatures even further."

Niki folded her arms across her chest and waited for what Ted guessed was the order to move forward with her suggestion.

"Sounds like an *excellent* suggestion, First Officer Tesler. Ah, make it so." He didn't know what the normal ship command protocol was for a request to execute an order, and the only anecdote he could come up with was from *Star Trek.*

With that, she pivoted on a heel and marched back to her console. She mouthed a few words to Jessica, and then rapidly tapped on her keyboard.

They all turned their gazes to their feet when they felt the rumble below, as if they could see through the floor to confirm the engines had started. Then, like they'd been given a nudge, they were pushed forward, and then to their port side. Ted watched a small island off their port-side slip past their bridge windows, slowly at first and then more rapidly with each passing moment. They were now moving, in a circle.

"Thanks, First Officer," Ted said.

She acted as if she hadn't heard him.

Ted returned his focus to the group. "So, unless they're all in one enclosed location, how are we going to get them into—"

The radio blared, "Bridge, we're under attack."

~~~

The two remaining officers in their group were following the staff captain's orders: each monitored a blockade, so that if any other survivors showed up, they could easily let them in. It was what they added to his orders that led to someone's death.

Not having a key card to the luxury suite, and not wanting to be stuck outside if one or both of them had to rush in, they inducted Boris into doorman service, and tasked him with holding open the cabin door. And being there if they needed their quick retreat.

"I have almost two hundred cruise days with this company, and you want to make me a blooming doorman?" he complained. But they ignored his complaint.

Boris wasn't about to indulge these tossers, no matter what they commanded. *What were they going to do to a guest?* he reasoned. Besides, they had ample barricades to keep the nutters back. And unless they were stupid, they could easily retreat without his assistance. So while each officer was staring through cracks in their barricades, Boris snatched one of the cabin's life-vests and wedged it under the door to keep it open.

He returned to a soft arm chair to continue watching BBC on the telly. The fact that their now deceased captain had lied to their ship about not getting satellite wasn't that much of a bother to him. He was just glad they were getting the news, no matter how ghastly it was.

Penny couldn't take the telly's drumbeat about death and destruction. She preferred escape in fantasy stories over anything scary from the news, or the movies. She wouldn't go with him to watch action-thriller pictures; he always had to call his mates. So while Boris was immersing himself in the news, she grabbed her new chum Evie, and they retreated into the
~~~

master bedroom to lie down on the two sofas.

Al, the doctor, who was really a vet, bothered him once more to check on his wounds, which were itchy, but fine. Then Al excused himself to check on the ladies. That's when Boris heard a commotion outside the cabin.

Holding the volume button, Boris waited for it to slowly cycle from 28 down to 5. He turned his head toward the door to see if he could tell what was going on. He certainly wasn't going to get up out of his seat, if he didn't have to.

One of the two officers burst into the cabin, ripped open the door to the loo, dashed in, and slammed the door behind him.

The volume was low enough now that Boris could hear someone yelling outside the cabin, "Bridge, we're under attack."

That's when it went balls-up.

Boris bolted upward, his knee instantly buckling and shooting ice picks of pain throughout his body. With only one good leg to support all of him, he toppled in the other direction. His size and gravity worked against him, and he tumbled back onto the chair. And then over it.

When he came to rest, once more on the floor, head pointed to the ceiling, feet shooting straight up into the air, propped up against the overturned chair, he heard the only sounds which now completely terrified him.

"No," he whined, flipping his gaze to the open cabin door.

From his sideways view, just like he'd experienced earlier in the cruise, he watched with horror as the same band of loony dogs, led by the same little devil-poodle, raced through the door and headed directly for him.

He closed his eyes and waited for more pain.

~~~
~~~

Al was much more at ease looking after his animal boarders than nursing humans: his animal patients did what he asked and were rarely fussy, whereas his human patients were impossible, with only one exception.

Boris complained loudly every time Al attempted to check on him. This was fine because his wounds were superficial. His wife, Penny, whined every time he checked on her, but she had an anxious stomach and excused herself once again, dashing back into the luxury suite's bathroom. Evie was his third patent and the easiest to deal with, but there was little he could do with her. She'd cut her foot badly on some broken glass in their escape to this part of the ship.

Evie never so much as winced when Al bandaged her, even though he could see by her expression that it was painful. Al did the best he could with the supplies at hand. But her cut was deep and would require stitches when or if they could get out of this mess. All he could do was tell her to avoid moving and keep her leg elevated, which she did without complaint.

While waiting for Penny, he started again to wonder about his dogs: he didn't know where they were; if they'd hurt anyone; and if they'd find them before they did. Ever since their last escape, he'd been a nervous wreck not knowing. But he was also exhausted and since he had to wait, he took up a chair near Evie, on the other side of the bedroom. Then he closed his eyes.

He wasn't sure how long he nodded off, but some noise startled him awake. There was a click across the room and he watched Penny lumber out of the bathroom door, and walk his way. Her features were ashen: she was obviously sick. As he watched her lumber toward him, part of him started to wonder if she was infected. If she was, what could he do? They probably needed to isolate those who were infected, but hadn't yet shown signs. That sure wouldn't go over well.

Another reason why he preferred dogs.

Al was about to instruct his patient to lie down when he heard a loud clatter outside the cabin. Then he heard their barks.

It was his dogs.

Seeing their bedroom door was open, and Penny was closer to the back slider, Al yelled to Evie to take Penny outside. Now!

Al dashed the other way, toward the bedroom door.

Penny scrutinized Al, in slow motion when he passed her. But when she heard the dogs, she became immediately animated, and raced for the back slider. Evie was already working on the latch.

At the bedroom entrance, Al first caught Boris, upended in a seat, on the floor. Then he saw the dogs bound through the cabin entrance. Boris would have no chance of getting away. So Al yelled and flapped his arms to attract their attention, knowing movement and noise would do the trick.

The lead dog—*that awful little poodle called Monsieur*—took the bait first, turned the corner and leapt through the door, right at Al. He turned on his hips and batted the pup away from him with his right hand, and the dog tumbled halfway toward the slider.

It recovered way too fast.

The little dog, who was now almost completely red and brown, must have caught the women's scent—*they were still not outside yet*—and dashed in their direction. The slider was open, but based on Penny's slow speed, he knew they wouldn't make it in time. Then all the dogs would get them and the two other passengers outside, who were staring through the windows wide-eyed. He couldn't let more people get hurt from his animals.

He ignored the other dogs, which he knew were no more than two seconds away, and catapulted himself toward the poodle, who was getting traction on the blue and white carpeting. Last time he sprang for the poodle, he was too slow. This time he was quick enough.

He reached for and snagged one of the little poodle's hind legs, and clasped onto it with all his strength, not worried about hurting the animal. But just then a giant weight hit him in the small of his back, knocking the wind out of him. He knew this was Max, the big German Shepherd.

Then a trumpet-sound of loud screeches and growls rang in his ears, right when he felt his neck explode. But he ignored this.

Al even ignored the poodle, who whipped around and bit him multiple times and then struggled against his unyielding grasp, shrieking from anger.

Al was focused on one thing: the ladies. When he finally saw they'd successfully exited the room and slammed the slider home, he let go of the vicious dog and accepted his fate. He turned his gaze to the poodle, right when it dove at his face; its little fangs found his eyes.

~~~

"It's dogs!" Deep hollered breathlessly on the other end of the radio. "Someone attacked in hallway. Now in eight-zero-zero-zero."

Ted reached down below the workstation where he was sitting, snatched the small footrest he'd been using, and pushed up from his seat. He hobbled to the bridge hatch, David already there clutching his table-leg club.

David snapped a curious glance at Ted's clutched foot-rest.

"I gave my table leg to Flavio. Come on. Let's go."

David drew open the hatch and they slipped into the hall.
~~~

Ted scanned forward and then to the starboard side, along the long hallway, toward Eloise's cabin and that blockade. One of the ship's officers, was curled up in a little ball on the floor, whimpering. That must be the one Deep said was attacked.

"He's just scared," David whispered.

"So am—" Ted bit his tongue when he heard the growling and other unspeakable sounds coming from the Queen Suite.

They tiptoed, into the suite and saw Boris pulling himself up off the floor, using an overturned chair. His face looked tortured and paler than normal.

David caught movement outside on the balcony, and started in that direction. Ted limped over toward the bedroom, where the ghastly noises of dogs fighting and chewing were as loud as ever.

He caught a glimpse of a body on the floor and the dogs going at it, when one of the dogs turned in Ted's direction.

Then a loud bang on the other side of the room distracted the dog, who turned toward the noise. That's when Ted moved faster than he thought he could. He darted three steps forward into the bedroom, hurled his foot-rest at the far wall and reached inside the bedroom.

He grabbed the door handle as his foot-rest clanged off the wall, adding to the racket inside. Without even looking—he didn't dare—he yanked so hard on the door, it slammed shut and sent him to the floor.

One or more of the dogs immediately banged loudly on the other side.

When he caught David escorting his wife and the others back into the cabin, Ted laid his head down. He was tired.

78

Deep Freeze

"Look, they're already settling down," David exclaimed, his head pressed up against the glass, hands cupped around his face so he could see.

"I know." Molly didn't need to look: she knew this would happen once they directed the cooling to that enclosed bedroom. Mostly she didn't want to look: her stomach turned cartwheels every time she thought of the dead vet, all ripped apart. He was a nice young man she'd just been speaking with earlier. Just picturing his face sapped her of her remaining energy. Her back slid a little against the slider, the rest of her weight balanced on her cane. She even started to go wobbly, like she might fall over, and there were no chairs out here to sit down on. They had used them for the blockade.

"Are you all right, Dr. Simmons?" David asked, his firm hand grasping her arm at just the right time. "Let's go in and sit for a moment."

She wanted to say, "Yes that's what I need, because I'm a tired old lady." All she could manage was, "Yes."

She remembered being led inside the luxury suite to a chair, although moments were starting to blur.

An open bottled water appeared on a table in front of her, as did David and Ted. They were all sitting at the dining room table now.

She snatched the bottle with a shaky hand and took a large gulp.

She heard her name mentioned a few times, but didn't hear the context. And then a question, directed at her. She looked up.

David repeated his question. "Can we help you into the other room to lie down for a while?"

She felt better now, though chilly. A little uncontrolled shudder erupted inside of her.

"I'm fine now, David. Thank you. I just had to sit a spell. Please keep talking though. Hearing your voices helps."

Ted had popped up out of the chair while she'd said this and put a man's jacket around her shoulders, before he sat down again in front of her and beside David.

"Thank you, dear. Please stop making a fuss over me. I'm feeling so much better, just sitting and talking."

She looked down for her cane and saw that it was resting against her chair. One of the boys must have put it there.

"That's the Rod of Asclepius, the doctor's symbol, isn't it?" Ted asked, smartly trying to get her mental faculties regrounded on terra firma.

She picked up her carved cane and held it up so both of them could see it close. It was a gift from her son. Her mind wondered what happened to him with all of this craziness happening. He was a Doctor without Borders, now somewhere in Africa. And the cane was something hand-carved by a local African artisan. She hoped he survived this thing. A wave of sadness overwhelmed her then, when she knew there was a good chance he did not.

So much death right now.

"I've always wondered what the two snakes crawling up a pole had to do with being a doctor." It was David, who was also trying to bring her back from now an emotional cliff.

"Well..." She wiped a tear from her cheek, and then gazed at both men and then finally the cane. She knew this story well. "Some say that these are not snakes, but Guinea worms." She looked up again to see Ted had a slight grin—he obviously knew this story, but wanted her to tell it.

"You see there's a parasite called a Guinea worm, a fascinating two-foot-long creature that escapes their host by punching through an ulcerous blister on the infected's skin, over the course of a few days." She was feeling better already.

"You couldn't yank it out at one go-round, since the parasite would snap in two and the remnant inside the body would die and cause a fatal infection. So the thousand-year-old traditional treatment was to wrap it around a small stick, and then slowly turn the stick, winding it around the stick, until you were able to pull out the parasitic worm and kill it. So you see, these aren't snakes, but parasitic worms."

That's when it hit her. She quickly turned in her chair and gazed at the outside. It was getting dark. She turned back to the men.

"I think we don't have any more time. We need to recall the three teams and get them back before it's dark."

"Why?"

"Because parasitics love the night, and I have a feeling that ours will too."

~~~

Jean Pierre held the door closed and waited. TJ was on the other side but had been gone for much longer than she had
~~~

been previously. Usually she'd just stick her head in, sniff and say whether or not the area was clear. Although at this point he wasn't sure if the longer time was good or bad.

Just previously to this, they'd found their first parasitic, but that was inside a cabin, on deck 7. It was then they decided to skip the cabins for now, and just focus on the public spaces. The cabins were secure, either keeping the parasitics inside or protecting the non-infected from any parasitics that might try to attack from outside. So they would make sure the "outside" was clear first. Then they'd work on the individual cabins.

Ted and the others had come up with a plan to air-condition the uncleared areas and the cabins and with each area cleared, they'd turn off the air. It was getting cooler inside, but it was not cool enough. They had to clear out more of the ship before turning the air on at max, or risk burning out their compressors.

Jean Pierre examined the colored printout of the deck plans, with his own markings, and saw they still had six more decks to go, including this one. At this rate, they'd be at this all night, even without the one-by-one cabin checks.

There was a triple-tap on the other side of the door. It was TJ.

He unlocked the door and pulled it open, and she slid out, still wearing her slinky outfit.

Her face told him the answer to the question he always asked. There were no parasitics there, or non-infected. He marked an "X" over Giovanni's, their premium Italian restaurant. That left one final place in the stern of deck 6. The Wayfarer Lounge.

TJ was already headed there, marching ahead of him. She had quickened her pace.

She was an amazing woman, especially now, with everything going on.

If she were not married, he would have been interested.

He stopped this line of thinking. This is what got him

into trouble years ago. It's why he told everyone he was gay. And why he pretended to live that life. The company was tolerant of everyone's lifestyle, but it was a big no-no to fraternize with the crew, and most especially the passengers. And women all loved the uniform. So he thought it was just easier to tell everyone he was gay. From that moment forward, women treated him different than the other male officers, thinking he was no longer a threat. The fact was, he loved women. And he especially loved driven women like Theresa Jean.

He noticed she was out of sight, so he double-timed it until he saw her again. She was there at the Wayfarer Lounge entrance, back to him, focused on something in a dark corner of the floor.

Jean Pierre was about to say something when she held up a hand to silence him. It was then he noticed she wasn't trying to focus on the floor, but something else. She beckoned him forward.

When he was beside her, she leaned over to him and whispered. "I think they're here. Please go back there." She pointed to some place diagonally across the hall. "I'm going in, but prepare to run back to that last restaurant."

He nodded, and stepped backward quietly, not moving his eyes from the dark opening of the lounge. He couldn't see in, but he thought he could hear something now. Some guttural sound. And while he was thinking of it, he caught a whiff of the most horrible smell. *Like a slaughterhouse.*

Once TJ saw he was at the place she had suggested, she turned and walked inside.

It felt like she was gone for an eternity, but he knew it was only a few short moments. She appeared out of the shadows, looking calm but focused. She reached to one side of the hallway and gave a short tug at one of the two double doors. Then she tugged at the other. Both began their slow swing inward, guided by her, until both were closed. She held both of the handles, her biceps and shoulders tensing.

She turned her head toward him, threw a scowl and mouthed the words, “Come here.” She wanted him to lock the door.

There was a thump on the other side of the door. And then another.

He jogged over, his right hand in his pocket, feeling for the keys. Like the other main public spaces, this door required an old fashioned metal key. The restaurants were on one electronic master key, and the lounges and theater were on another.

There was another deep thump on the door, followed by several more.

He had the keys out and then fumbled with the first, which he knew wasn’t the right one because of its shape. It was one of the four longer ones—he couldn’t remember which one it was.

“Would you mind hurrying? They’re there, and they’re waking up now.”

“Merde!” he mumbled, his hand shaking.

He slipped in one and turned.

Wrong key.

Almost in response, the doors thundered; their vibrations caused more tremors in him.

He slammed in the next key and turned.

Nope!

“Please hurry,” she said. Her shoulders were hunched and she was digging her heels into the carpet. The doors moved back and forward.

They were pulling from the other side.

The next key slid in and it turned slightly, but no further.

The doors rattled hard. And TJ grunted. He could tell she couldn’t hold it much longer.

Then he remembered this door’s lock was backwards. It was the only one in the ship like this. He slammed the last key back in again, but this time he turned it the other way, just as the doors were being pulled inward. The lock started to engage, but stopped short. With the two doors opening and now at an angle, there was no way to fully engage.

He grabbed her wrist and the handle with his free hand. "One more tug," he said and they both pulled, while he put pressure with his other hand on the key.

The doors gave in their favor, just a little. It was all they needed.

Finally, it clicked home.

TJ let go of the door and they both fell backwards onto the carpet, breathing heavily.

"Oh merde. That was close." He huffed. "How many are there?"

She didn't answer right away. Her chest rose and fell rapidly like a sleek ship in rough seas. Finally, she gave him a grin. "All of them."

Jean Pierre detached his radio from his belt, put it to his lips and whispered, "We have found the parasitics. Repeat, we found all of the parasitics. They are in the Wayfarer Lounge. Repeat, commence Operation Deep Freeze on just the Wayfarer Lounge.

He put the radio down on his lap and smiled at Theresa Jean. "Merci!"

The Journal of TD Bonaventure

DAY TEN

I AM UTTERLY EXHAUSTED.

THE PLAN, OR WHAT WE CALLED OPERATION DEEP FREEZE, WENT OFF WITHOUT A HITCH… WELL, MOSTLY.

WE WERE ABLE TO FIND MOST OF THE HIDING PARASITICS—THAT'S THE WORD MOLLY GOT US TO USE WHEN DESCRIBING THE FULLY SYMPTOMATIC INFECTED, AT LEAST THOSE WHO APPEARED TO BE COMPLETELY CONTROLLED BY THE T-GONDII PARASITE.

WE WERE INCREDIBLY LUCKY: MOST OF THEM WERE IN ONE LARGE LOUNGE THAT WE WERE ABLE TO LOCK UP. WE GOT TO THEM JUST BEFORE THEY WERE GOING OUT TO HUNT. THEY WERE JUST WAKING UP WHEN TJ FOUND THEM.

THE REMAINING PARASITICS WE ROUNDED UP CABIN BY CABIN, KNOCKING THEM OUT AND THEN TRANSPORTING THEM TO THE WAYFARER LOUNGE WITH THE OTHERS.

AND WE'VE BEEN ABLE TO KEEP THEM THERE THESE PAST FIVE DAYS. AND AS LONG AS THE AIR-CONDITIONING HOLDS UP, WE CAN KEEP THEM UNDER CONTROL.

BUT EVEN COUNTING OUR MANY BLESSINGS, OUR LOSSES WERE STAGGERING.

BARELY FIVE HUNDRED GUESTS AND CREW SURVIVED, MANY OF THEM INJURED, SOME SERIOUSLY. THE REST ARE EITHER PARASITIC OR DEAD. OUR BEST COUNT OF THE DEAD WAS OVER THREE HUNDRED AND FIFTY. IT'S MIND-NUMBING TO EVEN THINK ABOUT. WE'LL HAVE TIME FOR THAT TOMORROW MORNING, WHEN WE HOLD THE BURIAL AT SEA AND MEMORIAL SERVICE.

AND YET IT COULD HAVE EASILY GONE THE OTHER WAY.

WE ARE AT LEAST ALIVE AND WE HAVE CONTROL OF THE SHIP AGAIN. MOST IMPORTANT, MY WIFE IS ALIVE, EVEN THOUGH SHE IS PARTIALLY SYMPTOMATIC FROM THE PARASITE.

SHE CONTINUES TO CHANGE: GETTING STRONGER, SEEING AND HEARING BETTER THAN EVER BEFORE—SHE COULD BARELY SEE PAST HER FEET BEFORE ALL OF THIS. BUT OTHER THINGS HAVE CHANGED IN HER AS WELL, MANY NOT GOOD.

SHE'S DIFFERENT IN WAYS I CAN'T POSSIBLY EXPLAIN. IT'S AS IF A PART OF HER PERSONALITY HAS LEFT HER, EVEN THOUGH SHE SAYS SHE HAS THE SAME FEELINGS SHE DID BEFORE.

YET BECAUSE OF WORRIES ABOUT MY SAFETY, WE SLEEP IN SEPARATE CABINS.

AND SO, EVEN THOUGH I LONG FOR HER, WE SPEND ONE MORE NIGHT APART.

I DO NOT KNOW WHAT THE FUTURE HOLDS FOR TJ AND ME, FOR OUR SHIP, AND CERTAINLY NOT FOR OUR WORLD. SO WE WILL TAKE IT ONE DAY AT A TIME. GOODNIGHT.

.

79
The New Normal

He scratched around the bandage covering a large portion of his forearm. The bite wound itched like crazy now, which was a far cry better than how it felt a few days earlier.

Nurse Chloe had told him that bite wounds would hurt more than any other cut or wound he'd sustained before, because of the amount of skin surface broken and possible nerve damage.

Pain was not part of his worry. Of course, it hurt. But he'd felt much worse from many previous injuries, including a bullet to the brain, which still caused him migraines. What Flavio feared more than anything, was what would happen after the pain went away.

Would he become infected, and if he did, would he turn into one of those damned *parasitics*, as Dr. Molly called them?

No matter how much the nurse tried to reassure him that he was most likely not infected, he became sure that it was just inevitable.

With each flash of anger or each moment he wanted to

slap someone for being stupid—this happened daily—he'd stop himself and wait for some sort of change to begin. But it never came.

And when he'd see Mrs. Williams, during their daily campaign to root out any other parasitics hiding in the ship's shadows, he'd pull her aside and ask her to smell him. It sounded strange when the request came out of his mouth, but he saw what Hans could do and knew she could do this as well.

He didn't dare ask Hans for the sniff-test, because Hans was feeling all high and mighty about his status as one of the few people on the ship who could recognize the difference between an infected and a non-infected. He didn't want to add to that man's ego. And he just didn't like him. Mrs. Williams was more discreet, and like him, less emotional about such a request.

Yet each time she would grant him a sniff, she'd shake her head, telling him, *No, you're not infected*. But her reassurances didn't assuage his anxiety about becoming one of them.

He glanced up and scanned the crowd attending the service and saw Mrs. Williams standing back in the far corner of the open forecastle. Her arms were folded around her chest, nose-plug clipped to her nose—*too many non-infecteds for her to smell*—and her normal-looking sunglasses covered up her abnormal eyes.

Mr. Williams stood nearby, but they almost didn't seem together.

"And now we take a few moments of silence to honor our friends, our family, and our crew members we lost in the attack."

Flavio pulled his gaze away from Mrs. Williams and visually addressed his staff captain, who had just lowered his own head. Everyone else did as well. He searched the faces of his fellow crew members and passengers, feeling the weight of the pain of their losses.

Vicki, who stood beside him, also lowered her head. She reached up with both of her hands and grabbed one of his, squeezing it tight. Tears slid down her cheek, serenading her quivering chest. She was a big crier.

She was one tough lady, but the death of the captain and her close friend Zeka were very difficult for her to take. This was hard on all of them: they all lost someone they knew or cared about.

Everyone did but him.

Flavio had been purposely detached from most people. It was the thought of losing people he cared about that drove his personality. It was much easier not to care. And ever since he'd lost much of his family to a war, he had made the decision to just turn off his feelings for other people.

He had always smiled and was cordial to the passengers and crew, when it was appropriate. But he rarely asked anyone anything personal. The less he knew about people personally, the simpler it was to remain detached. This detachment worked well for a long time. Then Vicki came into his life.

Vicki Smith from England was the first woman in a long time that he gave a damn about. And it was obvious that she liked him...

What are you thinking, Flavio? he scolded himself.

There was no time, especially now, for relationships.

He told himself to let go of her hand, but he couldn't. She needed someone's hand to hold onto. And if not his, whose would it be?

A light bell-chime rang out from the ship's loudspeakers.

All their heads rose. Vicki released his hand and then wiped more tears away, smudging her thick mascara even more. *She looked so sad.*

The bell-sound rang again.

She flashed a smile at him. It was a facade. She was genuinely hurting inside. And because of this, he started to hurt as well. She returned her gaze to the staff captain, who was finishing up the service.

"Almighty God, we commit the remains of our brothers and sisters to the deep, for their eternal sleep. Protect their immortal souls. Amen."

Dozens of crew and passengers followed the staff captain to the port-side rail of the forecastle. Each held boxes of various sizes, which contained the remains of one or more family members, friends or crew. Once at the rail, each dumped the cremated remains over. Like clouds of chalk, billows of gray rained down onto the frothy waters below, and then disappeared, as if they never existed before this.

Meanwhile, the bell rang every five seconds.

Vicky startled him by wrapping her arms around his trunk. "This is so bloody hard," she sobbed.

Flavio hesitated, and then reciprocated, squeezing her back. It felt good to give comfort to someone... Someone he cared about.

He held her tight against him, while her body trembled in his arms, not even caring if she spotted his uniform with her mascara.

Out of the corner of his eye, he caught a glimpse of someone running. It was Mrs. Williams. She pushed through the exit, with Mr. Williams chasing after her.

~~~

Not everyone attended the burial at sea services. A few of the passengers still didn't seem to understand that their luxury cruise had permanently ended days ago.

Josef Rauff was emblematic of this mindset. Each day, while many of his fellow passengers chipped in to help the crew, he chose to lounge in his own ignorance, bathing in the blissful sun's rays. And at least until four days ago, he had
~~~

drowned himself in generous helpings of the ship's alcohol. That was until the staff captain cut him and everyone else off.

And what right did he have to do this, when they paid big money to go on this cruise? And that wasn't the only thing now lacking on their ship.

Normal services were now nonexistent. Restaurants were closed, there were no shows playing at the theater, their Internet and satellite TV didn't work, and finding someone to serve them even a soda was impossible.

"Where the hell are the servants?" he croaked to no one in particular.

Apocalypse or no apocalypse, the crew's job was to wait on him and his fellow passengers. It was what he paid for. Yet the service now was inferior even to those big cruise lines serving the masses.

"Dammit!" Josef pounded his lounger's armrest, generating tsunamis in the flab of his belly. "I want some damned service."

A shadow appeared in front of him, blocking his sun. So he shot a scowl of hatred at the silhouette.

"Get out of the way," he spat. "If you're not here to get me a drink, I don't want what you're selling, *Grunzschwein*."

"Hey, dude," said the young American, his high-pitched voice thick with scorn. "You know people died?" He pointed forward, in the direction of the burial at sea service he'd just attended. "And most of the crew is out there—"

"Get out of here, you idiot. Before I..." Josef shot his fist in the air to finish his sentence.

"German prick," quipped the American, who turned to walk away.

Josef snapped. He bounded out of his lounger, tripping over an empty table next to him. He tumbled, but remained vertical just long enough to tackle the American's legs. Josef bellowed his anger, in a combination of screams and growls.

Other passengers, having been attentively watching

Josef and the American's interaction, assumed it wouldn't go too much further. That was until they saw the big German tackle the other man. Most still remained in their seats, but a couple of men popped up to intervene, arriving just as the German was yelling something inarticulate which sounded like obscenities.

The situation changed dramatically when they tried to separate the two men.

Each Good Samaritan held onto a shoulder of the German, while the American slithered his legs out of the man's grasp. But then the German turned to the first man, hyper-extended his neck and then sank his teeth into the man's hand. Both yelled and attempted to release themselves from the German.

"Oh my God," yelled the American, now gawking a few inches away, "he's one of them."

Josef responded by growling, red and foamy spittle, glaring reddish eyes of malevolence at each of the frantic witnesses, before setting his sights back on the man he'd just bitten.

Most every passenger, at first casually watching the show, fled the sun deck. They ran break-neck for the exits, fearing a repeat of what happened here five days ago.

The American man, who'd tried to calm the German down before getting accosted, had had enough of this. He snatched a small table, kicked over from their scuffle. And while the parasitic German tried to lunge at the man he'd bitten, the American drove the table hard into the attacker's skull, subduing him.

The other passengers and a couple of crew, seeing the parasitic man was now unconscious, ran over to help out.

They would drag the man to the elevator and place him into an ice box they'd set up just for this type of incident. There he'd remain until he calmed down. Then he would be separated and placed in with the rest of the parasitic population on deck 6.

~~~

"The infected are not like any of us. We must remember that," said the very British-sounding animal behaviorist. "They're very much like animals, driven by instinctual needs: hunting, food, sex..." "Did you say sex?" a male voice cut in. "Why yes, of course," responded the British woman. "The Pyschotics have a strong sex drive, and we must—"

"—useful?"

Ted slid the headphones from his ears and glanced up. "Sorry?"

"I asked if you've found anything useful?" Jean Pierre strode through the door of their newly created communications room, formerly the master bedroom of 8000's luxury suite.

Ted laid the bulky headphones on the desk, pulled his blue Cubs hat off his head, and massaged his temples. He waited for Jean Pierre to settle into one of the hard chairs set up by the door, knowing their conversation would be a long one.

After running his fingers through his hair, Ted put his hat back on. "David left just a few minutes ago to have lunch with Evie. So I'll report what he found first." He turned about ninety degrees in his chair to address his captain.

"He only found one working television broadcast today. It's RTP from Ponta Delgada. But it's a taped talk show, being replayed over and over again. And it was in Spanish, which of course neither of us speak. More troubling, as of today, none of the satellite channels are working: even the BBC is off the air now." Ted paused to let that point sink in. It was a shock to David and him as well.
~~~

Since they were both asked to check on the radio and TV broadcasts, and Buzz had set up the suite's master bedroom as their communications center—he said this was because of the ease to connect to outside antennas—they'd been listening and searching for updates as to what was going on in the world outside of their ship.

Listening to radio broadcasts was not necessarily Ted's forte, nor was watching TV for David. But both wanted to contribute. And it helped Ted gather more data about the parasites' progression outside of their ship, so that he and Molly could help the acting captain decide on their next steps. And as Jean Pierre explained it, David and he were now considered trusted members of his bridge crew.

"Keep in mind, this ship is given a package of satellite broadcasts from a third-party company that Regal European subscribes to. So it's entirely possible that there are many broadcasts out there and we just don't know about them, because only our package has gone down. Buzz will be rigging up a new antenna system for us and he says he'll be able to hack some of the satellite TV systems out there. But it won't be for another day or two, since you've got him doing so many equally important tasks to get the ship systems back up."

Jean Pierre nodded to all of this, and then leaned forward. "So what about the radio?"

"Well, that's another story altogether. I've listened to hours of various commercial broadcasts and some ham radio as well." Ted stretched over his desk and grabbed a yellow pad, with scribbles all over its pages. He sat back in the chair and starting with the first page, he flipped through the pages quickly until he stopped about twenty pages in.

"Okay, best I can gather, reports of parasitic attacks have sprung up on every continent. It's pretty much the same story everywhere, only different gradations of chaos. The worst are London and Paris, both of which are mostly black now."

"Black? You mean as in nothing?"

"Correct. No commercial broadcasts whatsoever. Only intermittent shortwave broadcasts from there. Parasitic animals and humans control these two cities, roaming the streets freely."

Jean Pierre fell back into his chair. "I guess we should count our blessings then."

Ted had thought the same thing. They were in an environment they could better control. "Correct. Although there are places out in the Western US, including near our home in Arizona, where the Rage disease hasn't really taken hold. Only sporadic reports of animal attacks. But I expect that to change fairly soon." Ted tossed the yellow pad back onto the desk. "It's pretty much a shit-storm everywhere else."

"So we're completely on our own," Jean Pierre stated rhetorically.

"I'm afraid parasitics in control of our towns and cities is the new normal for the world." Ted examined the man who had assumed command of their ship, and therefore their lives. He appreciated the man's pragmatic processing of everything. And he felt lucky to be included in their tight circle to help him craft future decisions. And it was nice being one of the few in the know.

Realizing he forgot something, Ted popped forward in the chair. "Sorry, I forgot to mention one other broadcast you should know about." He snatched the pad back and moved to a page that was marked by a paper-clip.

"Here it is. Every couple of hours, with the last one about an hour ago, there's a shortwave broadcast in both Spanish and English from *L-Ha-D-Core-Vo?*" He said it phonetically. "I know I'm saying it wrong." He turned the pad around so that Jean Pierre could see it written carefully in his block-styled lettering.

"Ilha De Corvo. Yes, it's the northernmost island in the Azores archipelago."

"Makes sense. They're saying that they have fuel for any

ship that needs it and that they'll exchange fuel for any supplies, especially food. But here's the weird thing." Ted looked back up to Jean Pierre. "They say they don't have the Rage disease on their island."

"Have you spoken to them?"

"No. I didn't want to presume. And who knows if it's not just BS."

Jean Pierre's radio chirped at him and he answered it in one motion.

"Sir, this is Mr. Agarwal. We have another report of an attack on the sun deck, with a passenger turning parasitic. He's in the cold room right now, with the other one."

"Thanks, Mr. Agarwal." He clipped the radio back onto his belt.

"Damn, that's three cases in the last thirty-six hours, right?"

Jean Pierre nodded. "That's actually why I wanted to speak with you. I have some ideas on how we should manage the passengers and crew going forward. I hope you don't mind, but I've asked Dr. Simmons to join us. I need feedback from both of you before I announce new rules to everyone at tonight's meeting."

"That sounds good, Captain. It will give us a chance to share our idea about what to do about the parasitics."

80

Empty

It was a full house, with standing room only ten minutes before the doors closed. Every passenger and all but maybe the dozen or so skeleton crew who had to man the ship's critical systems were there. The only thing they were told on the intercom or from the door-to-door messages delivered by crew was that the meeting was mandatory. Short of being deathly ill, in the infirmary or one of the parasitic population, literally every person on their ship was required to be at the Tell Tale Theatre at 19:00. Ted was quite sure no one, aside from a few select bridge crew, had any idea how much their lives were about to change.

On stage, a line of seats facing the audience were occupied by their acting captain, Jean Pierre; security director, Wasano; first officer of navigation, Jessica; acting engineering director, Niki; acting medical director, Chloe; and special envoy to the captain, Molly. Ted—he didn't think he had a title yet—sat at the end, beside Molly. They all remained in their seats, silent, just waiting for the meeting to start.

Ted leaned forward in his chair and stared at his wife. She was hiding in the fold of a giant stage curtain, in a dark corner of the stage. She wore her now normal uniform: running outfit, nose-clip and sunglasses. Her breathing was more rapid than even normal. But with her changes, that could be nothing. It was the tension in her neck, head turning toward each cough or word spoken, and the stiffness in her posture which told him that she was distressed.

It was a complete role reversal. Before all of this, it was he who would have been hyperventilating with such a large crowd only a few steps away. Now it was his wife that couldn't stand to be around people.

She slid farther into the curtain's protection, no longer visible to him or anyone else.

Jean Pierre rose from his seat and proceeded to the lectern. Ted's watch, synchronized with the captain's, read 19:00.01.

"Good evening. For those of you who don't know me, I am Jean Pierre Haddock, acting captain of your ship, the Regal European *Intrepid*." He paused for a moment and then continued.

"The people behind me are the current members of my wardroom. That means, they speak for me. They, along with several other members of my crew and a few passengers, were the reasons why we are all still here today, alive and having this meeting. When you see them, you should thank them for their selfless commitment and for their sacrifices."

He didn't intend to pause for more than a moment before moving directly into the main reasons for their meeting. He needed to get through the part that would be most difficult for most of this audience to hear. And even more difficult for them to accept.

But several of the audience stood up unexpectedly and cheered loudly. Then every one of the nearly five hundred people inside joined in and cheered for their good fortune and the people who got them here. He allowed it, because they probably needed it.

He waited impatiently for the applause to ebb. When it didn't, after two solid minutes, he raised his hands, palms out, and said, "Thank you... Thank you. Please, hold your applause."

Finally, they stopped and everyone who had a seat, sat. And other than a few murmurs and coughs, it was quiet again.

"I would ask you to hold onto your applause and your comments until the end of our presentation. We have much to cover.

"The purpose of this meeting is to give you an update on what is happening aboard our ship, the status of the world around us, and our plans going forward.

"First, because I know many of you have concerns about the Rage disease, I've asked Mr. Ted Williams to speak to you and help you to understand better what it means to each of us on this ship." Jean Pierre turned to face Ted.

Ted rose and walked up to the lectern, his head still pointed in TJ's direction. She still wasn't visible.

Some of the crowd started to mumble questioning comments, obviously not making the connection between the man they knew as TD Bonaventure and the name Ted Williams. A few started to clap.

Jean Pierre, who stood just aside and behind the lectern, took a step forward and leaned into the microphone, "Again, I'd ask you to please hold your comments and applause until after the formal part of this meeting has concluded."

Ted nodded and mouthed "Thank you" to him, before bellying up to the lectern. He wore the same suit he wore during the formal night and his public toast. His hair was tightly combed and perfectly in place. Gone was his handlebar mustache and the grin he often wore when he spoke in front of people. Even four nights ago, when he was tasked with speaking on behalf of their now deceased captain, at this very same theater, he at least tried to mix some humor into his talk.

He was dead serious tonight.

"Thank you," he said in his normal American voice, no longer pretending to have any sort of a British accent. "As the acting captain said, my actual name is Ted Williams. Many of you may know me by my pen name. But I'm not speaking to you as an author or entertainer, but as a member of the *Intrepid* crew. With the assistance of Dr. Molly Simmons—our resident parasitologist and other recent addition to this committee—the captain wanted me to explain what has been occurring on-board and outside this ship, as it relates to the Rage disease."

While speaking, Ted had been addressing four imaginary points of his audience—something he learned from a speech coach when speaking to large groups—so that it appeared as if he was personally addressing each person in the audience, even though he couldn't see any of their faces. When he glanced to his right and down, he caught a glimpse in his periphery of TJ, still standing just inside the folds of the theater's curtains. She was visible because she was now trying to see Ted, and she acknowledged his gaze with a small glint of a smile... and tears. He quickly flashed back a slight grin and then returned his serious focus to his audience.

She was so sad.

He took a deep breath, recollected his thoughts to make sure he would cover all of the points Jean Pierre had wanted, and then continued. "We have all experienced the so-called Rage disease firsthand, and the effects of the parasite known as *T-Gondii*. What you probably don't know is that everyone who has become symptomatic, and appeared to have gone crazy, was already infected before they boarded this ship. They did not contract this parasite from a bite, or from something they ate on the ship, or even breathing in the air. Again, everyone who was already infected picked up this parasite before they stepped on board. They just didn't know it.

"The disease transformed most of the infected into

what we are calling parasitic; in other words, someone controlled by the parasite. This parasite was benign to most people, before a small bacteria, spread by volcanic clouds all over the world, woke up the parasite and caused so many of our fellow passengers and crew to become parasitic and thus seemingly crazy."

This is where Ted diverted somewhat from the truth, at Jean Pierre's insistence. "The good news is that we don't expect any more flare-ups of the disease. Pretty much everyone who was going to contract the disease and become symptomatic has already... become symptomatic. That is showing signs of the crazy behavior."

In truth, Molly explained to the captain's wardroom that they could expect as much as an additional 20% or more of their ship to, at some point in time, become symptomatic. There was just no way for them to tell for sure, without doing a blood test for each person on the ship. And they needed equipment they didn't have for this. Those who were either slightly symptomatic or who didn't pass TJ's smell test were going to be separated from the non-infected. But that would be addressed individually with each person another day.

"I will be happy to answer all of your questions afterwards. So please hold them until then. I return you to the captain. Thank you."

Ted abruptly turned and walked back to his chair. And before the audience could react and begin to disrupt his delivery of this meeting with their questions that they were supposed to hold for the end, Jean Pierre took over.

"Thank you, Mr. Williams. Again, I would ask you to hold all questions and comments until the end of this talk.

"Next, we have a short, five-minute video presentation."

Jean Pierre also abruptly turned from the podium and returned to his seat, just as the lights were dimmed on the stage. The curtains drew back, revealing a large rectangular screen that hung just above the heads of each of the wardroom members, all of whom remained almost motionless in their stage seats. They wouldn't be able to see the video, even if they turned to look at it, because they were too close. Not that any of them needed to see it, as each had previewed it at least once.

A blast of light exploded onto the screen and Ted's *TD Bonaventure* voice erupted from the speakers, narrating scenes from a real-life apocalypse they weren't going to want to hear. Using video clips that Ted, David and Deep had grabbed from previously available satellite broadcasts, TD Bonaventure described a world that had permanently changed in just ten days. All major cities around the world had already fallen or were about to fall to the parasitic animals and people. Normal services were gone: TV and Internet were down, as far as they knew; no planes were flying or trains moving; stores had been emptied, as food and other supplies had stopped being delivered; all communications other than rudimentary radio transmissions were down, including with their head office or any potential ports; and finally, medical services were difficult to find at best because most people were hiding, dead, or had become parasitic.

"For all of these reasons, the crew of the *Intrepid* have decided to remain at sea indefinitely... Or until we can find a safe place to port.

We will continue to work tirelessly to keep you safe, and to survive, even if our families and friends in the outside world do not."

Ted's crude mind kicked in, thinking, *We should have played the Rolling Stones' "You can't Always Get What you Want" at the end.*

The movie stopped, the spotlights were brought back up and the stage curtains slowly closed. Jean Pierre rose once again, just as a member of their security team breezed over to Wasano and whispered into his ear. Jean Pierre watched this, while pretending that it wasn't distracting, as he stepped up to the lectern.

Already, there was a loud groundswell of conversations which had burst out around the theater. Many in the audience were sobbing from the video.

"Friends." He held up his hands again to quiet the crowd. "Friends, I know this information is difficult to digest. It was for each of us as well. But it is a fact that the world we presently occupy has completely changed. The good news is that this ship is our safe haven. And until we've identified a safe place to port, this will be our home, for a while."

He knew he should have stopped for a moment or two and let them take a breath. But he thought while they were shell-shocked, it was best if he'd plow through with the rest. They had a lot of time together to process all of this, and it would not happen in one night.

"Because the world around us has changed so much, and so that we can be assured of survival, we all must make changes on this ship. As your acting captain, the one who is in charge of your welfare as long as you're on board, I am instituting some new rules."

He turned because of a loud conversation behind him was taking attention away from him. He glared at his acting security director who was just thanking the guard he was speaking with, and signaled Jean Pierre that he needed to now speak to him. Jean Pierre returned his attention to his audience.

"In a moment, you will each be given a set of rules of conduct, which will help you to understand what will be expected of you during your extended time on board the *Intrepid*.

"Here are the most important changes... As of today, you are no longer considered guests of this ship; each of you is now a member of my crew. And as a member of my crew, you will at some point be assigned tasks to do. Additionally, because we do not know when or if we will ever get supplies again, our food will be strictly rationed. All the other restaurants will remain closed, and we will all eat out of the same dining room."

He let this sink in, and then continued more slowly. "There will be no misconduct or breaking of any rules. You will not hoard your food or any other of the ship's supplies. Anyone who does not wish to abide by my rules, and make no mistake, these are my rules, will be dropped off on one of the islands, with none of the protections you now enjoy."

Wasano cleared his throat loudly. Jean Pierre cocked his head back and acknowledged that he saw that Wasano was standing and furiously signaling him.

Jean Pierre held one hand out to tell him to wait, and then turned back to his microphone.

"We are now passing out the list of rules and in a moment, we will take questions. Please excuse me."

Jean Pierre stepped away from the lectern, Wasano meeting him part-way.

Although Wasano tried to speak in hushed tones, the theater became incredibly loud, so Wasano spoke louder than he probably should have to be heard. Everyone on stage heard at least his side of their conversation.

"Our fuel tanks are almost empty," he told the acting captain.

"How much time?" Jean Pierre asked.

"At most… five hours."

81

Alone

TJ pulled the door closed behind her and sobbed into her palms. She felt utterly alone.

She found her bed, in a cabin separated by what felt like miles from her husband, when it was only a few decks.

She was absolutely exhausted, having not slept for many days now, even though her new body demanded sleep, and lots of it now. She literally could sleep for a week and it still wouldn't be enough.

As she stared at the ceiling in the dark—she could make out every detail—she longed for her husband and for his touch.

She pulled the necklace out of the folds of her running shorts. The clasp broke and it was the only way she could prevent losing it, and yet keep it close to her. Her fingers ran over each of its intricate curves and angles, knowing its shape and look so intimately now.

She considered the reasons behind Ted buying this: he had thought of her as a warrior, because she had always insisted she was a warrior, taking the job of a warrior, until her fears took that away from her. Now she was afraid of nothing. Almost.

She wished she could go back to being that fearful person.

Her previous fear of animals was a distant concept. The only fears she held were not being able to be with people, without wanting to hurt them. And most of all, she was terrified that she'd never be with her husband again.

She tried to tuck these fears back into the dark recesses of her mind. Before all of this, she was really good at repressing her fears, or at least hiding them so she didn't have to deal with them. So she would try to do this now.

She focused on his face tonight. He looked so handsome, with his perfectly shaved face. Even his mustache was gone. She grinned to the darkness at this.

TJ kissed the necklace, and then placed it above her heart, until finally she drifted off.

~~~

Ted let the door to his empty cabin slam shut, and all at once, he felt like he would collapse from fatigue. He'd been working for endless hours on the video project, the monitoring, the endless wardroom discussions, the confabs with Molly and Chloe. But, it was that image of his wife, with tears streaming down her cheeks, that sucked every last bit of energy from him.

When the meeting concluded, he tried to find his wife, but the endless questions poured out and Jean Pierre asked him and the others stay and answer them for an hour. So he did.

After an hour or so, he did what Jean Pierre asked and told the audience that they were concluding the meeting, because the acting captain couldn't be here to attend to a
~~~

problem on the bridge. So they would have to reconvene again soon. And fellow crew members would be in touch with each of them soon.

They concluded and the wardroom members broke free and met up with Jean Pierre and Niki, who also left early.

That was when they heard the details of the problem. Their fuel problem was real, though not quite as bad as they'd first heard: Niki was able to change the efficiency of some of their systems to buy more time. They also turned off all air conditioning throughout the ship, except in the Wayfarer lounge where all the parasitics were still being held. Even with that, they had maybe a day and a half of fuel left.

It seemed fortuitous that Ted had found the group who had fuel for trade. They made contact and were set to meet in the morning. If all went well, they'd avert one more disaster.

And what a disaster it would be: if they ran out of fuel, not only wouldn't they be able to go anywhere, but their parasitic problem would come back. And even though they had them locked behind doors, there was no way those doors would hold back the strength of two or three of them, much less a few hundred.

Ted looked over at the empty space where TJ should be lying beside him. She'd separated herself from him, out of fear of what she might do. And he was pretty sure that's what she was crying about tonight. His own tears welled up as he patted her side. "I miss you, darling," he whispered.

That's it; I can't sleep, he thought.

He was wired for sound, though his body was exhausted. He couldn't sleep now, even though his body demanded it.

He often found peace and the ability to sleep when he wrote. So he grabbed his Mont Blanc box and pulled out the pen she had given him for their anniversary. *Right when this whole thing started... It was on Day Five, the day I lost her...*

A couple of tears crept out, and he furiously wiped them

away.

Ted pulled out his journal, and reread his last notation. He examined his pen, with “T.D. Bonaventure” embossed on its shaft.

He clicked off the pen cap and slipped it onto the back of the pen.

Another tear burst out and was immediately wiped away.

He paused for a moment, thought about it, and began to write.

The Journal of TD Bonaventure
DAY FIVE Cont…

Part III
SYMPTOMATIC

"Your eye is the lamp of your body.
When your eyes are good, your whole body also is full of light.
But when they are bad, your body also is full of darkness."

Holy Bible, NIV, Luke 11:34

PRELUDE

When the Rage Began

Before the earth-rattling crash, twelve year-old Dominic Sanchez cast his fishing line into the bay. Almost immediately he got a nibble.

His audience was two of the multitude of stray cats which populated his island. Each meowed its anticipation at what it knew would be coming soon.

“Hey Pedro,” he said to the scrawniest of the pair, “hang on. Let me reel ‘em in first.”

Little Pedro continued his pleading, rubbing up against Dominic’s leg for added measure, to remind Dominic that they were waiting to be fed. The larger of the two cats, Beatriz, sat patiently, knowing that Pedro would do the begging for both of them.

Dominic yanked on the rod ever so slightly, snagging the hook deeper into his prey. When he knew he had it, he reeled in the fish. From the line’s light drag, he suspected it wasn’t very big. And barely a minute later, he pulled the little thing out above the water, where it flopped spasmodically.

“Good news, Pedro. You and your wife eat first. This one’s too small for me.”

Pedro and his mate both mewed in anxious anticipation.

The palm-sized Corvina was expertly unhooked and tossed to his two furry friends, whirring behind him. The fish bounced once on the wood dock, before Pedro and Beatriz pounced on it. Each immediately snagged a piece from the fish, before nearly a dozen other cats dashed onto the dock to join in the feeding frenzy.

“Hey fellas,” Dominic yelled at the approaching clutter, scooting away the biggest of the bunch, already attempting to not only take the remaining Corvina, but the pieces his buddies had pulled from it. "Don't be greedy. Pedro and Beatriz have first dibs on the little fish. And then I get the next one."

Pedro and Beatriz held tight to their tidbits of food and bolted away from the now lifeless carcass, and the swarms of fur around it.

Dominic re-baited his line, getting ready to cast once more. He figured this time, he'd set it out much farther, where the larger schools of fish should be. Hyper-extending his arm over the frantic felines battling for the bony remnants, he shot his friends a quick glance before relaunching.

Pedro ignored the world, already preening himself after inhaling his small but satisfying first meal of the day. Beatriz seemed riveted elsewhere, probably longing for what was coming next.

This time, Dominic put his whole body into his cast, sending his line perfectly into the air.

He snapped his head forward in the direction his lure should land, then immediately convulsed; his shoulders stiffened, his mouth slacked open.

The weighted hook bulleted through the air, targeting its mark perfectly. But on its downward arc, it bounced off the steel hull of a giant fuel barge headed straight for him.

He was so stunned, he let go of his pole and it too sailed outward, plopping a meter or so away into the small bay.

The cats and he scattered down the deck, sure the barge would hit them at any second.

The moment he had turned to run, his ears were assaulted with a grinding noise of metal against sand, and then rocks. Halfway down the wood dock, he was buffeted sideways, and his ears were pummeled by the sounds of boards splintering into thousands of pieces.

Dominic did his best not to trip and fall, while the longer-than-he-ever-remembered dock twisted below him even more.

When he reached the point where the dock's twisted

wood met the concrete breaker, the torturous noises had already subsided. He turned to see how far away it was, instantly relieved. The black barge had halted midway through the partially destroyed dock. His breathing became erratic with worry, as he scanned for a sign that they were okay. Then behind the sea wall, a calico tail tentatively approached, telling him his friends were fine.

After a long minute, when there was barely a rattle or squeak from the incoming tide's pushing the stationary ship against the mangled dock, Dominic began to wonder why there was no activity on the deck of the barge. He'd seen this very craft come into the town's small port a few times. The moment its mooring lines were accepted, the small crew would buzz around topside like ants at a picnic. Dominic studied these things because he was going to be a captain of a ship when he grew up.

He glared at the dead ship before him and was surprised that still no one appeared to come topside to see where they had crashed. *Where are they? They couldn't be asleep, could they?*

Dominic spun around to see if anyone else had heard the crash, still not sure what he should do next.

He was all alone.

The creaking and rattling from the ship's hull rubbing against the dock almost felt like it was offering him an invitation to come on board. He had never been on board such a large ship.

Not being one of those boys who only read about things in books, Dominic started back down the dock. But because of the crash, the wood dock had been pushed up in an incline and now led all the way to the deck of the awaiting dead ship at the other end.

Dominic's skin tingled at the thought that maybe everyone onboard could be dead for some reason. *Perhaps the captain had died of a heart attack: old people were always dying of heart attacks.* The cool breeze taunted his crawling skin further. His imagination produced an image of what the captain's dead body might look like, draped over the pegs of the ship's steering wheel.

An upturned board and his lack of attention caused Dominic to stumble.

It didn't slow him down. Dominic leaned into his ascension and mounted the dock's steepest incline, which appeared to lead directly to the ship's edge. It looked like he could literally walk right onto the ship's forecastle, which was his plan.

Without even looking at it, he passed by the familiar stenciling on the ship's side, announcing, "Ramirez Fuel Services SA, Punta Delgado, Spain."

Once at the newly created dock-edge, now bunched up and ragged, he hopped over the two inch span and landed on top of the deck. He froze and listened for someone to tell him to leave. Anyone.

He'd never been on top of a fuel barge, not really having any interest in this type of ship: he wanted to captain a cruise ship or a large luxury yacht. His only boating experience so far was rowing a neighbor's small row boat.

Other than the ship rubbing against the broken mess of what was left of their dock and a stiff breeze whistling its own tune, all Dominic heard was Pedro's purring right below him. *This ship is a ghost town.*

He shuddered at this thought.

His gaze drifted down to his buddy, about to ask if he was ready to explore the ship, when he noticed he was standing in a large puddle of red, starkly cast against the ship's white decking.

It was blood. Lots of blood.

~~~
~~~

Vila de Corvo's PCP Police Chief, Salvadore Calderon, slammed the door of his Skoda. Almost immediately he blew out an exaggerated whistle at the sight before them. "Well Tomas, here's one more thing you wouldn't see on the mainland."

Tomas Novo, the youngest of his two agents, who had pleaded with him to be released into a larger, more exciting police unit on the Portuguese mainland, said nothing. The young man adjusted his hat and waited for his superior. When Sal took up a place beside him, he too gawked at the wrecked hundred-year-old dock and the ship that caused the damage, wedged into the middle of it. Tomas asked, "Do you think she'll leak?"

"I'm more worried about why I don't see any of the crew, and what caused the crash," Sal said. His voice scattered into the wind as he stomped onto the dock. It felt as if it was moving with the tide.

Sal considered his own questions, and then wondered if this day could get any stranger. He and his agent had just returned from investigating two separate animal attacks and then a report of some crazy woman killing her husband. Now this. Their small station was barely two kilometers away. So when they heard the crash, it seemed like the whole town had poured outside of their homes and shops to see what all the clatter was about.

"Tomas, get on your radio and have Val call Ramirez Shipping in Puento Delgado. See if they know their ship has crashed onto our shore.

His junior agent started hollering inaudibly into his radio, while Sal mounted the inclined dock, which ended at the starboard bow of the ship.

Sal tried to block out Tomas' voice to listen for any other sounds. Other than the wind and the creaking of ship against the broken dock, he heard nothing.

When Sal hopped onto the barge's deck, he immediately knew something was very wrong, and drew his service Berretta in response.

Tomas hollered something else into the radio and froze beside him upon seeing his superior's drawn weapon.

Sal pointed, without saying anything. A puddle of blood and the bloody sneaker prints of a child led toward the open doorway a few meters ahead.

When they heard a little boy's scream, they both went running.

They followed the bloody trail, but with each of their footfalls, Sal felt his anxiety spike. Twice he glanced back at Tomas to confirm it wasn't some hallucination. He felt like he was seeing things lately, so maybe he was imagining some of this. Each time Tomas met his gaze with the same "this is some crazy shit" look, he knew it was real. He wanted to say to him each time, "Well you wanted some excitement... here it is." But he held off saying anything until they finished running the insanely long distance from the bow to the doorway.

It was an entrance into the bowels of the ship, where the blood-trail stopped. The door swayed slightly from the ship's rocking motion, forced upon it by the incoming tide.

Sal was a little out of breath and was relieved when looking back, that his young agent was as well.

"It sounded like a male child to me," Tomas stated, obviously trying to smooth out his own growing anxiousness.

He was right, it was a young boy, and the shriek sounded familiar to him as well. He probably knew this kid, because he knew everyone in their town. "Follow me," he said and then glared at his deputy. "Don't shoot unless you have to." He didn't want to get shot in the back by the nervous young man.

Tomas nodded, holding his service weapon down with both hands.

The entrance led into a dark stairwell, which almost

immediately descended into a dank murk. A blinking light below flashed a momentary view of the emptiness.

An animal screeched a hollow bray, like it was injured and angry.

It was close.

Sal had a sinking dread that this might be another animal attack, although he had no reason to connect the two attacks on his island with this crash. His heart began pumping ample amounts of adrenaline to his systems. Something else seemed wrong.

Was it him?

In all of his years in police work, he remained safe by being careful to avoid risky situations. Only when one of his men was in peril did he put himself into peril and then, only after he waited for the last possible moment. He felt different now. He felt like he didn't care, even if it was risky. Worse, he was looking forward to whatever was down there. His heart pumped happily; his chest heaved joyfully. He should have been terrified, just like his agent was.

Then he heard another bray, much closer now. A form appeared in the yellowish light of the flashing strobe. It wasn't an animal. It was a man. It was Old Man Ramirez, the captain and owner of this ship. Ramirez lifted his gaze up the stairwell to meet Sal's and screeched at him. Sal knew then that Ramirez was making the animal sounds he had heard, like he was the animal. Ramirez' eyes blazed red like two turn signals with each flash of light; they appeared to blink at him. Ramirez then turned and disappeared.

Sal didn't hesitate. He stepped into the darkness.

82

The Vote
Eleven Days Later

"It's their blooming eyes," Boris bellowed. His face twisted into a frown, which Chloe Barton couldn't see in the darkness. "Their damned red eyes. That's how you know they're animals."

"But they're not animals, they're still people..." Chloe pleaded. "They're infected with a disease and they're just not in control of what they do."

"Suppose you'd say the same thing about pedophiles: it's not their fault, they don't know what they do. So what? Should we feel sorry for them because they're diseased?" This came from an officer on the other side of the group. She didn't know him.

Chloe sighed, feeling like she was swimming against the current in a river of piranhas. "I'm not saying that. I'm just saying that killing them all isn't the answer. And it's not who we are as people."

Boris burst out of his aluminum chair, almost knocking it down. "Hon, I'm saying that's exactly what we are. The sooner we kill all of the parasitics, the better. For all of us."

"Shhhh. Someone's coming," one of their group huffed.

Every one of their group held their breaths. All heads turned to see who it was. A single set of footsteps, barely heard over the stiff sea breeze, grew louder with each footfall. Someone was definitely coming their way.

Chloe shrank back into the group, not really wanting to be seen by anyone, especially another officer. As the head of the ship's medical clinic, it didn't feel right to be at a Resist Parasitics meeting. She glanced at the faces, most cloaked in shadows. She knew many of them; it was hard not to, with so few of the original crew left. Some she didn't know, because they either worked in areas she'd just never visited, or they were originally passengers, like Boris.

She was amazed by people like Boris, who she understood to be infected with the parasite which had turned many men into monsters. He just hadn't become symptomatic yet. But he could at any time. Then what would he do, order his own death? Highly doubtful. It was just his fear talking.

They were all fearful, especially of what lay ahead of them. It seemed like they had some control of things, but this control felt tenuous at best. So everyone wanted safety and they were willing to sacrifice anything to get it, including every sense of morality they had. Well, she wasn't going to be a part of this. She didn't have an answer yet for their parasitics, but she wasn't going to stand for genocidal murder. It just wasn't right.

The footsteps were almost upon them, now echoing off the pool decking.

A few of the craned necks retracted back from the edge of the outdoor movie theater screen, seemingly satisfied with the footsteps' owner.

"It's just Bohdan. He's one of us," said someone she

couldn't see.

Bohdan Oliynyk was a despicable man, of the lowest order. A Czech from engineering, he'd been in two days ago, complaining of a sore throat. When Chloe said that she was in charge of this medical center, he refused to leave until a male doctor would see him, saying that he never trusted the words of a woman who wasn't even a doctor.

Luckily for Chloe, a male nurse, who was a passenger volunteer, saw him, diagnosed him as having acute pharyngitis, and gave him some antibiotics and sent him away.

She had hoped he would have remained sealed in engineering. She shrank further into the darkness.

"Good timing, Bohdan." Paulo from security and the organizer of this meeting spoke up. "We'd just been discussing whether or not we should treat the crazies like good, misunderstood people or just kill them. We were close to voting. Do you want—"

"Let's vote. No more discussions," Bohdan stated.

"Okay, all who want to do nothing about the crazies, locked away in our lounge, where one day they may break out and eat us all, say 'Aye.'"

Only one other person, a meek-sounding man, said "Aye" along with Chloe.

"All those who want to terminate the abominations before they kill us all, say 'Nay.'"

A resounding "Nay" sounded from the group.

"The Nays have it. Now, let's discuss how we should do this."

Chloe stood up from her chair and couldn't disappear from this place quickly enough. As she stepped away, trying to hug the shadows, she heard Bohdan speak up.

"I have a way to do this and I can do it tomorrow morning."

83
Ted

She stood over him while he slept. His cabin was void of light, and yet she watched and listened to him mumble something from an ongoing nightmare.

She slithered out of her long sleeve athletic jersey and then her shorts. Pulling the covers back, she slid into his bed, inching her way toward him. Her hand found him, knowing what he liked.

After a few seconds, he moaned softy. She smiled at this.

She guided herself on top of him and moved her hips slowly. His moans grew in response and he began to move with her.

“You're all mine now,” she whispered.

His eyes popped open and he glared at her. Her grin was Grand Canyon-sized, and equally rapturous. He knew her contagious smile all too well. But this one was different. It felt wrong.

He didn’t know why, until it became obvious.

It was pitch-black in the cabin and yet the features of her face and body were absolutely clear. She looked perfect: equal portions of delicately strong and delightfully sexy.

She grinned even more at his revelation, if that was possible. She moved her hips faster, and he saw that he was matching her motions. They were one. Even her eyes—both ruby-red now—pulsed in perfect synchronicity to their movements and their heartbeats. His breathing grew more rapid, as did hers, as if he were breathing for her.

Or is she breathing for me?

The logical side of his brain was stuck on figuring out how he could see her in the darkness. He couldn't resolve this, even if he accepted everything else. And yet her ghostly outline was as clear as if there were a full moon somehow casting its eerie glow on her. Some of her details even seemed as clear as they would be during a midday sun.

But how?

"You're wondering how you can see me," she stated, as if she could read his thoughts too.

He froze.

The chasm-sized smile slid off her face. "Don't stop dear, we're just getting started."

He could feel his mouth fall open, now gaping.

She leaned over him, pressing her bare chest against his, and softly took in his lips with hers. She kissed him passionately, but then abruptly pulled back. "You're one of us now."

She drifted farther back from him, but her legs and thighs remained clasped around him. Her hands still clutched his hips, and then locked into him even tighter. She wanted him to know that she had total control over him and his movements.

She was so strong now, so much stronger than he thought she could be. And he knew that she could crush him, snap him in two if she wanted to. But she didn't; she just wanted him to know that she had that kind of power over him.

He accepted it.

She released one hand from his hip. It slowly rose in the air above him, as if floating, her fist and forefinger becoming a pointer. She was guiding his glare to the other side of the bed, to what was supposed to be her side.

He turned his head in that direction, anxious to find out what she was trying to tell him. Gone was the shock that he could clearly see his cabin in total darkness, because he knew what she said was right. He had somehow become like her now, and this terrified him.

Even though each of her features and many of his cabin's details were crystal clear, he couldn't quite make out the moving form beside him. Blinking away at the darkness, he couldn't tell what it was, only that there was something under the covers, on her side of the bed. Then based on its size and shape, he knew it wasn't a something; it was a someone. They weren't alone now.

Repelled by this, he tried to move away from the writhing mass, which he could now see more clearly and even hear its rustle. But she held him down, still controlling him, demanding he see this. He gave up.

"Open your eyes, dear," she commanded, her voice sultry but serious.

It was then he realized his eyes had been closed. He didn't want to see who or what was in the bed with them. And whatever it was now rustled even more. And it groaned.

He flicked open his eyes, piercing the darkness once more. And he saw the form was out from under the sheets, sitting up in their bed.

Recognition slapped him in the face.

It was Jean Pierre, their acting captain. The same man she had been working with earlier on an FBI investigation, just before she had changed. Jean Pierre was here, in their bed.

If that wasn't enough of a shock to his system, he

realized that something was terribly wrong with this man.

Jean Pierre was gasping for breath. Gagging. At the same time, his hands were clasped around his neck. Thick streams of blood seeped through the gaps in his fingers. A dark red liquid coursed down his formal clothes and pooled all around him.

His face was a surreal death mask of terror. He tried to cry out for help, but it came out as a slight whimper. "Hellllpa."

"Oh my God, what did you do?" Ted barked as his eyes drilled into hers.

She bellowed back in laughter. "You did this, Ted. You're a killer now, just like me."

He coughed, because his mouth was full of something soft… chewy. He spat it out; a fleshy mess plopped into a puddle pooled beside him. *The pool was blood… Jean Pierre's blood.* And its sticky warmth coated his mouth, his body and now… hers.

At that very moment Ted was both excitedly aroused and utterly terrified. "Nooooo!"

She cackled in response, until her laughter fractured and faded into an almost scratchy-sounding voice that demanded, "Ted, are you there?"

Her voice became more distant, almost disconnected from her, like she was a ventriloquist throwing her words out into murk, where they became consumed by the night.

Once again, a scratchy call to him from the other side of the room, only louder this time, "Ted, are you there?"

The staticky voice chimed once again, "Ted, are you there?"

He flicked his eyes open and closed, and then open again, because he could no longer see her in the darkness. He couldn't see anything.

His right hand shot out of the covers and he felt along the wall, in a desperate search for the switch.

Clicking it on, blinding white light burst throughout his

cabin. He drilled his eyes forward to where his wife had been. She was no longer there. He snapped his head to his left, expecting to see the bloody man—*who was it again?* He was gone too.

It was Jean Pierre. That's who was there.

It was all just an awful nightmare. Nothing more.

"Ted, are you there?" called the portable radio on his nightstand. "This is Captain Jean Pierre; please answer if you can hear me."

The Journal of TD Bonaventure

DAY TWELVE

LIKE MOST PEOPLE IN THE WORLD, THIS DAY BEGAN AFTER A NIGHTMARE. FOR ME, THE NIGHTMARE ENDED WHEN I WOKE UP; FOR MOST EVERYONE ELSE, THE NIGHTMARE CONTINUES.

MANY ONBOARD OUR SHIP ARE CAUTIOUSLY HOPEFUL THAT WE'VE PUT OUR NIGHTMARE BEHIND US. MEANWHILE, THE REST OF THE WORLD IS STILL CLOAKED IN UNENDING DEATH AND DESTRUCTION. EVEN IF WE SURVIVE THE COMING DAYS, THE NIGHTMARE WILL STILL BE ALL AROUND US, LIKE THE DARK, FOREBODING CLOUDS NOW BLANKETING ALL THE HEAVENS. WE'RE NOT SURE IF THIS IS NORMAL AZURIAN WEATHER OR A SIGN OF MORE DARKNESS YET TO COME.

STILL THERE IS REASON FOR HOPE.

WHEN THE RAGE HIT US LIKE A TIDAL WAVE, IT APPEARED THAT WE WOULD SUFFER THE SAME FATE AS THE REST OF THE WORLD. I ADMIT TO LOSING HOPE AT TIMES, FIRST WITH SO MANY PASSENGERS AND CREW LOSING THEIR LIVES AND THE REMAINDER TURNING INTO SOME NEW FORM OF MONSTER, ALL SEEMINGLY CONTROLLED BY A SIMPLE PARASITE. THEN WE CONFIRMED THIS WAS HAPPENING EVERYWHERE.

FROM ONGOING NEWS REPORTS, UNTIL WE STOPPED RECEIVING THEM, THE SAME TIDAL WAVE OF MADNESS WASHED OVER THE WORLD, LEAVING ALMOST NO ONE UNAFFECTED. BILLIONS OF RAGE-FUELED ANIMALS AND MILLIONS OF BLOOD-THIRSTY HUMANS ATTACKED ANYTHING WITH A HEARTBEAT THAT WAS NOT ALREADY INFECTED. INDEED, THE PROSPECTS FOR ANYONE'S SURVIVAL

LOOKED BLEAKER THAN AT ANY TIME IN HUMAN HISTORY.

STILL, AS A SCIENTIST, IT'S HARD NOT TO LOOK WITH AWE AND APPRECIATION AT WHAT MAY BE THE DAWN OF A NEW SPECIES. THESE PARASITICS (THAT'S WHAT WE CALL THOSE WHO ARE FULLY CONTROLLED BY THE RAGE DISEASE) ARE SURE TO BE THE NEW APEX ON EARTH, THE TOP DOG IN THE FOOD CHAIN. AS A LIFE-LONG ATHEIST, I BEGAN TO ACCEPT THE FATE THAT HAD BEEN DEALT US HUMANS: EXTINCTION WAS LIKELY JUST AROUND THE CORNER.

AND YET, I CANNOT DISCOUNT THE THEORY THAT SOME PROVIDENTIAL HAND WAS AT WORK HERE, AS ILLOGICAL AS THAT MAY SOUND.

HOW ELSE DO I REASON THAT MY WIFE AND I ENDED UP ON ONE OF THE FEW SURVIVABLE PLACES TO WEATHER THIS KIND OF APOCALYPSE? BEING ON A CRUISE SHIP AFFORDED US CONTROL OVER OUR ENVIRONMENT, WHICH ALLOWED US TO TILT THE EVOLUTIONARY SCALES BACK TO OUR FAVOR. TALK ABOUT TRUTH BEING STRANGER THAN FICTION. I CERTAINLY COULDN'T HAVE WRITTEN THIS NARRATIVE: AN AUTHOR WHO WROTE A BOOK ON THIS VERY APOCALYPSE AND A PARASITOLOGIST (AN EXPERT AT WHAT'S GOING ON) SERENDIPITOUSLY APPEAR ON THE SAME SHIP, JUST AS THE WAVES OF ATTACKS ON THE MAINLAND WERE STARTING.

BEING ON A SELF-CONTAINED SHIP REMOVED US FROM THE PREDATOR-TO-PREY IMBALANCE ON THE MAINLAND, WITH TEN THOUSAND MAMMALS—MORE THAN THE MAJORITY OF THEM INFECTED—TO EVERY HUMAN. YET BY HAVING JUST A FEW ANIMALS ON BOARD, WE COULD USE WHAT WE LEARNED FROM THEM TO HELP US SURVIVE THE WAVE OF HUMAN PARASITIC ATTACKS THAT FOLLOWED NEXT. WE FOUND OUT, QUITE BY

ACCIDENT, THAT WE COULD CONTROL THE PARASITICS BY LOWERING THEIR BODY TEMPERATURE, AND THIS COULD BE ACCOMPLISHED BY DROPPING THE OUTSIDE TEMPERATURE USING THE SHIP'S AIR CONDITIONING. COULD ALL OF THIS SIMPLY BE FORTUITOUS?

THEN THERE ARE THE UNASSAILABLE TRUTHS CONCERNING MY WIFE, WHICH CANNOT BE EASILY EXPLAINED AS RANDOM CHANCE.

TJ CONTRACTED THE VERY PARASITE AT THE ROOT OF THIS WORLDWIDE APOCALYPSE FROM AN ANIMAL ATTACK YEARS AGO. AND YET IF SHE HADN'T, SHE WOULD HAVE SURELY DIED WHEN SHE FELL FROM THAT ZIP LINE. AND BECAUSE SHE BECAME SYMPTOMATIC, EVERY ONE OF THE SHIP'S SURVIVORS HAS HER AND HER NEW ABILITIES TO THANK, AMONG THE MANY REASONS FOR OUR MAKING IT THIS FAR. IT'S TRUE THAT HER "ABILITIES" DID NOT COME WITHOUT COST—MY HEART STILL BREAKS AT OUR INDEFINITE SEPARATION.

BUT THAT'S A WORRY FOR ANOTHER DAY.

AND AS EXPECTED, WE HAVE ANOTHER CHALLENGE AHEAD OF US, BUT AT THE SAME TIME, A POTENTIAL SOLUTION. FORTUITOUS OR PROVIDENTIAL? I'LL LET YOU BE THE JUDGE.

WHEN HALF THE POPULATION OF OUR SHIP APPEARED TO GO INSANE AND STARTED ATTACKING, TWO OF THE PARASITICS GOT ONTO THE BRIDGE AND DESTROYED SOME OF OUR CONTROLS. IN THE PROCESS, OUR SHIP DUMPED MOST OF ITS FUEL INTO THE OCEAN. WE DIDN'T REALIZE THIS UNTIL AFTER WE HAD TAKEN BACK CONTROL OF THE SHIP.

ONCE AGAIN, THIS WOULD PROBABLY HAVE BEEN OUR END: WE NEEDED THE AIR CONDITIONING TO KEEP THE PARASITICS' BODY TEMPERATURES LOW ENOUGH THAT THEY'D REMAIN

IN A SEMI-HYBERNATIVE STATE. AND WE NEEDED FUEL TO RUN THE AIR CONDITIONERS AND THE REST OF THE SHIP'S SYSTEMS. AND WITH THE WORLD IN CHAOS, INCLUDING ALL OF THE MAJOR PORTS, SAFELY FINDING THE NEEDED FUEL WOULD HAVE BEEN NEARLY IMPOSSIBLE AT BEST. THEN IT WOULD SEEM PROVIDENCE'S HAND OFFERED US A SOLUTION.

AMONG THE LOUD QUIET OF THE WORLD'S NOW EMPTY AIRWAVES, I FOUND A BROADCAST FROM AN ISLAND WHERE THEY SAY RAGE HASN'T HIT AND ITS OCCUPANTS HAVE THE FUEL WE NEED, IN EXCHANGE FOR A LITTLE OF OUR FOOD. SURE, IT SOUNDS TOO GOOD TO BE TRUE. AND PERHAPS IT IS.

ASSUMING THEIR INTENTIONS ARE GENUINE AND WE HAVE WHAT THEY WANT, I SUPPOSE A DEAL SHOULD BE MADE. WHO KNOWS, MAYBE THIS ISLAND WILL END UP BEING OUR NEW HOME.

CERTAINLY WITHOUT THIS ONLY OPTION, WE WILL BE DEAD IN THE WATER IN A FEW HOURS. AND THAT MEANS WE WOULD LOSE ANY CONTROL WE HAD OVER THE PARASITICS. GAME OVER.

THEN THERE'S THE NEWEST CHALLENGE: INDUCTION OF ALL PASSENGERS INTO THE CREW. IT WAS A BOLD MOVE BY OUR CAPTAIN. AND NOW, WE ARE NO LONGER A CRUISE OF LEISURE: WE'VE BECOME A FREIGHTER OF HOPE, FIGHTING FOR A COMMON GOAL, SURVIVAL. NO LONGER WERE THERE TWO CLASSES OF PEOPLE: CREW, WHOSE JOB IT WAS TO SERVE, AND THE PASSENGERS, WHO EXPECTED TO BE SERVED. EVERYONE WAS GIVEN A JOB TO DO, AND EVERYONE WAS EXPECTED TO DO IT, OR THEY WOULD BE DROPPED OFF AT THE NEXT PORT.

ALONG WITH OUR RATIONED FOOD, THIS WAS ALL THE NEW NORMAL. WE ALL WORK MANY HOURS TO HELP ALL ON BOARD SURVIVE UNTIL THE NEXT

DAY AND THAT MAKES OUR DAYS PASS BY QUICKLY, LEAVING LITTLE TIME FOR ANY OF US TO WORRY ABOUT WHAT'S GOING ON OUTSIDE THIS SHIP.

WHEN I DO TAKE TIME TO PONDER OUR WORLD, WHICH IS ACTUALLY PART OF MY DUTIES, I CAN'T HELP BUT THINK OF MY WIFE, TJ, AND WHEN I CAN SEE HER AGAIN. IT'S WHAT I LOOK FORWARD TO.

AND TODAY AFTER MY REGULAR MEETING WITH MOLLY, WHO SAYS SHE HAS AN "INCREDIBLE REVELATION" SHE'S DYING TO TELL ME ABOUT, I WILL GET TO SEE TJ BRIEFLY. THEN SHE AND THE OTHERS WILL ATTEMPT TO MAKE A TRADE. I'LL BE HELPING WITH THAT ONE VIA THE RADIO.

BUT THE BEST PART OF THE WHOLE DAY WILL BE SEEING MY WIFE.

I GUESS LIFE HAS COME DOWN TO LOOKING FORWARD TO THOSE SMALL THINGS… SMALL TO SOME, BUT GIANT TO OTHERS.

84

TJ

She awoke with a startled shake. Not from the room's coolness, but shock at finding herself sitting on the edge of her unmade bed, in the dark of this foreign cabin. TJ had been doing a lot of this since her rebirth: finding herself in places she didn't remember getting to.

She glanced down at her Orion necklace, currently lacking all luster. *There was no light in the cabin to reflect,* she told herself. But it was still clear enough, as if illuminated by bright moonlight. She had it cupped in her open hands, watching it move up and down with the rapid heaving of her chest.

She pressed her palms, and with it her necklace, back onto her breasts and allowed her eyes to shut, in a desperate attempt to recall the wonderful dream she had just had of Ted, before the evil within her invaded this rare respite with her husband and forced her awake.

The features of his face came to mind...

He no longer had a mustache!

She smiled at this.

Then she remembered the blood.

Her eyes flicked open and she pushed away the images. Looking down again, she shuddered, at once realizing she was squeezing much too hard upon the delicate gift commemorating their 20th wedding anniversary, given to her only a few long days ago. She was terrified she would smash one of the last tangible connections she had between her, her husband and her old life. But there were far more terrifying things than this.

Pulling at the elastic of her compression shorts, she slipped the necklace inside, feeling comfort in it resting against her skin—since the chain broke, it was the only way she could keep it secured to her. She shot up from the bed, her feet once again finding the path she was sure she was wearing into the carpet by now.

The pacing up and down the length of the cabin was one of the few actions she felt in control of; it was her way to physically force back the mental tides raging within her, all of which desired to burst out and consume what little remained of her old human self.

Her mind was an ongoing battlefield where a war was being fought between the armies of good thoughts or memories and evil aspirations or desires. Whichever side won would claim her soul.

At times, she was able to recall the delicate trickle of the lovely memories of Ted, her family, their home, and even her work. It was only during those times that she could actually find some peace and with it, sleep. But sleep, like the comforts of her old memories, was fleeting and brief.

During the remaining moments—the majority of the time—her thoughts were a windswept mental seascape of sin, a tempest of anger, a downpour of hatred, a hurricane of murderous rage, a destructive desire for blood. And when these thoughts were allowed into her mind, she felt like she was set on an unstoppable course to kill, or to maim, or to at least hurt whoever got in her way. It was during those times, times like now, that she would find herself wide awake. Hyperventilating. Although she was always breathing as if she were hyperventilating. One of the many things that had changed in her.

And it was all the changes that had manifested themselves inside her, and were still occurring, that led her to separate herself from Ted. He didn't understand. But how could he? She didn't really understand—was trying to understand—what was going on inside her brain and body.

She had told him that she had to remain separate, because she didn't feel he would be safe around her. And this was partially true, because she was afraid that her terrifying desire for human flesh would be unstoppable in close quarters. And when either passion or anger sprang forth, it brought with it an overwhelming sensation, even an unquenchable thirst, for murder and blood. And these desires could arise with the simple whiff of her next meal, all because of her new ability to smell everything...

Like some goddamn dog... Scratch that, like some damned hound from hell.

Great, just like me to develop a dog ability.

Most things simply smelled bad, like the body odor of another infected. But a non-infected's smell was frighteningly the complete opposite. Because of this, she worried that even the mere aroma of the uninfected could set her off. And it was why she wore a swimming nose-plug: to stem the smells of those who were not infected, like her husband.

But weren't these all just excuses?

After all, a part of her—an ever-shrinking part of her—that was still human and still loved him and badly needed him didn't really believe she would allow that evil part of her to take total control and hurt him. Although she reasoned thus, with each internal battle between good and evil, and with each noticeable physical change, she was a little less sure of this.

The largest part of her worry of their being together was that he would see the changes in her. And not just the physical.

It was her internal battles that she wanted the most to hide from him. She feared—one of the few fears she possessed anymore—that he could see some horrendous evil inside of her. She couldn't stand to see him repulsed by her becoming some sort of monster. That's really what kept her away. So she told herself, and him, that this separation would only last until she could figure this thing out. And get control of it.

This made sense to both of them, since she always had control of things. Even when she was deathly afraid of animals, she remained in control by staying out of situations where fear would rear its ugly head. In this way, she didn't allow fear to control her. Amongst all of the new changes in her, she'd lost her fear of animals, along with all the other normal human fears. Ironically, the less fear she felt, the more she felt like she was losing control.

Something outside of her consciousness was fighting for possession of her mind and body, tempting her with euphoric tastes and desires, and alluring her with fantastic abilities. But she would continue to fight for her humanity, even though she didn't know what it was going to do with her next. She wasn't going to let it win. Whatever *it* was.

"Yeah, I know what you are," she stated out loud so it could hear her. As if it worked that way.

She guessed that she must have been originally infected with this parasite when she was viciously attacked by that crazed dog. Ted said the dog's saliva could have introduced the parasite into her bloodstream. He had also said that this parasite had been around for centuries; it just wasn't as widespread until recently. And when the thermo-bacilli were spewed into the atmosphere, that's what ignited this whole apocalypse upon them.

She once more was surprised to find herself stopped, mid-step from her pacing, standing before the cabin's full-length mirror. There, she examined herself.

TJ found comfort in the darkness during moments like this, even though in this mirror, she could see the details of her own face and body. The colors were all different without light. She wasn't sure if there were any colors in the darkness, with her mind filling in the colors, albeit poorly.

Once again, she marveled at the physical changes which had occurred, as she focused on her chest rising and falling.

She had to admit that she was thrilled to have gained the ability to see not only long distances, but in the dark as well. Her whole life—at least for as long as she could remember—she was plagued with grotesque nearsightedness, barely able to see past her own two feet. She always wore glasses, giving her a bookish look during puberty. Later in life she found the freedom of contacts, and that's when the boys started to notice her more. Later still, as she got older, she could see a little better at a distance, while at the same time losing her ability to see things close. But all that changed with her rebirth. But with her new sight abilities came her creepy red eyes. Or at least one red eye.

She leaned over to the light switch, flipped it on and completely blinded herself.

After shaking away ghostly white flashes, she resumed her place in front of the mirror, where she examined her eyes again. She had to force herself not to squint against the cabin's bright lights.

Both Dr. Molly Simmons and Ted had explained that it had something to do with the loss of melanin. Gone were her blue eyes. One now was a pinkish-blue and the other a bright crimson—like blood. The same hue as those of her symptomatic brothers and sisters who seemed to have turned crazy after their own rebirths. They told her that the loss of melanin drained her of her color. But it wasn't just her eyes; it was her skin too.

In the stark lighting of this cabin, she now looked like death warmed over. And with each day, her skin lost more of its life. She was becoming some sort of albino. Although never dark-skinned—far from it—she at least had had a little pigment, especially in contrast to her blonde hair. She had even hoped to add to her skin's color on this cruise, by spending time in the warmth of the sun.

But I can at least do something about my outward appearance.

She shed her clothes and stepped into the cool spray of the shower—the lever at its coldest setting—and she washed away the grime that clung to her, more naturally than before.

After drying off, she slid on a fresh set of exercise clothes, her normal uniform now. The material breathed, allowing her to stay cool, which was of the utmost importance now. And because it was so form-fitting, she felt she had a free range of motion, which also felt important if she had to use her new abilities.

After pulling her hair into a tight ponytail, she grabbed the bottle of self-tanning lotion from the counter. She procured this from the same place she'd found the swimmer's nose plugs: the ship's gift shop. After shaking it up, she squeezed a healthy portion onto a palm and then smoothed it into one arm and then the other.

Not bad, she thought after examining her work.

She applied lotion up her shoulders, around the exposed skin of her chest, and then felt skilled enough at this to apply some to her blanched face.

She scrutinized herself in the bathroom mirror.

This might actually work.

After making sure she was well covered, she applied just a little makeup, finding a rosier color of lipstick than she would have normally worn: like the rest of her skin, her lips needed all the help they could get.

Finally she stepped back and analyzed herself against a mental picture of what was previously "normal," turning and tilting her head at different angles for confirmation. She felt like she was ready.

85
Molly

Dr. Molly Simmons removed her glasses and attempted to rub away the fatigue nested in her eyes. Last she looked, her scleras were as red as the irises of her parasitic subjects. It was no use. She was done.

She gave up holding herself erect, now allowing her body to tilt backwards in the reclining chair the captain had given her. This gift was so she could do her work better. "Work? Ha!" she chided herself.

I'm supposed to be a retired parasitologist. Key word is retired.

With her eyes closed, and her back finally supported for the first time in hours, Molly considered what led to these late hours of work on a former luxury cruise ship.

Before retirement, when she had been working regular hours—another oxymoronic concept for a scientist at any age—all she did was research, usually for corporate laboratories, whose sole interest was in finding the next big cure for the various parasitic illnesses. After she retired, she wrote a few papers on some of the potential coming crises that could come from some of the bigger parasitic challenges, including the subject of her current research, Toxoplasmosis. It was her futurist predictions that garnered her some of her notoriety.

With this notoriety came offers to speak, but she rarely accepted them. After all, she was retired. She did accept a couple of offers so she could also to visit her daughter in Northern Florida. Most recently it was the opportunity see her granddaughter in France, whom she hadn't seen since before she was married. So she traveled across the Atlantic to give a speech to a bunch of stodgy old men—there were few women in her field in Europe. And that was the extent of her "work," at least before this cruise.

When she had worked, there were few pressures other than those of self-imposed deadlines. She had loved every moment of what she did, even the long hours in her lab. She hated her work now.

The self-imposed pressures to find answers for her captain, her new author-friend Ted Williams and all the people on her ship were almost debilitating.

She breathed out a long groan, an equal mixture of frustration at being in this position and the extreme exhaustion she was feeling. The lack of sleep was at the root of all of this.

She'd slept little on this ship. How could she, as she was spending every waking moment reacting to one colossal problem after another? That was the nub of it. Proper research was never done during a crisis. It should be conducted in the vacuum of discovery, with lots of time. No matter the problem, she knew she could discover an answer, if given enough time. And it was often the motivation that drove her. That and a good laboratory.

She snickered at this, since her laboratory now was a videotape room and a couple of video cameras trained on her subjects.

Molly let her mind wander as she felt the weight of her eyelids, relishing these rare moments of peace and self-reflection... *And no back pain,* she thought.

It must have been the angle in which she was resting in this chair, and the pillows she had jammed around it. Her disease-riddled back often screamed at her to change position every few minutes. Rarely could she consciously remember not feeling that screaming pain. Not even in the soft beds the ship provided. She could almost fall asleep here. But her mind was racing too much.

So she took this opportunity to reflect on something delightful: her travel abroad and seeing her granddaughter's new family. *Hard to believe that it had all started three weeks ago. It felt longer.*

Molly's granddaughter Lola and her French husband Claude had encouraged her to accept the speaking engagement and go on this cruise. That's exactly what Molly did, first spending time with Lola and Claude on his family's winery in the Loire region of France.

She caught her breath when her mind wondered about their current fate. She now illogically reasoned that they'd be safe there; that they'd be left untouched by this apocalypse. She couldn't bear to think otherwise.

After her visit, Molly was the guest of the Universitat de Barcelona, Spain, speaking to some of the world's leading parasitologists at an annual conference. She had warned them all about a pending crisis, saying that all the signs were there, with increased animal attacks, along with widespread paranoia and schizophrenic behavior in humans. She shook her head at how right she was about that.

After this, she headed to Malaga to board the cruise ship, with the single goal of relaxing while sailing across the Atlantic. She had brought a couple of books to read, but mostly she would enjoy the pleasure of being waited on by someone who wasn't one of her family members. The whole trip would have culminated with Molly meeting up with her daughter in Florida.

But then the world fell apart.

She sprang forward in her chair, sling-shotting her spiking anger toward her desk, so she could address the perpetrator of this apocalypse. She stared down at her desktop; a printout of the giant-sized protozoa gazed back. "It's all because of you!" She punched the color-enhanced photograph, a close-up of a toxoplasma gondii parasite. "You're the cause of this whole mess." Her forefinger sliced down on the parasite's picture, as if it were that easy to do harm to this microscopic monster.

Her anger quickly subsided, and so did the rest of her energy. With this and her quick movements, the chronic pain in her back had returned in full force. She tried again to alleviate this, by falling back again into her chair and the comfort it provided. There was a reason why she had retired: she was too damned old for these late-night research events. *But there was no use in complaining about this, was there?* she again chided herself.

This time, she sat up more gingerly and leaned into her desk, organizing the papers which currently littered its top.

The recent online research papers Mr. Buzz had found for her on university databases had proven invaluable to her research. He was somehow able to rig up a way to connect up to their servers even though he said most of the Internet was down. She didn't exactly understand how it all worked, only that Mr. Buzz said he used some sort of mesh network connection to search and find digitized texts, studies, and other useful information, based on some select keywords Molly had given him. All of which he had printed for her.

She had just read through a majority of the recent batch. With these, she was able to compare the most current T-Gondii research studies with what she and Mr. Deep had observed. She sat up straighter in her seat, now looking at her pages of notes chronicling what they now knew based on their own empirical observations.

So much had changed with what they'd learned over the six days of their observing the parasitics they had locked up in the ship's largest lounge.

At first, they seemed no more than wild animals, uniquely focused on destruction and murder. At least that was what they had all first thought, even Molly. They had destroyed pretty much everything in their path. They were still cleaning up and fixing large parts of the ship, with some repairs expected to take weeks or longer to complete. The lounge where they were being held was emblematic of this: most of the seats were ripped apart; the batting covered everything, like a heavy snowfall. And as driven as they appeared to be by destruction, they were perhaps even more driven by their appetites.

They ate more food by body weight than what they did as humans, from the limited evidence they had so far. Molly immediately guessed this was because of their highly increased metabolisms, which had to be working overtime to maintain their accelerated activity and newly elevated body heat.

And in spite of the inactivity her ship had forced upon them with the cold temperatures, the parasitics' physical needs to fuel their accelerated metabolisms still meant lots more food. This explained their early rampage and eating of fellow passengers and crew.

Of course, they couldn't very well feed them live humans… She snickered at the thought of feeding some of the more problematic passengers, like Hans, to them. So they turned to raw meat, which seemed to be the only food they'd eat. But this changed fairly quickly after the first day. And it made complete sense.

As was the case with mammals in the wild, when their body heat was threatened, and after they had satiated themselves, they were forced to find ways to maintain their body temperature, and often go into a hybernative state. And that's what their parasitics had done.

But their parasitics were much more than wild animals. They were humans, and now humans with extra abilities.

She shuffled through her neatly hand-written pages, to re-examine her notes from last night.

It was her worst fear that these parasitics, who at first appeared to be just irrational animals, would start to use their cognitive abilities and apply them along with their new abilities.

And now they had proof that this was happening, along with one more new ability they had learned about last night. She needed to share these with Ted.

"Oh no!" she quipped, turning around to look at the clock by her bed. She was going to be late for her meet-up with Ted.

As she moved toward the bathroom to clean up, she shuddered at her thoughts about what these new discoveries would mean for all of them.

86

In The Air
Flavio & Vicki

"And when the whole thing was all sixes and sevens; Sean went all monkey on the zombies. And then Liz just smiled at him, as if it was the most adorable thing she'd ever seen." Vicki snorted at her story. But then something remarkable happened: her laughter exploded and seemed almost uncontrollable. But just as quickly as her jovial wellspring had burst, she cut herself off. "I'm sorry, I just loved that part..."

Flavio couldn't help but flash his own huge grin at her as she continued her narrative about some unknown scene from her favorite movie, *Sean of the Dead*, which he had never seen. And he wasn't really paying attention to her scene descriptions, much less trying to understand the movie she was describing to him. He was too enamored by her performance and her genuine enthusiasm. It was one of the most beautiful sights he'd witnessed in recent memory. Not that he could remember many beautiful things. But he could stare at her for hours.

It wasn't just that she was attractive—she certainly was.

It was her passion and her laughter. It was so genuine and contagious. He felt the worries of his world drift away when she laughed. And she laughed all the time.

He had never met someone who was always in such a good mood, when he so rarely was in one himself. Sure, she had her down moments, like everyone else and most especially lately. But hers never lasted very long before she'd bring up some funny anecdote from her past or from a movie that taught her some life-lesson; something that had meaning and why the world was a better place than all of them thought because of that little snippet of human understanding she'd uncovered from something otherwise so trivial.

Flavio knew if the world *was* a better place, it was because of her being in it. Period.

"Are you even listening to me?" she asked, her face still wrinkled in a happy grin.

No, he wasn't. At least not completely, but he didn't want to generate a frown from her lovely face. "So why you love movie about zombies so much?"

"It's not the zombies really. I mean come on; the whole zombie-thing is pretty lame. You see, it's not about zombies; it's about the friendship with your mates and it's about love in the worst of times and it's about looking out for one another, all told through Sean and his girlfriend Liz and his best friend Ed. And I'm reminded of this often... with you and me."

"So that makes me Sean?" He glowered at her, not really meaning it the way he said it, and knowing the unintended connotation of what followed. But he didn't mind.

"Only if it means that I'm your girlfriend." She smiled and reached out and touched his hand.

At any time in the past, at a moment like this, when a woman would try and get close to him, Flavio would head for the exit. But nothing in him was yelling, "Run!" Quite the opposite. He wanted this, too.

He returned her smile with his own and covered her

much smaller hand with his. Then he turned somewhat serious. "You know I have no girlfriend since my wife died."

His mouth started to dry up a bit. And he felt droplets of perspiration slide down his neck and puddle around his collar. For any normal adult male it would have been nerves causing this. Sure, he *was* a little nervous, but not for the reasons most men sweated during these moments with someone they were attracted to. And at the same time he felt confident he was exactly where he should be. He was mentally preparing himself to head down a road he hadn't traveled down in a while. He was about to dust off an old emotional road map that he had folded up many years ago and put away for safekeeping.

He *would* unfold it now.

He *was* ready.

He was the one that asked her out on this "coffee date," even though she used her own credits to purchase their coffees in the MDR. Every passenger was allotted one cup of coffee per day as part of their daily sea rations. He told her that it was sensible they'd share theirs together, in the open area of the Solarium. It was far more than common sense that drove him to ask her on this date.

"I do know this," she said softly. "We'll take this as slowly as you need."

"Don't need slow. Life too short." He abruptly leaned over the table, almost knocking his half-full cup of coffee over, and kissed her. It was the first time he had kissed a woman since his wife.

He sat back down and was greeted by the same captivating smile that he now knew he would look forward to every day, no matter what that day brought them.

Then he remembered where he had to go and his whole demeanor changed. "Sorry. Have to go."

Vicki looked at her watch. "Oh yeah, your new job. Do you know what it is?"

"No, but it better be good or I complain to captain."

Flavio squeezed her hand again. They exchanged quick grins and he dashed off.

~~~

Jessica

"I think you're all set, Jessica," proclaimed Deep, his grin stretching ear to ear. "You now have all of the ship's video feeds available on your console." He stepped away from her console to give her room to approach and give it a try.

Jessica returned a weak smile and approached her console before she halted. She already knew how to work the controls and trusted that if Deep said it was fixed, it must be fixed. She really didn't want to play with it right now, like he wanted. She just wasn't in the mood.

She attempted a smile again. "Thank you so much, Deep. I'll test it out later, if you don't mind."

"Oh sure. I know you have lots to do. I'll come back tomorrow and help you with anything else you may need."

"Hey, what about engineering? We have a long list of things that need fixing." Niki scowled, her words almost sounding like grunts.

Deep stared at the woman who was much taller than him—most non-Indian woman were—acting a little stunned by Niki's hostility. "Ah, Bu-Buzz," he stammered, "...is working on these, I think. I'll ask him when I see him later today." He turned back to Jessica, his facial features softening again.

"Anyway, I'll see you later." Deep's all-white smile re-enveloped his face. It was a nice face, and in spite of what was going on, it felt reassuring to have someone looking out for her.

"Thank you, Deep. You're a life saver," Jessica answered. "And thanks for the coffee."

"Sure," Deep said under his breath, while he grabbed his
~~~

small bag of tools and beelined it to the bridge exit. And just as quickly as he had entered, he was out the door. It felt to Jessica as if some warm Indian breeze had blown through the bridge and was then gone in an instant.

"You know that boy just wants to get into your pants? Of course, he's not the only one." Niki flashed her cohort a mischievous grin.

Jessica glowered at Niki. Deep's infatuation with Jessica was widely known around the ship and Jessica really didn't mind it. He was sweet and a good friend, and she needed friends right now. She also didn't mind the chiding from others, including Niki. Except now, when each day was filled with a greater realization that she would probably never see her family again. She reminded herself that it was just Niki; this was the way she was.

Although Jessica had rarely worked directly with Niki, since Niki's position originally kept them on different decks, she was recently reminded why she didn't care for Niki: it was her acidic personality.

That and the fact that she's so damned butch.

That's when she was hit by what Niki meant by the second part of her statement. With this and seeing the knowing grin on Niki's mug, which then grew upon recognition that Jessica had just caught on to her pass, Jessica turned beet red.

"Ah... I..." she stammered. "You know I'm straight... and *married*, right?" Jessica held up her ring finger to buttress her argument. But the small diamond in her engagement ring, under the bridge's muted light, barely glinted a rebuttal.

"Hey, Sunshine, don't get your dainty little panties all bunched up. I'll stop hitting on you. But Deep is another story. He brings you his coffee allotment and then goes out of his way to make sure your console works, when so many other things on the ship need work. Just saying, you're going to have to do something about him."

Thankful now to be on this otherwise uncomfortable

subject, but off one far more uncomfortable, she quickly answered. “Deep is sweet. He knows it’s been a tough time for me.”

“It’s tough on all of us,” Niki chortled. “But I suspect it’s toughest on the guests who now must work as crew.”

87

New Crew
Hans

"This sucks," Hans huffed. He reexamined his list, once again counting the number of cabins they had left to do. "Forty, forty-one... We have forty-one more of these damned things. And we've already been to this one before."

"Yeah, but then we're all done with this project," Frans stated, a little too enthusiastically.

"Sure, but then the captain will make us his personal slaves on something else. Don't forget we're supposed to be guests of this cruise line, not workers. I wouldn't have gone on this cruise if I had thought we might be forced into working. And all because we have special gifts."

"You mean because we're infected."

"I still don't believe that. We've been given special abilities. Though I would sure like some of the other abilities too. You know, like the super strength that that tow-headed woman has. Then we wouldn't have to take any more crap from the captain."

"Just knock on the door," Frans said, obviously annoyed by the whole conversation.

"Fine," Hans huffed back. He balled up a fist and thumped hard on the solid cabin door. "How do you say this *Schlitzauge's* name anyway, little brother?"

"I think, Ya-kO-bus," Hans read it phonetically and partially nodded his own acceptance to his pronunciation.

The door opened with a light squeak, and a single eye revealed itself through the dark slit. Then part of the man's face.

"Jes?" asked the sleepy looking mug attached to a single blinking eye, still shrouded in darkness behind the door.

"Are you Yakobus Wahid, currently working as a room steward on deck 7?"

"Jes... What is this about?"

Hans gave an exaggerated sniff, immediately crinkling his nostrils like he'd taken a whiff of something malodorous and then turned to glare at Hans, who nodded affirmatively back at him.

"Congratulations." Hans handed Yakobus a pre-printed piece of paper. "You've been given a new cabin, one much nicer than someone of your status would have normally been given."

~~~

Jaga

Jaga looked again at the piece of paper to confirm it. He'd examined the damned thing maybe a hundred times already. And each time he did, it made less sense than it did the first time he looked at it.

"Here it is, little buddy," he said to Taufan, "our new home."
~~~

He didn't understand why he had to move in the first place. There was nothing wrong with the arrangement he currently had. He liked having roommates. And since Asap went all crazy and disappeared and Catur was gone, Yakobus and he had more room than ever before.

Now he was forced to leave his home of several years. No explanation. No reason. Just some big German dude and a smaller version—probably brothers—who showed up unannounced at his door last night. They were part of the new crew: guests recruited into service by the captain.

Jaga's first thought was that he was about to be fired for having a ferret on board, and for the trouble he caused. But nothing was ever said about this. Just the late-night knock on the door. Yet that wasn't the most bizarre part of the German brothers' visit.

After they had knocked on his door and confirmed he was in fact himself, they then did the most peculiar thing: they sniffed him. The two brothers then looked at each other, acting like he had body odor or something—even though he had just showered—and then nodded at each other. Then the big guy said to his brother, "Number 3626" and his brother pulled out a sea card from a box, handed it to Jaga and said, "Congratulations Jaggamashi, you're now in cabin 3626. Enjoy your new quarters, but move in by early tomorrow morning."

It was all so strange.

And he wasn't the only one. Many of the other crew—the ones who had been around for a while—were moved as well, some to this side of the ship and others to a cabin more forward.

"It makes no damned sense."

Now he was going to be living here, in a guest cabin, very much like the nice guest cabins he cleaned... or rather, used to clean, as he was also told that he was going to be given a new job too. Apparently the guests, or rather new crew members, would be cleaning their own cabins. There were more important jobs each of them would be doing. Though he couldn't imagine what else the captain would have him do.

He wondered who would visit him in the middle of the night to deliver that message. And what sense did it make to take him away from something he was good at? And he loved it too, seeing his guests happy during their vacations. He had received a lot of praise from corporate about this and it was the reason why he was given so many cabins to service.

He wasn't good at anything else. He never had much use for school and he didn't have any skills, other than taking care of his buddy. "Right, Taufan?" He scratched the tuft of fur below the ferret's mouth to encourage a response. Taufan gave a little groan. Jaga took that as a "Yes!"

He pulled the new sea card that he was given from his pocket and slipped it into the door. He was almost surprised to see the lock turn green and click open. Pushing in on the door, he was immediately dumbfounded. This was a giant room, far bigger than what he and Taufan needed. Why would they give him this big room, for no reason at all?

He looked down at his ferret, almost expecting help from him with this quandary. Taufan bristled in his arms: his buddy was asking to be released. No doubt he wanted to examine the room for himself.

"And look Taufan, you have a window."

Jaga allowed the cabin door to slam shut and then he let go of his ferret.

Taufan burst out of Jaga's arms and darted across the room to the large window, immediately enthralled with the island they were fast approaching.

Maybe he should look at this as a positive. Maybe a little change was good. "Why go to all of this trouble unless it was a good thing?"

Taufan chittered his response at the window.

It still didn't make any sense, but at least Taufan approved.

88

Flavio

He was on a quick breakfast mission for Thai food, if he could just find some. He needed to eat quickly to be done in time for his meeting, which he guessed other crew members like him would be attending, all to receive their new job reassignments, whatever they were. “Dammit,” he cursed under his breath.

He found himself standing in front of the locked entrance to the crew mess. A recently printed sign—*definitely not there yesterday*—was taped to the door, to remind him and others why they were locked out:

> *From the Captain:*
>
> *Everyone, including all original and new crew and all officers, is to take their meals in the Main Dining Room.*

Flavio remembered hearing this, but it didn’t register until now. *They damn well better have my Thai food,* he thought. But he knew that that had changed too, like everything else on the ship.

He smiled at this last thought, thinking of Vicki. Not all changes were bad.

Someone cleared his throat and Flavio turned away from the door to see a tiny junior officer standing behind him. The man's shoulders drooped under Flavio's shadow, as he hulked over the officer. "Sorry to bother you, sir," the officer said, peering almost straight up at Flavio. "I was just coming up to get you. You are wanted in the MDR by the captain. He's waiting for you right now."

All of this struck Flavio as strange.

He had thought he was meeting in a group, all to receive their new jobs from someone far below the rank of captain. He certainly didn't expect a private audience with the captain himself.

And how did this junior officer know he'd be here? The officer had said, *"I was just coming up to get you,"* which must have meant that he was coming up to his new cabin, since he was no longer in his normal cabin on this level, having been given one of the guest cabins, with a fantastic view and a great bed, several decks above them.

Then it struck him.

Flavio tilted his head upward, glancing at one of the hundreds of the ship's cameras mounted on ceilings throughout the ship. He nodded his understanding at the one less than a meter away, peering down at them.

But there was one more unexplained oddity that Flavio just couldn't wrap his mind around. This officer referred to him as "sir." Since Flavio was not an officer, he should have just been referred to by his last name, Petrovich. That was normal decorum on an RE ship, unless that had changed too.

Flavio recast his gaze back down to the diminutive officer. The man was patiently waiting for an answer or some sort of acknowledgment. "Thank you. I go now."

It was all Flavio could think of saying. His mind was having difficulty keeping up since so much was changing, so very rapidly: he had actually slept an entire night for the first time in memory, he didn't have a headache, he felt genuinely happy and to top all of this off, the captain of his ship was waiting for *him*.

Flavio shook his head, turned and started toward the MDR. He heard the soft shuffle of the junior officer's feet behind him when he entered the crew stairwell. It was obvious that the man had a mission to make sure that Flavio made it up to see their captain. Flavio was going to make sure the man was going to have to work a little to complete his task.

Some things don't change, he thought to himself, as a smirk crept onto his face.

It didn't take long, because Flavio double-timed it to the MDR, his destination. A part of him wanted to see if his shadow remained glued to him, though he wasn't sure why. And afterwards, he felt a little silly for doing this.

One doorway later, he stepped into the MDR. Behind him were the sounds of the diminutive officer hacking up a lung. Flavio chuckled to himself.

If I were in charge of crew exercise, you would be the first person who would have to run laps, he thought. His smile-lines moved higher.

Flavio found the captain right away. The man who only a few short days ago was the staff captain until he was elevated in title when his superior was brutally murdered by the parasitics. Jean Pierre stood up from his chair and greeted Flavio with a broad and welcoming grin.

"Flavio, thank you for meeting me on such short notice. I know this may seem like it came out of the white."

Flavio wasn't sure what the captain meant by this, but he heard the captain often said things that didn't make sense.

"I wanted to personally thank you for all that you've done the last few days. Your tireless work has been above and beyond. I would have preferred doing this more formally, out of respect for your recent contributions in saving this ship and so many people on board. But we have little time. And I need you now."

Flavio was taken aback by all of this, still standing and facing his superior, when he realized the junior officer that had been dogging him, still breathing heavily, moved into his periphery. The officer handed Captain Jean Pierre a small box and then moved away.

The captain turned back to Flavio and held out the case, now opened. It had officer bars in them. He looked back up at the captain, whose smile had grown ocean-wide.

"Flavio Petrovich, you have been promoted to Second Officer, effective immediately. And I would like to offer you the position of Deputy Security Director… Assuming you want it?"

Flavio was flabbergasted. This was Director Wasano Agarwal's previous position, before they found the then security director killed a few days ago.

Another crew member appeared from behind him—Flavio never remained this long with his back to a doorway. For the first time in recent memory, he was startled, actually flinching a little. The man was from laundry and handed Flavio a fully pressed officer's uniform. Flavio mindlessly took the uniform while staring at the captain, unsure what to say or how he should react.

Before all of this happened, when he was just a lowly waiter, rarely noticed by any of his superiors, he would have been sure that this whole presentation was all a way for corporate to reward him without giving him the raise that he'd deserved for all his years of service, but never got. And that was because he was already at the top of his ranking, without being an officer. Then he considered the truth, the real truth about their situation.

Neither he nor anyone else would ever be getting paid again, certainly not from a corporation made up of people who were either dead or crazy and running around the head office, murdering and eating their fellow corporate executives.

Flavio shook himself from his mental meanderings and saw the captain was waiting for a reply.

"Guess my overtime work paid off," he quipped.

The captain chortled. "That and your unique skill-set, which are needed far more now than they were in your previous position… Can I take this as a yes then?"

"Yes, of course, sir. I am honored, Captain." Flavio firmly shook the captain's hand.

"That's wonderful. Now, I apologize for the lack of ceremony, but we just don't have time for such niceties now."

Flavio was happy for that. He hated recognition ceremonies, which he had always thought were set up more so for recognizing his superiors who loved to self-congratulate each other and hear themselves make speeches. This was better. Much better.

He wondered what he was supposed to do next, his eyes wandering down to the captain's table, where he had stood up from. There at his place was an empty coffee cup and a half-eaten Danish. There were other place settings at the table. And he had kind of hoped to have been invited to sit with him and have a meal as well, but knew that was asking for too much.

"I'm sorry I cannot join you for a meal. And I'm afraid you'll need to be brief as well. As part of your first assignment, please change into your new uniform and at zero-eight-hundred, you'll need to meet us at the deck 1 port-side gangway. That's forty-five minutes from now."

89

Speed

Ted sat enveloped in a bubble of his own personal disquiet. He stared into the large space of the Solarium, lost in thought. With his Cubs baseball cap tugged down tight around his head, the bill covering all but the day-plus stubble carpeting his chin, he was almost unrecognizable, unless someone stopped and really took a look at him. Incognito was preferable at this moment, because he was too busy dealing with what felt like an immense crush of weight bearing down on him. It was the summation of all the ship's worries and his knowledge of how bleak their future currently appeared. Even though he tried to convince himself otherwise.

Assuming they were able to make a deal for fuel, they'd eventually run out. Then what? And food was going to be their bigger problem, even if they didn't part with much of it, which they most assuredly would do if they were going to make a deal for the fuel.

And assuming they were able to solve the insurmountable problems of their fuel and food, how could they survive this world now owned by the parasitics? He didn't even dare allow his thoughts to fall onto his wife, TJ. Each time he went down that road, he'd eventually drive off it, into a ditch of despair, heading down a hole of hopelessness, where his psyche would be crushed beyond repair.

Then his bubble of blues was pierced.

Some lumbering idiot clobbered into his table, jostling the two cups of coffee on top, sloshing out some of their coveted contents.

Ted shot his glare upward, a fusillade of profanities loaded up behind his tongue, ready to be launched at the person who did this. His lips were pursed, his nose drawn up. Then he held his breath.

"Oh dear me. So sorry, Ted," Dr. Molly Simmons gasped. "I get clumsier with each day."

Ted's anger withered immediately. "It's all right. Please sit. I've tried to keep your coffee warm, but..." He pointed to the upside-down saucer resting on top of a coffee closest to the empty seat, drops of black liquid dripping from its edges.

"Oh, thank you. So sorry I'm late—don't get up."

Ted halted, halfway out of his chair, then lowered himself back into his seat, abandoning his effort to help her into the empty chair awaiting her.

He watched her slowly pull the chair farther out from the table, turn it toward her and then fall into it.

Just before she was done adjusting her seat, a couple walked by their table and glanced first at Molly and then at Ted. Ted could see the spark of recognition in their eyes, but he turned away before he'd confirm it and they passed by without saying a word.

It was another reason Ted didn't care to meet in the Solarium. This place was way too open. It may have been less populated than in previous days, since the cessation of food service in all restaurants except the MDR. And since most every passenger was given a job, there was less time for leisurely sitting and resting in an area designed solely for recreation. More than anything else, Ted was afraid their open conversations would be heard by others. But Molly liked this space. So this was where they met each day.

She argued that it was warm and the canopy of glass brightly illuminated the space, even with their recent days being heavily clouded over.

"Oh, that's so good," Molly said, taking in her cool coffee in short sips, as if it were hot. In fact, it had lost most of its heat a half an hour ago, when he brought their coffees down from the MDR for their daily meet.

"You're not drinking yours—say, you look tired... Are you all right, Ted?" Her ancient-looking features were twisted with concern.

"Yeah, I'm fine. And yes, I need more sleep. Speaking of sleep, what about you, Molly?"

"Me? Don't worry about me. I'll get all the sleep I need when I'm dead. I'm too busy for sleep." She took a big gulp of her coffee, her eyes still uncomfortably riveted on him.

"All right, then. So how are our monsters sleeping?"

Her eyes dropped from his, to the cup she was holding. "Well... that's why I'm late." She set her cup down and then looked back up to Ted. Her persona instantly changed from enthusiastic to something more serious. "As a scientist, I have to tell you I'm both excited and terrified by what we're witnessing. I cannot explain it, except to say..."

She looked down again, took a deep breath and then exhaled. She lifted her gaze back up to Ted's again.

"I think we're looking at the next stage of human evolution. Assuming I believed in macro-evolution the way it's taught in schools nowadays... Scratch that, *was* taught in schools."

Considering his own dour mood, Ted almost needed to debate her point about evolution, sensing—and needing—another sermon from her about God's providential hand changing the events around them in His favor, and theirs. He was just too tired to get into another weighty metaphysical discussion. He chose to buttress his own hopelessness instead, "All right, so it's survival of the fittest. So who's going to be the fittest in the end, us or them?" He knew the answer.

She smiled a little at his question. He was pretty sure that she enjoyed having someone who could engage her intellectually, especially someone who possessed a similar love for science, like Ted did. "Short term, we may survive this, if providence still chooses to lay His hand upon us, like He has so far."

Ted couldn't help but smile at this, knowing she would go there. *Maybe I wanted this discussion after all.*

"But long term, the future probably belongs to our parasitics." She cast her gaze back down, almost as if she were embarrassed to having just given such an ungodly forecast of the future, because surely God couldn't support these evil creatures over his beloved people.

And even though he knew she had to say this if she were being faithful to science, it still shocked him. Molly was someone who he'd come to know had a rock-solid hope in tomorrow, buttressed by her faith in a God that loved His children. Ted wasn't so sure about the whole creator thing.

He had admitted to her that he was much more agnostic than atheist. Until recently, he had always believed in the human condition, and that through science and the good nature of many, humankind would be able to figure a way out of this mess before something ended it for them. Even in his fiction, he offered hope for his characters. But it was getting harder to believe in humans when there weren't that many around anymore.

He realized Molly was watching his reaction to her words now. "I've been wondering the same thing. What recent finding makes you believe this?"

"Oh yes, I hadn't told you yet. As you know, we learn so

much each day as we study them.

"We're already aware that parasitics have an ability to use their muscles and tendons like those of a chimpanzee, giving them, from our observations, two to ten times normal human strength."

"I think you told me it had something to do with our brains getting in the way of our latent strength, as a means to protect our bodies."

"Yes, think of all of the reports you've read of a meek housewife lifting a car off her injured husband, or the daughter lifting the farm tractor off her father and so many other instances which prove this point: it's during times of extreme stress, or anger, that we can be at our strongest."

"And with parasitics, that's all the time, except when they're hibernating," Ted added so she knew he was following.

"Precisely."

"Okay, so what's the newest revelation?"

"Yes, sorry. You'll recall we've observed the parasitics hibernating in cylindrical groups that rotate periodically, sending those on the edges to the center, so as to maintain their body temperatures above the ambient temperature in the lounge."

Ted did remember this and found it fascinating. "Yes, I do. It seemed odd, but made sense when you first reported it. I was worried that if enough of them warmed up too much, our efforts to lower their body temperature would fail."

"And until last night, they seemed to remain in this rotating hibernative state, efficiently transferring their body heat to the others—"

"As if they were waiting us out, knowing the low outside temperatures were not going to last," Ted added. His dour mood was kicking back in again.

"Perhaps."

"You said, "Until last night." What happened last night?"

"Two recorded events, which have me troubled. The

first occurred yesterday morning. Each cylindrical parasitic pod has kept one parasitic in the center, so as to warm up its temperature even higher. We only noticed this because yesterday, one of the parasitics darted from the center of a pod and tried to attack one of our guards on morning feeding duty. It was close, but our guard retreated behind the door, just in time."

"That shows strategy. Not something we expect from them," Ted interjected.

"Precisely. The second event which has me a little frightened is actually tied to the first. Last night, at the start of the second feeding, it happened again. Like the first attempted attack, a parasitic leapt from the center of its pod. Also like the first, it was a little clumsy and not particularly fast. But this time, halfway up the aisle, it literally shot up the remaining distance like a cheetah. I have never seen a human move that fast before. I had Mr. Deep rewind and replay this part over and over again, because I just did not believe what I was seeing."

"So you're saying they're becoming not only stronger than us, but faster too?" Ted's stomach was a boiling cauldron of acid right now.

"Precisely. Of course, this is just one incident, but I think you understand why I'm so worried now."

Ted thought about the repercussions of what this meant to all of them. It was too awful to consider right now. Parasitics with lightning speed?

~~~

TJ rapped on the window with two knuckles, generating a loud enough sound on the other side that it startled the store clerk. The man was self-jolted from his seat, dropping the clipboard
~~~

he'd been holding.

He snapped his head in TJ's direction and then yelled inaudibly, "We're closed."

She knew what he said, even though his voice was almost completely muffled by the glass. But she wasn't taking no for an answer. So she acted like she couldn't hear him.

She mouthed, "What?" and raised her arms up as if she didn't know what he was saying.

The man violently shook his head and abruptly returned back to his work, yanking his clipboard from the floor, and continued to examine it and his inventory. At least, that's what she guessed he was doing.

Her anger grew. She hit the glass harder this time, causing the whole frame to shake. She was pretty sure if she struck the glass just a little stronger, it might break. *Don't want to do that more than once*, she thought while glancing at the broken window panel to the left of the door, now covered by plywood.

The clerk rose from his seat this time and stomped over in her direction, his shoulders stiff and aggressively pointed at her. As if he were going to win this showdown.

She almost guffawed at this.

The clerk plunged his metal key into the lock, turned it and cracked the door open. "We closed. Not sure when open again, but you—"

It was pure reflex, because without thinking, her hand shot through the door crack in a blur—much more quickly than she would have thought herself capable—and grabbed the man's forearm.

His eyes went wide and he looked down at his arm, convulsing with a jerk when he saw that she was clutching him, almost like he didn't know it was her who had a grip on his arm. He attempted to tug away, his face twisting into comical proportions as he pulled with his whole body. Her hand remained, an immovable vise clamped around his arm.

Then she squeezed harder, just to demonstrate she was in control. But she felt his tendons beneath her hand about to give, so she loosened her grip.

"Owah. Why you do this?" he whined, his face turning red.

TJ had planned a much more diplomatic approach, but when this guy stomped over to the door, it pissed her off. So she abandoned diplomacy for something more dramatic. And now she was short on time and just wanted what she came here for.

With her free hand, she pulled off her sunglasses and glared her scary eyes at the man. "If you don't let me in and give me what I want, I'll snap your arm off and eat it for breakfast." She said this deadpan, not really meaning it. She really had no desire to eat this man's arm.

The man's giant white orbs welled with tears and he tried once more to unsuccessfully yank his arm free.

Then she let go.

The man tumbled hard to the floor and he tried to desperately waddle away from her.

TJ snapped her sunglasses back on, slid into the shop, closed the door and locked it, using the key still inside. Then she glared at the man, who had shrunk into the recesses under a display of Regal European T-shirts.

"Look, I was just kidding about hurting you. I just need one thing. Give me that and I'll go away. I promise." She flashed him a smile to show she was sincere.

The man glowered at her from behind the T-shirts, hesitant to trust this offer, seeking comfort behind the clothing.

"Ya-ya-you promise to la-la-leave, if I give you what you want."

"Absolutely." She flashed a bigger smile at the man, like she meant it. In fact, she actually did: she was done dealing with this little man. If he didn't help her, she was just going to look and take what she wanted herself.

She glanced around the store and quickly saw the display. “Right there, that’s all I need. Please get me that. I’m late, and then I’m going to accompany the captain to get us the fuel our ship needs. *Please*.”

The man tried to right himself, but started to fall back over again.

Again she reacted so lightning-quick, lunging forward and yanking him up, she even surprised herself. The man squeaked in amazement, again drilling his tear-filled eyes at her, like she was some sort of freak. Now she genuinely felt bad for putting this man through such terror. “Sorry, thought you were about to fall. Just trying to help.”

She let go when he felt steady on his feet. He backed away from her and moved toward the display she had pointed to.

“Yes, that’s what I want.” She motioned past him, her smile leading the way.

He turned to the display, anxious to get away from this crazy woman.

Once he was at the display case, he wasn’t paying attention and drove his knee into it, sending two other table-top displays onto the floor. “Dammit!” he huffed, and glanced at TJ, who remained in her place.

“What color?” he asked almost inaudibly.

“Blue.”

The clerk reached inside, snatched two boxes from under the glass, and marched over to her, holding the boxes out in front of him like a shield of protection. “Here are two sets. Pa-please go now.”

She accepted the boxes, unlocked and then backed out the door.

“Thank you for your help.”

90

Meet Up

Ted stood, arms wrapped around his chest, his back holding up the room's aft wall, while tapping a nervous foot to the floor. She was late.

He looked at his watch—that he had never worn, until a few days ago—to confirm this. It was ten minutes past their meet time. This really annoyed him because it meant that he had less time with her before they both had their duties to attend to. They had so little time together these days.

He drilled his eyes through the all-glass conference room door, catching glimpses of people flashing up and down the aft stairwell, a few feet away.

She was never late before...

That was before all of her changes. He was the one who was usually late. It was his wife who reminded him constantly of his appointments. It was one of the reasons why he started wearing his watch, a gift from her a while back. When she had recommended he bring it on this trip, he questioned her about it. "Who wears watches anymore?"

"Remember, you won't be carrying your phone with you everywhere, and I don't want us to be late for shows, or our dinner with the captain."

"That's what I have you for," he told her. He was only half kidding.

"But I might not always be around... I may be lounging at the pool while you're writing. Please bring it."

It seemed like a little thing back then, barely a few days ago. Now every decision they'd made, and would make from here on out, felt doubly important.

An attractive blonde, about TJ's height, breezed up to the door, and he held his breath. But it wasn't her. To confirm this, the woman moved quickly past the door.

When he called her this morning on her house phone—he was allowed certain privileges being a member of the wardroom, including use of the house phones, which were still designated for emergencies—she at first didn't sound interested in meeting. He recalled this conversation too... "Good morning, how are you?"

"Fine," she said, absent all emotion.

"Are you sleeping?"

"Some."

"Can we meet?"

"I have to help with the fuel negotiations."

"You know that I know that. Please, I need to see you."

She paused for a moment, and then her tone changed. "Yes, I'd like that."

He had remembered this conference room was kept empty for important ship business and that it wouldn't be used just before this parley with this guy on an island who had fuel. So he set it up here.

Finally, he saw her slowly come up the stairwell and stop a few feet before the door, where she gazed inside and saw him looking back at her. It was hard to see her clearly, because the door was covered with smudge marks, probably from people looking in, and a recently erected sign on the other side that said, "This room is reserved indefinitely for the Bridge Crew."

She approached the door and pushed it open, and that's when he could see all of her.

He immediately had a flashback of the sexual dream that turned into a nightmare this morning, recalling both his arousal and his terror all at the same time. His heart raced again.

She looked absolutely radiant in her usual outfit: compression shorts and short-sleeve running shirt, complemented with color-coordinated running shoes; blond hair pulled back into a crisp ponytail; nose-plug winched around her nostrils, and its skin-colored tether loosely ringing her neck. She wasn't wearing her necklace, but she said the clasp had broken and she was afraid of losing it now.

He noticed right away two monumental changes in her appearance since the last time he had seen her.

First, her skin glistened a radiant brown; she'd been rapidly losing melanin, causing her skin to look a more deathly pale shade each day. But the biggest change was her eye color.

They were blue.

Not her normal blue, but not red or pinkish either.

Her smile made his heart sore. She seemed genuinely happy to see him.

And then she did something unexpected: she stepped up to him, wrapped her arms around him and squeezed him tight.

"I've missed you," he said into her ear.

"Me too." Her voice was nasal-sounding. She was also sweaty, like she had just completed a run.

He gazed into her eyes for just a flash and kissed her. That's when she went rigid and pulled away.

"Geez, you'd think we could afford to turn the air on in here," she joked, probably to cover her change. But her voice too sounded strained.

"You know, the whole fuel situation..." That's when he saw her cover-ups.

Her eyes weren't really blue; they were purple: she was wearing blue contacts, which couldn't completely counteract her red eyes. And her tan was from a bottle and not real. He could see now she looked more gold-colored than brown, like he had originally thought. He glanced at his hand that had clasped her shoulder and noticed some of the tanning cream had come off. He rubbed it around his fingers for further confirmation.

He glanced back up at her, but his gaze drifted higher, catching what he thought were a couple of white hairs hiding behind the blond strands in her well groomed eyebrows.

"Guess I could never fool you, Ted. Does it look that bad?"

"No... I guess a part of me wanted to believe that you were the same. You know, before your changes."

"Yeah, me too. But we both know I'm not. I'm completely different than what I was before all of this."

The truth was a bitter pill that he didn't want to swallow, but now he was forced to.

They held their silence for an uncomfortably long period of time. They had never had an uncomfortable moment of silence between them before, savoring each other's presence so much that periods without conversation were just as glorious as those infused with rapid dialog. That had changed too.

"I love you, you know," he said.

"But that's not enough anymore."

There it was. The fact that he didn't want to admit, but she put it out there. It was like a knife thrust directly into his heart. "Just don't give up on us."

"I haven't. In fact, knowing you are there is what has kept me... human."

At last, something to hold onto. They weren't lost, yet. He could still hope that she held on, as long as she remained "human."

There was a loud beep-tone, followed rapidly by another one. This was the prelude to an announcement. Before the apocalypse, these were often ignored because they were usually just outside of earshot and it was known that each was some sort of fun declaration about the day's drink special or an upcoming show. Now, the announcements brought him anxiety, even those he already knew about.

"That's the captain, telling everyone to get inside and to remain there until after we have concluded the trade and we've left the port."

"It's also why I have to go," she said.

He knew this too, but he didn't want their time to end, especially on her last hopeful comment. Then he considered what she was about to do.

"Please be careful." He thought about Molly's comments about the parasitics maybe having super-speed. "You may have new abilities, but you can't outrun a bullet."

This comment made her stop—she was already headed to the door. "Are we expecting trouble?"

"Ahh..." They weren't, but he was still skeptical of the whole thing. "No. Just promise me you'll be careful and not take any unnecessary chances."

She flashed her purplish eyes his way and gave him a slight smile. It felt genuine. "I promise. Bye."

She turned and was out the door. Gone.

91

The Parasitics

Whaudeep Reddy floated to the door and opened it just one second after Molly's faint knock on the other side. He didn't want her to wait long without protection. The area around the deck 8 Monitor Room, like most of the ship, was secure. But after everything that he'd seen, he didn't want to take any chances with this nice, elderly woman. So many images of violent murder were welded permanently inside his head, replaying themselves over and over, day and night.

"Oh my, you're so kind. Thank you for moving so quickly, Mr. Deep."

Deep offered an arm to help her inside, but she refused and hobbled under the aid of her odd-shaped cane. Once she was inside, he stuck his head out the door, to make sure no one else was there. His skin bristled at the thought that another one of those parasitics might be dashing down the hall, all because he wasn't at his seat watching for them, and warning the ship. He hadn't slept much worrying about missing the next attack. And with all that he'd learned from Dr. Molly's and his own observations, his anxiety grew with each passing day. Something was coming. And it was coming soon.

He checked in both directions: of course, the hallway was clear.

After securing the door, making sure it was properly latched, he turned to watch and wait for Dr. Molly to take her seat. *"Shuffle-thump, shuffle-thump,"* she worked her way to the chair beside his. The one with the two plumped-up pillows to comfort her aching bones.

Deep thought that she really should have an escort when she made her way forward, across the span of the ship, to the MR. With her reviewing tapes and making notes about the parasitics as often as four times a day, and for hours at a time, he was worried for the woman's health and safety: it would be so easy for her to trip and fall on her way to the MR.

But all his proposals for assistance were resisted by her, often with her stating adamantly that she didn't need any help, nor did she feel it was right to bother anyone else with such a request. Even when he offered to come and escort her himself, she said, "No!" And that it was her call, not someone else's. He at least got her to agree to call him first when she was headed toward the MR. That way, he could watch her like a hawk from his MR chair when she started her trip to the MR, just as he also did when she left the MR. At least he could do that for her.

Deep couldn't help but appreciate the work ethic of this woman, who was probably older than his own grandmother. And it wasn't that she had great stamina, as he often saw evidence of her exhaustion, especially now. Each time they met, she looked more and more the part of the elderly woman. He knew it was her scientific drive to understand their monsters, coupled with a general feeling of alarm that they had a very limited window to do so. Regardless of her reasons, Dr. Molly Simmons was someone he'd grown to care for and greatly admire.

He flashed an unseen smirk at her back, as she was getting set in her seat. He didn't want to rush her. So he'd wait until she was done fiddling with her cane, even though he felt building apprehension at being away from his monitors.

It was almost zero-eight-hundred, which was their normal feeding time. But after yesterday's two incidents of attempted attacks, right at feeding times, they had moved this morning's feeding time up a half hour or so, to see if the parasitics were going to try something right at 08:00 or would they wait for the guard and feeder's entrance around 08:30? And with the new information from last night, which he hadn't yet shared with Dr. Molly, there was no way to know what they'd do next.

He could see she was done fiddling with the pillows in her seat.

"Are you close enough to the monitors, ma'am?" he said softly, just behind her.

She turned her head and shoulders back toward him and glared a look that said, "I'm not so feeble I can't move my own damned chair!"

He nodded and whipped around her, dumping himself into his own seat. He typed a couple of quick commands on his keyboard and waited for her to start the review of some of the key video snippets he had compiled. He'd already seen the live feeds playing on four of the monitors, including the main screen.

Before she'd start looking at the video, she would examine his notes scrawled on the clipboard which he had left in front of her: a detailed summation of any interesting developments since her last review, the parasitics' movements and any thoughts about what he saw. She'd given him instructions on how to write research notes about their empirical observations. And he tried to follow her direction to the letter.

He was anxious for her to get to the newest

development, at the end of his notes, which both surprised and terrified him. But she always did a review of their previous notes first, to make sure she didn't miss something, before she worked her way to the most recent point. He waited for her to get to that place, studying her facial features, while his mind wandered, thinking about how much had happened and what they'd seen so far in the few short days they'd been observing their parasitics...

Once they had control of them, Dr. Molly had been tasked by the captain to examine all of the live and taped feeds from the four cameras they had trained in and around the Wayfarer Lounge, where the parasitics were being held: two inside the lounge, one covering the main entrance, and one on the back stage—it was pitch black back there, so it was as if they had no camera there. None of the feeds had audio, so they could only rely on the video and the first-person reports from the guards who watched the doors and the volunteers who fed these monsters.

Since they had locked the doors on the parasitics and turned down the air conditioning to keep it icy cold, sending them into a form of hibernation, they had gained a lot of knowledge about them from the two cameras.

Deep had been on watch almost the entire time and had reviewed every moment of tape himself, including those from Fish's short shifts. He also read every one of Dr. Molly's notes. So he knew exactly what was going on.

Until an hour ago, most of the parasitics were asleep and naked. But it wasn't always this way.

During the first day, after the temperature in the lounge had dropped, the parasitics then mostly lay in their places and fell into some sort of quasi-sleep. Dr. Molly explained it was similar to what bears do in the winter. She said it was a semi-hibernative state, where they were very aware of what was going on around them, but as long as they didn't sense a threat, they remained where they were.

She said this was occurring for several reasons: they needed the rest to replenish their energy; their bodies needed to fix what was broken or damaged; and they needed to wait until it was warmer, so that their body temperatures could rise to their new normal levels, which was considerably hotter than our own normal.

After the first few hours of that first day, something unexpected, but wholly explainable occurred: they started to cluster themselves into pods, intertwining arms and legs so as to almost become one.

By the second day, all their clothes had come off, apparently for two reasons, one very odd and the other sensible.

Deep's cheeks always flashed red when he thought about this, and he was enormously embarrassed when he was present with Dr. Molly while she watched this with him.

Almost all of them had copulated together, often with whomever they were next to. Dr. Molly suspected that most of the time it was not the normal partner they were on the ship with. At first, Dr. Molly said she had thought this was part of their innate desire to indulge in their primal behavior, based on who biologically had the greatest sex drive. But the longer she studied the parasitics' behavior, the more she said she suspected there was a purpose to this behavior: the parasites inside each host wanted their hosts to reproduce.

She said this was especially odd, since it didn't fit the T-Gondii's normal life cycle of trying to end up in the guts of cats, where they could naturally reproduce. So her hypothesis—he loved that word—was that the volcanic bacteria that spread world-wide had somehow mutated or genetically altered the parasites which were controlling their parasitics, along with most of the human and animal population of the world.

But their parasitics' behavior wasn't just filled with sleep and sex. They had witnessed several murders as well.

Like the sex, Dr. Molly at first thought this was part of each person's basic needs being exaggerated by the parasite. And that this was just the parasitic's period of rage being expressed by murdering another parasitic that was in its way.

When it happened, it was quick and violent.

What changed Dr. Molly's opinion, at least somewhat, was after seeing what they did with the bodies: each was eaten.

So even though parasitics were undoubtedly driven to kill non-infected humans and consume their flesh for sustenance, they were not opposed to consuming each other, if it was necessary. Dr. Molly later said that she believed they were choosing to kill the weaker of their group, perhaps those with mortal injuries.

Whatever the reasons were, it was too gruesome to watch. And like the sex parts, Deep often averted his head or partially closed his eyes so he didn't have to witness this. His own fear was that these images would become commonplace to him and at some point, he'd find them no longer disturbing.

Luckily for Deep, these two behaviors seemed to stop about as abruptly as they began, but they also couldn't really tell.

That was because by the end of the second day, the parasitics started to use their already-shed clothing to cover themselves, like a large blanket. It was then that they realized the parasitics were both protecting their body temperatures and maybe even trying to raise them. Several other interesting developments immediately followed.

The pods became more defined, with 20 to 30 parasitics coming together in an almost perfect circle. It was hard to count the exact numbers, because most of these were under the shroud of their shed clothing. And the lounge's two cameras could only see so much.

By the third day, it was obvious each pod had its own structure. And that was when they noticed the pods were periodically rotating those from the outside in and moving those on the inside out.

It was only last night that they'd observed that one individual parasitic was being kept in the middle of the pod. Dr. Molly guessed that it all had to do with retaining that parasitic's higher body temperature so that it could use its new abilities for something they didn't yet know. At the beginning of the fifth day of their captivity, they'd found out what that was. That's when the attacks came.

Dr. Molly had thought the attacks were random; at least, at the time it *did* seem that way. The two attacks were against the guards, who were there to oversee the feeding and protection of that area. Each guard was attacked during the feeding times, when the guards entered the lounge. The first attack almost seemed telegraphed, with the parasitic grunting its intention before it started moving. The guard had barely opened up the door when he heard and then saw the parasitic running in his direction. He simply slipped back behind the door and closed it before it could get to him.

The second attack was much more of a surprise. The guard entered with another feeding volunteer—a newly recruited crew member from the guests that volunteered for this duty—who carried the food. The attacking parasitic dashed from its pod, which was also closer to the intended target. And it did so, as told by the guard, without any sound. The feeder reacted quickly and ran back out the door, although he tripped over his own feet at the door's threshold and fell just outside the doorway. The guard was two seconds slower, having followed the same path, but he didn't see the feeder at his feet, causing him to tumble even harder. Luckily, another guard was able to secure the doors before the parasitic hit. But the falling guard sustained a broken leg and messed-up ankle. It could have been much worse.

This morning's attack, the third one was the most odd...

"Fascinating…" Dr. Molly said, obviously reaching the end of his notes. She turned to him with a slight smile. "Thank you, Mr. Deep, for such a concise rendition of the last few hours' events. Can you please play me the recordings of the last attack?"

He had the two main camera recordings all cued up and clicked a button to start the recordings.

"This is the pod, Dr. Molly." Deep tapped on the screen at the pod that seemed particularly active, bristling with movement under its clothes-tent.

It came from the pod farthest from the main entrance door. The parasitic leapt out of its pod, this time headed toward the port-side lounge exit. And like the other two attacking parasitics, it first wobbled when it rose while it gained its stride. But even more so than the last one, halfway to the door, it moved with blinding speed. That was, until it hit the door head-first. Both the door and the parasitic sustained heavy damage. The parasitic fell to the floor from what looked like a broken neck and never moved again. The door held, but the frame was bent at an odd angle and the door itself was partially twisted inward; enough that it exposed light from the other side.

This was very scary to Deep for multiple reasons. Primarily because it was a fire door: a solid steel protective barrier, and all it took was one former human to almost take it down.

She had him play the tape back twice and each time she "hmmmm'd" out loud, seeming to pick up a new thought or a new piece of evidence to support her latest theory, which he desperately wanted to hear.

"Did you report the door?" she asked.

Her question jostled him a little, because he had lost sight of the obvious: if that door was not impenetrable, then these parasitics could get out.

He didn't hesitate, flipped a switch, snatched the

microphone and clicked it open, "Attention Maintenance. This is Deep from the MR. We need a maintenance crew to the port-side crew entrance of the Wayfarer Lounge. There may be a breach in the side lounge door, holding back the parasitics.

Deep's eye caught movement on one of his monitors and he let go of the mic button. The main monitor was set to live stream from the camera right above the main entrance, facing aft. The same pod that sent the dead parasitic to attack the door was bristling with new activity. And then one of them leapt out of the pod.

"Look Dr. Molly, it's happening again."

92

Ágúst

The man formerly known as Second Officer Ágúst Helguson gave the order to the pod: a short but rapid gagging sound, which he knew to mean several things to the pod he commanded. And like all decisions and thoughts, he considered this one and what led up to it.

As before, he was more of a manager now than a leader and he was fine with that. When he was a mere human, he commanded many people, but only after receiving his orders. There were times he made decisions as the safety director of the *Intrepid*, but even those were a programmed result of a problem he had already encountered or was trained for.

And the few times he didn't know the answer, he relied on those around him, unafraid of delegating the many tasks given him to others who would complete the task more competently than even he could.

His life now was really no different, even if he was very different. Just like before, he reacted to outside stimuli, as well as deducing what might happen and his mind—because of his knowledge—would automatically generate the result. But it wasn't just his learned knowledge at work. There was something else.

Another being inside his mind was calling the shots. But it wasn't so bad, because this other being also gave him certain abilities that he never enjoyed as a mere human.

Besides no longer having an upset stomach or an irritable bowel, problems which used to plague him constantly, he had lost all his fears. He had none now. For instance, he used to worry what others thought of him, sometimes spending sleepless nights contemplating what he said or did, or what he was about to say or do. Not any longer.

Besides lacking worry, he had lightning-quick reflexes, twice his normal strength, an increased intellect and excellent eyesight. And he never had to second-guess himself, because the parasites inside him told him what to do and when to do it. So did Eloise.

The woman known to her dead relatives and a few on board this ship as Eloise Carmichael now had a hold over him he couldn't resist. And he didn't really want to.

When Eloise first spoke to him, it was right after his changes started. It was a confusing time for him, as his mind was filled with such tumult. The ship was in chaos, his colleagues panicking and he just didn't know what was going on inside his brain and body.

It was the reflexive nature of his former personality, which was afraid of what they thought of him. He didn't really fear it, only what was going on inside of him. But when they saw his red eyes and reacted with such horror, he thought he needed to do something to help his ship be safe. That was his job, after all.

When the task of securing the anchor release was offered and no one volunteered, he did. He could prove to them that he was still the Ágúst Helguson they trusted and do his job. But then she called to him.

He still couldn't explain it now, as he thought about it, but when he was running to get to the anchor release, he could feel her in his mind. As he got closer, the feelings were stronger. And when he saw her, he disregarded all he knew and learned, giving it all away to her. She told him what to do and he did it, even though some little part of him told him it was wrong.

But then she was gone and so was her pull. And his human side, even though it was barely there, called him back to his duties. It was a horrible time for him, because he was torn by two sides pulling equally then and he didn't know what to do. He felt sick and tormented by good and evil. And he was so exhausted. So he sought rest and somehow ended up in this lounge.

That's when everything once again became clear to him.

It was perhaps his fatigue at first, then it was his need to eliminate the confusion—the being inside him was offering the answers—but once he was in the lounge, with all the others, he had submitted to it. And he'd found Eloise again.

Previous to his changes, he was uncomfortable with women, having had sex only once, and it went badly. He had believed that sex was something that you only shared with a married partner; it was not something to be done with someone you casually bumped into.

Yet, when they discarded their clothing—he couldn't remember who told him to do this, his inner being or hers—he found her and she him and never questioned it. As it was with every part of his becoming something new, innately he knew he was being called to do this, so it must be right.

Immediately, he felt an even stronger intuitive connection with Eloise. He seemed to know her thoughts and she his. This was when the greatest changes took place in him as he accepted everything the parasites inside him and she told him. This included his command over the others.

He automatically came to know a new language and

they listened to him and followed his commands without question. Unlike his human life, where he second-guessed his every decision and worried that others did as well, he never questioned anything. It was what was commanded of him and so therefore it was what he should do.

Today, he had a new command, a new purpose for their people. He knew what they had to do and how to do it. And so before they expected any of the humans to enter the lounge for their feeding, he heard in his mind and he then commanded that one of their strongest test their strength against the fire door on the far side of the lounge. He knew from his time before this would be difficult. But he also knew that if the right amount of pressure were applied to the right point in the door, it would start to give. And so the command was issued and carried out perfectly.

They knew they could exit out this door and so all they had to do was wait for their next feeding to start the next part of their plan. That was now.

Eloise bellowed a long single grunt, jostling Ágúst from his contemplations. He was given what his next command should be.

Ágúst immediately gave a series of short grunts that sounded like a seal barking.

The command's recipient burst from the pod that had physically prepared him for this. He dashed to the door.

Ágúst didn't even look to see if he executed his command. He knew he would. It was time for the next part of their plan. He bellowed his next command, knowing that this would soon lead to their freedom.

93

Ship Reps

When Flavio turned the corner at deck 2, they were all there, waiting. They reacted to his arrival, their gazes rising to acknowledge him. He instantly felt out of place.

Before all of this, he was a waiter, for God's sake. And a damn good one. But by some twist of fate, he was now the second in command of all the ship's security. Worse, he was a damned second officer, now part of that clan of folks he used to revile because they cozied up to corporate, so as to garner all of the increases in title and pay that weren't normally afforded to the likes of other crew, like him. But that was before; now he was not sure if any of his previous perceptions of reality were correct.

He only knew that he now had a job to do and that his captain had asked him to be here and to do this job. And because he accepted, with God as his witness, he was going to do it. And he'd be as good an assistant security director as he was a head waiter.

I'll be better!

At least that's what he told himself until all their eyes fell upon him.

He fidgeted with the buttons on his new uniform as he closed the distance between them. His new uniform fit well, perfect even. It just felt weird to be wearing it and the bars that had to be paraded so loudly on top of each shoulder.

Waiting for him was the captain, Mrs. Williams, and his new boss, security director Agarwal, who now wore three bars on his uniform.

The captain spoke first, “I know introductions are not needed, as we know what Mr. Petrovich has done for all of us this past week. But I did want to recognize Mr. Flavio Petrovich for taking the role of assistant security director and joining us here today.”

There was a short clap from everyone, as each scrutinized him.

This was absolutely the one thing he didn't want.

“Way to go, Flavio,” TJ announced with a smile behind her sunglasses. He was surprised to see that she looked less pale to him, like she was dead before and had come back alive today.

“Thank you, Mrs. Villiams,” Flavio said and then nodded at her. “And thank you, Captain and Mr. Agarwal. It is my honor to serve you and my ship.”

“I believe you know how to handle this weapon," Wasano handed him an M4 rifle. Flavio could see Wasano had another slung behind his back.

Flavio accepted the rifle, grabbing the stock with one hand and the rail with the other; the butt found a familiar place underneath his pit. He pointed it at a crate on the floor, away from the group. “It's not like my dependable AK-74.” He pulled back the charging bolt and examined it to see if there was a round in the chamber. There was. He let go, letting it slide back into its place, and flicked the safety back on. “But this will do.”

Flavio slung the weapon to his back, the same way his

superior had his. “What's our mission, sir?”

Captain Jean Pierre looked like he was going to answer, but then he stopped and motioned toward the movement coming from the stairwell. It was five other security personnel, who appeared to be joining them.

“Very good. Now that we are all here,” the captain lifted his voice, addressing their whole group, “we are waiting for the all-clear from our OOD on the port-side swing deck, as well as Ted Williams, who will be our base operator on the bridge. So far, we have not observed any activity out on the dock. We can't tell if anyone is alive. It's possible the radio broadcast is just repeating itself and the people who broadcast the signal are either dead or have left. And in fact, it does appear that this town hasn't sustained the chaos, fires, or death that everyone else has. It looks like the town has simply been abandoned.”

“Maybe they heard British chef Jon is here to serve them food.” Flavio instantly wanted to take this back, while he had to forcibly hold back a snicker that wanted to come out. He was shocked that the quip came out of his own mouth. It was like his old self was rebelling, not wanting to give into his new position.

“Officer Petrovich, do you have a question for the captain?” Wasano asked with a scowl.

“Sorry, sir. Only wanted to know, if guns for people or crazies?” Flavio coughed once in his hand, hoping his misplaced comment didn't get him into too much hot water.

“Maybe both. We just don’t know. Any other questions?”

“No sir. Thank you.”

While they waited several long minutes for the all-clear, Flavio examined each of the people in their group of ship’s representatives, starting with Teresa Jean Williams.

Normally she would stand out in a crowd, especially wearing the only thing she seemed to wear now, very tight athletic clothes. Compared to the three officers in their formal white on blue uniforms and the other security in their standard uniforms, she looked out of place. However, he knew Mrs. Williams was FBI, and he had seen her in action. And although he still didn't completely trust her because of her recent changes, she seemed uniquely qualified to be a part of this group.

He suspected that the security director was capable. Wasano had already proven himself pretty solid under pressure. On the other hand, he knew nothing about the other security personnel, but he suspected that none had experienced any extreme pressure, much less being in a fire-fight. What kind of pressure does security see on a cruise ship, except dealing with drunkards and minor rule-breakers?

It was then Flavio noticed that each of the security team held their long flashlights as their only weapon. The largest of them had a stun gun holstered to his hip. Flavio always suspected there weren't many firearms on board. Seeing just the two rifles appeared to buttress his suspicion. He also suspected that no one but maybe Wasano and certainly Teresa Jean—who carried no weapons of her own—had any firearms training.

At least I won't be accidentally shot by my own people, he thought. This was not an uncommon problem with troops in their first battle.

He guessed then, that their real mission was to show force and more importantly, to protect the captain. This he knew he would do with his life, if necessary.

Flavio understood that they were there to make a deal with the locals of this town, assuming they were still alive, by exchanging some food for their fuel. But he also suspected that these people were probably the local thugs who had taken control during the chaos. They probably then cleaned up any evidence of their actions, so that they could lure an unsuspecting ship in under the promise of trading for fuel.

What is it the Americans say... It's not my first rodeo.

Flavio thought back to his time in the Romanian Army. Even though the Russians were on everybody's minds, it was usually the local mob or Bratva, or “brotherhood” as the Russians called it, who were most likely to fire upon them, even if you gave them what they wanted. Flavio's fear was that this group had no intention of making a deal with them. So as much as he respected his captain, the man was not accustomed to these kinds of situations. Neither was the security director.

Flavio was beginning to feel very glad he was asked to accept this position as he might be the only one with the experience to deal with what could become a bad situation.

Their radios chirped at the same time. A female voice crackled through. "I see someone coming. Suggest you put your earpieces on.”

Flavio didn’t have one, but he watched the captain, security director and Mrs. Williams plug their earpieces into their ears and into their radios, silencing the static.

He was glad for this, because he wanted to be completely focused on what was going on around him. He had a sinking feeling that he was going to have to use all of his experience and skills today.

94

The Island

Salvadore “Sal” Calderon marched down the dock—*his dock*—alone. He wore his dress blues for this occasion and his reflective sunglasses, even though the sky was darker than normal.

He stopped when he was halfway down the dock and glanced up at the giant cruise ship ported in front of him. He couldn’t help but smile. He was amazed at how his plan had worked out so well. He had hoped that he'd be able to snag maybe a freighter or at least a smaller cruiser or two. Never in his wildest dreams did he expect a cruise ship to fall into his trap.

The food problem *was* getting bad and if this didn't work, they were going to have to take more aggressive actions and attack one of the neighboring islands. Of course, this was fraught with much risk, as they didn't know what to expect from the other populations, whether they were affected by the disease or unaffected. He had minimal manpower and few weapons. That meant his people could be wiped out in even a small battle, regardless of their capabilities. The last thing he wanted to do was leave the protection of his island, over which he at least had control. He just had to satiate his ravenous people before things got desperate. So he had to explore all options.

With only a few men he could trust to carry out his orders, he had started the planning for an incursion into Ponta Delgada on Ilha das Flores, the closest island to them. It was less than half an hour away by the only boat they had which could make the journey. They would pull up to the port and blast away any competition with their large weapon. Assuming it was then clear, they'd raid the port of what they needed and bring back fresh supplies to his island. If none of his plans worked, the final fall-back was to abandon his island altogether. Even though it was worst case, he had to still plan for this.

But then they received the reply.

A couple of days after Sal took complete control of the island, he learned the world around him had completely fallen apart. So he'd come up with the brilliant idea of setting up a beacon; a repeating radio broadcast that offered up the one resource they didn't need but had lots of, heavy fuel. Only big ships, like freighters and, of course, cruise ships ate up the stuff. The P-114 military patrol boat they had taken burned marine diesel. They had plenty of this already. So with his radio rig at the police station, he set up his broadcast and went fishing, using his heavy fuel as bait.

After the tidal wave wiped out many coastal communities on this side of the Atlantic, along with many of the ships already at sea, he wasn't sure what was still out there. He figured there had to be other semi-protected ports or bays, like theirs, which weren't too badly damaged, along with their ships. And he knew it was possible to survive a big wave at sea.

When he received his first and only nibble, claiming to

be coming from a cruise liner, he thought maybe it was a joke. Or someone else's subterfuge. But to hear that a giant cruise ship had answered their call was simply too much to expect. Although not familiar with this particular ship, he had seen other Regal European ships ported on Sao Miguel, plus he'd read enough about them to know there had to be at least 1000 passengers and crew on board. And that meant lots of food for his people.

When he spoke to the captain of the *Intrepid*, Sal did his best to make it sound like a simple trade. "We just need a little food for our starving island, and you can have as much fuel as you want." Sal suspected a captain of a luxury cruise ship would be naive and not expect anything other than what he had heard. Still, they would be ready if the crew of the *Intrepid* offered up any resistance.

He heard a foot-shuffle coming up behind him, knowing instantly who it was. Sal turned to see Tomas hurrying up the dock in his direction, and he was happy to see that Tomas was following his instructions to the letter: his young agent wore his cleanest uniform and wasn't carrying his service weapon. Sal knew he could count on Tomas setting up everything else as requested. He was a smart boy, who understood well the penalty for disobedience.

"Everything is set, sir," Tomas stated this like a private to his drill instructor, only without any exuberance.

"Good boy," Sal answered, turning back toward the cruise ship, waiting for its hatch to open, and for the fly to get completely ensnared in his web. He licked his lips with utter anticipation, savoring in his mind what his next meal might taste like.

"You really think they will go for it?" Tomas asked, his voice stoic and professional, as always.

"They're here, aren't they?"

"Yes, but what makes you think they will make a deal with you?"

Sal hadn't yet revealed the main goal of his plan to Tomas, much less the mechanics of it. It wasn't necessary and he was pretty sure Tomas would resist him if he understood their ultimate goal. His best agent only had to follow orders. And he was good at that. He had others, with far fewer moral impediments and unique skill-sets, like him, to do his dirty work. "Simple. I'm going to accept whatever they offer, in return for all the fuel they want."

“Isn't that kind of craz—” Tomas stopped himself, obviously seeing the wisdom in not infuriating what he must have perceived as his power-crazed superior. “I mean, wouldn't it be better to hold back some of the fuel, out of the prospect of getting another ship to come here?”

The poor boy was just as naive as everybody else in this world. That is, everyone who used to be in this world.

Sal learned long ago, but it was made even more obvious very recently, that whole world was populated with naive people, who never would have conceived that something like the Rage disease would appear and change everything and everyone. People were like sheep, never able to think past their next latte, or their next sexual escapade, or even their next paycheck. The world’s population had been weak and ripe for conquest. And now it would be controlled by special people like him—those who had the abilities and weren’t weighed down by the moral entanglements to use them, for their own purposes.

As much as he wished Tomas was of the same mindset as he, sadly he wasn't. And while Sal still needed the boy, he had to use care in not sending him over the top by telling the boy their ultimate plans. He knew Tomas wouldn’t be able to handle it. Besides, Tomas would find out soon enough what they’d planned to do with the cruise ship. And when that happened, he’d either be on board or Sal would kill him. It didn’t matter either way.

“Look, there’s someone on that balcony, off the bridge.

She's looking at us through her binoculars."

Sal had already seen the woman. His eyesight was far better than the younger man's.

He looked in her direction and waved a friendly hello to the woman.

95

Wayfarer Lounge

They had both been dumbstruck when the parasitic had leapt from its pod.

It was 08:15 and just like the last attack, a lone parasitic dashed from the same pod, closest to that slightly damaged rear door. But unlike its dead predecessor, it slowed down before hitting the door, holding up right before its fallen brother, who lay lifeless a meter in front of the damaged door. With one arm, it effortlessly snatched and dragged the dead parasitic back to their pod, where it discarded the body at the pod's edge and moved away. What happened next was horrific.

The Americans had something called Shark Week on one of their TV channels that fascinated Deep and several other crew. It was supposed to be real-life, even though much of it felt professionally edited—something he understood quite well. What wasn't edited were the videos of schools of sharks being chummed with fresh blood and guts. It was like this, but worse. And in a way, what they had watched seemed less real.

Almost immediately after the body was dumped on its

periphery, the pod buzzed as if it were an angry beehive. The pod convulsed and shimmied upward, at first moving amoeba-like slowly as a single form toward the body. Then the form broke apart into its many individual parts, which swarmed their fallen parasitic. Each frantically pounded and tore at the body, separating limb from limb, breaking up their comrade into multiple pieces.

Deep dared not blink for fear that he was going to miss the tornado-like blurs on the screen. Seconds later, all the parasitics rose back up from where the body had been and then rapidly regrouped until the pod was whole once more. The re-formed pod then finally settled back down, although it still seemed to gesticulate in an almost anxious anticipation of another feeding.

Nothing from the dead body was left behind, except for an almost imperceptible stain that could have been easily mistaken as a normal part of the loud carpet.

Both Deep and Dr. Molly sat in stunned silence and were so completely focused on the gruesome sight in the left-hand corner of the main screen, that they had forgotten about the parasitic that initiated the feeding of one of their own and then moved out of their way.

But then they caught the flash of the lone parasitic, once again dashing off to the right. It was so fast, the camera couldn't resolve its ghostly image, until it collided shoulder-first with the damaged door. It bounced off, falling to the floor.

Both Deep and Molly waited breathlessly to see what the parasitic would do, paying no attention to the new damage done to the door.

"Look Mr. Deep. He's injured pretty badly."

Deep saw this too; its right arm was broken and bent at an odd angle. "But that's on the other side of where he hit the... What's it doing now, Dr. Molly?"

Deep didn't see her shake her head, keeping his eyes riveted to the same scene she was.

The parasitic rose from the floor, seemingly unaffected by its injuries, only taking a second to examine its target. It then backed up farther and then sprang. It moved even quicker than before.

This time they couldn't see which part of its body hit first. Deep instinctively knew that it went for the door at its weakest point and this frightened him to his core. It struck the door with so much more force that the wall around it shuddered.

Without the audio, they couldn't hear the impact, but they could imagine it. The door was now bent far enough inward that they could see the emergency light, fixed to the wall on the other side.

Like the first one, this parasitic collapsed to the floor, perhaps suffering a similar fate, after serving its purpose for its fellow parasitics.

"Was he commanded to do that?" Deep asked, but he didn't want to hear the terrifying answer. It was one thing to have a bunch of wild animals reacting to genetically innate desires and inner demons. If they were only like other wild animals, they could control them because humans were always smarter than wild animals. But if the parasitics were thinking, calculating and able to call up any one of their group to use their superhuman strength and sacrifice themselves, without fear or thought, humans were doomed.

Deep stared at Molly, seeing her eyes darting around the monitor's screen, as if she were some old computer using all of its processing power to calculate what the hell was going on.

She obviously wasn't ready to output, because she was still silent.

"Look," she whispered.

He did, his eyes first searching the monitor and then finding them.

"Ma'am, what are they doing?"

Molly squinted to try and better see the two figures standing in the very back of the lounge. One was the older woman Deep had recognized as the one who was running around the ship naked, attacking many passengers and crew. She was the one they called Eloise. Standing beside her was Ágúst Helguson, their missing safety director.

Wearing what appeared to be layers of other people's ill-fitting clothes, they were standing against the farthest corner wall of the lounge, almost completely hidden in the shadows. Eloise was telling Mr. Helguson something, as if she were commanding him to do something.

Mr. Helguson nodded. Then the former safety director opened his mouth and appeared to scream something.

"Mr. Deep. Warn our security now." She scooted up out of her chair. "Tell him not to go in!"

It was too late.

96

Ted

Ted flipped the channel selector to security channel two, or SC2, to make sure no one from their away team or Jessica was speaking. He had thought he'd seen the captain's lips move. His radio speaker emitted nothing but staticky silence. With his eyes riveted on his video monitor, his thumb and forefinger tensed over the channel selector. His attention was elsewhere.

He wanted to turn back to SC1 to eavesdrop on the conversations between the guards just as they were preparing for the feeding of their parasitics. Molly had told him that they were going to do this later than normal, because of the two attempted attacks on their feeding crews yesterday. Since it was a few minutes after eight, he was anxious to hear what would happen or what was happening.

The split screen monitor in front of him flashed two video streams, which seemed to change little: one from inside of the deck 2 port-side gangway and one just outside of it. The outside view revealed maybe a third of the island's dock, just outside of their hatch. Nothing was moving there, except the occasional gust of wind.

The inside view showed the members of their ship's away team, which included TJ. Everyone, with the exception of his wife, shifted weight between their feet or incessantly fussed over their clothing. Flavio checked and rechecked his rifle before slinging it behind his back once more. Supposedly the rifles were a show of force, which the captain said he didn't believe they would need. Almost all of them seemed anxious.

TJ, on the other hand, was a sculpted statue of patience. The only part of her moving was her chest, constantly heaving for air to fuel her racing metabolism. Otherwise, she carried the look of someone impatiently waiting for their number to be called at DMV. In other words, impatiently annoyed.

All were waiting for the verbal thumbs-up from Jessica, who was watching from the port-side swing deck. He suspected this would happen pretty soon since she had already instructed them to put on their earpieces moments ago. That way, the team could silently listen to any alerts either Jessica or Ted gave them. Jessica was primarily the eyes for this trade, since she had a complete view of the whole port and what lay beyond it. Ted was a backup set of eyes on the cameras and to relay any relevant reports from anyone else.

Three members of the team, TJ, Jean Pierre and Wasano, had inserted their earpieces. Then they had Jessica and Ted each do a system check to adjust their volumes. Then silence. The next word would come from Jessica, letting them know it was time to go.

Ted was surprised when he had been told that their earphones didn't have mics on them: they had to speak into the actual portable radio transceiver, which had to be inconveniently lifted from their belts to do so. It seemed silly to have inferior equipment such as this. Even the standard cell phone comes with ear buds and a microphone for hands free conversations. Of course, the away team would not be conversing with him or anyone else on the radio, unless everything went south, and then it probably didn't matter if they had microphones in their earpieces or not. The captain, the security director and TJ would be listening in for one reason and one reason only: warnings. If Jessica or Ted saw anything that would be a threat, they would warn them. And the more Ted thought about it, the more that he was convinced that he was making more out of this than was necessary.

The trade *would* happen, because it had to happen. So surely they'd figure out a way to make it happen. Their situation was that dire.

When Ted arrived, after his meet with TJ, engineering head Niki announced to him that she was going to have to increase the temperature in the Wayfarer Lounge and several pre-designated cabins at least three degrees every fifteen minutes and that all electrical systems were off. Only their most critical systems were on and running on battery power. Further, if they left this port right now, they'd have less than one hour of propeller use, at ten knots, before they'd run out of fuel entirely. She said that was enough to maybe get them to the next closest island and that was all. They had to make a deal and it had to happen now.

Ted decided very little was going on in the two areas he was tasked to watch. And because he wasn't expected to say anything other than if he saw something wrong, and that wouldn't be until after they opened their hatch in a little while, he chose to switch back to SC1 and listen in on the chatter about the feedings. He would switch the radio back to SC2 the moment he saw movement from the away team. Until then, he wanted to hear what the parasitics were up to next.

Immediately he heard the anxious guards, who sounded like they were sending in their feeding team right now.

"—imple. You all ready, two?" asked a familiar sounding Brazilian voice.

Ted suspected this was the guard named Paulo that he had run into a few days earlier, when trying to alert then

Captain Jörgen to the dangers in Gibraltar.

"Jes, one. We have your back."

Even though he was staring right at it, Ted was startled to see some movement on his monitor. The team must be getting ready to exit. He needed to switch back to SC2, even though the feeding was supposed to happen right about now.

"This is Feeding Team One. I'm ready with my feeder to go in. Going silent."

"Two here. We're silent."

Ted's hand found the selector, while he focused on his wife, as she held up her portable to her mouth. He needed to switch now.

"Attention!" a frantic voice hollered. "We may have a breach on the port-side—"

Ted switched the channel.

"—ed are you there?" TJ asked.

"I'm here. I'm watching."

He could see a female security guard, operating controls on a small panel rising up to her belly. She flicked a switch and the hatch began opening.

"I just wanted to thank you for meeting me earlier."

"You're welcome. I—"

"Let's keep the chatter down to only warnings from here on out. Okay?" the captain offered his soft reprimand.

"Yes, sir," Ted quickly responded. He could see TJ nod her acceptance as well.

"OOD, everything look good still?" Wasano was holding his unit up to his mouth.

"Yes, sir. It's all clear. I see two men. Another has joined the first on the dock after going into a small building at the other end. You're good to go."

Ted desperately wanted to switch back to the other channel to hear more about the warning.

"Ted, do you see anything out of the ordinary?" Wasano asked.

Ted wondered what the hell was ordinary, for comparison. “No. I see less than you do. I can’t even see the two people Jessica mentioned.”

Jean Pierre nodded and then held up his walkie. “We’ll see if we can move him into your view.” Then he added, “I want all eyes and ears on these people.”

The three with portables all refastened them to their belts and waited for the gangway bridge to unfurl itself onto the dock.

Ted knew he had to stay on SC2 for the duration, as well as watch them, even though any of his efforts felt superfluous. But at that moment, more than anything else, he wanted to desperately hear about the breach.

97

A Deal You Can't Refuse

Jean Pierre strode to a stop, holding up at least fifty meters from the two men waiting for them. A quick glance at their exit confirmed that they were in view of the ship's camera. He wanted as many eyes on them as possible. But the main reason for his abrupt stop was to move the negotiations in their direction.

He'd read endless books about negotiating at the insistence of his father, who wanted him to take over the family business, and Jean Pierre knew that a big part of starting a negotiation was controlling the negotiating venue. The venue favored this unknown group, because Jean Pierre's people and their ship were in unfamiliar territory. And since the stakes of this meeting were so great, he thought he'd try to get things started by forcing these unknown men to walk to him. It was a little thing. But sometimes the little things made a difference.

The two men, midway on the dock, both wearing formal police uniforms, shot each other looks of surprise and then returned their gazes back to *Intrepid's* away team. It was obvious they didn't expect this.

Intrepid's security director, Wasano, took his place right beside Jean Pierre, with his weapon moved from his back to his chest. Having a weapon was mostly as a show of force, indicating that they had the means and the will to use force, if they needed to. Wasano whispered, "I'm glad to see they're both police."

Jean Pierre also had this thought. At least at first. Then his mind started a game of devil's advocate: *Couldn't these men have stolen their uniforms from dead police officers?*

If this were true, they were probably in big trouble. If not, they'd probably make a deal.

His mind wasn't done: *If they're police, why aren't they armed?*

Many European countries didn't arm their officers and so this alone wasn't strange.

But in a new world, where crazed animals and people could attack at any moment, wouldn't you have weapons?

He remembered the radio broadcast, where the man said that Rage hadn't touched his island. Still, he did expect them to be carrying weapons.

But...

Enough! he thought, no longer entertaining these ideas.

Maybe the opposite was true and these men were trying not to show themselves as the thugs anyone would have assumed they must be. Perhaps they were leaders, just like Jean Pierre, only trying to manage a crisis on behalf of their people. People were starving, from what their leader said on the radio.

One of the two police officers smiled from behind his oversized sunglasses—the kind he'd seen daily on the cruise ship, often worn by men and women twice this man's age. This man also had more ornamentation than the other and so Jean Pierre assumed that he was the other's superior.

The leader and the younger man beside him proceeded

to walk in their direction. They were coming to Jean Pierre on his own terms.

The negotiations had begun.

"It looks like they have fuel, sir," Wasano again whispered, making an obvious attempt at not letting the wind carry his voice to the other side.

Jean Pierre had also seen the fueling barge on the other side of the dock when they pulled up to the port. "Let's hope it's full of what we need."

As both men waited for the two officers to arrive from their slow march, Jean Pierre admired the little town in front of them. It wasn't the usual touristy town, whoring useless knick-knacks to ships full of people. It still had the flavor of the more familiar Azores villages. But this one existed to serve only its residents, who were mostly retired, government employees like these two men, and a few others who must have had some sort of employment, though he didn't know what that might be. When the small military base, somewhere on the other side of the island, shut down a few years ago the town's employment engine mostly died with it.

He had never been here and doubted any cruise ships had before them. The dock was way too small for a ship their size. The *Intrepid* didn't really fit. They had to jerry-rig some of their mooring lines to the side of the ship to moor them to a buoy, just off the tip of the dock.

The small size of their town and its even smaller population mix might explain why Rage hadn't hit their island. It was a logical explanation.

Just then, something rubbed up against his leg, jolting Jean Pierre from his thoughts. He looked down, expecting a sickly looking rat, which were way too common for his preference around ports. Instead, it was a black cat. It purred away like a little motorboat, doing side-swiping passes against his leg. The cute little thing looked up at him and meowed softly. Then it ratcheted its head forward, hissed loudly and then scurried behind him, out of his periphery.

"Captain Haddock, I presume?" asked the clean-shaven leader, with a welcoming grin and an outstretched hand. "I am Vila de Corvo's PCP Police Chief, Salvadore Calderon, and this is my best agent, Tomas Novo, at your service."

"Yes, I am. Greetings Chief Calderon and Agent Novo," Jean Pierre replied, shaking each man's hand. "This is my security director, Wasano Agarwal."

"Ahh, a French captain? Thought all of you were from Iceland."

"Belgium, actually. Regal European has"—*his mind flashed, HAD*—"captains from all over the world. So tell me about your fuel."

"Ha-ha, right to the point. Okay..."

The man seemed very composed, as if he just didn't care whether or not they made a deal. But he also seemed to be hiding something. And Tomas, his police deputy, or what he called "Agent," looked decidedly ill at ease: the man's face was as serious as death and his eyes darted everywhere and nowhere.

"Here's the deal," stated the chief. "The fuel barge you see here crashed on our shore a few days ago, carrying in it heavy fuel and MGO. We don't need heavy fuel and we already have an ample supply of diesel fuel for our boats. What we don't have is food, and I'm guessing you do, looking at the size of your ship. So here's my offer. We want three-quarters of all of your food. In return you can fill up your ship with all the heavy fuel you want." His smile remained, seemingly a permanent fixture on his face when he wasn't speaking.

Jean Pierre knew that this was just the first offer in their negotiations. But he also knew that he couldn't really spare that much food and he didn't really have anything else to bargain with. He also knew that every moment he waited here brought them another moment closer to running out of fuel. And that surely meant they were doomed. He had little time to stand around wagging their tongues with back and forth offers and counter-offers. He needed to close this deal. Now.

"That's crazy. We're a cruise ship of 3000 people"—he had decided it was better to exaggerate their actual population—"and we're low on supplies already after being at sea for over ten days. If we gave you three-quarters of our food, we'd all starve in a couple of days.

"We'll give you one quarter of our food and we'll take not only all the heavy fuel our ship will accept, but also your MGO as well.

"That's my final offer."

Jean Pierre shut up and willed himself not to breathe another word before Calderon did. This was another negotiating technique he'd learned: the one who said something first usually lost.

"Would you mind if I speak to Tomas about this in private?" asked Calderon.

"Of course," Jean Pierre replied, still acting as if everything was fine, although he was now starting to wonder if he pushed it too far. He was prepared to give away whatever he had to, in order to secure the fuel.

Wasano leaned in and muttered, "Sir, can we even afford to give away one quarter of all of our food? With so many mouths to feed, I fear we'll run out without any other options for finding food."

Jean Pierre remained stoically silent and waited to answer his security director, while he carefully watched Calderon for some sign as to what they'd do next. Calderon instructed Agent Tomas something. This appeared to light a fire in Tomas, who then turned and ran back down the dock.

Jean Pierre still didn't respond to Wasano's unanswered question, as he watched Chief Calderon return. He had planned to explain his future plans to everyone in the next couple of days. But only after they had their fuel.

The chief's smile rose higher on his face. "I sent my man

back to get help to unload the food."

"So you agree to our terms?" Jean Pierre asked.

"Yes, of course." The chief thrust out his hand.

Jean Pierre couldn't hold back his own smile and vigorously shook Calderon's hand. *The man has quite a grip.*

Only then did Jean Pierre realize he must have been more nervous than he thought, because his palm felt hot and sweaty compared to the chief's cool and dry hand.

He then saw a dozen men already moving toward them. Jean Pierre had two thoughts then. *They must have been desperate for a deal as well. And he should have offered one fifth of his food instead.*

"My men will come in and inventory your food. And maybe you can help us with the offloading?"

"Of course. My procurement manager has already prepared an inventory for you and awaits your men inside. And what about the fuel?"

"As you can see, it's already making its way. Prepare for it on your starboard side."

He could see that the barge had started up its engine and several crewmen were already untying the mooring lines.

Jean Pierre breathed out a deep sigh. He was actually starting to believe this was all going to work out.

~~~

Even before the black cat had darted from the captain's legs, Flavio was anxious. This had quickly progressed to worry.

Like TJ, Flavio had been asked by the security director to hang back from the "negotiations" and to watch for trouble. He had done this, scrutinizing not only his captain, security director and the other two, but also the several men flooding into a small building at the beginning of the concrete dock they
~~~

were all standing on. He also eyed the men on top of the fueling barge, just a few meters away. He felt certain that something was about to happen, at any second.

Then the cat appeared by the captain's legs. At the time, he thought nothing of it, even though it was black—he never believed in the old wives' tales. It was when the cat reacted to the leader of this island group with a hiss that something in Flavio's brain said this was all wrong. He knew dogs were good judges of character and wondered if the same thing were true about cats. That's when something *did* happen, which he would have never suspected.

The cat dashed in his direction then, rather than scurrying past him, it leapt onto his leg. As if he was some sort of damned tree, it dug its sharp claws into him. Because he was trying to be hyper-attentive to his surroundings and he felt sure that something was going to happen, he tried to ignore the cat, thinking it would eventually jump down. Instead, it started to scale his leg like a kitty-climbing wall, each paw's needle-like talons pricking his skin with each slow pull.

Flavio released his tensed fingers from his rifle, slung it around his neck and rested it on his chest. His hands found the soft little creature and he gently encouraged it to stop its trek upward and to release. He knew if he yanked it off, he'd lose some of his treasured skin in the process. Surprisingly, the cat let go and slowly walked along his straightened forearm, purring its delight at him.

"Looks like you have your hands full with a new girlfriend," chortled TJ.

An uncontrollable smirk cracked his facade. "Yes, Mrs. Villiams. I have a vay with women," he said, purposely emphasizing his accent.

He let the animal down and silently cursed either the blood or perspiration trickling unseen down his pant leg. At least it hadn't done this around his white-shirted upper body, which would have shone through. He glared at the cat, which was indifferent and continued its purring and rubbing up against his leg. Then it parked itself up against his shoe, where it proceeded to preen itself.

"Now she has to take a bath after you're done with her."

"Ha-ha-ha." He was not amused, even if he couldn't help but feel something for the little animal.

"Hey Flavio," TJ huffed. "It looks like JP made a deal."

Flavio glanced up, forgetting his new friend, and saw she was right. They were shaking hands and the other police officer—if they really were police—was returning with close to a dozen men from the building at the other end of the dock.

Flavio leaned in closer to TJ. "Do you smell anything about these men or this place? You know, are they infected?"

She removed her nose plug again—he'd seen her do this a few times earlier in the ten-plus minutes they had been out there. She shook her head. "I smell you now, but barely. It's hard to smell anything with this stiff breeze."

TJ slipped back on her nose plug, just as the captain and security director returned.

"Okay, a deal has been made," Jean Pierre announced, sounding somewhat jubilant. "They're giving us all the fuel we need, in return for one quarter of our food."

"Sir, you don't trust them, do you?" Flavio interrupted.

"Doesn't matter, Mr. Petrovich. I'm asking you and Mrs. Williams to escort some of their men to our procurement officer, who is waiting for you on deck 1, in the refrigerated food storage area. You both will be my eyes to make sure they don't try anything... funny. We're almost out of fuel and as you can see, their fueling ship is already moving to our starboard side to begin refueling. So I want this to go smoothly but quickly. Is that understood?"

"Yes, sir," Flavio said.

"Aye aye, captain," TJ stated.

Jean Pierre smiled and then followed Wasano up the

gangway and back onto the ship, while Wasano spoke with his refueling crew on his radio.

Flavio didn't care for the brevity of all of this. The negotiation, the execution of the deal. It was happening way too fast. No time for planning and no time to consider the consequences if something happened. But his captain gave him an order and he would follow it.

As he followed the two men inside, he heard TJ, behind him now, casually announce the details of the deal on her radio.

He had to admit, he was beginning to feel very glad to have TJ with him. He felt surer by the minute that he was going to have to rely on her more than he wanted to imagine.

98
Otto

"Are you sure dis is all right?" gasped Otto. The rotund German had to stop again to catch a breath and wipe off the sweat rolling down his face. His heart raced like a freight train moving uphill, and he wondered if he might suffer a heart attack if he continued at this pace.

"You work for me now, lazy tourist. You do what I say," his new boss, Bohdan, huffed back.

The two other black-jumpsuited crew members chortled their amusement at their supervisor ordering around the former guest of their ship. The insults didn't really bother Otto; he just wasn't used to this kind of physical labor. Most days, he sat at a desk at his office in Munich, where all the running around was done by the younger associates of König AG, his namesake engineering firm.

Now, he was the errand boy for these three mechanical crew members, who seemed like they were up to no good, even though they swore otherwise. But what could he say? He was literally threatened with being kicked off the ship if he didn't do his duties. And he assumed the captain supported this way of thinking, based on his public statement and having crew with these attitudes. The man at the top is always responsible for his people's actions.

At some point soon he would have to talk to the captain. Not to complain. But to promote the fact that a man with his skills could be put to better use than running physical errands. He would need to do this soon though. Because he wasn't liable to live through this kind of work much longer.

"That's enough. Rest over!" Bohdan bellowed. "We don't have much time to complete our work."

Otto exhaled his frustration, bent over to pick up the full 5 gallon water bottle and pulled upward. His back protested with a stabbing pain, a threat it was about to go out or just a warning—he didn't know. Somehow he was able to hoist up the heavy bottle to his side hip with both arms. He took a wobbly step forward. Then another.

"Come on, lazy tourist. This way," his immediate supervisor demanded. Bohdan was already many steps ahead of him, the others in tow, beckoning their struggling new crew member forward.

Otto wasn't sure what they were having him do, but he felt pretty sure it was not part of their normal duties. He had lots of evidence for this.

Their entry to this restricted area, off engineering, was done with some stealth. They pretended to be nervously fiddling with some controls, near a small access door, making sure they were not being watched. Only then did they produce a key card—Otto suspected the one he was given wouldn't work on that same door—and entered the tight access way. Through this, they had made their way up and over to where they were now.

Twice they stopped because they thought they heard someone else in the metal tubular walkway, crowded with cables and ducking. When they realized it was nothing, Bohdan moved them farther forward, but they were always looking back behind them, watching and listening for someone else who was never there. These were not the actions of men just doing their jobs.

Otto decided it was better to bite his tongue. He'd do what they told him to do, and then he'd tell captain all about this. Maybe he could garner some favor by reporting what their errant crew members were doing in the dark shadows of his ship.

"Here," Bohdan commanded one of the two crew members; their names, also Slavic sounding, escaped him. And unlike all the crew before all this craziness started, many, like these men, no longer wore name badges. Otto first assumed they were recent recruits, like him. He understood that lots of the existing crew were being relocated to different positions and even different departments, based on the ship's needs. For instance, he had heard of room stewards going to engineering or wait staff going to mechanical, which was the suspected job path of these men. Except they at least had the right color uniforms, which he did not.

The crew member Bohdan had been commanding set down his tool bag, opened it up, and pulled out a small reciprocating saw. The other crew member, the largest of the two, already had a drill out, and started drilling holes into the top of a long span of aluminum tubing running along the confines of the small access hallway they were in. Otto was no expert on the mechanics of a cruise ship, but he knew this to be duct work for the ship's HVAC system.

The moment the driller finished making four holes, the other crew member with the saw began cutting from hole to hole. And within less than a minute, a rectangular cutout was made.

"Are you sure this will work?" asked the driller.

"Yes, have faith, my friend," Bohdan reassured him, standing about five meters forward from their newly made hole. "We will be safe again after this. Now, make your next holes here." He tapped an area a little more on the side of the same aluminum ductwork.

Once again, the driller expertly completed his work, this time drilling four holes in the upper-side of the tubing. And the moment he was finished, the other worker stepped in and sawed another square piece out of the tubing.

Two holes, but for what? Otto wondered.

Both Bohdan and the driller moved back toward Otto, near the first hole's location, where Otto was standing hunched over, still collecting his breath. "Okay Anton. You grab the water bottle from fat boy."

This insult bristled Otto and he was immediately reminded of the nursery rhyme taught to him by his mother after school kids picked on him for being overweight: "Stöcke und Steine brechen meine Knochen" (Sticks & Stones may break my bones), "aber Namen können mich nicht verletzten" (but names will never hurt me).

It still hurt.

Anton, the driller, who originally carried the bottle up the access way ladder, once again effortlessly snatched the water bottle from Otto, hoisted it up and over the ducting, above the first hole. Then he lowered it, neck first, into the small hole at the top of the ductwork. Gently he let go and the bottle's weight pushed down on the soft material, making it and the brackets supporting the ducting crinkle slightly. But it held.

He still had no idea what the hell they were doing there... *Creating some sort of flood in the ducting? It made no sense.*

"Your turn," Bohdan demanded. Then Otto realized Bohdan was speaking to him. "Take this." He held out a thick plastic bottle that rattled, which he must have pulled from the small satchel he'd been carrying, demanding Otto take it.

Otto did as instructed and waited for his boss' next

command, not sure he wanted to know where this was going.

"Pay attention now," Bohdan instructed. "Don't breathe when you do this. When I tell you... Open bottle"—Bohdan demonstrated by pretending to twist open the cap—"and pour in 10 or 12 tablets. Then close. Then quickly move forward from here"—he pointed to the end-point of the access way, only a few more meters away—"and we'll follow you from behind. Okay?"

Otto wasn't terrifically worried at this point, thinking this was just some sort of stupid joke three men were conspiring to do together and he figured they were already saddled with Otto. So they'd get him to come along for the gag, making him the mule to slug the water bottle around for them.

But then Otto caught a glimpse of the bottle's label and he saw what it was. He glanced up to Bohdan. "What could you possibly need hydrogen phosphide for?"

"Not to worry, tourist. We just killing some pests," Bohdan stated resolutely. The other two giggled.

That's when Otto panicked.

99

Flavio

Flavio had two immediate problems upon entering the ship. First, his new friend the black cat had followed him onto the ship, shadowing his every step. More importantly, he didn't know any of the names of the four men and one woman who were security and were waiting just inside the ship. He wanted to get everyone set before the men from the island came on board to do their inventory and start the process of collecting the agreed-upon food from their ship.

Cat meowed much too loudly and Flavio immediately felt the prickles of what he was sure was the other security guards' scorn as they eyeballed their new second in command, who just allowed an animal to follow him on board.

"I need four security to remain here and stay on radio channel"—he turned to TJ—"what channel are we on?"

"It's SC2, sir," answered one of the two women in his detail, with a dark complexion and strong South African accent. "We were already instructed to remain on comms. Ms. Kashatri, Mr. Akashi, Mr. Ivanov and I will remain at this hatch, sir."

Flavio allowed his gaze to hover on the guard, surprised at how competent she was. He assumed most of these guards were not going to be professional after seeing the way their former security director ran things on this ship for the past year.

"Thank you, Ms..." his eyebrows raised up, exaggerating his question, as he waited for an answer.

"Sorry, sir. Violet Johansson, sir."

"Thanks again, Ms. Johansson. Can two of you also work the metal detector machine right now? I want to make sure our guests don't have any weapons."

"Yes, sir. We were instructed to do that as well."

In fact, Flavio could see that two had already taken their positions at the machine.

"Okay, I can see I not needed here. Could whoever is left come with Mrs. Villiams and me and escort their men down to deck 1?"

"Aye, sir" came from a heavy-set guard. Then all eyes turned to watch the men from the island approach and mount the gangway leading up to their hatch.

"Mrs. Villiams, could you go and stay out of sight, but smell each man after they come through metal detector? I have feeling about these men."

TJ nodded and without a word, stepped through the metal detector. It immediately emitted an ear-piercing beep-tone and she reacted to it immediately, doubling over and clutching her ears, as if in pain. Flavio squinted to see where in her skimpy outfit she could possibly be carrying any metal on her, while she scurried through and disappeared around the wall leading to the stairwell landing.

His newest friend Cat continued her incessant purring. He couldn't have this, when he was trying to do his job as each of the island men scaled the gangway single file. He didn't want Cat hurt, but he couldn't deal with it right now—not even sure what he'd do with it after all this.

Flavio scooped up Cat—*Vicky missed her cat and would love it* sprang to his mind. He held it out to a portable fabric curtain that was used with others to partition an area for private screenings of passengers who set off the metal detector. Cat grabbed hold of the curtain and began to climb up it, leaving small holes where each of its claws had been.

Flavio quickly returned to the exit and stepped up to the first man who had come on board.

"I am Flavio Petrovich, second in command of security for the *Intrepid*. I'm here to make sure your men don't get lost on way to and back from our food storage. Dah?"

"Ain't... that sweet... We have... tour guides," huffed the squat man, who looked homeless, but well fed: his thick jowls waddled as he spoke, stopping every other word to take in a gulp of air with his giant mouth; his huge belly protruded out from a stained T, which seemed several sizes too small; and he was entirely plastered in a thick sheen of perspiration and dirt. Each of the man's wide nostrils appeared extra flared. And Flavio caught a flash of something white inside, but the man turned before he could see better.

"Please proceed through metal detector. Then wait for me with your other men."

"So long... as we get... our food... mate," said the man, flashing a set of equally dirty teeth. He then lumbered, as instructed, through the metal detector. No beeps or anything. Flavio stood in the way of the next arriving man, while he watched the squat man continue into the hallway, scanning his surroundings. Squat man abruptly stopped, a smile slithering onto his mug at the entrance to the stairwell. Flavio knew right away what the man was leering at: TJ. Flavio felt his stomach turn when he attempted to imagine what the man's sewer of a mind must be thinking right now.

Flavio turned to and spat out a retread of his directions to all of the other men, who all nodded their acceptance, each then processing through the metal detector and each finally lolling in the hallway with the others.

Not once did the metal detector chime an alert. And TJ didn't show or indicate any sort of alarm. After the final man, she popped her head out from the wall's edge to look back; finding Flavio's gaze, she gave him a thumbs-up.

All appeared right, but Flavio couldn't shake the sinking feeling in his gut that they were missing something.

100
Entropy

Otto glanced again at the bottle and then back at the tablets he had just poured out into the HVAC ductwork, then at the three grinning goons: two preparing to run back to where they had just come and one trying with difficulty to yank the cap off the water bottle. The obvious intent was to release its contents down the ductwork, so it would make its way... *To the tablets.*

Otto was a civil engineer who built exquisite German bridges and perfect German roads; he was not chemist. But he took enough chemistry in his primary schooling to know when water mixes with aluminum phosphide, it will produce either toxic phosphine gas—often used on ships to kill rats—or if there's too much gas, or a flame introduced to it, an explosion.

Bohdan had told him that they were "killing some pests." He suspected that these goons were planning to kill the parasitics the ship was holding in the big lounge. There had been many rumblings by former passengers and existing crew about how twisted it was to keep monsters on board the ship. Some of the more vocal folks advocated poisoning their food, or just tossing them overboard. Part of him didn't disagree with the idea: the parasitics posed a huge threat to everyone on the ship and if all of the crew—including the new inductees like him—were able to vote on it, Otto felt sure they would have unanimously voted to get rid of the parasitics. He had even heard Bohdan mention a meeting last night that Otto now felt certain was to give this man the go-ahead to take this very action. But this much gas would kill many of the non-infected people on the ship too.

It was also then, during his brain's rapid-fire assessment, that Otto connected the fact that Bohdan instructed him to move forward after planting the tablets. They were planning on running back the other way, leaving Otto to die from inhaling the toxic gas. Otto would be their fall guy. The one they could point their fingers at as the instigator of this crime.

"Come on, Anton. Finish it," Bohdan yelled at the big man, who couldn't seem to get the cap off the bottle by tugging at it through the little hole they had made on top of the duct-work. *They weren't the brightest bulbs in the pack.*

But somehow he did. Otto could see the air bubbles shoot upward in the clear bottle, indicating that water was pouring out into the ship's ducting.

Otto knew at that point what was going to happen and there was little he could do to stop it.

Maybe one thing.

Otto subconsciously patted his left pocket to confirm the presence of one object he needed. It was there.

His next decision was his last, but it gave him much satisfaction: in spite of the captain or his crew's stupidity in assigning Otto with such menial duties, he alone was the only person who could mitigate the loss of life Bohdan and his crew were going to cause. Knowing this made it worth sacrificing his life for all those he'd save, even if he suspected no one would ever know he was the hero.

As quickly as he could move, he jammed the open bottle of tablets sideways into the hole, so that all of the tablets would come in contact with the water. He could hear the water's effect on the tablets he'd already poured out and white vapor began to billow out from the hole.

"Come on, let's go." It was Bohdan's voice.

"What about the fat man?" asked one of the workers.

Otto was already running in their direction. And because of Otto's movement toward the three men, each of whom had turned to consider the man and the question, all were momentarily puzzled enough by Otto's movements and hesitated.

It was just enough time.

"What the fu—" Bohdan breathed before being hit by all 122 kilos of Otto König.

~~~

"Pull back! I repeat, exit the lounge immediately," Deep hollered once again into his radio, even though he knew it was no use. The guards had explicit instructions to turn off their radios during feeding sessions, so as to not to risk startling or otherwise awakening the parasitics. Neither the guard entering the lounge nor the other two guards outside the main entrance would hear Deep's warning.

The radio silence was supposed to last from the moment just before they opened the main door to begin feeding until the feeding was completed and the door was sealed tight. Physically switching off their radios negated any chance that someone would forget and cause a loud tone or voice, or that some other crew member would call out on SC1. Their reasoning was that the other two guards were already monitoring through a crack in the main entrance, watching the backs of the two who were tasked with feeding the parasitics.

The radio silence was supposed to be for the feeding
~~~

team's protection. But now that rule put everyone in jeopardy.

Deep hesitated with the channel selector. He wasn't yet ready to alert the security on SC2 because they were too far from their location and had their hands full with the trade out on the dock. That left the general security channel, SC3. If there were any other security personnel left who weren't either part of the away team or the feeding team, this is where he'd find them. Those team leaders who were not on shift were supposed to have their radios on and switched to this channel. That was assuming there were any team leaders left. Deep wasn't sure how many they had after the first wave of Rage took the lives or humanity of so many crew members. And those who were left, he feared, would be helping the away team. He'd try anyway, switching the channel from SC1 to SC3. "Attention all security, this is Monitor Room Supervisor Whaudeep Reddy. I have a priority one message for all security personnel: we need additional security support to the Wayfarer Lounge on the double. Repeat, all security personnel, turn to SC1 and report to the Wayfarer Lounge on the double."

Deep switched back to SC1 and repeated the same message he did before.

He expelled a monumental sigh, lowered the microphone from his mouth and fell into his chair. All they could do now was watch, hope and pray there would be no attack. Because if there was, this time, he didn't think they'd fare well.

From the main entrance camera, Deep and Molly could see an armed security guard, followed by the feeder, carefully move inside the lounge. From the inside, long-view camera, in the back of the theater, they could see the two men enter tentatively. The security guard had his rifle at the ready. His charge, the feeder, carried two heavy shoulder bags of raw meat: the only food stuff the parasitics seemed to eat now.

At least it wasn't people, Deep thought.

The security guard halted just forward from the main

entrance camera. He raised his rifle to his cheek and gazed through his sights.

After the last two attacks, the guard assigned to feeder detail was given a rifle and instructed to use lethal force if he felt either his or the feeder-volunteer's life was in danger.

Molly didn't like this at all, but Deep was glad for it, especially right now.

They literally held their breaths and scrutinized both monitor views, hoping nothing would happen.

The guard, with his weapon firmly pressed against his chin, rotated his torso like a gun turret. He seemed ready—almost pleading—for any threat from the parasitics to give him a reason to pull the trigger.

Neither the guard nor the feeder seemed to have heard Deep's calls on the radio, nor the other two guards at the door, who Deep could see just through the crack in the main entrance doors. It seemed like business as usual, just tenser than previous feedings.

Deep's fingers were interlocked in a prayer-like death grip, now white with the tips angry-red. He mentally pleaded with them to finish soon.

The feeder had held up behind the security guard, who signaled with one finger, his okay to move forward. The feeder nodded, accepting the quiet command from the guard that neither Deep or Molly could visually make out, but knew was given.

The feeder took several quick steps forward, walking past the guard, who trained his weapon on the closest pod, only a few meters down the aisle, which led directly to the stage.

Heavy-breath—"Mr."—*another heavy breath*—"Deep?" Dr. Molly panted.

Deep exhaled a long chest-full of air. "Yes, ma'am." His eyes moved from screen to screen to screen.

"Are we missing some of our parasitics?"

He snapped his head to face her. "What?" He heard her. He just didn't understand the question.

She sprang out of her seat, leaned over the long desktop separating them from the monitors and tapped the main screen. "This pod is definitely smaller." She moved her finger an inch over and tapped again, "And so is this one... In fact, all of the pods now look to me..."

"Like they're smaller in size. I... Hey, you're right. But where could they..." His head snapped again in her direction and hers to him.

Together, they yelled out, "The stage!"

Deep pounded his keyboard with a computer command, sending the dark stage camera view from a smaller monitor to the largest one. The video feed showing the volunteer gingerly lowering his food bags to the floor disappeared and was replaced with one that was thick with blackness.

At first glance, it was easy to assume that whatever the largest monitor was displaying was devoid of any light, as if it were turned off. Deep even shot a glance down to the power indicator light, to make sure it was on.

It was still green.

Then they saw the blackness on the screen was actually bristling with some sort of activity, like flashes of static. They could almost feel it more than see it, because when they focused on a perceived ghostly movement, the screen was still black.

Then there was a painfully quick splash of light through the center-break in the curtains. For just a moment, it appeared as if there were a multitude of people standing up on the stage. Like the final act of some giant talentless show, involving all the ship's bad actors; a curtain call to a horrific ensemble, that wouldn't receive an encore.

Then it was gone.

All at once, the curtains parted wide and out poured an uncountable number of parasitics. A geyser of terror sprayed into the lounge.

They'd been assembling there, waiting for this moment; when the main entrance was least secure; when the guard and feeder were preoccupied; and all timed to occur after they had found a way to open up the other door.

They had planned this.

~~~

Otto held tight, not letting go of the men. He had his arms wrapped around all three. They kicked and punched, but he held on. Otto knew this would be his final heroic action, not that he was feeling particularly heroic at this moment: his mind was filled with revenge. He'd take these horrible men with him. He was most impressed that he had no fear and felt deep satisfaction knowing the other three did.

Gas billowed all around them. The three men in their black jumpers coughed and choked as they struggled to get free of Otto's grasp. And in their struggles, they breathed in more of the toxic gas. Otto wedged his eyes and mouth shut, holding his breath, not because he thought he would escape death. He was certain this was how it would end for him. He just wanted to make sure these men felt death's sting before he did.

Finally, as the men quickly succumbed to the toxic effects of phosphine gas, searing through their lungs, eyes and skin, Otto couldn't hold his breath any longer. It was time.

He let go of the three men, fluidly snatching the cigar lighter from his pocket, and held it out ready before he was forced to suck in a deep breath of the caustic fumes. *I shouldn't have waited so long,* he thought.

With his eyes still shut, Otto involuntarily thrashed. He felt vital blood vessels and maybe even some organs inside him
~~~

begin to burst. He had maybe a second or two.

Otto had two final seemingly disjointed thoughts: this was a real-life example of entropy, as in this was the point in their closed system when disorder began; and he wished he could have taken out his cigar and lit it before this.

He clicked on his cigar lighter at the same time he flicked open his eyes to see what it would look like. The effect was instantaneous: his eyes caught the beautiful blue flame, followed immediately by an all-consuming white light and then nothing.

101
The Trade

Minutes before their boat shook from the phosphide gas explosion, TJ had been eyeballing the disgusting men from the island carefully, even taking in another whiff of each. But other than their hideous body odor—which made her wince—and their revolting sidelong glances at her, she couldn't find anything out of the ordinary. Yet she couldn't shake a feeling that there was something wrong with these men.

Before they started their trek down to deck 1, all their eyes were trained on either her chest or crotch, their hideous minds actively molesting her. She understood this and even expected it because of her chosen outfit. Still, it incensed her.

Pushing aside her anger, she focused on the first two men who boarded, but held back in the procession to the food storage: one was a stocky pervert with a bulging belly and other was skinny with a drawn face. They seemed different than the others in a way she couldn't place. She wanted to take just one more whiff of these two, to see if she missed something, but watching them ogle her spiked her anger further. And she was afraid if she did take another whiff, she'd lose control of her anger and just kill these men.

This caused her to question whether she was actually receiving some input from her heightened hearing, sight and smell, all instructing her that something was wrong. *Or is it the Rage disease in me, trying to wrestle allegiance of my senses so it can use them for its evil mission?*

The men followed Flavio and the ship's other guard down the stairs to deck 1 and then finally they turned onto the I-95.

The squat man at the end of the line continued to turn back and glare at TJ. Although all of the men looked like they'd lived on the streets this whole time, Squat was the most disgusting of the lot. His black-as-night eyes glared evil thoughts, while his tongue constantly protruded out of his muck-filled beard. And multiple times he'd made a lip smacking sound that turned her stomach. She was about to grab his flabby mug and pull it right off his stump of a body.

When she made the turn onto the I-95, she decided that however she was able to, she was going to have to kill this man first. That's when she was struck by how empty this place was.

The main artery to the entire ship, where its vital crew members circulated from every part of the ship, through its smaller capillaries, each carrying the life-sustaining resources or services that made this ship function, was dried up, as if the heart of the ship were no longer pumping.

In fact, she knew this was by design. The captain had ordered all crew to be in their places before these men entered their ship.

Up ahead, several crew were already speaking to Flavio, who introduced them to the men.

TJ slid by them all and found Flavio deep in the hallway where most of the refrigerated food was stored. He had stepped away to allow the crew and the men to inventory and transact their business.

"You look out of breath," he said to her, genuinely worried about her.

"I always look out of breath." This was true. She wasn't out of breath; it was just that she breathed much more rapidly than before. "I cannot place it. Either it's their smell—which is definitely off—or it's their mannerisms, or it's something else. But there is something wrong about these men. Especially those two."

She pointed at the squat and skinny man.

~~~

Vlad Smirnoff—no relation to his favorite vodka that shared his name—knew he probably should have worn his clean jumper today, after seeing his fellow crew in their best. His mama drummed into him at an early age to always wear clean clothes because, "you never know if this was your last day." He had no idea how right she was.

Instead he listened to his best friend, who ranted, "To hell with them. I'm not dressing up for extra duties." Their extra duties were to assist with the refueling of their ship. They weren't part of the normal refueling crew, but everyone was pulling multiple duties and multiple shifts lately. He often didn't listen to Sven, who always mouthed off about corporate, but for some reason he did today. Part of him wanted to be rebellious, like Sven. The rest of him just wanted to be home.

Vlad stared out the porthole in their exit, watching the refueling barge tie up alongside them.

"Out of the way," commanded one of the normal refueling crew, who rudely pushed Vlad aside. He guessed it was to confirm it was okay to open up the door.

He glanced back at his friend, who was slouching off to the side, acting disinterested. Sven was always trying to act
~~~

tough, whereas Vlad just wanted to get this job done. Especially now. The stakes were high, from what the captain told them: they needed this fuel; it was as vital to the ship as their own blood was to them. And if they didn't get this fuel, their situation was pretty hopeless. The captain didn't say that last part, but Vlad knew this to be true.

Without the fuel, they'd never get to the next port, much less make it back to their families. None of the crew had heard from their families in days. They had no way of knowing if their families were even still alive with everything going on in the world and on this ship, from crazy people, and crazy animals, to cities burning and chaos everywhere.

It didn't help to know, as the captain liked to tell them, that their situation on board was much better than the rest of the world. He suspected that might be true, but that meant his family had it worse.

Their ship was currently consumed by organized chaos, with short-staffing and passengers becoming crew to plug up the holes. It kept their minds off their families but it also added to their exhausting duties. Sven and he had to train two men and a woman earlier this morning while they did their normal engineering jobs. The woman was pretty bright and seemed eager to learn, even though she didn't speak Czech or much English (the only two languages they knew). Although she did teach Sven and him a few words in German. The other two men were a different story.

They ignored most of what Sven and he had instructed, nodding their heads occasionally, but often making comments under their breaths in German, which neither of them understood. He suspected they were unkind comments, because at one time the German woman said something scornful to the two, then smiled at Vlad and said, "Please make more teach."

Sven hit Vlad in the shoulder, shaking him from his daydream, just noticing that the door was sliding open.

"Ready?" Vlad asked his friend, who nodded back with zero excitement.

Their job was to help the others with the fuel hoses, which sometimes got quite heavy. They'd be setting up two hoses, one for each kind of fuel, going to two different fuel tank fittings on the side of their ship. Normally it was two *Intrepid* crew, assisting two or three crew of the fuel barge. But there were at least two or three times more crew members here today, all waiting to hop onto the barge and get the refueling done quicker than normal, as if they were racing against the prospect of the men on the fueling barge changing their mind.

He started moving with the others toward the gangway off the hatch, which was a narrow balcony-like walkway running forward from its opening. From there, they'd have to hop down to the deck of the barge and not fall off. Vlad was deathly afraid of heights, but even more afraid of falling in between the two ships and drowning or getting crushed to death. He felt his anxiety soar as he stepped outside and saw the drop.

Then, probably because he didn't have any time to think about it and the others pressing against him, he hopped the four or five feet to the barge as if it were a normal day's activity. He landed in a crouch so as to not damage his knees or tendons. Standing up straight, he looked back to see Sven was already behind him.

"Piece of cake," Sven muttered, although he often said this when it wasn't.

Vlad looked back along the span of the barge's deck and noticed many more workers than he expected. He counted maybe a dozen, even though there were usually only a couple of men needed to do this job. Even with double or tripling the workers to accomplish the task faster, it didn't account for the total number of personnel here. A couple of them wandered over to meet with the *Intrepid's* crew, who were already grabbing hoses. The remainder of the barge crew, if that's what they were, jumped up *Intrepid's* gangway and entered their ship. It made no sense.

"Come on. We're up," Sven said, slapping his shoulder.

Vlad caught the scornful gaze of his new superior, at least for this shift, who was waiting on them to help him lug the heavy hose. And so he trotted over to help hall it over to the connector fitting on their ship. Another oddity was that their supervisor was manning the hose, not the barge worker, which was usual protocol. Vlad turned back a couple of times to see if Sven noticed any of these oddities too.

"Don't you see it?" Vlad asked him and was surprised to see a man, who he guessed was one of the barge workers, in between Sven and him. The man wore sunglasses so he couldn't tell if he was staring at him or at where they were connecting the hose.

Then they stopped, with the *Intrepid* crew member who was their direct supervisor busily connecting the hose fitting and then giving the okay to the barge's control operator, topside and behind them. Their supervisor waved as if the operator wasn't paying any attention to him because his waves became more furious.

Vlad glanced back to find the operator staring at his shoes. Until there was a loud whistle—maybe from his supervisor—and the operator looked up, glaring hatred. Then the operator pounded something on a panel and Vlad immediately felt the flow of hot fuel running through the hose, through his work gloves.

Vlad checked again with his supervisor to see if it was all right to drop his portion of the hose, but then he did this anyway because the damned thing was getting hot.

Oddly, he didn't see his supervisor at all, like he had disappeared. Vlad was about to search for him when he heard a commotion behind him, followed by a gurgling sound. Swinging around to see, he found Sven clutching his neck, his face twisted in wide-eyed confusion. Blood was trickling out from his fingertips, like he had cut his neck or something.

In shock, Vlad was about to yell for help, when his attention was pulled to his right, were he was met by the toothy grin of the barge worker who had been between them. He held a large cleaving knife up, its silver blade coated in red. *That's Sven's blood on it!*

The yell, which was stuck behind his swollen tongue, erupted the moment the worker plunged the cleaving knife into Vlad's chest. Just as abruptly, it was yanked out and Vlad was kicked to the deck. He laid there in shock, his brain not fully registering or unwilling to register that he had just been stabbed and would die there.

He felt more like a witness than a participant to everything unfolding on the deck: a set of gloved hands pulled against his chest in a futile attempt to stem the blood flow; some *Intrepid* crew who had earlier come out to help were also lying on the deck motionless; the barge worker who had stabbed him was climbing up the gangway into their ship.

The fuel barge was all a ruse. They used it to penetrate their ship. They were all going to die.

Vlad maneuvered himself to see his friend.

Sven wore a death mask: his eyes blank and fixed upward in a perpetual gaze at the darkening heavens, his hands loosely covering his throat which still trickled blood.

Vlad knew that would look the same in a matter of moments.

He turned onto his back and glared at the sky.

The thick clouds churned above and rapidly darkened around the fringes. With each blink they choked off more and more of the sun's light.

Screams in the distance.

The blackness rained down upon him, enveloping him.

Just before his last blink, he heard an explosion.

~~~

The skinny man walked right into the refrigerated liquor storage area, as if it was his own personal stash. "Now we're talking," bellowed the squat man, whose hairy belly pushed farther out from the bottom edge of his sweat-soaked T-shirt. He strutted into the room after his buddy, like a passenger who had paid for one of the top suites and expected top-flight service, when TJ guessed he wasn't much more than a second or third-tier henchman.

Intrepid's procurement manager and his assistant in training followed from behind. She heard the manager argue about whether liquor was part of the trade or not and then the room went quiet.

"Where's the rest of their group?" asked TJ, swinging her head around.

"There were eight men total," responded Flavio, stepping up to one of the three open refrigerated rooms. He ducked in, stepped out, and shook his head.

TJ jogged over to the third room, looked in and then returned to Flavio.

A glass bottle shattered in the liquor storage room.

They dashed inside where they found Skinny, in the back, standing over their procurement manager, a clear knife being pulled from their man's chest. TJ knew he must have been hiding this and because it was plastic and didn't set off the metal detectors. Skinny made a motion like he was about to drive it back in. Squat, on the other side of the room, had the assistant by a shirt collar and was reaching for his own plastic knife.

Flavio reacted without hesitation, shooting Skinny once in the head, pivoting on a heel to take out Squat. But TJ already had him down on the floor, the knife kicked away and the assistant duck-walking the other way.
~~~

Squat tried to wriggle free, but she pushed him down harder. Then he laughed, bellicose-like. "It doesn't matter. You and your people will be dead soon enough." She drove her knee hard into the man's arm, snapping it with a loud crack. But rather than crying out, the man laughed harder. "Hah-hah-hah-ha."

"You think you can hurt me? No, I'm going to hurt you," he boosted.

TJ glowered at his black-as-oil eyes and sneering face. She was about to say something, when she caught only a flash of his other hand, swinging around, followed by the ear-rattling blast of Flavio's rifle.

The bullet shattered the man's left shoulder and he dropped the knife that he had somehow gotten hold of while TJ was torturing him. She felt the squat man finally give up the fight. His breathing escalated to the point he sounded like he was hyperventilating.

Squat closed his eyes and smiled a wide smile. "Oh yeah, you can kill me. But it won't matter." His voice was even sounding. Controlled.

He paused a long while, and both TJ and Flavio waited, not sure if he were about to pass out or what. TJ shook the man, like a ragdoll.

Squat flipped open his eyes. For just a moment, TJ thought they flashed red, before returning to their oily blackness. "While you're feeling me out, my men are taking over your bridge and will blow your engine so you can't go anywhere. And when we're done, I'm going to eat you two for breakfast, with a little hot sauce on—"

Flavio drove the butt of his rifle into Squat's face, his nose making a satisfying cracking sound. He went limp.

"I had enough of you," Flavio added.

TJ handed him her radio. "Have Ted check on the engine room and the refueling team. I'll head to the bridge. You go to the engine room. We need to stop these attacks."

"Wait!" Flavio warned. While holding the radio, he slung off his pack, reached in and grabbed his two Moraknivs, handing one to TJ. "Take this just in case." She accepted, sliding it behind her back, into the fold of her compression shorts.

He attached his to his belt, while re-securing his pack and rifle. Bounding up, he had the radio to his mouth, intending to start transmitting, when the whole ship buffeted and shook. A tremendous boom echoed deep within the ship's skeleton and under their feet.

That's when they both ran.

102

The Explosion

The explosion not only incinerated the four men involved in the giant fireball, it also blew apart all of the aft ducting, thus severing A/C in the ship from the midway stairwell to the very stern. The fireball melted much of the plastic jacketing which protected the wiring and cabling that ran the access-way. As plastic and other flammables continued to burn, the concentrated heat fairly rapidly melted off the remaining protective coating from the wiring connecting every system in the stern. Then various systems started shorting out and shutting down. The heavy-duty power cabling was the last to fail.

With little more to burn, the fire was out, but the phosphine gas continued to billow out from the aluminum phosphide dust still being exposed to the air coming from the incoming A/C ducting. The lethal combination of toxic phosphine gas and air conditioning would have been deadly to everyone in the stern if all the vents had not been closed.

This was by design, as Regal European programmed this

feature into its ships to lessen the severity of a fire. The thinking was that if all venting were closed, the hot air and smoke from the fire couldn't travel through the air ducting, and there'd be less circulation of air, lessening a fire's spread.

As it turned out, most of the vents were already closed, so as to lower the load placed on the ship's A/C compressors until they had received fuel. Once the power was cut to the aft decks of the ship, the remaining vents closed, too. This combo may have saved a hundred lives from the effects of the phosphine gas, but it also saved the parasitics in the Wayfarer Lounge.

There was still some leakage of the phosphine gas, as vents were not completely air-tight, but the small amounts that found their way into cabins, although disturbing, would not be deadly.

With all the vents closed, the phosphine gas had nowhere else to go. So it continued to billow through the small, seven foot by seven foot access way. It moved forward, following the same course Otto and the other dead men had come from, traveling rapidly along and then down the tubular structure.

Originally used to kill rat populations, the phosphine gas then rolled down five decks until it held at deck 1. It grew thicker and thicker, patiently waiting for any unsuspecting rat or person to wander in.

The deadly gas only had to wait two minutes to kill its first of many victims.

~~~

"Are we under attack?" bellowed Ted.

Alarms rang out and lights flashed all over the bridge.

"Captain," hollered Niki, ignoring Ted's question. "I'm
~~~

losing power readings for all aft decks."

Ted instantly knew what this meant. No power equaled no air conditioning. No air conditioning meant the couple hundred parasitics they were holding were going to wake up.

"What about the AC?" Ted asked, thinking instantly that it was a stupid question.

"Compressor is still operating at twenty-five percent. But I can't tell if any of it is getting to our guests. If power goes out, vents close... I now have zero—repeat—zero readings coming from anywhere from the midway elevator going aft. So I have no idea if they're getting anything."

Wasano had popped in from the port-side swing deck, where he had taken over monitoring the dock from Jessica, so she could return to her station as OOD.

"Ted, get on the horn with all our security personnel on SC3," Wasano stated. "Let's get people to all decks mid-way and find out what happened." He said this and immediately called out on presumably another channel.

Ted had turned down the volume on SC2 to talk to the bridge crew, but when he turned it back up, he heard the frantic call from Flavio. He spun it to its max setting so that everyone could hear.

"—under attack. At least six men are headed to the bridge and there are others headed to the engine room. We are under attack. I am headed to engine room."

The captain flew to Ted's right and picked up one of the phone lines to another section of the ship. He was immediately speaking to someone.

"Flavio, it's Ted. Where's my wife?"

"Please contact refuel team," Flavio continued. "Attack came from there and food area. Mrs. Villiams is coming to bridge. I am—hold on." Flavio yelled something, followed by a single gunshot. *Bang*. "Sorry, must go," he said and disconnected.

Ted didn't wait; he flipped to SC3, eyeing Wasano hurry

across the bridge to the starboard side. "Attention all security personnel. We are under attack from a group from this island..." Ted held open the transmission, but put his hand over the microphone.

"Wasano, did you catch all that from Flavio?"

Wasano was still moving toward the starboard swing deck. Opening the door, he barely paused, said, "Yes" and shut the door behind him.

Jessica marched to the left of the captain and even though Ted was not too familiar with the bridge, he knew where she was going. "Stop!" he hollered at her before she punched the ship-wide alarm button.

"I just heard on SC1 that the parasitics are trying to break free. Let's not incite them any further with that loud noise. Remember what happened with the birds."

Ted remembered he had the mic still open, wondering what he should tell security on SC3.

Wasano popped back in from the starboard swing deck, holding binoculars. He looked like he was in shock. "They're all dead," he huffed.

The entire bridge held its collective breath for a moment, considering what was just said, and then the frenzy continued.

"Ted," Wasano continued in his normally controlled voice. "Call E1 and tell all engine room personnel to exit out the aft crew stairwell to deck 3."

Ted followed his directions, letting go of the mic, shutting off his transmission and flipping the channel selector to E1, Engineering.

Ted transmitted, "Attention all engine room crew. The engine room is about to come under attack by outside forces, who mean to hurt you. Please evacuate the engine room immediately. Repeat, evacuate the engine room immediately through the aft crew stairwell and continue to deck 3. Go up the crew stairwell to deck 3 and await other instructions."

While the captain was speaking to someone named Ms. Johansson, Ted wanted to see and hear what was going on with the parasitics, as well as talk to his wife. But he couldn't do everything at once. He switched the radio to SC1 while he attempted bring up the cameras on his monitor. He typed in one command after another, but he couldn't find any cameras working in the stern.

103

Violet

When Violet Johansson first heard the dull thrumming boom, followed by the shudder underneath her feet, she dropped down to her knees. The memory of a terrorist bombing in Istanbul, during one of their ports of call, was still fresh in her head. Pretty quickly, she realized that this was different and she went into action.

"Mr. Ivonov," she bellowed, "please check the inside door again and make sure it's secure. Ms. Kashatri and Mr. Akashi, please secure the outside door."

"What was that, Violet?" begged Ms. Kashatri.

"I'm about to find out." Violet picked up the direct line to the bridge and pressed the plastic button. It immediately flashed red and her receiver made a dialing tone.

The plastic button turned solid green.

It clicked a connection, meaning someone picked it up.

"Port-side gangway, Ms. Johansson calling," she announced.

"This is Captain Haggard, Ms. Johansson. Are you all

right?"

"Yes, Captain." She was a little surprised the captain himself answered and not the OOD or someone else. "We were just trying to find out what just happened, sir."

"We don't yet know, Ms. Johansson, but I would ask that you secure your area. And do not let anyone onboard without a second officer or higher's approval. Is that understood?"

She watched the gangway door shut, her team doing exactly as requested. "We are already secure here... Ah, sir. We also heard what sounded like gunshots. What can we do here, sir?"

"Hold on," the captain asked. Then she could hear voices from the bridge and the words "They're all dead" from her new security director.

Violet could feel goose bumps blossoming down her neck, in spite of her perspiring a lot. Then she started to shake. She was absolutely terrified by the time the captain got back on the phone.

She heard him take a deep breath before speaking. "Ms. Johansson, we believe the islanders are trying to damage our ship. Hold position. However, I do need one of your team to check on the starboard exit. The crew doesn't answer our calls. There may be combatants there, so be vigilant and be safe. If possible, secure that exit. If not safe, just report back with status."

"Aye, sir." She sucked in several breaths of her own before placing the receiver back in its cradle.

Then she turned to face her team.

They eyed Violet, their saucer-eyed faces were deadly serious. Expectant.

"I think we're under attack," she said. "The captain wants us to protect this exit, but he also wants one of us to check the starboard exit, which isn't reporting." She turned to the tall Russian. "Mr. Ivanov, I'm asking you to go, but the captain warns that there might be combatants there. Don't take any risks, but..." she paused. "If you're able to secure the outside exit, do so. Then return and report."

"Aye, Ms. Johansson."

Igor Ivanov didn't hesitate. He cracked open the interior door, waiting for Violet to come from behind and get ready to secure it behind him. When she was there, he checked the area just outside the interior doorway,

It was clear and so he slipped through, Violet immediately closing it and locking it.

~~~

Igor Ivanov felt the door close behind him. When he heard its lock click from the other side, he knew right away that this was a bad idea.

There was almost no place to hide. As the Americans would say, he was a sitting duck.

A good span of the port-side hallway, leading forward and aft, was open in both directions. The stairway landing was wide open and directly in front of him. And the opening into the starboard hallway and then starboard exit was right there as well, open all the way to the outside. And that's when he saw the dead crew member.

Igor immediately took cover behind the hallway wall's edge, in the event a bad guy came out of that gangway door or the stairwell or elevators. He also knew that he'd achieved one part of his mission of finding out the status of the starboard exit and their crew: it was unsecured and their crew was dead. But he was not to take any risks and moving beyond this point was risky. He knew he should have knocked on the door and retreated back to safety.

But then what?
~~~

Was he just to let these murderers do what they wanted? And how long could the four of them remain locked up in their area? And didn't this also mean that the rest of the ship needed help? He could not just do nothing. Then he looked down.

On his hip was his only weapon, a stun gun. Yet they had real guns—they had heard the shots. That's a fight he'd lose every day.

But there was no one in sight and his mission wasn't done.

Igor convinced himself to take one quick look at the starboard exit, close it and then return for a full report to the captain. Maybe then the captain would advise them how they could fight back.

Igor again checked the hallway aft and forward, before proceeding into the stairwell and elevator landing. He walked quickly, while still keeping an ear to anyone coming up from deck 1 or coming down from deck 3, just above. Other than a distant murmur below, he heard nothing else.

At the starboard hallway, it too was clear, so he continued into the starboard gangway area, holding up at the threshold.

Like his team did on their starboard side, it was here where he could secure this area with a large wall and doorway that slid into place. But that would have still exposed them to further penetration from the outside. He needed to secure that exit. In between him and the exit lay the bodies of several of his crew. Then one of the bodies moved.

Above a fallen crew member, another man was bent over... *eating him*.

It still didn't feel real seeing a person casually kneeling over and chowing down on another person, even though he'd witnessed this a couple of times during the last parasitic attack. But here was this man munching on a dead crew like he was enjoying a late morning buffet. In an unseen hand the cannibal must have had eating utensils too, because the blur of a clear-plastic knife appeared, swinging at the dead man's arm, cleaving off another piece of muscle.

Igor gasped. This he'd not seen before. He'd only seen them use their fingers and mouth to tear at tissue.

Just then the cannibal stopped, swung his head up and glared right at Igor, his red eyes ablaze.

Igor sucked in a huge breath. He must have made a noise watching this and now he was caught, backing up.

Equally surprising and new was the cannibal's speed, because no sooner did Igor turn a shoulder with the intent to run when the knife-wielding cannibal leapt off the dead crew-member and was there, vice-gripping him with one hand and plunging his clear plastic knife into Igor's gut with the other.

Igor acted on pure adrenaline; his stun gun out, he jammed it into the side of the cannibal's neck and clicked the button, releasing 60,000 volts into its carotid. The cannibal let go of Igor and the knife and pulled away slightly, causing Igor to fall onto his back, with the knife still protruding out of his gut.

The cannibal convulsed twice more, while standing, like he was doing some macabre dance routine. But then he rapidly regained control of his muscles and nerve endings, even though he'd received a four-second jolt, which should have been enough to knock down a moose. The cannibal came at Igor again.

This time, the cannibal-monster, with red eyes practically pulsing at him, led with his blood-coated mouth open wide, blaring an inconceivably loud bray. Igor attempted to scoot away, but the cannibal was too fast. Igor turned to his side to make himself a smaller target and to block with an arm, as the cannibal came down on him.

Once again, Igor's reflexes were his friend at that moment. And perhaps so was the cannibal's one-track mind, set on sinking his teeth into the Russian. Somehow, Igor was able to move his stun gun around and jam it into the cannibal's mouth as it tried to clamp down on his other blocking arm. He clicked home the trigger, this time holding it down as long as there was a charge left, and watched the cannibal dance some more.

It may have not been the best idea, but when terror and adrenaline are cascading throughout your body, your thinking is far from logical. With his blocking hand, he yanked the now red-colored knife from his belly and shoved it, with all of his remaining strength, into the dancing cannibal's neck. Then he let go.

The cannibal danced for almost twenty more seconds, violently writhing on the floor, before he was finally silent. At the same time, Igor felt very, very tired, even though he had a raging fire in his gut. He laid his head on the floor, staring at the overhead lights. Sleep sounded to him at that moment. But then he remembered. He lifted his head and glanced at the wide-open exit, that he was supposed to secure.

"Fine, first door. Then sleep."

~~~

"How long has it been?" Violet asked no one in particular.

"About ten minutes. I think," said Ms. Kashatri.

"He should have been back by now." She knew she couldn't leave him out there, no matter what happened to him. She'd read about American military never leaving a man behind. She always thought that was a noble endeavor and vowed herself then to do the same for her people. "Mr. Akashi, I'm going out to check. Please secure this door behind me."

Violet stuck her head out the door; looking ahead, she saw him immediately. She pulled herself back in. "I'll need your help," Violet whispered now. "Ms. Kashatri, man the door."

She popped her head back out, checking in all
~~~

directions. She whispered again, “Come with me” and darted out the door. Mr. Akashi followed.

Violet quickly saw that there were several dead bodies and their own Igor, who also looked dead, in a pool of blood. A large bloom of red covering most of his white shirt told her it was his. The door to the outside starboard exit was shut. She also heard someone coming up the stairs.

“We need to drag him back,” she said, grabbing one of Ivanov’s arms, Akashi grabbing the other.

In the process of lugging Igor Ivanov’s giant frame across the floor, Violet could see he was still breathing, though barely.

They made it back inside their area and secured it, leaving a long trail of blood.

She had no idea if he’d survive, but she didn’t leave anyone behind. Not today.

104

Coordinated Attack

The explosion sent Jay Falcone down onto his knees. Jay cocked his head all the way back and studied the ceiling, certain this was the explosion's origin and it would collapse on top of him.

Jay continued to gaze upward into the murk, just noticing there were only two small lights on in the whole theater. He couldn't remember if this was new, or if it had been the same the last time he'd done this.

The explosive tremors quickly subsided, but then they grew again. Now, the growing rumble and its accompanying noise—like the shuffling feet of hundreds—were coming not from above, but from the stage area. Jay turned his gaze to the growing tremors, wondering if this was the prelude to another explosion.

He had no idea how much worse it would be.

Only a few days ago, after a marathon day of poker, capped off by winning the ship's poker tournament, Jay celebrated with the Bucket of Beer special and an unfunny comedy show, featured on this very stage. This current performance was far more mesmerizing. And in response, Jay's mouth dropped open. His brain just couldn't accept what his eyes were hollering at it: a multitude of naked men and women were dashing across the stage.

Frozen in his place, Jay didn't budge even as the first of these naked performers, racing in his direction, touched down on the carpeted aisle. When they began to yell their torturous screams and they were close enough for him to see their red eyes, that's when Jay sprang.

Boom.

In his panicked dash, Jay caught just a glimpse of the guard's rifle crashing in front of him. Then beside him.

Boom-boom-boom!

Even in his youth, Jay was not much of a runner. Yet he'd already passed the guard, allowing his gaze to hang on the man one last second before he bounded out the door. Jay didn't dare look back any longer.

The guard—Jay had already forgotten his name—remained on a bent knee, discharging his rifle, now on automatic fire. In Jay's final glimpse, before turning to face the main entrance, he caught a white streak hit the guard so hard, it knocked him backwards.

Jay had just enough time to take in the faces of the two wide-eyed guards before they disappeared behind the closing doors—his only way out of this.

The realization hit him at the same time Jay felt something barrel into his back with the power of a freight train, sending him careening hard into three overturned seats. Coming to rest on his back, neck ratcheted up, he watched multiple blurs of white, brown and black whisk past his field of vision. His sensory world was awash with the banshee-like cries of these human-animals, their mind-numbing pounding on the door and then the face of one of these bare-skinned monsters.

At one time it was a woman, and a pretty one too, with

its long red hair and attractive figure. Now this woman was the stuff of nightmares: it brayed at him, its mouth opened wide, its red eyes blazing absolute hatred. Without warning, it stuck its thumb into his left eye socket. Jay attempted to react, lifting a hand to protect his other eye, but she struck again with the force and speed of lightning.

His mind—since he had no eyes to see—filled with flashes of bright light and equally searing pain. All he could do now was scream his blind terror.

The she-beast did its best to silence him, but his escalating screams of panic and pain lasted the longest minute of his shortened life. He sensed its teeth, followed by many others, violently rip into his skin, all of them pulling and tearing at the flesh of his arms, legs and chest, until at long last, Jay felt nothing.

Then, like Jay, the lounge was plunged into darkness.

~~~

Dr. Molly watched with dread as both an observant scientist and a feeling person.

Her eyes welled with tears, which she couldn't hold back when she saw the pain on the volunteer's face, as one of their parasitics viciously attacked him and literally ripped him apart.

The scientist in her marveled at the speed and agility of its assault, as well as its vindictive voracity to rob the man of his eyesight before it ate up his life. It was as if the parasitic was punishing him for gazing at its nakedness, even though Molly would have thought that parasitics no longer cared about these things: parasitics weren't burdened by such human frailties as pride, fear or empathy.

Molly had never seen this kind of action in the animal or parasitic kingdoms before: animals and parasites killed for food
~~~

or to fulfill what they were genetically programmed to do. The only beings who killed for revenge or sport were humans. Molly was observing the worst of combinations: human anger and cunning, mixed with animalistic reflexes and strength.

The parasitic woman then appeared to call out to the others, as many joined her to pounce on the man, ripping at him and feeding on him, while he was obviously very much alive and screaming in pain.

She shuddered at this whole episode. These creatures were advancing in so many more ways that she could have guessed.

So riveted was she by what was unfolding, Molly was barely aware of Mr. Deep continuing to holler on his radio. He had finally connected with security and mechanical. But it would do no good. She knew after observing this attack that once this new species was free on their ship, they were all doomed. There was no place to hide, as these parasitics would eventually break down every door to get to their prey. They were as smart as humans, now coordinated, bloodthirsty and lacking all the human hang-ups. In short, they were the perfect killing machines and they would prevail over their human forebears. And there was nothing she or anyone else could do about it.

Molly felt gutted. Every muscle and bone in her old body cried out in physical and emotional agony. She just wanted to give up…

But they weren't.

She looked up from the big monitor, her watery eyes blurring the scene on one of the other monitors. Blinking away her sense of doom, she could see something was going on outside the lounge.

She scooched forward and sat up in her seat to see better.

At least my fellow humans are not giving up yet, she thought.

She always had hope in and a strong belief for what would come after this life ended. She'd just been losing hope in humans in this life. Ted said he had really believed in the human spirit. She hadn't been so sure anymore. And yet, here was her proof.

Security and volunteers from around the ship were arriving at the main entrance and the side door, to try and shore them up. They were all working together to try and save their ship and seemed to be holding back the horde.

The side door was their biggest problem. There was too much damage, caused by just two parasitics. Now there was an uncountable horde, pushing, pounding and beating the door down.

And yet Molly could see her fellow humans on the other side, trying to stab the parasitics with poles and she suspected, because they didn't have cameras back there, they were employing the same techniques that they were at the main entrance: heavy items and wedges. Was it even possible?

Then the four monitors on which they'd focused all their attention, went black.

Molly steepled her hands together and said a silent prayer, tuning out the horrific screaming coming from Deep's radio.

105

Last Stand

When Paulo Oliveira saw the stampeding horde of crazies overtake their people, he was sure they waited too long to shut the lounge doors. But somehow, they did, just as their non-human bodies struck the doors, one after another, delivering an inconceivable amount of pounding and shaking.

He and Jason Anderson, a new addition to his security team, took multiple steps back and watched the doors shudder and shake. They could feel the tremors below their feet and all around them. And it continued to build. When Paulo heard a cracking sound, he knew either he had to turn tail and run or do something before they broke through.

Then the lights went off and the entire area was plunged into darkness. The pounding continued unabated, though. When the emergency lights popped on, Paulo knew what he had to do.

"Help me," he barked at Anderson.

They grabbed a heavy coffee table, just outside the lounge entrance, and drove it hard into the door.

Others joined them, some from security and some from mechanical, all grabbing heavy pieces of furniture and moving them to the door.

"Wait! We need to wedge them," announced a slight man from mechanical, his grease-covered hands demonstrating. The man looked around the area for something, until he was jolted by a vision from another sitting area.

"Here. Help me now." The man grabbed Paulo's elbow and pulled him with him to another elaborate wood table with curved feet.

"You break. We use under door as wedge."

Paulo understood right away, nodding. He turned the heavy table on its side; the glass top slid off and broke into a hundred pieces, some long and lethal-looking. He searched for the weak point in the legs and drove his foot into that point, separating two legs at their joints. Pulling one away, he handed it to the small man from mechanical, who dashed to the door, then around the group of helpers pushing furniture toward the doors, stopping before the table Paulo and Anderson had just used to buttress one of the doors. Already two more were on top.

The small man stuck the curved wedge under the door and kicked it a couple of times. "One more," he yelled.

Paulo bashed the table into three curved wedge pieces and ran over to the small man, handing him one of the pieces. Paulo took another and used it like a hammer to pound the already set wedge in harder, while the little man set up the one he'd given him under the other door. Paulo pounded at that one as well.

"Thank you," Paulo announced with a smile.

The man didn't smile back; he stood up and said, "Come with me, need others." He grabbed the other pieces from Paulo. "Side door bad. Must fix before they break out." The small man grabbed a tool bag he must have left on the floor and ran to the crew access door at the far side of the hall.

"Stack up more furniture against here," Paulo yelled to the now twenty men and woman who had showed up to help, while pointing at the bottom of the doors. "Then, I need a dozen of you to wait here."

Paulo dashed back to where he had broken the tabletop and carefully picked up pieces of the thick broken glass. He pulled off his button-down work shirt and wrapped the pieces inside. In a quick dash back, he passed his dozen-plus volunteers and yelled, "Follow me."

Paulo didn't look back as he ran to the side entrance to the back of the lounge, used only by crew and performers. A thousand memories raced through his head as he opened it and held it for the others to follow.

A couple of years back, Paulo had an affair with one of the young performers. He had used this entrance to visit with her before and after her performances. And inside was one of the few places he knew where they could be intimate together and no one would know.

At the back of a dark hallway, barely illuminated by the single emergency bulb in the corner, was a storage closet. When he and Lucy had their affair, this room had just been cleaned out. Last he had seen, housekeeping used it for storage. He was counting on this.

Flicking on his Maglite, illuminating the door handle, he held the bundle of wrapped broken glass under an armpit and fished for his keys. Once open, he flashed his light inside. "Eureka," he said. He laid the broken-glass bundle down and entered the storage room.

Paulo came back out with several push brooms. "You," he said to one of his volunteers, "twist off the brooms from the handles."

Another trip back into the room and he came out with a pile of rags. "Okay, some space please." He plopped his pile next to his shirt bundle, which he opened. Snatching an extra-long piece of glass and a rag, he stood up straight.

"Okay, watch," he said while slicing the rag into three long pieces. He wrapped one of the pieces around the base of the long splinter of glass he was using as a knife. "You," he said to a woman nearest him, "make more long pieces like this out of these rags." He flipped the glass-knife around and handed it to her.

"Okay, I need a broom handle." Someone handed him one.

"Now," he reached into his shirt and grabbed another fragment. "We're going to make spears. Tie the glass like this to the ends of the broom handles. Do it now and then meet me in back."

Paulo then left them, holding his newly-made spear, hoping they'd follow his lead. He turned a corner and felt his hope die.

The small man was stabbing a crazy trying to get through the top of the broken door. It wedged its way through the opening at the top of the door and grabbed the small man and tossed him down, either knocking him out cold or killing him.

The crazy turned just as Paulo drove his spear into its eye socket. He pulled back and then kicked the naked crazy in the head with his boot, just for good measure.

He turned to face the door, as it was literally being pulled off its hinges.

Paulo jabbed with his spear, getting several.

Then others joined in, also jabbing and slashing with their own homemade spears.

The ship should have killed them all, rather than believing they could hold them. There was no holding back these beasts. He knew they'd eventually get through.

Even though Paulo's brain rapid-fired these thoughts, he felt no anger at his ship's officers for their ignorance. In fact, for some strange reason, he was filled with pride right then.

Rather than abandoning him, as he probably would have done after seeing their situation was so hopeless, one after another of his volunteers showed up with their homemade spears. They stood toe-to-toe with the beasts, stabbing and slashing at them, probably killing quite a few.

Never did his volunteers falter. They held until the very end, when the door came off and they were overwhelmed.

106

Jaga

Jaga was rattled awake. He gazed into the darkness, disoriented and just trying to get his bearings. His hand touched emptiness, where there should have been a table and his flashlight. This tool allowed him to quietly navigate his way in between his roommates' bunk beds to the bathroom door at the end of their cabin. Now, his table and flashlight were gone.

An ember of fright started to glow red in his gut.

Next, he turned to his left and felt around for Taufan, who often slept by his head, but his ferret wasn't there either. And the cabin wall that was always there was gone: the bed went on forever, as did emptiness above.

The smoldering coal of fright burst into a hot flame of alarm.

He swung his legs out of his sheets and onto the floor, his feet instantly sensing a supple carpet as opposed to the rubberized flooring that he was used to. The same rubberized flooring that his roommates constantly made a fuss about Asap not cleaning when it was his turn was gone. "Guys, are you there?"

Silence.

The fire of alarm in his belly now exploded into a wildfire of panic.

He heaved out breaths and took in short puffs of putrid air. Looking for some shred of recognition, he noticed a small shaft of light, cleaving its way from behind a curtain, where there shouldn't have been one. A flood of images dashed through his head: he was in a new cabin; he'd lain down on his new bed, relishing its softness; he must have fallen asleep, even though he didn't intend to; he didn't have any roommates anymore and he was split up from his best friend Yacobus; Catur was dead and Asap was a monster now.

He dashed over to the curtain, desperately wanting the light of reality to confirm that this wasn't just some nightmare, but then hesitated.

Do I really want reality or to fall back into a dream?

The curtains flew open, and a foggy beam lit his new cabin. The air inside had substance... *Smoke!*

A quick sniff only made him cough. It smelled a little like smoke, but also something else... *Dead fish?*

He looked for a vent, not remembering where it was in this room, his eyes now sore, like they were burning. He found it above the bathroom and scrutinized it for a second. Little wisps of white smoke leapt in from the register.

It was enough. Something was happening, and he only knew he had to get out.

Taufan!

"Taufan? Taufan, where are you buddy?" he yelled out, now feeling overwhelmed by a raging bonfire of panic. He had to find Taufan and get out now!

"Taufan, please, where are you?"

Jaga slipped on his sandals, glad that they were by the bed, right where he left them.

He padded over to the closet. There was no time to

change out of his pajamas, but he'd put on his house coat if it was cool and because of its special pocket.

"Taufan," he pleaded, almost in tears. "Please, say something."

He froze.

Was it the squeak of his sandals on the carpet or did he hear his little buddy?

Squeak-squeak-squeak.

Jaga heard the muffled cries coming from the closet. He flicked on the light switch, but nothing happened—*the power was off.* He tossed open the bi-fold glass door way too hard, and Taufan shot out, hopping once on the carpet, and bounded into his arms. He barked once and then gave out a slow whine; his body shivered. Jaga kissed his head, but took no time to relish this moment.

"We need to get out of here, Taufan," Jaga announced, as he held him with one hand and rifled through his canvas duffel bag in the back of the closet. He had thrown it there when he arrived.

Of course his robe was near the bottom.

Upon grabbing it, Jaga slipped one arm inside and then moved Taufan to his other hand and slipped in the other arm.

"Okay, my friend. Time for a ride," he coaxed, holding Taufan over the giant-sized pocket. He had sewed this into this house coat so he could carry his ferret around with him, without anyone knowing he was there.

Taufan hopped in, still whining.

The air in his cabin was getting very stale and hard to breathe. But he needed something more.

Jaga held a sleeve over his mouth and searched the cabin once again, until he found it.

A quick shuffle to his table, which was lower than his previous table and probably why his hand couldn't find it. Right in the center was his large black Maglite, a gift from a passenger some years ago, and his sea card. He snatched the heavy flashlight, thinking he might need it if there was a fire, and then shuffled back to the door.

Just before opening, he heard voices. Lots of them.

A swarm of people were just outside his door, milling around and speaking to each other in short agitated sentences.

"Jaga, hello," called out a familiar voice from the crowd, which he recognized as a mix of passengers and crew. *Or should that be new crew and old crew?*

It was Samuel Yusif, from Somalia. He didn't bump into Samuel much, because he worked in the kitchen, but he liked him. "Hey Samuel, is there a fire?" Jaga jammed the Maglite in between the door and frame, now wondering why he didn't grab his sea card too. He stood up again to find Samuel there.

"We just trying to figure this out ourselves too. Dis smell like burned garlic... After de explosion, we see gas in cabins. Come out here. That when—"

"Explosion? What explosion?"

"Some say it bomb."

Jaga was puzzled by this, now realizing that the explosion must have been what woke him. "Hey look, the smoke is coming into the hallway." Jaga pointed to a vent in the hall. The same white smoke was wafting out of the vent, but not like a regular fire. This was something else, like a gas.

"It's poison," someone yelled out.

"Maybe," Jaga hollered over the din of harried conversations, "we should get into the stairwell. The ventilation is best there. And if we have to, we can run down stairs and away from the gas or smoke, if it isn't safe." He wasn't about to call it poison, just because someone said this. But he wondered if it was.

His words were having an effect, because the people in his hallway were already moving down the hall and turning into the stairwell.

"Aren't you coming?" Samuel asked, following the group.

Jaga glanced at his door, propped open slightly by his flashlight. He was going to grab his sea card, but now he was having second thoughts. If this was a poisonous gas, the last thing he wanted to do is breathe any more of it. And right now his skin and throat felt prickly, like they were burnt. *Probably just my mind playing tricks on me, but just in case...* He snatched the flashlight from the door, which instantly clasped shut. He'd get another card, or ask someone to let him in again, if given that chance. "I'm coming."

The group of ten or so people, now his neighbors, had already filed into the landing area in between the midway elevators and stairwell. He quickly followed, anxious to get away from the poisonous gas that was slowly leaking into their cabins and hallway.

"I'm so glad you here, Jaga," Samuel stated. "Now what we do?"

The others cut off their conversations and looked to him. He found this odd, because other than a few friends, people rarely found what he had to say interesting, much less important.

"I think we wait here. The gas doesn't seem to be moving fast, and I'm guessing that's because the power outage and probably the explosion automatically closed the vents. We have good ventilation here. So I would suggest we wait for the captain or crew to instruct us and we listen."

So they quietly waited. But rather than an expected announcement, they heard something strange above them.

"Do you hear that?" someone whispered.

It was like animals... Hundreds of breathless animals, in a stampede.

107

Engine Room

The experienced engine room crew calmly followed protocol immediately upon feeling the explosion rock the ship, even before they received any confirmation from their engineering chief. In anticipation of a gas explosion or even a terrorist attack, they attempted to do what they were supposed to do first: secure all doors. The automatic systems took care of the rest. The protocol and automated systems were designed to lower the possibility of a fire spreading and/or cut off any access terrorists might have to their engines. However, many of the new and inexperienced crew members did the opposite. They panicked.

Bobby Gibson, a retired banker from Cheltenham, ran as fast as he could for the nearest exit, which thankfully was right in front of him. When his new supervisor, Edger Ivonovich, had abandoned him to follow some sort of "emergency protocol," Bobby figured he'd take his chances topside. He'd get out of here and face the consequences later.

At the small steel door, there was a placard that read

"Deck 1" with an up arrow. That's all Bobby needed. He heaved up on the metal handle until it budged, slowly at first, then finally sliding all the way up with a large clank. He pulled on the same metal latch to open the door, but it was stuck. So he yanked at it with all of his might, and then tugged again, until something in the door and in his back gave way with a loud *thunk* sound. He held onto the latch, while taking in several rapid puffs of air. Besides whatever he pulled in his back, his chest was beating so fast now, he thought it might explode.

A noise behind him caused him to turn back. He didn't see them, but he could hear frantic voices coming toward him. *Need to move quickly.*

Another tug at the door caused it to swing open. Without hesitating, he stepped blindly into a soupy fog on the other side. His skin burned immediately, as the fog—*or was it smoke*—surrounded him. *If there's smoke, there's fire,* he thought. Yet this smelled like melting fish guts. Something was wrong here and he had to find another way out of the engine room.

Bobby took a quick turn, attempting to return to the way he had entered. He took one step and he ran into something solid; a pin-prick of pain shot through his forehead. He couldn't see a damned thing in this smoke and his eyes were on fire. So were his lungs. He took another breath and coughed hard.

Now really panicking, he spun farther left on his heel, thinking he had turned prematurely, took another step and this time ran face-first directly into a sharp but equally solid object. Bobby lost it at that point.

"Help me!" he screamed.

Gagging on the smoke, he thrust out his hands and desperately tried to feel his way to the opening. Every square inch of his skin felt on fire. "Hell—cough-cough, plea—cough-cough."

He found the opening, thrusting his two arms out to

confirm it, and then dashed for it. This time he forgot to lift his feet over the threshold of the bulkhead door, designed to be air and water-tight. His feet remained inside the access way, but his body continued moving forward, until he hit head-first on the grated walkway. Bobby no longer felt panic, nor the sting of the toxic gas.

As he slowly died, the toxic gas, finding its release, billowed inside the engine room, filling it up fast.

~~~

Flavio dispatched another one of the island men. This one was loitering by the main entrance of the engine room. At first he was going to shoot him with his rifle. Quick and easy. But he opted for a more silent method and withdrew his Morakniv.

Flavio surprised the man and before he could react, Flavio sliced across the man's neck and then drove his knife down, deep into the man's chest, at the same time shoving with all of his weight to knock the man onto his back. The man did what all do: he clutched his hands around his neck to hold back the flow of blood. With one gloved hand still on the knife stuck in the man's chest, Flavio placed the other over the man's mouth to keep him quiet, while Flavio waited for him to die and searched for the others.

It took less than a minute for his target to stop moving. There was no one else around.

Glancing back down at the dead man, Flavio was momentarily jolted. The man's eyes were blood-red. They were just like Mrs. Williams' eyes. That meant that his man was symptomatic like her.

He hesitated before extracting his knife, wiping the blood off it onto the symptomatic's chest. Immediately, he felt a sigh of relief. He probably couldn't win a hand-to-hand battle
~~~

with one of these things. Mrs. Williams could certainly kick his ass if she tried. And certainly any somewhat able-bodied man with double or triple their normal strength would be a difficult force to stop. Worse would be several of them at once.

No more stealth, he reasoned, sliding his knife back in its sheath attached to his belt. He left his small pack by the door, stood up and brought his rifle back around, at the ready. He flicked off the safety, did another scan of his surroundings, and then clicked open the main entrance door to the engine room.

His gun was thrust inside, but he held up there, listening. The fluorescents above revealed a misty wasteland. Some sort of fog held to the floor, covering four or five bodies. One wore a black jumper like he'd expect of the crew that worked here. His head looked bashed in and his throat looked ripped out. This told Flavio that more of these island men were symptomatic or parasitic. He wondered if the two men they had confronted in the food area were as well, even though Mrs. Williams said they were not. But she also said something was wrong with them.

As the fog started to inch its way out the door, surrounding his boots, Flavio scrutinized the other bodies. They were the island men, wearing the same dirty clothes and sunglasses—*many of them had sunglasses, just like Williams, to hide their eyes*. He could only see two of them clearly. Their faces were covered in red sores and their mouths were wide open, like they had suffocated. Their throats were swollen to twice their normal size.

The fog crept up his knee. And that was close enough. He withdrew his rifle from the opening and stepped back, quickly shutting the door and closing off the gas.

He had seen this stuff used before, to kill rats as well as people. He hesitated, thinking about what would happen if someone else happened to open the door. Whoever was in the engine room was probably dead already, or would be soon, and it wasn't worth risking any others. He flipped his rifle around to his back and undid his leather belt.

It took only a minute to tie up the handle of the door, just enough so that no one would accidentally stumble inside.

He then left the engine room, with the intent of going to try and help TJ with the men targeting the bridge. Even as talented as she was, she'd still need help.

While running, he reported the probable death of all of the engine room crew and the island men who were trying to target that area. He also announced his intent to help Mrs. Williams and that some of the islanders were symptomatic.

Flavio made it to the deck 2 landing, telling Mr. Williams that he intended to ascend the stairwell all the way to deck 8 and then forward to the bridge.

"Flavio, don't go that way," Williams warned. "The parasitics are breaking free directly above you. Suggest instead you—" Flavio clicked off the radio.

Right above him were the sounds of many people—he now suspected the parasitics—coming down these stairs, and they were less than a deck away.

108

TJ

After hearing and feeling the explosion, TJ wasn't sure what to expect. The words of the disgusting Squat man rattled in her brain: "While you're feeling me out, my men are taking over your bridge and will blow your engines so you can't go anywhere." In addition to the perversity of this man, the sheer temerity of these people to come on board and believe they could do what they wanted to her people, pissed her off to no end.

TJ was ready to kill and she didn't care what the repercussions were. She was done holding back, repressing her desire to kill. These men needed to die in the most gruesome ways and she was going to enjoy every moment of it. Then she was going to come back to where they were holding Squat and pop his head like a pimple.

Her smile grew, as did her stride, as she turned off of I-95, hoping this shortcut would get her to the bridge before the islanders did, or at least before they were able to take out the bridge door.

She turned into the extra-dark crew stairwell, barely lit by emergency lights. She punched through the murky area, ascending three steps at a time, and was on deck 8 in barely a blink or two. It was almost frightening how quickly she could move now. At the top step, she froze and came to an abrupt stop.

Before her was a man dressed just like Squat and Skinny: a sheen of dirt, grime and sweat coated his skin, face and clothes. This one had a broken ankle; his foot was bent at a ninety-degree angle. He sat on the decking, legs splayed, making a meal out of someone's arm.

The man looked up, glared at TJ with his red eyes and brayed a series of cackles at her. TJ instantly knew that this meant, "Stay away, this is mine."

Below his elbow, in puddles of blood and muck were his sunglasses. *Some wore sunglasses and some were wearing black contacts,* she reasoned.

But why no smell?

But there was a smell; in between the non-infected blood, she could smell it.

She pulled out the knife Flavio had given her from the fold of her shorts and thrust it into the ear of the dirty parasitic. His head flopped over and the half-eaten arm he'd been munching on, tumbled to the floor. With her other hand, TJ wiped the sheen of dirt and sweat from the man's face and smelled it, and then him.

Also remembering something she saw in Squat, she pushed the dead man's head back and glared into his nostrils, which were flared like the others'.

Then she understood immediately: The nostrils were filled with cotton so they couldn't smell. Their own smell was someone else's dirt and sweat. They were using a non-infected's body odor and dirt to cover the island's infected. These men were infected and symptomatic like her, although some like this one, looked parasitic, all to overtake their ship.

And so they wouldn't go crazy until they needed them to, they shoved cotton up their noses, so they couldn't smell their own scent masks.

"Those..." So many expletives rapid-fired out of her brain at that moment, they got stove-piped at her tongue and wouldn't come out. She stepped forward, crunching the dead man's sunglasses under her feet, turned the handle and threw back the door, not caring whether she was stealthy or not.

She was going to wreak havoc upon these men.

TJ leapt into the hallway and ran around the public stairway to take the starboard hallway toward the bridge.

She turned the corner, past the entrance of Eloise Carmichael's cabin, and dashed toward the men already there and setting up explosives at the bridge entrance.

One of the men's radio was hollering at him and he picked it up to answer it, when he saw TJ. The man dropped his radio and stared at the beautiful blur coming right at him. His lips attempted to form words, but all that fell out was, "Look at—" before TJ struck him like a wrecking ball, crashing him hard into cabin 8000's doorframe.

TJ was able to stop right where she'd struck him, sparing herself from a potentially concussive blow. But something hit her as strongly as the man she'd run into, who now writhed in pain on the floor. The man was not infected. And that meant that only some of their group were infected and others weren't. This was puzzling.

It was a flash of movement, just out of her periphery. She snapped her head in that direction. There, a few feet from her, was a smiling face, pointing a revolver; the revolver's chambers were filled with .357 cartridges; it clicked. Before she could react, the smiling face pulled the trigger.

109

Tomas

Tomas Novo, Via de Corvo's only surviving agent, listened patiently to his boss ranting on the radio.

"Team A. Team B. Report goddammit, report!" Sal hollered, spewing spittle and anger at the radio. Not getting a response, he was naturally inspired to take action, as he always did. He pulled back, portable in his palm. Then, because he got no response, he smashed the radio against the rough stonework of the building they were in. The radio splintered into a multitude of now useless pieces. Sal glared at the cruise ship out the window and then at the broken parts of what was his radio.

Tomas sat quietly behind his boss, unwilling to offer even one thought or suggestion. He'd wait until he was asked. And he certainly didn't want to venture a guess now, when he was so mad. When Sal got mad, people died. And Sal was as angry as Tomas had seen him in several days.

It was a common theme with his boss: he'd lose his temper and then break something, or someone. Only then was he able to collect his logical thoughts and refocus on the task at hand.

Tomas knew enough to let him be and wait for the anger to pass and his logic to return. Until then, he didn't make a peep.

"Tomas? Hand me your radio."

Tomas popped out of his seat and took the few steps to Sal. He laid it down on the table between Sal and the window, through which he still stared at the elusive object that had been avoiding his capture. That was the root of his anger, not being able to easily seize the *Intrepid*, even though he had thought it would be so easy; even though he had made all the plans he made. He just couldn't wait to get his hands on it and enough food to supply his people for at least a year or two.

Tomas quickly pulled back and returned to his chair.

Sal picked up the radio and studied it, like it was some sort of puzzle box he wasn't sure how to open.

This often happened after his explosion of anger. He'd almost get delirious with anger and then confused afterwards.

"Why?" Sal paused, as if he wasn't sure what words to add to the end of the sentence. Though Tomas was pretty sure what the question was: "Why don't... they answer?"

This is where Tomas had to be extra careful.

He'd seen this very thing happen with the other agent, maybe two days after the barge crashed into their island. Sal went on an anger bender, smashing a car with a cricket bat, all because he couldn't find the keys, which it turned out he left in his desk in the station.

After ten minutes of Sal assaulting the car with the cricket bat, the other agent, went inside, grabbed Sal's keys and came back out to offer them to him. When Sal stopped his tirade and just stared blankly at the car for an untold amount of time, he finally said, "I wonder where I put my keys."

The other agent said, "I've got 'em right here, sir," jingling them like a trophy.

Sal looked at the keys and then the agent, and then proceeded to beat him to death with the cricket bat.

Tomas and the others in town knew then that Salvadore Calderon had become mentally unstable and a psychopath.

From this incident and other people's trial and error, Tomas learned to give an answer that sounded logical, but wasn't complete either. The combination seemed to force Sal to think more about it. This, for some reason, reconnected his logical thoughts and brought him back to someone Tomas could deal with.

Sal had sent in two teams so far. Team A was supposed to go to the bridge, blow the door, and take the captain hostage for later torture. Team B was to blow the ship's engine—Tomas never told Sal that there were two engines—and thus disable the ship, so it would have to remain at their dock permanently. Then they'd take over the ship and take its food, as they wanted.

Neither team had reported on their radios, which they were supposed to do after they blew their explosives and completed their missions. They heard one explosion. But nothing since.

"Maybe," Tomas offered, "the teams are trying to be quiet and not alert the *Intrepid's* people as to where they are."

Sal stood almost completely unmoving, other than his breaths. Then he turned to Tomas and said, "Okay, it's time to send in Team Z now!"

At first, Tomas thought maybe Sal wanted him to take his radio back and call in the order, but then Sal did this himself. "Team C, send in Team Z. Make sure they have taken down the ship before entering."

This part was disheartening, even though Tomas knew where this was going. Tomas somehow hoped he was wrong about Sal, even though he knew better.

It was just that, as insane as this man was, he still in a sick way cared for him like a father. And he knew that Sal cared for Tomas like a son. It was the real reason why Tomas had, in fact, never been seriously threatened by Sal. Even though Sal did threaten him with death or dismemberment, and did so to so many others, Tomas never really believed it.

He went along with Sal all this time, always hoping that he wasn't really going to kill all these people. But when he called for Team Z, as in the last group from A to Z: the final solution, Tomas knew the die was cast. There was no going back.

As he listened, three of Sal's four men who were Team C, opened the doors of the three shipping containers—hidden in plain sight, behind them on the dock. Then the fourth member of Team C blasted a horn on the other end of the dock. That was the signal.

The mob of people, some thirty men and woman, stampeded out of the three shipping containers and raced down the dock with one intent: kill everyone on the *Intrepid*.

Tomas saw them race by the little building they were in, yelling their battle cry, and Tomas lowered his head.

He couldn't do anything about this, but he could do something about his boss. He knew right then what he would do next, and when.

"Come on, my son. It's time for the last part of my plan. You and I are up."

110

Flavio

At first, Flavio pointed his rifle up the stairs, but then he second-guessed himself: if there were hundreds of parasitics pouring down the stairs, he didn't have enough ammo. He spun around, looking for a way out, and saw only the starboard gangway area was open; he'd have to get the door closed… They were already here. He spun back, flicked his rifle to full auto and readied himself. Their feet were visible in between the steps and then he saw them, when they hit the mid-deck landing.

He clicked the safety back on.

It was just a bunch of scared people. That's all.

He recognized the leader of the group as Jaga, who recognized him as well.

"They're coming." Jaga jumped the last step, then moved to his left. "The crazies are above us." Jaga was headed down to deck 1 next.

Flavio had an idea.

"No. Go there." He pointed to the starboard gangway

area. “Slide interior door closed and be quiet. Go now!”

Flavio didn’t even wait for them, he sprinted to the port-side interior door, which led to the exit his security had secured. Before pounding on it, he eyeballed the fresh blood streak leading inside and wondered if they were all right. “It’s Flavio Petrovich… Ah, Second Officer Petrovich. You there?”

Flavio could hear the rumble above, coming down the stairs, while the dozen or so friends of Jaga were making their way to the starboard exit area, albeit much too slowly.

The door slid open. “Hello, sir,” said Violet Johansson.

He wanted to ask them about the blood streak, but there was no time. “Open interior wall and hide. Then when I tell you, open exit door.”

“But the islanders… They’re on the other side.” Johansson shot him a look of curious fear.

Flavio could hear them pounding on the other side of the metal hatch. This made his plan even better.

“Trust me. This work for everybody. Open *exactly* when I say, but everyone must hide now or you die.”

She nodded.

He took a few steps toward the starboard exit, just outside the port-side hallway. Doing a quick check, he could see Jaga’s group was having difficulty sliding the interior wall closed. As he laid his rifle down, he looked back to the port side. They were pushing their wall open, but not fast enough. “Hurry!” he yelled to both sides.

Above, he heard a collection of animalistic grunts and fervent barks and the shuffling of a multitude of feet. They were close and moving fast.

Flavio needed to get ready.

He lowered his pack and withdrew an air-horn. He thought he might have a need for this and was right.

They were right above him now.

Johansson had the port side ready. They were hidden and Flavio could see her hand on the control pad button that would open the hatch. The pounding from the other side seemed to get louder.

When he looked starboard, he was shocked to see their wall was still half open, with Jaga and another tugging, until one lost his footing and fell to the floor.

They were sitting ducks.

He stabbed the switch on the compressed air can with this thumb, sending it through the horn, causing it to emit a horrendously loud blare. Then he released his thumb. "Come and get some fine Romanian meat," Flavio yelled.

The stampede swung into his view, but stopped at the mid-deck landing. A horde of parasitics filled the stairs leading up and out of sight. In front of the horde was Ágúst Helguson, his pale face highlighted by a ring of red around his mouth. Helguson glanced at Flavio, who just glared back at him. Helguson turned to his right and saw all the people trying to hide in the semi-open area.

The horde of parasitics behind him were like an enormous pack of mad pit-bulls, snarling their anticipation at taking a bite out of a neighbor that'd been bothering them. All appeared to be held back by Helguson, as if they were waiting for his command.

Jaga and his people were easy pickings and so was Flavio, but he was just one person. The target was obvious.

Helguson turned back to Flavio, a grin slowly formed on his red-rimmed mug. He then abruptly pointed at Flavio and barked like a seal.

That was his cue.

Flavio had a long piece of duct tape fastened to the side of the airhorn. He pulled one side of the duct tape across the top and fastened it to the other side so that it put pressure on the button. The air-horn blared again while Flavio bolted to the port-side exit. "Now. Open door!" he hollered at the top of his lungs.

Johansson must have heard him because the port-side

gangway exit slid open, revealing a mob of people, who all looked crazed themselves.

Flavio ran right at them holding his blaring airhorn up—the condensed air canister was cold as ice now.

The mob held at the door, even though they had easy access, apparently completely thrown off by Flavio's actions and the loud horn. Then they saw the hordes of parasitics flooding their way.

Flavio tossed the airhorn over the mob, past the gangway and onto the dock, where it bounced once before coming to rest, still blaring its call to all parasitics. Flavio leapt toward the mob, which had already course-corrected and was running the other way, no doubt because of the horde less than two seconds behind them.

Flavio felt a little like a gymnast as he nailed his jump, sailed above the gangway bridge railing and disappeared over the side of the boat, out of sight. While soaring, he reached back and just barely snagged the protective netting used to keep passengers from falling overboard. He clanged hard against the side of their ship, just above the water line.

111

TJ

The bullet had sliced through her cheek and scratched her cheekbone, but she didn't even feel it. She only knew it and reacted.

What happened next required no calculation; it was entirely impulse that moved TJ to spin on a heel and fling herself around.

The second bullet went way wide.

The smiling man attempted to correct on his third shot, while he squeezed the trigger, but she was much quicker, with her left wrist blocking his gun away and her right hand simultaneously slicing with her borrowed Morakniv—she didn't even remember unsheathing it—connecting a blood line from the man's cheek, down his neck and ending at his chest. In a blur, the knife was pushed back the other way and buried deep into the exposed side of the man.

As he tumbled to the floor, something inside TJ snapped. A stream of blood sprang from her cheek, rolled down her neck and covered her shoulder, but she still didn't feel her injury.

At that moment, she had clarity of purpose. Her anger past the boiling point, but there was so much more to it than anger. She had only one thing that mattered at that moment and nothing in this world could dissuade her: she was going to murder the other four men.

As if she stepped away from her conscious self, no longer an active participant in what happened next, she sliced and punched and kicked and bit at these men. As much as she was insane with madness, she was also filled with a strange calmness that warmed her whole body like an internal radiator.

Stoking this fire was an unquenchable hunger that wanted it all. Until this moment, she had tried so hard to repress this desire, but she gave into it now. And even though she could smell and taste that some of these men were infected like her, she didn't care. She indulged in their warm blood and the gore, as she ripped and tore and at one point, dismembered her enemies.

In barely the time it took to pull in a breath, there was only one standing: the one she first ran into. His whimpering cries sounded like a call to her and she wanted him even more because of it. Clutching his broken chest and limping slowly on a shattered leg, he didn't get far, tripping toward the floor. She bolted so fast to him, she caught him before he hit the floor, while at the same time, slicing her knife across his neck in one fluid motion, severing his carotid and most of his windpipe. It was better treatment than he deserved.

She held his shuddering body, his brown eyes fading and artery spurting a fountain of blood onto her face and into her mouth.

Ohhh, the taste.

She saw two more appear, while she licked her lips and drank down some of the man's life. She let him drop to the floor, while fixing her sights on these two, who looked familiar.

One called to her, as if to taunt her.

She'd take the bait.

~~~

When Ted heard the gun shot, knowing that his wife TJ was coming to the bridge, he was worried. With Wasano carrying his rifle behind him, Ted pushed open the door just as a blood-soaked TJ removed herself from a body in front of them, to race starboard down a hall to attack another.

Her speed was mesmerizing, grabbing the man before he fell from his nasty compound fracture. But it wasn't to save him. It was to drain the life out of him.

He watched her in disgust, as she sliced open the man's neck and even gulped at the spray of his blood.

Ted couldn't believe this was his wife. She looked like a wild animal who wore a coat of other people's blood.

It was even more eerie when she fixed her wild eyes on them.

"TJ, can you hear me? TJ, it's all right, honey."

Her eyes blinked from Wasano to Ted, to Wasano and back. Then she was focused on just Ted.

She looked like she might attack him.

Ted felt movement beside him and saw that Wasano was a foot away, lifting his rifle and pointing it directly at her.

She let the dead man drop at her feet, his blood coating her face, rivulets of red ran off her chin. Her mouth dropped open, as if she were about to say something. Her red eyes glared like two bullet-points, focused by the whites of her sclera, both drilling into him like a target. This was no longer his wife.

Wasano flipped off the safety. She darted forward. Wasano fired.
~~~

112
Eloise

Freedom was the simple goal she had had for her people and they had just achieved this now that they had broken out of their confined area. And in their pre-programmed exuberance to follow sound, her people had gone even farther, or Ágúst had led them farther.

Eloise was the last of her people to leave the ship. All the others had unwittingly followed the loud horn-noise, leading them off the ship to another group of humans. She had wanted them to leave the ship anyway, but only after they had killed and fed on the crew. Finding the island was just a bonus. Being on a large island would mean greater opportunities for feeding, where all their feeding opportunities were very limited on this ship.

As she approached the port-side gangway, she couldn't help but revel in what she saw before her.

Even the heavens above grew angrier by the minute. A clattering echo of thunder warned the world below—her world now—of the next stage of their continuing wrath.

The dock below was filled with her people, now ravaging the humans outside, after having escaped from their human captors on this ship. This island was now their island.

Standing at the edge of the gangway, she felt a sense of pride in her people.

But something is wrong, she thought.

The smells were wrong.

Beyond the gangway bridge, she noticed maybe twenty-five or more who weren't her people out on the dock, but they didn't smell like humans. In fact she couldn't smell any humans outside now, when she had approached this exit. Not one human. And she should be able to smell many humans, even in the distance, if this island were big.

The falling rain made it more difficult for her to catch the scent of humans.

And then she did.

Just then she got a whiff of strong human scents, but they weren't coming from outside.

She spun around to face the ship's interior and sniffed again. *The human scents are here, in this room,* she thought.

Her head snapped back to take in the air from this direct area, now catching more of it. There was more than one in here, but she couldn't see them. She screwed her eyes to any detail that would point her to them. Then she saw the human blood—she could smell this as well. A trail of red that began at the stairwell landing, stretched through the hallway, through this area and then led to a curtain on her right. Just then the curtain moved.

Knowing they were there, she should be able to hear them, hiding behind there. *As if they could hide from me,* she boasted to herself. But with the loud noises outside, she couldn't hear anything in this room. When her surroundings were quiet, she could hear their heartbeats.

But she did hear something and spun to her left. There

she saw a human's hands clinging to the ship, just outside the opening. And another one, hiding just inside the door, behind the controls for the door.

Then she knew.

This was a trap.

And where was Ágúst? He should be here, with her. She selected him and told him what to do after he had become. She gave herself to him. She rarely did that when she was a mere human.

She turned back to her people, who weren't as enraged as before, because the horn-noise had stopped. They had ceased fighting with the others from the island, because they were all of the same kind.

But Ágúst was not anywhere to be seen.

She called out for him, bellowing a long, guttural grunt.

Her people and the island people looked up at her and regarded her cries.

Then she heard him. Ágúst was not outside with her people; he was still inside.

~~~

Ágúst couldn't explain any of it, but he knew this was right.

He had pointed them in the direction of the trap, sensing what the human called Flavio was trying to do. He was trying to lead them off the ship, even though Eloise's instructions were for them to take over the ship and kill the rest of the humans. But he couldn't let that happen.

Ágúst had thought he had lost his human self when he had consumed their flesh and gave himself to her. But when they had broken free and he was leading their people, killing anyone and everyone that was in their way, he understood that he still had a choice. And he chose his humanity, even though
~~~

so little of it remained.

When they were following the group of humans down the stairs and came upon Flavio, he realized that all of those people they were following were infected too. Flavio wasn't infected, and he was leading them in.

And so he had chosen to send his people off the ship and save the humans and give them a chance at survival. And when they took the bait and left the ship, he was happy. He didn't even know he had that feeling still.

And so he hid with the small group of infected crew, on the other side, and watched them all leave.

But Eloise stopped.

She was too smart for their simple tricks, even if the rest weren't. And as he watched her consider their trap, he knew that she knew. And he knew she could smell them there, hiding from her.

It was when she called out to him that Ágúst knew what he had to do.

He stepped from the shadows and made his way to her, while her back was still to him and she was facing outside. When she called for him, he responded with his call in their language that he knew she would understand. He told her, "I've been here the whole time."

She spun around quickly to see him, her glare questioning. Unsure.

That's when he used his newfound speed and bolted for her.

She saw him, but didn't really know what he was doing until it was too late.

When he hit, he wrapped his arms around her and drove her out of the ship, onto the gangway bridge, where they both rolled down it, entangled in each other.

While he had a chance, knowing that she would kill him for this, he looked back and saw Flavio climbing back up into the ship.

"Close up, now!" Ágúst bellowed.

Ágúst caught a knowing grin from Flavio, who understood his sacrifice. But it didn't feel like a sacrifice. It was just the right thing to do.

As Eloise wiggled free from him, he watched the door to the ship shut them out.

He turned back to face Eloise and his fate, which he knew would come as quickly as her vengeance.

As a mere human, he was always afraid of death and everything else that was a part of him being human. He wasn't now.

He faced his death, remembering his life as a human and how he saved his ship.

113

Tomas

The cold drizzle quickly grew into a driving rain which pelted the windows so hard, Tomas feared they might break. He wasn't much of a ship's captain, having piloted the P114 only one other time, after his boss gave him a crash course on its operations. Trying to keep an eye on where he was going, he looked all around for the windshield wipers and couldn't find them. Then Sal's hand appeared silently from behind him, making him jump.

"It's right here," Sal stated, twisting a knob on the console that sent the blades slashing back and forth violently.

They rounded the stern of the *Intrepid*, now getting the full view of the giant cruise ship.

"You seem jumpy. No need to be. We'll succeed, just as planned." Sal's voice was smooth and in control now, not at all like he was earlier. This was also the time when he was most aware of everyone around him.

Tomas also knew his boss was spewing bluster. Sal had expected to be in complete control of the cruise ship by now.

But somehow the ship's crew had thwarted Sal's every move. They weren't even supposed get any fuel from the barge, which was only a ruse to allow their armed crew on board, or what Sal called his version of a Trojan horse.

But that obviously didn't work either.

Tomas was pretty sure it was just Sal's way of being vindictive when he sent all of his crazy people to board the ship, with the idea that they'd kill everyone in sight. Not only were they not able to board the ship, but in addition to the thirty-plus crazy people on their island, the ship dumped over one hundred more on them. They were already running out of food for their current crazy residents, as they were down to only a few uninfected humans. That's why they needed this cruise ship.

~~~

"You little people can't win. We're superior to you," snarled Squat, his reddish eyes bouncing from Flavio to TJ. "You know what I'm saying, honey. Right?" he grinned at TJ when he said this.

It was just reflexive recoil when TJ socked him with her balled-up fist. A smile crept up her face, though she tried to hold it back, so that she wouldn't pop the new stitches in her cheek. She rather enjoyed this, desperately wanting to put on a world of hurt on this dirty, sneering perverted man, who happened to be a symptomatic like her.

Squat attempted to wiggle his hands and legs free from his tightened table restraints. His head was strapped down as well, an extra measure by Flavio, not trusting the thick straps to completely hold the monster down.

They were tasked by the captain to get information from this man they called Squat, and to do so 'by any means.'
~~~

'Any means' gave her a lot of latitude in the interrogation and she planned to take full advantage of this order.

"You're wasting your time. You know I don't feel pain. And at some point I'll find a way to get free. Then I'll kill and eat each of you. But you..." again he turned to TJ, "I'll lick you first, before I—"

TJ struck him in the Adam's apple, her hand stiff like a chopping knife.

A spate of uncontrollable coughing erupted from Squat.

TJ let her smile curl up high, feeling the tug of her stitches reach their limit, while readjusting her crutch under the other armpit.

"Just tell us why you wanted our ship and our food. We have little raw meat and that's what you eat, right? And why hurt engines?" Flavio asked, scrutinizing the small, bulbous man with the deep-set scar in his mug.

"You..." Squat was trying to say something, but then burst out into a fit of laughter and coughing.

"This get us nowhere," bellowed Flavio. "Answer questions or I just kill you myself."

"You people really are"—he cleared his throat—"stupid, aren't you? You said it yourself. We only eat raw meat."

Once again, he leered at TJ, his tongue sticking out slightly. "Aside from this tasty one, I was going to have the pick of any of your passengers. And with three thousand, we weren't going to go hungry for a long time. And you brought your own food. We just couldn't believe our luck when you showed up. It was like a farmer bringing us fresh farm animals and the animals agreed to fatten themselves up with their own food. You were so gullible to think that we would give you fuel for just a little fo—"

TJ had had enough. This time, with her free hand, she struck him with a heavy metal tray she'd found on the table next to them, almost falling over in the process.

~~~

Tomas had pretended not to know Sal's real plans, mostly to protect himself. He figured if Sal cared enough not to let him know that they were planning to eat everyone lured to their island, he must want him around for a while.

But it had gone too far and he was just tired of being scared all the time. He lived in constant fear of his boss' anger or one of his boss' lieutenants or of one of the crazies, who he knew wanted to kill him and tear him apart. He was done accepting his fate.

When this cruise ship thwarted their actions, he thought there might be a chance, a way for him to stop this monster and for him to get off this island and go someplace safe.

He shuddered in anticipation.

"You're shivering. You should have brought a jacket," Sal said, his attention mostly on the *Intrepid* off their port side.

"All right, hold up there." Sal pointed to a spot on the starboard side of the *Intrepid's* bridge. "Guess I don't need these things." He pulled off his sunglasses and tossed them onto the small table beside Tomas. Sal flashed his dark red eyes at him. "I'm going to make our demands known," Sal said, snatching a bullhorn from a rack before punching open the door of their little bridge.

A swirl of rainwater poured in and then the door slammed shut.

Tomas watched his boss splash his way to their weapon on their boat's forecastle, all loaded and ready. Sal turned back to Tomas and held up his palm, indicating he wanted to stop here.

Tomas pulled the boat's throttle all the way back, causing them to slow to a couple of knots. He reversed the
~~~

engines to halt their drafting, when he heard his boss's voice over the bullhorn.

"Ahoy there, Captain Jean Pierre Haddock of the *Intrepid*. This is Salvadore Calderon. We met a short time ago. Apparently I didn't make my demands clear; instead I attempted subterfuge, when clearly I'm dealing with an intelligent man. So I'll make myself perfectly clear now and I'm only going to say this once, so you better be listening, Captain Haddock of the *Intrepid*. You are to surrender your ship in the next two minutes or I will sink it. Is that clear enough?"

Sal placed his bullhorn on the wet ground by his feet, horn down, stood back up, straightened himself and then swung the 12.7 mm machine gun around so that it was pointed right at the cruise ship.

Tomas mentally counted down sixty seconds.

Ninety seconds later, the *Intrepid's* captain appeared on the swing deck about thirty feet above them. He too had a bullhorn in his hand. He held it up, causing it to squeak first. "We don't negotiate with terrorists. Leave now and our security will not shoot and destroy you." He put his bullhorn down and appeared to wait for Sal's reply.

Tomas knew this game. It was called the game of chicken. Whoever chickened out first and pulled their car aside before both cars careened into each other, head on, was the loser.

The captain's response must have incensed Sal, because he kicked the bullhorn, sending it clattering against the other side of the boat he couldn't see. Sal first aimed at the captain, but then lifted the barrel high in the sky, aiming the large gun over the ship. That way, the captain could see Sal was purposely trying to miss, but only this time: the equivalent of accelerating your car to force the other guy to chicken out faster. Sal fired, sending twenty tracer rounds over the *Intrepid's* bridge.

Tomas needed to end this game now, before it was too

late.

He stepped out into the rain, slowly pacing to his boss, who had his back to him, all his attention focused on the *Intrepid's* swing deck.

Tomas focused on Sal's head, willing it to not turn back to him.

The rain hid his splashing footsteps, bathing the world around them in a loud, pattering drumbeat.

When Tomas was halfway from the bridge to Sal, he drew his Beretta, hidden beneath his shirt, and held it low and slightly behind him, so that Sal couldn't see it.

Sal huffed and murmured a fusillade of words under his breath, all of them not good. He was getting very angry again. This time, Sal swung the gun down, aiming the sight's crosshairs at the *Intrepid's* bow, right around its water line. The rounds were armor piercing, so Tomas imagined they'd go through their hull fairly easily. The *Intrepid* wouldn't survive if Sal fired the gun from bow to stern, even if he only sent over half of the rounds he was loaded for.

Tomas was three meters away now, raising his pistol and aiming directly at Sal's head.

Sal pulled back on the machine gun's charging bolt once again, readying the 12.7x108mm rounds for their intended destination, obviously figuring if he couldn't have this ship, he wouldn't let anyone else have it.

Two meters away, Tomas clicked the safety off.

"Really?" Sal yelled loud enough that Tomas could hear him in the rain. "Do you really think you could fool me, Tomas?"

Tomas halted, his arm starting to quiver, along with his nerve.

"I knew this was what you were planning..."—Tomas wasn't sure if he was pausing for effect or thinking out loud—"That's why I removed a round from the chamber... You'll now have to chamber a round before you can shoot and you know in that time, I can turn around and rip your throat out. Or Tomas, you can lay your gun down and join me."

Tomas thought about what Sal said, now unsure if Sal was bluffing or not. Tomas always checked the chamber of his weapon before he holstered it and Sal knew this. But Sal had him remove his weapon and holster earlier and Tomas was so nervous about hiding the gun under his shirt, he didn't remember checking it.

He pulled the trigger anyway.

The sound was hollow, but his bullet struck home with all the force he needed.

Sal's head buffeted back, but he didn't go down. Sal turned and faced him, his evil-looking eyes taunting him for more.

Tomas didn't hesitate. He put another round in Sal's head and four more into his body, until the man went down for good. Sal had been super-human, but he could still die like all humans.

Tomas dropped his Beretta, pulled his head up and immediately saw that a rifle was trained on him from the swing deck. He dropped down, ducking out of sight, and scooted over to the bullhorn.

He shook off its coating of water and held the bullhorn to his lips. "Please don't shoot me. I'm not one of them. He forced me to be here."

Raising up, unprotected by the hull, Tomas held both of his hands high in the air. He waited to be fired upon, not really caring anymore.

114

Four Orders

Jean Pierre made Tomas wait almost eight hours before allowing him to come aboard. It wasn't to punish or some sort of plan to wear down a potential combatant. Jean Pierre and his crew simply had a lot of work to do first, before they'd let anyone else on board.

In suite 8000, the captain convened his wardroom and invited his assistant security director and his environmental compliance officer to join them. He first discussed their preliminary status and then he went into his four orders, making sure they all understood and gave him their feedback. He sent them on their way and returned to the bridge.

At precisely, 10:30 AM, Jean Pierre stood in front of the ship's intercom and clicked the microphone button.

"Attention all crew of the *Intrepid*, both new and old. It is now safe to come out of your cabins as the danger has passed. I will address you all in the coming days and explain in more detail what has happened and what our situation is, but there is much work we must do right now.

"To this end, I have issued four orders to all of my crew, and that includes you. The first two have already been given to my most senior crew and they are executing them as I speak. The last two relate to everyone else who is currently on this ship.

"The four orders are as follows: first, to put a safe distance between us and the island's port; the second, to make sure we are properly fueled and then detached from the refueling barge on our starboard side; the third is to make sure there are no more combatants from the island or parasitics on board; and the fourth order is to clean up the mess.

"Because you are all a part of my crew and we are all in this together, I'm making you aware of all my orders. Again, only my third and fourth orders apply to everyone hearing this.

"We believe the immediate threat is over. The parasitics, which we had been holding in our Wayfarer Lounge, are no longer on the ship. Additionally, even though we let several on board, there should be no more guests from the island"—Jean-Pierre chose not yet to reveal their symptomatic nature—"on board.

"I won't lie to you; many have perished at the hands of the islanders and the parasitics. And many of them were killed as well. But the threat has passed.

"That's where you come in, and this leads to my third and fourth orders, which I am now giving to each of you.

"Everyone with a last name beginning with the letters A through L is on search patrol. Everyone with a last name beginning with the letters M through Z is on clean-up patrol.

"First, to the search patrol. Your job, beginning at the conclusion of this announcement, is to scour every cabin and every room on the entire ship, from deck 3 all the way up to the highest observation deck. You are looking for any islanders or parasitics. If you see either, alive or dead, do not engage them by yourselves. Call attention to any of our personnel wearing Regal European Blue. They will have our security staff toss them off the ship.

"For our clean-up patrol, your job is equally important. Besides cleaning up the debris in the areas that were damaged, so as to minimize any future hazards, you will also help us with identification and disposal of any bodies. If you find a dead body, please do not touch it yourselves. Report this to one of our personnel wearing Regal European Blue, and they will tell you what to do.

"Our personnel wearing Regal European Blue are already making their way to various locations. If you're unsure what to do, simply ask them.

"For both groups, consider this the ultimate scavenger hunt, where the prize is not a bottle of wine or fine dining, but all of our survival. Your work in the next few hours may be just that important.

"Those are my orders. As a member of my crew, I expect each of you to follow them. Thank you for your cooperation.

"This is your captain, Jean-Pierre Haddock. Out."

~~~

Flavio was tasked to lead a team to carry out the captain's first order: giving them a safe distance from Vila de Corvo's port. This order posed their biggest challenge. They certainly didn't want any more unauthorized boardings and having their port side moored to this dock left them too exposed and vulnerable. And that's where their challenge initially appeared greatest. On this, they realized quickly they had caught their biggest break.

Flavio had personally just dumped all of their parasitics out their exit and onto the dock, with another thirty parasitics, all of whom were hungry, angry and anxious to get back on board and make a meal out of his crew the moment they opened up their gangway again.
~~~

He was told that they couldn't just abandon the mooring lines, because they had a limited quantity of the specially designed rope on board and they had already cut one free when they had to flee the Port of Malaga.

And since there were no shoremen on the dock to disconnect the lines from the dock, that meant Flavio had to lead a capable team of men and women, only a few of whom were expert in detaching the heavy mooring ropes from dock's bollards, onto the dock.

Flavio wasn't sure what they would do if the parasitics swarmed the dock. And that's when he saw they had caught a giant-sized break. Before meeting his team at the port-side gangway on deck 2, Flavio first checked out the dock from the deck 10 outside running track.

The heavy downpour of cold rain must have driven away the mostly naked parasitics. They were now gone, except for a few bodies, and so was the rain.

Now, just before opening up the door, he checked once more with Ted on the radio, who had eyes on the dock from the port-side swing deck.

"Okay, open up, Ms. Johansson," Flavio stated, rifle at the ready.

The door slid open and Flavio stepped out onto the gangway bridge and searched their perimeter.

It was clean, other than the three dead parasitics and two dead islanders, who must have killed each other in the initial waylay. There were no other signs of anyone, anywhere.

He stepped up to the first body, giving it a kick, to make sure it wasn't faking it. In the distance, he heard something.

Flavio held a bald-fist up in the air, letting everyone know to be quiet and wait for him.

Mixed in with the growing commotion building on the ship, as their search and clean up teams started spreading out, finding their way topside, he heard something else. From the island, he heard an occasional scream or even grunt. He assumed this meant that their parasitics had gone on to feed on the rest of the islanders, who were probably easier to get to than the passengers of a sealed up, steel cruise ship.

He stepped over to the next body and gave it a kick. None of the others stirred, not even a little.

But then one did.

Flavio flipped off the rifle's safety and pointed at the clothed form on the deck, surrounded by a puddle of red. It was breathing. With his finger on the trigger, ready to put an end to its obvious suffering, he recognized quickly it was Ágúst Helguson, the parasitic who singlehandedly saved their ship.

Flavio cupped his hands around his mouth before he spoke, so that only those in the gangway could hear him. Just above a whisper, he said, "I need a medical team here."

He turned over the former second officer, who looked unconscious, but whose chest was still moving.

Three people, who represented their medical team, all recently recruited crew, took over and went to work on attempting to save the near dead man.

He's a parasitic, no longer a man, Flavio corrected himself in thought.

At the top of the gangway, he stated loud enough so all could hear, "Okay team, it is clear. Work quickly and quietly!"

~~~

Wasano was charged with carrying out the captain's second order, making sure they were properly fueled and then detached from the refueling barge. It was also to protect their engineering chief, "at all costs."

The captain was concerned that they were running out of engineering personnel, since most had either been killed or had become monsters. As many as half of their remaining
~~~

engineering staff died when toxic gas was released into the engine room by their own crew, in a traitorous attempt to kill the parasitics on board. When they were safe, Wasano planned to demand the captain hold a trial and punish any of those involved who were still alive.

The shortage in capable engineering crew meant that Niki Tesler, their punk-haired chief of engineering, was almost as important to their ship as the captain, when it came to crucial ship-knowledge which couldn't immediately be taught to someone else.

"Okay, first officer, can we get started?" Niki requested.

"Captain?" Wasano asked on his radio. His ear-piece immediately squawked back with the captain confirming from above that it was all clear.

"You're good to go, security chief."

The door opened with a gnawing creak, revealing a slaughter fest outside. There were over a dozen of their crew murdered and lying topside on the fueling barge. And as bitter a pill as it was, they were not going to collect these men and women and hold a proper burial at sea, like they did earlier for those who died during the first wave of attacks. Instead, one of their team was tasked with taking a picture of each dead crew member, for later identification, and then several of their team were tasked with tossing the bodies overboard.

The captain's orders were explicit when it came to this. There simply wasn't enough time. And their medical director said the bodies were too much of a health hazard to hold on board for later burial.

The rest of the team scurried out to each of the hoses, Niki behind them barking off directions to pull one hose off, which represented their heavy fuel. And then to attach the other hose, which was for their GMO. Niki told them that they had enough heavy fuel to last them for months, if they were judicious in its use. And so all they needed now was the GMO. They'd be done in less than an hour.

They had also decided to anchor the fueling barge off the dock and moor it to a mooring float, so that they'd have access to it later, if they needed it. There was no telling when they'd ever see another place to refuel.

As Wasano looked over the activity on the barge and most especially Niki, he didn't even want to consider the idea of returning to this place. As far as he was concerned, they couldn't leave soon enough.

115

After-Effects

Finally, when they had powered away from the Via de Corvo's dock and completed their search of the entire ship for the dead, confirming as well that there were no more parasitics or islanders on board, they invited the man they knew as Tomas Novo to board. He was promptly arrested.

Ted and TJ had been asked to be a part of their interrogation of Mr. Novo, so they could decide what to do with him after this. The security director and the captain would be conducting the interrogation.

Ted was the first to arrive at an unmarked room, next to the also unmarked brig, on deck 1, where they held the symptomatic islander whom Flavio and TJ had interrogated earlier.

While Ted waited for the others to arrive and for their "guest" to be escorted in, Ted reviewed his notes from the day. He planned to move these details into his log when he had a chance.

One thing bothered him, and he wanted to know the

answer before anyone arrived. Each number in his notes, he mentally added to the last one, scratching a sub-total to the right of each number on the page. At the bottom of the second page, he wrote a final number and circled it. 215. That was preliminary number of reported dead their teams had found, which included both infected and non-infected, regardless of whether they died from the parasitic or islander attacks or succumbed to the toxic gas, or even somewhat more natural causes. These were rough numbers, but from what he remembered, that meant their total crew now, both existing and newly recruited, was somewhere south of four hundred.

He wondered how many crew it took to run a cruise ship this size, questioning if they had enough, even after the newly recruited were made useful.

The door clicked open and the captain walked in.

"Hello, captain," Ted welcomed.

"Ted," he acknowledged. His tone and face were of someone very tired and heavily burdened. It was the same look Jörgen had before he was viciously killed. Ted knew this to be true of any leader of a large group which experienced much hardship. And they certainly had.

The captain took a seat and glowered at Ted, like he wanted to tell him something horrible, but he wasn't sure if he was willing to at this point. But then, in a blink, he finally decided not to.

"How is your ankle?" the captain asked. His face and body language all at once were more relaxed, though he still showed concern.

"It's fine. I'm more concerned about TJ, and of course, all the others with much greater injuries than mine."

His face immediately switched back again to that of the leader who felt crushed by the burden of knowing some secret which caused him great pain. It hit Ted that whatever Jean Pierre was unwilling yet to tell him probably concerned his wife. And it was bad.

Jean Pierre tried to hide his emotions again, only partially masking his true mental state with a forced grin. “She’s one of the toughest people I’ve ever met. She’ll be fine. Doc Chloe says she’s already healing, thanks to... well, whatever is happening to those infected like her.”

“I know, I checked in on her earlier. Doc gave her a heavy sedative to knock her out for a while. That’s why I’m surprised she was joining us on this... interview of our guest.”

“We’ll only need her for one purpose, to confirm whether or not Mr. Novo is a bad pear—”

“You mean apple.”

“What?”

“You meant, whether or not Mr. Novo is a bad apple.”

“Yes,” his brow furrowed, and once again the whole complexion of the man changed. “And we can dispense with the pleasantries. This will be at minimum an interrogation and at worst an execution. You’re here for one purpose too: yours is to observe and to render your opinion, only after we’re done and only when I ask for it. I trust your opinion, Ted. But I will be the one who decides what happens to Mr. Novo. Are we clear?”

“Very.”

The door opened, and in walked TJ, cleaned up and now wearing a light jacket, zipped up over her running outfit. Last time Ted saw her, she lay on a cot in their medical clinic, half asleep and still covered in dried blood, which was caked over her multiple scratches and two bandages covering her bullet wounds: one on her cheek and the other on her leg.

She limped in, assisted by crutches, looking dazed. “Hi Ted,” she smiled and sat in the chair next to his. The only blood on her was that blood that still stained her nose plug, firmly clipped to her nose.

Before the door could close itself, Tomas Novo, in handcuffs, was led in by Wasano.

Mr. Novo was seated in a heavy chair in the center of

the room. Wasano pulled out another set of handcuffs and clicked them around the chain of the handcuffs he already wore. The other end quickly clasped to the arm of the chair.

"I told you this is not necessary. I'm the one who killed Salvatore," pleaded Mr. Novo. His accent seemed strange. Ted guessed that was his Portuguese, with which Ted had little familiarity. "I will tell you whatever you want. Just please don't send me back to that island. I've been trying to leave it ever since I was sent there."

Their interrogation, which turned out to be more of an interview, went well as the man gave them every detail about how he first came to the island as a lowly deputy, or what they called an agent. And how he'd been trying to get transferred to Lisbon, but his boss wouldn't let him leave the island.

Then he told them about the barge that crashed into their town and how over three-quarters of their town went crazy or at least showed signs of the Rage disease.

Tomas said that he wasn't completely opposed to Salvatore's methods to segregate the infected from those who were not infected, like him.

Each time Mr. Novo mentioned the infected or what he called crazy-people or the Rage disease, he'd eyeball TJ, who remained quiet the entire time, only twice pulling off her nose clip, sniffing and then turning to the captain with a head shake, which Ted guessed meant that Mr. Novo wasn't infected.

Tomas said that he noticed that his boss's behavior had been changing, that he showed less compassion and constant anger. One night, Mr. Novo said he followed his boss and witnessed him torture and murder a man who was showing signs of the disease. It was also the first time he saw that his boss was one of them, with red eyes and pale skin, just not as out of control as the others.

Before this, he had just assumed his boss was fighting a cold.

Mr. Novo then went on to the elaborate plan that his

boss and two other men had come up with to lure in a ship, like the *Intrepid*, pretending that they were offering fuel for food, when in fact, the offer of fuel was only to trap a ship and hold the people for food.

He'd been trying to find a way to leave them, but he was under the constant threat of death. It wasn't until he was alone with his boss that he found a way to stop him.

Wasano showed him a picture of the squat islander TJ had tortured earlier and then interrogated with Flavio. Then, he had heard from Flavio that the islander boasted about the plot that Mr. Novo just confirmed. Mr. Novo not only ID'd the men, he gave them the names and details of these men.

"So where did you get the military ship?" asked the captain.

"Oh, you mean the P114?" asked Mr. Novo. "My boss stole it from the closed military base on the other side of the island."

"The former US military base, closed years back?" the captain asked.

"Yes. We were looking at the base as a place where we could keep the crazy people separated from the ten or so regular townspeople, like me, and the fifteen or so men, like Salvatore, who showed signs of the Rage.

"We went there a few days ago and happened to arrive the same time as that patrol boat. We're not sure where it came from, because Salvatore and his men killed the two military guys and took the boat. He told me it was to limit the threat and because he really wanted the boat." Tomas was looking down at his handcuffs and then had a thought. "Hey, you can have the boat if you want. I can show you how to work it." He glanced at the captain. "Although you probably already know how."

"Did you find any supplies there?" Ted asked, forgetting he was supposed to be quiet and just listen.

"Not that I saw, or was told, but the whole base was

intact. And it didn't look like the tsunami damaged it at all. I wondered why we never used it for the crazy people. Until your ship answered Salvatore's call. Then, only after he released them today, did I understand why he wanted them kept close."

Mr. Novo fell silent, but so did everyone else.

Because it was the captain's show, everyone looked to him, waiting for some cue as to what he wanted to ask next.

Jean Pierre's eyes were drilled into the floor in front of him, his face drawn down into a scowl, like he was calculating something in his head. Then he arrived at an answer, his head popped back up and he asked, "Mr. Novo, will you take us to this base tomorrow?"

116
News

TJ Williams frowned at her reflection in the mirror. She was already getting used to the stranger staring back at her each morning, but she wasn't used to all of the added effort she had to go through to cover it up for the benefit of others. Dabbing at her lips with Hollywood Red, her preferred shade of gloss—*actually their preferred shade*—she tried to figure out some sensation which seemed out of place. It began in her stomach. This quickly grew into a scratchy feeling in her throat. She swallowed back the raw bitterness, like something trying to come up. "Oh no." She bent over and puked in her sink.

"What the hell?" she asked herself, pushing up from the cool basin, holding back the next wave of nausea that wanted to take possession of her. She scrutinized herself once again in the mirror, focused on every detail or nuance in her face, looking for some sign to tell her what was going on. *Am I getting sick?* she wondered.

As she examined her tongue for spots, her neck for swelling, her head for heat, she began to panic. Illness for people who were symptomatic meant a fever. A fever meant becoming parasitic. She did not want to turn into one of those things, not after fighting so hard to remain human.

She thought she had become one, when she took those men's lives, consumed some of their blood and then almost attacked her husband. But Wasano's bullet brought her back. She wanted to avoid another episode, at all costs.

A quick look at her clock confirmed she could make it to the medical clinic before she met with JP, who had something important to tell her before they sent a team in to inspect the military base. She would thankfully sit that one out and maybe take some time to apologize to her husband. The last three times he'd seen her, she was either crazy or drugged.

Doing a final check of her look and outfit, she noticed right away she'd forgotten her contacts. *No time,* she told herself. She'd wear sunglasses; otherwise she looked fine.

The sunglasses went over her eyes and she slipped out the door, now only needing one crutch to move around. She bounded down the hallway, so focused she didn't even hear Jaga yelling her name from a cabin door close to hers.

In the two minutes it took her to drop down the two decks and get into the RE Medical Center door, the nausea had a firm grip over her once again.

~~~

"What is it?" Vicki asked. She flopped her head up to look at him, her eyes expectant, a giant smile was plastered her face. Flavio thought then, if she didn't like the gift, it was worth it just for *that* look.

"Maybe you open up and you find out," Flavio stated, trying to make his words sound matter-of-fact, as if this box wasn't anything more important than a lost hairbrush he'd found or a stick of her favorite bubblegum. But it *was*
~~~

something he knew she would love.

"I can't believe you bought me a prezzie." Vicki flashed him another smile and turned to address the box. Each of box's flap corners were tucked in under the next, loosely sealing the top closed, but for a small square hole in the middle. She stuck her forefinger into the hole and felt something soft. And then that something moved.

She pulled her finger out and glowed at him. "You didn't?"

Flavio shrugged. At this point, he just wished she'd just open the damned box.

The box meowed at her.

She opened it up, reached in and pulled out Cat, immediately plowing her face into its soft belly, Cat purring in response.

"Watch out. She has sharp claws and—are you all right?"

She held the cat under her chin, like she was using it as a chin-rest. She stared at Flavio, tears flowing from her eyes. "How did you know I missed my kitty so much? I think I mentioned her only once to you."

He just smiled, remembering when she had told him how much she missed her cat. *Why spoil it with words,* his mother used to tell him.

"Flavio Petrovich, I think I may be in love with you." She leaned over to him and kissed him softly.

"Where *did* you find her?" She sniffled.

"It followed me inside, after climbing up my leg."

She sniffled some more. "Look at me, blubbering like a baby."

She put Cat back into its box and looked up at him, her face serious. "Okay, so tell me you'll be safe?"

"I will."

She hugged him, unwilling to let go.

"I promise," he said, meaning it.

"And thank you, Flavio."

He felt like fist-pumping right now, but he knew that would be a little much. So he offered a simple "You're welcome," kissed her again, and walked out the door. Then once it closed, he dashed down the hallway and up the stairwell. He was going to be late for a private meeting with the captain, if he didn't hurry. He smiled the whole way.

He made it to cabin 8000 with a minute to spare and reached to knock on the door, just as Mrs. TJ Williams was coming out. She glanced up at him, surprised he was there, tears streaking her face. She hesitated in between him and the doorway, as if she was shell-shocked. She looked completely unsure of what she was supposed to do next.

"Mrs. Villiams, are you okay?"

She remained that way, not responding. And Flavio had no idea what he could do to help or comfort her. Unlike Vicki crying tears of joy, this woman was very upset about something she heard or saw.

"I..." Her gaze fell back down, like the words were stuck behind her tongue and she couldn't figure out how to unstick them. She looked up again. "I'm sorry." She then turned and walked off, dragging her crutch behind her.

He watched her move away, shocked himself at what he saw. This woman was one of the strongest he'd ever met, but at that moment, she looked helpless.

Flavio now considered the fact that he was meeting the captain next and he was likely to hear whatever the captain had told Mrs. Williams, and the reason for her distress.

Flavio was rarely nervous about anything. But at this moment, he felt his stomach turn loops.

He knocked. "Captain? It's Flavio Petrovich."

"Please come in, Flavio."

He did.

"Flavio, please sit down. I need to tell you something that only three other people currently know, but it will affect everyone on this ship."

117

The Island

Less than an hour later, TJ, Flavio and Wasano left on the P114 military craft, piloted by Mr. Novo, to the other side of the island to inspect Layes military base. Ted didn't know this at first, only that TJ never showed up for their breakfast date at 8AM. He asked around and no one knew where she was. When he went to her cabin, she didn't answer. The only person who had seen her was Jaga, their room attendant when they first boarded, and now in a cabin next to TJ's temporary cabin on deck 3. Jaga said only that she seemed upset and was limping away as fast as she could and didn't hear him calling her. Jaga also said he was sure that TJ had gone "downstairs."

There were only two destinations she'd have any business with downstairs: deck 2's exits or deck 1 and the RE Medical clinic. He had heard the military boat leave, but she didn't indicate anything about being on it, so he concluded she must have gone to the clinic. And Jaga said that she looked upset and in a hurry. Maybe she was sick. That's when he became worried.

Now Ted was dashing down the stairs and through the small deck 1 public area to see Chloe in Medical.

Ted heard her voice when he knocked.

"Oh Ted, I'm glad you're here. I wanted to talk to you about my results for the T-Gondii blood test. Do you have a few minutes?"

Ted watched her carefully, not answering right away. He had been working with her regarding the parasitics, running ideas and theories back and forth. She was incredibly bright and would have made a brilliant doctor, if their normal world hadn't ended. Instead, this young woman was receiving one of the finest crash-course educations on medicine.

She looked up from her notes to see why he hadn't answered.

"Did you see my wife today?" he asked, scrutinizing how she responded next.

She looked down and away from him—a sure sign she was hiding something. "Ah, yes, I did. But..." She hesitated and gave him a tentative glance, "you really should talk to her."

"What's wrong? Is she all right?" He was really getting worried.

"She's fine, just a little nausea."

"Nausea?" He looked up, trying to remember if other symptomatics complained of nausea, other than at the onset of a fever, and that was not good. "Are you sure she's okay?"

"I'm sure."

"Okay, can you at least tell me where she is now?"

"I only know that she went to see the captain after me. She had an appointment with him, in fact."

"Thank you." Ted turned to leave.

"Ted, what about my data on the Toxo test?"

He would normally have been interested, but he had only one thing on his mind: his wife. Ted gave her a smile. "Sorry. Maybe later?"

~~~

The P114 drafted with ease through the waves tossed up from the windward side of the island.

Tomas drove them around a breaker wall into a small bay with a beach, but no dock. Lush trees surrounded both sides of the beach and the rest of the area was thick with vegetation growing all around multiple buildings that spread out over a large area. A giant fence appeared to bisect part of the island, separating this base from the larger section of land stretched all the way around to the other side, where they left the *Intrepid* anchored. Apparently, no road on the mostly rural island connected the two sides.

Flavio looked back at Mrs. Williams, who seemed to be gazing out into nowhere.

He thought about what the captain said and thought about her and all of the others who would be affected. He couldn't imagine what she was thinking right now. He felt such sorrow for her and Mr. Williams.

They beached only a couple of minutes later.

Flavio gazed at Mrs. Williams and her leg, where he understood Wasano had shot her to keep her from attacking them. She still favored it, although less than he would have expected. But now Flavio had such empathy for her, he worried about her getting it wet.

"Mrs. Villiams, can I help you to the—"

She didn't wait for him to finish, jumping off the boat into the water, which was chest-level on her. She thrust a full canvas bag above her head.

Flavio jumped in next, holding his rifle above his head before plunging in, soaking himself up to his waist. He turned back to see his security director doing the same thing as him, only he was almost completely submerged.
~~~

For a moment Flavio wondered if Mr. Novo was going to leave them there, stranded. But he too jumped out, carrying a rope attached to the bow. He lumbered through the water, then up to the beach and tied the line to a piling attached to a large rock, just out of the water. He'd obviously been here before, just as he had said.

Once they were all of the water, Mrs. Williams called to them, "Come on, let's get started."

The captain's instructions were to follow her around and make sure the place was clear of parasitics or other threats and that it was securable.

She retrieved a clipboard and pen from the top of her soft canvas bag. Immediately she started scribbling notes on the pre-printed pages.

As they went from building to building, she furiously dashed down notes, occasionally asking one of them to assist her with a measurement.

Wasano left Flavio and Mrs. Williams alone while he walked the entire fence line to make sure there were no breaches.

For the next two hours, Flavio continued to keep an eye on their surroundings, sometimes vaulting himself into crawl spaces or inspecting dark corners and generally assisting her with whatever she asked. She seemed to know exactly what she was looking for.

When she was done, they sat on the stoop of one of the houses nearest the beach and waited for the security director to return. Meanwhile, she examined her notes and he watched her. He couldn't help but say something.

"I feel such sadness for you, Mrs. Villiams."

She looked up at him, laying her clipboard aside. She was no longer wearing her sunglasses, either losing them or finding no more need in wearing them to hide her eyes. Besides, it was a dark and overcast day. Her reddish eyes no longer looked eerie or horrific. To Flavio, they looked beautiful but burdened.

"Please Flavio," she said softly. "After all we've been through together, would you do me the favor of calling me by my first name or just TJ?"

He nodded.

Ever so tenderly, she laid her hand on his. "I know you know why we're here. And soon everyone else will know. I also suspect, by your comment, that you must know about my personal situation. I'm asking you to please say nothing to my husband. I want to tell him myself."

He tried to grin, but his frown didn't want to budge. "Captain made me swear not to mention it, even to Vicki. I'll keep your secret, Mrs... Teresa Jean."

"It's better this way, you know... for everyone."

She smiled at him, but he knew it was covering up her own sadness.

He wanted to comfort her. And if they had been like this any longer, he would have. But right then, he heard Wasano trudging back along the beach.

She released her hands from his.

Wasano signaled for them to meet him in the boat and Flavio waved back, acknowledging this.

She watched him as he stood up and he then offered to help her up, but she shook her head.

And then he knew.

"You aren't coming back with us, are you?"

"No, I'm not, Flavio. There's lots of preparation needed. And I want to get a head start on it."

Flavio looked back at the boat and then at her. "Will you be all right?"

"Yes, I will." She held out her hand and Flavio held out his, thinking she was going to shake his, but she pulled herself up so that she was standing toe to toe with him. She leaned up and kissed him on his cheek.

"You're a good man, Flavio. The ship is lucky to have

you. Look after my husband, will you?"

He gave her a weak grin and nodded.

She sat back down on the stoop and waved at him.

He turned back to the boat, slowly making his way through the sand and then the water.

Taking a hand from Mr. Agarwal, he hoisted himself up onto the boat. At the same time Mr. Novo, who had already brought in the mooring line, started up the engine and reversed them back into the bay.

As they turned in the bay to head back to their ship, Flavio watched TJ Williams—*Teresa Jean*, he corrected himself.

She was still sitting on that stoop, staring out at the beach.

It was the last time he saw her.

118

The Meetings

After Flavio said goodbye to Teresa Jean, he considered what had happened to the world, in light of what that meant for Teresa Jean and Ted. He then vowed to himself to never let anything go unsaid between Vicki and him. And when he returned to the ship, he literally ran to Vicki's cabin, proclaimed his love to her and asked her to marry him. Even though he wanted to tell her what had happened, he could not reveal the truth until after the captain's message was delivered four days later. On that morning, everyone would know the basic truth, including Ted.

Each day since Flavio's return, two tenders of men—all of whom only knew a little of the truth, but were all sworn to secrecy—along with food, bulk materials and other supplies were transported to the island. Each day, the tenders would return with just the men.

Each man, upon return to the ship, was escorted back to their cabins on deck 2, where they ate and slept, isolated from the rest of the ship, and under the watch of armed guards. The only other crew member allowed into that section of the ship was Buzz at the same time the first tenders were sent out, only so that the monitor cameras could be disconnected. Their mission was kept hidden from everyone.

Meanwhile, the *Intrepid* was slowly being cleaned and fixed up as teams of crew members worked tirelessly to bring her back to full functionality. Everyone was working on something, night and day, so that there was little time for anything but eating and sleeping.

Flavio was tasked during the day with training new recruits to become security. During the afternoons and evenings, he held personal defense classes for the whole ship. Often forty or fifty attended each of the two classes.

He was given the freedom to teach as he wanted, but the captain had told him to focus on giving each crew member the tools to take care of themselves if a parasitic attacked. He did as instructed, using his personal knowledge of going toe-to-toe with some of those things. But he knew it probably wouldn't do any good: as fast as they were now, Flavio was pretty sure in most every circumstance, it was a losing proposition against one. And there'd be no chance against two or more. The only tool that worked and gave you a fighting chance was an automatic weapon, like his. But since there were only three automatic weapons on the whole ship, Flavio had to do his best instructing them how to use knives and clubs.

Still, all who attended thanked him, saying they just wanted to feel safe and in control, and he gave them that power with his instruction. Flavio had to admit that this filled him with immeasurable pride.

Every moment Flavio wasn't working or sleeping, he spent with Vicki, treating each like it might be their last. That was the secret gift that Teresa Jean gave him and he hoped Vicki would be the benefactor of TJ's gift as well.

The whole time, he thought about Ted and Teresa Jean during the quiet moments or just before sleep, when Flavio was forced to deal with his own guilt.

Two days before the meetings was the only time he had seen Ted. They were passing along the promenade deck, going in opposite directions. Flavio watched Ted, but Ted stared into space, marching at his usual quick pace—his limp from his sprained ankle was almost imperceptible now. Flavio had to step in front of him, because Ted was so lost in his thoughts that he didn't even hear his own name. Flavio wanted to let Ted be, but he needed to talk to him, even though he didn't know what to say, because he really couldn't say anything.

"How are you, Mr. Villiams?"

He gave Flavio a vacant stare. "You know... And would you please call me Ted? After all we've been through together."

Flavio smiled at the memory of being asked the same thing by Teresa Jean. "Your wife... She..." He couldn't bear to say it. He couldn't say it without revealing more than he should. "Please let me know if you need something, Ted."

Ted nodded, gave him a little smile and walked away.

Like any known moment in the future, neither work nor joyous play could slow down the steady march of time. The day he dreaded was now. The morning of the meetings arrived.

Flavio was to be at the meeting run by the captain. Ted was to run the other.

The announcement came at 7:30AM, just as previous announcements and fliers had warned all crew to be prepared to listen then. The captain stated that there would be two mandatory meetings held in thirty minutes. The one held in the Wayfarer Lounge, which had been miraculously cleaned out and ready in time, was to be attended by everyone whose cabins were in the aft half of the ship, from the mid-way stairwell to the stern. The second meeting, held simultaneously, was in the Tell Tale Theatre, and was to be attended by all cabin holders from the forward stairwell to the bow.

No one but Flavio, Wasano, Ted, the captain and now all but five of their security personnel, which had blossomed to twenty-five, knew the content of the meetings' message. Rumors had spread that it had something to do with the military base, especially since many could see the tenders going back and forth. And certainly those crew who saw the supplies being loaded could surmise that the men who were traveling on the tenders and kept in isolation were making the military base habitable. But for what, they didn't know. Flavio was amazed that the captain kept this secret so under wraps.

As the people filed into each room, his security personnel's job was to get them to their seats quickly and quietly. Thirty minutes prior, immediately after the announcement, some of his security personnel had gone to each of the aft cabins to make sure their occupants attended the meeting in the lounge.

Other security corralled the few stragglers into their respective rooms, so that on the hour, it appeared to Flavio, that everyone was where they should be.

At that moment, Flavio for the captain's meeting and Wasano for Ted's meeting, locked the main entrance doors, so that no one could leave until it was time.

~~~

Ted marched over to the lectern on the stage, taking quick measure of his audience. All looked nervous. He wasn't. It seemed like another lifetime ago when he was often filled with overwhelming panic at having to speak to a large group. Now this felt like an old hat: snug, comfortable, ready to do its job. The speaking wasn't the issue; it was the dread of delivering this message. He'd been dreading this since the day the captain told him what was going to happen next. At that moment, he
~~~

put on his speaker's hat and delivered.

"Good morning." He paused to make sure everyone was paying attention. They needed to hear what came next.

"My name is Ted Williams and I'm here on behalf of our captain, Jean Pierre Haddock, to make a special announcement that affects everyone on this ship. At the same time I am speaking to you, the captain is delivering almost the same announcement on the other side of the ship.

"First, so you know, the ship has all of the fuel it needs and we've removed the island threat." Normally Ted would have paused here to allow this good piece of news to sink in. But he moved directly into the first part of the secret he'd been carrying.

"Additionally, the threat of parasitics attacking on board is behind us... for now. It's true, we have removed the parasitics from our ship, but the parasitic threat still dwells here. That's because anyone who is infected with the Toxo parasite can become parasitic the moment their body temperature rises to ninety-nine degrees. Many of us have witnessed this firsthand, with a passenger seemingly okay one minute and then the next minute, they seem crazy, with murder on their minds.

"Today we will remove that threat from this ship for good. All of you in this room are currently staying in forward cabins, but your being invited to this specific place wasn't for your convenience. It was for one simple reason: none of you are currently infected with the parasite."

~~~

Jean Pierre paused to let it sink in.

"Yes, what I'm telling you is true. Everyone in this room is currently infected with the Toxo parasite. Many of you know
~~~

this and have known this. But for some of you, this is the first time you've heard this, because you may not be symptomatic yet. Then again, a few of you are already symptomatic and you've noticed the tell-tale signs like the red eyes, pale skin, thoughts of violence, confusion and unreasonable anger."

The room filled with murmurs and mumblings from almost everyone in the room.

Jean Pierre stopped and held up his hands. And when they didn't immediately settle down he yelled, "Quiet! Listen. Every single one of you will, at some point in the future, experience some or all of these symptoms. And as someone who is infected, when your body temperature hits ninety-nine degrees, you may become parasitic. And if you do, you would be a threat to everyone on this ship who is not infected. And that means *you* are a threat to this ship.

"As the captain of the *Intrepid*, I cannot allow this threat to persist on my ship. Therefore, I have arranged for temporary shelters and supplies for each of you at a secure military base on the other side of this island. We will begin moving you there in a few minutes. Your personal belongings have already been packed up for you and are waiting on a tender, which will deliver you and your belongings to the island. And before you ask, this is not negotiable." He took a deep breath. "If you do not comply or you resist leaving this ship, you will be shot. Please begin leaving now. You will be escorted by our security now.

At that moment, Flavio clicked open the door lock and hollered, "Follow this man right here, now."

A security guard held up a sign that had a number 1 on it. Other guards had placards with other numbers on their signs.

~~~
~~~

Ted held up his hands to quiet the crowd.

"People... This is happening right now."

The theater was filled with whispers, weeping and a few angry comments. Two people rose from their seats and started to march toward the entrance, but Wasano took a step in front of them and pointed his rifle. The intent was clear: you intend to interfere, you will be shot.

"Everyone, remain seated until this announcement is over. Security is now walking down the aisles, passing out lists of those people infected who are moving to the island. If you don't find a name on the list, then that person is not infected. If a family member or a loved one is one of those who is infected and therefore going to the island and you are not infected, you will not be allowed to accompany them to the island. This is for your safety and the safety of those on the island. At some point in the future, we will set up a method of visitation to the island. Believe me when I say this was a hard decision which affects everyone."

Ted was about to say, "My wife is there too." But he didn't want to blur the line. It was true, he'd suffered by being separated from her since she'd nearly died and become symptomatic. And he hadn't seen her since she was on the island preparing it and planning to help those who were infected and forced to go there, so they could prepare for their life as an infected person.

But then Ted expected her to return to the ship, as the one exception to the captain's rule, not only because she had proven herself multiple times, but because they still needed someone symptomatic to be able to periodically sniff-test each of their crew to make sure no one became infected, no matter how unlikely that might be.

119

New Life

51 Days Later

Flavio came home to find his wife Vicki standing just inside the door, wearing a giant smile and the short blue dress he loved.

"Ahh… Hello," Flavio responded, his smile only crawling up one cheek. "Did I do something?"

She snickered, "Well yeah, I'd say you did."

She held out her hands and he accepted them.

"Come here." She led him into their cabin, body-blocking something she didn't yet want him to see. When she moved to the side, she revealed their coffee table covered in a checkered tablecloth, with near formal settings, including nice silverware, two covered plates—he could see they were heated—and a Guinness beer, with beads of sweat rolling down its neck. He could smell the delightful Thai spices in the air.

"Did you do something?" he asked sure that something was wrong; otherwise she wouldn't have gone to such trouble.

"Yes, I did!" she proclaimed, practically hopping.

"What's that at the edge of the table?" she asked playfully.

He looked at her and then at the table and now saw something there. He walked over and picked up the only foreign-looking object from her table setting.

Then it hit him. He snapped his head back to Vicki and now her entire face was enveloped with a smile. "Does this mean..."

She nodded, hopped twice and then leapt onto him. "We're preggers."

He spun her around, but then thought twice about it, letting her down easily. "Sorry. You must be careful now."

She punched him in the arm. "You can be so daft sometimes. I'm fine. Ohh, and that's not the only big news."

Flavio was already feeling lightheaded about her pregnancy announcement. He wasn't sure he could take any other big news.

"Come here." She grabbed his paw and led him to the bathroom.

"What?"

"Take a peek, but don't be too loud; you don't want to wake them."

He screwed his mug at her, like she was playing some sort of gotcha game and he was about to walk into it.

"Go on..." she insisted.

If it makes her happy, especially in her condition, he thought and pulled open the bathroom door.

In the corner, where they had been keeping Cat—she insisted on calling it Liz—was not only Cat, but five little kittens.

"Isn't that cute? Liz had little babies."

All Flavio could think of was how they were going to hide six cats now; one was hard enough.

"Can you put in a request for a family cabin now, or do we have to wait until little Flavio is born?"

He ignored her request. Of course he'd put in the request. But something struck him as odd.

He stepped into the bathroom and knelt down to closely examine Momma Cat and her kittens that were blindly suckling on her. Cat looked over to Flavio and meowed at him and he saw it again. It was one of her eyes: it had turned red.

~~~

The tender slashed at the surging sea and Ted tried not to feel nauseous, not usually getting seasick, especially after living on a ship for over two months. But he knew it was not just the rocking seas that jolted his sense of balance; it was the thought of seeing his wife after two months. But that wasn't all.

It was the sense that this meeting, rather than being a joyous celebration, was instead a goodbye.

Ted was no idiot. He knew that they had no need for a symptomatic on their ship anymore: Chloe had fully developed a blood test for the Toxo infection. A simple prick of a finger and a little droplet of blood was all that was needed and already the captain had ordered mandatory testing once every two months for everyone on board. And those who tested positive would be escorted to the island.

So the only reason why TJ could return to them was eliminated by Chloe's new test. But Ted still held out hope.

The captain had even agreed that she could come on board and stay for short visits. It wasn't a permanent solution, but it was a start. But only if he could convince her to come back.

Their last conversation on the radio told him she was thinking otherwise. She was cold and seemed unconvinced by his logic.

The boat came down hard off the crest of a large wave, rattling his bones in the process.

Ted looked up and saw the ring of the beach, past the
~~~

breaker wall, almost completely covered in dots: no doubt the residents waiting to greet all of the visitors on their first visitation tender since the infecteds were relocated fifty-one days ago.

He glanced back and saw all the happy faces pointing at the beach, some even waving, as if they could see their spouses, loved ones or friends from this distance.

Ted returned his gaze, trying to do the same thing and sort out which one was his wife.

TJ always stood out in the crowd to him, even if she wasn't the most glamorous or the most classically beautiful. Most would consider her a beautiful woman and many had made comments to him and to her about her features over the years. But to Ted, her beauty and presence was so much more than that. She had a radiance that shone brighter than any physical beauty could.

Pretty quickly, he could identify her, standing alone at the top of the beach's littoral plain. She was covered in a hooded white robe that whipped around in the wind.

Ted found that his heart was racing, beating so hard it hurt for him to take breaths. He couldn't wait to hold her, to gaze into her strange new eyes and see the love she'd always held for him.

The tender slid onto the beach and a crewman tossed a line to a waiting person, who tied it off on a pylon to the left of TJ. She stood there stoically, a pylon more unmovable looking than the inanimate post beside her.

Ted was the first off, hopping with both feet into the water, not caring about getting wet. He shuffled through the water, then ran up the beach, desiring to the embrace her. He dashed by others, as if they didn't exist; his gazed was glued to her.

Still she remained, unmoving and seemingly unaffected by him.

When he was a countable number of steps away, a glint

of light illuminated the darkness inside her hoodie that otherwise shrouded her head from him. He caught just a glimpse of her familiar smile creep up her unfamiliar face.

He halted only a few feet from her, because she still hadn't moved. *Was she unwilling or unable?* His squinted to see more inside the covered murk of her hooded robe, for another glimmer of his wife, standing there in this foreign form.

Finally, she lifted her hands up to the hood's edges and pulled it back to reveal her newly striking features. It was purposeful and it sucked his breath away.

Her hair was cut short, just over her ears and it was ghostly white-colored, like fine strands of silk; her eyelashes, thinned to the point of being hidden against her skin were also white; her skin's pigment was completely bleached away; her lips, also almost invisible; both her eyes blazed like two blood moons cast against pools of white. And yet, they were the two most beautiful eyes he had ever seen.

A teardrop fell out of one of them. Then another. And another, until they both showered like a summer rainstorm.

"Oh, Ted," she cried and in a single bound, she leapt onto him, wrapping her arms around him.

Not expecting this, he almost fell backwards, but he dug in and held tight to her slight frame, not wanting to let go. Her lips found his and they remained passionately locked for one all-consuming breath.

And then she released herself, exhaled and pushed away from him. He let go and she dropped into the sand and stepped back, breathing heavily while wiping at her eyes.

Normally tears would have streaked her makeup, but she wasn't wearing any. Her face almost instantly returned to its natural state just before the tears, without any normal rosy flare in her cheeks or any of the other tell-tale signs that she had cried. It was like it didn't happen, even though he could still taste the proof of their saltiness from that moment.

Her robe had opened some during their embrace and

the wind whipped up again attempting to open it further. She immediately subdued it before more of her was exposed, palming her belly softly with one hand and tugging roughly with the other at it, where it criss-crossed her bust. Underneath the robe she was wearing a sleeveless olive T, rather than her usual—at least it was usual when he last saw her—sports bra. Most noticeably missing against her pale chest was her Orion necklace that he had given her over two months ago for their anniversary.

His eyes must have been hanging there too long, because she pulled with both hands now on the robe's edges, covering herself to her neck. "I lost it," she blurted. "The new chain you gave me broke." She said this without emotion, as if she were speaking about something that was meaningless.

He really didn't care about the necklace, not much anyway. But he couldn't help but feel like it meant something, a metaphor for their relationship... *Was it truly broken? Lost?*

Almost in reply, barely loud enough to be heard over the excited chaos around them from loved ones and friends embracing, just like they had been too many moments ago, she said, "I'm not going back with you. I have to stay here."

There it was, now stated in no uncertain terms. And as much as her words hit him like a punch to his solar plexus, he knew this was how it had to be.

Even if she agreed to come back with him, she'd never be allowed to stay. And it was foolish for even him to think this. She might still be his wife and it was obvious that she loved him, as evidenced by her tears and passionate embrace, but that didn't change what she was now: a predator, who could no more occupy his cabin than a leopard.

Her delicate lips opened slightly, quivered, but then held firm. Then they quivered again before she said, "You know I'm still in love with you?"

He smiled. "Yeah, I'm sure of that." He wanted to ask her something, but he wasn't sure how to. "Are you... Okay? I mean, are you happy here?"

Now she smiled. And it was genuine.

"Yes, I'm fine. And for the first time since this whole thing started, I'm at peace."

Ted couldn't help but cast a questioning glance, because he really didn't understand. But he desperately wanted to. He was trying to think how to ask it, when she volunteered to help him understand.

"I had thought it was some sort of inner evil—that I was evil and that part of me was trying to take over my humanity. It's not. I'm not evil and it's not an evil being: it's just a disease that was making changes in me. And yes, these changes brought temptations of doing evil things. And at times, they were overwhelming and felt uncontrollable. But I always had a choice, just like I did before I was infected. I chose not to do evil things to others. I chose not to be a monster. Anyone afflicted with this can also make that choice.

"And Ted, I'm helping others here to make the right choice. Some have chosen the easiest way, and they often end up becoming monsters; others have chosen the harder path. It's always their choice.

"The disease does change you in many ways, both physically and physiologically, as we both know. In a way, it's just like say, cataracts changing your eyesight. Barring some sort of surgery, you'd have to just adjust to your new condition. In our case though, the condition offers some benefits too and we have to adjust to them all." She hesitated, her eyes getting watery again.

"None of this changes my feelings for you. My heart will always belong to you and to you alone... But I also know we can't be together, like we were."

"I understand," he said. "It's not just us. There's no possible union for infected and non-infected people... But it still hurts."

"For me too... We can still visit, like this. I *do* want to see you again."

"Okay."

They held onto their silence for a while. It was not unlike so many of their times together in the past, when they'd talk for hours and just stop and enjoy their silence together.

But this too couldn't last.

"I need to go. I'm working with Boris and Penny, who are having a difficult time coping with the changes she's going through."

"Until the next visit then," Ted said, stepping into her with his lips pursed.

She reflexively scrunched up her nose, obviously attempting not to smell him. But she kissed him softly and then quickly turned and ran the other way, into the village.

He watched her disappear behind a stand of trees, then into the arms of Penny, who was standing with her husband on the stoop of one of the many buildings clustered around the beach.

Ted breathed out a long sigh. This wasn't the life he wanted, but it was one he could accept. He would count the days until his next trip here.

Until then, he knew everything would be all right.

Epilogue

Four Years Later

Ted rubbed the gray beard carpeting his face, while keeping his other hand tightly on the tender's wheel. The waves were extra choppy today so he had to keep a tight hold of the rudder. They'd lost one of their tenders a year ago, killing their pilot and another crew member, not to mention dumping their supplies into the ocean. The captain said the rudder probably got away from him in the cross current. Ted wasn't about to be another one of the *Intrepid's* many casualties.

This month's load of supplies was similar to what he brought on most of his trips. Salt and some other recyclables. For the first two years, they were exporting their food supplies to the colony. But now it was the other way around. They would receive fresh meat from the livestock that the colony tended, fruit from their orchards and vegetables from their gardens.

Today, he had a new addition for their colony—the first person in memory who had developed an infection and then become symptomatic. The young boy, named Pasquale, sat alone in his thoughts, at the back of the tender, only Ted and a security guard—there for Ted's protection—to look after him. But soon Pasquale would be with his own people. They would teach him about living a life with this disease. If Pasquale was lucky, he'd get Ted's wife as a teacher. Ted prayed this would happen for the boy and TJ.

Once he maneuvered the boat around the breaker wall and into the bay, Ted did what he always did before each visit: he scanned the beach for his wife. There were quite a few colonists on the beach today, much more than normal. They must be there for Pasquale's benefit, to make him feel welcome.

Ted had gotten quite good at his landings, cutting the engine and drafting the boat to the same place each time. As he stepped carefully out and around to the bow, grabbing the coiled line, he saw several familiar faces waiting. Some waved at him.

Ted tossed his line and it was grabbed and tied off when the boat stopped. Ted hopped off from the bow, barely splashing at the waterline's edge.

Ágúst was the first person to greet him, his welcoming smile always genuine and wide. It was still hard to believe he survived the beating he took, though every time Ted saw him, his skin looked paler.

Frans was there as well, and so was Jaga. Little Taufan, who was all white now and apparently didn't run around much anymore, was at home nestled in his arms. Both wore big smiles as well. He noticed right away that Frans' eyes were like two bright cherries. Ted had heard that he'd become symptomatic and was following Ágúst and TJ's spiritual guidance. Jaga looked no different than before and he was glad for that. He'd never become symptomatic.

Ágúst motioned to Ted for the mail bag, which he almost forgot he was carrying. He hoisted it over to Ágúst, thus fulfilling his duties as the *Intrepid* postman.

Many others of the colonists had already made their way to the tender to collect *Intrepid's* supplies he'd brought over and then load the supplies Ted was transporting back to the ship. Ted was only half paying attention, constantly looking for the one face he really wanted to see.

At this point the colonists flooded Ted with "hellos" and a drumbeat of questions about the *Intrepid* and its people; where they'd been, what they were doing, and so on. Ted was happy to answer whatever he could. This was their time to visit as well as his. It was never too long, especially if TJ wasn't there. Sometimes she was and other times she wasn't.

"Sorry, Ted," Ágúst said in his always measured tone. "She's out hunting today. She's up in the hills now. She thought you were coming yesterday."

Ted nodded. A while back, for their tender's protection, they decided not to broadcast the day of Ted's supply run. They were still afraid of pirates after a previous attack.

"I thought as much when I didn't see her."

"She's doing well. She really is."

"Don't touch me," hollered a high-pitched voice from the tender. "I get out on my own."

"So that's our newbie?" asked Jaga.

"Yep, Pasquale. Seems like a good kid. Lost his parents in the first attack. A few weeks ago, he failed the blood test. Then one day, he started screaming from his cabin and we saw that he was symptomatic. He was immediately placed in a cooler. He's struggled a lot since then. I've been praying with him, but he really needs some help from one of his own kind."

"You know we'll take care of him."

"I know you will. Say, how are you getting along with your parasitic neighbors?"

"That's something I wanted to talk to you about. I would recommend that you only come in the morning, while it's still cool. They hunt now and I'm afraid it's just not safe for you so late in the day."

"Got it. I'll get going then. Thanks." Ted shook his hand. "And please tell her hello from me. It's going to be hard to wait another month before I see her again."

"I will, Ted. Peace."

Ted waved to everyone and made his way back to the tender.

As he stepped into the water, he saw something sparkle, even though the sun was well shrouded today. He reached in and pulled up a familiar object: it was TJ's Orion necklace, the one he had given her and she said she had lost some four years ago. She must have lost it right here.

He turned back to the shore and gazed out toward the hills, where Ágúst said she was hunting. He didn't know why, probably just wishful thinking on his part, but he felt like she was watching him right then. He held the necklace up in the air, moving it so that its diamonds would reflect the dull sunlight from above. Then he placed it against his chest and crossed his arms: the sign language symbol for "love." Then he pointed to the hills. "You!"

He held his gaze for just a second longer before turning back to the tender.

~~~

TJ stood high upon a ridge, looking down upon her colony's beach. She crossed her arms over her chest and then pointed her finger at the tender a couple of miles away, her face glowing with joy.

"What are you doing, Mommy?" the little girl asked. She had one arm wrapped around TJ's knee and she gazed up with her ruby reds at the person who was the center of her young life.

TJ removed a foot from the deer she'd just killed and
~~~

knelt down to pick up her daughter, marveling at how heavy a nearly four-year-old was.

"You see that man? The one now in that boat, with the gray beard and the blue cap, driving away?"

"Ah-hah," she said, not even having to squint to see him.

"That, my darling, is your daddy."

THE END

A Quick Word From The Author

Thank you for reading all the way to the end of *The Final Outbreak*. This has been an amazing journey for me, and I hope it has been for you as well.

In case you weren't aware, I'm an independent writer who relies on ratings and reviews to help get the word out about my books. This is why reviews are so important to me and why I truly need your help. Leaving even a short review would be greatly appreciated.

Michael

Please post a review on Amazon
http://www.mlbanner.com/final-outbreak-review

Is This Really

the end of the story?

Even though over a year of research and planning went into *The Final Outbreak*, the story was intended to be a three-book trilogy, and *The Final Outbreak* contains all three books of that trilogy.

But that doesn't mean the story is over.

In fact, if your feedback (through your reviews) makes it clear that I need to bring back the characters for more, I will. There are several follow up stories I have in mind, assuming the demand is there. Here are some of the many questions that remain unanswered…

What will become of the *Intrepid* and her crew?
What happens to Ted and/or TJ?
What about their daughter?
Can the island colony and neighboring parasitics coexist?
Will humans survive in this world?

Why do you want more?
Unleash your feedback (in your review):

http://www.mlbanner.com/final-outbreak-review

Other Additions to This World
Regardless of what happens to the characters in their own part of this world, I plan to open up this world (called Madness World) to other stories, not only written by me, but other authors. If you're interested in what's coming next, be sure you're receiving one of my *Updates*. Have ideas for a story in Madness World? Contact me directly at mlbanner.com/contact-author/

Updates on Rage Disease
The T-Gondii parasite is very real and so are many of the effects from its infection. This is why I created a website for news and info, which include real-life reports about the Rage disease and the T-Gondii parasite, as well as updates about the stories set in Madness World. Fill your need for more madness here:

MadnessWorld.Info

More Discussion Possibilities
Interested in discussing Madness World's stories and its characters? For instance...

What do you think is Ted and TJ's daughter's name?

Or who was *your* favorite character?

This is your chance to join in the discussions. Post your questions here to get my answers and those of other *MADNESS* readers:

https://www.facebook.com/MadnessWorldInfo/

FREE BOOKS

Sign up for ML Banner's *Apocalyptic Updates* (VIP Readers list) and get a free copy of one of my best-selling books, just for joining.

In addition, you'll have access to our VIP Reader's Library, with at least four additional freebies.

Simply go here:
http://mlbanner.com/free
(give us an email address to get your free book)

WHO IS ML BANNER?

Michael "ML" Banner is an award winning & international best-selling author of apocalyptic thrillers.

Six of his books were #1 Amazon best-sellers in one or more genres. He's won two Readers Favorite Medals for different genres: a silver for *MADNESS* in 2018 in Horror and a gold for *Highway* in 2016 in Thrillers. His work is both traditionally published and self-published.

Often his thrillers are set in far-flung places, as Michael uses his experiences from visiting dozens of countries—some multiple times—over the years. His last two transatlantic cruises were the foreground of *The Final Outbreak*.

A serial entrepreneur, having formed multiple businesses over the years, he founded and still runs SmallBiZ.com, which helps small businesses create and maintain entities, forming almost 100,000 entities over its 20 years of existence.

When not running a business or writing his next book, you might find Michael hunting, traveling abroad, or reading a Kindle with his toes in the water (name of his publishing company) in the Sea of Cortez (Mexico). That's because he and his wife split time between the deserts of Arizona and the beaches of Mexico.

Books By ML Banner

For a complete list of Michael's books, and his upcoming books,
go to MLBanner.com/books/

MADNESS CHRONICLES

MADNESS (01)

A parasitic infection causes mammals to attack.

PARASITIC (02)

The parasitic infection doesn't just affect animals.

SYMPTOMATIC (03)

When your loved one becomes symptomatic, what do you do?

The Final Outbreak (Books 1 - 3)

The end is coming. It's closer than you think. And it's real.

HIGHWAY SERIES

Highway (01)

A terrorist attack forces siblings onto a highway,
and an impossible journey home.

Endurance (02)

Enduring what comes next will take everything they've got, and more.

STONE AGE SERIES

Stone Age (01)

The next big solar event separates family and friends, and begins a new Stone Age.

Desolation (02)

To survive the coming desolation will require new friendships.

Max's Epoch (Stone Age Short)

Max wasn't born a prepper, he was forged into one.
(This short is exclusively available on MLBanner.com)

Hell's Requiem (03)

One man struggles to survive and find his way to a scientific sanctuary.

Time Slip (Stand Alone)

The time slip was his accident; can he use it to save the one he loves?

Cicada (04)

The scientific community of Cicada may be the world's only hope, or it may lead to the end of everything.

Connect With M.L. Banner

Keep in Contact – I would love to hear from you!

Email: michael@mlbanner.com
Facebook: facebook.com/authormlbanner
Twitter: @ml_banner

Made in the USA
San Bernardino, CA
18 November 2019